THE
SUNDERED
SEA

ZIPANGU

HANSE   JIQAL

★ HALDHEIM

GEUMJOSEON

GEUMSEUONG ★

SHENZHOU

THE
HANHAI
SEA

★
SHANGAN

SOUTH WESTERN ROAD

MARAKAND

★ INDRAPRASTHA

TAPROBANA

HIND

THE
LAKSHAD
SEA

KEY
~~~~ ROAD
~~~~ RIVER
★ CITY
ABC COUNTRY

By Cassandra Clare

CHRONICLES OF CASTELLANE

Sword Catcher

The Ragpicker King

THE RAGPICKER KING

THE
RAGPICKER
KING

Cassandra
Clare

NEW YORK

Published in the United States by Del Rey, an imprint of Random House, a division of Penguin Random House LLC, New York.

DEL REY and the CIRCLE colophon are registered trademarks of Penguin Random House LLC.

Hardback ISBN 978-0-525-62002-0
International edition ISBN 978-0-593-97684-5
Ebook ISBN 978-0-525-62003-7

Endpaper maps: Sarah J. Coleman/Inkymole
Case illustration: Charlie Bowater

Printed in the United States of America on acid-free paper

randomhousebooks.com

2 4 6 8 9 7 5 3 1

First Edition

Book design by Susan Turner

For my grandmother Isabel

You shall leave everything you love most:
This is the arrow that the bow of exile
Shoots first. You are to know the bitter taste
Of others' bread, how salty it is, and know
How hard a path it is for one who goes
Ascending and descending others' stairs.

—DANTE, *Paradiso;*
translated by Allen Mandelbaum

THE RAGPICKER KING

Prologue

Artal Gremont, heir to the tea Charter of Castellane, had never much liked the ocean. It was the source of his wealth, of course. The millions of crowns' worth of tea and coffee that were carried in sleek ships across the seas to the Castellani port had made his family richer than Gods. In theory, he appreciated the convenience of the sea; in actuality, he found it flat, featureless, and dull.

Then again, Gremont found most things dull. People tended to be dull and generally limited in their thinking. Most parties were dull. Being the son of a Charter holder in Castellane, with money but no real power, had been equally dull. And when he'd tried to make life more interesting, he'd been exiled, sent off by his parents to oversee the tea business in foreign climes. That had been *exceedingly* dull.

Now, however, things were starting to get interesting. With his father dead, he had inherited the tea Charter and been recalled to Castellane, his exile ended. He'd booked passage on the next ship leaving Taprobana harbor: one of Laurent Aden's galleons, which at the moment was carrying a shipment of teakwood to Castellane. The ship had six tiny passenger cabins, up near the stern, though the captain's vast quarters hogged all the windows. Gremont's room was little better than a closet with a berth built into the wall and a table bolted to the floor to prevent it from sliding when the ship rolled.

Dull, dull, dull. Gremont paced the floor of his cabin fretfully. There was nothing to do on the bloody boat, and his anxiety was building. When he got like this, he often *had* to do something to make himself feel better. It was a need, like other men felt for food or water.

Alas, Laurent Aden ran a tight ship and had little patience for Artal's preferences. A young stowaway had been discovered last week after they'd left the port in Favár, but at least Artal had been able to have a little fun with her before Laurent found out about it and had the girl removed from Artal's quarters posthaste. Words had been exchanged that were not particularly polite, and Artal had been given to understand that if he engaged in any more such business while on the *Black Rose*, he would be unceremoniously dumped off at the next port, charter or no charter.

He did not know what had happened to the girl, and did not care. She had gotten blood on his favorite jacket, which had annoyed him. Though not as much as being trapped in this cabin was annoying him now.

Laurent had told him not to wander the ship, but fuck Laurent. Gremont yanked open the door of his cabin and made his way out into the narrow passage that ran the length of the ship. He plucked a glass windlamp from a nail on the wall. Best if he strode purposefully, he thought, making his way across the ship toward the stairs that led up to the weather deck. A purposeful stride tricked people into thinking you were on important business.

He passed the ship's galley, where the cook was asleep in a chair, a wooden bucket of half-peeled potatoes at his feet. Thank the Gods, they only had a few days left at sea. Gremont was vilely sick of salt beef, boiled potatoes, and suet.

Up on the weather deck, the air was clear. The moon hovered

close to the horizon, creating a white path that stretched along the water. Rope for the sails lay in neat coils like sleeping snakes.

Some might have admired the view, the stars picked out across the sky as bright as nailheads, the water like hammered glass. Gremont merely glared at it all. The sea was a barrier between him and Castellane, between him and reclaiming all he had lost in exile.

The creak of a board underfoot alerted him to the fact that he was not alone. He turned and for a moment saw nothing; then she appeared, shadow evolving out of shadow. (The first time he had seen her do this, he'd nearly fallen over with shock; he was more used to her brand of magic now.) She wore her assassin's gear: Every bit of her was covered with smooth black fabric. It rendered her faceless, which Gremont found unnerving despite the fact that he knew perfectly well what she looked like beneath the disguise.

"I came to congratulate you on your upcoming nuptials, Artal," she said. Her voice was low and husky. If he hadn't known her gender, he doubted he could have guessed it.

"I don't suppose there's any point asking you how you got here from the continent," he replied sourly. "Flew on a bat, eh?"

She chuckled. "You are amusingly bitter for a man about to make a very advantageous marriage."

He snorted. "You know I had my sights set higher than Antonetta Alleyne."

"I know your sights were set as high as Anjelica of Kutani. But her family would never have accepted you; she is royalty, and royal blood demands royal blood to match with."

"I suppose you would know."

She scoffed and sprang lightly to the railing of the ship. She balanced there easily, though the thought of the long drop to the water made Gremont queasy. "Don't be sour, Gremont. I do hope you are not having second thoughts about our arrangement."

Gremont felt a slight chill run up his spine. He knew she held magic, though he had grown up believing that all but small magics had died with the Sundering. The first time she had proved this wrong had shocked him. He still bore the scar upon the back of his hand—a glossy patch of burned skin that resembled a starfish.

Even now, he feared her, though the fact that she knew it galled him. "I have not," he said, "had second thoughts."

"Good." She gazed down at him, eyeless and faceless, a dark shadow against the vast blue of the night sky and the sea. "I hope you are made of stronger stuff than your father was. He gave us assurances of his loyalty, too, but planned to betray us in the end."

"He was always weak," Gremont muttered. His father had never lifted a finger to save him from exile, and Gremont had never forgotten or forgiven it. His mother was just as weak, but one expected less from a woman, and at least she adored him blindly. "You do not need to remind me that if certain strings had not been pulled, I would not be returning so soon from exile. I am well aware where my loyalty lies."

"Glad to hear it," she said, "for a new opportunity has presented itself. A chance for you to show your cleverness. Your dear lady-wife-to-be, Antonetta of the silk Charter, has certain information, it appears. There is someone else we need on our side, and she knows how to find him."

"Antonetta? Really? I hadn't thought she carried any information in that empty head of hers."

"Even a mouse can come upon a precious crumb. Regardless, once you are married, I grant you entire permission to get the truth out of her. Using any means you might prefer."

"Really? Any means?" Gremont smirked. "I will not let you down, my lady."

"Try not to get too carried away, Artal. For now, Liorada Alleyne is more afraid of us than she is of House Aurelian, but if that calculus changes, it could spell trouble for all our plans. Your marriage to Antonetta is one more lever we can utilize to threaten dear Liorada. So keep the girl alive, won't you? As a favor to me."

"Of course," said Gremont. "Far more fun to keep her alive

anyway. My very own amusing toy. We'll see what she's like when her silk is torn."

The dark figure chuckled. "How nice to see you happy, Artal. But remember. There are many on the Hill who would like to see us fail. Many still loyal to House Aurelian. Do not forget to wear your amulet. It is more powerful than you think."

"Indeed." Artal lifted his hand to touch the pendant she had given him in Taprobana before he'd ever set foot on this ship. "I would be a fool to scorn its protection. And you would not have approached me if I were a fool."

She said nothing. A little insulted, Artal looked up, wondering at her silence, and saw that she was gone. He raced to the railing and leaned over it, but he saw only darkness and water below, and the moon's white path laid across the sea, pointing the way to Castellane.

CHAPTER ONE

In the Hayloft, Kel and Conor were practicing their swordplay.

It had been some while since there had been time for practice, and both were a little rusty. Still, the moves came back as they always did. Muscles had their own memories, as Jolivet often said. Kel had begun the morning feeling stiff, his body half asleep and his joints objecting to being stretched. Now, after an hour or so of drills in the space they'd trained in since they were young boys, he felt flexible, his muscles fast and liquid.

The flat of his blunt-tip sword slammed against Conor's with a metallic ring. Kel pressed his advantage, but this time Conor leaped out of the way, jumping onto one of the hay bales that, scattered about the room, served to create a changing terrain for practice. He raised his left hand, signaling a time-out.

Kel let his sword arm fall, rolling his shoulders back.

Conor raked a hand through his sweaty dark hair, frowning. "We need to do this more often," he said. "I can barely recall what to do with my blade. Too many late nights at the desk, exercising nothing but my writing hand. I've turned into a pudding from inaction these past months, Kellian."

"I wouldn't say a *pudding*," Kel objected. Conor was as trim and fit as ever. Busy as he was, he still swam and rode his horse Asti nearly every day. Besides, hadn't the Queen been fretting that he was too thin just the other day? If he was having trouble, it was far more likely to be the late hours and lack of sleep causing it.

Not that Kel would ever say so. Conor was willing to hear things from Kel that he would never stand for from someone else, but the subject of the great change in Conor that had begun three months ago—his strange new dedication to his role in actual governance—was off limits even to his Sword Catcher. Kel guessed it was because the whole business was a sort of penance for Conor, but it was only a guess. It had to be. Conor would not speak on the subject, and Kel did not press.

"We can certainly train more often, if you'd like," he said now. "You can join my sessions with Jolivet. I stand ready," he added, "to assist with all pudding-avoidant activities."

He raised his sword, indicating the time-out was over. Conor laughed and spun down from the hay bale, bringing his blade across in a sideways strike. Kel responded with an overhand cut, the swords slamming together with the satisfying sound of steel on steel. Kel danced backward, out of harm's way, as Conor came toward him.

They had been practicing such sword-work together for so long that they knew each other's ways: Conor tended to be too reckless, Kel too careful. They were comfortable enough to carry on a conversation even as they parried and redoubled, lunged and feinted.

"Are you feeling ready?" Kel asked. "It will be the first Dial Chamber meeting since—in nearly four months."

He had almost said *since before the Shining Gallery slaughter*. Though Conor was willing to speak of the attack on the Palace and the murder of the little Princess from Sarthe, he did not like to be reminded. He had nightmares, still, about it, and woke up screaming; Kel, who slept in the same room with the Prince, would remain awake when that happened, tensed and waiting for Conor's breath to even out. For him to sleep again.

Parry, riposte. Conor ducked nimbly back, his face expressionless. "A bunch of cowards," he said, referring to the Charter holders—the eleven most powerful families in Castellane. "Half of them seem convinced they'll all be murdered the moment they set foot in Marivent." (To be fair, Kel thought, the last time they'd all come to Marivent for a banquet dinner, they nearly *had* all been slaughtered.) "Of course, they won't *say* that's the problem. They fuss about being busy or having strange ailments. But Mayesh has put about rumors that I have a significant announcement, so this time curiosity drives them."

Despite the fears of the aristocracy, Conor had been determined that the monthly Dial Chamber meetings be reinstated as soon as possible. He had gone to each of the holdouts individually to point out that they could not hide themselves away like rats but must present a unified, stalwart front. There were always going to be spies—especially now, with Castellane being squeezed like a grape in a wine-press by Sarthe's demands. Should the spies return to their homelands with the information that the ruling class of Castellane were terrified, it would only go worse for them all in the end.

"And it's quite an announcement," Kel said.

Conor tried a vertical cut; Kel defended with a parry *quarte.* Conor gave him a sharp look. "You're worried," he said. "Do you think I'm doing the wrong thing?"

"No," Kel said. "But the nobles may disagree. The last time you told them you were marrying to solve the nation's problems, it ended badly."

Badly being an understatement. *Badly* being the slaughter in the Shining Gallery that was the cause of Conor's nightmares. And the reason that Kel not only did not ask questions, but also kept secrets. Far more secrets than he had ever wanted to keep.

"Well, this decision was not only mine. It was also Jolivet and Mayesh's. And my mother's. As for my father . . . Well, they will get no answers on that front."

Indeed not. The day after the slaughter, the King had entered the North Tower. He had not left it since. Food was brought to him there; he did not emerge, did not speak, did not respond when spoken to. Mayesh had named it a kind of shock—catatonia, he called it—and said that, like an illness, it would heal in time.

Yet the extent of the King's withdrawal had been kept a secret. Besides Kel, only Conor, Mayesh, Jolivet, and the Queen knew he did not speak, that the "King's orders" that emerged from the North Tower were actually Conor's orders, crafted with the advice of Mayesh and Jolivet.

"Yes," Kel said. "It is something of a shame. You have fended off war with Sarthe all this time with extraordinary diplomacy." *Late nights of work, carefully crafted missives, apologies that admitted no culpability, accommodations without capitulations.* "But you will not get the credit. Not from the families."

"Perhaps not," Conor said. "But I am the one with experience of blackmail." His smile was a blade. "Sarthe does not care about the death of the Princess. They care about the leverage it gives them to make demands. And once a blackmailer gets their hooks in you, it won't end neatly. They'll keep coming back, always wanting more, no matter what you give them. Sarthe will not just go away one day the way Prosper Beck did."

Prosper Beck. Sometimes Kel found it hard to believe the criminal he'd once bargained with for Conor's safety and sanity had simply left Castellane. It was the existence of Beck that had pulled him into the Ragpicker King's shadow world in the first place—Beck had set himself up as a challenger to Andreyen, and the Ragpicker King had employed Kel to find out who on the Hill was bankrolling Beck's various criminal enterprises. Beck had seemed to Kel a crueler, more dangerous version of the Ragpicker King himself, someone not held back by Andreyen's peculiar code of honor. A wild card, capable of anything.

Conor was still talking about Sarthe; Kel forced his mind back to the present. "The only thing that will make the Sarthians stop is if we show that we are too powerful to bully. If we secure money and warships through this marriage, Sarthe will realize it is too dangerous to try to bleed us dry." His gray eyes flashed. "That reminds me. Speaking of marriage, Artal Gremont should arrive soon. Then we will all have to prepare for what will surely be an interminable show of triumph as Lady Alleyne prepares to marry her daughter off."

Kel moved to parry Conor's jab a moment too late, and Conor tapped him with the protective cap of his sword as if to say, *Pay attention.* Kel said woodenly, "Indeed, this will be the culmination of her plans for Antonetta. I wonder what she will find to engage her once the ink on the certificate of marriage dries."

"I assume she will do all she can to meddle in the affairs of Gremont's tea Charter as well as her own," said Conor. "I will have to keep an eye on the two of them. That much power concentrated in one family is likely trouble. At least Antonetta is not ambitious," he added, "though her mother may prod her to make trouble."

Not ambitious. It was what everyone thought of Antonetta; only Kel knew they were all of them wrong. He remembered her telling him that she wanted control of the silk Charter, and at another time she had told him that her mother did not think it acceptable for an unmarried woman to control a Charter. If she and Gremont married, though, each of them would hold their Charter individually until it became time to will the Charters to a new generation. That she was willing to marry a lout like Gremont in order to control the most valuable Charter in Castellane spoke quite a bit to her ambition.

"Then again," Conor added, and the tip of his sword came up under Kel's to lightly scratch his shoulder; Kel went still to acknowledge the scoring of a point. "I think often of what old Gremont said before he died. No one is really to be trusted."

Kel almost closed his eyes as he remembered the old man's words. He had been there when Gremont passed away, the only one at his side as he went through the gray door, and Gremont had not even known him. Had thought he was Conor.

Place your trust in no one, he'd said. *Not mother, not Counselor, not friend. Trust no one on the Hill. Trust only your own eyes and ears, or else the Gray Serpent will come for you, too.*

The words were meant for Conor. It was advice Kel had passed on, in the terrible days after the slaughter, when Conor did not sleep but only paced the floor in their apartments. When Kel had told him of Gremont's speech, a ghost of a smile had passed over Conor's face.

"Good enough advice," he'd said, "but I have already learned it. I place my trust in no one—save you, but then, you are my eyes and ears, are you not? Not my Counselor, or my friend, or even my brother. You are more like myself. And I will need you even more now. Not just to protect me, but also to look and to listen. To tell me what you see and hear."

And Kel had said nothing. He could not tell Conor he was lying to him, too—even if it was for his own good. Not then. Not now, either. He kept his silence and his counsel, telling himself that it was all for Conor's own good. That Conor would know the truth someday and forgive him for the betrayal.

"Oh, it's so good you're here," said Antonetta Alleyne, struggling to sit up against the massive pile of cushions that dominated her gilt-carved bed. "Did anyone but Magali see you come in?"

Lin Caster shook her head. She'd had a brief battle with Magali, the parlormaid, at the front door; Magali had been determined to relieve Lin of her coat and medical satchel, and Lin had refused to part with either. A silent struggle had ensued under the watchful eyes of what seemed to Lin at least two dozen portraits of past Alleynes.

Lin had never gotten used to the Alleyne house's interior. It was not grand and empty, the way House Roverge had once been, but rather stuffed full of *things:* landscape paintings, massive silver epergnes overflowing with silk flowers, gilt clocks, and marble busts of poets and playwrights past. Every bit of furniture that could have been gilded had been, and if it had not been gilded, it had been capped with white lace like a virgin bride.

The maid finally gave up her siege of Lin's belongings and led her up a gilded staircase to a long hall carpeted in knotted silk. As Lin ascended the stairs, she passed a dozen silver-framed mirrors that gave her back her reflection: her red hair coiled close to her head in braids, her simple dress of Ashkar gray, the worn leather satchel in her hands. She was certainly the plainest and most unadorned thing in the house.

She could not help but recall the first time Antonetta had summoned her. She had been surprised to receive the request, given the Alleyne family's exalted status, but Antonetta had been firm: She wished for weekly visits from Lin—absolute discretion required—and the visits *must* be at a specific hour and day. She had not said why, but in talking to Kel at the Black Mansion, Lin had come to understand it was the time of Lady Alleyne's weekly card game with the ladies of the Hill, which meant Antonetta's mother would most likely not be at home.

Lin had liked Antonetta Alleyne when she'd first met her—not surprising, since Antonetta had snuck her into the Palace under the watchful eye of the Castelguards—and had only come to like her more during their weekly meetings.

Antonetta was kind, if a little scattered. She seemed to Lin a rabbit among the jackals of the Hill. She actually required very little in the way of medical care. Usually they would spend a few hours together chatting and drinking one of Lin's medicinal teas. In Lin's opinion, Antonetta was paying for the company, not for the services of a physician.

She found Antonetta half lost among a massive influx of fabrics: Silks and satins in a rainbow of colors hung from dressing-rails and even the curtain rods at the windows. Every surface was piled with papers: menus, invitations, lists of items still needed. Antonetta herself was propped against a mound of silk pillows that formed a sort of barrier between her and the head of her bed, which had been carved into a pretty but uncomfortable-looking gilded rose.

If anything, Antonetta's room was less extreme in its decoration than the rest of the house. The walls were painted pale pink, like the inside of a seashell; silk flowers still cascaded from vases, and scroll-armed sofas were upholstered with fabric depicting pastoral scenes of shepherdesses and farmhouses. Still, there were *fewer* silk flowers, and no marble busts whatsoever.

Antonetta dismissed the maid with a brief, "Leave us, Magali," and gestured for Lin to lock the door behind her before approaching the bed. Antonetta's hair, down, was a riot of golden curls nearly the same color as the silk bedclothes. She wore a pale-blue dressing-gown with lace at the sleeves and a woebegone expression. "Have you anything for a headache brought on by the stress of planning for an engagement party you wish was not happening?" she inquired.

Lin sat down on the bed by Antonetta's feet and began rummaging through her satchel for an extraction of willowbark. She could not help but smile at the title of a leather-bound book that lay open on the covers nearby: *The Cold Heart of the Lonely King*.

"Is it still next week?" Lin said sympathetically. "It does seem like it's coming up awfully fast. And he hasn't even reached Castellane yet, has he?"

"His ship docks in five days," Antonetta said without enthusiasm. She looked hopefully at Lin. "Perhaps I could develop a mysterious illness, something that would prevent me from having to see him? At least for a month or two."

Lin handed the small sachet of willowbark tincture to Antonetta. "It would only be putting things off," she said. "I wish . . ." She left the rest of the sentence unfinished. She already knew that the man Antonetta was engaged to marry, Artal Gremont, not only was much older than her but had an unsavory reputation as well. Kel had hinted at doings so unpleasant that Gremont's family had been forced to send him away to foreign shores—and given the sort of misbehavior the nobility of Castellane got away with regularly, they must have been wretched doings indeed.

Lin worried, too, at how resigned Antonetta seemed about the whole situation. It was something her mother had arranged; Antonetta had had no say in it, and there was, she insisted, nothing she could do to change her mother's mind. Lin knew all Antonetta had wanted was to remain single and hold the silk Charter herself, as her mother did. But Liorada Alleyne, it seemed, did not trust her daughter: She had told Antonetta that unless she agreed to marry and carry on the Alleyne bloodline, she would leave the Charter, and all the power that came with it, to a distant cousin, cutting her own daughter out completely. Now Antonetta's hope seemed pinned on the possibility that Gremont was as unenthused about the marriage as she was and would leave her mostly alone, allowing her to lead the life of a wealthy lady of the Hill without too much interference.

"I hope he either already has a mistress or takes one soon," Antonetta said now. "If he was very attached to her, he might hardly bother me at all." She looked at Lin. "Do you think it's possible?"

"Unfortunately, how to convince one's husband to take a lover is outside my experience," Lin said with a wry smile. "Take that and put it under your tongue."

"You *are* demanding," Antonetta said. "At least after I'm married, I'll still be able to see you. I can't imagine what kind of man wouldn't let his wife visit a physician."

"I suppose the kind who might be planning to hurt her himself," Lin said carefully. She had treated many such women, who insisted their injuries came from their own clumsiness, though they were well aware Lin knew better.

Antonetta snorted. "Gremont wouldn't lay a finger on me if he wanted to stay in Castellane," she said. "Assaulting a noblewoman is punishable by exile—even if the attacker is her husband."

If only the ordinary women of Castellane had such protection, Lin mused, but she pushed down the thought. Better that some women were protected than that none were.

Hoping to change the subject, Lin pointed at the book lying open on the bed. "Is that any good?" she said. "It sounds like a Story-Spinner's tale."

"It's about Prince Conor," Antonetta said with a sideways smile. "Most of the Story-Spinners' tales are, you know."

Lin felt herself going red. She always did when the Prince of Castellane was mentioned; it was very inconvenient. She began rummaging through her satchel. "Surely not all of them."

"Oh, yes," said Antonetta. "*The Seven Skeletons of the Prince's Seven Brides, The Prince with a Heart of Ice and a Crown of Gold, The Prince in Silk and the Lady in Rags*, and *The Naughty Prince's Cruel Laws—*"

"Those titles seem very long," Lin observed.

Antonetta shrugged. "Everyone likes a Prince, especially when he's unmarried." She idly examined her nails. "Though he won't be unmarried very much longer."

Lin couldn't help but look up at that. "What do you mean?"

"Conor is entering into an engagement," said Antonetta, watching Lin's face closely. "It's all been arranged. He is to wed Anjelica of Kutani."

There seemed to be a rushing noise in Lin's ears. She could not help but think of the last time she had seen the Prince, in his carriage outside the Sault. Of the last words he'd said to her. *Then I am cursed to think only of you. You, who think I am a loathsome person. A vain monster who could not resist showing off and who, in doing so, has made you wretched.*

She had never had a chance to reconsider those words. Certainly not a chance to tell him she did not think he was a monster. That evening, *it* had happened—the massacre. The Shining Gallery slaughter. The Great Betrayal. There were all sorts of names for the attack on Marivent that night—the night Lin had declared herself the Goddess Returned and the Roverge ships had burned in the harbor. She had woken up the next morning to see black flags flying from the parapets of Marivent, had heard the dirge-bells ringing out across the city, and had thought that it somehow had something to do with *her*—with her crime, her great lie.

I am the Goddess Returned.

But of course it was not that. Mayesh had come to her house, his face like a skull's, seeming to have aged another ten years overnight. He had looked at her and said, his voice weary with strain, "A bloodbath at the Palace. And now this." He had not sounded angry, even. Only very tired.

She had made him *karak* and forced him to tell her what had happened—the attack, the death of the little Princess from Sarthe, what this would mean for Castellane—and all the time she had held herself back from asking: *Has he been hurt? IS HE HURT? Is the Prince all right?*

She had no right to ask. No right to be worried about Kel, either, though she had been. She had put her hands under the table, to hide that they were shaking, until he was done with the story.

"We cannot afford war," he'd said, and she'd realized he was talking not about Castellane but about them, the Ashkar. "If Castellane is attacked from outside, it will become a passion to purify that which is inside. They will begin to ask themselves: *Who are they, these Ashkar, who are among us but not of us? Where do their loyalties lie?*"

"They won't. You've done so much, *zai*. So many gains made, even in the last twenty years—"

He'd looked at her then, his eyes hard. "Do you say that as my granddaughter Lin or as the Goddess Returned?"

She swallowed hard. "I could tell you—"

"Don't," he'd said. "I don't know what you hope to gain from all this, but don't tell me. It is better if I do not know."

She had known then that though he and the Maharam might detest each other, they were in agreement on one point: Lin Caster was not the Goddess Returned, and no good would come of her saying she was.

"Lin," said Antonetta fretfully, "what *are* you thinking about?" She leaned closer. "Does the news about Conor . . . bother you?"

"I once treated a man with an awl through his head," Lin said. "I do not bother easily."

"Good, because I would like to ask you to do something unpleasant."

"What sort of unpleasant?"

"I would like you to come to my engagement party—"

"Oh, no," Lin said, recoiling. "No more parties on the Hill. The last one—"

"I heard you danced very well," said Antonetta. Lin gave her a hard look, but Antonetta's eyes were wide and innocent. "I need someone there who is sympathetic, Lin. Please. Someone who is on my side."

"What about Kellian?" Lin asked. "Won't he be there?"

It was Antonetta's turn to look away. "Well, yes, but he will be in attendance on the Prince. Conor likes his friends around him at parties."

Of course, Lin realized. Conor would be at the engagement party. A small part of her shrank from the idea of seeing him, but a greater part whispered: *Go. Go and face him. Soon enough you will face the Exilarch and the Sanhedrin. You must not be thinking of the Prince of Castellane when you do. See him one last time and put him behind you.*

"Please," Antonetta said again. "I will lend you any of my dresses. Whichever one you like. You will look absolutely stunning."

And it will be easier to put the Prince behind you while armored in a glorious dress, Lin thought. "Oh, well, if you truly need me, Ana," she said with a reluctant smile, "I will certainly go."

ALL THAT IS GOOD COMES FROM THE GODS. ALL THAT IS EVIL COMES FROM MEN.

Kel could not help but stare at the words picked out in gold tesserae across the interior of the domed ceiling of the Dial Chamber. They seemed to carry a sinister weight they had not conveyed three months ago, the last time the heads of the Great Charters of Castellane had met together in this place.

He was not sure precisely why. In the end, Conor's announcement went over rather better than Kel had expected. At first, voices had risen in protest after Conor gave the news of his engagement. Kel could hear snatches of conversation, objections—*it was a marriage that got us into this in the first place*—and complaints about not being consulted. Conor sat patiently—patience, like a new coat, sitting awkwardly on his shoulders—until the noise died down.

He said, "Our new partner knows of the situation with Sarthe. They have pledged a dowry of one hundred thousand crowns, and the use of their fleets in case of war. They have ten thousand warships. Sarthe has none; they would have to beg, borrow, or steal the use of them, and if they chose to do so, they would find our harbor full of ships ready to blast them to Hell."

His eyes were narrowed to silver slits, and Kel could not help but think how much care had been put into the preparation for this moment. Sleepless nights considering whether this was the right thing to do. Consultations with Mayesh, hours spent locked in the North Tower with the Counselor and Legate and those maps, endless maps with pins in them. Every pin an army. And for every pin representing the armies of Castellane, ten more representing the armies of Sarthe.

In the end, there had been no real question.

It was Cazalet who spoke first. As it should be, Kel thought; the other families took their cues from him. "An admirable decision, Monseigneur," he said, "and one clearly made with the benefit of Castellane in mind."

If a fuss had been brewing, it subsided. Ciprian Cabrol looked genuinely pleased. "Brilliant stuff," he said. "Sarthe cannot stand against such combined forces. They dare not even try."

Even Lady Alleyne had accepted it gracefully. After all, Antonetta was engaged; Liorada had no further hopes of marrying her to Conor. She had abandoned her dream that her daughter might be royalty and accepted that it was likely she would only be very, very rich.

Kel had half hoped that Antonetta would be at the meeting, but she was not. He had seen her only a little since her engagement had been announced, only a week after the Shining Gallery murders. She had not come to the Palace at all, and when he had seen her at House Cabrol one night, she had only smiled very brilliantly and said that the wedding required a lot of preparations. She was much busier than she had imagined, and did he think that it would be a problem to have pink roses on the altar, because pink roses were her favorite but in the Castellani language of flowers they suggested impermanence of affection?

He had only just managed to get away without saying something he shouldn't. He could still remember her, months ago, begging him to do something to stop the marriage—but he had been wearing his talisman at the time. She had thought he was Conor. Which meant that Kel was not supposed to know she had—at first—not wished for this engagement; he could not mention the fact without betraying his Sword Catcher vows.

Suddenly, he found he was desperate to get out of the Dial Chamber and into the fresh air. The meeting over, several of the Charter holders were clamoring around Conor. Between the heaving shoulders of those trying to get close to the Prince, Kel could see only the bright splash of his red velvet cloak and the wink of the ruby in his crown.

A movement near the door caught his attention. Legate Jolivet, the leader of the royal guard. His hair seemed to have grown grayer since the Shining Gallery, his profile more angularly hawkish. He had said very little during the meeting, though he had been intimately involved with every decision the Prince had made over the past months.

In the chaotic days after the slaughter of the Sarthian Princess, along with her bodyguard and ambassadors, Marivent had waited breathlessly for word from Sarthe. To show good faith, it was Jolivet who suggested they send a message to Sarthe immediately, detailing what had happened—truthfully, he had emphasized; the tale of what had occurred would be everywhere soon enough, and the King in Aquila would soon discover any lie. The only untruth had not been in the words, but in the implication that the King had penned the message himself. Conor had done it, and then signed his father's name.

When the reply arrived, it was terse and cold. Writing from his palace in Aquila, King Leandro d'Eon said that Sarthe had sent its Princess in good faith. That calamity had befallen her at Marivent was the fault of Castellane. To prevent war, an honor price must be paid.

He named a figure of one million crowns. Even Mayesh's expression had changed at that. "He can't be serious," he'd said. "One could sell all of Castellane and not raise that much. No country save perhaps Kutani could part with that much gold and survive."

"D'Eon is saying he wants war," Conor had said wearily. "He is offering a way out, but it is not a real offer."

"Or a real way out," Jolivet had said. He had looked around the room at them all, his expression imperturbable as always. "We will not pay. We will find another road."

And so they had, though Jolivet did not seem overjoyed at the plan's apparent success. He jerked his chin at Kel, indicating that Kel should follow him out of the room, and left.

Kel slipped away through the crowd. Outside the Star Tower, it was a hot, bright midday. A haze hung over the city that fell away below the Hill, turning the ocean to a distant green smudge.

He found Jolivet standing in the shade of the wall that surrounded the Queen's Garden. He wore a flat expression along with his Lion Ring and the gold braid on his uniform. When Kel drew close, he said in a low voice, "I suppose you will be taking the news of this meeting to the mansion."

"I see no reason to conceal it," said Kel. "The city will know soon enough, and the Ragpicker King before anyone else."

Jolivet grunted and crossed his arms. "I suppose you and your friends have made no further progress."

Kel bit off an annoyed retort. Of all the people in Castellane, he certainly would not have chosen Legate Jolivet to be the only one outside the Black Mansion to know his secret. But he'd had no choice in the matter. Jolivet had nearly ordered him to throw in his lot with the Ragpicker King in the hope of finding out who had orchestrated the Shining Gallery murders.

Kel belonged to the Palace; he was Palace property. If Jolivet ordered him to do something, it would have been in the nature of a small insurrection to refuse. He could have gone to Conor, but in his heart he was in agreement with the Legate. Whoever had executed the attack on the Gallery had a bigger target in their sights than the visiting Sarthians.

Kel had followed one of the assassins out of the Gallery, trapping them on the roof. He still recalled what the black-clad figure—face and body entirely hidden, identity unguessable—had hissed at him as he stood, incredulous, sword in hand.

You stand upon the threshold of history, Sword Catcher. For this is the beginning of the fall of House Aurelian.

Conor was the only child of a King who was himself the only survivor of three sons. If the line of Aurelian was to end, it meant Conor's death. And Kel was sworn to prevent that. Even if it meant following the orders of Jolivet to keep his activities a secret. Even if it meant joining forces with the Ragpicker King—the biggest criminal in Castellane.

"Progress is slow," Kel said. "We are chasing ghosts. No one seems to know anything of the attackers. Thirty men must have died that night, yet there have been no whispers of anyone missing. And the Ragpicker King has access to many whispers."

Jolivet grunted again. "Nothing happens with no warning," he said. "Only the warnings may not take the form you imagine. Anything unusual or amiss in the city is worth noting." He glanced toward the door of the tower; Ciprian Cabrol, Joss Falconet, and Lupin Montfaucon had emerged and were walking in their direction along the path of crushed stones, their heads bent together as they spoke.

"Cabrol," Jolivet muttered in his gravelly voice. "What d'you think of him?"

Kel hesitated a moment before replying, watching the three men as they slowly drew closer. Against the white backdrop of Marivent's towers, they resembled birds of bright plumage. Montfaucon was elaborately dressed as always, in trousers and a doublet of bright yellow, like a golden oriole. Joss wore a suit of cardinal red, embossed with a stitched design of coppery serpents. Beside him, Cabrol was the most plain of the three, in dark gray, though his tunic had a kingfisher-blue underlining that flashed when his sleeves fell back as he gestured.

"Hard to trust him," Kel said quietly, "after the way he gained the dye Charter."

Until three months ago, the dye Charter of Castellane had belonged to the family Roverge, whose son, Charlon, had been one of Conor's close friends, along with Joss and Lupin. On the night of the Shining Gallery slaughter, the whole of the Roverge fleet had burned in the harbor, wiping out their fortune. Within days they were gone from the Hill, taking only a few belongings; the rest of what they had would be sold to pay down their vast debts. The Charter itself belonged to the crown and the Council, and was given over to a family chosen by Cazalet (and approved by the King in theory; Conor, in reality): the Cabrols, prominent ink merchants in the city.

There were three in the family: Ciprian, the eldest son; Beatris, his sister; and his elderly mother, who had been little-seen since the changeover of power. Ciprian was arrogant and good-looking, and he seemed to have entirely expected to be handed the reins to one of Castellane's most profitable Charters.

And perhaps he had reason. After talking to Lin about the destroyed fleet, Kel had cornered Mayesh in the North Tower. "We are all aware that the Cabrol family burned the Roverge ships, aren't we?"

"Oh, yes," Mayesh had said. He'd been studying a map of Sarthe. It was studded with different colored pins, though Kel could not make out their code. "It is an open secret, Kellian."

"And nothing will be done?"

"The Roverge family had many enemies." Mayesh moved a pin. "They threatened and intimidated anyone they saw as rivals; the Cabrol family was only the most recent of their victims, and the first to have fought back. Their behavior would likely have landed them in the Trick if they had been other than who they were. Many on the Hill and among the merchant guilds consider this Benedict's comeuppance." He looked curiously at Kel. "How did you *think* Charter seats changed hands?"

"Not like this," Kel had said. He'd thought of the harbor on the night of the fires, of the sea full of dye, of waves that broke in foam colored in yellow and scarlet, turquoise and violet. For days after, the smoke had hung in the air over Castellane, turning the sunsets into painterly displays of wine red and gold. A victory banner for the Cabrols. "They may have their power now, but it will matter how they got it. It always does, in the long run."

Mayesh had smiled a little at that. "An astute observation, Kel. You have identified one reason that nobles are not constantly blowing up one another's ships for Charter seats."

"Is there another reason?"

"Black powder is expensive," Mayesh had said, chuckling, and gone back to his map.

"Anjuman!" Joss called out. He was grinning his usual easy, lazy grin. "I suppose you already knew Conor's big news, eh? No wonder you looked half asleep the whole meeting. No surprises for you."

Kel made a mental note to adjust his *listening calmly but with interest* expression. Clearly it was not conveying what he had hoped. "I knew, yes. It was no simple decision for Conor. He has wrestled with it."

"Indeed," said Montfaucon with a chuckle. The yellow of his suit was almost alarmingly bright against his dark skin. "He barely escaped the manacles of matrimony once. Now he willingly walks back into the prison."

"Conor rarely just walks anywhere," observed Joss. "I would say he is striding back into the prison with purpose aplenty." He turned to Jolivet. "Would you agree, Legate?"

Jolivet muttered something about needing to review his troops and slipped away.

Cabrol looked after him with a raised eyebrow. "A lighthearted individual," he said dryly. He had unusual coloring: dark eyes and hair the color of Castellane's red roof tiles. "I have usually found soldiers to be good company in a tavern, but I would say the Legate is an exception."

"Soldiers can be good company when off duty," said Kel, wondering why he was about to defend Jolivet, but unable to help it. "Arguably, Jolivet is never off duty."

Cabrol transferred his raised eyebrow to Kel. "I suppose that's true. One certainly cannot doubt his loyalty to the city or the crown. Or Conor's," he added. "He is clearly marrying for the good of Castellane. And he will be sure to earn the gratitude of the people for it. Even those of us on the Hill."

His voice was smooth, his tone light. Kel did not trust him for a moment.

"Gratitude." Montfaucon waved away the concept as boring. "Listen, Anjuman, I'm having a gathering at the Caravel tonight. Liquor and hourglasses on me. Bring our young Prince along with you. He needs to have a bit of fun."

"Indeed, and not much time to have it in," Joss said, laughing. "Besides, he's been working himself to death since—" He broke off, a little awkwardly, which was unusual for Joss. He was rarely awkward. "Well, for the past few months. He deserves to enjoy himself a bit."

"I'll tell him about tonight, Lupin," Kel said. He realized he could not recall the last time Conor had gone to the pleasure houses of the Temple District—with his friends or without them.

Montfaucon pointed a white-gloved finger at him. "Tell him it's important," he said. "There's someone I wish him to meet."

Joss, having regained his composure, slapped Montfaucon on the back. "Montfaucon's infatuated with a new lover," he said. "Been very secretive about him. Won't even tell us his name."

Montfaucon shrugged, though he was clearly pleased with himself. "I told you, he goes by his Arena name. The Gray Serpent."

Cabrol laughed and said something about how surely Montfaucon could not reasonably, in the throes of passion, be expected to call his lover "the Gray Serpent," but Kel barely heard him. Too shocked to speak, he stood where he was, motionless, staring into the past.

Marcel

On Anchor Street in the Maze, almost up against the walls of the Sault, stands a temple over whose front doors have been carved a frieze of dancing skeletons. It had once been the fashion to worship Anibal, the God of death, and it was to this purpose that the temple had been dedicated long ago, when the area that was now the crime-riddled Maze had been swampland and shacks. A million black-clad worshippers had worn down the wide front steps with their comings and goings over the years, even as worshipping the death God fell out of popularity and those who prayed to him began to be looked upon with suspicion.

Finally, when worshippers stopped coming in earnest, the Hierophant, chief priest of the city, had padlocked the doors, covered the windows, and declared the temple closed to the citizens of Castellane. The place is not a ruin, though; fear of Anibal and his wrath has kept vandals away.

Marcel Sandoz, professional drunkard and poppy-juice addict, often drowses on the steps of the old temple. Superstition means that few bother him here, even in the small hours of the night. Lost in his usual colorful, poppy-addled dreams, he is imagining himself in a meadow surrounded by laughing girls in bright silk dresses when he hears the strangers approach.

He blinks his eyes open, wincing at even the dim light. Perhaps the noise was part of his dream, he thinks, or perhaps he heard the Shomrim calling to one another on the Sault walls. But the hard ache in his head and the cold stink of the stone beneath him soon dispel that notion. This is reality, and the footsteps are only growing louder.

On hands and knees, he crawls up the last steps to the portico, where he hides behind a column of chipped marble. Vigilants, he guesses. They were always hurrying him along as soon as he found a comfortable place to sleep. But as three shadowy figures ascend the temple steps, a chill runs down his spine. They aren't wearing the usual Vigilant uniforms of red and yellow. Instead, they are dressed all in black as though they mean to disappear into the night.

One of the figures—a man whose shaved head gleams in the moonlight—speaks in a language that is not soft like Castellani, but full of hard edges and grunts. Strange, Marcel thinks. Travelers from Malgasi are rare. It is a secretive kingdom, east of Sarthe, about which dark rumors swirl. "*Cza vayuslam. Vaino sedanto anla.*"

In a cold voice, the slimmest of the figures—a woman—says, "Bagomer, remember what I told you. You need to practice your Castellani."

Thickly, the bald man says, "I was just saying, my lady, that the temple is unused. No one will bother us here."

"It's quite grim, isn't it," she says, sounding pleased. Marcel is able to see what she wears now—a close-fitting suit of all black, tight as a snake's skin, as if she has been painted with black oil. A hood covers her hair, but the face that looks out from the darkness is as pale and bony as the skulls of the dancing skeletons above. "Janos," she snaps at the second man, across whose face a wicked scar leaves a puckered line. "Get a message to Artal Gremont.

Tell him that the Princess of Malgasi, heir to the Belmany throne, has arrived in his city. That should bring him running."

As Janos nods and melts away into the night, Marcel feels a terrible fear grip him. Princess of Malgasi? If there is one thing he knows after living most of his life in Castellane, it is that no sensible citizen wishes to get caught up in the affairs of royals. Not ever.

Belly-down like a snake, he begins to wriggle away across the portico. Unfortunately for him, his bare, dirty foot collides with an empty bottle lying in a drift of garbage. It rolls across the marble with a scraping sound.

Marcel lumbers to his feet; he means to run, but his heavy legs will not obey. He sees the two figures on the steps glance up at him. Sees the face of the woman—the Malgasi Princess—twist in annoyance.

A great, invisible hand seems to seize him and catch him up. He thrashes, but to no avail. He is flung down on his back, the cracked marble of the steps biting into his spine. As he stares up in terror, the figure of the Malgasi Princess looms over him, a cruel smile twisting her predatory features. "Look at this, Bagomer," she says. "A little Castellani mouse."

The man behind her on the steps grunts again. "Get rid of him," he says. "Before anyone sees."

There is blood in Marcel's mouth. He sputters around the copper of it, tries to push himself up on his elbows. "Don't hurt me, please. Please. I'll go. I won't tell the Vigilants nothing—"

"No," the Princess says with an almost dreamy look. "You won't."

The last thing that Marcel ever sees might well have been a vision out of one of his poppy-juice dreams, all color and fire and danger. The foreign Princess holds her hand up, palm out, and from the center of it comes a bolt of flame: gold and red and bronze at the edges. *Magic,* Marcel thinks, and barely has time to gape at the beauty and the surprise of it before he is charred away to ash.

CHAPTER TWO

I keep telling you," said Jerrod, "use the edges of your feet, not the points of your toes. You're Crawling, not dancing."

Kel glanced down in order to glare at Jerrod and immediately felt a little sick. He'd never realized before he started Crawler training—learning to shimmy up and down walls with only the barest of hand- and footholds—how much heights bothered him.

It had never really come up before Jerrod had gone to work for the Ragpicker King and offered to teach any of his current team— Kel, Merren Asper, and Kang Ji-An—his Crawling skills.

Only Kel had taken him up on it, which was somewhat ironic. On the face of it, Kel had less reason than his friends to trust Jerrod Belmerci, who—when he had worked for Prosper Beck—had once ambushed Kel in an alleyway. They had papered over their differences, though, and it had been Merren and Ji-An who had been stiff with Jerrod at first. Their loyalty to Andreyen was paramount, and Beck had been a threat to the Ragpicker King until he had abruptly departed Castellane, leaving Jerrod unemployed.

It was Andreyen who had calmed their doubts, assuring them that Jerrod would be more of a useful asset than he would a drawback. He had even ordered the construction of a model climbing wall, made of smooth granite with irregular indentations, which was installed into the solarium. (Jerrod had suggested they construct the climbing wall above the interior river, feeling the crocodiles would give Kel additional incentive not to fall, but Andreyen had nixed that idea. "Those crocodiles are expensive," he had said, "and eating Kel would certainly give them indigestion.")

"And don't look *down*," Jerrod now said. "I've told you before never to look down. And don't look sideways. Or up," he added. "Don't look for the handholds. Feel for them."

Glaring directly in front of himself, Kel adjusted his position. When he'd arrived at the Black Mansion and found Andreyen closeted in a meeting, Jerrod had suggested they get in some Crawling practice. Kel, still antsy from the Dial Chamber meeting and with the words *the Gray Serpent* echoing in his head, had agreed—though he was beginning to regret it now.

Crawling required all one's concentration, so he'd hoped it would calm him. When he was a boy in the Orfelinat, clambering up rocks with Cas, he'd dreamed of one day being a Crawler. It had seemed the peak of what a Castellani orphan could achieve: perhaps not a mastery over one's own life, but at least a mastery over the city's vertiginous peaks—its sloping roofs and towers, its arches and high windows.

He missed a foothold now, slipped a little, and swore. It was one thing to feel for a handhold with well-chalked fingers and another entirely to try to wedge one's shoe against a vertical wall—

"Lean *into* the wall," Jerrod called, sounding exasperated. "Visualize it below you— Oh, hello," he added in an entirely different tone. "Meeting's over, I take it?"

Kel couldn't help himself; he looked down. The floor of the solarium seemed to blur under him, and he slid halfway down the wall before he was able to arrest his fall with an ungraceful scrabbling at the nearly featureless surface. *Embarrassing.*

He dropped the rest of the way, landing nearly on top of Jerrod, who ignored him. He was looking at the Ragpicker King, who had just come into the room, flanked by Ji-An and Merren. Ji-An wore her usual silk jacket and trousers, embroidered with peonies. Her black hair was gathered up on her head, held in place by a copper clip. Beside her, Merren looked the student he was in faded black, his blond hair bright as Antonetta Alleyne's.

Kel pushed the thought of Antonetta to the back of his head. He noticed that Jerrod did not seem to be looking at Andreyen so much as staring at Merren—though Merren was, as usual, oblivious.

"What happens if you fall all the way from the top?" Merren inquired, craning his head back to look at the full height of the climbing wall. "Is there some special way Crawlers learn how to land so they don't break their legs?"

"No," said Jerrod. "He'd just break his legs. That's why I'm trying to teach him not to fall."

"Do try not to break him while he's still useful," said Andreyen. The Ragpicker King's green eyes gleamed in the solarium shadows. "I assume you are here to tell us of the Dial Chamber meeting, Kellian?"

Kel tried to brush the chalk from his fingers. Ji-An was glaring at Jerrod, which she always did. He had worked for the Ragpicker King for three months now, gathering intelligence from all over Castellane—even deep in the Maze—but Ji-An still did not trust him.

Jerrod didn't seem to mind—though it was hard to tell when things bothered him. Half his face was covered with a hammered-steel mask. Now that he kept his head bare around Kel and the others, it was easier to see the thin scars that unspooled like thread from beneath his mask, marring his temples and cheekbones. Kel wondered often what could have made such a wound as the one Jerrod Belmerci was hiding.

"Yes," Kel said, having gotten off as much of the chalk as he could. His fingers still felt unpleasantly dry. "But there is something else I have to tell you—"

The words *the Gray Serpent* were on his tongue, but Andreyen held up a hand. "Go in order, please," he said. "The meeting, from beginning to end."

Kel sighed inwardly but did as requested. As they all took seats on the stone benches surrounding an ornamental pond, he ran through the events of the Dial Chamber meeting: the nervous attendees, Conor's announcement, the reactions of the Charter Families.

"Your Prince is marrying again?" Jerrod raised his eyebrows. "I suppose nobody brought up how well that plan went the last time."

"Actually, Montfaucon did, since he has no tact," said Kel. "But the situation is different from last time. Now it is a matter of preventing war, and both the Queen and Bensimon agree it is the best course. If anyone wasn't truly relieved, they did a good job of acting."

"Surely they did not need to act. No one profits from war," said Merren.

"Not true," said Andreyen. "*Someone* always profits from war. Still." He sat back. "Kutani is the richest country in the world. They will have more than enough gold to pay any blood price Sarthe is demanding, or for an army to hold off Sarthe if that is what it comes to. I am impressed that Bensimon and the Queen were able to secure such an alliance."

"Conor did a great deal of the negotiating himself," said Kel, and when everyone looked at him sideways, he added defensively, "I've told you. He's changed."

Ji-An had taken a pack of cards from her pocket. She spread them out on the stone table beside the pond. "I have seen Anjelica of Kutani," she said, to Kel's surprise. "At the Court in Geumjoseon. It was an official visit. She is . . . beautiful." She looked down at the cards, then placed the Lion atop the Weeping Girl. "So beautiful that it is almost too much. Prince Hui, all he wanted was to marry her. He would have done anything, I think. His father forbade it. He said such beauty could only cause trouble."

"It is curious," said Andreyen, resting his chin atop the head of his cane. "Anjelica of Kutani should have her pick of any suitor. Why our rather troubled Prince?"

Kel felt himself stiffen. The observation cut too close to questions he himself had; Conor had not shared the details of the arrangement, and he had not asked. "I do not know what Castellane is offering Kutani," he said. "It must be something they believe they cannot get elsewhere."

"Despite the Prince, Castellane remains a valuable ally," Ji-An pointed out. "Especially for a trade-dependent country like Kutani."

"Malgasi will be angry," said Merren. A leaf had caught in his curling hair. He reached up to free it, and Jerrod's eyes followed his movement. "Did they not want Aurelian to marry their Princess? Now he is to marry once more—and once again, not to Elsabet Belmany."

Kel spread his hands wide. "Officially, Bensimon would tell you that Conor wedding a Princess of Malgasi would pin Sarthe between two allied countries. They might feel threatened, perhaps even need to go to war."

"And unofficially?" asked Ji-An, crossing the Prince of Swords with the Dark Widow.

"Unofficially? Conor despises the Belmany family. Not only because they are dishonest in their dealings, but specifically because of the way they have tormented and murdered their Ashkar."

"That's interesting," Andreyen murmured. "There are few royals out there who would care much about the Ashkar. I suppose Mayesh is doing his job."

"Imagine Conor Aurelian having a moral qualm," wondered Merren. "I always thought of him as qualmless."

"I don't think that's a word," said Kel. "Also, it's practical as well as moral. Not only are the Malgasi royal family unpleasant on the face of it, but their subjects seem to have noticed. Jolivet's sources tell him a revolution could take place any day."

"As an anti-monarchist, I am technically in favor of revolution," noted Merren.

Kel smiled but could not forget King Markus hissing at the Malgasi Ambassador: *You would cage your son as you caged me!* A dark current ran between the courts of Malgasi and Castellane, a history of blood and secrets that were locked away in the mind of the now-silent King.

"What of our friend the Legate?" said Andreyen. There was a little edge to his voice; the Ragpicker King understood that the arrangement with Jolivet was a necessary one, but Jolivet represented one side of the Law and Andreyen very much the other. He would never really consider the Legate a friend. "I assume he was at the meeting. Has he any insights for us, or directives?"

Kel shook his head. "He is impatient," he said. "The Arrow Squadron has interrogated everyone in the city they can find who had a grudge against Sarthe. They have learned nothing."

"And so he leans on you?" The edge was still in Andreyen's voice. "Is he not worried that if he leans too hard, you will break?"

Kel could not help but remember something Andreyen had said to him earlier, when they had been alone. *I fear you cannot hold all conflicting things within yourself. Being a Sword Catcher, and also this.*

Kel only shrugged. "Jolivet seems to feel we should know more than we do at this juncture—"

"Oh, he thinks it's easy, does he?" said Ji-An. "Having us do his job for him?" She shook her head. "No one in Castellane is talking. Not to the Hill, and not to us, either. There are no clues—"

"Well," said Kel. "As to that. Montfaucon is hosting a gathering at the Caravel tonight." Merren glanced over; his sister, Alys Asper, owned and ran the Caravel.

"And?" said Jerrod. "Shall we all go drown our sorrows with the dissolute nobility?"

"I doubt that would be as much fun as you think," said Kel. "Anyway, Montfaucon invited us all there expressly to meet his newest lover, someone known as the Gray Serpent."

"The Gray Serpent," Andreyen murmured. "Gremont's last words?"

Kel nodded.

"You think the Gray Serpent is a person now? Not a metaphor? Not the snake-headed boatman of the tales?" asked Andreyen.

"The Dark Guide," said Merren. "He ferries souls into the underworld."

"Gremont spoke with such urgency," said Kel. "I have long wondered why he would waste his last breath reminding me of a fable. But perhaps it was no fable. Which means I will be at the Caravel tonight."

"Does that mean you will be attending with the Prince?" inquired Jerrod. "Or *as* him?"

"Neither," Kel said shortly. He always said as little about Conor as he could get away with. He was not here to report on the Palace, and even if Conor would never know it, even if it might never matter, keeping Conor out of the discussion as much as possible felt less like a betrayal. "I'll be there as Kel Anjuman. If this Gray Serpent is a person, then I'll follow him, see what he does."

"I don't like Alys being near to all this," said Merren, frowning. "I should tell her—"

"Tell her what?" asked Jerrod. "That you believe Lord Montfaucon might know someone involved in the attack on Marivent? Telling her that will bring her closer to danger than telling her nothing."

Merren set his jaw in a stubborn line. "I still want to be there tonight."

"You shall be," said Andreyen. "And *you*"—he indicated Jerrod and Ji-An—"will go with him."

"Do we have to wear disguises? I hate disguises," said Merren glumly.

"No," said Andreyen. "You needn't wear one. You should remain outside the Caravel—"

"Merren could be a courtesan. He's attractive enough," said Jerrod absently.

"I just said he didn't need to wear a disguise; pay attention, Jerrod," said Andreyen, not without a flicker of amusement. "You three stay with the carriage, where Kel can signal if he needs you. Ji-An can drive."

"I disagree," said Jerrod.

Ji-An shot him a dark look.

"Well, if you change your mind and decide you need costumes this evening," said Kel, "I may have a pirate's hat I saved from the Queen's last nautically themed ball. Jerrod, let me know if you need it."

Jerrod glared at him darkly. Merren said, "Kel, at the Dial Chamber meeting . . . was there any mention of Artal Gremont's planned arrival?"

Kel shook his head. "He's still at sea. Literally, I mean, not figuratively."

"He is cutting it rather close, isn't he," said Merren, "if he plans to marry your friend Antonetta before the end of the month?"

"Merren." Kel tried to catch his friend's eye, but Merren was looking studiously in the other direction. "Are you still planning on killing Gremont in revenge?"

Merren blinked rapidly. "I have not made what you might call a concrete plan. I prefer spontaneity."

Jerrod looked worried. "Merren, Artal Gremont is very well connected. He's about to be a Charter holder, which is as close to being royalty as you can get without being royalty."

"Ah, yes," Merren said with an uncharacteristic bitterness. "He destroys my family and is rewarded with a Charter. It couldn't have gone to some other Gremont?"

"It seems his mother is bestowing it upon him as a method of getting him out of exile," said Andreyen.

"Be that as it may," said Jerrod. "Merren, murdering him would put you in a great deal of danger." He looked at Kel. "Tell him, won't you?"

"I think Merren is a careful person," said Kel. "And Gremont does not deserve better."

"Thank you," Merren said, looking gratified.

"Is that really what you think?" said Jerrod, looking annoyed. "Or do you just want Antonetta Alleyne's future husband dead?"

Kel smiled tightly. "Why must it be one or the other?" He turned to Merren. "Do what you think you must," he said. "Though it would be better if I knew none of the details."

Ji-An raised an eyebrow. "Because then you'd have to keep secrets from Antonetta Alleyne, and that troubles you?"

"Why would that trouble me?" said Kel, feeling very tired indeed. "I keep secrets from everyone."

It was always a test, going through the gates, Lin thought. Not a test of herself, but a test of the Sault and its mood toward her: the Goddess Returned they had not expected, had not—in many of their minds—truly asked for.

Two guards were at the gate today: her old friend Mez and Adar Gamel, one of the younger Shomrim. He had just turned eighteen, the age when he could begin his guardian duties, and was still gangly as a new colt. He did not like Lin and did not bother hiding it.

"Greetings, *Goddess*," he said as she passed, infusing the word with mockery. Mez smiled at Lin, clearly embarrassed by his companion's tone.

"Lin," he said. "Out visiting a patient? Is all well?"

"Very well, Mez."

"The Maharam wants to see you. He said to let you know when you returned."

He gave a half-apologetic shrug as if to say he had no idea what this summons was about. Lin did not doubt this was true. She smiled at Mez and, ignoring Adar's glare, swept through the gate, cutting across the Sault toward the Etse Kebeth. She did not hurry away, not wanting to show any outward sign of distress. Inwardly, her stomach felt knotted up like rope.

She still remembered the night it had happened—her announcement, the flaming of the ships in the harbor like stars exploding. There had not been doubters that night, save her grandfather, but time had passed and things had changed in the walled city.

Mez and Adar seemed to sum up the divided opinion of the Sault. Some believed her to be the Goddess or thought she should at least be given the chance to prove herself. Others felt it was clear she was lying. They did not say so to her face, but the whispers ran through the streets like poison: What second miracle had she performed, since that first one? And why, of all the Ashkar women in the world, would the Goddess have chosen *Lin Caster* to herald her return?

As she cut across the Kathot, she saw Arelle Dorin sitting on a stone bench, surrounded by other young women. Lin gave them a wide berth. The last time she'd met Arelle alone in the street, the other girl—whom Lin had known all her life—had looked at her coldly and said, "The Sanhedrin's coming soon enough. Enjoy this while you can."

She was right, too, Lin thought. Not that she was enjoying this, but that the Sanhedrin were coming. It was something she tried not to think about. She had the time she had, and access to the Shulamat during that. She could not think about the future.

In the meantime, Lin occupied a liminal space: not quite the Goddess Returned, but not her old self, either. She was now allowed access to the Shulamat, to the books and tools she needed for her studies. She came and went with little questioning. She continued to see her patients, for had the Goddess not been a healer? She had her defenders: Chana, Mariam, Mez. One day, she had opened her door in the Sault to discover a silver bowl on her threshold. It was inscribed with the words of a spell meant to ward off the *shedin* and *lilin*, evil spirits who sickened babies and snatched old people from their beds. She was not sure if it had been placed there to protect her or to protect others *from* her.

Either way, it was doing nothing to keep away the dreams that had haunted her for months now. Strange dreams of the Goddess herself, of the flames rising and surrounding Aram—and sometimes dreams that made even less sense: of a man throwing a book into the sea, of a Malgasi man finding something golden and dangerous inside a cave. Even last night, she had dreamed of a dark-haired woman with fire spilling from her hands and of a man turning to ash against a white marble pillar.

The Shulamat was quiet at midday, still under the sun like a sleeping cat. Lin cut through the dusty, washed-stone interior, passing the gold lattice-gate behind which were the Shulamat's books. Books she had held in her hands now, feeling their weight, the texture of their bindings. Smooth leather sometimes, or heavy silver, carved and inscribed, or stiffened fabric whose glued-on precious stones were beginning to fall away. Three months ago, she could never even have imagined touching them. When she did, it was all worth it: the resentment and hostility, whatever damage she had done to her own soul with her lies.

(And then there was her most precious volume, which she had reclaimed after the Maharam had confiscated it: *The Works of Qasmuna*, so rare and so forbidden that she kept it wrapped in black velvet. The Prince had given it to her personally, and she could not help but see his face every time she opened the pages.)

She made her way through corridors spangled with dust motes that shimmered in the syrupy sunlight and passed out into the enclosed garden behind the Shulamat. Here the air smelled sweet, for honeysuckle crept down the stone walls, and the ground was carpeted with blue lupin and yellow crocus. Fruit hung heavy from the pomegranate and date trees that lined the paths.

She could see the Maharam, standing in the shadow of a plane tree. He was not carrying his staff; he seemed absorbed instead in scattering seeds for a boisterous group of sunbirds. A few of them hopped away as Lin approached, but the Maharam did not look up. Instead he whistled, and a sunbird with a bright-red head hopped closer to him, nearly sitting on his slippered foot.

Lin did not greet the Maharam, merely stood patiently (a task made easier by the fact that her skirts had become caught on a prickly *sahja* cactus) waiting for him to speak. At last he said, "Have you ever wondered at the purpose of this garden?"

Before three months ago, I was not allowed *in this garden.* But Lin only said, "Must a garden have a purpose, other than to be a peaceful retreat?"

The Maharam reached into the pockets of his voluminous robes and took out another handful of seeds. "When the first Exilarch, Judah Makabi, fled Aram, he took with him not only its people but also the seeds and fruits of the plants that grew there, in order that none of them might vanish from the earth. Everything that grows in this garden once grew in Aram. King's crown and white anemone would carpet the mountains, and roses and tulips the valleys. We preserve them all, growing them where we can, so they can be carried back to Aram when it is restored." His dark eyes studied her. "Your task, of course."

Lin heard a snort from behind her. She turned and saw Oren Kandel passing by them on the path. She had, of course, seen a great deal of him since she had assumed her new role—such as it was. The Maharam had appointed him as caretaker of the Shulamat, and he was always there, glaring from the shadows. He walked off stiffly now, a burlap sack over his shoulder.

"Do not mind him," said the Maharam. "One must have patience with those who are not ready for her return yet."

"Some people accept change more easily than others," said Lin, matching the Maharam's bland tone with her own. There was no use in saying that if the Maharam himself were not such an obvious doubter, things would be different for her in the Sault. He knew that; and besides, she did not entirely blame him.

He was not wrong to doubt.

"The Sanhedrin are coming," said the Maharam rather abruptly. "In a week."

Lin caught her breath. Everything in the garden seemed suddenly too vivid: the brightness of the flowers, the precise, sharp-edged black shadows cast across the dusty earth. Even the scent of the honeysuckle seemed suddenly cloying. "I thought you said it would be several months before they arrived—"

She cut herself off, but the Maharam looked pleased nonetheless. Too late. He said, "They move at their own discretion. Perhaps they have taken a special interest in you."

"How flattering."

"One week," the Maharam mused. "That would mean they are not so close that it would be impossible for me to send them a message and tell them not to come. If, perhaps, you had changed your mind about the test."

Why would I do that? Lin almost said, but she could not deny that her heart had leaped at the suggestion. Not to have to stand before the Exilarch and his court, not to have to lie to the Sanhedrin . . . She did not have a miracle in her pocket this time—a once-in-a-lifetime bit of knowledge regarding the burning of a fleet of ships, a coincidence of timing . . .

She had only herself, and what she had learned. She knew it would not be enough.

And yet. The Maharam was looking at her with kindness. The look of the old man who presided over weddings, blessed babies, and fed sparrows and sunbirds from his own hands. If she asked him to tell the Sanhedrin not to come, that she had been wrong about who she was, then he would be kind about that, too.

But the rest of the Sault. Her friends, neighbors, patients. They would always regard her as a liar. She would escape exile, but she would be shunned. Those who had doubted would be vindicated, but that did not bother her as much as the knowledge that those who had believed would be heartbroken.

And there was still Mariam. Mariam, who was not yet healed. But a week was not nothing; a week was time . . .

A sunbird had alighted on the Maharam's shoulder. It cheeped thoughtfully. "Let me know what you decide, Linnet," said the Maharam. "I assure you, it is your choice."

Well, of course it is, Lin thought. The Maharam was too canny to want the weight of the decision, or its consequences, on him.

"Many thanks, Maharam," said Lin, who had finally freed her skirts from the cactus. One of her fingers, pricked, had begun to bleed; a small drop of blood rose against her skin, bright as the Prince's rings. "I shall think on it carefully."

Kel arrived at the Caravel alone on Asti. He had left Conor in the Star Tower, flanked by Lilibet and Mayesh, still finalizing the arrangement for the Kutani Princess's arrival. "I suppose Montfaucon will be annoyed I'm not there," Conor had said, though he did not seem terribly bothered about it. "But this is more important."

Kel found himself feeling oddly bereft as he set off down the Hill. It was better in many ways, he told himself, to have a Conor who found his responsibilities more compelling than his enjoyments. And yet—Kel missed him, especially with the prospect of a night spent with the nobles of the Hill in front of him. Conor was the only one of that group he truly liked—save for Falconet, sometimes.

Kel determinedly set himself to enjoying the clear bright night regardless. The stars were a fisherman's silver net flung across the sky; the air was still, translucent enough that he could see the dark profile of the Orfelinat, his first home, perched on its sheer cliff above the ocean.

He found the Caravel alight, windows and doors flung open, the sounds of merriment spilling onto the street. Passersby looked on, curious, as Kel left Asti with the footmen and ducked inside. Wondering who he was, no doubt: a nobleman, even a Charter member? Or perhaps they'd noted his Marakandi colors: green velvet trousers, celadon silk shirt, and figured waistcoat studded with green gems—though they were not real emeralds, only colored paste. False as his name, his relation to the Palace.

The interior of the Caravel had been decorated in the colors of House Montfaucon, which happened to be silver and violet. The courtesans wore versions of the Montfaucon livery, and their eyelids were colored with metallic lavender. They darted among the guests with liquor and food, trailing silver scarves. Montfaucon, in purple moiré silk, was moving through the crowd, clearly in his element: greeting some, snubbing others. Since it was his own guest list, Kel could only assume Montfaucon had invited them in order to snub them, which did seem like something he would enjoy.

Kel let his gaze drift over the crowd and saw only familiar faces, save for a few of the courtesans. It had been a long time since he'd visited the Caravel, he realized. Nearly four months. The feel of the place was strange to him now, in a way he could not quite describe. On stage, a group of workmen were hammering together a sort of wooden structure that Kel couldn't identify.

Kel swept his gaze across the room and saw familiar faces from the Hill; most already seemed to have gotten well into the plentiful wine on offer. He did not see Ji-An or Jerrod anywhere, but he did spot Merren in conversation with Alys on a red settee. Kel did his best not to look at them too closely—a goal made easier when Ciprian Cabrol and Joss Falconet approached him. Both carried silver goblets of a milky liquor. Joss wore black velvet, Ciprian a modest gray that did not suit him.

"What are they building up on the stage?" Kel asked, trying to sound drawling and unconcerned.

"Perhaps he wishes to show this Gray Serpent off against some sort of fanciful backdrop," Joss said. "Montfaucon has always had a theatrical disposition."

"Is this truly his debut?" Kel asked. "Montfaucon has not so much as brought him out for a card game before?"

Ciprian shook his head. "Montfaucon has never been so secretive about a lover before."

It was odd, Kel thought, how Ciprian spoke of them all with such familiarity, as if his family had always been on the Hill.

Joss took a sip from his cup, his dark eyes thoughtful. "Apparently, he used to be an Arena fighter, before it was outlawed. He killed so many in combat that they started calling him the Gray Serpent, because he sent souls to the underworld."

Ciprian frowned. "Excuse me. I must pry my sister Beatris from the grip of Esteve. He constantly corners her and lectures her about horses."

"For Esteve, that is the language of love," said Kel. Ciprian made a disgusted face and shouldered his way into the crowd.

Joss grinned. "I rather prefer these new dye merchants to the old ones. They're more fun."

Kel raised an eyebrow. "What, you don't miss Charlon?"

"I've had penetrating leg wounds that I've missed more than Charlon," said Joss bluntly. "And the Cabrols seem to have settled in without a hitch. One has to admire the ruthlessness."

Kel glanced over at Ciprian, who had an arm around his sister's shoulder—she was dressed all in white and yellow, like a daisy—and was glaring at Esteve. Behind him, someone had begun to tunelessly play a lute. The room was tightly packed, the noise of the construction on stage deafening. Kel caught a flash of red hair in the crowd and thought for a moment: *Lin?* But of course it was not her. It was Silla, wearing only a number of cleverly knotted violet and silver scarves. She looked like a drawing of a sea sprite, trailing the foam of the waves. She beckoned to Kel with a crooked finger, her head to one side.

"I see you have to go," said Joss, "which is rather too bad. I was going to ask you when the Kutani Princess is arriving."

"A few weeks, I think. She is already on the way, but it is quite a sea voyage." Kel hesitated. He did not want to be distracted by Silla, but he could not push too hard with Falconet on the question of the

Gray Serpent, either. It would only bring suspicion. Nor did he wish to enter a conversation about Conor's engagement. "If you'll excuse me?"

Falconet flicked his gaze to Silla and smiled knowingly. "Of course. Who am I to barricade the path of young love?"

Kel clapped a hand to Falconet's shoulder and pushed into the crowd. *Young love.* Silla and he had only ever been commerce, of course, but then love and commerce were nearly the same thing on the Hill. There was no point in being annoyed with Falconet about it.

He reached Silla, passing Gasquet, who was sprawled in a plush chair, a handsome young man perched on the arm. Kel wondered if Montfaucon had invited every member of the Charter Families; certainly he could not have expected Lady Alleyne or Lady Gremont to attend. Lady Gremont was elderly and respectable, and Lady Alleyne took only rich lovers. Both would have felt obligated to seem shocked by the debauchery of the Caravel, though Kel would have wagered they'd both seen more scandalous things in their lives.

Kel realized with surprise that he had forgotten to remove his gloves when Silla made a circlet of her thumb and forefinger around his wrist, where the skin was bare. She looked up at him from beneath silver-and-violet-painted eyes. She had used the paint cleverly, creating the illusion of a shimmering mask. "Come," she said. "I want to talk to you."

He let her lead him from the room. As they left, Kel caught a glimpse of Montfaucon, who seemed to have inserted himself into the conversation between Esteve and Beatris, but there was no one with him who could credibly be an ex-gladiator named the Gray Serpent. Where was Montfaucon hiding him?

"You *are* distracted," Silla said. A little sharpness cut the honey of her voice. "And it's been such a long time since I've seen you."

She'd led them into one of the velvet-lined alcoves in the heart of the Caravel. Each one was no bigger than a closet, but they were all plushly upholstered, with soft walls and a pillowed chaise. Mont-faucon used to joke about these rooms, saying they were for cus-tomers who lacked either the cash or the commitment to take a courtesan upstairs.

Silla drew the sheer curtain closed across the alcove entrance and turned to Kel. Violet tapers shed a reddish light, deepening the shadows. "I've missed you," she said, taking hold of his hands and placing them on her hips. "Have you missed me?"

His gloved fingers slipped over the fabric of her scarves reflex-ively. It was strange, touching her and not touching her at the same time. He could feel the shape of her but not the texture. He let his hands travel, leather against silk, her body curving under his hands. When he kissed her, she was already leaning up into him.

Kel was used to being able to lose himself in a kiss, a touch. The pleasure that caught him up, blurring the sharp edges of thought and memory. He was jolted now by how distant that feeling seemed. He was aware of Silla's touch, her taste, but just as aware of the fact that one of his boots was laced too tightly and he had a crick in his neck.

His thoughts scattered themselves, following different paths: Was he missing a chance to lay eyes on the Gray Serpent? Were Ji-An and Jerrod outside with the carriage as promised? Should he have left Merren, who should have been with them, on his own? Obviously, he had his sister, but—

Silla drew back, looking up at him. Silver paint made half-moons of her lowered eyelids as she said, "There is something wrong. Kel, I *know* you. Don't think I don't know you. I was your first girl."

"And you'll always be that," Kel said. He still had his hands at her waist. He might as well have been holding a log. He let her go and stepped back.

"Is this because of the Prince?" she asked, raking lilac-tipped fingers through her red hair. "I knew that night I shouldn't have gone back with him, that you shared a room with him, but—"

It took Kel a moment to even remember what she was talking about. The morning after the Roverge party, Silla creeping out of Conor's bed at dawn.

He shrugged. "You make your own decisions. You owe me nothing at all."

"I like you," she said. "Most customers, it's a transaction. An investment. But you . . ." She sighed. "I don't suppose you'll believe me, but the Prince did not . . . he did not want from me what most men or women do. He asked only for me to be there and be silent. He did not even say much to me. Only went to sleep, and I watched him until I went to sleep, too."

Kel sighed. "Silla, don't you see, that is what makes it strange for me. These things are private to Conor. He would not want me to know them."

"He called me by a name that wasn't mine," Silla said. Some of the metallic paint on her face had smeared; silver tears appeared to be trickling from her eyes.

Kel held up a hand. "I don't want to know." This was not entirely true, but he had done enough behind Conor's back these past months. He did not want this on his ledger, too.

Silla frowned. "I used to understand you."

Kel almost said, *I used to understand myself.* It was on the tip of his tongue—and then a hand twitched the alcove curtain aside and Kel found himself staring into the face of Antonetta Alleyne.

She was very pale, almost as if she had powdered her skin the way some of the older women on the Hill did. But there were bright spots of color on her cheeks as she looked from Kel to Silla and said, "Oh, my goodness, I'm *so* embarrassed."

Silla ran her hand down the front of Kel's waistcoat. "You could join us, Demoselle."

Antonetta gave a bashful laugh; only Kel would have seen the flash in her eyes. "Gracious," she said. "How very shocking. I shall have to tell Magali. She will positively faint." She waved at them vaguely. "Do carry on," she chirped, and vanished from the alcove.

Kel swore and detached Silla's hand gently from his waistcoat. Thoughts of the Gray Serpent momentarily fled, he darted after Antonetta.

He caught up with her in the narrow, wood-paneled corridor that led back to the main rooms. When he called out her name in a low voice, she didn't turn. He jogged ahead and planted himself in front of her, blocking her way forward.

"Ana," he said. "Listen to me—"

Assuming a look of saintly patience, she crossed her arms over her chest and regarded Kel with a level stare. He could not help staring back. He had not been this close to her since the awful night in the Shining Gallery. She had not dressed herself in Montfaucon's colors; she wore scarlet silk like a banner of rebellion, and dark-red ribbons had been woven through the heavy mass of her curling golden hair.

"Antonetta," he said. He was close enough to smell her perfume, to see the ever-present locket nestled in the hollow of her throat. The locket that contained the grass ring he'd given her when they were children. He could hear his own blood pounding in his ears. "I didn't think you'd be here tonight."

"I'm an engaged woman now, Kel Anjuman," she said lightly. "I have more freedom. I need not fear society's scorn, only my future husband's—and he is not here."

"That will not always be true," said Kel. He hardly remembered Artal Gremont; he had seen him only when he'd been a child, before Gremont had been exiled from Castellane. He'd been a big man, with slablike hands. When Kel pictured those hands on Antonetta—*following the rise of her breasts, the curve of her waist, big meaty fingers digging into her silk-covered flesh*—he wanted to throw up. Though Alys would make him pay for it if he ruined her carpeting.

"I know that," Antonetta said sharply. "I will know the moment he sets foot on the Hill. Believe me. Until then . . ." She glanced around. "I might as well see the world."

"This isn't the world." Kel was still looking at her; he couldn't *stop* looking at her. It was like not being able to stop eating when you were starving. Of course, people died of doing that. "This is a place of . . ."

"Desire?" she said lightly.

Kel shook his head. "Loneliness."

She glanced away.

"Antonetta." He took a step toward her. "Let us not be angry with each other. You do not *have* to marry Gremont—"

"Yes," she said, and to his surprise, she looked angry. He was used to Antonetta giggling or being dismissive or even haughty; angry was new. "I do. You know the way things are for Conor. He must marry whoever is chosen for him. For me, it is no different. Two Charters will be united. He will hold the tea Charter, and I will hold the silk Charter, and together we will control both. That is all my mother cares for."

"Conor could put a stop to it," he said. "He could free you—"

She was wearing white silk gloves. Her hands gripped each other tightly, two still white birds. "I will not beg him for help."

But you did ask him. I know you did. Though it had not been Conor she had asked. It had been Kel, bearing his talisman, pretending to be Conor. As was his duty. And he had answered her as he thought Conor would have answered her, because answering her as himself was not a choice.

But Conor had changed since then. "I will ask for you, then."

The look she gave him was alive with ferocity. "You shall do no such thing," she said furiously. "Do I want to marry Gremont? No. If I escape wedding him, will the next man my mother selects be just as bad? Most likely." Voices rose in the main room—some kind of cheer that nearly drowned Antonetta out. "The silk Charter should be mine by rights. If the only way my mother will give it to me is if I marry, then he will do as well as another."

"He is not a good man," said Kel. "It is why he was exiled." He wanted to tell her what Gremont's crime was, but he had sworn to Merren he would not speak of what had happened to his sister.

"I know that. Of all people," she added in a low voice, "I thought you, at least, did not believe me completely foolish."

A feeling like despair seized him. She was so close that he could see her pulse beating in her throat, the rise and fall of her locket with her quick breaths, yet she felt as distant as she had ever been.

"You pretend to foolishness," he said. "It is your armor."

She raised her head at that and looked at him, her blue eyes so dark they seemed black in the low light. "We all have armor," she said. "As if you do not have yours, Kel Anjuman."

He choked on the words he could not say. *I am the Prince's armor. I cannot have my own.*

"Antonetta—"

She took a step back. "You are not my father, not brother or lover," she said. "You have no rights here."

And with that, she pushed past him in a rustle of silk and was gone. Back to the main room, where he could not be seen to follow.

Kel stood motionless for a moment, where he could still smell the lingering scent of her perfume. Where he could imagine her still there with him, a handsbreadth away.

But he had a duty to his friends. A duty to his Prince and city. He could not mope about in a brothel like a lovesick student preparing to write reams of poetry about his delicate feelings.

Kel stomped his way up the Caravel's stairs in a very poor mood. He wished he had not thought the word *lovesick*. He prided himself on never having been in love, and his situation with Antonetta could not change that. *You have no rights here*, she had said, and she was utterly correct. He had no rights where she was concerned, and no chance to be anything other than a friend—one her husband was unlikely to be enthusiastic about.

He could not love her; therefore, he did not love her. So he told himself as he arrived at the library door. He could hear raised voices from within. One sounded very much like Montfaucon's. Under other circumstances, Kel would have made himself scarce, but there was no chance of that now. What he needed to know was more important than manners.

Kel opened the door quietly. The lamps were not lit; the city light that poured through the windows was the only real illumination. It turned Montfaucon and the man he was arguing with into silhouettes, like clever paper cutouts.

"Raimon," Montfaucon was saying, "you're being unreasonable—"

Raimon snorted. He was a head taller than Montfaucon, solidly built, with white flecks in his dark, close-cut hair. The moonlight picked out the lines in his face—a harsh spiderwebbing. Kel was surprised; he looked quite a bit older than Montfaucon. "Am I some kind of joke to you, then?" he was demanding. He had the accent of lower Castellane: the docks and the Maze. "I'm not bloody going on some stage and hitting people for the benefit of those posh fuckers you call your friends."

"It's nothing to do with thinking of you as a joke." Montfaucon's voice was a soothing purr. "I want them to see how skilled you are. To see the great Gray Serpent in all his glory."

"I am not that man anymore."

"You are still a fighter," said Montfaucon. "One I wish them to admire."

"You wish them to admire *you*," said Raimon. Kel, in the doorway, ducked his head to hide a smile—not that either of the men had noticed him yet. Raimon certainly seemed to know Montfaucon well. Kel wondered how long they'd known each other. Which made him think of the Shining Gallery slaughter. His smile vanished.

"I'm leaving," Raimon growled. "I never wanted a part of this in the first place, Lupin. You told me yourself, city business and Hill business should stay separate."

He turned on his heel, brushing past Kel in the doorway, as if his presence there was of supreme unimportance. As he shoved his way into the corridor, Kel caught sight of a dark tattoo on his neck, above the collar of his shirt—the inky S shape of a hook.

Not a tattoo then, but a brand. The Tully brand that denoted a convicted criminal.

Montfaucon turned on Kel, scowling ferociously. "What's wrong with you, Anjuman? Why've you been standing there like an idiot during what was obviously a private conversation?"

Kel was too distracted to answer. A Tully brand—so Raimon was a convict, then? That was interesting. It was difficult to find employment when you bore a prisoner's brand. Many such men and women turned to mercenary work to keep food on the table.

With a disgusted noise, Montfaucon shoved past Kel into the corridor and hurried downstairs. Kel waited a few moments before going after him. He doubted Montfaucon would take well to being followed at the moment.

He found the main room of the Caravel in chaos. Raimon was not there, and Montfaucon was on stage arguing with a bulky man, stripped to the waist, carrying what looked like a bear mask under his arm. "I don't care if he's run off," the man was saying, "or if there's no one for me to box. I expect to be paid—"

"I'll box you," called someone—Ciprian?—drunkenly from the crowd. Everyone was milling; Kel looked briefly but did not see Antonetta. Good. She was the only one likely to notice if Kel left. "Let me on stage!"

"I won't fight amateurs," said the man with the bear mask, clearly outraged. But the crowd had already started shouting— *Fight! Fight! Fight!*—which was bad luck for the bear man but excellent luck for Kel. He pushed his way through the distracted crowd to Merren, who was in a corner talking to a courtesan named Audeta about the chemical composition of perfume. Audeta looked as if she was considering fleeing. "Merren," Kel hissed, grabbing his friend by the back of his coat. "We're leaving."

"Oh, thank the Gods," said Audeta. "Kel, why is Montfaucon trying to get someone to fight that bear?"

"You'd have to ask him," Kel muttered, and he hauled Merren away through the crowd.

Outside, the footman wanted to know if he should fetch Asti, but Kel was already hurrying Merren across the street to where a black carriage with scarlet wheels waited, Ji-An perched atop the driver's seat. She gestured to Kel just as the carriage door flew open and Jerrod leaned out, saying, "Someone just took off in Montfaucon's carriage, so move it, you loitering bastard! *Come on!*"

Hoping the footman would chalk his behavior up to "strange things rich people do" and think no more about it, Kel dashed across the road and leaped in through the open carriage door just as the wheels began to turn. They rattled away into the Castellane night.

Laurent

There have been sea caves along the rocky coast of Castellane for as long as anyone can recall. Historians generally agree that they have been there since the naval battles of the Sundering, and that part of the reason for their enormous size was the subsequent mining of Sunderglass from the rock, which left the coast wall pocked with holes like Detmarch cheese.

Every few years, an enterprising crusader among the Castellane merchants decides that it is time to clear the caves of smugglers and their loot once and for all. These attempts are never very successful: The piracy and privateers have been there as long as the caves themselves, and any official in Castellane who might otherwise be interested in clearing the caves has long since been bribed to look the other way. The legal business of trade is far too entangled with its illegal cousin, smuggling, to ever be extricated from it. Then of course there are the superstitions that hang about the caves like sea mist: that their depths are haunted by the souls of dead sorcerers, who would sicken and kill any who disturb them. It is a convenient tale for the smugglers, who want to be left alone and cheerfully repeat the tales of vengeful ghosts to anyone in the Maze who will listen.

The cave in which Laurent Aden has chosen to berth his ship, the *Black Rose,* is one of the largest of its kind. Vast and hollow as the inside of a drum, it is dimly lit by veins of glowing Sunderglass weaving their way through the rock. The towering masts of the galleon are lost in the shadows overhead; the ship bobs quietly in the dark water. If one were of a suspicious mind, one could imagine the ghosts of dead Sorcerer-Kings among the stalactites above. But Laurent Aden is not of a suspicious mind, and he knows perfectly well that the flitting shadows are bats.

Generations ago, a long wooden dock had been built along the curving side wall of the cave to facilitate the loading and unloading of illegal cargo and the comings and goings of crewmen. Aden, unwilling to go far from his ship, has spread a Marakandi rug on a portion of the dock, onto which he's placed two chairs and a small table. The table holds a bottle of wine, already open, and two fluted glasses.

He's only just settling himself in one of the chairs when he hears the splashing sounds of the small boat entering the cave and tying up nearby. Boots ring on the dock as the newcomer to the cave paces toward him; when the long shadow of his visitor falls across him, Aden looks up, feigning surprise as he takes in the familiar figure: the polished leather boots, the brass-buttoned admiral's coat (no doubt thieved from some actual admiral), the piercing, steady eyes.

"Prosper Beck," Aden says. "I wasn't sure you'd come."

Beck makes a small sound of annoyance. "Why wouldn't I?"

"I heard you had left Castellane."

"I see." Beck leans his folded arms on the back of the second chair. "Rumors of my departure have been greatly exaggerated."

"Have they? You've been absent from your normal headquarters, and your usual operatives—Bron, Kaspar, Jerrod Belmerci—all seem to be employed elsewhere now."

Beck shrugs. "They'll return when summoned. They all knew my leave of absence wasn't permanent."

It is clear more information is not forthcoming. "In that case, you'll be glad to know I've held on to your goods for you. Thirty-six crossbows, hidden under an order of teakwood for House Raspail." He lifts the bottle. "Shall we drink to a deal concluded?"

The corner of Beck's mouth quirks up. "Alas, I cannot remain long. Duty calls."

Aden shrugs and takes a swig from the wine bottle. He makes a face. Bitter. "Very well. But there's something you should know."

Beck has begun to turn away but stops and swings around to look keenly at Aden. "What is that?"

It is nice to hear Castellani again, Aden thinks. The language of his birth. Sometimes he goes months now without hearing it. "I know," he says, choosing his words carefully, "that you have much invested in the fortunes of Castellane. I thought it might interest you to know that in the time we've been docked here, my men and I have seen foreign soldiers coming in and out of the caves. Now, pirates I'd expect—all manner of ruffians really—but not soldiers." He takes another swig of the wine. "I thought you ought to know."

Beck's light eyes narrow. "Foreign soldiers? Not Castellani?"

"No. Malgasi would be my guess."

A look of surprise passes across Beck's normally impassive face. "Soldiers of Malgasi. You're sure?"

"No, I'm not sure. But that's who I think they are."

"Interesting. Very interesting," Beck murmurs in a voice so low, Aden guesses he isn't meant to hear the words. "But—enough about that. I'll be sending my men to collect the goods from you later tonight. If I might inquire, how long do you plan to remain in Castellane? Or is your business here concluded?"

Aden smiles down into his wine bottle. "It's not concluded. No, I may be here some while."

For the first time, Beck grins. "I don't suppose your desire to remain has anything to do with a certain Princess from Kutani, does it?"

Aden knows better than to show when he is caught off guard.

He busies himself in studying the label on the wine bottle, though he could not have said what information it held. After a moment, he says lazily, "I'm here on my own business. Nothing to trouble you."

"Hm." Without another word, Beck turns and walks away along the narrow dock. Aden mutters and reaches for the wine bottle, only to sit back when Beck whirls around to look at him again. "Artal Gremont." The cave walls amplify Beck's words, making them resound as if they stand inside a temple. "You brought him to Castellane. On your ship."

Aden groans silently. "For better or worse, yes. He slithered off into the city the moment we arrived here."

"And what did you think of him?"

Beck's tone is studiedly neutral. Aden hesitates only a moment before he says coldly, "I took Gremont on board because he was willing to pay handsomely for a passage to Castellane. And I regretted it immediately. The man is a pig with no redeeming qualities whatsoever. In fact, he gives pigs a bad name. If you were thinking of doing business with him, I'd advise against it." He taps his fingers against the side of his chair, remembering the stowaway on board the *Black Rose,* what Gremont had done to her. How—if Laurent had not arrived in time—Gremont might even have killed her. "He likes to hurt people. People weaker than him. He's . . . not a careful man."

Beck stands still for a long moment, haloed in the light from the Sunderglass above. "Thank you," Beck says eventually, with a nod. "For the advice."

Aden sits lost in thought as Beck strides toward the nearby boat and clambers in. He can hear the sound of low voices in conference, muffled by the lap of water. He raises the bottle again and takes a second swig of the liquid. It is still bitter.

CHAPTER THREE

As Second Watch began and the lamps in the Kathot were doused for the night, Lin left her house and struck out across the Sault for the House of Women.

She found Chana Dorin waiting for her in the kitchen with a mug of *karak*. Chana had been rubbing balm into her hands, arthritis having swelled her finger joints until they looked like knots in wood. She had already heard that the Maharam had asked to see Lin that afternoon, and she demanded a full accounting of events.

"That old fool," she snorted, once Lin had recounted the conversation in the garden. "Did he *really* tell you to have patience with those unready for the Shekinah? As if I haven't spent the past three months telling you to have patience with *him*."

Lin smiled a little. It was true. The Maharam might be the most powerful man in the Sault, but Chana clearly felt that, in the wake of Lin's announcement, he was behaving like a petulant child.

"He offered to tell the Sanhedrin not to come and test me. I think he was trying to be kind."

Chana snorted. "There is no kindness in telling the Sanhedrin you lied about being the Goddess Returned. You are not a liar." She looked closely into Lin's face. "Few know of the good you have already done for Mariam, and I believe there is so much more good you can do for our people. There is a reason you stood up in that moment at the Tevath and claimed your power. Do not let fear take that reason from you now."

The earnestness in Chana's voice seemed to strike at Lin's heart. What would Chana say if she told her that she had stood up in that moment because she knew that the ships in the harbor would burn at the hour of midnight? That she had learned of the plan to burn them, in fact, in the house of the Ragpicker King, a man of distinctly low moral character? It helped that the Laws he was breaking were not Ashkar Laws, but there would still be many questions if it was found that Lin was regularly visiting the Black Mansion.

It was at the Black Mansion that she had learned of Ciprian Cabrol's plan to burn the Roverge ships. That burning was the one reason most in the Sault credited her claim, even with hesitation: *When the Goddess returns, she will come in fire.* It was close enough, and how else would she have known?

She knew she could not tell Chana the truth, and it weighed upon her. Chana's belief weighed upon her like a chain around her neck. Like Mayesh's medallion. Though Mayesh was a different tale entirely.

"I ought to go see Mariam," she said, and bent to kiss the older woman's cheek. Chana smelled of *karak* spices and strong medicinal herbs. As Lin drew back, Chana took light hold of the sleeve of her dress.

"The Maharam is just a man," she said. "He is not the Goddess, nor even the Exilarch. He is afraid the life he has always known is going to change, and you represent that change. All the things that have always made him important will no longer do so."

"But if he believes in the Goddess, he must also believe in the future she brings," said Lin. "In Aram, he would be honored for his service to her."

Chana's smile was mournful. "He has only ever sung our songs in a strange land," she said. "He may fear he will find Aram foreign.

The cantillations of a faraway place may not be music he can imagine."

A faraway place. The words echoed in Lin's head as she made her way down the hall to Mariam's room. It was late and the lamps were low, but she would always know her way around the Etse Kebeth, even in the dark.

Aram was meant to be more than a faraway land in the heart of every Ashkar. It was meant to be an imagined perfect home, far different from the uninhabitable slag heap it was now.

Still, when Lin tried to picture Aram, she could only conjure up visions of green hills and placid sheep. A storybook land, not real. She had never truly imagined leaving the streets of Castellane. In that way, perhaps she was not so different from the Maharam.

Before Lin went into Mariam's room, she took her brooch from her pocket and pinned it to her sleeve, close to the pulse of her wrist. The Arkhe stone in it shone, but it was the lifeless shine of reflected light. No gleam came from within the stone itself. Lin tore her gaze from it, its darkness emblematic of her failure.

She found Mariam in bed, reading a thick tome full of painted fashion plates. She sat up when Lin came in, her thin face lighting up, her blankets slipping about her shoulders. She wore a nightgown of thick needlecord despite the warmth of the night. "Lin! I've been missing you."

Lin felt a wave of guilt. She knew she should be visiting Mariam more often, but between her studies of magic, her frequent trips to the Black Mansion, and her responsibilities as the Goddess Returned, she often felt she was living three lives.

Mariam must have seen something in her face. "No, don't— *don't* feel badly. I didn't mean it that way." She set her book down and gestured for Lin to join her on the bed. "Come. I want to hear everything you've been doing."

Lin settled onto the worn coverlet, legs drawn up under her. She and Mariam had spent hours of their adolescence like this, trading bits of gossip and fantasy and imagination. Stories they had heard or invented. Places they wished to travel; whether they wanted to marry someday, and if so, to whom. Whether, if magic really worked, they'd rather have the power to fly or become invisible. But what could she tell Mariam now? *As you know, I have been trying to teach myself magic using the books from the Shulamat, but I keep running into the same walls over and over again.* Or: *I am terrified of what will happen when the Exilarch comes.* Or: *I do most of my work in the Black Mansion of the Ragpicker King, but I pretend I am out visiting patients.*

"I was at House Alleyne," she said instead. "With Antonetta."

Mariam's eyes flew wide. "You were up on the Hill? Is there any news about the Prince's engagement? It's all anyone's talking about in the city."

Lin wished she had taken Chana up on her offer of tea. Her mouth was dry. She said, "Antonetta didn't mention it. To be honest . . ." She leaned in conspiratorially. "We were discussing a different wedding. Antonetta's fiancé is arriving in Castellane soon."

Mariam wrinkled up her nose. "Is she still marrying the toad?"

"Alas, yes. And her mother is throwing an engagement party to celebrate the toad. And—Antonetta asked me if I would come."

"I thought you swore you'd never go to another party on the Hill."

"I know, but . . ." Lin threw up her hands. "I just can't leave Antonetta to face it all alone. I'm not sure there's anyone else in her life who understands."

"You're a good friend," said Mariam. "As I have cause to know."

"I'm not sure I am Antonetta's friend," Lin mused. "I am her physician. Though I am fairly sure she keeps our appointments because she wishes to talk, not because there's anything wrong with her."

"I would say that makes you her friend," said Mariam. "But I am no expert on such distinctions. I *am*, however, an expert in the field of fashion." Her eyes sparked in her thin face. "What will you wear to your second party among the nobility of Castellane?"

"Oh. *Ugh*. I don't care what I wear," Lin said. "I'm not interested in impressing any of those vacuous popinjays on the Hill."

"But you are the Goddess now," Mariam said. "You represent the Ashkar and the people of the Sault. You cannot go to the Hill in a burlap sack."

"My grandfather represents the Ashkar and the people of the Sault."

"Mayesh represents what we are," said Mariam. "You represent what we can be. Our strength."

Her eyes were shining, and Lin could not help but think of Mariam's past—of what had happened to her in Malgasi, how her family and community had been destroyed for the crime of being Ashkar. How much it meant for Mari to think of the people of the Sault as protected. As safe.

"All right," Lin said. "I'll let you dress me like a doll. I know you want to."

"I *do*," Mariam agreed.

"But first—" Lin held up a hand. "Before we are sidetracked into talk of frills and furbelows, it's time again, Mari."

"Now?" Mariam tugged at the cuffs of her dressing-gown. "The same thing again?"

"I'll try to do it quickly. It isn't hurting you, is it?"

Mariam shook her head. "No. And I always feel better afterward. But it is . . . odd." She raised her chin as if in defiance of her own illness. "I'm ready."

"Lie down," Lin said, and Mariam did, arms straight at her sides. She gazed at Lin trustingly as Lin placed a hand over Mariam's heart. She was so thin, Lin could feel the bones of her rib cage. Mariam's heart pulsed under her fingers, a steady beat.

Look within. That was what all the books said: This was the first step. To reach within oneself, to find the power inherent in every soul.

But it was not enough. The sorcerers of old had augmented their abilities with the use of Arkhes, Source-Stones, which were able to store power, like water in a reservoir. When great magic needed to be done, they could draw on that stored power rather than draining their souls to destruction.

Lin was blessed to have a Source-Stone, the Arkhe in the brooch at her wrist. But despite her access to the books in the Shulamat, despite all her studies, she had been unable to determine how to store power into the stone. It was meant to glow like a lamp, suffused with energy, but it remained dead and blank as a fish's eye.

Sometimes, when she used her own energy to do the small magic that she could, she could feel the stone reaching out, as if it were searching for something—a source of power, or another stone like itself? Once the world had been full of them; now, as far as she knew, hers was the only one in existence. She felt almost as if she were failing the stone in her brooch, consigning it to a lonely existence without power or companionship.

Do not think about your failures, she told herself. *Think about Mariam. Think of the words you would use to describe Mariam. Fall into that sea of words, as the Goddess fell into a sea of stars.*

Mariam. Friend. Sister. Loyal. Promise.

Heal.

Slowly, Lin's vision softened. The shadows in the room thickened, and the points of light—Mariam's single candle in its silver holder by her bed, the faint illumination that came through the curtained window—grew brighter and more blurred. The talismans—all for health and life—bound to Mariam's wrists, around her throat, began to glow like points of blue fire.

Lin slowed her own breathing, letting her concentration on Mariam sharpen. She repeated Qasmuna's words to herself, memorized from her most precious possession: the book the Prince had given her. They made a soft litany:

The Word is the sum of human will. Magic cannot exist without the Word because it cannot exist without will.

Of course, the Word had been lost long ago, wiped from the memory of the world after the Sundering. But will and volition—

those still existed, and Lin focused all of hers on Mariam. Between one blink and another, her vision changed. She saw words written across the scene in front of her, as if they had been scrawled on a painting. Words like *sickness*, *pain*, and *poison*.

She reached out with her mind, using all her will to erase those words. To replace them with other words: *healing*, and *cure*, and *remedy*.

Mariam's body arched as smoke poured between Lin's fingers. It seemed to rise out of Mariam's body, from her heart, curling upward through the air: a dark, acrid, diffuse *stuff* that Lin called smoke because she could think of no other word for it. Mariam exhaled as the smoke left her.

And it was over. The world had gone back to what it was, a place of ordinary light and shadow. Lin drew her hand back from Mariam's chest; her palm was red, as if she had held it over a fire, the result of drawing on her own life energy to heal Mariam. She knew from experience that it would hurt for some hours before subsiding.

"Ugh." Mariam sat up, her thin brown hair tumbling around her face. Her color was already better, her movements easier. Her expression, though, was resigned. "I hate knowing that stuff was *inside* me."

"Don't think of it like that." Lin had explained before: This was Mariam's sickness she was drawing out. It did not live inside Mariam in this form; it took on this dark, shadowy aspect when forced into the open. "How do you feel?"

"Better." Mariam took Lin's hand. She held it tightly; Lin forced herself not to react to the pain as her palm stung. "I don't mean to complain. I know that what you are doing for me is— It's a miracle, Lin. I would have been dead months ago if not for you."

"It needs to be a better miracle." Lin could hear the harshness in her own voice; she could not stop it. It was half a miracle at best, she thought, if such a thing was possible. She had to draw the smoke from Mariam's lungs every fortnight, or she would sicken badly again. She simply did not have enough power within herself to do more, not without extinguishing her own life. "I need to make sure you are entirely better and can manage without my interventions."

Mariam only smiled. "Well, that's true. If the Prince is getting married again, my services will be sorely needed to make dresses. Think of the parties and parades! So if you could make the miracle happen in the next, oh, fortnight or so, that would be awfully convenient."

"I don't think miracles work quite like that," said Lin, but she was smiling, because Mariam always made her smile. Mariam believed in her not for the reasons Chana did—because she yearned for the return of the Goddess in her lifetime—but because she had always believed in Lin. If Lin said she was the Goddess, it must be true, because it was Lin saying it. And Mariam's faith did not weigh Lin down; it was not something for her to carry. Rather, it had always carried her.

Ji-An drove as if Gentleman Death himself were at her heels, and Jerrod, Merren, and Kel, crouched inside the carriage, were flung repeatedly into one another. Kel was fairly positive Merren was praying—though to whom, he wasn't sure.

Raimon indeed appeared to have appropriated Montfaucon's carriage, Kel noted—a steel-blue calash driven by matched bays. It was much lighter than their own, but they had reached the city traffic now. Even if Raimon had demanded the driver go hell-for-leather, the crowded streets would have prevented it. Ji-An slowed down, bringing their carriage in behind Montfaucon's, to the undoubted gratitude of Andreyen's horses.

Merren and Kel peeled themselves off the carriage floor. Merren groaned about his bruises as Kel peered out the window. A low red moon hung over the city, tinting the streets a pale cerise color. The Broken Market was in full swing, and the Ruta Maestra was crammed with stalls, naphtha torches blazing as buyers wandered the wide avenue, hunting for bargains.

They had slowed to a crawl, and Kel cranked the window down, trying to catch sight of their quarry. The steel-blue carriage had come to a halt at the side of the road. As Merren demanded to know what was going on, Kel realized it had paused before one of the Story-Spinners.

A hand emerged from Montfaucon's carriage, and a shower of silver talents caught the naphtha light. Kel heard male laughter, the crack of a whip, then the bay horses started off again. Kel barely had time to catch hold of the window frame before their own carriage was once again lurching over the cobblestones, twisting this way and that to avoid pedestrians while keeping the calash in view.

"If Ji-An flattens any pedestrians," wondered Merren, "do you think they'll be able to trace it to us?"

They hurtled onto Ruta Taur, which cut up through the Silver Streets. The noise of the Ruta Magna fell away; here, among the placid homes of guildmasters and shopkeepers, there were far fewer foot travelers. The carriage slowed, Ji-An keeping a sedate pace so as not to alert Raimon.

Ruta Taur meant "street of towers," and indeed, the tall, thin houses showcased fanciful towers along the edges of the rooflines. They were built in rows, their sides close up against each other, with no space between them.

Montfaucon's carriage had come to a halt in front of one of the row houses. It disgorged Raimon, who descended swiftly, after exchanging what looked like angry words with the driver. As soon as the door closed, the calash hurried off.

Their own carriage was only a little way behind, and Kel waited for Raimon to look back at them. But he didn't turn his head, only went up the front stairs, unlocked the front door, and slammed it behind him.

"We needn't have hurried," Merren said, picking himself up off the floor again. "He was only going home in a snit."

"He might not have been," Kel pointed out, though he, too, would have bruises tomorrow.

Ji-An rapped her whip against their window, presumably to quiet them. She led the Ragpicker King's carriage silently around the corner and onto a darkened side street of smaller houses. On the corner was a shophouse, the lower floor selling copper pots and pans.

There was a flash of movement; Ji-An had leaped down from the driver's seat. The carriage door opened, spilling Merren and Kel out onto the paving stones. Jerrod, somehow, had regained his seat and was able to descend the steps of the carriage in relative dignity. Kel stretched, relieved at no longer being tossed around the carriage's interior like a child's bouncing ball.

"Thank you," he said to Ji-An. "I have long been hoping someone would shatter my legs into multiple discrete pieces."

"I am pleased to make your dream a reality." Ji-An didn't have a hair out of place, somehow. She looked as neat as ever, and even a bit smug, the collar of her closely fitted silk jacket flipped up around her pointed chin.

Merren sat down on the curb and put his head between his knees. "Is that how carriages are driven in Chosun?" he said weakly.

"It is how carriages are driven in Castellane," Ji-An retorted. "Get up, Merren."

"Let him sit," said Jerrod. "Kel and I will do a bit of Crawling. See what we can see through the windows." He cracked his knuckles, grinning in Kel's direction. "Ji-An, you and Merren stand watch. If Raimon tries to leave his house or anything suspicious happens, whistle like a mockingbird."

"I'm a city boy," Merren complained. "I've no idea what a mockingbird sounds like."

"It sounds however it wishes to." Jerrod glanced around the side of the shophouse. "Kel, are you ready?"

Kel was not ready, but it seemed the time had come to put his lessons to use. "Merren and Ji-An, try not to stand out or do anything peculiar to attract attention."

Kel and Jerrod slipped around the corner to the Ruta Taur. All was as it had been before, except now lamplight spilled from the upper windows of Raimon's house, casting a dull illumination across the pavement.

"Now," Jerrod said, "like we practiced," and he began to scramble up the façade of the house. Kel followed, digging his fingers into the gaps between the bricks. As the street fell away below them, he tried to recall the varied instructions Jerrod had given him in the Black Mansion. *Do not expect to dangle from your fingers; that will get you killed. Let your body lean into the wall. It's all about how you distribute your weight. You can balance on a single nail if you hold yourself correctly. And don't behave like a fool.*

Jerrod was a great deal like Jolivet, come to think of it—at least as far as instructional technique went.

The sand-lime bricks were rough under Kel's fingers. He leaned into them, imagining that the wall was lying flat on the ground and he was Crawling across it, gravity pulling his body toward the house's façade. He passed a window, unlit, and glanced inside: He could see the shapes of furniture, an unlit fireplace along one wall. Several more windows went by, though there was nothing interesting to be observed: a kitchen with copper pots, a tepidarium with tiled walls.

"Here," he heard Jerrod whisper. He was balanced on an ironwork railing just above him; it was very small, just wide enough for the two of them to stand on, but not wide enough for Kel not to feel faintly sick when he glanced down at the street below. Apparently, he'd forgotten his last lesson: *Don't look down.*

He soon saw why Jerrod had paused. They were just below a window from which lamplight spilled; Jerrod was gazing inside with an impassive expression. Kel, balanced beside him, looked through the glass.

Inside was a bedroom, decorated in shades of red. Raimon had changed out of his party clothes and was pacing the room wearing only a pair of simple drawstring cotton trousers. Thick ropes of pinkish-white scars scored his shoulders, back, and legs—the mark of his previous life as a professional fighter. And on his throat, clearer now that Kel was closer to it, the brand of the Tully. As they watched, he stopped, rubbed his forehead unhappily, and returned to pacing.

"Now what?" Kel whispered to Jerrod.

Jerrod shrugged, a complicated maneuver while still clinging to the building's façade. "Now we go in."

Kel hesitated. "He knows me. At least, he knows I was at the party."

"We'll be very subtle," Jerrod said. "I'm a Crawler. I'm an expert at moving without a trace of noise. He won't even know we're here until we're on him."

"All right," Kel said. "Let's go, then."

Jerrod peered down at the sill below them and drew back one of his feet with care. He closed one eye as if sighting the distance, then swung his foot at the windowpane, which shattered with a sound loud enough to wake up the entire neighborhood.

"Without a trace of noise?" muttered Kel. Raimon had turned with alarm toward the sound.

"Direct approach is sometimes best," Jerrod grunted, and threw his entire body through the window into the bedroom beyond. Kel followed Jerrod, taking as much care as he could not to tear his clothes or his hands on the broken glass remaining in the frame. He rolled across the floor and came up quickly on his feet, only to discover that Raimon had turned and fled.

Kel exchanged a startled look with Jerrod. Raimon had been a vicious fighter in the Arena, vicious enough to be gifted with a nickname synonymous with death. So why had he run? Wouldn't he stand and fight to defend his own home?

But there was no point hesitating. Kel raced after Raimon, Jerrod close on his heels.

The house was tall but narrow, and it was quickly obvious that Raimon had nowhere to run but up or down; thankfully, Kel could hear him clattering about below. It sounded as if he was descending the sharply curving stairs two at a time. Kel and Jerrod raced after him. They were younger and lighter on their feet, but the former gladiator was shockingly quick for his size, and they were unable to get a hand on him as they corkscrewed their way down the spiral steps.

They burst into the ground-floor receiving room—a wide space with a fireplace taking up much of one wall. Uncomfortable-looking gilded chairs were set about as if ready to receive guests, though they were dusty, as if they had not been used in a long time, if ever. Over the fireplace hung a battered assortment of weapons, the kind often used in Arena fighting: a hand-axe, a longsword, a wicked-looking flail.

Raimon stood in the middle of the room, a bronze spear gripped in his hand. From the way he carried himself and the way he held his weapon, Kel could tell he knew how to use it.

"Stop." Kel flung up his hands. Jerrod, at his side, was breathing hard. "We just want to talk to you."

Raimon sneered. "Do you think I don't know—"

He broke off, staring, and Kel realized he was getting his first real look at who had broken into his house. His gaze slid from Jerrod to Kel and back again, and a look flashed across his face. One that surprised Kel.

Relief.

Who did he think we were? Clearly, Raimon had expected an attack. He hadn't been surprised, but he *had* been terrified. Now, though—

He gave a hoarse laugh and raised the spear. "Idiots," he said. "You're idiots. Do you have any idea what you've done?"

"I'd say we're pretty clear on it." Jerrod's voice was calm, but he had rocked forward onto the balls of his feet, ready to rush at Raimon.

Raimon drew his arm back. A shadow rose up behind him. Kel felt his eyes widen as something silver flashed at Raimon's throat.

A metal chain. It looped his throat, jerking him backward off his feet. He fell hard, the spear clattering out of his hand. Over him stood Ji-An, holding the looped chain in her hand.

She placed a booted foot on Raimon's chest and glared at Kel and Jerrod. "What are you waiting for?" she said. Raimon made a noise; Ji-An kicked him lightly. "Get over here and help me tie him up. I really don't know how you two ever get anything done."

"We're really very sorry about this," Merren said.

Raimon glared at him. The big man was tied to one of his own gilded chairs with Ji-An's metal chain. To no one's surprise, she had turned out to be a master of knots, looping the chain in such a manner that Raimon's struggling only tightened the bonds. Upon realizing this, Raimon had gone still. He wasn't gagged—Kel saw no point, when they wanted him to talk—but he'd been silent since they'd subdued him.

The subduing itself had not been easy. Raimon now had a black eye and a lower lip that was rapidly swelling. Kel himself had bruised knuckles, and Jerrod was limping slightly.

"No, we're not," Jerrod said to Merren. "We're not sorry."

"We broke into the man's house," Merren protested. "He could have fallen down the stairs and died."

"I could have," agreed Raimon.

"Well," said Ji-An. "That would have been your own fault."

"We're very sorry," Merren reassured Raimon.

Raimon slewed his gaze around to the others. "Who *are* you?" he demanded. "You two—" He indicated Kel and Merren. "I saw you at the Caravel. Thought you were nobles. But nobles don't do their own dirty work, do they?"

"Sometimes they do," Kel said. "But that's not the point. I saw your face, before. You were afraid when we broke in, then you looked relieved when you got a good look at us."

"Of course I was relieved," said Raimon. "You have to admit, you're not that frightening."

"I wouldn't continue in that vein if I were you," said Ji-An, twirling a slim knife she'd taken from her boot.

"Let me guess," said Raimon. "This is some trick of Lupin's. He wants you to drag me back to the Caravel—"

"This has nothing to do with Montfaucon," Kel interrupted. He was getting fed up. "All we need or want is information. Give us that, and we will happily leave you be."

"And if I don't?" Raimon snarled. In that moment, he was very much the Gray Serpent. Banked fury smoldered in his eyes, and Kel could see how he might once have dominated the Arena.

Merren had left Kel's side. He crossed the room to a low table and began to busy himself with a lime-green glass decanter.

"If you don't," Kel said slowly, knowing he was taking a chance, "I might need to inform Legate Jolivet that you were involved in the Shining Gallery slaughter."

Raimon blinked at him slowly. He was expressionless, but his hands gripped the arms of his chair so tightly that his knuckles had turned white as milk. "Fuck you. I'm no murderer. I don't know who told you this horseshit, but they're lying."

"Did you think no one would investigate what happened?" Kel was aware his friends were staring at him, and he hoped they had the will to just go along with whatever he said. "A Princess of Sarthe and two ambassadors are murdered on Palace grounds, along with several of our own people, and you thought no one would look into it?"

"If I thought about it at all, and I'm not saying I did, I'd have thought the Vigilants would look into it," muttered Raimon. "You don't look like Vigilants to me."

"We're not," Kel said. "We are an elite unit, tasked with discovering who committed the atrocities in the Shining Gallery. Unlike Vigilants, we can move undetected through society, gathering clues."

Jerrod made a coughing noise. Ji-An rolled her eyes; only Merren seemed unruffled by Kel's string of lies. He had returned, having poured red wine into a glass of Detmarch kristal. He offered the glass to Raimon, who indicated his bound hands. Merren held the glass up to Raimon's lips, letting him drink. Loosening his tongue with wine, Kel thought; it wasn't the worst idea.

Raimon finished the liquor in two swallows and sat back, a flush on his cheeks. He nodded at Merren—a curt acknowledgment, though not a thanks. "Elite unit or not"—he indicated Kel and the others with a jerk of his chin—"you are in over your heads."

"No need for you to worry about that," Jerrod said. "We want to know who's responsible for the slaughter. Old man Gremont died with your name on his lips. *The Gray Serpent.*"

Raimon barked a laugh. "The Gray Serpent died a long time ago, when he was cut from the Arena. Too old to fight, they said." He narrowed his pale eyes. "I'm just an ex-fighter trying to get by."

"You have an awfully expensive house," said Kel, "full of expensive things, for an old fighter just trying to get by."

"I make do," said Raimon.

"I think," said Merren, "he's asking you a question. How'd you make the money to pay for a mansion on the Ruta Taur?"

"What d'you think, idiot?" Raimon said. "No respectable citizen wants to hire someone who was in the Tully and fought in the Arena. Sometimes you can get work beating up drunks in the Maze, but it doesn't pay much. You know who pays? The nobility. And they'll spend a lot of gold to find someone to get their hands dirty on their behalf. I've only used what I had: contacts with mercenaries who could get things done. Ex-fighters, ex-prisoners. No one looks out for them. Someone had to do it."

"You're a true benefactor," Jerrod muttered under his breath.

"So you had a reputation," said Kel, as evenly as he could. "And someone came to you, asked you if you knew anyone who could carry out the Shining Gallery slaughter."

Raimon rocked forward in his chair, his muscles straining against the ropes. "It wasn't supposed to be a slaughter!" he said hoarsely. "They fucked me over. Liars! They were liars!"

"Who f—ah, who did you wrong?" asked Merren. Kel saw Jerrod hide a grin. Sailors swore, and nobles swore like sailors. The middle class—guildmasters among them—were far more prudish.

"It was just supposed to be embarrassing," said Raimon, his gaze far away. "That's all. Just show the little Sarthian chit that we didn't want her folk traipsing through here, acting like they owned the place, cluttering up our harbor. She was supposed to run back to Sarthe with her tail between her legs. They came to me, asked me to round up some of my old friends from the Tully—folks living low, avoiding the Vigilants. Knew they'd be desperate for the work. Hard to get hired for much when you've been officially exiled."

Raimon was almost breathless, the words spilling out of him. Kel didn't dare interrupt him; it was almost as if he had forgotten where he was, or who he was talking to. As if he'd been desperate to spill this information to someone.

Raimon went on. "My friends, they did what they were supposed to do. Dressed up, got into the Gallery, waved their swords around. Yelled a bit. They were told . . . we were all told . . ." He struggled for the words. "There'd be a way out."

"A way out of the Gallery?" Kel said, surprised. "But once the front doors were blocked, there's no other entrance."

"That's why they fought like they did," Raimon said hoarsely. "They were trapped. They wanted to get out."

I don't believe you. There was a fury rising in Kel, a rage that felt like sparks alighting through his veins, prickling his skin.

"Bullshit," he said. "The Sarthian Princess. She was only twelve years old, and she was murdered. Pinned to a wall with a crossbow bolt. What does that have to do with escaping?"

"None of my men would have done that—"

"Who hires a pack of criminals to frighten a child, anyway? Who would expend the money, the planning, on such a thing?"

Raimon tried to shrug again. "People want all sorts of things," he said. "And many nobles hate Sarthe. I didn't ask questions."

"Then you're a fool," said Jerrod, to Kel's surprise. "A fool who got his friends killed. Why would you trust a noble, no questions asked?" He narrowed his eyes. "Was it Montfaucon who hired you?"

Raimon gave a hoarse laugh. "Lupin could care less about politics," he said. "He's my protection. Once it all happened, once my people were all dead, I realized—I was the loose end. I knew what had happened. No one was supposed to know what had happened and survive. I needed to be close to someone in power. Lupin had approached me before. He likes to shock his friends, and what could be more shocking than a branded pit fighter? He'd have taken up with a crocodile if he thought it would make for a better party."

This struck Kel as a remarkably accurate assessment of Montfaucon. "Right," he said. "So Lupin Montfaucon had nothing to do with the plan. But there were others who knew about it. Gremont warned me about you at the party, just after one of your mercenaries put a sword in him. He said you would come for the Prince. Was that ever a part of the plan?"

Raimon looked horrified. "Harming the Aurelians? No. Gremont was part of the group that hired me, but he got squirrelly. Thought the plan seemed dangerous. Everyone was afraid he'd crack, tell on the others. He knew about me, knew I'd provided the mercs. He must have thought I was behind the bloodshed. Stupid old fool."

"Not that stupid," said Jerrod. "He led us to you. Maybe he realized in his last moments that you were the only one who would talk."

Raimon snorted. "Or he knew you wouldn't dare tie a Charter member to a chair and torture them for information."

He had a point, Kel thought. "So who *did* hire you? Which of the Charter Families knew about this, besides the Gremonts? You must have had a contact. Someone told you Gremont was getting squirrelly. Someone who paid you."

Raimon dipped his head. "A woman," he said. "Called herself Magali—"

The front window exploded. Shards of glass flew, shedding illumination, a crazy-quilt of reflected fire. Raimon's body jerked as a silver crossbow bolt slammed into his chest, pinning him to the chair. Its fletchings, three black feathers, quivered from the impact.

Kel felt a sharp sting below his ear, like a horsefly bite. He could hear Ji-An swearing and Merren asking if everyone was all right, if anyone was hurt, but he barely registered the words. He was already bolting toward the front door, his hand to his neck. He knew those fletchings. They matched the ones on the bolt that had killed Luisa.

He burst out of the house and glanced around. The shot had obviously come from across the street, probably from the roof. Without hesitation, trusting that his body would obey Jerrod's training, he ran toward the nearest house.

His hand came away from his neck gloved in blood and he cursed to himself. A stray bit of the glass from the window must have cut his skin. There was nothing he could do about it now; he wiped his hand off on his trousers and began to scale the façade of the house.

He was fast, very fast for someone who had only been Crawling up walls a short time. But not as fast as the assassin, it seemed. He reached the roof, a flat expanse of black tiles, and pulled himself onto it. It was empty. There was no sign of movement, and he felt the sinking sensation that he'd already lost his target.

Someone slammed into him from behind, sending him crashing to the hard tile of the roof. The wind knocked out of him, Kel could only gasp for air as a dark shadow loomed over him, blotting out the moon.

A very familiar dark shadow. This was surely the same person he'd met on the roof of the Shining Gallery, the one he thought of as the Dark Assassin. He had nearly forgotten how eerie the figure was, how—covered in close-fitting black material—it seemed faceless, inhuman, a blank where an identity should have been.

At last Kel had his breath back. He started to get to his feet, but the Dark Assassin didn't seem to like that. Kel found a booted foot on his chest, pressing him down.

And when it spoke, it was in the same guttural hiss that revealed nothing of the person speaking—man or woman, old or young. "Stop following me, *Királar.*"

Flat on his back, Kel cursed the night, his choices, and the murderer who seemed to have taken a personal dislike to him. "I didn't follow you here," he said. "*You* followed me."

"Oh?" The Dark Assassin sounded almost amused. "Does your Prince know where you are, Sword Catcher? Should you not be by his side?"

That hurt, more than the boot to the chest. "I do not need to be beside him to protect him," Kel said through his teeth. "Nor need you pretend you care about his fate." He recalled the last words the Dark Assassin had spoken to him on the roof of the Shining Gallery, voice gloating: *You stand upon the threshold of history, for this is the beginning of the fall of House Aurelian.*

"Oh, I care about his fate very much," purred the assassin. "And yours, for they are intertwined. You are his shield, his unbreakable armor. You die that he might live forever."

Kel stared past the Dark Assassin, at the stars fretted across the sky like glimmering needlework. *You are my unbreakable armor. And you will not die.*

It was what Conor always said to him at the end of their litany; as he said it now, he heard Conor's voice, the reassurance in it.

The assassin hissed a laugh. "You have been trying to find out who was responsible for the bloodbath up at the Palace."

Kel glared silently. There was something, he thought, about the way the assassin spoke—the words were accentless but strangely formal, as if Castellani was not their first language.

"I suppose," Kel said, "that now is the part where you tell me that I'd better stop investigating, or you'll kill me."

"I might kill you regardless," said the assassin pleasantly. "In fact, you're lucky that I have a use for you, Sword Catcher, or you would be dead already."

"A use for me?" Kel echoed, but between one blink and another, the Dark Assassin had darted off, racing across the rooftop at great speed. Kel sat up in time to see his assailant leap to the roof of the neighboring house and from there to the house beyond. By the time Kel had clambered wearily to his feet, he had lost sight of the Dark Assassin against the night sky.

Lin

The woman in the bed has the hollow, drawn look of impending death.

Lin knows it well. When you are a physician, death walks at your side, solicitous and inquiring. You learn to recognize the signs of his arrival long before the patient does: the first spatter of blood into a white handkerchief, the persistent cough that lasts into summer, the faint yellowing of the eyes.

Lin takes Domna Delores's pulse—light and rapid—and listens to her chest with the auscultor, but she already knows. Knows from the red spots on the woman's cheeks, from the tightness of the skin on her bones, the shadows beneath her eyes. Consumption, in its latest stage. She will die of it soon.

From her satchel, Lin draws the only medicine that will help now: morphea grains for the pain. As she begins to explain how to dissolve the grains in water, Domna Delores lays a hand on hers. The sick woman's fingers are fragile as hollow reeds.

"Tell me, Doctor. Are you Ashkar?" she asks.

Lin hesitates for a moment, taken aback. Surely her clothes— neat, plain, gray—make it obvious? And surely the woman knows what kind of physician has been recommended to her?

"I am," Lin says. She does not elaborate. Every Ashkar knew this hesitation, the space between declaring one's identity and the reaction to it. Would it be anger, rejection, curiosity?

Domna Delores's eyes fill with tears. "So was I, once."

A long silence. Lin looks a second time at the dying woman's small, sunny flat. It is clean but plain and tiny: There is a single small table, and only one chair. No signs of books, music, color. To Lin, the room seems to sing of loneliness, an unadorned, unaccompanied life. "You chose to leave the Sault?"

"No. I was exiled."

Lin draws in a sharp breath. "Oh. I am so sorry."

She can think of nothing else to say, but it does not matter. A feverish energy seems to take hold of Domna Delores; words spill out of her, a tale of love and punishment. An Ashkar girl, a Castellani boy. She had fallen in love, and when it was discovered, she had been exiled by the Maharam—not Davit Benezar, the current leader of the Sault, but the one who had come before him. A man Lin had not known.

Unusually, the boy had stood by her, and Delores had married her sweetheart. He was a shipbuilder, and they had always lived in sight of the walls of the Sault. Every time she saw the gates and the guards, Delores had felt the knives of loss turn in her chest. Her sister, her mother and father, her friends. All of them still alive and in the same city in which she lived, but none willing to breach the boundaries of the Law to communicate with her. She had even tried approaching her sister once in the marketplace, but the other woman had fled from her as if she were poison.

Later, when her husband died in an accident at the Arsenale, Delores had been left utterly alone. She had never made friends in Castellane. Others had kept their distance, made uncomfortable by her Ashkar background. She had found work at a stall in the market with her skill as a needlewoman, sewing on buttons for widowers, embroidering family crests into the linens of merchant families made good.

Life had passed her by quietly: a lonely, solitary thing. On windy nights, she would take herself to a tea shop close to the Sault and listen for the music that carried over the walls, the cantillations of the holy night as the Maharam called out questions and the men and women of the Sault responded: *What is life? It is a narrow bridge. Why will the Goddess return? To heal the world.*

"If you give me their names, perhaps I could tell you of your family," says Lin gently. "It is most likely that I know them, or my grandfather does."

But Delores—a Castellani name that means "sorrow," Lin knows; she cannot help but wonder what name her patient had been born with—only shakes her head, gripping Lin's hand tight. "No," she says. "No. It is too late for all that. Tell me of the Sault. Do the almond trees still flower in the Kathot?"

So Lin sets aside her morphea grains for a different treatment, one that will sustain her patient now more than tea or bread. Yes, she says, the almond trees still flower in the main square of the walled town-within-a-city. The Shulamat glitters gold under the sun, and the physick garden grows green and strong, and children dare one another to climb the walls as they always have, and come to Lin afterward with skinned knees and sheepish looks. And on holy days, of course, there is honey bread and spiced wine, and music at night when the waggons of the traders return from the Gold Roads . . .

Delores closes her eyes, a slight smile on her thin face, and Lin lets her voice trail off into silence. The next time she comes, she resolves, she will bring her patient a honey cake, or an egg bread studded with raisins. One cannot erase the bitterness of exile with the sweetness of sugar, she knows, but it is better than nothing at all.

CHAPTER FOUR

I t would be difficult," Kel said, poking at his noodle soup with a ceramic spoon, "to regard this evening as an unqualified success."

"Perhaps a qualified success?" Merren suggested.

They were in Jerrod's favorite noodle shop on Yulan Road in the heart of Castellane. After Kel had descended from the rooftop across from Raimon's house, he'd found the others waiting for him impatiently in the carriage. Broken glass littered the street in front of the house where Raimon lay dead, and they were all eager to be gone as soon as possible. As soon as Kel slid into the carriage, Ji-An took off at speed; this time, no one complained about her driving.

They'd finally stopped at a public cistern, where Ji-An leaned against the carriage as the others washed the blood off in the lukewarm water. Merren scrubbed ineffectually at the dried scarlet flecks on his hands until Jerrod, wordless, tore a strip of cloth from his own shirt and used it to scrape Merren's hands clean.

Kel had frowned as he explored the gash along his own neck with his fingers. It was longer than he'd realized, and though it was shallow, it had soaked the strip of cloth around his neck. It seemed to have stopped bleeding, but he didn't like it. A mark he'd have to explain at Marivent was inconvenient at best.

Merren said, "Who do you think killed Raimon?" He lowered his voice. "Not the Vigilants?"

Jerrod snorted. "No. They knock your door down and arrest you; they don't shoot at you through a window. Someone wanted to shut Raimon up before he talked to us."

Ji-An tugged thoughtfully at her braid. "Which might mean someone followed us from the Caravel. Did you find anyone on the roof, Kellian?"

"That was some brilliant Crawling by the way," Jerrod noted. "Getting up and down that wall so quickly. Must be all that Sword Catcher training. Most of my gang couldn't have done it."

"Shut up, Jerrod. I want to know if Kel found the assassin on the roof," said Ji-An. Her glance at Kel said: *You saw something, didn't you?* Kel thought of the figure in black, outlined against the curved rooftops of the Ruta Taur: faceless, almost voiceless.

"Let's not talk here," Kel said. "We're exposed on the street, given the attacker's expertise with a bow and ability to track us."

"I know where we can go to talk," said Jerrod. "Yulan Road."

"Wonderful," said Merren. "I love noodles. Though I'll be needing my hand back, Jerrod."

Expressionless, Jerrod returned Merren's now-spotless hand to him.

They had been to the Yu-Shuang Noodle House often in the past three months; Jerrod still liked to meet colleagues and informants there, and Ji-An and Merren liked the food. As did Kel, who realized as soon as he entered that he was starving. The scent of garlic and steaming pork hung in the air like a fragrant cloud.

The staff knew Jerrod, and once everyone had ordered, they waved him toward the booth in the back where he usually held court. Ji-An had come in last, having paused on the road to fix a broken lace on her boot. Now she made a face at Merren, who had just made his comment about considering the evening a qualified success.

"What part might be considered successful?" Ji-An demanded, licking her spoon. She had an incorrigible sweet tooth and was consuming a pudding of egg custard, dusted with sugar. "The part where our one connection to the Gallery slaughter was assassinated while we were questioning him? The part where we had to flee before the Vigilants came?" She sounded resentful, though not of Merren; Ji-An wasn't one who enjoyed running from a confrontation.

"While we were questioning him, not before we questioned him." The night's events didn't seem to have spoiled Merren's appetite. He was on his second plate of vegetable dumplings, lightly dotted with carmine splashes of hot oil. He licked his thumb and said, "We did learn some useful things—"

"There is something I have to tell you," Kel said.

"You're arresting us all in the name of the Arrow Squadron?" said Jerrod.

"What— No, of course not. Have you been expecting me to say that?"

"Every time I see you," said Jerrod. "I keep waiting for the other shoe to drop."

"Jerrod, you have an untrusting personality," said Kel. "It's about the killer who shot Raimon."

He told what he knew—not just what had happened tonight, but the first time he had seen the Dark Assassin, on the rooftop of the Shining Gallery. How he had seen that the crossbow bolts were the same, with their characteristic gray-and-black fletching.

"Why didn't you tell us before?" demanded Ji-An. "About what happened during the Gallery slaughter?"

Kel shrugged uncomfortably. "I didn't like that they'd spoken to me as if they knew me. Like they did tonight. I felt . . . implicated, I suppose."

"You are implicated," said Ji-An. "But that isn't the same as responsible."

"I felt as if I should know who it is," Kel said, hand tightening around his cup of rice wine. "Or at least I should have a good guess. But I don't."

"Lin," said Merren, his voice warm, and for a moment Kel thought Merren had lost his mind and decided the Dark Assassin was Lin. Then he realized Merren was, in fact, greeting Lin Caster, who had just arrived, wearing her gray physician's tunic, her bright hair tied at the back of her neck with a ribbon. Over her shoulder was her medical satchel.

"What are you doing here?" said Kel. "Not that I'm not glad to see you."

"I sent for her," said Ji-An, and Kel realized she had not, in fact, paused outside to fix a broken bootlace. "I didn't like that cut on your neck. It looks as if someone's tried to slit your throat."

Kel touched a hand to the gash on his neck and winced. "That was . . . thoughtful."

"It's not that I care about you," said Ji-An. "It's that I don't want you to fall under suspicion at the Palace."

"Clearly." Kel spoke gravely, shifting over in his seat to make room for Lin, who settled herself beside him and began examining his neck.

"It's a very clean cut," she said. "Not bad, but something very sharp made it."

"Glass," offered Merren.

Lin darted a look at Kel with worried green eyes, but didn't ask what had happened. "It's just above the artery. A bit deeper and . . ."

"I would have bled out," said Kel, "rather dramatically, on a rooftop. An unpleasant surprise for the homeowners."

"Nonsense," said Jerrod. "You'd never have made it up to the roof in your weakened state."

Ji-An ignored their banter. "Someone who could follow us like that person did, without us noticing, is very good at what they do. I don't like it." She tapped her nails against her teeth, looking thoughtful.

Lin, having told Kel to hold very still and not talk, had taken out a salve from her bag and was brushing it along the cut on his neck with her fingertips. It stung like the contents of a wasp nest.

"It won't hurt for long," Lin said. "And look—the cut's already closing. By the time you get back to the Palace, it'll just look like a scratch." She was leaning in close to him, smelling pleasantly of soap and crushed leaves. Kel was sure he stank like rain gutters and sweat. He closed his eyes to let the sting fade as the others filled Lin in on the evening's activities.

"Montfaucon wanted his lover to fight a boxer who was dressed like a bear?" she said at one point. "Why?"

Nobody seemed to have an answer for that, and the conversation moved on. After Lin had screwed the lid back onto her salve jar and put it away, she said, "I'm sorry to hear of that man's death."

"Raimon? I would not weep for him," said Jerrod. "He almost certainly knew more than he was admitting about the Gallery attack."

"I don't know if he did," said Kel. "He sounded genuinely bitter against those he felt had tricked him and his friends. Which leaves us to ask: Who hired them?"

Ji-An pushed her empty bowl away. "Let us consider what we do know. Raimon was paid to hire a group of criminals he'd met in the Tully years ago. Most had been released, but under order of exile, which is why nobody has noticed they were missing. They were already in hiding. The criminals believed they were supposed to frighten the Sarthian Princess, not kill her."

"So he claimed," muttered Merren. "That poor girl."

"I thought you hated royals." Jerrod looked bewildered.

"I don't want them *murdered*," protested Merren.

Jerrod shook his head. "I really don't understand your politics."

"Stop." Ji-An made a shushing motion in their direction. "These criminals, his Tully band, didn't believe they were on a suicide mission. They thought they were going to escape."

"Right," said Kel. "Which means they had no real passion for punishing Sarthe; they did this for money, at the behest of a group whose motivations we do not yet know. Old Gremont was part of this group, but regretted it before his death. The mercenaries were not so much the guilty parties themselves as tools in the hands of the guilty parties."

"Well, we got a name, if only a first one," said Merren. He had finished his dumplings and regarded his empty plate sadly. "Magali."

"There is a Magali who works for the Alleynes," said Lin. "I remember taking note of her name. It's unusual."

"Not that unusual," Kel said sharply. "There's no reason it need be Antonetta's housemaid."

Lin raised an eyebrow at his vehemence.

"And yet," said Jerrod, his dark eyes thoughtful, "there is—was—a Magali who used to frequent the Maze in order to borrow money from some of the less scrupulous lenders. She had a gambling habit. More of a problem than a habit. Bets on the games in the Arena. Didn't care who was fighting—crocodiles, humans, giraffes—she'd place a wager on it."

"There are giraffe fights in the Arena?" said Merren, eyes wide. "I love giraffes. They always look surprised to be up so high."

"Shut up, Merren," said Ji-An, turning to Jerrod. "Why didn't you mention this before?"

Jerrod shrugged. "Like Kel said, there's more than one Magali in the city. I hadn't thought about her for a long time, but what Lin said reminded me, as this Magali bragged about having a job up on the Hill. I never quite credited it, but it sounds like she was telling the truth."

"If it's the same Magali at all," said Kel tightly.

"Does this mean the Alleynes are our malefactors?" said Ji-An. "Since Magali is their servant?"

"It's quite early to decide that," said Lin. "I doubt the Alleynes have much idea what Magali gets up to in her spare time. Antonetta certainly doesn't."

She smiled reassuringly at Kel, in a way that made him glance away quickly.

"I didn't realize we were all such admirers of the Alleynes," said Ji-An. "One of us is going to have to talk to this Magali person—"

"I need to speak to the Legate first," said Kel, and everyone looked at him in surprise. They all knew of Jolivet's role in their investigation, but Kel rarely mentioned him and had certainly never invoked him before as a reason for delay.

"I suppose," Jerrod said, "if we're starting to circle this close to one of the Charter Families, the Legate will have to know."

"The Alleynes do seem as if they might not be trustworthy," said Merren. "They *are* allying themselves with the Gremonts."

Kel said nothing. He didn't quite trust his voice in the moment.

Lin said, "I assure you, marrying Artal Gremont was not Demoselle Antonetta's choice."

Kel could hear Antonetta's voice, soft at the back of his head. *Do I want to marry Gremont? No. If I escape wedding him, will the next man my mother selects be just as bad? Most likely.*

Most likely not, Ana, he thought now. He was not certain it could be worse, and he felt wrenched and sick inside. If he were someone else, he could offer Antonetta another option. Though he supposed it was the height of presumption to assume she would want to marry him, even if desperate.

Lin glanced at him before turning back to Merren. "I'm a little curious that Raimon told you so much so willingly. Did you put something in his wine, Merren?"

Merren blushed. "Of course I did," he said, and Kel recalled Merren fussing with the decanter. He felt a mild annoyance with himself; he ought to have guessed, as Lin had. "My own mixture. It forces—well, *inclines*—one to tell the truth."

"That was a clever thought," said Jerrod, and smiled at Merren. He had a way of smiling, Kel had noticed, that seemed unique to Merren; he certainly never smiled that way at anyone else.

Ji-An stretched and yawned. In fact, they were all exhausted, and they wearily gathered up their things before leaving the spiced heat of the noodle shop for the humid night outside. Kel offered to walk Lin to the Sault gates—he needed to return to the Caravel to retrieve Asti, regardless, and he knew Lin would more easily avoid trouble from the Vigilants if she was accompanied.

As for the Dark Assassin, Jerrod and Ji-An both agreed that someone with skills like that must be known in the criminal under-world; Jerrod, seeming aggrieved that he did not already know who it was, promised to seek out answers among his connections. "Being able to Crawl is one thing," he said, "but to aim like that is another. They shot Raimon through the heart from a rooftop across the street. Not many can do that."

He sounded almost admiring.

"Remember," Kel said, "we are trying to catch this person before they kill again, not trying to hire them, Jerrod."

Jerrod grinned, the moonlight winking off his mask. "We caught you and then we hired you."

"You didn't hire me; Andreyen did. And I don't think they'd make a good ally."

"You're just taking it personally because they tried to kill you," Jerrod said with a grin.

"No," said Kel, thoughtful. "They didn't. That's the odd part. They could have killed me easily enough. But they said I was of use to them."

"Well, that's ominous," said Ji-An. "Try not to be too useful, if you can."

Kel smiled crookedly. "I'll do my best."

It was Third Watch now, and the moon had set. The streets of Cas-tellane were dark, and as quiet as they ever got. They were not de-serted, as Kel walked Lin home through the lamplit shadows of the curving streets, but those abroad at such a late hour seemed to know it was a hushed time. The costermonger pushing his cart did not whistle; the maidservants on their way to light the morning fires at the noble houses where they worked did not chatter among one another. Even Kel, when he spoke, did so in a low voice.

"I suppose," he said, "I should not ask what it is like."

"That depends on what *it* is," said Lin, a little amused. It was not like Kel to be oblique.

"Being the Goddess," he said. "I was thinking on it in the noodle shop. We summoned you so casually for healing, and yet—you are not simply the healer you have always been, are you?"

"No, I am," she said. "I am that person. I am just also . . . something else."

She had tried to explain it to Kel and the others in the Black Mansion, the day after it had all happened. She had been honest in what she told them: In her desperation to get her hands on books in the Shulamat in order to heal her friend, she'd made the claim that she was the Goddess whose return was prophesied in the lore of the Ashkar people. It would be temporary, she had told them, and they should not consider it in dealing with her, for it was a thing that would matter to Ashkar only, and they were not Ashkar.

None of them had really batted an eye—save Andreyen, who had peppered her with questions, mostly about the books they both wanted—yet here was Kel, suddenly curious.

"Did Mayesh say something about it to you?" she asked. They were walking west on the Ruta Magna, and in the distance she could see the harbor, or rather the abrupt end of the city that signaled the place the sea began. The horizon was a single blue band, ocean and sky united. As a child, she had wished she could leap from the walls of the Sault into that blueness—that limitless expanse that seemed to promise an unimaginable freedom. And she had wondered, too: Was the Goddess, somehow, on the other side of that light? In her own limitless expanse, but of darkness, closed off from the world Lin knew?

"I asked him about it," Kel admitted. "He made it clear he had no plans to discuss it with me." He looked a little abashed. "Did I do wrong?"

It was interesting that abashment came easily to Kel; Lin could not imagine the Prince seeming sheepish or unsure of himself. Two boys, raised in the same room, side by side, so close in looks, and yet so entirely different.

She wondered what would happen if she were to ask Kel about Conor. Was the Prince pleased about his engagement, the coming alliance with Kutani? Did he know the Princess at all? Had they exchanged letters, portraits? She felt a little wrench in thinking of it, of Conor admiring the famously beautiful Princess. Perhaps he could not wait for her to arrive. Perhaps he was counting the hours, the minutes.

She forced her mind away from those thoughts, though not away from the Prince entirely. Kel had said Prince Conor had changed; that one sentence refused to leave her. Changed in what way?

But the Prince was a topic that Kel did not like to discuss. He saw it as a sort of betrayal; he was already torn enough over keeping his activities in the city hidden from Conor. *Prince* Conor, she reminded herself. Kel might call him by his first name, but it was not her place to do that.

The Prince was not the only topic Kel Saren avoided. Lin had not missed the way his careful pleasantness turned to tension whenever Antonetta Alleyne was mentioned. When it had been suggested that the Alleynes might be implicated in the Shining Gallery plot, Kel had gone stone-faced, which for him was the equivalent of an apoplectic fit. She wondered what he would say if she told him she saw Antonetta often, that they even spoke of him sometimes, and that Antonetta was as flustered by mentions of him as he seemed to be by mentions of her?

But what would be the point? A Sword Catcher could not marry, and Antonetta was committed to Artal Gremont. She and Kel were similar in that way, Lin thought: They lived within walls both real and imagined, bound by the expectations and plans of others. And as for whose faces they saw when they closed their eyes at night, they kept that to themselves.

"No," she said. "No, you did not do wrong, though I could have told you Mayesh would have sent you packing if you asked him anything."

Kel pushed his dark curling hair off his forehead; there were light scratches, probably from flying glass, at his left temple, and small nicks and tears in his fine clothes. "It wouldn't be the first time the Counselor has kicked me out of his office for asking troublesome questions."

Lin laughed. Kel was good at that, making her laugh. "The whole business— It's hard for me to talk about, I suppose," she said as they passed a candlemaker's shop. Candles had been left alight in the window overnight, an advertisement for the merchant's goods: fat white pillars and braided, multicolored tapers burning softly behind the glass. "Not because it is forbidden or because I am ashamed, but . . ."

"Because though you are pretending to be something you are not, you still feel a responsibility."

Lin nodded. "I walk around the Sault, and I can tell the others are seeing me—but also seeing someone else in my place."

"Yes. You behind the Sault walls, me behind the walls of Marivent—and here we are, of course; too bad. I was enjoying our talk."

Indeed, as if he had conjured them up by speaking of them, the walls of the Sault loomed over them. They were not quite close enough for Lin to see who was guarding the gates, but the ever-torches burned in their holders on either side, as they always did. In their light, Kel's eyes were very gray. She recalled him saying they had once been another color, before they had been changed to look like Conor's. She could not help but wonder what color.

He said, "I have always wondered what it says over the Sault gates. I've seen the words before, I am sure of it. But I cannot recall where."

"On my grandfather's medallion, perhaps," Lin said. "The one he wears as Counselor. They are in our Old Tongue."

"I thought all Ashkar spoke the same language?"

"We do, though accents, dialects, can differ." Lin was thinking of her parents, of the bits of Shenzan and Malgasi and Hindish incorporated into the near-incomprehensible trader's patter of the Rhadanites. She had never learned it herself, nor the written language of signs and symbols that only the Rhadanites could read. It had always been Josit who was interested in all that. "But there is a difference between the language we speak daily and the words of prayers and songs. Words like Sanhedrin, or Shekinah, are in the Old Tongue. Over the gates is written our Great Prayer. *Oqodemshe, thān Ashkar, Mayyam khaf, anokham miwwod.* 'Hear, oh Ashkar, She is One, She will return.'"

"So the Great Prayer speaks of the Goddess. But what does that mean, *She is One?*"

"It means we do not believe in many Gods, as you do," Lin said. "We believe only in one. It is what makes us what we are, that faith. And so the words of the Great Prayer are a safeguard. They are etched into amulets worn against the skin, woven into clothing, inked as tattoos. In times when the Ashkar have had to hide who they were, they were often written on strips of paper cunningly concealed inside a pen, or an earring, or the heel of a boot. As long as you carry the Great Prayer with you, she protects you. And you never forget you are Ashkar."

Kel was silent for a moment. His face was grave in the light of the ever-torches.

"I never knew any of this," he said at last. "I have known Mayesh all my life it seems, yet I did not know this."

"We are not meant to tell such secrets to *malbushim.* I have come to know my grandfather better these past months, and to understand that while he speaks *for* the Ashkar at Marivent, he does not speak *of* us at Marivent."

"No," said Kel. "He is an interesting man, Bensimon. I do not think there are many people for whom he lets down his guard."

"I think I am like him in that way," mused Lin. "But around you, around Merren, Ji-An, even Andreyen and Jerrod—they do not care if I call myself Goddess or Queen of the Harbor or—or Princess of Potatoes." Kel grinned. "They know who you are, too," she added, "Sword Catcher."

"That they do," Kel said. "Now, if you'll excuse me, I must rescue my horse from a brothel. Not a sentence I ever thought I'd have to say aloud. And for the Gods' sake, don't tell Mayesh about any of this," he added, turning to go. "He'll have my head, and play *boules* with it on the Palace lawn."

By the time Kel returned to Marivent, the sun was beginning to rise over the Narrow Pass. Having brought Asti to the stables and rubbed her down with a few handfuls of hay (she was quite resentful about having been left behind at the Caravel, and snorted when he tried to give her an apple), he discovered a note from Jolivet tucked inside the feed trough, which simply read, *I shall expect a full report tomorrow.*

Kel tore the note into small pieces, scattered them, and headed for the apartments he shared with Conor.

He was already rehearsing the version of the evening he planned to share with Conor. He would keep it as close to the truth as he could. Not only was that the safest way, but it also assuaged the part of his conscience that stung like a cut when he had to lie.

He would tell him about Montfaucon, Kel thought as he entered the rooms, and the boxer dressed like a bear, and Esteve's interest in Beatris Cabrol. That he had talked with Silla. Or perhaps he would not mention her. That Conor had not slept with her was a surprise—but it had been the night of that miserable party at the

Roverges', hadn't it, and Conor had been wretched at the time. And, Kel thought, it really was none of his business.

The rooms were cold, the fire having burned down in the grate, and dark, too. The only illumination was the dawn light that spilled through the windows like thin blue milk. Conor was at his desk, as he often was these days, but as Kel came closer, drawing off his gloves, he saw that the Prince was asleep, cheek pressed to the top-most of a pile of papers, as if he'd laid his head down for just a moment and fallen asleep instantly.

Kel hesitated. In sleep, Conor's face was wiped clean of tension and consideration, and he looked as he had when they were boys. Not innocent, or wicked, either, but curious and expectant. As if there were much to look forward to. Kel could still remember what he had thought the first time he had seen the Prince. *I want to be like him. I want to walk through the world as if it will reshape itself around my dreams and desires. I want to seem as if I could touch the stars with light fingers and pull them down to be my playthings.*

He knew better now. The world did not reshape itself around anyone. No matter how powerful you were, there were forces more powerful than you would ever be. It was true in the city and on the Hill.

He laid a hand on Conor's shoulder, felt him begin to stir. "It's me," he said. "Con. You've been working too hard."

Conor sat up, rubbing at his eyes. "A Prince's duties are never complete."

That's not what you used to think. But Kel did not say it aloud. He merely slipped an arm around Conor's back and said, "Come. I'll help you to bed."

Lin

"Come now," says Lin, as if coaxing a child. "Show me your wrist."

"It's fine," the girl sitting across from her—Silla, that was her name—says. "I needn't have any treatment. No leeches and things. It'll get better on its own."

Lin smiles. "I don't use leeches; ask any of the other girls."

Silla sighs dramatically. She is a pretty girl, with red hair a few shades lighter than Lin's own, dark eyes, and a sulky mouth tinted red. She wears a silk dressing-gown with long flared sleeves, and as she turns her head, Lin sees the dark marks of bruises on the other girl's throat.

She feels her smile vanish and plasters a look of professional blankness onto her face. "It won't hurt," she says, and with another sigh, Silla pushes up her right sleeve, baring a long, slender arm. A delicate arm, made for languid gestures, marred now by an ugly bracelet of bruised, puffed flesh around the wrist.

Lin takes the other girl's hand and hears her suck in her breath as she examines the wrist as carefully as she can. Not broken, at least. Just a bad sprain, as if someone had caught Silla by the wrist when she tried to walk away, grabbed her hard, and twisted . . .

"When did this happen?" Lin demands, hot anger coursing through her.

"Just today." This seems true; the bruises look fresh.

"Who did it? You must tell Domna Asper. She won't stand for it."

"Alys hasn't got much choice." Silla looks glum. "Not when it's nobles, like the Prince and his friends—"

The blood seems to stop in Lin's veins. Suddenly nauseated, she hears the pounding of her heart in her temples. "Prince Conor did this?"

"No—oh, no," Silla says, seeming genuinely dismayed. "He drinks and gets ridiculous like they all do, but he's not unkind. It's been nearly ten years he's been coming here with his cousin, and never a bad word about either of them."

Lin expels a breath of relief. There is still a tight knot in her chest, but it has loosened slightly. She knows Prince Conor frequents the Caravel; Kel has told her as much. They both do. It is safer, Kel explained, than dalliances with the young men and women of the Hill, which could lead to awkward entanglements. This way, with the transaction up front, is easier.

Still. Ten years. She cannot help but think of Conor at that age, when he'd been all long legs and arms and big gray eyes under a thick mop of curling dark hair. Kel had told her frankly that he'd been terrified the first time he'd visited the Caravel; she wonders if Conor had been, too.

"So who was it?" Lin says, removing a roll of bandages from her satchel. "Who did this to you?"

"Artal Gremont," says Silla, after a long pause. The spilling of secrets must not come easily to her; her job tends to entail keeping them close. "Alys knows. I told her."

"Artal Gremont?" Lin demands. "I didn't even know he was in Castellane yet. Antonetta didn't tell me."

Silla snorts. "The moment he landed in the city, he came straight to the Temple District. All he seems to want to do is stagger drunkenly from one bedroom to another. None of the girls can stand him. And Alys looks at him as if she despises him, but only when he's not looking. She says we have to make nice—he has powerful allies."

"He's powerful himself." Lin begins to bind Silla's wrist. "He's about to take over the tea Charter. And marry into the silk Charter, too."

Silla rolls her eyes. "He did say something about needing to have all the fun he could before the walls of matrimony close in on him. But he's the sort of man to see courtesans behind his wife's back. I think he was just whining for sympathy."

"Ugh," Lin says. "Alys won't make you see him again, surely?"

"No. But she can't keep him away from the Caravel. There are other girls, the kind who cater to men who like to inflict pain. I suppose he'll see them. But they'll have to pretend they truly hate what he's doing; he won't enjoy it otherwise. He wants to cause misery."

And this is the man Antonetta is supposed to marry? Lin thinks. Should she warn Antonetta? Would it do any good if she did? Antonetta seems so removed from this world of the Caravel; would she even understand? Her determination to marry Gremont regardless of how awful he is seems immovable.

And marriage is a different thing for those on the Hill, she thinks. What Gremont felt no compunction about doing to a powerless girl in the Temple District was not what he might feel comfortable doing to the heir to the silk Charter fortune.

She has finished bandaging Silla's wrist; as she bends to put her things away, Silla says, in an uncertain voice, "You know Kel Anjuman, don't you?"

Lin pops back up in her chair. "Did Alys tell you that?"

Silla nods. "I used to see him all the time. He was one of my more regular clients. Then he stopped coming around—but so did the Prince, and I thought perhaps he simply goes where Conor goes."

It is odd to hear someone call Conor by his first name so casually, but the thought does not linger long in Lin's mind: She is stunned to hear that he's been forgoing the Caravel. Perhaps everything Kel has said about him is true. Perhaps he has changed.

"The last time I saw Kel, he made it clear to me our interactions were finished," Silla adds. "It is a shame. I had hoped, perhaps . . ."

Lin looks away, wanting to hide her expression from Silla. "I can imagine it is hard to have hopes when the object of your affection is one of those on the Hill."

"Oh, affection." Silla waves the concept away with her uninjured hand. "I'm fond enough of him, but I never imagined marriage or anything like that. But I had thought he might want a mistress—an official one. The dream of every courtesan is to become a mistress. One gets a house in the Silver Streets, a carriage, and a bit of money to save. Independence. It's a decent living if the man's kind."

"And Kel is kind," Lin agrees, picking up her satchel. "But you will find another kind patron. I am sure of it."

Silla only smiles at her faintly; Lin knows her words probably carry little comfort. They are worlds apart, she and Silla, but as a doctor and a courtesan they share the same knowledge: that kindness is rare as gold in Castellane, and real goodness rarer than Sunderglass itself.

CHAPTER FIVE

I t's black," Lin said.

Mariam shook her head. "It's dark blue."

Lin glared at the gown hanging from the rail on Mariam's wall. "It's *black*. Which is not a color Ashkar are allowed to wear outside the Sault, Mari."

"It's marine blue," Mariam insisted stubbornly. "It's supposed to be the color of the sea."

"Hmph." Lin brushed her hand down the material of the dress. The silk was smooth and heavy in her hand; she could feel the weight of its richness, its luxury. Tiny jet beads cascaded across the front, a scatter of stars. The neckline was modest enough, but the back seemed dangerously low. "You made this in two days?"

"I adjusted it to your measurements in two days," Mariam corrected. "It took me two weeks to make it. It was meant to be for Demoselle Mirela Gasquet, but her mother decided it was too revealing."

Lin eyed the back again. "If it's too revealing for a daughter of the nobility, it's certainly going to be too revealing for *me*."

Mariam rolled her eyes. "It's the fashion. At least try it on."

There was no arguing with Mariam when she was in this sort of mood. Lin stripped down to her smallclothes and shimmied into the heavy dress, standing patiently while Mariam did up the hooks along the side.

"Lovely," Mariam said when she was done. "Oh, Lin. It's so pretty."

Lin looked in the mirror. She had to admit Mariam was a dress-making genius. The dark satin was as close-fitting as a glove. The beads that shimmered and drew the light seemed to illuminate the most sensual parts of her: flare of hips, curve of waist, rise of breasts. When she turned, she nearly gasped: The back of the dress was cut almost to her waist, showing a moon-pale expanse of skin.

"I feel practically naked," Lin said, awestruck.

"Which is why you will be carrying this shawl," said Mariam, producing a soft black shawl woven with a pattern of silver flowers. Somehow it did seem to match the dress. Lin took it and threw it about her shoulders, causing Mariam to sigh.

"Really, the dress is better without the shawl," she said, "but if you feel you *need* to wear it . . ."

"I need to wear it," Lin said firmly. "Oh—and shoes."

"Demoselle Mirela had me make a matching pair of *pasifles*. They're over here, I think," Mariam said, waving off Lin's offer of help as she rummaged around a pile of fabric remnants. She sighed again as she straightened up, two silk slippers in her hands. "I do wish I could go with you. See everyone admire you in your dress."

As she handed over the slippers (which were very clearly black, like the dress), Lin felt a wave of guilt wash over her. To her, attending this party was an obligation, one she was dreading. (Again, the little voice in her mind reminded her that the Prince would be there, that she would see him, that he would probably have forgotten her.) But for Mari, it would be a treat, a chance to see the glittering beauty of the Hill.

And the treachery, Lin thought, remembering the little Princess from Sarthe. The cruelty. Mariam was kindness personified—easy sport for the wolves of the Charter Houses.

"You're too good for the people on the Hill, Mari," Lin said.

Mari looked as if she wanted to argue, but she stopped herself. She twisted a bit of her skirt between her fingers and said, "It hardly matters. I mean, I *couldn't* go—and besides, there's something else I'd like to do tonight."

Lin finished wiggling her feet into the slippers. "What's that?"

"The books that you've been reading," Mariam said. "The ones about"—she lowered her voice—"magic . . . I want to read them, too."

Lin was surprised. "Really?" Mariam had never evinced any interest in this aspect of Lin's studies before.

"I'm so grateful for all you've done for me, Lin." Lin started to protest, but Mari waved her words away. "*But*—I feel as if my fate is entirely out of my own hands." Her dark eyes searched Lin's face. "Do you understand that?"

"I understand that feeling," Lin said. "Only most of the books are—" *Stored at the Black Mansion,* she was about to say; she had never felt truly safe keeping them all in her house since the time the Maharam had barged in and confiscated her precious tomes. He'd had to give them back after the Tevath, but the memory stung.

"I don't care if they're forbidden," Mariam said. "Lin, the only choice I *can* make is to rely on you to save my life. And I do—I trust you entirely—but surely it cannot help either of us for me to know so little. I want to understand what you're doing. What is happening inside me."

Lin felt a lump in her throat. "Mari—"

There was a perfunctory knock on the door; a second later Chana was peering into the room, her eyes bright under the scarf that bound her hair. "Oren Kandel is outside," she announced without preamble. "Lin, he has a message for you from the Maharam. He says it can't wait."

Lin's hands flew to her bodice. "I can't meet the Maharam wearing *this*."

Chana shook her head. "He said no delay, chicken. Better to meet the Maharam wearing that dress than to keep him waiting. Just keep that wrapped around you." She waved a hand at Lin's shawl.

Lin turned to Mariam, who was looking anxious. "Mari," she said slowly. "That foreign tea you were looking for—I have some on my kitchen table. It's only one flavor of tea, but it's a good one."

Mariam mouthed *thank you* to Lin as Chana fussed her out of the room and down the hall. Lin barely had time to wrap the shawl more tightly around herself before she'd been hurried outside, where Oren was waiting for her in the street.

His dark eyes seemed alive with hostility as he watched her approach. "The Maharam has requested I bring you immediately to the Shulamat, *Goddess*."

Oren flicked his gaze over Lin, from her bare head to her slippered feet, and it felt like a garden rake scraping her skin. She could feel the hunger and loathing in his eyes as he looked her over. As if he were starving but the only food he could find was something he detested.

Lin crossed her arms over her chest. "And what is this about, Oren?"

He smirked. "The Maharam will explain."

There was no point arguing. Oren had the upper hand and was clearly enjoying her discomfort. Lin resisted the urge to pull her shawl even closer and followed him without another word.

They set out into the blue twilight. It was the time just after sunset when the sky was not yet dark, but shadows had begun to gather thickly into corners and beneath trees. The air was velvet-soft, carrying a trace of salt so vivid it seemed as if one could taste it.

As they walked, Lin's mind raced. Could it be the Sanhedrin? But the Maharam had said they would not arrive for at least another few days, and besides, the Sanhedrin were a full caravan of dignitaries. The gates would have been thrown open for them, the Sault's council of elders assembled to greet them. It was not the sort of event that could have passed unnoticed.

Had the Maharam decided it was time to stop hinting around and demand that she admit she was not the Goddess Returned? She wondered if he had spoken to Mayesh. The two men disliked each other, and they had clashed before over Lin, but surely the Maharam would not take action against her without Mayesh's knowledge. Her grandfather was too important a man for that. And Mayesh would have warned her—despite the distance between them, he would have warned her. He was still angry at her, he had been since the Tevath, but he had also kept her secret. He had not told anyone he disbelieved her claim to be the Goddess, though she knew he did. That had to count for something.

They had reached the Kathot, the main square of the Sault. The flowering fig and almond trees at its heart cast great shadows across the flagstones, and hawk moths rustled in the darkness. The blue tesserae atop the dome of the Shulamat glowed under the light of the dimming sky. As Lin lifted her heavy skirts to make her way up the steps, she thought of the pride, mixed with resentment, she had always felt at the sight of the temple. Pride in the beauty of the architecture and in her people's knowledge and history. They had fled Aram with nothing, and built so much; they carried their wisdom, their traditions, as if they were precious goods, passing them down like heirlooms from one generation to the next.

Yet those same traditions had blocked her from the knowledge she desired. *I would not have claimed what I did*, she thought, *save that I had no choice.*

She raised her chin, straightened her spine. Stepped around Oren, entering the Shulamat before him. The Goddess did not follow a man like Oren Kandel.

She moved down the central aisle of the Shulamat, to the raised dais where Maharam Benezar sat, Oren hurrying behind her. The

Maharam was in his usual chair, his staff across his lap. At his shoulder stood a stranger.

The stranger watched Lin as she made her way down the aisle. He looked older than Lin, but was still a young man—twenty-nine, perhaps, or thirty. His hair was the color of bronze: a dark, tarnished gold. His skin had probably once been fair but was deeply tanned. He was clearly Ashkar; wrapped around each wrist and crisscrossing up both forearms were the slender black leather straps of the Rhadanite traders. He bore their markings as well—inky tattoos written in their pictographic shorthand—on his arms, his hands, and his throat where the laces of his shirt were open. He was plainly dressed in the dust-stained linens of a traveler, his boots thick brown leather.

Lin looked from the stranger—expressionless, his posture ramrod-straight—to the Maharam. She could hear Oren behind her, breathing harshly. A flash of terror went through her, sharp and hot as a razor's bite. She had thought only of the Sanhedrin, but this was a traveler come with news. News from the Gold Roads. News for her.

"Josit," she whispered. "Has something happened to my brother?"

The stranger glanced at Benezar. "She has a brother?"

Confusion cut through Lin's anguish. Before she could repeat Josit's name, the Maharam said: "Lin. This is Amon Aron Benjudah. Our Exilarch." His deep-set eyes bored into her. "He has come to test the Goddess Returned."

Lin's stomach cartwheeled in a mixture of relief and shock. This was the Exilarch? She had seen pictures of Exilarchs, of course—men in rich robes, bearing medallions of silver. Yet here stood this stranger, in much-washed linen and a buckskin vest, sleeves pushed up, one bootlace partly untied. His bronze hair was thick and untidy, his cheeks grazed with stubble. Nothing about him spoke to his high position. Amon, she knew, was the name he used ceremonially, but the common people referred to him by his birth name, Aron.

"Now?" Lin kept her voice low, hoping it would not tremble. "Surely the test cannot be now. I have had no time to prepare."

"Is preparation necessary? Should the Goddess not simply be . . . the Goddess?" Aron's voice startled Lin. It was deep, rich, and musical. The voice of a descendant of Judah Makabi, the protector of the Goddess, who had gone with her people into exile.

Lin did her best to remain expressionless. She said, "It is written in the *Book of Makabi* that when the Goddess first returns, she may not even know herself."

"So it is," said Aron dryly. "It is good to see you know your holy books, Lin Caster." He glanced past her, his eyes narrowing. "Leave us, Kandel."

Oren glanced beseechingly at the Maharam, who shot him a quelling look. "Do as the Exilarch says."

As Oren walked away, slump-shouldered, Aron Benjudah stepped down from the dais, quashing Lin's hopes that he would be short. He wasn't. He was at least a head taller than she was. His amber gaze ran over her, taking in her silk-slippered feet, the richness of her satin dress. His look was absent both the hunger and the fury that had been in Oren's eyes. It was cool, calculating, adding her up and assessing. "Is there," he said, regarding Lin steadily, "some sort of festivity in the Sault tonight? One I am not aware of?"

Lin raised her chin. There was no point in lying. "A festivity, yes. But not in the Sault. On the Hill."

"On the Hill? Where the nobles of your city live?"

"You do know," said the Maharam, "that her grandfather is Mayesh Bensimon? The Counselor to the King?"

"I know Mayesh well," said the Exilarch, to Lin's surprise.

"He hopes she will follow in his political footsteps," said the Maharam. "He likes her to accompany him to the Hill now and then. Acquaint her with those close to the throne." His tone was dry.

"Interesting," said Aron. "Mayesh always had something of an unorthodox perspective. Unless he's changed. It's been seventeen years since I saw him last."

"He has not," Lin said shortly, "changed." Though her mind was racing—how had her grandfather known the Exilarch seventeen years past?

"He is at the Palace now," grunted the Maharam. "I am sure he will wish to see you, Aron."

"All in time," Aron said. "I have other concerns in the Sault."

"Many matters of justice await your judgment," said the Maharam. It was customary for the visiting Sanhedrin—and for the Exilarch, their leader—to take up cases brought before them for the application of Law. Often these were disputes of property or custom: anything the council of elders felt was beyond them to decide.

"Indeed," said the Exilarch, but it was clear his mind was elsewhere. He approached Lin consideringly, as if she were a horse for sale in Fleshmarket Square. "Maharam," he said, without taking his eyes from Lin. "You know I must."

"Yes," said the Maharam, his thick brows drawn together. The Exilarch's attention was still on Lin, who fought the urge to knot her hands at her sides.

She would not show that she was anxious, she told herself as he came closer. She would not let him intimidate her. She had experience of princes. They were just men, like any other men.

"Lin Caster," Aron said. "I am your Exilarch, your *gadol hador*. Look up at me."

She raised her face unwillingly. He was only a few inches away from her. This close, she could see that his eyes were the color of desert sands, as if they had been dyed by the arid landscapes he had passed through on his travels.

The room was utterly silent. She could hear her own breath as their gazes connected. She did not think she had ever been looked at so closely. Aron seemed to be taking her apart with his eyes, as if he could crack open the shell of her with the force of his will and examine every component of her being for the truth or lies contained within.

Lin's heart seemed to beat with a sort of sickly dread that whispered to her: *He is who he says he is. The Exilarch, the descendant of Judah the Lion. He is seeking in me some sign that I am who I say I am: the Goddess Returned, the one who is destined to reunite with him. Surely there is meant to be some spark of the divine, some flame that is lit when the Exilarch looks upon the Goddess for the first time. Surely he expects to feel something.*

It seemed quite clear to her he felt nothing.

He stepped away, breaking the contact of their eyes. Lin wanted only to drop her gaze, but she forced herself to stare straight ahead, her heart hammering in her chest.

Aron's voice was flat. "Well, you are not the first who has claimed the stature of Goddess Returned since the Sundering. You are not even the first this year. I have learned to temper my expectations. So have the Sanhedrin, which is why they chose, in the end, not to accompany me here. If you pass the first of the tests, I will summon them."

Otherwise, it would be a waste of their time. He did not say it, but it was clearly what he was thinking. Lin felt a flare of annoyance before telling herself she was being ridiculous. He was right to be cautious. She knew that better than anyone.

"The first test?" she echoed. "How many will there be?"

"Let us concern ourselves with the first now," said the Maharam. "If it does not go well, after all, there will not be another. You will be notified when it is to take place."

Lin swept a small curtsy. It was a bit of Castellani decorum, not Ashkar custom, but it hardly seemed to matter. "I would appreciate some advance notice," she said, "as I must concern myself foremost with the care of my patients."

"Foremost?" The Exilarch raised his eyebrows. "Above your duty to your people?"

Lin set her jaw. "These are lives, Exilarch," she said. "And as the

Goddess herself said, we who are Ashkar hold life above all other things. Above even duty."

I will not let one single patient die to please you, she thought. *No matter what it costs me.*

The Exilarch only narrowed his eyes, as if he guessed what she was thinking. Without another word, he turned his back on her. From the dais above, the Maharam gestured at Lin; she was dismissed. It was over.

As she left the Shulamat, she paused at the top of the steps to catch her breath. Had she been holding it? She wasn't sure; her head was pounding. All she could think was that she must do as much for Mariam as she could before her first test took place. Afterward, it seemed clear, it would be too late.

"I shall drink myself into a stupor tonight, I think," Montfaucon announced.

Kel looked over at him without much interest. He was crammed into one of the smaller Palace carriages with Conor, Falconet, Montfaucon, and Ciprian Cabrol, on their way to House Alleyne to celebrate Antonetta's engagement. Not that Kel saw much to celebrate.

"So, an ordinary night for you, then," said Falconet dryly. He was dressed in his best, as they all were. In Falconet's case this meant an ivory silk shirt with slashed sleeves showing ice-blue velvet beneath, and gloves with a frill of ivory lace at the wrists. Montfaucon wore poison yellow, and Cabrol his usual linen.

"I mourn my great love, Raimon," said Montfaucon portentously. "Had I known when I saw him at the Caravel it would be the last time—"

"You would not have encouraged him to publicly fight a man dressed as a bear?" said Ciprian.

Conor stretched and yawned. "Ciprian, let him be. Montfaucon, you fall in love every two weeks."

This was true. Kel strongly suspected that Montfaucon was not so much mourning the death of Raimon as he was trying to milk every drop of drama there was to be had out of the situation. Murder was exciting even to the jaded denizens of the Hill. According to Montfaucon, the Vigilants had been investigating Raimon's death, largely under the assumption that he had been killed by an old enemy from his Arena days.

As much as he doubted Montfaucon's sincerity, Kel still couldn't look at him when he talked about Raimon. As Montfaucon launched into an explanation of why Raimon was different from any other lover he'd had, Kel glanced over at Conor, who was slumped in the corner of the carriage. He wore a cloak of black swan feathers tipped in gold. Rings flashed on his fingers; his crown was a thin gold circlet from which a pendant diamond glittered against his forehead. There were shadows around his eyes: kohl or exhaustion, Kel couldn't tell.

"I'm too sensitive," Montfaucon said. "That's the problem. I feel the pain of others deeply. I worry about our dear Antonetta, being forced to marry Artal Gremont."

"You don't think exile might have improved him?" Kel said. He doubted it himself but wondered if Montfaucon knew anything he didn't.

"Not from what I've heard," Montfaucon said grimly.

Before Kel could ask exactly what he'd heard, Falconet, turning to Conor with his usual flashing smile, said, "It's your fault, you know."

Conor raised his black eyebrows. Kel said, "How's that?"

Falconet smiled. "If our Prince had not made it clear that he would never consider giving Lady Alleyne what she wanted and marrying Antonetta, perhaps she would not have chosen this particular alliance for her daughter."

Conor looked at him coolly. "I have chosen instead to make an alliance that will benefit our nation, not Lady Alleyne."

"Lady Alleyne will find some way to turn it to her benefit in the end, I'm sure," said Cabrol. "She strikes me as a very practical woman."

"Practical is one word for it," said Montfaucon. "She's the sort who's happy to smile and stab you in the back at the same time. Ice in her veins."

"A good quality," said Cabrol, "for the head of a Charter Family. Is her daughter like her?"

"No," Kel said flatly. "She isn't."

They all looked at him—even Conor. Luckily, Kel was saved having to explain what he meant by their arrival at the Alleyne manor.

A double line of servants bearing torches in gold holders flanked the walkway that led to the front door. Inside, they were guided into the Alleynes' ballroom, which had been elaborately decorated with yet more gold—dangling chandeliers, immense vases holding sprays of silk flowers, stacks of plates and goblets shimmering with rims of diamonds. A stage at one end of the room was half hidden by billowing ivory silk curtains embroidered with designs of coffee and tea leaves. *The union of silk and tea Charters. Charming.*

Beside it, a statue of Turan, God of love, bore a tray holding glasses of green wine from Hanse. For a moment, the loud room full of chattering nobility seemed to fall away from Kel; he forgot the reason he was here, remembering only a scene from memory, many years ago. Antonetta's debut ball, the first time he had seen her as her mother and the Hill wished her to be: icy with diamonds at her ears, glittering in gold and silk. A hard smile like a knife's edge. Beside the statue of Turan, she had looked at him with lifeless eyes and said, *I know my mother spoke to you. She was right. We are not of the same class. It is one thing to play in the dirt as children, but we are too old to close our eyes to reality.*

"There he is," Conor said, at Kel's shoulder. Feathers from his cloak rose up around his face like wisps of black smoke. "Artal Gremont. Just as I recall him." He narrowed his eyes. "Slightly repellent."

"Only slightly?" said Falconet, in a tone of somber amusement.

Kel followed their eyes and saw Lady Alleyne by a banquet table laden with pastries, wearing a dress that itself looked like a confection: cream lace and silk, tightly corseted, her hair swept high and dressed with garnets. She was laughing with a man Kel recognized immediately, though he had not seen Artal Gremont in many years.

He had been a burly young man and was still big, with shoulders like planks of wood and a thick neck. His clothes had a faintly military flair, though Kel was sure he had never been near a battle, with gold braid and a stiff upright collar whose tips prodded his jowls. The years that separated him from the young man he'd been when he left Castellane made him resemble a portrait whose paint had smeared, blurring its clarity.

Cabrol said nothing; he had never known Gremont, and was gazing around the room, clearly bored. Montfaucon, too, had his eyes elsewhere. "Sancia Vasey looks particularly delightful tonight," he said.

Sancia, positioned near a display of silk violets that matched her dress, glanced over at Conor and the others and winked. Her lids had been painted silver; the wink flashed like a knife blade under candlelight.

"I see you're already moving on from Raimon, Montfaucon," Conor noted dryly.

"It's what he would have wanted for both of us," Montfaucon said, and departed in a cloud of swirling yellow. After a moment, Falconet followed him, arrowing his way toward a group of young noblemen playing dice in the embrasure of a large window.

Kel turned, meaning to make a wry comment to Conor, but the words died on his lips. Gremont was bearing down on them, grinning broadly. Up close, Kel could see a thick chain hanging around his thicker neck, a gaudy medallion, set with a winking ruby, hanging off it.

"Conor," he said in a booming voice as Conor looked at him with a dry, nearly invisible dislike. "*Monseigneur,* that is." He chuckled. "My apologies. The last time I saw you, you were ten years old and had just fallen into the fountain in the Queen's Garden."

"I expect I was drunk," Conor said pleasantly. "I was often in those days."

Gremont, looking nonplussed, chuckled again. "Well. Youth is the time for wildness."

"Some of us are still young," said Conor. "Time is a cruel master, is it not, Gremont? And you have stayed away from Castellane for quite some time."

"My dear city," said Gremont. "She has welcomed me back handsomely."

"It must be nice," said Kel, "to have whatever business has kept you away so long cleared up."

Gremont waved a hand. "Youthful hijinks, as the Prince said. I never understood what all the fuss was about." He leaned in conspiratorially. "I've been asking around about where a man can go to have a good time these days. Is the Pearl still open in the Maze? That was quite an interesting establishment."

"Oh, no," said Cabrol. "The Caravel is the place to be nowadays."

Gremont grinned unpleasantly. "I'm partial to the Caravel. Perhaps we can all make a visit together sometime soon. Before the prison gates of marriage close upon me." He laughed aloud; Kel fisted a hand at his side. Somehow, he was sure Gremont knew exactly who owned the Caravel and was taking special pleasure in thinking about inflicting himself upon her. "And you, Monseigneur," Gremont added to Conor. "Congratulations on your upcoming nuptials. Word of the beauty of Anjelica Iruvai has made its way as far as Taprobana and Favár."

"I do not think I'm very popular in Malgasi at the moment," said Conor lightly.

"Oh, the Malgasi admire strategy, Monseigneur, and aligning yourself with Kutani was a masterstroke. Besides, the news of the moment is that Elsabet Belmany is considering marriage to Floris of Gelstaadt."

Conor and Kel exchanged a look. It had not been long ago that the Malgasi Ambassador had demanded furiously that Conor wed Elsabet, the heir to the Malgasi throne.

"How interesting," Kel said. "Between his great height and her fierce beauty, they are sure to produce a brood of absolutely terrifying children."

Conor hid a smile. Lady Alleyne's voice trilled from across the room: "Artal! Artal, could you come here for a moment?"

Gremont looked torn. It was clear he would have preferred to stay near Conor, who gave him a tight smile. "Do go on," he said. "I must take myself off across the room to inquire of Sieur March-bolt about his health."

Gremont looked puzzled. "Isn't he dead?"

"All the more reason to be solicitous," said Conor, and walked away.

Gremont, bereft of the presence of royalty, smiled tightly at Kel and Cabrol. "I remember you," he said. "That foreign cousin of the Prince's. Anjan or something. And you"—he tipped a nod at Cabrol—"the new holder of the dye Charter, if I'm not mistaken?"

"Correct," said Ciprian. "I hope you weren't too attached to the last one."

Gremont snorted. "Not at all," he said, "but I hope you'll excuse me. My future mother-in-law requires my presence."

"Well," said Ciprian as Gremont wended his way across the room to rejoin Lady Alleyne, who was snapping her fan in annoyance at his dawdling. "He seems charming. Surely the fair Antonetta cannot be delighted to be saddled with a husband who regards marriage as prison."

Husband. Kel felt sick, but before he could say anything in return, the inhuman wailing of a dying swan echoed through the room. Everyone turned to look at the stage, from which the noise had emanated.

Kel stared. The curtains were drawn back, and three musicians were standing on the stage. One carried a viola, another a cornet;

the third held a *lior* and was tuning its strings, which had caused the terrible screeching sound. Realizing everyone was staring, the musician nearly dropped the instrument, but that was not why Kel was staring.

He was staring because the three musicians, all dressed in Alleyne livery, were Jerrod, Merren, and Ji-An.

Jerrod

Two days before being forced to pretend to be a musician at Antonetta Alleyne's engagement party, Jerrod is handing over a half-crown to a criminal informant in the Yu-Shuang Noodle House on Yulan Road.

Jerrod watches through weary eyes as the little man scuttles out the door. He hasn't been one of the Ragpicker King's usual informants, but he brought the news that the well-known privateer Laurent Aden is holed up in a sea cave along the coast. This is, in Jerrod's estimation, a mildly interesting piece of information. Not urgent, but something Andreyen would want to know, if he didn't already. The Ragpicker King has worked with Aden in the past and, for all Jerrod knows, might find him useful in the present.

Jerrod likes to be here, at his usual booth in the Yu-Shuang Noodle House, for four hours every Sunday afternoon. He never knows exactly who might show up, but the Ragpicker King pays well for information that doesn't waste his time. Gathering these reports and judging their usefulness always fell to Jerrod. Ji-An just frightened everyone away, and Merren was too interested in individual stories and would keep informants talking for hours. Jerrod smiles slightly, thinking of Merren, then starts in surprise when someone slides unexpectedly into the booth across from him.

Jerrod hates being surprised. Merren is bad for his concentration.

"Jerrod," says the newcomer. "It's been a while."

Jerrod gazes narrowly at the large, pockmarked man across from him, and his heart sinks a little. He knows what this means. "Kaspar," he says. "I thought perhaps you'd left town since you stabbed the Prince's cousin."

Kaspar is clearly not amused. "I cooled my heels in Jahan for a while, but I'm back now." He slides a piece of crumpled paper across the table. "A message for you."

Jerrod unfolds the paper. He recognizes the cramped printing, the handwriting of someone clearly trying to disguise their penmanship. *I may need you soon. Be ready, and tell Maeva, Bron, and the others to be ready, too.* It is signed, below, in printed capitals: *PROSPER BECK.*

CHAPTER SIX

L in was already in a bad mood.

The moment the carriage Antonetta had sent for her had swept up to the front of House Alleyne, it had been surrounded by torch-bearing footmen, all in rose and gold. They had been so eager to help her out of the carriage and light her way to the party that she had become flustered and left Mariam's shawl behind, doubtless shoved halfway down the back of the carriage seat.

She hadn't even noticed until she'd entered the ballroom and seen the eyes of the nobles thronging the place turn toward her. Their gazes were half hunger, half consideration, like the stares of vultures wondering if a bit of carrion was dead enough to eat.

She recognized only a few among them—Joss Falconet, sharp-featured and handsome, was in conversation with Lupin Montfaucon and a young woman in a purple dress. Montfaucon looked vexed. Lady Alleyne, Antonetta's mother, was laughing with a thick-necked man wearing a gaudy pendant on a chain. Lin narrowed her eyes; that pendant was very interesting. Very interesting indeed, but at that moment, the man turned away, and she could no longer glimpse it.

Meanwhile, there were three people that Lin did *not* see. The Prince. Kel. And, most surprisingly, Antonetta.

It was Antonetta who had asked her to come, Lin thought, so the first reasonable thing to do would be to find her. She put her chin in the air and strode through the ballroom, aware at every moment that most of her back was bared to view.

She was halfway across the room when she saw Kel, leaning against a raised wooden stage. On the stage were Merren, Ji-An, and Jerrod, awkwardly clutching musical instruments. Lin had just stopped to stare—she couldn't help it—when she heard her name hissed in a low voice.

"Lin. *Lin*. It's me."

She turned, searching the crowd. Nobody she knew seemed within earshot. Joss Falconet, his black eyes gleaming, winked at her, but he was too far away, and besides, the voice had been female.

"*Lin*. Behind the curtain."

Lin whirled. "Antonetta?" Behind her, a heavy ivory curtain against the wall rustled as if in a stiff wind. Lin gave a quick glance around to see if anyone was watching before ducking behind it.

She felt faintly ridiculous, but there was more room behind the curtain than she would have guessed. It hung stiffly away from the wall, creating a narrow tunnel between the heavy fabric and the patterned silk wallpaper. Halfway through the tunnel was Antonetta, her back to the wall. She wore a dress of a deep rose silk, so close-fitted that it made Lin feel positively modest by comparison. A net of diamonds held back her hair, and around her throat was a choker of rubies, dripping gold chains that connected to a gold belt around her waist, effectively enclosing her upper body in a sort of glittering cage.

"What are you *doing*?" Lin whispered, edging nearer. She was positive their slippers must be visible under the hem of the curtain. "This is your engagement party!"

"Well, I don't want to be at it," Antonetta said rebelliously. "I hate him, Lin." Lin didn't have to ask who she meant. "Gremont's horrible. He smacked Magali—she's off somewhere crying—he flirts with my mother, and he kicked Puggles."

"Puggles?"

"The stable cat at Marivent." Antonetta shook her head, making the diamonds in her hair glint like raindrops.

"Still, you can't hide here all night," Lin pointed out.

"I know. My mother's already searching for me. Pecking about like a bird looking for a delicious bug." Antonetta looked gloomy. "If I have to marry Gremont, I have to marry him. But it's too much to expect me to put on this *show* of being happy about it. In front of—in front of everybody."

Everybody? Lin wondered. She was fairly sure Antonetta had been about to say a specific name before she'd caught herself.

"He talks to me as though I were a child," Antonetta went on. "And the way he looks at me—ugh!" She shuddered. "He brought this necklace for me from Taprobana. Insisted I wear it. I think it looks like a slit throat, don't you?"

"I think," said Lin, "that if you don't want to marry him, you have to tell your mother now."

Antonetta exhaled. "She won't change her mind. He's already promised that he'll give her at least a dozen of his tea plantations to turn over to silk production. It will mean thousands of extra crowns in the coffers of the silk Charter. I can't imagine what anyone else could offer that would compare."

Lady Alleyne is selling her daughter, Lin thought in disgust. "But surely if she knew how miserable you were, she'd change her plan—"

"She wouldn't. Besides, it may have begun as her plan, but I have my plans, too." For a moment, Antonetta's eyes glittered like a cat's. "But Gremont is trying to change the game."

Lin was bewildered. "What do you mean?"

"Nothing. Nothing." Antonetta shook her head. "Do you have anything with you that might calm me down?"

"Oh—I didn't bring my satchel. And honestly, I wouldn't recommend anything stronger than a glass of wine. Stay here; I'll fetch you one."

Sneaking back into the party was easier than creeping behind the curtain had been. Peering out from her hiding place, Lin saw that everyone was staring toward the musicians on the stage. She took advantage of their distraction to slip back into the party and saunter toward a servant holding a tray of delicate glasses, each half filled with pale-red liquid.

She'd just taken one when a voice behind her said, "Fancy meeting you again."

She turned to see a familiar young man. Dark-red hair, black eyes. A bitter turn to the corner of his mouth.

"Ciprian Cabrol," Lin said. It was Ciprian whom she'd overheard planning to blow up the Roverge ship in the harbor; it was thanks to him she'd been able to convince the Sault that she was, in fact, the Goddess—for had she not predicted the fire, the explosion? Had the flame not seemed to come at her bidding?

Not that there was any reason for him ever to know that.

"How interesting," he said. "When we first met, I did not realize who you were—the granddaughter of Bensimon. You did not let on."

"It did not seem relevant at the time. And considering where we both were . . ." In the Ragpicker King's mansion. Him seeking explosive black powder; her, illegal magic.

"Indeed," he said. "A secret we must both keep."

"I suppose I should at least congratulate you," she said. "You hold the dye Charter now. You have what you wanted."

He looked at her narrowly, and she realized that, though he hid it well, he was quite drunk. "Just what I wanted," he said, "but not in the way I wanted it. I always thought that living on the Hill would be freedom, but it is its own sort of prison. Once they get their claws in you, they never stop squeezing."

She blinked at him. "Who? The Charter Families?"

But Cabrol did not answer. He shook his head as if to clear it and wandered off back into the crowd, moving carefully.

Very strange, Lin thought, and turned, meaning to return to the curtain and Antonetta. But she had not looked behind her; she stumbled into someone immediately, spilling the contents of her wineglass all over the front of a fine silk shirt.

Her hand flew to her mouth. "Oh—I'm *so* sorry—I—"

"What an interesting way to greet your Prince, Lin Caster," said a horribly familiar voice.

Whatever words she'd meant to follow her apology died before she could speak them. She looked up into a pair of cold gray eyes, her heart sinking.

It was Prince Conor.

Later, Kel would recall having rushed up to the stage in the Alleyne ballroom in a panic, though in fact he had done his best to saunter aimlessly across the room, attracting little attention. He snatched a glass of green wine from the statue of Turan on the way, admired a few of the draperies, then slid up to the edge of the stage.

"Merren," he hissed. "*Merren.* What are you *doing*?"

Merren jumped. Clearly he hadn't noticed Kel approaching; he'd been too engaged in playing about with his *lior*. At least it was no longer making horrible noises. As a result, the assembled nobility had lost interest in whatever was happening on stage and returned to their drinking and amusements.

Merren knelt, making a show of fiddling with the instrument. Kel saw Ji-An and Jerrod glance over at him; Jerrod wore a hooded tunic of gold linen that half hid his silvery mask. Ji-An, in a jacket and trousers of rose silk, went back to industriously examining her viol.

Merren kept his eyes on the *lior* as he replied. "What if I told you we were trying to make a few extra crowns on the side?"

"Andreyen pays that badly?" Kel snorted. "I wouldn't believe you, and you know it."

"We wanted to clap eyes on the mysterious Magali," Merren admitted. "Make sure she's the same person Jerrod knows from the Maze. Since there's a Magali that works for the Alleynes, it made sense that she'd be here tonight." He peered into the crowd. "Have you seen her?"

Kel looked upon him darkly. "Aren't the agents of the Ragpicker King not supposed to be active on the Hill?"

"Andreyen didn't ask us to be here," Merren said, his pale-gold hair falling into his face. He pushed it back. "It's a fact-finding mission, that's all."

"Well, I *haven't* seen her," Kel said. "Where Antonetta goes, Magali usually follows, but I haven't seen Antonetta, either. You know who I have seen? Artal Gremont."

Merren still didn't look at Kel, but his *lior* gave off an agonized twang as he fumbled at it. "He won't recognize me," he said. "It's been too long. I think he only saw me once, anyway, out the window of a carriage."

"Still, being in the same place with him, are you sure—"

Jerrod interrupted. "If you are looking for Demoselle Alleyne," he said, "she is behind that curtain."

He pointed toward a curtain of ruched ivory silk that hung against a nearby wall; Kel suspected it concealed an exit from the ballroom. He frowned at Jerrod.

"Are you sure?"

"Quite. She's been there for a while," Jerrod said, though he was looking not at Kel but at Merren's bent head.

Kel considered arguing, but there seemed no point. He'd already been up at the stage for too long; he would soon draw curious eyes. Also, Jerrod was notoriously stubborn, and it wasn't as if Kel was going to be able to convince the three of them to abort their mission at this stage.

Besides, Kel admitted to himself as he walked away, his interest in Antonetta was stronger than his suspicion that Jerrod, Ji-An, and Merren were looking for trouble. He placed his still-full wineglass on an ormolu table and—with a quick look around to make sure no one was watching—ducked behind the ruched curtain.

He did not see her at first—the curtain was thick, the light dim—but he smelled her perfume. Lavender and honey. He pushed deeper into the tunnel between the curtain and the wall and there she was, turning to look at him, her eyes widening.

"Oh," she said, pitching her voice low. "I thought you were Lin." She frowned. "What are you doing back here?"

For a moment, Kel couldn't speak. The way she looked seemed to cut at him like a blade. She wore the deep rose of the Alleyne family— a close-cut dress that held her body like a lover's hands. Over her hair was a shimmering gold net threaded with diamonds, and the pupils of her eyes had been turned to diamonds by posy-drops. Around her throat was clasped a gold *collier* set with rubies and trailing gold chains hooked to a belt around her waist. It looked to Kel as if the chains were meant to skim the curves of her breasts where they rose above the neckline of her silk dress. He could not help but imagine her naked, rising from her bath wearing only the ruby-dripping collar, like the Goddess Cerra rising from the sea to seduce Aigon, God of waters.

"I *said*," Antonetta whispered, "what are you *doing* back here? Did Lin tell you where to find me?"

"I haven't even seen her," said Kel, glad for the dimness of the enclosed space. He hoped it hid his expression. "And I could ask you the same. I'm sure you're supposed to be attending this party in a more . . . visible capacity."

She glared at him.

"Let me guess," he said. "You'd resigned yourself to marrying Gremont. But now that he's here, you've had to face how horrible he really is. Sadly, you can't spend the rest of your married life hiding behind this curtain."

"Don't be so sure. It's a very nice curtain."

"Antonetta—"

"Shh." She put her finger to her lips, painted carmine pink. "Be *quiet.*"

Kel lowered his voice, which made her lean in closer to hear him. He breathed in lavender honey. "Ana. You say you have to marry Gremont. You say you have no choice about it. But I *know you*," he said with an almost savage force. "You have spent the last ten years lying with your smiles. With your every breath. What prevents you from pretending now? Why are you hiding? You've never hidden from anything."

For a moment, her diamond-pupiled eyes seemed to glitter. "You can be cruel, Kel Anjuman."

"Not like Gremont."

"You really want to know?" She hissed the words between her teeth. "Even though there's nothing—*nothing*—you can do about it?"

"Yes," Kel said. "Tell me."

Antonetta said, "Gremont has insisted that, as a term of the engagement, he be given the right of first night. That there be witnesses to the consummation of our marriage."

Kel said nothing, but put a hand out to steady himself against the wall.

"All eleven are supposed to watch us," she said. "All the other Charter holders."

Kel said, through what seemed to him a mouth full of acid, "That's barbaric. He has no right to ask for that."

"He has every right," she whispered, and he could not help but remember her words in the Caravel. *You are not my father, not brother or lover. You have no rights here.* Perhaps that was why she was telling him this. Because there was nothing he could do, nothing he could say to anyone.

"No one has invoked this Law in a hundred years, but it's still the Law." He had heard many different tones animate her voice through the years. He had heard her happy and disappointed and angry and affectedly foolish, but he had never heard her sound so . . . flat. "After we marry, I belong to him, and he can display me in any manner he chooses."

"Ana. What if he hurts you?" Kel said, giving voice at last to his deepest fear. "He likes causing pain—"

Antonetta raised her face to look up at him. The glitter in her eyes—surely it was tears? Or perhaps only the posy-drops? "He won't lay violent hands on me. You know the Laws. I could have him hauled before the Judicia. He'd risk being exiled again," she added. "No. I am not worried about him causing me physical pain."

"There are other kinds of pain," Kel said. "He wishes to humiliate and control you—"

"I am aware of that." She fixed him with her cool blue eyes. "I can manage that. And besides—what *could* you do about it, Kel?"

It was like having a knife dipped in acid twisted deep in his side. He thought he might have actually flinched.

Kill him, Kel thought. Slip into his bedroom in the dead of night and cut his throat wide open so that it gleamed with scarlet like Antonetta's ruby collar. She did not know he was a Sword Catcher; she did not know what he could do. What he was capable of.

And he could not tell her. Only endure her looking at him, half wearily, as if she could not imagine a world in which he might be any help to her at all.

He did not remember leaving her. Only that one moment he was with her behind the curtain, and the next he was back in the ballroom, the sounds of festivity assaulting his ears like weapons. He saw Conor, like a bird of dark plumage in his swan cloak, deep in conversation with a slim, beautiful girl with a fall of scarlet hair. Distantly, Kel realized the girl was Lin. He had not known she would be here tonight and neither, judging by his expression, had Conor.

More figures moved around the room in the dance, like clockwork dolls set in motion. He cut a path through them to the stage, where the three "musicians" were playing—the sound uneven, though not as terrible as he'd expected.

Merren glanced at him as he approached and must have seen something in his face, for when Kel arrived at the stage's edge, Merren was already kneeling, still plucking the *lior*, a question in his eyes as he looked at Kel.

"Forget anything Jerrod or I may have said about the dangers of murdering Gremont," Kel said, his voice low but surprisingly steady. "Go ahead and kill him."

Merren did not look surprised. He did, however, look relieved. "I'm so glad you said that." He exhaled. "You see, I've already poisoned his wine."

Lin stood frozen. The party seemed to fade away around her, as if she were traveling away from it, hearing its noises in the distance. It was a blur of murmuring sound and color, and in the middle of that blur, she stood alone with Prince Conor, whose silk shirtfront she had just covered in wine.

"I see," he said, "that I have been anointed by the Goddess. Is this ceremonial or merely a comment on my personality?"

His voice. She had forgotten his *voice*. How it was rough and soft at the same time, like the lap of a cat's tongue. He wore a cloak of black feathers, clasped at the throat with a silver brooch carved in the shape of a lily. It was like something out of a Story-Spinner's tale, a garment that seemed as if it ought to be enchanted. His hair was the same jet-black as the feathers and fell in waves over his forehead. His face was thinner than she remembered, dominated now by his eyes, fiercely gray and surrounded by coal-dark lashes.

She had remembered him as beautiful, but not as beautiful as this. As forbidding, but not as forbidding as this.

Somehow she found her voice. "How fortunate," she said, "that you are so encrusted with jewels, no one is likely to notice the stain."

In fact, his shirt was black; the stain was only a greater darkening rather than a bloody discoloration, the wetness making it cling to his skin. Without a word, he reached out, took the empty glass from her hand, and set it down on a small table nearby.

The colors and sounds of the room around them began to come

back to her. Music had begun—a sweetly discordant tune. The musicians seemed out of practice, but the crowd of partygoers began to come together in pairs, laughter rising as the dancing began.

She expected the Prince to turn on his heel and walk away. Instead, he held out a hand. "Dance with me," he said.

Lin's mouth went dry. "But— Everyone will see us."

He looked impatient. "And? You are the granddaughter of my Counselor. No one will question it. They will assume we have matters to discuss."

Still, she hung back. "Do we? Have matters to discuss?"

He said nothing, only remained as he was, his hand extended. If she did not take it, she realized, people really *would* stare. One did not refuse a dance with the Prince of Castellane.

She reached her own hand out. It was immediately enfolded in his. His grasp was careful, his fingers long and sparkling-cold with rings. He drew her closer, and they began to dance. Lin did not know the steps, but the Prince—*Conor, he asked you to call him Conor*—clearly did.

"Relax," he murmured. "I know you can dance."

She felt the blush spreading across her face. The last time she had danced, here on the Hill, she had been the only one dancing. She had danced the story of the Goddess Adassa with Conor watching her, the heat of his gaze like a brand. She remembered how it had made her burn, made her dance more wildly, as if she could show him her rebellion, her fury, with every movement of her body.

Where had all that bravery gone? She tipped her head back, looking up at him squarely. Around them couples whirled and turned to the music. "I was very sorry," she said, "to hear of the tragedy in the Shining Gallery. The little Princess—"

"Whom I treated cruelly. I know. You needn't say it. They already say it in the city, in the streets. There are Story-Spinner tales about it. *The Bloody-Handed Prince*, that sort of thing." He held his left hand up, where his rings glittered—little points of scarlet. "Perhaps they recognize, as you did, that I am a broken person."

Her own words, flung back at her.

I think you are a broken person. I suppose it is not your fault.

How she had regretted what she'd said, hoped he'd forgotten it, as he'd surely forgotten her. But the cold in his voice was the way she imagined snow in Detmarch might feel. Her grandfather had described it to her once, saying that breathing the air in winter there was like swallowing the oil of mint leaves. A cold that burned.

He hates me, Lin thought dismally, and nearly stumbled, the next step of the dance catching her off guard. But Conor steadied her, setting his free hand at her waist, his long fingers curling around so they touched the bare skin at her back.

She heard him catch his breath. His fingers were wands of fire against her skin. She thought she had never felt anything so intensely.

Save when he kissed you. When you ached for him. When you would have let him do anything he wanted.

She shoved the thought away hurriedly. "You are angry," she said. "But it does not matter what I think about the little Princess. What is important is whether you think you treated her cruelly."

His lip curled at the corner. Disgust? Amusement? "You speak as Mayesh would," he said. "And here is what I would say to him. I do not have the luxury of introspection. What matters is what the Charter Council thinks of me, what the people of Castellane think of me, and what our foes abroad think of me. What you will soon discover about being a leader, Goddess, is that you are only a vessel for your people's hopes and fears, their dreams and desperations. What *you* want does not matter."

"Is that why you asked me to dance?" Lin said as he turned them again. She was aware of other couples. Some she recognized, like Antonetta and her soon-to-be husband, standing stiffly beside each other—it seemed Antonetta had come out from behind the curtain at last—or Lupin Montfaucon with a girl in a purple dress. Most she did not. "To impart your thoughts about leadership?"

"I asked you to dance because I was curious," Conor said. He did not sound curious; he sounded dispassionate, as if nothing she might say signified much. "If I asked you for help, would you help me?"

Her gaze flew to his face. She could read nothing there. "Would I . . ." Her voice trailed off. As they had left things, she had never imagined he might want her help again. "You require a physician?"

"Not I," said Conor shortly. His grip on her waist tightened; she doubted he even knew it. She could feel the tremble in his muscles, as if he were feverish. As if it were killing him to have to ask her for help, she thought, when he so clearly hated her. He must be choking on the words.

But what could drive him to this? In her bewilderment, she forgot to look at him covertly, staring at him openly. At the silver circlet binding his brow, at the shadows beneath his eyes, the hollows below his cheekbones. The feathers at his collar brushed his jaw like a lover's kisses.

"It is not for a physician to ignore anyone in need," Lin said slowly. "But I have other responsibilities now, and I must do nothing my Prince would forbid me to do."

"But I am your—" Conor began, then caught himself. "Ah. You mean your Exilarch. Mayesh told me he would arrive soon to test your claim that you are a deity." Lin winced a little; he spoke with worse than contempt. Cold dismissal. "And if he determines your claim to be false, what happens then?"

"Surely you are not concerned for me?"

At that, he did smile—a savage wolf's smile. "For you, no. For him, perhaps. Has anyone warned him you tear princes into little pieces?"

"If that is what you think of me, then why are you asking for my help?"

"It is a good question," he said. He drew her a little nearer, his lips close to her ear. She breathed in the scent of him. Skin, leather, musk. "You know," he whispered, "I do not have to *ask*."

Lin caught her breath. The ache in the pit of her stomach was almost pain now. "If you—"

The music stopped. Conor released her immediately, stepping back; her skin felt cold where he had touched her. "You should go," he said.

Despite everything, Lin scowled at him. She could not help it. "I did not come for you," she said. "Antonetta invited me—"

"Be that as it may. Your grandfather is waiting for you by the door, I believe." He swept her a slight bow. "Goddess," he said, and strode away, into the depth of the crowd.

Lin looked toward the door, only half believing it, but there he was. Mayesh stood near the ballroom entrance, his arms crossed over his chest, his gaze fixed upon her. He did not look pleased.

"What do you mean, you *already* poisoned him?" Kel demanded.

Merren stared industriously at his *lior*, as if racking his brain as to what could be the matter with it. "What it sounds like. Wait for the wedding toast. I poisoned the groom's cup."

"*Merren*," Ji-An hissed. "We need you over here! Playing music!"

"I thought you hadn't made plans—" Kel started, but Merren was already on his feet, playing his instrument, moving back toward the center of the stage. Kel caught a hard glare from Jerrod before he turned and walked away from the raised platform.

A few people looked at him curiously, as if wondering what he'd wanted with the musicians, but most were far too caught up in their own business to notice. Montfaucon and Falconet competing to impress Sancia Vasey; Cabrol with his back against a silk-papered wall, a wine bottle in one hand; Beatris Cabrol dancing with Alonse Esteve. And Conor, Conor in his black feathered cloak, dancing with Lin. Kel narrowed his eyes. Their bodies were close together as they moved through the steps of the quadrille, but neither looked happy. Then again, neither looked as if they wanted to run away, either. They seemed two people bound together by an invisible net, something only they could see. That only they could feel.

He was not the only one watching them. And though he knew Conor better than anyone, he doubted he was the only one to sense the tension between them. Lady Alleyne had her eyes on the Prince, her mouth set grimly.

And then, beside her, Kel saw Antonetta. She was standing with Artal Gremont as, in groups of twos and threes, noble families came up to offer them congratulations.

Kel thought of it all—the First Night, the poison, the cage of gold imprisoning Antonetta—and felt an overwhelming urge to vomit. It propelled him out of the room and onto a long balcony that ran the length of the ballroom. He gulped in lungfuls of fresh air before leaning on the parapet; his head was throbbing as if he'd drunk too much wine. The balcony was raised off the ground only a little bit. From here, he had a view of the jagged mountains that rose between Castellane and Sarthe, and the dark fissure of the Narrow Pass that was the only way between them.

"Kellian?"

Conor's voice. Kel knew it without having to turn around; it was the voice he knew best in the world besides his own.

Conor joined him at the stone railing. "I had wondered where you'd gone," he said. "Tired of the show?"

"It was more than a little unbearable," Kel said. "The years do not seem to have improved Artal Gremont."

"No," Conor agreed. He set his hands on the railing. His rings glittered in the moonlight. His profile was fine and sharp, his posture all coiled tension. Something was bothering him. The dance with Lin? Kel considered asking him about it, but something in Conor's expression forbade it. "Do you know of the Exilarch?"

Interesting. "Yes. The Prince of the Ashkar people. He is always a Prince, never a King, is my understanding, for he cannot supplant their Goddess."

"Indeed. I have seen etchings of the Exilarchs, I recall, in history books. Old men with great medallions. Rather like Mayesh." Conor looked up at the stars. "A strange evening," he said. "Marriage on the Hill is a bloodsport, is it not?"

"For you no less than anyone," said Kel.

Conor laughed without humor. "But I am marrying the most beautiful woman in the world. Have you not heard? None should have cause to pity me. And gold will flow into the coffers of Castellane, and there will be peace and all will be well—"

Kel could not stand the bitterness in Conor's voice. "And you will still wake up every night screaming," he said.

"Perhaps," Conor said. "But after my marriage, you will not be there to hear it."

Before Kel could reply, he heard footsteps behind them—a deliberately heavy tread. Boots on stone. Someone wanted to be sure they knew he was approaching. He turned, expecting Falconet or one of the others, and instead saw Jolivet.

In the harsh moonlight, the Legate's face looked craggier than ever. His hair had been black when Kel had first come to Marivent; it was almost all gray now. He was not in uniform but was still in Palace colors: a red doublet, black trousers, his lion ring gleaming on his hand. He said, "Have you asked him already about the Princess?"

It took Kel a moment to realize Jolivet was addressing Conor.

Conor frowned. "No. We were speaking of other things."

Jolivet looked disapproving. He said, "This is important. For your safety, Monseigneur." He turned to Kel. "The Princess Anjelica arrives in three days—"

"Three days?" Kel was astonished. Why had Conor not mentioned how soon she was arriving?

"Yes. We have kept the time of her arrival quiet, for reasons I am about to explain to you." Jolivet paused. "Do you know of the privateer Laurent Aden?"

Kel nodded. Everyone knew Aden. He'd been a pirate before he'd gone into private work for the Kutani Court. He'd only made a name for himself in the past five years or so, but his exploits were already legendary in the city. Less so on the Hill, where privateers who were not in the employ of Castellane, and the toll they took on profits, were generally loathed. Still, Kel could recall being a boy at the Orfelinat, where he had dreamed of being a pirate with his friend Cas, thieving from the rich to give to himself. "He's meant to be a sort of clever trickster, isn't he? There's a story about how he disguised himself as the captain of a merchant vessel so convincingly that he was able to off-load all the goods before the first mate caught on. And by then it was too late. Aden had escaped."

"If even half the exploits credited to him are true," drawled Conor, "then he may be the wiliest privateer since the days of the Empire."

"Indeed," Kel said, "but what does that have to do with the arrival of the Princess?"

"You do recall my fiancée is meant to be the most beautiful woman in the world," Conor noted, an edge of amusement to his voice. "Well, it appears pirates are not immune to her charms."

"This is beginning to sound like a Story-Spinner tale," said Kel. "Has he kidnapped her and taken her away on his galleon?"

"No," said Jolivet, "but he would like to. It appears he fell in love with her at some point, and since then she has been his obsession. Information came to us from Kutani that he was hoping to intercept her ship as it enters the harbor here in Castellane and take her away with him."

"Really," Kel said a little dubiously. "Why try to seize her as she lands in Castellane? Why not attack in his natural habitat, at sea?"

"Her craft will be guarded by Kutani warships on its journey," said Jolivet. "But of course, by tradition, warships are forbidden from entering our harbor. It may be that Aden judges that she will be least protected as she approaches the Royal Docks."

"But we can arrange for that not to be so," said Kel. "We can station soldiers—"

"And we will," said Jolivet. "We will also have ships at sea, guarding the harbor entrance. And yet, if Aden slips by somehow, there may still be violence. Nothing we cannot subdue, but . . ."

"Conor must be protected," said Kel. "I understand."

Jolivet nodded. "Castellane needs her Sword Catcher, Kel."

Conor shook his head restlessly. "It should be me," he said. "What was it you told me when Luisa arrived? I should not begin an engagement with a lie?"

"In that case," said Kel, "it was Sarthe telling the lie. Perhaps we have all learned something from that." He laid a hand on Conor's arm, the soft feathers of the Prince's cloak tickling his palm. "I will go. I am your shield, Con."

The balcony door opened again, and Conor glanced irritably toward it. "Is *everyone* at this party planning to join us here?" he muttered as Sancia Vasey appeared framed in the doorway. She was smiling, her coppery hair tousled.

"There you are, Conor," she said in a playfully scolding tone. "Didn't you promise to dance with me tonight?"

Conor's face changed instantly, as if he had put on a mask for the Solstice Ball. Gone was everything real in his expression—hesitancy, annoyance, weariness. In its place there was only a sort of bland amiability.

"So I did," he said, "and as they say, a Prince always keeps his promises."

"Do they really say that?" Sancia giggled as Conor came toward her. "I thought a Prince *never* kept his promises."

Together, Sancia and Conor ducked back into the ballroom, leaving Kel alone on the balcony with Jolivet. He frowned at the Legate. "What was that?"

Jolivet looked at him without expression. "I'm not sure what you mean."

"Why did you bother making Conor ask me if I'd escort Anjelica Iruvai? I am a Sword Catcher. You can simply give me orders. It does not matter what I *want* to do."

"That was not for you. It was for Conor. That should be obvious," said Jolivet. "And besides, I needed to speak with you—no, not about the Princess." He waved away Kel's next question with an impatient gesture. "About Magali Berthe. You wished to question her." He glanced toward the door, as if to make sure no one was listening there. "She will be at the Arena on Ellsday. It will give you an opportunity to question her away from Lady Alleyne's watchful eye."

"Jerrod did say she was always borrowing money to gamble on Arena games," Kel acknowledged.

"Even more important to question her, then. If she's in debt and desperate, she would be far more susceptible to outside influence."

"She won't want to talk to me about it," Kel noted.

"How fortunate that you're an excellent actor," said Jolivet. "Do your best to charm her. Much depends on it."

A loud cheer went up from inside. The lines seemed to deepen at the corners of Jolivet's mouth. "Ah," he said. "The wedding toast."

Wait for the wedding toast.

With Merren's voice echoing in his ears, Kel pushed past Jolivet and dashed into the ballroom. The crowd had pushed together into a tight knot surrounding the banquet tables. Kel shouldered his way among the nobles. He used his elbows liberally, which resulted in angry grunts and mutters. The smell of damp wool and silk, sweat and perfume, was overwhelming. Over the heads of the throng he could see the stage, where Merren stood with Ji-An and Jerrod, their instruments dangling in their hands, forgotten.

At last he was at the front. He could see Conor, with Falconet and Montfaucon, clapping in a desultory fashion. Most of the nobles held empty glasses in their hands; they would be filled just after the toast.

In front of a groaning banquet table, Antonetta stood beside Gremont and her mother. Antonetta's lovely face was set like a doll's, her lips curved in a painted smile, her gaze blank. Artal rested one big hand possessively on her back. In his other hand, he held a ceremonial wedding goblet, its rim studded with emeralds, as Antonetta's matching goblet was studded with rubies.

I poisoned the groom's cup.

Kel did not move as Gremont raised the goblet and spoke in a booming voice. "I hope you'll all join me in toasting to the alliance between House Gremont and House Alleyne. May it bring health and wealth to all of us, especially wealth."

An even louder cheer went up. With a sly wink to his captive audience, Gremont tossed back his wine, draining his glass to the dregs.

Lin crossed the room to join her grandfather, who stood glowering, the great circular medallion that hung against his chest resembling a massive, glittering, watching eye.

He smiled when she came close, laying a fatherly hand on her shoulder. Lin was not fooled. He was furious. "What," he demanded, "are you doing here?"

"Antonetta Alleyne asked me to come," she said. "In the capacity of her personal physician. The Law allows physicians of the Ashkar to travel abroad at night; you know that."

"Does it also allow them to wear whatever colors they like?" snapped Mayesh.

"My dress is marine blue," Lin said coldly. "The color of the sea."

Her grandfather snorted. "Antonetta Alleyne will manage without you," he said. "Come."

Lin went. She cast a single look back over her shoulder as they departed the ballroom, searching for Antonetta; she was standing with her mother and Artal Gremont, looking blank-faced. Lin could not see Conor among the crowd, or Kel. Perhaps they were together.

Outside, the moon had risen. It was high and full, casting a bright light over the city, and over the royal carriage that waited for them outside the mansion. As Mayesh hurried her between the ranks of torch-carrying servants, he asked coldly, "If you are here as Antonetta's physician, where is your satchel?"

Lin said nothing. She wondered if her grandfather would point out that by the standards of the Ashkar, she was also half naked. She wondered if she would step on his foot if he did.

They reached the carriage, and a driver in Aurelian livery held a door open for Lin. She thanked him despite his connection to the Blood Royal. It was not *his* fault the heir to the throne was a bastard.

Once inside the carriage, she faced Mayesh as they rattled off down the Hill, her chin set. The harsh moonlight spilling through the windows made his face look more lined than she remembered. "You," he said, managing to make the word sound like an insult, "have a tendency to look after other people without considering what the consequences will be for yourself. Antonetta cannot protect you from the Laws that govern our curfew. Only I can do that."

Lin raised an eyebrow. "Is that a threat to leave me to the Vigilants?"

He ignored this. "You should have told me you planned to come to the Hill tonight. If there had been an incident, I would have found out when you were already in the Tully."

Lin said nothing.

"You are not usually so reckless," he said. "I heard you met with Benjudah this afternoon. Has it made you afraid? Perhaps you are worried about what will happen when you fail the first test."

Lin laughed. "You're not even going to do me the kindness of saying *if*?"

"It would be unkind to pretend."

The carriage tilted as the slope grew sharper. Lin braced her hands against the seat cushions to keep herself from tipping forward. "I assume I will become an object of pity. A pathetic, mad girl who believed she could be the Goddess of the Ashkar people."

"Really?" Mayesh looked at her with a hard gaze. "Do you think that's all that will happen? Do you think you'll be able to continue to practice as a physician?"

"I am prepared for that," Lin said calmly. Inside, her stomach felt as if it had shrunk back against her spine. She had never considered such a thing; she forbade herself from considering it now.

"There are worse punishments. What if they exile you?"

The carriage evened out as the Hill gave way to city streets. Though it was late, the roads were still crowded with pedestrians—many, no doubt, on their way to the Broken Market that ran the length of the Ruta Maestra. Through the window Lin could see the flicker of lamplight and the gleam of the dark-green Fear River. "The Exilarch told me I'm far from the first woman to make this claim. If every other girl had suffered exile as a punishment, surely such news would have reached our ears."

"Perhaps not all of these girls had grandfathers who knew the Exilarch when he was a child."

Lin narrowed her eyes. "He mentioned that," she said. "I did not get the impression he recalled you fondly."

"I am sure he does not."

They had reached the Ruta Maestra. The carriage slowed to a crawl; on either side of them were the stalls of the Broken Market, selling items that had once been whole and were now in need of repair. Lin saw a doll with a shattered china face propped against a ripped cushion; its one eye seemed to follow her. Above them, the unbroken moon gazed down on the ruined things humanity made.

She sighed. "What did you do to make him dislike you?"

Mayesh was silent a moment—long enough that Lin wondered if perhaps he would not answer her. Then he said, "Years ago, Aron Benjudah was a friend of the Maharam's son. Asher."

Lin stared. Everyone knew the tale of Asher Benezar, who had studied forbidden magic when he was still a boy of fifteen and had been exiled for it. It was not known what had become of him, and the Maharam would not speak his son's name. It was a story that had taken on the character of a myth—something from the *Book of Makabi*, a long-ago happening. It had not occurred to her that Asher might have had friends who were still alive, still young, today.

"In Aron's view," said Mayesh, "I did not do enough to prevent the Maharam from exiling his son."

"But you spoke for Asher," Lin said, forgetting, in her surprise, to be angry. "You argued with the council. We have all heard the tale. You told the Maharam that exile was too cruel a punishment. It is why—" *Why you are no longer friends,* she almost said, but she held the words back; they seemed too hurtful.

"Aron was only a boy of eleven at the time," said her grandfather. "He was badly hurt by the loss of his friend. He fastened on me as someone who could have changed the course of things if only I had tried harder." He was not only talking about Asher now, Lin thought. "I tried to be there for him as much as I could, under the circumstances, but he was the Exilarch's son. They never stayed in one place very long, and after Asher was exiled, they left."

"You think he will judge me differently," Lin asked, "because he resents you?"

"I like to think not. I only knew him as a boy; I hope he has grown to be a fair-minded man. But I thought you should know the history."

"I am not going to change my course, *zai*," she said, reverting to the old, childish name for "grandfather." She was weary, and they were nearing the walls of the Sault; she could see the gates and the ever-burning torches. "I am glad you were there for Asher Benezar in his time. I wish you had tried to be there for me and Josit, long ago."

"Well," he said, looking as tired as she felt, "I'm trying now."

Antonetta

Late on the night of her engagement party, after all the guests have gone, Antonetta goes out into the garden behind the Alleyne manor. It is here, where grass and flowers grow in thick, disorderly hedgerows, that she once played with Kel and the others when they were children. As precise as she is about her home, Liorada Alleyne has never paid much attention to her vast garden, and the riot of trees and flowers provided excellent hiding places for games of bandits and prisoners.

The sky is already beginning to lighten in the east, heralding the dawn. The air smells of damp grass and white flowers. Antonetta wends her way down the gravel path that leads to a small grotto beneath an overhang of rock. Here they had played on hot days, for a small rill of water runs through the grass and the space is always damp and cool. Antonetta still goes there sometimes to be alone—but tonight, there is someone else already there.

She pauses, bewildered, one hand raised to catch at a branch above her head. "Conor?"

She sees the flash of his eyes in the dimness as he looks up at her. He has thrown his cloak of black swan feathers onto the ground and is sitting on it, his back against the stone of the grotto.

His clothes are rumpled, his shirt reeking of spilled wine, the dark kohl that rims his eyes smudged in a way that gives the impression of dark circles.

He is still beautiful, though, the disarray only enhancing the air of careless dissolution that he cultivates anyway. For years, Antonetta has been resentful of his beauty, because it matters so little for him. Conor Aurelian would still have all the power he had, and all the adoration, if he were plain as unsalted bread. For a Prince to be beautiful is like an extra row of beads on an already thickly embroidered dress. It is a matter of degree, not necessity, in a world where Antonetta's looks spell out her entire future.

"My apologies," he says, sitting up straight. "I had only intended to be out here for a few moments. I must have lost track of time."

Antonetta ducks under the branch she's holding. She has taken off the ruby choker Gremont gave her, but she is still in her silk dress; she feels suddenly overdressed, and resents Conor all the more for that. Still. To have the chance to talk to him alone—

"You are the Prince, Monseigneur," she says. "If you wanted to stay out here all night, it would not be my place to forbid it."

"I suppose not." He doesn't look particularly pleased at the thought. In fact, he looks miserable. He holds a feather from his cloak between two fingers, spinning it back and forth. As he looks down at it, she catches the flash of his resemblance to Kel, which always feels like the bite of a blade in her skin. Kel, who is beautiful in such a different way, who is warm where Conor is icy and removed. Kel, who lies because he has to, not because it gives him pleasure.

Conor releases the feather, which floats lightly on the air. He says, "I suppose I needn't ask why you're out here. I would commiserate with you about your marriage to Gremont, but I suppose neither you nor I ever expected that we could marry for love."

I saw you dancing with Lin, she wants to say. *I saw the way you looked at her, and the way she looked at you. It must tear you apart not to get what you want.*

Instead, she says, "The Princess of Kutani is rumored to be the most beautiful woman in the world; I don't think anyone would ever say something like that about Artal."

To her surprise, Conor laughs. In that moment, she sees neither Kel in him nor even his grown self; she sees the boy she'd known once, who never wanted to be the bandit king or the captain of the pirate ship, and was always content to have others take those roles. "Indeed," Conor says, "he has neither looks nor personality to recommend him. Is there some good quality of his I am overlooking?"

Antonetta sits down on the grass: not too far from Conor, but not close, either. "I think you know there isn't. I'm sure he's told you about his First Night demand."

Conor nods.

"I had rather hoped the rest of the Hill would shun him for it," she said.

"I fear you greatly overestimate the morals of the Hill. Some are horrified, indeed; most regard it as not their business or their problem. And a few of the worst are enthusiastic about it. Indeed, Esteve said something about how you have to watch horses in the act of mating in order to be sure of the bloodline."

Antonetta wonders if she might throw up, but it passes after a moment. She has known people to do and think much worse, in the end.

Conor turns toward her. "Ana, do you want me to intervene? I understand Gremont has made it a condition of the marriage, but it will not be your only chance to marry. The Charter Families may look askance if I interfere, but they look askance at half of what I do regardless—"

She can tell he is serious. Serious enough that she cannot give him a real answer, not now. "Why are you being so nice to me?" she says instead.

He blinks. "We're friends. We've always been friends."

"But that isn't precisely true, is it?"

He sits back slowly. His boots have torn a number of the swan feathers free from the fabric of the cloak—Antonetta doubts he'll be able to wear it again—and they float around his feet and legs, light as smoke on the air currents. "What do you mean?"

"I was fifteen," Antonetta says. "You were the one who told my mother that it was time for me to stop spending all my time with you and Kel and Joss. That if she ever hoped I would have a future on the Hill, she would do what was right and ban me from Marivent until I learned how to be a proper lady. When I asked my mother whether you would miss me, she laughed and said that you gave her no indication that you would." She tugs a handful of grass free from the ground; the sharp scent of torn greenery assails her.

When Conor speaks, his voice sounds strange. "And this has been bothering you all this time?"

"Don't make it sound like it's childish. It altered my whole life. I had friends, a happy life; then suddenly, I had neither. Suddenly everything my mother had ever disliked about me was proved right in her eyes."

"Antonetta." Conor pushes his hair out of his eyes; it is a habitual gesture he and Kel share. Or perhaps Kel has simply learned it from Conor; it is hard to know with them where anything originates. "If I'd known—" He shakes his head. "I managed the situation poorly. I was fifteen and an idiot. Just know that when I went to your mother, I meant to protect you."

"From what?"

Conor sighs. "Charlon. He wouldn't stop talking about you. I began to realize that as we had all grown up together, Kel and Joss and I had come to think of you as a friend and equal, but Charlon thought of you as property. There was no way to keep him away from you without enraging him—a rage he would have taken out on you. There was no way to watch him constantly. That was what I thought."

"I could have looked out for myself."

"I know that now. But I didn't then. I am sorry, Antonetta. It should have been Charlon I sent away. I didn't know how—but that is no excuse."

I am sorry, Antonetta. She stares at him. These are words she never imagined him saying, never imagined he *could* say. It feels as if everything around her is changing. She has been so angry at him for so long, and done so many things because of that anger. She does not regret those things yet, but she fears that she will. "You made that decision for me then," she says. "You do not need to make any decisions for me now. I will manage Gremont."

He nods slightly. There is enough light now that she can see the color of his eyes: gray, like storm clouds. Like Kel's. "What is your plan? For you have always been someone with a plan, Antonetta."

She looks down at the shredded grass in her hand. "Something you may not know," she says slowly, "is that part of the marriage contract is an agreement that, after a year of marriage, my mother will pass the silk Charter to me. My reward for doing all she wishes."

"Is the silk Charter really worth all that to you?"

A question only a Prince would ask. "My independence is worth all that."

"But you'd still be married to Gremont—"

"You've met the man." Antonetta digs the toe of her satin slipper into the damp ground. "He's the sort who has so *many* enemies. On the Hill and in the city. Who's to say what might happen? And by Law, if something did befall him, well . . . Both Charters would come to me, wouldn't they?"

Conor raises his dark eyebrows. "Not precisely. No one person can control two Charters. You would need to will one to someone else."

Antonetta smiles. "Yes. That's what I thought."

"And I would have to approve the transfer of power," Conor adds. There is a gleam in his eyes as he looks at her, a sort of restrained amusement. "Of course."

Still smiling, Antonetta says, "I truly don't think that would present much of a problem, Monseigneur."

CHAPTER SEVEN

Despite her late night, Lin rose early the next morning, put on a plain gray dress, and pinned her silver brooch to her shoulder.

The Exilarch was here, in the Sault. She had been able to put the fact out of her mind at the party, but she had woken up with the knowledge pressing down on her, an oppressive weight on her chest. *The Exilarch is here. I have not much time to help Mariam.*

Since most of her books of lore and magic were at the Black Mansion, she set off across the city. Usually, she loved mornings in Castellane. The heat of the day had not yet set in, and the breeze was fresh and cool. Colorful birds chirped from the wrought-iron balconies of houses whose bright paint had been dimmed to pastel by salty air. The Broken Market had melted away into the shadows, and the stores lining the Ruta Magna displayed the riches of their wares: heavy silks, translucent porcelains, gorgeous brocades, sculptures made from jade and ivory in the shapes of foreign Gods. Though perhaps all Gods were foreign to the Ashkar.

But this morning, when she arrived at the Black Mansion, she found it in an uproar. She had gone first to the laboratory to retrieve her books, but it was empty; upon hearing shouting, she made her way to the Great Room, where she discovered the Ragpicker King sitting calmly in a chair, his blackthorn cane across his lap, while Merren—to Lin's surprise—made angry noises and clutched madly at his tousled blond hair.

Kel was also there, which Lin had not expected. He was leaning against a wall, as was Ji-An, who looked bored as usual. Jerrod stood hesitantly in the middle of the room, as if he wished desperately to approach Merren, but did not dare.

"He should have *died*," Merren shouted. "I can't understand why he didn't die! It was enough aconite to kill a horse!"

Lin glanced around the room, puzzled, but everyone else seemed to know what he was talking about. "Who should have died?"

"Gremont," said Jerrod, as Merren aimed a kick at a nearby chair. "We tried to poison him at last night's party."

Lin looked accusingly at Kel, thinking of their walk together before the party. "You didn't tell me that was the plan."

"I didn't know until I got there," he responded, sounding aggrieved.

"You *said* I ought to kill him," Merren objected. "Last night."

"And *you* said you'd already poisoned him anyway," Kel pointed out. "Also, it was the heat of the moment."

"Murdering a Charter holder is serious business," said Andreyen. "As we have discussed before."

"Murdering *anyone* is serious business," said Lin. "I don't understand—I know he's awful, but what's he done to Merren?"

There was a moment of awful silence. The anger drained out of Merren's face. He sat down heavily in an armchair. He looked very young suddenly; Lin could imagine him as a boy with a cap of fair curls, his small hands stained with alchemical solvents, his voice rising with excitement as he described some new experiment.

Ji-An sighed. "This is ridiculous," she said, and, turning to Lin, she recounted the tale of Merren's past: how Gremont had raped Alys, his sister, and arranged the imprisonment of his father. It was a grimly awful tale, and Lin felt her stomach shrink back against her spine. *Oh, Antonetta,* she thought.

"Merren," she said when Ji-An was done. "I'm so sorry."

Merren only nodded. He looked exhausted. Jerrod stepped forward to lay a hand on Merren's shoulder.

"I think I know why the poison didn't work," Lin said.

Merren's eyes flew wide, and Kel let out a low whistle. Only Andreyen looked unsurprised.

"He is wearing a protective amulet," Lin went on. "A bit like Kel's talisman—powerful old magic. I glimpsed it around his throat last night."

"That ugly necklace?" Ji-An made a face. "Well, I can shoot him with an arrow if poison won't work—"

"No," said Merren, in an uncharacteristically cold voice that made Jerrod look down at him worriedly. "I want him to die by my hand. Not someone else's."

"I'm not even sure an arrow *would* work," said Lin. "The amulet isn't a protection against poison. It's protection against *danger.* Anything that might threaten him. And it is from a time when amulets were far more powerful than they are now. The arrow might break before it ever struck him."

Kel said, in a peculiar sort of voice, "If Conor had a talisman like that, he might not even need a Sword Catcher."

"I'd be very curious as to where Gremont got it," said Jerrod. "Very curious." He looked down at Merren. "There is only one thing to do, then. We must steal the amulet—"

"Stop." Andreyen's voice, cut steel, sliced through the conversation. The room fell silent. "All of you. Cease this foolishness immediately." He rose to his feet. Lin forgot sometimes how tall he was, tall and rangy as a shadow elongated at dawn. "Amulets can be powerful and complex. In the old days, there were some so powerful that any action taken against the wearer would be turned back on the attacker sevenfold." He turned to Merren. "You trust me, do you not?"

Merren nodded. Andreyen knew a great deal about amulets, Lin thought, though that did not really surprise her; he had always been fascinated with magic. It was why he had approached her in the first place.

Andreyen's voice softened. "I will look into this amulet business. Specifically, its origin. Something like that would be illegal to sell. If he bought it, I should be able to trace the acquisition. In the meantime, turn your attention *back* to the matter of the Shining Gallery." He brushed his fingers along the head of his cane—a habitual gesture. "And indeed, I wouldn't be surprised if we find Gremont's name somewhere in this Gallery business."

Kel uncrossed his arms. "You think Artal Gremont could be implicated in the massacre? I'd love to see him swing from the Tully gallows, but he was in exile when it happened."

The Ragpicker King smiled his long, unnerving smile. "And now he has returned, precisely because his father was killed that night. His exile was ended by his inheritance. Always look to who benefits from a crime when seeking the culprit."

There was a short silence. Merren looked disappointed, but Lin knew he would not speak up against Andreyen, whom he adored as a sort of father figure—though truly, Andreyen was not *that* much older than any of them.

"Well, then," said Jerrod, "we have our next move in the investigation. The Legate told Kel that Magali Berthe will be at the Arena croc fights on Ellsday. We can find her there."

"And do what? Interrogate her?" Lin asked.

"Talk to her. She'll speak with me. I'm from the Hill; she's known me for years," said Kel. "If there are any changes to the Ellsday plan, let me know through the usual channels." He smiled crookedly. "Alas, I must depart. I have to retrieve a Princess in two days, and there are many preparations to see to."

x x x

Two days later, Kel, dressed as Conor and bearing his circlet and talisman, rode along the Ruta Magna in the Palace's open-topped carriage. The great road that ran from the Narrow Pass to the harbor was lined with the citizens of Castellane, who had turned out in great numbers to celebrate the new Princess's arrival.

It was almost as though they had forgotten that three months ago, there had been an entirely *different* new Princess—one who had barely lived a week in the city before being murdered. Public memory was short when it came to an excuse to celebrate, Kel thought, remembering to incline his head gently every once in a while to acknowledge the presence of the crowd. They cheered as the carriage went by, waving the golden chrysanthemums that had been passed out that morning by Castelguards.

Though they held tightly to the green stems, the flowers would not be thrown until the Princess showed herself. *She* was the one they were desperate to see. Would she be beautiful? Glorious? A credit to the city? Today, the Crown Prince would be eclipsed. Kel could only feel relieved about it.

Queen Lilibet had stayed back at the Palace to ready everything for the arrival of Anjelica Iruvai. Jolivet, too, had remained behind, which struck Kel as strange. Usually, the Legate would have been present at a moment like this. He wondered if it had anything to do with the Shining Gallery investigation.

He felt the incipient beginnings of a headache, a buildup of pressure behind his eyes. He should not be thinking about the investigation. He was Conor now, doing what Conor would do in this situation. He needed to be alert not just to danger but also to the authenticity of his portrayal. He owed it to Conor and to his oath.

As they approached the curve of the harbor and turned toward the Royal Docks, Kel saw that they, too, had been prepared for the Princess's arrival. The wood had received a coat of gilded paint, and climbing roses had been wound over and under all the beams, then the blossoms had been painted—gold again, the color of House Aurelian. Kel thought the whole thing resembled a gold dinner plate, adrift on a blue tablecloth.

It was quiet as the carriage drew up and Kel dismounted. Lilibet and Jolivet had argued that morning: The Queen wanted the Prince to meet the Princess alone, without soldiers or counselors to spoil the mood, while the Legate had pointed out that they were sending the Sword Catcher precisely because there was possible danger, and having guards present would only be good sense. In the end, they had compromised. The mounted members of the Arrow Squadron made a scarlet crescent behind Brigadier Benaset, seated on Jolivet's white stallion, though they did not approach the wharf.

From here, Kel could see the curve of the shoreline all along the harbor they called the Key. The commercial wharves had been shut down for the day, and crowds of onlookers massed on the wooden platforms, gazing out to sea, their arms full of flowers. The taverns along the Key had thrown their doors open, and the sound of festive music drifted across the water. Only the armored ships moored off Tyndaris served as a hint that Castellane was prepared for an attack.

Someone in the crowd cried out. A speck had appeared on the horizon, growing quickly in size as the steady wind carried it toward the harbor. It was a clear day, the kind where heaven and sea met seamlessly at the horizon. The great ship from Kutani could be seen in all her splendor, moving across the harbor like a dowager queen sailing across a ballroom floor. Her red-orange sails made Kel think of spices—a spill of saffron and turmeric.

As the great ship neared the shore, Kel craned his head back to see it. The soul of the boy who had once, with his best friend, Cas, wanted to be a pirate, soared at the sight: polished, gleaming wood and brass, vast sails, the prow carved into the shape of a brightly painted mangrove tree. Men and women crowded the decks.

The massive ship stopped short of the dock. Uncertain muttering whipped up among the Arrow Squadron. Kel stood, feeling like an ass, as the Kutani boat drifted just offshore.

After some moments, a small *dow* boat was released into the water. It oared smoothly to the dock, where a single man—of medium height, with a smoothly shaven head and lean, handsome features—disembarked. His tunic and trousers were white linen; over them he wore an open robe the color of sumac, threaded through with gold. The deep color set off his dark-brown skin.

The sunlight glinted off his gold spectacles as he bowed to Kel, as was Kutani custom; Kel bowed in return. "I am Kurame Iruvai," the man said. "This dock is too small."

"You are Anjelica's brother?" Kel realized, belatedly, the import of the purple-red robe, the gold bracelets at his wrists, studded with scarlet bloodstones. And Kurame's familiarity: Of course he resembled his sister. "Then you are of the Bloodguard."

Kurame inclined his head. "I am. But this dock remains too small. My sister cannot disembark here."

"Can't she?" Kel was frankly amazed. "She seemed ordinary-sized, from her portrait. Not a giantess of any sort."

A smile touched the corner of Kurame's mouth. "You will see what I mean, if the problem can be rectified. If not," he added thoughtfully, "perhaps we must return to Kutani?"

Kel turned to face the Arrow Squadron and summoned his best version of Conor's imperious tone. "We need to move the dock. Now."

There were some muttered protests, but the dock had been designed to be mobile. Kel retreated to the shore as the Arrow Squadron waded into the water, muttering furiously as the lapping tide splashed up to ruin their scarlet-and-gold trousers. With a great deal of heaving on ropes, the dock was towed aside, leaving a clear path from the water to the land.

Kurame, meanwhile, had returned to the *dow* boat, where he seemed to be reading a book. Benaset, who had remained on horseback, glared. Kurame ignored this with a truly magnificent indifference. Kel, who was beginning to sweat in his heavy clothes, considered whether Kurame might be his personal hero.

When the dock had been relocated, the boat drew near. A massive gangplank was lowered, the Arrow Squadron staring up in frank amazement at the shining expanse of wood. Two long columns of Kutani courtiers lined up along either side of the walkway. Each carried a branch bearing the scarlet flowers of the flame tree. The women wore simple shift dresses of gorgeously printed cotton with rich decorative borders of gold and silver thread; the men wore white linen, with bands of more colorful fabric at their wrists and ankles.

Kurame's small boat had come to shore; he climbed out and made his way to where Kel was standing. Two more of the Bloodguard—both handsome young men with a family resemblance to Kurame—marched down the walkway, heads high, swords glimmering at their waists. Like their brother, they wore the gold bracelets of their rank. As they reached the foot of the gangplank, they bowed to Kel and stepped aside, one to the right and the other to the left. They reminded Kel, somehow, of a double line of Lutan's priests moving aside to allow the common folk to view the holy flame of the Temple.

He craned his neck back as movement stirred at the top of the gangplank. Something moved into view—something so massive that for a moment, it blocked the sun. Making its way down the wooden gangway was an elephant—massive and gray, with huge dark eyes lashed like a girl's. Saddle-cloth of amber brocade draped its sides; its tusks were painted silver, and strands of tinkling silver bells wreathed its head and ankles.

Kel's mouth fell open. He heard Kurame laugh delightedly. "I told you," he said.

As the beast came nearer, Kel saw that lashed to its back was a basket-seat, woven from strips of mangrove wood. Inside the basket sat Princess Anjelica, her back as straight as an arrow.

She, too, wore a sheathed dress, but hers was of gold brocade, and over her slim shoulders hung a translucent cloak of gold and scarlet Marakandi *sef*, creating the effect of dragonfly wings. Her cloud of black curling hair was bound in a shining net. She glanced down at Kel from her perch, and he caught the fleeting glance of her dark eyes.

He drew in his breath; he could not help it. She was beautiful in a way that was like a blow. Kel had seen portraits of her, of course, and had heard all the tales of her loveliness. She was famous for it—and rightly so, it seemed.

But Kel had always thought of beauty as something to admire and enjoy. He had not realized there was a kind of beauty that was painful to look upon. That brought an ache to the back of the throat, as if he were listening to music that was profoundly sweet and sad.

And she looks sad, he thought. *No, she looks anxious.* She was looking around the harbor, half expectantly. He could see her tension. *She, too, is expecting an attack from this spurned suitor of hers.* But there were no ships on the horizon, no sign of any craft between here and Tyndaris bigger than a fishing vessel.

She rose to her feet and bowed—not to Kel, but to the people of Castellane who had gathered to see her. A great cry rose up. Cheering, they hurled their flowers into the air—a plumed cloud of saffron.

Then she called out—a sharp single word, clearly a command—and the elephant began to kneel. It sank down gracefully before Kel, extending one foreleg, bent slightly. "She wishes you to join her," said Kurame, a hand on Kel's shoulder. "Climb up."

Here goes nothing, Kel thought, and clambered up onto the elephant's sturdy leg.

Lin read for several hours in the Black Mansion before it was necessary for her to leave and go on rounds. She only had a few patients to see today, but given the crowds that would be clogging up the roads in the city, she was anxious about getting to them on time.

To her surprise, she found Andreyen waiting for her on the front step of the Black Mansion. He was leaning on his cane, gazing out at the Scarlet Square and the city beyond. His expression was especially opaque today—not that it was ever easy to tell what the Ragpicker King was thinking.

"You are worried," he said. "Is this because Benjudah has arrived in the city?"

She gave him a curious look. Few *malbushim* even knew that the Ashkar had a leader, and if they did, like Conor, they called him the Exilarch. Then again, Andreyen had known about the forbidden books in the Shulamat. His pursuit of knowledge about magic had taken him closer to her people than most.

"Yes," she said. It was something of a relief to state the plain truth. "It is his task to test me. To see if I am the Goddess I claim to be. When he discovers I am not—"

"I have a suggestion for you," Andreyen said, still gazing out across the city. "I imagine you are trying to learn all you can before you, as you predict, inevitably fail at whatever challenge he sets you." He turned to her. "You can lay your hand on magic, Lin. Concentrate not on faking your way through these tests, or on the time you imagine is growing ever shorter before you. Concentrate on *passing* the test. I believe you can."

Lin was too astonished to say anything in reply, and indeed he did not seem to expect one, but went back into the Black Mansion, closing the door behind him.

She had been right about the difficulty of traversing the city. It was nearly midday, and the crowds were out in full force; all of Castellane had heard of the beauty of the foreign Princess and were eager to celebrate her arrival. (Save those young girls mourning that the Crown Prince would soon be married and unavailable to them; they wandered the streets disconsolate, wearing red ribbons pinned to their chests to symbolize broken hearts. Lin thought they were ridiculous.)

White jasmine was the flower of Kutani. Every balcony seemed to sport a plant pot from which white jasmine flowers spilled; every door was a wreath of the blooms. The air reeked with the rich, buttery-sweet scent. Alongside the jasmine were displayed yellow roses, the flower of House Aurelian, and colorful silk flags of Castellane flew from every window.

The closer Lin came to the Ruta Magna, the more densely crowded the streets became. Castellani had turned out in celebratory colors: bright red and gold, of course, as well as lime greens and raspberry silks saturated enough to look edible. Women wore crowns of flowers; the men pinned sprays to their buttonholes or pockets.

Lin realized she was terribly underdressed. But then, she was obviously Ashkar: people's gazes slid over her and away, dismissing her, just as they usually did. The Ashkar were not expected to celebrate things like royal marriages. After all, they were not really citizens of Castellane.

Lin soon found herself entangled in a group of drunkenly boisterous students, carried along for several blocks, and deposited somewhere near the Street of Singing Women. Irritably, she dusted off her clothes and cut across the Temple District toward the Fountain Quarter, where her first patient, Zofia Kovati, lived.

She found Zofia in high good humor. Zofia had been a pirate in her younger days and still wore a black eyepatch. Today she wore a military jacket buttoned over an old-fashioned taffeta dress with full skirts.

"There'll be music in the streets tonight," Zofia said a bit dreamily, as Lin knelt to feel the swelling in the old woman's frail ankles. "Clever of the Aurelians to marry the Crown Prince off to the girl from Kutani."

"Yes," Lin said. Clever and cold. Conor did not love this Princess, though perhaps if she was as beautiful as rumor had it, he would come to eventually. Her stomach tried to give another sick little lurch, but she ignored it and picked up her auscultor.

"I was in Kutani, long ago," Zofia said, still in the same dreamy tone. "In Spice Town. The houses there are like castles. The sand so fine and soft you can sleep on it like a mattress. Even commoners are draped in silks and velvet, gold rings in their ears, on their fingers. The gardens are like paradise."

The thrum of Zofia's voice came through the auscultor, along with the sounds of her failing heart. When the heart began to die, Lin knew, fluid built up around the muscle, slowing its function further, causing the body to retain water and salt. A Castellani doctor would bleed Zofia's swollen arms and legs, as if they were the cause of her ills and not a symptom. They would tell Zofia she could be cured.

Lin knew better than that.

She put away her auscultor and took out the usual medication. *Digitalis lantana.* "One tablet each morning with water," she instructed. "And I shall leave several talismans for you, too, here on the nightstand. Wear them close to your skin."

Zofia looked impish. "Can I dance? In the streets tonight, there will be dancing to celebrate the royal marriage."

"Of course you can dance. In fact, I recommend it." Lin slung her satchel over her shoulder. "I prescribe moonlight and music and a handsome young admirer to swing you about."

Zofia cackled as Lin took her leave. If anything, it was hotter outside than it had been before. Lin walked close to the buildings, keeping to the shaded areas as she headed toward the Temple District. Children gathered around the public cisterns, splashing themselves with water. There would be swimming in the Fear River, cold sherbets sold from stands that seemed to appear magically on every corner when the heat rose above a certain temperature—

Lin sensed movement on her right side and turned her head just as a carriage pulled up alongside her. It was not just any carriage. This was a Marivent carriage, all red lacquer, with a gold lion blazoned on the side. The driver, perched in his seat above, wore Palace livery; he was staring straight ahead, his expression dour, as if he did not see her.

The carriage door swung open. The man who leaned out had graying hair, a hawk's profile, and a narrow, hard mouth.

Lin stopped in her tracks. The carriage halted beside her.

"Legate Jolivet," she said. She looked up and down the street; there were a few pedestrians making their way toward the Ruta Magna, but they studiously avoided glancing in the direction of the carriage. Palace business was Palace business.

The Legate inclined his head. "Domna Caster."

"Shouldn't you be with the Prince?" she said. "On such an important day as this?" *And a dangerous one.* Mayesh had always said that for royalty, appearing in public was a matter of risk and reward. Exposed to the public, they were in danger, but to hide from the public was to risk their ire or contempt.

He raised a thin eyebrow. "Kel Anjuman has the situation well in hand, I assure you."

Ah. When Kel had said he needed to retrieve a Princess, Lin had assumed he would be going to the docks *with* Conor. Not going in Conor's place, a Sword Catcher acting not the part of protector, but the part of Prince.

"Come." Jolivet gestured impatiently, indicating that she should get into the carriage. "Your presence is requested by the Palace."

"By the Prince, you mean," Lin said.

Jolivet simply stared at her, his expression stony. She knew she ought to be afraid, but something inside her rebelled. She was a physician, on rounds. She had other patients, people who depended on her. Unlike a certain Prince who clearly could not imagine that she had responsibilities more important than his whims.

"Mayesh Bensimon is my grandfather," she said. "He will not like to hear of you treating me this way."

"Mayesh would tell you that you were being foolish to deny the Palace, if that is indeed what you are doing," said Jolivet. The signet ring on his hand flashed as he gestured dismissively. "Believe me. I know him well."

He was right. Lin gritted her teeth together. She had the urge to kick the wheels of the carriage and scream, but that would do no good either way.

She raised her chin and matched the Legate's gaze, stare for stare. "I suppose," she said. "But I will need to be back at the Sault before dark."

He smiled thinly. "As you wish, Domna," he said, and reached out with a callused hand to help her into the carriage.

Elsabet

A faint aura of neglect reigns over the former temple of Anibal on Anchor Street. Inside, the corners of the *cella,* the great central chamber, are thick with dust. Tiles are missing from the ornate mosaics on the floor, and matted spiderwebs hang like seafoam from the candelabras.

Yet the northern part of the *cella,* where the altar rises, has been recently swept. On the altar, surrounded by glowering statues of the God of death, is a tall priest's chair, and in the chair sits a woman with long black hair and sharp, aquiline features. She wears a scarlet gown, close fitting as a glove, as if she has been dipped in blood. She is a Princess, and very far from her native land.

She gazes without expression at the two men standing before her. One is Artal Gremont, looking unpleasantly sweaty. The other refuses to be referred to by his real name: The Princess has taken to calling him Seven, as that is the position of his chair on the clockface of the Dial Chamber.

"So the Prince is set on this alliance with Kutani, then?" says Elsabet Belmany. "He cannot be turned aside?"

"I've always thought of him as weak-willed," says Seven, who knows Conor better than Artal, "but he's been remarkably firm on this. It doesn't help that he has the backing of all his usual advisers. Bensimon, Jolivet—they're all keen on this match."

"Of course they are," Elsabet breathes. Spineless opportunists, all of them. Everyone knows Castellane runs on greed the way the human body runs on blood and humors. Each person surrounding the Prince sought only to enrich themselves with gold; they have forgotten the more valuable offerings of royalty: nobility, stern pride, the steely rule of Law, and the courage to lead a nation into battle. "Annoying," she says, "but as we suspected. It is the Sword Catcher who concerns me at the moment. He continues to be a thorn in our side."

Artal's forehead creases. "Is that the one that's supposed to be the Prince's cousin? He doesn't look like much of a threat. I could easily hire a mercenary to put an end to him—"

"He's a better fighter than he looks," says Seven, shooting Artal a sideways look of contempt. "And besides—our lady wants him alive."

Elsabet flatters herself that she finds most people easy to read. It is clear to her that Seven is none too fond of Artal and is barely tolerating his presence. She hides a smile. Seven thinks a great deal of himself, as all the Charter holders do, and it amuses her to see him discomfited. "I do want Kellian Saren alive," she says. "But I also want him out of the good graces of the Palace."

"It's not the Palace that protects him," Seven says, "it's the Prince. He loves him like a brother. Won't hear a bad word about him. I've tried."

"But with what evidence? Surely the Sword Catcher has been loyal. And if he failed in some small way, surely the Prince would forgive him?"

Seven inclines his head to acknowledge the truth of Elsabet's words.

"Still," she muses, "a Prince must acknowledge treason. Where a friend could forgive a betrayal, a ruler cannot countenance an act against himself, for it is an attack against his country."

"You mean because he is working with the Ragpicker King?" says Seven. "And not with Conor's knowledge, as far as I can tell."

Elsabet watches a black spider scurry across the broken-tiled floor. She says, "That is not enough. In Castellane, the King in the City and the King on the Hill have long had more of a connection than most people know."

Artal and Seven exchange a puzzled look; clearly they do not know what she means. Nor do they need to; they are merely rich men, not royal ones. There are some secrets it is unnecessary for them to know. "But working with the Ragpicker King— Well, it sounds to me as if he begins to chafe at his servitude. He was born to die for someone else, to uplift them with his blood. He surely has come to resent it. We can play on that. We will watch him, observe him. He will make a mistake." She turns to Artal, who has begun to look glazed. Alas, complex machinations are somewhat beyond him. "In the meantime, Artal, you know your task. We have reason to believe your pretty fiancée knows where Prosper Beck can be found. I shall rely upon you to convince her to tell."

Artal grins. "Wonderful," he says. "I'll enjoy that very much."

CHAPTER EIGHT

Jolivet was silent all the way to Marivent. The carriage took side roads, avoiding the main streets where the celebration was now in full swing: Lin could hear the sounds of it—distant shouts blending together like the roar of an unseen waterfall.

Since he was ignoring her, Lin felt free to stare at the Legate curiously. He really *did* look like a raptor up close, with his curved nose, receding chin, and nearly unblinking eyes. No wonder the people of the city called him the Eagle of the Fall, though she had never been sure which Fall they meant exactly—the fall of the cliffs away from Marivent? Or a more metaphorical fall, the fall of the Empire long ago? For there had been Legates back then, too, enforcing Laws for Emperors.

Jolivet seemed to relax minutely when they reached the Palace. Kutani flags fluttered from atop the North Gate, and inside the walls of Marivent, red-liveried staff were hurrying to and fro, carrying pots of flowers in brilliant shades of coral, peach, and tangerine. Wires bearing golden chimes were strung between balconies; gold bunting hung above the doorways. Had all this been done this morning? Or last night, when she was sitting up with a patient in the Sault?

The carriage drew up in the courtyard of the Castel Mitat. Jolivet helped Lin descend and hurried with her into the small palace.
It seemed deserted, quiet enough inside that she could hear the
faint carillon of the chimes outside, shimmering on the air.

When they reached the door of the Prince's chambers, Jolivet
knocked, and there was a flurry of sound behind the door; it cracked
open slightly and a woman in a white mobcap appeared. Lin remembered her—one of the hurrying servants she had caught a
glimpse of the night she'd come to Marivent to heal Conor after
he'd been whipped bloody.

It all seemed an age ago, now.

Clinging tight to her physician's satchel, Lin followed the mobcapped servant into the Prince's chambers while Jolivet remained
outside. The chambers themselves did not seem to have changed
much. There were the same two beds, the same marble tables and
crumpled-silk divans—though there was now a heavy desk pushed
against one wall, covered in a white hill of ink-scrawled papers.

A whirlwind of activity was happening in the center of the room.
And in the center of the activity stood Prince Conor, almost completely naked.

Lin dropped her satchel. Luckily, no one seemed to notice; it hit
the floor with a soft *thunk* as she stared. She knew, of course, that
the very rich had servants to help them dress, but she had never
pondered what that would actually look like before—or that it
meant that, of course, they would clothe you from the skin out.

Not that the Prince was *entirely* nude. He was in his smallclothes: short breeches of fine linen, cut on the cross to be close
fitting. Fluttering around him like anxious birds were a group of
servants: a tailor, carrying thread, needle, and seam-ripper,
another—the woman who had greeted Lin at the door—taking various garments from the wardrobe to hold up for the Prince's ap-
proval, and a third holding open a velvet box inside of which rested
a variety of glittering ornaments.

At the eye of the hurricane, the Prince stood calmly, utterly unselfconscious about his lack of attire. In fact, he looked half asleep, his eyes heavy-lidded, his black hair tousled and still damp from the tepidarium.

He did not seem to notice that Lin was there at all. No one did. And she realized, as if at distance from her own self, that he had put himself there for her to look at him. She knew him enough to know that. He meant to unsettle her. No doubt he imagined her as prudish—and indeed, compared with those on the Hill, she was, with her modest dress, her scuffed shoes, her plain unbound hair.

But she would not let him see she was bothered. She did not look away, but stared straight at him. She had seen Conor's bare skin before, when she had healed his whip wounds. But she had been a physician then, concentrated on the mending of torn flesh.

This was different. He was perfect, healthy, unmarred. His skin was a light brown, polished and unmarked. Lin was used to looking at human bodies dispassionately. Perhaps she had forced herself to forget how beautiful they could be. The lines of him flowed smoothly into one another—broad shoulders, a waist that tapered to lean hips, muscles that moved dexterously under his skin when he turned.

His skin looked as if it would be soft to touch, fine-grained as silk, but his body was hard and lean, doubtless made so by years of riding and hunting. And sword-training. Kel had said he was always training, and one could see the results. The muscles in his stomach were as clearly delineated as if their shape had been drawn onto him with ink. He had been blessed with his mother's beauty, too. Full lips, high cheekbones, and long fingers like poetry. Fingers that had touched her once—*finding the edge of her dress's neckline, where her breasts rose to press against the material* . . .

As if he could read her mind, Conor flicked his gaze toward her for the first time. He caught her eyes, and she could feel her cheeks burning as his mouth curled up at the corner.

"Delfina," he said, his voice low and lazy, "not that one. The black, with the silver buttons."

The mobcapped servant—Delfina—deftly switched out the garments in her hands and went to hold the shirt up against the Prince. He frowned into the pier glass that hung inside the wardrobe door and shook his head. Water dripped from his damp hair onto his bare clavicles as Delfina removed the rejected garment.

A body is just a body, Lin reminded herself fiercely as he stepped into a pair of sueded gray trousers. "Perhaps you could choose something in gold, or cinnabar," she said, crossing her arms over her chest. "The colors of Kutani. It might be appreciated."

The group of servants looked at her in alarm, as if she were a child who had poked a stick into a tiger's cage. Conor's gaze flicked over her as he drew down his shirt, covering—much to her relief, she told herself—his naked torso. "Oh," he said in a careless tone. "You're here."

It was a tone calculated to make her feel like a small pebble that had fetched up under his shoe.

"Well, you seem to have brought me here to watch you get dressed," Lin said. "I assumed you wished my opinion on your choice of outfit."

"Believe me," said Prince Conor, letting his hands fall to his sides, "I do not seek your opinion on sartorial matters."

There was a small whirl of movement as Delfina attended to his cuffs. There was a frill of lace on each one, shot through with gold thread. A gold waistcoat, thick with brocade, went on over the shirt. The lace at his throat foamed over the waistcoat in a cascade.

You wanted my help, Lin nearly said. *You asked me for it at the party.*

She didn't say the words aloud. Somehow she knew—just as she knew he was doing his best to unsettle her—that he did not want her to mention that.

The tailor had darted in now to make minute adjustments to the fit of his shirt. Delfina was carrying over a pair of boots, which looked to Lin to be nearly as tall as she was. "I asked Jolivet to pick you up while you were on your rounds, so you'd have your satchel with you. Although I see you have dropped it on the floor. How careless."

Lin glared at him, but he was studiously examining the velvet box of jewelry held out to him. After dithering between rubies and sapphires, he held out a languorous hand for rings to be slipped onto his fingers.

"Indeed, I assumed it was a matter of urgency," said Lin, "not a choice between red and blue."

He opened his eyes in mock-hurt. "Clothing is often a matter of urgency. Do you know what would happen if I wore orange in front of the Shenzan Ambassador? An international incident."

"No doubt," said Lin. "Speaking of political necessities, isn't there somewhere else you're supposed to be?"

Clink. The servant with the velvet box had dropped a ring. There was a scramble to retrieve it, during which the Prince regarded Lin steadily over the kneeling servants' heads.

"Delfina, my dear," he said as she rose with the fallen ring in her hand, "Alois, Ivèta—leave us. I would speak with my physician alone."

Delfina set the ring back in its box, and the group of servants melted away silently. As the door closed behind them, the Prince threw himself onto the nearest divan, boots in hand. As he began to lace one up his calf, he said, "As far as the world is concerned, I *am* at the docks, greeting the Kutani ship. Indeed, most of the Palace is there. This is as empty as Marivent is likely to be for quite some time. Which is why I asked you here now."

Surely he wasn't saying he'd sent Kel in his place so he could meet Lin at the Palace? She rejected the idea as ridiculous.

"You said at the party that you needed my help," she said. "And that it was not you that was ill. I think you'd better tell me what it is you do want. It may not be within my ability to grant it."

Having laced his second boot, Conor rose to his feet. He was not wearing a circlet, and black locks of hair fell over his forehead.

She thought of his swan cloak, how the feathers had kissed his skin. "I have every faith in your ability."

"The Exilarch—"

"Ah, yes," he said. "Your preferred Prince." His voice was light as the notes of a satirical song. "I considered that. So I am giving you a royal order. You will help me, and you are not permitted to tell your Exilarch about it. Which relieves you of any responsibility there. A neat solution, don't you think?"

Lin felt a rushing in her ears. She could hear Mayesh's voice, over the pounding of her own heart: *A royal order is a formal demand made by the Blood Royal. The punishment for disobeying it is death.*

But he wouldn't, she thought. Conor wouldn't. She searched his face for some sign that he was joking, but she saw nothing there. He was as unreadable as a message written in cipher.

"You're serious?" she whispered.

His expression did not change, and Lin did not notice his hands. They had clenched at his sides into white-knuckled fists.

His gray eyes were cool and distant. "You have not seen me for the past three months. I have become a far more serious person."

He is really doing this, she thought, incredulous. But why had she thought he wouldn't? In the end, he would always do as he liked.

In a dry voice she said: "You are telling me I must defy one of my Princes."

"So it seems. Obviously, I would rather it not be me. Now fetch your medicines, and I will take you to your patient. We have not much time."

Within seconds, Kel found himself seated, facing Anjelica. He gripped the sides of the woven basket as the elephant rose and they sailed together up into the air.

There was a great deal of yelling as the Arrow Squadron tried to circle around to follow the elephant, which had already started up the harbor path toward the city. The animal moved at a slow, stately pace, flanked on either side by the Bloodguard. The roar of the crowds rose; the slips between the wharves were full of flowers, floating on the surface of the tide.

Now, Kel thought, *I am Conor. Now I am the Prince, greeting my bride. Kel might wish to be kind, but Conor needs to be gracious. Gracious and clever. Kindness is not a part of politics, and this is a political alliance.*

Across the basket, Anjelica Iruvai regarded him through wide dark eyes. Kel inclined his head. "Be welcome to Castellane," he said. "I am glad to see you arrived safely."

"Yes, thank you, *Ufalme.*" The word for "Prince" in Kutani.

Her voice was soft and distant; she was even more beautiful up close. Her lids were painted with gold powder, her high cheekbones dusted with it. She had slender arms ringed with bracelets of copper and bronze; her hands were folded tightly in her lap. Kel, used to reading body language, could tell that the tension had not left her, though the harbor was rapidly receding in the distance.

He pitched his voice low. "*Ayakemi.*"

Princess.

A flash of gold. She was looking at him in surprise; she had not expected him to know any Kutani. It was a complex language, having developed out of the lingua franca of spice traders. Indeed, Kel had struggled to learn even a little of it.

"Someone has taught you how to speak properly," she said. "I am all amazement."

Kel grinned. Perhaps she was insulting him, or Conor; he didn't mind. He had never seen anyone so beautiful, and he was rather enjoying being on top of an elephant with her. As they turned onto the Ruta Magna and approached the thick of the crowd, he thought: *They will not be disappointed. They cannot fail to love her.*

So different from the arrival of poor Luisa, which had been a scandal. A shaming. Not so now.

"You are smiling," she said. Her Castellani was perfect, accentless. "What has pleased you?"

The crowd that lined the streets was roaring ecstatically. Roaring and hurling yellow roses and chrysanthemums. Some fell into the basket, scattering yellow petals.

"The people of the city love you," he said. "That is a good thing. Castellane was holding its breath, waiting to see its next Queen. They are relieved that you are beautiful."

Anjelica did not change expression, only regarded the wild crowds lining the streets with solemn gravity. The air was full of thrown blossoms; many had fetched up on balconies or tangled themselves in existing trellises. "That should not matter."

"It does, to them," said Kel. "Your elephant seems to know where he is going. Has he visited Castellane before? Avid sightseer, perhaps?"

"*She* is indeed clever. Her name is Sedai. She was a gift to me from a Prince of Hind." She reached to stroke Sedai's back. "She follows the Bloodguard. They know the way well enough. We have maps, you know, in Kutani."

They were passing the closed doors of the Sault. Kel thought of Lin's Ashkar prayer: *How shall we sing our Lady's songs in a strange land?* Anjelica, too, was a stranger here, in the place she had come to rule.

"*Ufalme.*" Anjelica held a small woven box. In it was an arrangement of nuts lacquered with sugar. She took one and popped it into her mouth, then offered the box to him. "There are those who say Conor Darash Aurelian carries ill fortune with him," she said, looking at him from beneath her lashes. "That he was glad when the little girl from Sarthe died, for Sarthe had shamed him by sending her."

Kel blinked. What she had said was not rude precisely, but it was unusual for royals to be so direct. He bit into a nut to buy himself an extra moment.

Then he swallowed and said, "Luisa did not die of bad luck." Why not match frankness with frankness? "She died because someone wished to cause war between us and Sarthe, and they may still succeed. I mourn the Princess's death, for her own sake as well as for the sake of Castellane."

Her eyes were fixed on his face. "Spoken like a clever Prince," she said. "But you are not the Prince, are you?" She studied him as if he were an interesting puzzle to be solved. "Conor Aurelian cannot tolerate walnuts. They make him sick. But you appear to be suffering no ill effects."

Kel felt the shock like a dull blow. She had offered him a walnut, and he had not remembered to refuse it. How could he, after his years of training, have made such a tremendous mistake?

I fear you cannot fold all conflicting things within yourself. Being a Sword Catcher, and also this.

He had never failed so badly at his sworn task. He said, "The allergy can take time to come into effect. I may be quite sick when we get to the Palace." He made a noise he hoped indicated oncoming stomach trouble.

She smiled slightly. "You forget your own magic," she said. "Those who know who you really are can see you as you really are. There is no purpose in lying to me, Sword Catcher."

In the hall, Lin and the Prince rejoined Jolivet, who clearly knew their mission; he led them down the curved stairs, through a narrow door, and down a second set of stairs, this one lit by lanterns. There were no windows, and the stairs opened out at the bottom into a long, stone-lined tunnel. Lamps blazed bright lines along the walls. They were underground, Lin guessed. She recalled Kel having said that the Hill was honeycombed with passages beneath Marivent.

If Jolivet was bothered by the chilly silence of his companions, he certainly did not show it. His boots clicked on the stone floor as they went, and the Prince's embroidered frock coat swirled around him in the faint breeze that blew through the tunnel. The lamps along the walls caught the gold embroidery at his wrists and made it shine.

Like manacles, Lin thought. But he was not a prisoner. *She* was. To break a royal order was treason. It meant the Trick, and the Trick meant death.

The Prince must know I will never trust him again after this, Lin thought. But then he already believed she did not trust him—did not even *like* him. She had refused to say she would help him, so he had chosen to compel her to give him that help. He was a Prince; what else had she expected? The anger she felt was bitter as a poisonous herb; she was furious not just at Conor, but at herself.

As they moved down the tunnel, Lin noted multiple doors set into archways along the wall. When they reached the correct one, Jolivet unlocked it with a large key that seemed to appear in his hand as if by magic.

They were once again at the foot of a staircase, this one spiraling upward. As they ascended, they passed several casement windows, and Lin began to realize they were inside one of Marivent's towers. The staircase ended finally at a metal door, hammered with a pattern of stars and constellations. Light spilled from around the door's edges, providing the strange illusion that it was floating in space.

Jolivet knocked in an odd sequence—three, then two, then three again. The door was opened by a Castelguard, who stepped out of the room to let them in. Prince Conor went first, gesturing for Lin to follow. The moment she was inside, Jolivet shut the door behind them.

Lin found herself in a brightly lit chamber. It was wide and circular, the roof above rising into shadow at the tower's point. Small, diamond-paned windows were set high up; the furniture was Valdish chestnut, gleaming a warm brown in the light of many candles.

A gold-and-silver orrery, displaying the position of the planets, rested on a desk; the walls were lined with books regarding astronomy, the positions and histories of the stars. A cabinet held a sextant and telescopes of varying sizes—some made of ivory or studded with gems. Finely drawn wheel charts and maps, showing the position of the stars and the paths of the planets, hung upon the walls. Everywhere were papers, covered in notes made in a close, dark, scribbled hand. Something gleamed among the papers, and for a moment Lin thought they were gems, scattered on the surface of the desk, but a closer look told her they were shards of broken glass. *Odd.*

As her eyes adjusted to the light, she saw Conor cross the room to a high-backed wooden chair by the window. Lin had taken it to be empty, but she realized as she followed Prince Conor with her eyes that they were not alone in the room. The chair was occupied. It was only that the man sitting in it was so still, she had not reacted to his presence. He did not seem to be moving at all—not even a twitch of muscle, or a breath. Despite the number of candles in the room, he was in shadow.

The Prince had stopped before the chair. Lin could not read his expression as he looked down at the man sitting before him. His face was still as a mask.

"Father." The Prince's voice was even and low. "I have brought a physician to see you."

Lin was too surprised to move. Her patient was *his father*? The King?

And why was the King so still, so silent?

"She is the granddaughter of Bensimon," added Conor. "You know, the one he speaks of often."

Still no response. The Prince beckoned for Lin to come closer. She found herself moving reluctantly to join him, facing the King in his great carved chair.

King Markus Aurelian. She knew what he looked like, of course, and not only because his face was on the half-crown coin. When she was younger, the King had still made public appearances. She recalled seeing him in Valerian Square—a tall blond figure, broad-shouldered, resembling his Northern mother. A bear of a man, her father had said.

He was a big man still. Yet somehow his skin seemed too tight on his bones. His hair was bone white, long, reaching past the blades of his shoulders. His veins seemed too close to the surface of his skin; she could see the spidery map of them, stark at his temples. Though he sat slumped, as if half paralyzed, his shoulders hunched, his black-gloved hands clasped the arms of his chair with a force Lin could feel in the pit of her stomach. It was as if he were gripping on for dear life, but who could hold such a grip very long? Yet he had been doing it since they had entered the room; she was sure of it.

Strangest of all was the look on his face. Not quite expression-less, not at all; his eyes were wide and seemed to stare fixedly past them, as if he saw something horrible in the distance. Lin almost wanted to turn around and look behind her.

"Don't bother," said the Prince bitterly. "He is staring at noth-ing. He is always staring at nothing." He waved his hand in front of his father's face, his mouth twisting. "Now you know," he said. "The King of Castellane, my father, has become a waxen, drooling doll. Vacant as an empty heart. All his great strength gone to ruin."

Yet this is the man who had you whipped till you bled, Lin thought. But she knew better than to say it; her own experience with her grandfather had taught her you could easily hate and love someone at the same time. Especially someone who was supposed to love you.

"Who else knows?" she said instead. "About your father's con-dition?"

"It is known that my father is unwell. That is what Kel would tell you, if you asked. Few know more than that. Bensimon and Jolivet. A few of the guards. My mother, the Queen."

The King stirred suddenly, a restless gesture. Lin looked quickly at Conor, but he did not seem surprised. He bent over his father, reaching as if to take his hand—

The King's arm came up with incredible speed, his gloved fin-gers curled into a fist. He swung at the Prince as if he meant to break his son's jaw, but Conor—clearly practiced at this—caught his father's wrist and held it tightly.

"Father," he said. "It's me. It's your son."

The King's blank eyes slewed in Prince Conor's direction. Lin could see red, angry-looking skin at the edge of his gloves, where they met his wrists. Years ago, she recalled, his hands had been burned horribly during an official ceremony; he had worn the gloves ever since.

"*Ryura hini*," Conor said softly, and Lin realized she knew the words. They were Malgasi. Mariam had murmured them to her, years ago, stroking her hair as Lin screamed through nightmares. *Ryura hini. Ryura.* Calm yourself. Calm.

The King's arm lowered slowly to his side. Conor released his grip on his father and took a step back. The King was still expressionless; bright-red spots burned high on Conor's cheekbones.

Lin thought of the broken glass on the desk. "How—" *How often is he violent?* she almost said, but changed her mind. "How long has he been like this?"

"Since the Shining Gallery," said the Prince. "That night, after the bloodshed, my father walked away from the Carcel and entered this tower. He has not left it since. He has barely spoken since. He has been"—he waved a hand, his rings winking brilliantly in the candlelight—"as you see. Most of the time."

"But he understands you, you think. You spoke to him in Malgasi."

"Would that I understood more of it. But yes. He fostered at the Court there when he was a boy." The Prince sounded impatient; the shadowlight threw the sharpness of his features into cold relief. The angles of his cheekbones seemed cut there by knives. "I cannot have Gasquet examine my father; Gasquet has no skill. Besides, he cannot be trusted. The world cannot know the King is ill. We have been at the verge of war with Sarthe these past months. If they knew—"

"But surely the Charter Families must have noticed he has not communicated with them, not appeared at meetings or communicated with Ambassadors?"

"I have forged all his letters," the Prince said dispassionately. "With your grandfather's help. Fortunately, we have not had to deal with Ambassadors coming in person. After the Shining Gallery, they have stayed away out of respect. Or fear, perhaps." He smiled a twisted smile. "I will stand beside you if you wish to examine the patient. If he tries to raise a hand to you, I will stop it."

"I have treated violent patients before. You need not worry."

His gray eyes raked over her before he turned back to the King. "Father. She is going to examine you now."

Clinging to the strap of her satchel, Lin advanced slowly toward the King. His eyes did not move to follow her progress, even when her shadow was cast across him. Conor stood close by, arms crossed, watching her as she fetched her auscultor.

Taking a deep breath, she leaned in close to the King. A faint scent rose from him, like old paper and char. Up close, she could see a little of his resemblance to Prince Conor. His eyes, too, were gray, clear as seawater, though the skin around them was seamed with fine lines.

Placing the auscultor against the King's chest, she listened. It was unnerving to have a patient who did not even seem to know she was there, but his heartbeat was steady, his breath sounds normal. The King's glands were not swollen, nor did his skin bruise when firmly touched. His eyes did not track the movements of her fingers, but that she had expected. He seemed far away again, and it was difficult to remember that moments ago he had lashed out at his son.

"He seems healthy enough, in body if not mind," she said, drawing back. "I assume he eats and sleeps?"

Prince Conor nodded. "There is a small apartment through there." He indicated a door, near invisible, set in the wall paneling. There were odd marks on the door, Lin noted. Black, like scorch marks. Perhaps the result of some old experiment. "The Queen sees to him, bringing food and water. Jolivet sometimes. I trust no one else."

"Could it be simply the shock of the events in the Gallery, affecting his mind?" Lin asked. "I have seen it before, in sailors who have survived shipwrecks but seen their friends drown. The mind can be wounded as well as the body—"

"It is not that," said the Prince. "You asked me before about his fostering at the Malgasi Court. My father did not return from there alone. He brought a man named Fausten with him. A strange little companion. He and my father spent hours locked in this tower, claiming to be unraveling the secrets of the stars. In his more lucid moments, my father asks for him. But Fausten is dead. My father had him executed months ago."

Lin said nothing. There were times when she knew she needed to let her patients and their families talk; they would tell her what she needed to know, given space to do it. This seemed one of those times.

"I wondered why he seemed to want to see a man he had distrusted enough to condemn to the Trick," Conor went on, naming the black tower where convicted prisoners of the crown were held before execution. "Then I realized it was not Fausten himself he was asking for, but rather something Fausten provided for him."

The Prince looked once more at the unmoving shell that was his father, then crossed the room to the desk and returned with a glass flask. In it was a few inches of dark-brown liquid. He held it out to Lin. "He calls this his *medicine*," he said, his lip curled. "It seems Fausten was giving my father this brew regularly. One of the guards told me. There is no more of it, though; I have searched Fausten's quarters, but it seems to have gone with its maker."

"And what is it?"

"That is what I wish you to discover. You are an Ashkar physician; you have knowledge of herbs and medicines. I wish to know what this is. A medication, a poison, or—something else."

Merren would say the difference between a remedy and a poison is only in the dosage. The thought of Merren brought the image of his laboratory to her mind: mechanisms to distill, to separate and concentrate ingredients . . .

"Something else?" she echoed. His gaze caught hers; she was aware again of how much his eyes were like Kel's, and yet how different. The same shade, but there were different patterns inside the iris. In his left eye, Conor had a small white spot, like a star, near the dark rim of his pupil. "If not a medicine or a poison, then what?"

"That can be addressed when we know what the mixture is." He held out the flask. Lin took it, and for a moment her fingertips brushed against his. The hard jolt of it went all the way through her as if an arrow had split her rib cage.

She snatched her hand back. *Stupid*, she thought a moment later; stupid to let him see how much he affected her. How ridiculous he must find her, she thought, and indeed his mouth had settled back into a hard, uncompromising line.

"Get word to me as soon as you discover anything," he said as Lin slipped the flask into her satchel. "You can send a message through any of the Castelguard you see in the streets."

"Thank you," Lin said tonelessly. "I would like a carriage. To take me back to the city."

"Now?"

"That is up to you," said Lin. "I wait on your pleasure, Monseigneur. You have made that very clear."

He grinned. It was a hard flash, like a knife in the dark. "You're angry at me," he said. "Good."

Lin looked at him in surprise. "Good?"

"It will keep you sharp," he said, and brushed past her, on his way to demand that Jolivet find a carriage to remove her from Marivent.

For a moment, Lin was alone in the tower with the King. It was like being alone with a statue, she thought, slinging her satchel over her shoulder. He was so unnervingly silent, without even the rustle of a sleeve as he moved, or the scrape of his boot against the ground.

She slipped the flask into the satchel and was about to go when the King gave a sudden, deep gasp. She whirled, her heart pounding. "Your Highness—?"

Still staring past her, hands gripping the arms of his chair, the King said in a low, toneless voice, harsh as the buzzing of a bee, "*Hollazekyer di niellem pu nag.*" His gaze flicked toward her. "*Hollazekyer di niellem pu nag. Hollazekyer di niellem pu nag. Hollazekyer di niellem pu nag.*"

"Your Highness—" she began again, but it was clear he neither saw nor heard her. He was repeating the same sentence over and over now, as if he could not control the words spilling from his lips.

Unable to help herself, Lin fled.

Antonetta

Antonetta had discovered the tunnel when she was fifteen. In her misery and loneliness after she had been abandoned by her friends, she'd taken to wandering the manor at night. Like most houses on the Hill, it had been built upon ancient foundations. In the cellar she discovered—hidden behind a painted panel—a tunnel hewn into stone. When she raised her lantern, she could see that it seemed to stretch on for miles, branching out into smaller corridors like coral growing under the sea.

She'd nearly gotten herself lost in the winding network of underground hallways before she'd learned to bring chalk with her when she went down there. She'd discovered that many of the other corridors led to doors that were now sealed, but the main corridor brought her eventually to an abandoned building in the Maze. She was never sure who had created the tunnels, although she had some guesses: an ancestor who wished to be able to flee the Hill in case of attack, perhaps, or one who'd been engaged in smuggling illegal goods. It was a delightful secret—one she once would have shared with Kel and the others. Now she keeps it to herself, and has used the tunnel often in the years since she discovered it. Neither her mother nor any of the servants has ever noticed.

In the months since she's been promised to Artal, she's taken to anxiously visiting the door to the tunnel, as if to reassure herself she still has a means of escape if needed. The concept of sexual activity with Artal repulses her, and the added insult of First Night—slobbering nobles like Esteve and Uzec and that weaselly Ciprian Cabrol looking on—even more.

She still recalls Artal standing over her, his breath stinking of brandewine as he winked and told her: "Don't say I haven't given you a choice. If you'd stop being so stubborn and set up a meeting for me with your friend Prosper Beck, we could make our nuptial night as private as you like."

Antonetta has told him over and over again that what he is asking for is impossible, but he hasn't believed her. She has not yet ascertained exactly who is pulling his strings, but she knows someone is. He enjoys dropping hints that he has powerful friends, for one thing. For another, he is too stupid to have come up with such a devious plan on his own. When Artal likes what he sees, he takes it, and that seems as complicated as his plans ever get.

But who could it be who stands behind Artal? What puppeteer directs him? Antonetta, sitting on the edge of an old cistern, gazes moodily at the door that hides the tunnel below. And most important, how had they gotten hold of that name, Prosper Beck? The name of the man who'd first taught her sword-fighting when she was just a teenager?

Her thoughts turn to Kel, to the look on his face when she'd told him about Artal's First Night plan. Shock mixed with horror and disgust. She would have liked to take it as evidence that he cared, but it was Kel. He might well have felt the same at the fate of a stranger. Empathy is a lovely quality, she thinks, swinging her booted feet in annoyance, but it does make it hard to know what he is thinking.

How well does he even know me? she wonders. He certainly

could not imagine the depths of rage and hatred she was capable of; she did not think anyone could. She has trained herself over all these years to keep those feelings hidden, never to let them show on her face, to always be smiling like a good girl should. She would smile her way through the wedding ceremony with Artal, and afterward, after the horror of First Night was done, she would smile her way through her revenge.

CHAPTER NINE

Kel let out his breath in a soft hiss. The Princess from Kutani had blindsided him, and it was not something that happened often. He felt both deeply annoyed and slightly admiring, as if she had beaten him with a sly move at Castles.

"You have been pretending all is well since we met at the docks," she said. "But if the Palace sent the Sword Catcher in place of the Prince today, they must have felt a serious danger loomed. If I ask the King or Queen, I suspect I will hear only lies. But you know. Tell me: What sort of danger am I in?"

"I suspect you know," he said. "Laurent Aden."

Her cheeks flushed. Anger or embarrassment, Kel couldn't tell. "I saw no signs of ships in the harbor. Not Aden's galleon or warships of Castellane."

So she was worried. She'd been looking. Kel said, "Visible warships would have alarmed the populace on a day when the Palace wishes them happy. But believe me, they were there. The cliffs on either side of the harbor hide warrens of caves and tunnels. Smugglers use them, but so does our navy—when necessary."

"He might have other ways of getting to me," she said. "He is a rich man. He can afford to travel the Gold Roads in luxury. As long as he is alive, Aden will pursue me."

"Castellane is a fortress," said Kel. "There are only two ways in—the harbor and the Narrow Pass. Both will be guarded. And Marivent is impregnable. The pirate is certainly alive, and just as certainly, he cannot reach you."

The tense line of her shoulders relaxed. "If you are sure he is alive— Well, then. There is something more. I know what will happen when I arrive at Marivent. They will wish to show me every nook and cranny of the Palace, every portrait and statue. But before I agree to remain, I need one thing. I need to speak to Prince Conor. Honestly and without the King or Queen there. Can you arrange that?"

Before I agree to remain. Kel had not realized it was any kind of an open question. He hesitated as they passed beneath the North Gate, their perch atop Sedai barely clearing the arch.

"Yes," he said finally. "With help from you, I can."

Many who came to Marivent were intimidated by the size of the place, the walls of sheer white stone, and the towers casting their shadows down over the city and the harbor. Kel remembered how he had felt, so long ago, riding through the North Gate as a child with Jolivet.

Anjelica did not seem at all intimidated, though; only watchful. She seemed to take everything in as they emerged into the grassy space past the gate, where a circle of courtiers, their hands draped with flowering vines, had formed a loose circle. In the center of the circle stood the Queen. Beside her was Mayesh, his medallion gleaming dully like the moon behind clouds. Kel did not see Jolivet.

Lilibet had already begun to step forward, smiling, when she caught sight of Sedai. A genuine expression of surprise crossed her face; Kel could not help a small feeling of amusement. Mayesh, of course, changed expression not one whit as Sedai came to a halt and Anjelica rose to her feet. She wore brocade slippers, Kel saw, and exquisite chains of gold and silver circled her ankles. Without a glance at him, she stepped out of the basket and made a chirruping noise: Sedai lashed her trunk backward and circled the Princess's waist. With a gentle motion, she lifted Anjelica and deposited her on the grass.

Anjelica bowed low to the Queen. Kel could not hear her greeting; he was busy scrambling off the elephant's back. He made a less elegant job of it than Anjelica had, as Sedai did not seem inclined to help him out. Fortunately, he managed a safe enough landing to keep his dignity.

Already the Arrow Squadron were pouring through the gates, making their own ring around the courtiers and the Bloodguard, who stood at Sedai's head, motionless.

The Queen glanced over at him for just a moment before returning her attention to Anjelica. "Welcome, *Ayakemi* Anjelica. A lovely name," she added, smiling as she held Anjelica's hand between her own. The Queen resembled a calla lily today, in a dress of green-and-white silk, draped in heavy folds to show the richness of the material. A rope of pearls dangled from her throat, and more pearls, worked with white gold, circled her brow. "But not Kutani, I think?"

"I was named for a musician my mother adored. Anjelica Kjell, of Hanse."

"Lovely, lovely," said the Queen, patting Anjelica's hand and releasing it. Behind her, Kel noted Mayesh turn to whisper in the ear of a Castelguard, who took off running. "I would love to take you on a tour of the Palace and grounds, my dear," Lilibet said. "I recall seeing Marivent for the first time myself as a girl, knowing I would be Queen of the place. It was not something that could be forgotten." She sounded wistful.

Anjelica smiled. "That sounds wonderful," she said. "Perhaps tomorrow. Today I would like to speak privately with my betrothed."

The Queen glanced sharply at Kel, as if to say silently: *What are you* doing? After all, the plan of action had been decided on already. Kel was meant to slip away while the Queen guided Anjelica about the grounds, allowing Conor to take his rightful place and join his bride upon her return from the tour. "But it has all been planned for you, my dear. A tour of the grounds, and afterward a small supper, only ten courses—"

Anjelica's pleasant expression did not change. Nor did the tone of her voice. It was the same measured music as she said, "I must admit, I am smitten with my Prince. I yearn for private counsel with him." She gazed limpidly at the Queen. "Surely you understand."

Lilibet looked utterly baffled. She turned stiffly to Kel. "Conor, dear," she said loudly, rather as if Anjelica were not there. "The Princess—"

Kel smiled so widely that it hurt. "Ought to have anything she wishes. I shall of course accompany her to her rooms and speak with her there. Bensimon, will you lead the way?"

"I truly hope," said Mayesh, "that you have an excellent explanation for what has just transpired, Kellian."

Kel and the Counselor were walking a few yards behind Anjelica, headed in the direction of the Castel Pichon. Anjelica was flanked on either side by her Bloodguard; Kurame seemed interested in the layout of the Palace and was pointing out towers and gardens to Anjelica as they passed them.

"I have an explanation," said Kel. "But I cannot promise you will find it to be an excellent one."

Mayesh gave Kel a hard look. "She guessed who you are, didn't she? Or did she already know?"

"She knew. She seems very well informed," Kel said. He wondered if he should confess his mistake with the walnut but decided against it.

Mayesh sighed. "Kutani is infamous for the quality of its spycraft. I suppose they must have been diligent in investigating Castellane after the . . . previous events. What does she want with you?"

"She doesn't want anything from me," Kel said. "She wants to talk to Conor. Alone."

"That's all she requires? For Conor to join her in the Castel Pichon?"

Kel nodded. "She knows her mind," he said. "If I had refused her request, she would simply have told Lilibet she knew who I really was and demanded to speak with Conor regardless."

They were crossing the wide lawn in front of the Castel Pichon now, the green shafts of grass muddled with the small white flowers that had appeared after a recent rain.

Mayesh gave a grunt. Kel sensed the Counselor had been surprised, and he did not like to be surprised.

"She was anxious at the harbor," Kel added, "when I told her Aden might put in an appearance. But she is not fearful or delicate. She may look like a flower, but I saw iron in her."

"There are different kinds of iron. There is the iron that binds and strengthens. And there is the edge that cuts." The old man looked sideways at Kel. "Which is she?"

"I cannot say yet. But Conor must meet her as she is." He glanced at Mayesh. "Tell him to come with his defenses down."

Mayesh grunted again and turned away, cutting back through the grass, headed for the Castel Mitat.

Kel put on a burst of speed to catch up with Anjelica and her brothers. He reached them as they arrived at the front door of the castle, a low square building with small towers at each corner of the roof. *Castel Pichon* meant "Little Palace," and it was traditionally the home of visiting royalty. Luisa d'Eon of Sarthe had stayed here for the brief time she had been at Marivent before the bloody slaughter that had claimed her life. And the life of her bodyguard, Vienne d'Este, who had been sworn to protect her and had died trying.

Kel forced himself to shake off these thoughts. He greeted the

Castelguards posted at the red door of the Little Palace and led Anjelica and Kurame inside. (Isam and Kito, her other two brothers, had remained outside to chat with the Castelguards.)

A short, tiled hallway gave onto a massive set of carved doors, and beyond those doors were the apartments that would be Anjelica's. As he filed in with Anjelica and Kurame, Kel experienced a peculiar, untethered feeling, as if he had fallen asleep and woken up in a foreign place. He was not Conor; he was not even Kel Anjuman. He was a commoner. He had no business entering the private apartment of the Princess of Kutani. Yet here he was.

Anjelica was silent as she gazed around the rooms. To Kel's relief, Lilibet had clearly redone the chambers since Luisa had occupied the space. In fact, they were not just redone, they were *overdone*, in just the way Lilibet loved. The walls were hung with saffron silk tapestries, and every surface had been upholstered in silk or satin, all in shades of orange, yellow, and red. A massive couch in dark-red velvet ran along one wall, and a carved daybed groaned under the weight of brocaded pillows.

"*Deela tie, zia,*" said Kurame. "She has certainly tried to make you feel at home."

Anjelica sighed. "It was kind of the Queen," she said, "to think of me, and I do love my homeland. But I do not need to live inside the national flag."

"Lilibet enjoys a theme," said Kel. "Possibly more than she enjoys anything else."

Anjelica shook her head. "It will all need to be redone."

"Lilibet won't like it," said Kel.

"I shall cover the costs myself. Surely she will accept that."

Probably not, Kel thought. Lilibet would take it as an insult and a rejection of her taste—which, to be fair, it was. But he could already tell there would be little point telling Anjelica that; she would believe him, but she would not bother herself about it. The Queen would get over it, she would say. And they were her rooms, were they not, to do with what she liked?

Kel almost envied her. It must be freedom, he thought, to care little what others thought of you. And then he saw her eyes slide past him and realized that Conor had come into the room.

He had dressed for the occasion. A frock coat that swept to his ankles, lined in bright silk; a figured waistcoat and a shirt of white samite, threaded with gold. Heavy rings on his fingers, each flashing a stone of a different color: poison green, sea blue, blood red. A circlet of finely worked gold glittered with pinprick diamonds.

For the first time, he looked at Anjelica. And Kel felt immediately that he ought not to be in the room; there was something strange about being here for their first meeting. Conor's gray eyes met the Princess's dark ones, and Kel could see the shock of her beauty strike him, as it surely struck everyone who looked at her.

But that surprise was fleeting. What came after was a mix of consideration, calculation, and a cool appraisal that matched Anjelica's own look. It was rare, Kel thought, for Conor to look upon someone so very much like himself. Someone who was also royal, also armored in privilege and beauty. Someone who was neither above nor below him, but exactly equal. Perhaps the situation was the same for her.

"Welcome, *Ayakemi*." Conor swept a bow that made his frock coat fly around him like dark wings.

Anjelica inclined her head. "*Mizuru*."

It took a moment for Kel to recall what the Kutani word meant. Not "Prince," as she had called him at the docks, but "betrothed." He saw Conor mark the choice of word, too, a flash of interest in his eyes.

I should leave them to spar, Kel thought. Indeed, Kurame had already left the room, having slipped away discreetly at some point. Kel made as if to follow him, but Anjelica held out her hand.

"I would prefer the Sword Catcher stays while we talk," she said, her gaze on Conor.

"Kel is welcome to know anything I know," said Conor. "But

chaperoning me is not his usual occupation. And I believe you made it clear you wished to speak to me alone?"

"I wish to speak to you honestly," said Anjelica. She sat down on the nearby daybed, folding her hands in her lap. "And I know what a Sword Catcher does. For years, he will have lived with you, slept beside you, learned with you, come to speak as you speak and dream as you dream. If you are lying to me, he will know it."

"And you think I would tell you, if he did?" said Kel, his voice carefully neutral.

Conor winked at him.

"I think I could read it in your face," said Anjelica.

I don't think you could, Kel thought, but Conor nodded in his direction, as if to say silently: *Stay.*

So he would stay. Kel leaned back against the wall as Conor turned his attention to Anjelica. "I must offer my apologies, Princess. I do not normally decline a chance to make a first impression. Unfortunately, it was not possible for me to greet you at the Royal Docks today."

Anjelica did not move. She was perfectly still, in a way Kel had rarely seen before: the line of her body utterly motionless from her straight spine to her graceful neck. She said, "I had assumed you did not come because of Laurent."

"Rather unfortunate you had to spurn a pirate," said Conor, "and not, perhaps, someone else with a less dangerous profession. A gardener, perhaps, or a cook."

"A Princess has little opportunity to meet gardeners and cooks."

"I would have thought a Princess had little opportunity to meet pirates."

When Anjelica shook her head, the gold net that held her hair sparked like fire. "I have seen many royal marriages. Some are good and some are bad. But I think the most important thing is that we are honest with each other."

"I thought we were discussing pirates?" Conor said lightly, and

Kel shot him a warning look. Anjelica was still a stranger; she might easily take Conor's light amusement, directed at everything in the world that he found ridiculous, as mockery of herself.

But if she was bothered, she was too well trained to show it. "It is relevant," she said.

"I trust that it is," Conor said. "So. Honesty among royalty. What will you think of next?"

"Only the truth," she said. "I am one of ten daughters of the Kutani King. Not the oldest, and not the most important. But I was considered the most beautiful."

"I, too, am my parents' most attractive child," Conor said.

Anjelica ignored this. "When you are a Princess who is not the oldest or the most dowried, you learn to be practical about each of your advantages and disadvantages. But there was a man who frequented the Court. Someone I saw often at parties and social occasions. Laurent Aden, the privateer. He courted me passionately."

Conor exchanged a quick look with Kel, who shrugged. For someone who spoke of passion, Anjelica's voice was cold and flat as a sheet of ice.

"I thought he truly loved me," she said. "Even when my parents found out and forbade me to see him, I held fast to the belief that he was true to me."

"Let me guess," said Conor. "He was only interested in enriching himself with your dowry? Men who make a living thieving often cannot put down the instinct, even in personal matters."

"It was worse than that," said Anjelica. "One of his sailors betrayed his plan to the Palace. Aden hoped that I would let him into the Palace; he would use that access to rob the royal coffers before escaping on the *Black Rose*. When this was discovered, he fled Spice Town, but before he did he dared to come to me and beg me to run away with him. I refused. I spat in his face. He said I belong to him, and that he would keep coming for me. He has not left me alone since."

"I quite understand," said Conor. "I, too, have had pirates obsessed with me."

A smile quirked the corner of Anjelica's mouth, but it vanished quickly. In a grave tone, she said, "You amuse yourself greatly, *mizuru*."

"I hope to amuse others as well," Conor said, not ungently, "though I am aware it may not happen." He sat down on the daybed, not close enough to Anjelica to crowd her, but not as far away as he could get, either. "You feel you need to warn me," he said. "You were afraid Aden would be at the docks today, and are afraid he may yet come for you."

"I thought you should know. He may not leave me alone."

Conor said, without a hint of humor, "We were made aware of the danger some time ago. There were fleets out looking for him today, but he was neither captured nor even spotted."

An odd look passed across her face. She said, "He is clever. I expect this is not the end of him."

"I told her this Palace is a fortress," Kel said. "She will be safe here."

"Surely you could not be afraid to tell me this," said Conor. "You cannot imagine I knew nothing of it. I was told that your reputation had been marred. That this was why your parents were willing to countenance your marriage to me at all."

Ah, Kel thought. So that's the reason—the thing Castellane had to offer to Anjelica that no one else did. A Princess's reputation was as important as her dowry; her botched alliance with the privateer would have rendered her unsuitable for marriage in the eyes of many royals.

It also explained why Conor had been reluctant to tell Kel the details of the alliance. It would have been Anjelica's secret he was spilling, not his own.

Anjelica flushed. Conor said, rather gently, "Do not be ashamed. I do not come to you unmarred by any scandal myself. Surely you have heard I murder all my fiancées?"

"Oh, yes," said Anjelica, "and that you drink, and gamble, and whore as well—though I have also heard that you have changed in these past months. But I suppose that is only ordinary behavior for a Prince."

"You shall have whatever you require, in the way of protection," said Conor, "though surely you would have expected that. I cannot help but feel there is something else troubling you. Something that is, perhaps, less easy to ask for than physical protection."

Anjelica raised her great dark eyes to his face. "Laurent considered himself a great romantic," she said. "He did everything to sweep me off my feet. He thought nothing of filling the harbor with flowers—paid for from the spoils of his piracy, no doubt. He lavished me with jewels and poetry. And all that time he was lying to me."

Kel thought: *It may not have been a lie that he loved you. In fact, I would very much guess that it was the truth.*

"When I think now of flowers and declarations of love, I think of lies. I know that what we are entering into together, you and I, is a business alliance. I know that we will also be encouraged to pretend otherwise. To make a great show of adoring each other, for the pleasure of the people and the Palace. I suppose what I am saying," Anjelica finished, "is that I am not interested in pretending to emotion we do not feel."

"I am beginning to see why most people do not find stark honesty an aphrodisiac," Conor said dryly. "Are you saying that in public, we must ignore each other, or perhaps stare at each other as if revolted? Because indeed, this may well present a public relations issue."

"We can pretend to the public," Anjelica said. "Just not to each other. You need not make any false pronouncements to me, or any great show of false passion." She looked straight at him. "If all this sounds horrible to you, you can send me back to Kutani."

Her head was held high, but Kel could tell from her voice that she was more nervous about Conor's reply to this than she was pretending. It was perhaps the first real crack in her armor he had observed.

"Not horrible at all," said Conor. "There is a cold practicality about it all that I find rather charming. Speaking of which, there is the issue of fidelity. Do you expect it?"

For the first time, Anjelica looked slightly discomfited. "I will do my duty by you," she said quietly, "in the matter of heirs. I will take no other man to my bed, for I understand that the lineage of the Aurelians must be protected. You may do as you like before we are married, as long as you behave with the utmost discretion. I will not be seen as a fool unaware of her betrothed's amorous activities."

Conor said calmly, "Discretion shall be my watchword. The last thing I should want to do is to cause you discomfort when you have been so honest with me."

She gave him a quick, sharp look, but even Kel could not see anything in Conor's expression to indicate displeasure.

Conor rose to his feet. "If that is all you wished to speak to me about," he said, "all I can say is that I am in agreement with you, and we shall proceed accordingly. I will leave you now, if you do not object, for I can only imagine you are tired from your journey."

Anjelica inclined her head. "Thank you."

Conor took several steps toward the door, then stopped and turned back to face her. "There are," he added, "two more things I thought I should mention."

She raised her eyebrows inquiringly.

"First, you have an elephant," he said. "I'd like very much to meet this creature. I've never met an elephant before."

A smile flashed across Anjelica's face. "I'm sure Sedai would be delighted."

"Second," he said, "there is always the danger that you might fall in love with me. I am very appealing."

Anjelica regarded him with great seriousness. "I shall," she said gravely, "let you know if such a thing occurs."

Conor swept a final bow and headed toward the door; Kel followed, pausing only a moment in the doorway to look back at Anjelica. She had not moved from the daybed; she looked a little lost, as if, having unburdened herself of a great secret, she was unsure what ought to happen next.

Outside the castle, the sun had begun to set. Kurame and the other Bloodguard had joined the Palace guards in a card game around a folding table. The air was full of the scent of night-blooming flowers, only just beginning to open.

Beside Kel, Conor took a deep breath. Kel turned to look at him. To Kel's surprise, Conor, too, looked unburdened—as if he had been relieved of something he was dreading. Which was strange; Kel could think of nothing about what had just transpired that would lift a weight from Conor's shoulders.

"Did that go the way you hoped?" he asked, truly curious.

Conor threw his head back, gazing up at the dark-blue sky. "I *like* her," he said, sounding pleased. "She's a delightful girl, don't you think?"

Lin

For the first time in a long time, Lin dreams.

The dream is vivid. She stands in a green valley, watching a man dressed in fine clothes, in the style of centuries ago, make his way toward a house that stands in the lee of a mountain. The door flies open as he approaches, and a woman and children run toward him with their arms outstretched.

But when he goes to embrace them, one by one they catch fire and burn. The man weeps, but he cannot seem to stop himself. Each member of his family that he wraps in his arms becomes a pillar of flame reaching to the sky.

The man falls to his knees among the pillars, his hands catching the grass alight. Soon the house is burning, too, and the trees, and everything green is turning to ash. Lin cries out in pity and horror and the man turns to look at her, seeming unsurprised that she is there.

"*Hollazekyer di niellem pu nag,*" he says.

Lin wakes, her heart pounding. Ever since she'd acquired the Source-Stone, she's had strange dreams, though they were rarely so clear. She'd really thought she was in the valley, seeing the fire. Seeing the greenery turn to ash.

She rolls onto her side; she keeps her Source-Stone on the bedside table, where she can always reach it. She picks it up now, turning it over in her hand. "What are you trying to tell me?" she whispers.

The stone, in its silver setting, weighs heavy in her hand. More so than usual, she thinks—although perhaps she is imagining things? She closes her hand around it, only to feel a jolt of emotion go through her. It feels like fear—a fear that comes from outside her. As if somewhere out in the night, a storm is gathering. But she has never felt this before at the advent of lightning or thunder. It is as if the stone is warning her of a threat, something dark in the city, something that sings with a high, discordant note like struck crystal.

Something unnatural and malevolent.

Wondering and worrying, Lin sets the brooch back down on the nightstand. She closes her eyes, visions of Source-Stones dancing in the darkness that come before sleep.

CHAPTER TEN

Two days later, Lin sat perched atop a wooden stool in the Black Mansion's laboratory. She was watching Merren with great curiosity as he unveiled the various tools he'd readied to test the substance she'd brought back from Marivent.

Wearing thick gloves to protect his hands, Merren lined up a series of glass jars along the edge of the table, each containing, he had explained, a different reagent. He had set up an alembic as well, with a flame beneath for distilling.

None of it was entirely unlike the tools in the House of Physicians, where ingredients were pulverized, chopped, distilled, aged, and purified into medicines. Merren had a set of different words for what he did and the things he used, though—*alchemy, retorts, cucurbit, anbik.* In the Physicians' House, everything was done as it had been done for hundreds of years. Merren seemed to be inventing his technique as he went along.

"You're very clever with all this," Lin said. Merren looked up and smiled, but there was a distance in his blue eyes, as if he'd only partially heard her. "Merren, is everything all right?"

He bent his fair head, grimacing as he added a drop of the vial mixture to a jar of yellow liquid. "I hate the fact that Artal Gremont is in Castellane and still alive. He squats like a toad on the Hill, and my hands—my hands are tied." Nothing had happened with the yellow liquid; Merren moved on to the next jar. "I hate to ask, but have you learned anything? About the amulet?"

Lin frowned. She had spent some hours in the Shulamat, studying spidery old illustrations of amulets and protective medallions from times past. It was not enough for her to feel like an expert, though. "It is a very old and powerful thing that he bears," she said. "The sort of object that would have been gifted to an emperor or king before the Sundering. A few such objects have survived the ages, but surely if the Gremont family had such a thing in their possession for generations, someone would have known it before now."

"Interesting." Lin wasn't sure if Merren was talking about what she'd said, or about the blue substance he'd just dripped liquid into. It seemed to be fizzing a bit. "So how did Gremont get his hands on it? It doesn't seem the sort of thing he would have picked up in his travels."

"I imagine it was given to him," Lin said. "But by who, and why?"

"And more important, how do we get it away from him?"

"I don't know yet. And Merren, Andreyen is right. Trying to take such a thing from its owner can be dangerous."

Merren looked grim. "It is bad enough for me, this waiting," he said. "I know Kel hates it, too. It tortures him. And it is even worse for my sister, having Gremont in the city—patronizing the Caravel, even."

Lin thought of Silla, of the fear and disgust on her face when she spoke of Gremont.

"I cannot decide whether he has forgotten Alys altogether," Merren said slowly, "or whether causing her discomfort gives him pleasure. But she cannot throw him out—not without alienating her other patrons from the Hill."

Other patrons from the Hill. Lin could not stop herself from wondering if Conor knew all of what Gremont had done years ago. Kel had not known either until Joss Falconet had filled in the details for him. She could not help hoping Conor did not know, and wished she didn't.

Nor did she really wish to think of Conor at the Caravel. Kel said he had changed. But would someone who had changed really have given her a royal order?

She pressed her fingers to her temples, feeling a headache beginning to start. "Where is Jerrod, by the way?"

Merren, adding a dropper of liquid to a jar of what looked like blue water, started a bit. "I . . . don't know. Off on some errand, I suppose. Why?"

"Because he seems to like to be wherever you are," Lin said with a little smile. "You could break his heart, you know."

Merren's cheeks had gone pink. Staring at the watery substance in the jar, he said, "Jerrod doesn't think of me that way. I don't think he even has feelings like . . . like that for anyone."

There was a noise at the door. Lin looked over, but there was no one there. Probably the mansion settling, she thought, but before she could say anything, Merren gave a shout.

The blue watery substance had turned an oily, opaque black. "Blackroot," Merren said. "The main ingredient in this concoction is blackroot."

Lin frowned. "I haven't heard of it."

"It's very strange." Merren seemed to have forgotten talk of Jerrod entirely. He was a pure alchemist now. "You are a physician; you know the old saying. The only difference between poison and cure is dosage."

Lin nodded.

"But that is not true for blackroot. A few grains of it will sicken. A dram of it would be enough to kill an ox."

Puzzled, Lin said, "And how much would you say is in this medicine?"

"A killing dose." Merren regarded the jar, which continued to boil away. "This is pure poison."

x x x

Kel was lacing up his boots when Conor came into their apartment, carrying a worn copy of *The Cold Heart of the Lonely King*. (He'd previously complained to Kel that the book had gotten none of the details about the true responsibilities of royalty remotely correct, but he hadn't stopped reading it.) Kel nearly leaped into the air, leaving the boots behind; he'd thought Conor had a meeting today. He'd been counting on it, in fact.

"Marvelous news," said Conor, flopping down on a divan and tossing his book aside. He proceeded to recount the tale of breakfast, during which Anjelica had horrified Lilibet by announcing that she was removing all the draperies from the Castel Pichon and replacing them with fabrics of her own choosing. "Every curtain, every bedspread," Conor reported with glee. When Lilibet had asked what Anjelica planned to do with the old fabrics, Anjelica had said she would either store them or have them distributed charitably to poor families in the city.

"*Maman* is livid," added Conor. "I'm sure she regrets ever agreeing to this marriage."

"I'm sure she never expected to have to sacrifice her draperies for the good of the kingdom," Kel said, but Conor wasn't paying attention; he had just noticed Kel's boots.

"Are you going riding?" he asked.

Kel briefly considered lying, then discarded the idea. "No, I thought I'd visit the Arena this afternoon. You know how dusty it gets." He indicated the boots. "You have that Dial Chamber meeting today; you won't need me. You were going to introduce Anjelica to the families. I'd just be in the way."

"You would," Conor agreed, "*if* the meeting were happening. But it's off. Cazalet has the lurgy or the dropsy or something like that." He sat up straight, tossing his hair out of his eyes. "What's on at the Arena?"

Fuck, fuck, fuck. "Crocodile fights," said Kel. "I think. Or it could be a poetry competition—"

"If it's Ellsday, it's the fights." Conor sprang to his feet. "Excellent. I'll go with you. We haven't sat in the box at the Arena for ages."

"I wouldn't think you should bring Anjelica there," said Kel. His hands, clammy now, slipped on his bootlaces. "I don't think she'd like it—"

"She won't mind. You heard her—she doesn't expect me to take her everywhere with me. In fact, she doesn't even want it. She'll be perfectly happy here, decorating her quarters. Which means I have a free afternoon, thank the Gods—and Cazalet." Conor grinned. "Besides, I've fifty crowns on Green Death already. I had Joss place the bet. Now I can collect my winnings in person."

There was no way to warn Ji-An, Jerrod, or Merren. Kel would just have to improvise when he got there. He supposed it was true what they said about the Gods: They struck most suddenly the moment you made plans.

In the days of the Empire, the Arena had been the center of the city. The Emperors of Magna Callatis had been addicted to bloodsport, and the people had loved it, too, for they had been taught that there was no greater glory than to fight and die for the Emperor—whether it was on a battlefield far away, or on the dusty sand of the Arena, for the Emperor's amusement.

There had been weekly shows of violence, where gladiators battled—sometimes each other, sometimes wild beasts. (Before the Sundering, it was claimed, a swordsman might be forced to fight a phoenix or a dragon; such battles never lasted long, nor did the human combatant often come out the winner.) Tigers from Hind, wolves from Detmarch, great apes and lions from the Sunlands to the south—the crowd would roar as they tore men and women apart and left the sands of the Arena soaked with blood.

The Empire had gone, but like the roads and aqueducts and sewers that kept the city running, the Arena remained. After the

Empire's fall, gladiators, now free men instead of slaves, continued to volunteer to participate in Arena battles, for the rewards—gold and fame—remained tantalizing.

It was Conor's great-grandfather who had passed Laws forbidding men to fight each other to the death for sport. There had been grumbling from all sides, but the animal fights remained, and King Marchal had brought in acrobats and dancers, musicians and acting troupes, from up and down the Gold Roads to perform in the Arena—free of charge for the citizens of Castellane. That had quelled the complaints.

The Arena had become a great leveler in the years since. Any citizen could come to be entertained, be they noble or merchant, guildmaster or street urchin. All of Castellane took a proprietary pride in the place, though it had grown grimy and worn down over the centuries. The outside of the circular arena was clad with marble, but inside the ancient stones were cracked and worn smooth, the bright paint that had once decorated the rows of seats faded to sun-worn pastels.

Kel and Conor entered through an archway, accompanied by Castelguards. There was a faint cheer from the crowd as they realized the Prince was among them. A few lewdly admiring remarks about Anjelica were called out, along with offers to buy the guards various alcoholic drinks. Conor, dressed in white linen like an Emperor of old, smiled as if deaf to their commentary, graciously inclining his head. He and Kel had been to the Arena many times before; Conor had once told him that it was good for the people of Castellane to see the royal family enjoying the same things they did.

A set of stone steps led up to the royal box—once the Emperor's seat, from which he could dole out death or mercy at a whim, but now merely a privileged viewing position. Kel and Conor headed up between their escort of guards, Kel keeping his eyes on the crowd as they passed.

He saw them, a flash at the corner of his eye: Jerrod, Ji-An, and Merren seated in the fifth row. He caught Ji-An's furious gaze, shook his head quickly. *I couldn't stop him from coming.*

Ji-An turned back to Merren and Jerrod; they began to whisper together. Kel cursed quietly to himself as he entered the royal box, hung with a bunting of yellow flowers. The stone benches here were cushioned, and glasses rested on a low, inlaid table, ready for wine. He took a seat beside Conor, scanning the Arena below. The seats were half full—whole families had come, with small children, spreading out blankets over the stone benches.

And then, down by the first row, Kel saw her—Magali—her crown of braided gray hair familiar even at a distance. But as long as Kel was with Conor, he could not get away to question her. What, Kel wondered to himself, were they going to do?

It was a hot day, the sun gleaming like a yellow diamond. Lin was on her way back home from visiting her patients (several of whom needed to be placated with apologies, since she had missed visiting them the day Conor had brought her to the Palace). She kept to the cooler sides of the streets where flowering fig and almond trees offered shade. The sky was cloudless above the Sault walls, the color of *techelet*—the ancient blue dye that even now was used to color holy tapestries and the garments of priests like the Maharam.

Once inside the Sault, Lin cut toward the Etse Kebeth, meaning to check in on Mariam, but she came to a halt at the edge of the Kathot, her eyes squinted against the sun. A dais had been set up, just as on the day of the Tevath, with the Maharam's carved seat atop it. The seat was occupied not by the Maharam, however, but by Aron Benjudah.

The Exilarch did not look as he had when Lin had met him in the Shulamat, dusty and travel-stained. He looked like paintings she had seen of Judah Makabi, the Lion, the first head of the Sanhedrin, dressed in a tunic of *techelet* blue, a sword slung at his side. Around his neck hung a heavy silver medallion, not unlike Mayesh's, though this one was set with deep-blue stones that matched his tunic.

Two small groups were clustered in front of the dais, and Aron seemed to be listening to them intently. A line of more Ashkar trailed from the dais nearly to the steps of the Shulamat. Lin had seen this before with the Sanhedrin: Aron was hearing cases and giving judgment, just as the King of Castellane had once done in the Convocat.

Seeing Mariam standing at the edge of a cluster of onlookers, Lin crept up beside her and tapped her shoulder. Mariam grinned upon seeing her. There was color in her cheeks, which was good, but her eyes looked too big for her face. Lin made a note to brew some gentian tea tonight. It would stimulate Mariam's appetite.

"I've never seen such a crowd on a Judging Day," Lin whispered. "Is something fascinating happening?"

"Oh, goodness, no," said Mariam, her eyes sparkling. "The Ohl family has a tree that's been dropping its fruit into Kep Chaiken's garden. The argument is over who owns the fruit."

"What kind of fruit?"

"Who cares?" Mariam elbowed Lin playfully. "Everyone's here to see the Exilarch. He's gorgeous. I'd watch him adjudicate a catfight."

Taken aback, Lin rose up on her toes to stare at Aron. The last time she'd met him, she'd been far too terrified to ponder if he was handsome or not. He was, she supposed, much younger than everyone had expected. He had tidied up his hair, which was now a neat halo of dark bronze. The planes of his face were strong, like the profile of a king on a coin. Square jaw, serious eyes. He seemed at ease dispensing judgment, gesturing fluidly as he talked. When the sleeves of his tunic fell back, Lin could see the Rhadanite markings on his arms.

Lin said, "What happens if the fruit falls into the public street? Or a squirrel steals it?"

"Legal chaos," said Mariam solemnly. "Don't you think he's handsome, though?"

"He holds my future in his hands, Mari," Lin said. "I haven't time to wonder whether they're attractive hands."

At that moment, Aron glanced toward them. Lin forced herself to meet his gaze, even as she thought: *Everyone here knows. They know the Exilarch must recognize the Goddess Returned, for the soul of the Exilarch is passed down through the blood, and the soul of the Goddess is eternal.* They would be watching her and Aron, watching for some visible sign of connection between them.

She tore her eyes from his.

"Are you all right, Lin?" Mariam said. "You seem troubled."

"I had a dream two nights ago. A bad one. It was so vivid." Lin recounted the substance of her dream to Mariam, though she did not mention that the words she'd heard the man in her dream speak had also been said to her by the King in the tower.

"He burned everything he touched?" Mariam said curiously when Lin was done. "I think I know why you had that dream. It's one of the stories from that book of yours. The one you lent me."

Lin frowned. "Which story?"

"I wish I had the book with me. It was one of the Sorcerer-Kings." Mariam lowered her voice. "The others called him the Phoenix King because he harnessed the power of fire. He cursed his enemies so that everything they touched would burn away. All sorts of odd things we read turn up in our dreams, Lin."

"Yes," Lin said slowly. "In fact, something a patient said to me turned up in my dream. It was Malgasi, I think. *Hollazekyer di niellem pu nag.*"

"What an odd thing to say." Mariam looked puzzled. "It's Malgasi, yes. It means 'They are trying to prevent me from becoming what I am.'"

Before Lin could reply, she was interrupted by a familiar hissing voice.

"Goddess," said Oren Kandel, his dark eyebrows beetling. "Pardon me for interrupting. There is an angry woman at the gates, looking for you."

"An angry woman? Did you get her name?" *A patient?* Lin wondered.

"No." Oren looked at her haughtily. Of *course* he hadn't gotten a name. "I believe she is from Geumjoseon."

Ji-An? Lin thought. She didn't have any current patients from Geumjoseon, so who else could it be? But wasn't Ji-An supposed to be in the Arena today, with Kel and the others?

Had something gone terribly wrong? Bidding a quick farewell to Mariam, Lin hurried from the Kathot. She thought she could feel someone watching her as she went. Aron Benjudah, most likely, but when she turned to look back over her shoulder, he seemed engaged in the business of judgment, and as utterly unaware of her as if she had been a passing moth.

"Here we are," Conor said. He was sitting back against the cushions piled on the bench in the royal box, a half-full wineglass in hand. "Like old times. Before I became, you know. *Responsible.*"

His tone was light, but Kel wondered if there was a sadness underneath it. It was hard to tell with Conor. He had always been able to retreat from unpleasant realities—into drink, into courtesans, into games of chance or indoor archery. Now that he was no longer allowing himself such strategic retreats, hard truth seemed to sink in at unpredictable times.

"You seem to have taken to those responsibilities," said Kel. He tried to force himself to focus on Conor—though it should not be a matter of force. Conor should be the center of all his thoughts. But his mind kept returning to Merren and Ji-An and Jerrod, and their broken plans. "I think far more than you imagined you would, at first."

At first. Kel knew what had brought on the great change in Conor, even if no one else did. He remembered the moment, outside the Gallery full of the dead, when Conor had taken hold of him as if he needed Kel to keep him standing upright. How he had whispered, every word edged in grief: *I went behind their backs out of vanity and pride, and now that pride is paid for in other people's blood. This—this is my mess. Mine to clean up.*

"Out of necessity," Conor said now, twirling the narrow stem of the wineglass between his long fingers. "Not out of choice. I wonder if the fact that it is a necessity limits how good I can ever be at it."

"Con. Everyone who takes on the responsibility of ruling does it out of some kind of necessity."

Conor raised his eyes to Kel's. They were ringed with kohl today, which made them look larger. More as they had when he was a boy—when he and Kel had been boys together, and Kel had dreamed of seeing as those gray eyes saw.

"Most people would not listen to my complaining sympathetically, Kellian," he said. "I am, after all, regretting the responsibilities that power confers. Look how quickly Artal Gremont came running back to Castellane once he knew the power of the Charter was within his grasp."

It was painful to hear Gremont's name. But before Kel could say anything, a grinding sound came from the center of the Arena. The Empire's system of hydraulics and pulleys still functioned, tended to by a team of engineers. Two slabs of earth drew back, revealing a watery pit below.

Savagely, Kel said, "Gremont is the sort who wants power for the worst reasons. Antonetta told me he plans to exercise his right of First Night when they marry. I suppose you know—?"

"I know," Conor said quietly.

Kel flung himself down on the bench beside Conor. "Then why don't you put a stop to it?"

"You think a man like Gremont will be angry with me if I tell him no," said Conor, "but you do not understand his mind. He will be angry with Antonetta. He will take that anger out on her."

"Antonetta said she was not worried he would harm her," Kel said, though he knew he had said too much as soon as the words left his mouth.

Conor only lifted an eyebrow slightly. "He will not hurt her physically—she is a noblewoman of the Hill, and they are not yet married. He would be a fool to do such a thing. But there are other

ways to harm. He could plan a lifetime of humiliations and cruelties
we might never see." He looked into his wineglass. "Better to let
him have that one show of power. You understand? It is not possession of her body he wants. It is power, and wielding it in front of
others."

"How do you know that?"

"I understand him," said Conor, his voice sharp, but the cutting
blade was turned inward, against himself.

"I cannot fathom how you can bear to," said Kel.

Conor set the wineglass down. "Believe me when I say I wish it
was not necessary." He sounded weary enough to make Kel feel
torn in half. Half fury that there was no way to stop Gremont, that
Conor could not do it, that Kel himself was helpless, alone with his
bitter fury and murderous rage. And half despair that these grim
calculations were ones that Conor was forced to make, that he had
no choice.

Another grinding sound ripped through the Arena. Iron port-
cullises at opposite ends of the field below heaved upward, and from
the dark space within came marching a long line of crocodiles, each
one with a steel ring around its scaled neck. A chain was attached to
each ring, the other end gripped by a masked crocodile handler. As
the soon-to-be-fighting reptiles entered the Arena one by one, they
were met with cheers and admiring cries.

Kel and Conor watched the parade for some time in silence,
Conor through half-lidded eyes. The animals would be paraded for
the admiration of the crowd, after which bets would be placed and
the fights would begin. Kel had little stomach for bloodsport, but
he had to admit that if he had to watch any animals fight, he would
feel the least sympathy for the terrifying monsters that lurked in the
harbor. He thought of Fausten, his scream as he had hit the water,
the splash and the silence that had followed.

"Sometimes," Conor said, breaking the silence—he seemed to
be speaking half to Kel and half to himself—"we must forget that
we are creatures with feelings. We must take the emotions we have

and bury them, or turn them to stone. And hope to the Gods it does the trick."

Kel wasn't sure what to say to that, but at that moment Benaset approached the box and cleared his throat politely. "Monseigneur," he said to Conor, "there's someone here to see you."

The Castelguard looked down at Lin—he stood upon the step above, adding to the sense that he towered over her—with a superior frown. "One cannot simply intrude upon the royal presence," he said, gesturing at the flower-draped box some feet above them. Lin could just see Conor and Kel, who seemed deep in conversation; neither had noticed her yet. "If you wish to lay a matter at the feet of the Prince, there are ways—"

Lin clenched her fists at her sides. She hated what she was about to say, about to do, but there seemed little choice. When she'd left the Sault, she'd found Ji-An outside, distraught. The other girl had begged her—

Well. That wasn't precisely true. Ji-An never *begged*. She'd told Lin of the wreck of their plan to have Kel question Magali in the Arena.

"The Prince just turned up," Ji-An said. "No warning at all, or any consideration for other people's plans—"

"That does sound like him."

"You're going to have to question Magali." Ji-An had taken Lin by the shoulders. "You're the only one she'll recognize, the only one she might talk to—"

"Don't be ridiculous." Lin had shaken her head. "She won't tell me a thing. *But*—I think I can help another way."

Which was how she'd found herself here, about to lie her way into the royal box at the Arena. Lin had never even been to the Arena as a spectator. She'd nearly choked on the dust when she'd first arrived, not to mention the strong smells of fried onions and sweaty bodies.

"Do you have no request?" the Castelguard asked, eyeing Lin—who had gone silent for who knew how long—with some puzzlement. "If so, I am going to have to ask you to remove yourself, Domna."

Lin took a deep breath. "I am the granddaughter of Mayesh Bensimon, the Counselor to the throne," she said, and saw the guard's face change as she'd known it would. "Please tell the Prince I am here."

The Castelguard looked irresolute. He cast his gaze over her, more closely this time, noting her Ashkar colors, her demurely braided hair. She could practically see the gears whirring in his mind. Clearly he did not relish the idea of interrupting the Prince, but neither did he wish to risk Mayesh's wrath by sending his granddaughter packing. With a shake of his head, he gestured for Lin to follow him.

Somewhere down in the Arena, Jerrod, Ji-An, and Merren were watching her as she hurried after the guard. She let that knowledge strengthen her as she approached the royal box. She could see Kel and Conor lounging on a long bench draped in rich fabrics, beside them a gilded table upon which was set a pitcher and wineglasses. The heady scent of Aurelian roses perfumed the dusty air.

"Monseigneur," the Castelguard said, "there is someone here to see you."

Lin held herself as calmly as she could as two pairs of gray eyes swept over her. The Prince's were heavy-lidded; he seemed to be squinting at her, as if trying to recall exactly who she was. Beside him, Kel had gone still, but it was the only surprise he showed. Lin forgot sometimes what a good actor he had to be, to do what he did.

"Domna Caster," Conor said, inclining his head. The sun sparked off the slim gold circlet that bound his brow. "To what do we owe this pleasant surprise?"

Lin spoke quickly. "Monseigneur. I bring word to you from my grandfather. He would have come to the Arena himself," she added, "but he is an old man, and the sun is too strong for him here."

Conor smiled a charming smile. She wondered if he had practiced it in a mirror. Like a painted screen in a theater, that smile, hiding the unknown. "Well, let her in, Benaset. One cannot disregard word from the Counselor."

Benaset stepped back, and Lin entered the box. Something crackled beneath her feet; she glanced down to see the floor strewn with dried petals. Conor was watching Benaset leave, his only movement the tap of his fingers against the arm of his chair. Kel was looking out at the Arena floor, but Lin could tell his attention was on her. Waiting to see what she wanted, what she'd do next.

Heart beating like the tap-tap of a timbrel, Lin said, "Sieur Kel Anjuman, please excuse us, but my business is state business, I'm afraid. I must speak to the Prince alone."

Kel glanced at Conor, who shrugged, as if to say: *This is not my doing*, and nodded. Kel rose to his feet. "It's no trouble, Domna. It gives me a chance to place a bet on today's fight. I have a good feeling about Green Death's chances."

Kel ducked out of the box, angling a quick smile of acknowledgment at Lin as he went. It was a comforting look: one that said they were in this together even as they went their separate ways.

The moment Kel had gone, Conor's whole demeanor changed. Lin saw the tension in him as he turned his full attention to her. "I told you how to reach me," he said. "Through the Castelguards, not like this—"

"I couldn't wait. I had to speak to you."

"Has something happened? Are you in danger?"

"Danger? No, not at all," she said, and to her surprise, his posture relaxed. "But the message. About the patient you introduced me to. I didn't want to risk it falling into any hands but yours."

"Then you'd better tell me what it is," he said, and gestured for her to take Kel's vacated place beside him.

Lin hesitated—but she could hardly refuse, and besides, this was all in the service of distracting the Prince. She settled beside him on the bench. It was a comfortable seat, padded with thick-napped velvet, the arms cushioned. The view over the Arena was sweeping; Lin felt she could see every bit of it spread out before her as a green flood of crocodiles, who had been marching on display, were led one by one back into the darkness of the pens below.

The sense of being pinned in the sky, looking down on the world below, was inescapable. The old Emperors had thought themselves Gods; it was easy to see why.

"An excellent view of a shabby place," said the Prince, and Lin realized he had been watching her take it in; she could see her fascination reflected in his face.

"Shabby now," she said. "But you can see that it was glorious once."

"I never thought of you as being particularly interested in the architecture of the Empire."

It was odd, Lin thought. Despite the clear urgency of her message, he didn't seem interested in hearing it, at least not immediately. "Everyone is interested in beautiful things," she said.

After a moment, he said, "Yes," in an odd sort of tone that made her look over at him. He was turned away from her, though, reaching to take a bottle out of the ice chest by his seat.

He placed it on the low table between them. The bottle glass was bright red, condensation already beginning to run down its sides. When he poured the liquid into two crystal glasses, it was nearly the same color, bright and deep as blood.

"Would you care for some *rabarbaro*?" the Prince inquired, sliding a glass full of the bright-scarlet stuff toward her. She took it automatically. The crystal was cold as ice against her fingers, a pleasant chill. "It is made from the roots of Shenzan rhubarb, to which the Sarthians add cardamom and lemon to lessen the bitterness."

Lin hesitated a moment. She rarely drank spirits; sweet wine at festivals and weddings was the extent of it. She took a sip and nearly choked; the tang of the rhubarb was almost eclipsed by the fire of the alcohol.

"It tastes of medicine," she said before she could stop herself.

To her surprise, the Prince laughed. He was holding his own glass between his fingers, the red of the liquid bright against his white linen clothes. She did not think she'd seen him in all white before. He looked like a dissipated priest. "I suppose it does. I hated the taste of it when I was younger—not *rabarbaro*, all liquor—but one gets used to it. And the effect is worth it."

Lin stared dubiously into her glass. She was about to set it down when, below in the Arena, she glimpsed Kel approaching Magali. Quickly, she took another sip, spluttered, and turned to the Prince, who was watching her with amusement.

"Your fa—" she began, stopped and licked her lips, tasting rhubarb. "The patient in whom we both have an interest," she corrected herself. "I tested his medicine. More than once. I wanted to be sure."

"Sure of what?" The Prince had drained his glass. It appeared to have no effect on him that she could see. He poured himself another, his movements casual, careless. Lin watched the splash of the red liquid in the crystal and wondered briefly if Ji-An and Merren were watching. Would they be wondering what on earth she was doing?

"The drug has a sedative base, but that is not all it is. There is within it blackroot. Which is a poison. And there is not just a small amount of it present. There is more than enough to kill."

The Prince went still. He sat back slowly, glass in hand. His gaze was on the Arena.

"But he has been taking this medicine for years," said Conor, finally. "If Fausten had meant to kill him, would he not have died long ago?"

"I cannot say what Fausten was trying to do. Or why the patient is still alive. I only know he is. And clearly it has affected him, though whether because it has harmed him or because he has developed a dependence on it, I cannot guess yet."

"A dependence? As if this stuff were poppy-juice? But addicts become desperate for the drug they take. They will do anything to get it. That hardly describes our patient."

"It does not," she said. "But not much is known about black-root, since usually any dose kills. If one survives taking it, it is hard to say what might happen then."

Conor was silent, his gaze inward and thoughtful. Lin took another sip of the *rabarbaro;* this time she did not choke. A warmth had started to spread out from her stomach, making her skin prickle. The sun, too, was strong on her skin, and Prince Conor's. It illuminated his face, making the white scar at his temple stand out like a twist of silver thread. His circlet seemed to glow among the shadowy locks of his hair; it was the sort of hair that was so dark, it would absorb the sun's heat. If one stroked one's hand through it, one would feel the sun-warmed threads against one's palm, hot and soft as black silk.

"Could the patient, perhaps, have built up a resistance to the poison over the years?" said the Prince at last. "Perhaps Fausten started with small doses and increased them over time?"

Lin blinked and set her glass down on the table. To her horror, it was empty. Somehow, she had drunk all the *rabarbaro.*

"It's possible. It's a common mountain plant in Malgasi; perhaps Fausten heard about it there, and uses for it beyond the ones we are aware of in Castellane. Unfortunately, there are few books on florticulture in the Shulamat—"

The Prince raised an eyebrow. "Did you say *florticulture?*"

"Floriculture," said Lin haughtily. "I said floriculture. The study of—"

"Flowering plants. I'm aware." The Prince looked at her closely. "Are you drunk?"

Lin frowned. "I don't know. I've never been drunk."

The Prince smiled. It was not his earlier, practiced smile. It was a real smile, with no edge of falsity to it.

"I'm a very busy physician," she said. "I don't have time to be drunk."

"Gasquet is a doctor, and he's drunk all the time," Prince Conor pointed out.

"Yes," said Lin. "But he is a very, very bad doctor. That's why you keep coming to me in emergencies. You've done it"—she counted aloud on her fingers—"three times now. *Three*."

His eyes sparkled. There was something heart-catching about his unstudied amusement. Though it had nothing to do with him personally, Lin reminded herself. It was as she had said before, about the Arena. *Everyone is interested in beautiful things.* Though it was unfair that he was a Prince and also beautiful. Like being very rich and very lucky; a person should really be only one of those things.

"I have an idea," he said. "There are plenty of *floriculture* texts in the Palace library, due to my mother's obsession with gardens."

"You've been to the Palace library?" Lin couldn't hide her surprise.

"The assumptions you make about me are truly bizarre," he said. "Apparently you think I am illiterate and are not afraid to say so to my face. It's . . . unusual."

"I just didn't think—"

"That I know how to read? Believe me, I'm required to—*and* in several languages. I *enjoy* reading. I could show you my favorite books, but you would probably tell me they were silly."

Lin made an indignant sound.

"There's a banquet I can miss, if I must, tomorrow night. Come to Marivent. I'll let you into the library. You can help me look for information on this root of yours."

There was a loud grinding noise. Two gates had opened in the pit. Through each slithered a massive crocodile—certainly among the largest that had marched around the Arena earlier. Now that there were only two, it was possible to see them in more detail: Elaborately worked collars encircled their necks, each collar attached to a chain. Their scales flashed; jewels were embedded into individual scutes, each jewel a symbol of a battle won. White scars showed along their hides, around their eyes and jaws.

At the other ends of the animals' chains were their handlers.

Massive men with oarsman's shoulders, they controlled their beasts with a mixture of strength and training. These were not crocodiles from the harbor of Castellane; they had been bred as fighting animals, and as such, responded to their handlers. Still, it was a dangerous job: Lin had once cared for a handler whose leg had been bitten off below the knee by his beast.

The handlers released the animals, who lunged for each other, jaws snapping. The acoustics of the Arena brought the sound up to the crowd, who yelled out the names of their preferred fighters— *Split-Tail! Green Death!*—though Lin doubted the crocodiles cared.

Amid the noise and motion of the fight, Lin caught sight of another movement. It was Kel, heading up the steps of the Arena, clearly having finished his conversation with Magali. Lin must have made a noise of surprise—she had nearly forgotten that her purpose in the box was to distract the Prince's attention—for Conor glanced at her and said, "Does it bother you? The sight of the crocodiles?"

"I am not afraid of them, no." The warmth of the alcohol was receding; she felt a bit sick. "It is more that I have no desire to see two living creatures, no matter how brutal they are, kill each other."

"It is unusual for one to kill the other." Prince Conor gestured toward the Arena floor. "You see that white circle chalked at their feet? Each crocodile tries to drive the other out of the circle's boundary. The one pushed out of the circle loses. They fight for territory just as people do. Murder is not the first step; the game of dominance comes before it. It is about what you can hold," he added, "even as another might try to take it from you."

"But they wound each other," Lin said. "They bite and slash and bleed."

"Of course." There was an odd light in his eyes as he studied her face. "I had forgotten you can be gentlehearted."

In the pit, the crocodiles circled each other, heads down, growling. Lin wanted to say, *I am always gentle, I heal, I am a physician.* She wanted to say, *I can see the shadows in your eyes, hear the bitterness in your voice when you speak of your father. I know you have nightmares. Kel told me. I feel for your wounds. How could I not?*

But she thought, instead, *He gave me a royal order,* and the taste of the *rabarbaro* was bitter in the back of her throat.

"Well," she said, rising to her feet, "not to Princes. Just crocodiles," and she slipped out of the box without looking back.

She passed the Castelguards on the long stairs and heard the crowd roar as she went; the beasts in the pit below had begun to fight.

Well done, Lin, Kel thought as he made his way down the Arena steps. Away from the shade of the royal box, the Arena was even hotter than it had been earlier, and more crowded. The air was thick and salty, as if the sea and air had melded at the horizon.

Lin had been nimble in getting him away from Conor. Clever to use her relationship with Mayesh that way. Though she'd certainly have to think up something that would keep Conor distracted for the next quarter hour at least.

He was aware that somewhere in the Arena, Ji-An and the others were watching him as he approached the lower tier where Magali Berthe was seated, alone.

Kel was used to seeing Magali on the Hill, clothed in the rose and silver of the Alleyne livery. Now she was dressed as an ordinary woman of Castellane, a shopkeeper or a publican's wife, wearing a plain brown cotton dress over a linen cotehardie. In her lap was a ceramic dish of sweet treats: fried milk, sesame *pasteli*, spiced biscuits from Hanse. She was staring fixedly at the crocodiles parading around the Arena floor.

Kel pushed past a knot of people—some of whom stared; perhaps they recognized him as one of the Prince's companions—and planted himself in front of Magali. She was gnawing a *macun*— a sweet-spicy toffee wrapped around a stick and popular on the Gold Roads.

Kel sat down beside her on the stone bench. "Domna Berthe," he said. "A fine day for the Arena, don't you think?"

Jolted, she turned to stare at him, nearly dropping the *macun*. In the harsh unfiltered light, he realized she was older than he'd guessed, closer to sixty than fifty, lines of worry etched deeply at the corners of her eyes and mouth.

"Sieur Anjuman." She inclined her head, but he could see her clearly wondering: What on earth was he doing here? Nobles were certainly not meant to make light conversation with servants, but then he was a *foreign* noble, wasn't he? Marakandi by birth—a little strange perhaps, in his customs. In the end, she said in a slightly sulky voice, "I am permitted to attend the games, Sieur. Today is my free day, and my lady gave me leave."

Kel said mildly, "You are a very loyal servant to the Alleynes. I suspect Liorada—your lady, that is—relies on you a great deal."

Magali seemed to puff up, like a long-haired cat. "Yes, she does. For everything."

"You have been her right hand," Kel said, keeping his voice smooth and gentle, "helping to raise her daughter, to maintain the household, plan her festivities, pen her correspondence . . ."

Magali nodded along, puzzled but pleased.

"And when she most needed your help, Domna Berthe, you assisted her in hiring mercenaries to murder the little Princess from Sarthe."

Magali went white. The ceramic bowl slid from her lap; Kel caught it before it shattered.

"My lady would never—" Magali began, but she didn't seem to know what to say after that. Her eyes darted around the Arena. Looking for exits, maybe?

"Don't run," Kel said in the same calm voice. "It will go worse for you if you do."

"What do you want from me?" she whispered. In the distance, a roar went up from the crowd to signal that first blood had been drawn on the Arena floor.

"Only the truth. To know what happened."

Magali shook her head. "You cannot ask me to betray my lady."

"Then I will tell you what I already know," Kel said, plucking a piece of *loukum* from the bowl he was somehow still holding. "You frequent these fights, here at the Arena. I can only assume that this brought you into contact with Raimon—also known as the Gray Serpent. You offered five hundred crowns to Raimon and his band of mercenaries to attack the Shining Gallery—specifically, the Princess Luisa and her delegation from Sarthe. Something went wrong—Raimon says a means of escape was promised, but none delivered—and the result was an all-around slaughter." He popped the *loukum* into his mouth, tasting sugar and roses. "Do you deny it?"

The dots of rouge on Magali's cheeks stood out now, like bruises. "Who knows this?" she whispered.

"Only a few," said Kel. "House Aurelian does not *yet* know— and if you do not want that to happen, then you must help me. Raimon named *you* as his contact, but I assume you were acting on behalf of your mistress. I cannot imagine where you would have gotten such money otherwise. And while I know Lady Alleyne hoped the Prince might marry Antonetta, I could not imagine why she would think harming the Blood Royal in this way—"

"She didn't!" Magali gasped. "Oh, this is wretched." She wrung her knobby hands. "That's not what she did. She would never do such a thing."

"But it was done."

"My lady is loyal to House Aurelian. The Sarthians sent this . . . this brat-Princess to humiliate us. To humiliate Castellane and our royal family. My lady only meant to humiliate them in turn. Since they sent us a child, the idea was to frighten her as a child might be frightened. It was meant to be a prank."

"It is rare," said Kel, "that one hires mercenaries to do one thing, and then they do another. They were there to kill."

"My lady did not give the mercenaries their instructions. She was not behind what happened, Sieur Anjuman. There were others—one who was giving instructions, demands—" Magali's voice had started to rise.

"Who?" Kel demanded. "Who was giving instructions? Who was in charge of all this, if not Lady Alleyne?"

Magali clamped her lips shut.

"You understand that what your mistress did was treason," said Kel. "And she will hang for it, for all she is a noble. She will not be able to protect you then. The walls of the Trick will close about you both."

"No." Magali blinked rapidly, shaking her head back and forth. "I am no traitor—"

"Then tell me," said Kel, low and urgent. "If your lady did not order the slaughter, *who did*?"

"Please," Magali gasped. "You must believe me. It was a day or two after the Gallery murders. I overheard my lady in her study. She was arguing with someone, saying, 'How could this have happened? Is this what you intended all along? This death, this destruction?' And a voice replied to her. Such a dark, rough voice as I have not heard in all my days." Magali shuddered. "It said, 'You are now implicated. Should you attempt to betray me, we will fall together, and your fall will be far harder than mine.'"

A dark, rough voice. Kel thought of the black-clad figure on the rooftop, the ragged voice saying, *You're lucky that I have a use for you, Sword Catcher.*

"And you've no idea who Lady Alleyne was talking to?"

"No. *No.*" Magali was breathing hard. "The visitor arrived masked and hooded, all in black, and left the same way, in an unmarked carriage, and my lady shut herself in her study for all the rest of that day. I heard her weeping through the door." Magali looked at Kel eagerly. "So you see? It was not her fault. Find the person who was threatening my lady, and you will find the one who planned the slaughter."

"A mysterious figure, all in black, who comes and goes in an unmarked carriage?" Kel's tone made Magali shrink back. "If I bring this tale to Legate Jolivet, he will imagine you have invented this individual, Magali, to distract attention and blame from Lady Alleyne. If you have no further proof—"

"There is one more thing." Magali's eyes were red-rimmed now. "My lady received a letter a few days ago. She flew into a rage over it. I—I may have fished it out from the rubbish. I wanted to know what had upset her so greatly."

"What did it say?"

"It ordered her to a meeting on Cereday night. On Tyndaris. To discuss *a matter of loyalty.*"

"Tyndaris?" Kel frowned. People tended to avoid the drowned island, save for religious pilgrims determined to visit the Chapel of a Thousand Doors, visible only at low tide.

"Yes." Magali's voice was firm. Kel knew lies and the look of them. She was not lying—of that he had no doubt. Nor did he sense she had anything more to tell him.

He rose to his feet, the taste of *loukum* oversweet and sticky on his tongue. "Keep this conversation between us, Domna Berthe. Or I will know it, and so will the Legate. Do you understand?"

Magali nodded; the spirit seemed to have left her, as if she had no energy for anything but agreement. Kel left her staring blankly at the Arena, with no sign that she was aware of the now-unchained crocodiles as they circled each other, each snapping at the other's sides with blood-flecked jaws.

Kel turned his steps toward the stairs that led back to the royal box, thinking of Magali, the fear in her eyes as he spoke of the Trick, the Law, the Legate. He had never really used his place as Kel Anjuman to threaten anyone before. He was surprised to find it did not bother him nearly as much as he'd thought.

Jerrod

Jerrod doesn't like it. He doesn't like it at all.

Ever since Kaspar had slid into the booth across from him at the noodle shop with the news that Prosper Beck was officially back, he'd been brooding. He had always known Beck would return and that, when that happened, his former boss would reach out for him again. He was Beck's man; he'd sworn it. But he'd underestimated how comfortable he'd gotten in his new life at the Black Mansion.

When Jerrod had joined Andreyen's team, he'd instructed himself not to form any attachments. Not to make friends, despite the deliberately congenial atmosphere. He'd failed parlously.

He supposed he'd secretly thought that the collegiality in the mansion was a façade, as false a front as the warehouse he was standing in right now, with its painted signs outside advertising a gambling parlor. Beck had once run games out of the place, but that had been a long time ago. Now it housed something quite different from games of chance.

What Jerrod had not expected was how genuinely attached to one another the group at the Black Mansion was. He had grown up around criminals; most were out for themselves because they had to be. When the Vigilants came, you ran, and you didn't look to see if your accomplice was keeping up with you. In fact, you might consider stabbing your accomplice yourself so he couldn't spill your name in the Tully.

Andreyen Morettus's crew were nothing like that. They looked out for one another. Jerrod was a little afraid they might even look out for him.

And then there was Merren. The others—Kel, Ji-An, Andreyen himself—might well have reservations about Jerrod. He wouldn't fault them for it. But Merren trusted him. For a poisoner who worked for a famous criminal, Merren was astonishingly trusting in general, but Jerrod liked to think—

Footsteps on the warehouse steps snap Jerrod out of his reverie. He has been waiting in the corridor; he goes now to the doorway of the small office and peers inside. The big man behind the desk wears his usual coat of scarlet and silver; somehow it makes his size look even more imposing. "I'm going to bring them in," Jerrod says.

He gets a curt nod in response, which is very in character for Beck. Jerrod makes his way back into the hall, where his two guests have just arrived.

One he knows by name and sight: Artal Gremont. Beside him is the Malgasi woman. Jerrod hasn't been told her name, only that she is someone significant in Malgasi circles of power, and that she is determined to talk to Beck. She has long dark hair and a narrow face and is dressed in severely cut black velvet. A gold chain gleaming around her neck is her only jewelry.

"The guard downstairs sent us up," says Gremont, unnecessarily. They wouldn't be here if Kaspar hadn't directed them.

Jerrod gestures for the two to go into the office and they pass him, neither really acknowledging his presence. He stands for a moment, his hand on the door. This is the closest he's ever been to Artal Gremont, and he is surprised at the nausea that twists in his gut. Jerrod has never thought much of the nobility. Though they operate within the bounds of the Law, they cheat and lie and steal just like anyone else. Their belief that they are somehow better seems to him distant and ridiculous. But Gremont is unusual—so loathsome the other nobles had taken the step of sending him away from Castellane. And he'd hurt Merren, the person in the world who least deserved to be hurt.

Jerrod steps into the office.

". . . And you know the city needs a leader," the woman is saying. She has a heavy Malgasi accent, which isn't surprising.

"We have a monarchy, here in Castellane, that functions well enough," says the man behind the desk. "And a King."

"The Palace is hopelessly corrupt," the Malgasi woman says sharply. Everything about her is sharp. She has the air of something rapacious, waiting to strike: a bird of prey, or a coiled snake.

"I won't dispute that." The man behind the desk folds his hands over his middle. "But there is another King here. The King in the City."

"He does the bidding of your Palace," she sneers. "More than you know."

Interesting, Jerrod thinks.

"The game is about to change, Beck," says Gremont, his voice oily. "And you do know what that means."

The man he calls Beck only shrugs.

"You refer to a redistribution of power," Jerrod says quickly.

The Malgasi woman flicks a look in his direction. "As you say." She nods. "Things are going to change, on the Hill and in the city. Some will fall, and others will be lifted. The Ragpicker King's day is over. We need someone independent ruling over your streets. Someone I can work with. Can I work with you?"

Small tendrils of alarm unfold in the pit of Jerrod's stomach, quickening his pulse. He'd expected the woman to make some sort of deal with Beck, perhaps buy something illegal. Weapons or the like. This—the implicit expectation that Beck would align with her against the two most powerful forces in the city—sets off every alarm he has.

The woman holds the gaze of the man behind the desk, her stare boring into him. At last, he says, "I'll have to think about it," his eyes sliding away from her. "Give me some time."

Her narrow mouth curls at the corner. "Of course," she says, and then seems to hesitate, as if something has just occurred to her. "Out of curiosity, why do you hate Conor Aurelian so very much?"

Jerrod tries to catch the eye of the man behind the desk, but it is too late. He raises his big shoulders in a casual shrug and says, "He is corrupt. All nobles are corrupt."

"Ah," the woman says, less of a word than a soft exhale. A moment later there is a flash of silver, as if a metallic bird had launched itself into the air. The man behind the desk falls back, clutching at his throat, where the hilt of a knife now protrudes.

Jerrod's hand is at his side before he has time to think, his palm brushing the hilt of his own dagger. Before he can grasp it, he feels himself knocked backward, his back slamming painfully into the doorframe. The woman looms up in front of him, her face inches from his, her raptor eyes gleaming. He's never seen anyone move so fast.

"Little minion," she says, her thin white fingers brushing against his chest. "Stop twitching. I'm going to let you live, and this is why: Go back to Prosper Beck—the real Prosper Beck—and tell him Elsabet Belmany is looking for him and doesn't suffer fools gladly. Nor will I easily forgive him for trying to palm me off with a trick." She grins, a flash of white teeth in the shadows. "Beck can expect to hear from me again, and next time, I'll turn Gremont loose on him. Gremont loves causing pain, and he's very good at it—aren't you, Artal?"

Gremont nods in the dim light, his face blank, and in that moment, Jerrod realizes how very much under the Malgasi Princess's control he is. He reminds himself to tell Beck of this later. It's exactly the sort of thing Beck will want to know.

A moment later, soundlessly, she is gone, leaving Jerrod alone in the room with Artal Gremont, who is gazing with a mild sneer at the dead body slumped across the table. This, Jerrod feels, is typical of the nobility: They are willing enough to order blood to be spilled, but don't enjoy seeing the mess.

"That . . . wasn't Beck?" Gremont says.

Jerrod sees no point in lying. "No."

"That was stupid," Gremont says with a little more force. "Stupid of your boss."

Jerrod lets his lip curl at the edge. "You'd better fucking hope you never meet my boss."

Gremont's eyes darken. Not that Jerrod is worried. His companion has charged Jerrod with delivering a message, and she wouldn't be pleased if Gremont interfered. Gremont knows it, too; he snaps a curse and turns on his heel, stomping out of the room like an angry, oversized toddler.

Jerrod has already stopped thinking about him. He crosses the room and bends down next to the dead body, looking at the pool of blood spreading very slowly across the table. Looking at the dead man's face.

Bron. He'd been one of Beck's for a long time, nearly as long as Jerrod. Jerrod remembered Bron learning how to be a passable Prosper Beck: what to say and what not to say, what to wear, the right accent. A little like Kel's job, Jerrod had thought, when he found out what Kel's job really was, and later he wondered if that was where Beck had gotten the idea.

Jerrod sighs. "May you pass through the gray door unhindered, my brother."

He touches the other man lightly on the shoulder, feeling the scratchy fabric of the brocade jacket of which Bron had been so proud. Feeling very tired, Jerrod sinks down into the chair opposite the dead man. He sits there a long time.

CHAPTER ELEVEN

The lamps were turned low in the royal apartments; it was past midnight. Kel sat on his bed, his back against a fortress of pillows, and watched Conor as he worked.

Conor seemed to be poring over a series of maps, looking at each one and taking notes in his fine, crabbed hand. (Kel knew Conor's handwriting as well as he knew his own: In most respects, it *was* his own. He had not been taught to write so much as he had been taught to imitate Conor's writing.) He had been doing it for some hours since they'd returned from the Arena, pausing only to stretch or splash water on his face.

"You should eat," Kel said, breaking the silence. "The meal Dom Valon brought won't be good for long."

Conor frowned at the plate near his elbow. "It's already congealed."

"Then ring for Delfina to bring you a new one." Kel swung his legs over the edge of his bed. "I was surprised to see Lin at the Arena today," he continued carefully. "And to see you laughing with her. I thought you didn't care much for her." *At least, I know you'd like me to think that. But I know well how rare it is for someone to truly make you laugh. And how rare it is for you to look at anyone the way you look at Lin.*

Conor shrugged without looking up. "She is the best physician I know. We're both evidence of that."

Kel let the words hang between them for some time. Then he said, "So you've decided . . . ?"

Conor set down his pen. "To seek her help with my father, yes. I've asked her to remake the medicine Fausten was giving him."

Your medicine, Fausten had shouted, just moments before the King had pushed him from the clifftops to his death below. *Only I can make it. If you kill me, your sickness will be worse. You know what is coming, my lord.*

"And you think that's the best course of action? Fausten was hardly trustworthy," Kel said.

"Trustworthy or not, my father was better while he was taking Fausten's potion. He is worse now. And we are running out of time." Abruptly, he looked up at Kel. "I don't expect to get back the father I once had, Kel. But even a father who speaks to me and can reason would be a great improvement. And we cannot hide him away forever. It makes the Aurelians seem weak."

The memories were coming thick and fast tonight. Kel recalled the words of the Dark Assassin, on the night of the massacre in the Gallery. *You stand upon the threshold of history, Sword Catcher, for this is the beginning of the fall of House Aurelian.*

"Well," Kel said, "this is not a sword whose thrust I can block for you. But I will help in any way I can."

Conor bit the end of his pen thoughtfully and said, "Take my place at the banquet tomorrow night."

Kel felt obscurely disappointed; he had hoped for a more direct action. "Are you sure? The last time I took your place at a banquet, it did not go well."

This was certainly an understatement. Conor shot him a wry look. "It seems vanishingly unlikely to happen twice in succession, don't you think?"

Kel couldn't help but laugh. "Do Jolivet and Bensimon know of this plan of yours? Or the Queen?"

"Jolivet knows. The others, not yet. If they ask why I'm not attending, tell them I'm drunk or in a brothel. Just don't tell them I'm meeting with Lin Caster in the hope of helping my father."

"I'm not sure they'll believe me about the brothel," Kel said. "You've changed your ways too much."

"Tell them I backslid. Or I backslid and then went to seek forgiveness from the Hierophant for my sins." Conor gestured vaguely. "You'll come up with something."

"And what shall I tell Anjelica? Your bride-to-be?"

"I'll tell her I won't be in attendance," Conor said, to Kel's surprise. "I can be straightforward with her. It's what she wants, which is a relief. Though I cannot tell her about my father," he added, tapping his pen against his teeth. "That would be going too far."

"I'm sorry you have to keep it all a secret," Kel said. He knew the weight that secrets carried.

At that Conor smiled—his rarely seen, plainly sincere smile. "At least I can tell you," he said. "You're the only one I can trust."

Like a once famous gladiator returning to the Arena to show that he had lost none of his skill, Queen Lilibet had unleashed all her talent for entertaining upon Anjelica's welcome banquet.

The Shining Gallery remained closed, its doors nailed shut since that terrible night, so Lilibet had decided to take advantage of the hot weather and hold this particular banquet out of doors, in the Queen's Garden, with its walls of greenery and central pool, black-tiled so as to reflect perfectly the changing colors of the moon. Tonight it was tinged slightly blue, like Valdish wine.

Outside the garden, in the buzzing twilight, Kel—with Benaset behind him, a silent guard—was waiting for Anjelica. All the nobility had already arrived. Only Anjelica was late, though no one was surprised. As the new Princess, she would be expected to make a memorable entrance.

Though Kel's view of the party was partially blocked by the

flame trees Lilibet had imported from Kutani to add to the decorations, he could hear the raised voices of the nobles and see dancing lights through the leaves, like the eerie candle-glow that sailors reported seeing far out to sea, leaping and frolicking atop the nighttime waves.

It was a hot night, and the fire-red outfit that had been made for Conor to wear was uncomfortably heavy with touches of velvet and brocade. It bore some Kutani influence as well: gold sea-dragons sewn up and down the sleeves and the plackets of the long scarlet coat, each of their eyes a fire opal. Around his throat and wrists were collars of gold, intricate with Kutani knotwork. Kel thanked Aigon for the night breezes; he would be sweating through his clothes otherwise. Not just from the heat, but from nerves.

Many years had passed since he'd panicked every time he was required to impersonate Conor. In the first years of being a Sword Catcher, it was what he'd hated most—far more than the idea of being in danger. Every impersonation was walking a tightrope: always remembering you were playing a part while also remembering every tiny detail that made you someone else.

He was not totally sure why his nerves were playing up tonight. Perhaps because the last time he'd impersonated Conor at a banquet, the bride-to-be had ended up pinned to the wall with a crossbow bolt, and he hadn't been able to stop the horror. Perhaps because Anjelica had so easily fooled him with her deceitful walnut trick. He grinned to himself in the dark. All right, it had been a *little* funny. Perhaps—

But Benaset was tapping Kel on the shoulder, muttering for him to straighten up and present himself properly. Kel turned to see Anjelica coming down the path from the Palace, making her way between the hedges with her Bloodguard brothers at her side.

Her dress was nominally in the style of Castellane, with a tight bodice and pleated skirt, beneath which sandals of dark-gold leather were visible. But the fabric was like no other material Kel had ever seen: It had the sheen of satin, seeming to pour over her body, as if her dark-brown skin had been painted with a fierce and uncompromising liquid flame. Around her throat glimmered a collar of brilliant orange citrines, and the same stones dangled from her ears. Her braids were wrapped with gold wires, and threaded along the wires were more gems: cinnamon-colored garnets and imperial topaz, yellow jade and ametrine.

Her beauty was as startling as ever. It made him think of the beauty of a sword, sharp and bright and almost stern. The kind of beauty that seemed as if it could cut.

She acknowledged him with a slight nod as she came near. Her brothers were walking close to her, their heads together in murmured conference. Their uniforms of cinnabar and gold seemed to glow against the dark night.

Kel offered her his arm, stiff with embroidery and jewels. "Greetings, *Ayakemi*," he said.

"And to you, *Ufalme*," she said, taking his arm.

"Conor sent his apologies," Kel said as they made their way down the path to the Queen's Grove, followed by Benaset and the Bloodguard, keeping a careful distance behind them. "That he cannot be here himself—"

"It does not matter." Her tone was dismissive. "But does he do this to you often, then? Schedule two engagements and send you to the one he would decline?"

Kel studied her profile. *Was* she angry? Conor had insisted she didn't mind, and indeed, if she was upset, she was hiding it perfectly. "I don't know whether you will believe me, but no. I can only assure you he would not be absent now unless he was required to be. And I do not think of it as something he does *to* me," he added. "This is my duty. My livelihood."

"I thought your livelihood was to catch swords. Or daggers, or poison, or whatever might be thrown at your Prince."

"Are you worried we are walking into danger?" Kel said. "Because of the last banquet held here? The Castelguards are well prepared—"

She shook her head, and the gems in her hair made a musical sound. "No. Only a fool repeats a surprise attack, for it is not a surprise the second time. My Bloodguard would protect me, in any case."

Kel glanced over at Kurame, who winked at him through the dark. Isam and Kito did not look nearly as amused; Kel suspected they were annoyed at Conor over what must seem like disrespect of their sister, and probably annoyed at him by association. Kel was, as always, a conduit through which feelings about the Prince passed and were transformed, like one of Merren's alchemical mechanisms.

At the end of the path, the Queen's Garden opened before them. A flourish of the *lior*—not, thankfully, being played by Merren this time—announced their entrance. The Bloodguard melted away into the shadows, though Kel was well aware that they were still close by.

Barely had they stepped into the grove than the fountain in the center of the reflecting pool shot forth streams of water colored in red, orange, and gold. The guests yelled and clapped—Beatris Cabrol, beside her mother, screamed aloud in surprise—and Lilibet, seated upon a golden chair beneath a canopy of cinnabar brocade, smiled. She wore her usual green, with a golden collar so high it nudged the base of her chin.

Everywhere were lanterns of pale-white parchment: hanging in the branches of the white-flowered almond trees, floating atop the reflecting pool like lily pads. The orange trees bore glimmering fruit: Dark-orange crystals and candied oranges hung from the boughs. On each of the tables scattered around the grass were vases of red and yellow Shenzan porcelain, from which spilled flowers native to Kutani: orange trumpet vine and scarlet arrowroot, the greenish-yellow petals of ylang-ylang, which gave off the strong scent of perfume, clashing with the odor of the citrus trees. Glass basins held pastries and candied fruits, atop which fat yellow bees—confusing the crystalline lantern light for day—buzzed and feasted.

If Anjelica was impressed by any of this, her calm expression did not show it. She kept her back sword-straight as they moved past rows of politely clapping nobles, on their way to a marble pavilion on which had been set a single table for their repast. It looked like a stage set, Kel thought, but perhaps that was not surprising. This whole business was a performance for the benefit of the Hill.

Many of the nobles gaped openly at Anjelica as she went by. They had all heard she was beautiful, of course, but seeing her up close was different. Kel wondered if they felt as he had on the docks, that this was a kind of beauty that caused pain. But his mind was only half on the question. He could see Lady Alleyne, who had placed herself near Lilibet, with Gremont standing beside her. But he did not see Antonetta. Surely she would be here tonight?

But even if she was, he thought, as he and Anjelica made their way up the steps to the pavilion, he was Conor tonight. He would not be able to approach her as himself.

Though what could he do as himself? She'd already told him he couldn't help her.

They reached the single table resting beneath a canopy of gold organza. Anjelica seemed to hesitate just for a moment before taking her seat beside Kel. Perhaps she, too, was uncomfortable with the performance.

Kel busied himself with formalities: the finger bowl with rose petals floating in it. A sip of scarlet wine, bitter on his tongue. Beside him, Anjelica rested her hands on the table. Around her slender wrists, bangles of coral and amber clinked like coins. Kel was terribly aware of all the eyes on them, the avid gazes of those desperate for a tidbit of gossip, a word they could spread about Castellane's soon-to-be Princess.

Kel cleared his throat. "You know," he said, "we have this pavilion to ourselves, whether we like it or not. The nobility of Castellane is free to stare at us, but I assure you, they cannot hear us. If you have questions, now is a good time to ask them."

"Not questions, precisely," Anjelica said, "but I wished to ask you for a favor."

"To ask me, or the Prince?"

"You, *koya-mitimi*. Or is it too difficult to be both the Prince and yourself at the same time?"

"I am very used to playing at being Conor. Walnuts notwithstanding."

She smiled faintly. "What about Kel Anjuman? Are you used to playing him? After all, that is not who you are, either."

Kel felt as if someone had put a hand on his solar plexus and pushed. He said, "I am used to that, too."

If the deliberate neutrality in his voice struck her, she did not react, only nodded. "You are right," she said, though he was not entirely sure what he was right about. "There is no reason to waste this evening." She set her glass down. "I need to arrange a meeting without the knowledge of the Palace, and I need you to help me."

Unable to stop himself, Kel swung around to stare at her. She looked back defiantly. She no longer seemed quite as distant and unearthly. He could sense the nervousness under her commanding tone, and it made her seem very human. "Me?" he said. "What would make you think I am the one to ask if you wish to keep secrets from the Aurelians?"

"You know about Aden," she said. Her voice shook slightly. "The pirate. The trouble I have had with him."

"You are not planning to meet with Aden, of all people?"

"No. *No.*" A look of indignation flashed across her face. "Someone who knows him. Someone who has promised they can make him leave me alone. Forever."

"Then why must this be a secret?" Kel plastered a smile on his face. It could not look as if they were having an argument; *that* would be a scandal. "The Aurelians would surely wish to help you rid yourself of this annoyance."

"They would," she acknowledged, "but they would send me into the city bristling with guards in a royal carriage, and the person

I am supposed to meet would flee. No one wishes for such attention from the Arrow Squadron."

"Then why involve me at all? Why not have your brothers take you? Simply claim you wish to see something of the city you will be ruling one day."

"They don't know the city at all—it would make no sense for them to show it to me! I need someone who is familiar with Castellane for the tale to make sense, and I would rather it was you than Legate Jolivet." She leaned closer to him. *That* would please Lilibet, who was surely staring and wondering. "The Palace guards are a gossipy lot, if they're anything like the ones in Spice Town. I need them to believe I am on a sightseeing tour, arranged by the Prince or the Queen. Something they won't question."

Kel hesitated.

"I can only tell you that this is in everyone's interest—especially the Prince's. And you, I think, are perhaps the only one here who puts Conor's best interests above all other things."

"And if I refuse?"

She sat back in her chair. "Then I will endeavor to slip away from Marivent on my own and make my own way in the city."

"You can't do that—"

"You cannot stop me."

Kel wanted to grind his teeth together. She was right, of course. He couldn't prevent her, but he knew from experience that creeping in and out of Marivent undetected was a difficult thing even for someone familiar with the Palace. Kutani's spies were good, of course, but there was always an element of chance—and for her to be caught would be disastrous for the alliance with Kutani.

And Conor needed that alliance.

"I will consider what you've asked me," Kel said. The nobles were stirring, getting to their feet. Soon they would approach to introduce themselves to the Princess. He and Anjelica would not be alone much longer. "And give you an answer in the next days. Do not act before I do."

"Then do not wait too long," said Anjelica with a sweet smile. She had turned to look out at the garden. "Who is that girl who is staring at you?"

Kel followed her gaze. It was Antonetta. She had come into the garden without him noticing and stood in the shadow of a flame tree, looking up at the pavilion. She was all in green silk, like the stem of a flower, with green silk ribbons threaded in her hair.

She met his eyes. The look on her face was hard to read. He would have guessed it was concern, but why would she be concerned for Conor? A moment later, Gremont had joined her, along with Lady Alleyne. They were both talking to her rapidly, and Kel could guess easily enough that she was being scolded for arriving late.

Then the nobles were swarming up the steps, ready to be introduced to Anjelica, and Kel could no longer watch Antonetta. First up to the table was Cazalet, with his pleasant smile and sharp, gleaming eyes. Then dour Sardou, who presented Kel with a wedding gift he claimed was—rather surprisingly—from Malgasi, and after him Raspail, whose gift was a wooden carving of Sedai. He must have had *that* made up in a hurry, Kel thought, but Anjelica seemed pleased.

In fact, she seemed pleased to meet each one of them. Whether she was or not, Kel couldn't tell, but she had been well trained in Spice Town. To each noble she said something warm and welcoming, dotted with personal asides—asking Ciprian Cabrol about a new sort of dye, and inquiring of Gasquet as to the health of his many brothers and sisters. In the few moments when she looked blank, Kel leaned in to whisper bits of noteworthy intelligence about each new arrival.

"Who is the man all in silver? He looks as if he might have Kutani blood," Anjelica murmured.

"Lupin Montfaucon? Textiles Charter. Cotton, linen. Not that they interest him."

"What does interest him?"

"Drink. Brothels. Gambling. He is a sybarite; his goal is pleasure."

"How typical of this city," Anjelica replied, but when Montfaucon came up, she was all delighted inquiry about his silver coat. With Joss Falconet, she chatted about spices; with Esteve, primed by Kel, she inquired solemnly about his obsession, the horses of Valderan.

Lady Gremont came up with Artal, who gifted Anjelica with a tea that had been created just for her, or so he claimed, and would soon be for sale in the coffee shops of Castellane.

"*Tĕ Anjelique*," Lady Gremont announced, looking pleased with herself.

"It seems the Princess's royal portraits did not exaggerate. Most are too flattering, and leave out the pox scars and lumpy noses." Gremont leered. "You must have been pleased, Conor, to arrive at the docks and find your betrothed more attractive than her likeness, and not less."

Lady Gremont, looking horrified, pulled Artal away before either Kel or Anjelica could reply.

"What an unpleasant man," Anjelica said.

"You've no idea," said Kel.

And then it was the turn of the Alleynes. Lady Alleyne bustled up in a whirl of calla lily silk, Antonetta close beside her. Lady Alleyne remained only long enough to be polite before descending the steps to speak with Queen Lilibet. But Antonetta hovered for a moment, her hands clasped, her eyes fixed on Anjelica.

"Now I see it," she said, the ruffles at her throat trembling. "For so long, I thought Conor and I would marry"—Kel nearly choked—"but you are so beautiful, Princess. I see that you are destined to be Queen of Castellane."

For the first time that night, Anjelica looked taken aback. "Oh, I—"

But Lady Alleyne had called for her daughter to join her. Antonetta hurried off in a swirl of blond curls and green satin. Anjelica turned startled eyes to Kel. "Were they betrothed?" she whispered. "She and the Prince?"

"No. Never," Kel said, too sharply. "Her mother spent her childhood filling her head with talk of Conor, that is all."

Anjelica shot him a long, considering look. "I see. So she is free to marry now?"

"No. She is engaged to Gremont. The unpleasant one."

"How unfortunate for her," she murmured. "Is she someone I can trust?"

Kel looked after Antonetta, who was chatting with Joss Falconet, seemingly admiring his fox-fur cloak. "Are you looking for someone you can trust?"

"If the nobles here are anything like the ones in Kutani," she said, "it is important to know who you can rely on."

Kel looked out over the lamplit garden, brilliant with light and shadow. "Well," he said, "if there are nobles in Kutani you can rely on, then they aren't much like the nobles here."

Anjelica looked at him curiously. "You paint a dark picture."

"Think of it this way," Kel said. "You will be Queen one day, so they will wish to please you, because to be close to the throne is to be close to power. And that, at least, you can rely on."

The library at Marivent was, as Lin had imagined, magnificent, but it did not dwarf the beauty of the Shulamat. And this pleased her more than she had thought it would.

She had nearly gone to Mariam to find a dress suitable to wear to Marivent, but at the last moment had stopped herself. She was not invited to the Palace as a member of the nobility; she was there to do work, and would be there in secret, to boot. She put on a plain blue dress, worn to gray at the cuffs and hem, braided her hair, stuffed her satchel with books, and walked out the gates of the Sault to the royal carriage waiting in the street.

They had arrived at the Palace not through the North Gate, but through a side entrance she had not known existed. Dusk laid its deep-blue shade over Marivent as she hurried across the grounds after Manish, the Castelguard who had retrieved her from the city. Fireflies, tiny needle pricks of flame against shadow, darted among the shrubberies lining the white stone paths. In the distance, she could see the cliffs, falling away to the aching vastness of the sea. The horizon's line between sea and sky was already softening; soon it would disappear altogether.

The library turned out to be located in the Castel Saberut, a rectangular pile of dark-gray stone with an endearingly round tower rising from its north side. As they approached, Lin could hear, in the distance, the sound of festivities—music and the loud chatter of voices. Through the thick trees, she could see the glow of golden lanterns hung high in the branches like translucent apples.

Manish left her at the doors to the castle, after telling her the library would be easy enough to find: It occupied the entire second floor. Lin hurried up a set of dimly lit stairs and through an archway to find herself in a vast, high-ceilinged room flooded with the light from a dozen carcel lamps. Light and books—so *many* books they dazzled, just as the riches of the Shulamat did. But in the Shulamat, the books were lined up neatly behind screens of golden mesh. Here, they were everywhere—piled on long tables, on the seats of chairs, and in stacks on the floor, some reaching higher than her head. The mess did not bother her. It provided a sense of abundance, like the sight of a table groaning under a mass of platters. *So. Many. Books.*

"The volumes are arranged by country." Conor's voice, the soft drawl as familiar as the sound of the ocean receding after a wave. Lin turned and saw him standing in the arch of a doorway that led, she suspected, to the round tower she'd seen from outside. "It is not the *easiest* way to find books. I believe it was my great-grandfather's design. He was rather eccentric."

He came into the room, and Lin realized he was not wearing a crown or circlet. He was as plainly dressed as she had ever seen him, all in dark red, the color of blood and Castellane. Black lace fringed his jacket at the wrists. He wore only a single ring, set with a pearlescent moonstone the size of a child's marble.

"I don't see how you find anything at all here," Lin said.

"Look down," said the Prince, and when she did, she saw that the mosaic floor—which she had thought a pattern of swirling tesserae, conveying no particular image—was, in fact, a map of Dannemore. Shelves of books had been placed atop the outlines of different countries. Valderan, Hanse, Marakand, Hind, Shenzhou—she crossed the floor and then back again, unable to prevent a smile. She had crossed all of Dannemore now, she thought, just like Josit. She wished she could tell him; he would laugh.

She reached the part of the map that had been Aram but was now uninhabited desert. There was no shelf here, no books. Aram existed only in history. That sobered her. She looked up and found Conor watching her; she could not have defined the expression on his face. There was a strange softness to the line of his mouth, but perhaps he was looking through her, at something else entirely.

He said, "Should I ask where you are supposed to be tonight, Goddess?"

"At home," Lin said. "Studying, or with my friend Mariam, perhaps. But there is no one keeping track of my movements that closely."

"I like the sound of that. Not to have anyone keeping track of your movements." The yellow light of the carcel lamps reflected off his mirror-gray eyes. "Come. I've gathered some books for us to look at already."

She followed him through the arched doorway into a circular room—they must indeed be inside the tower, for the roof sharpened to a conical point—whose walls were lined with books. It was much less cluttered here, though. Lin suspected it had been imagined as a reading room. Plush armchairs were placed here and there with views of the casement windows. More carcel lamps illuminated the space, creating a restful sense of warmth. In the center of the room was a round table stacked with books—and not just books. There was a bottle of wine and one of water, and plates of savory and sweet pastries: marzipan cut into the shapes of castles and stars, sugar-dusted *gibassié*, fried millet with rosemary and pepper, white-iced *rousquille*, and sliced figs and cheese.

For a moment, Lin was touched; the food was a thoughtful gesture. Then she told herself that she was being ridiculous: It was not as if he had laid out this feast himself. It had been a matter of a few words to a servant, no more effort or thought than that.

She turned to look at him. While she had been in a reverie about food, he had gone to stand before the open window. The blue of dusk had given way to darkness, though she could see lights moving outside and hear the blur of distant voices.

"There," he said. "That is where I am supposed to be tonight."

He was leaning on the sill of the window. There was a dormant tension in his posture, as if he were a hawk about to take flight. She could not see his face, only the curls of his dark hair. She moved a little closer until she could see that he was looking down on a garden, hung with paper lanterns that illuminated a riot of color: jessamy yellow, cinnamon red, saffron orange. Tables spilled food and flowers; there was a reflecting pool, blue as the moon above, seeming to glow from within. Dark figures, rendered anonymous by distance, moved among the flowering shrubs. The breeze was warm and carried with it the scent of eucalyptus and lavender.

"A welcome banquet for Princess Anjelica," he said. "Jolivet is taking no chances. If you look, you can see the Castelguards stationed among the trees."

Lin tucked a lock of hair behind her ear. "And you feel you don't need to be there?"

He made a restless gesture. The moonstone ring on his finger flashed; it was etched with a lion's profile, head back, mane flowing. What was it the sailors said? *Castellane roars, and the world trembles.*

"I ought to be there. But I find myself in a situation now where I must balance multiple needs at once. Kel can manage the banquet.

It is more important for me to attend to the situation with my father."

Lin couldn't help her next question. "And your fiancée doesn't mind the substitution?"

"Anjelica knows I have a Sword Catcher. And Kel is difficult to dislike."

"Do you think of yourself as easy to dislike?"

He said dryly, "Charm is a skill anyone can learn, but one must make an effort to be charming. And right now I have too much else to concentrate on." He indicated the books on the central table. "I've taken the liberty of gathering up our most comprehensive volumes on florticulture, if you'd like to have a look."

"Florticulture— Oh." Lin glared, made an impatient noise, and flopped down in a high-backed chair near the table. She could *sense* Conor's amusement from across the room.

The books were a motley collection: different sizes, different languages, different dates. For a short time, Lin lost herself in the research, turning to Conor—who had taken the seat across from hers and was watching her through narrowed eyes—only when she came across an unfamiliar language.

"Here," he said, pushing a small book across the table toward Lin. She glared down at the tome, so old that most of the ink had faded into illegibility. "Look at this one."

Lin picked up the book with a frown. It was a small volume, bound in cracked leather, the sort of thing you could buy in Fleshmarket Square. The title was printed in dull gold: *The Flower Book of Morwenna Aurelian.*

"Aurelian?" Lin looked up. "Who wrote this?"

"My great-great-grandmother," Conor said, leaning his elbows on the table in a princely disregard for manners, "and strictly speaking, she was breaking several Laws in doing so. But royals can get away with things ordinary people can't."

Lin shot him a look. "I've heard that."

He grinned and popped a fig into his mouth. "Queen Morwenna was fascinated by plants, especially those with certain properties. She kept a garden of them. She wished to know the history of every plant, its uses in healing and . . . in magic." He sat back. "I've found the book useful myself in the past. It has an excellent section on hangover remedies."

Lin rolled her eyes as she bit into a rosewater-soaked pastry, then suppressed a sound of pleasure at its deliciousness. *Concentrate on the book*, she told herself, though she was aware that Conor was watching her as she read.

Queen Morwenna had handwritten the text in a style long out of date and only barely legible. Lin found blackroot described near the end of the book: *Sports beautiful obsidian flowers, has no scent, blossoms and leaves are toxic to animals and people. Legend has it that, before the Sundering, blackroot was used to suppress the effects of magic. Sorcerer-Kings were known to have slipped it into the cups of their enemies before a duel, in order to blunt the edge of their power.*

She looked over the top of the book at Conor. "This is interesting," she said. "Blackroot *is* poison, that is in no doubt, but it also works to suppress magic. Is there some possibility that Fausten was trying to *undo* the effect of a spell?" She frowned. "But no, that couldn't possibly—"

"Let me see that." Conor reached out a hand for the book. As he did, the lace fell away from his wrist, and she saw the red mark of a burn on his skin, one that had not been there when she saw him shirtless in his apartments.

She must have betrayed something with her expression, for he shook his sleeve down quickly, covering the wound. But Lin looked at him squarely. "You have a burn on your wrist."

He shrugged. "It's nothing. A spill of candle wax." But he would not meet her eyes.

"Let me see it."

He set down Morwenna's book with a characteristic scowl. "If you insist," he said, and held out his arm to her.

She had not quite thought ahead this far. But Lin was a physi-

cian above all other things, and she had treated Prince Conor before. She took hold of his hand and turned his arm over so she could
study the inside of his forearm, where the skin was a shade lighter,
nearly as pale as her own. She could see the blue veins running like
a map beneath his skin, see the long delicate lines that crossed his
palm, the light calluses on his thumb and fingertips. His skin was
warm against hers.

He leaned in closer, looking down at the burn on his wrist just
as she was. The wound was pale red, almost glossy, unusually
shaped. Lin ran her finger lightly over the skin, feeling the smooth-
ness of the burn. She heard him suck in his breath and jerked her
hand back.

"Did I hurt you?" she asked, worried.

"No." There was a strangled something in his voice that made
her look up at him. He was staring at her, his eyes hot and silver, his
white teeth sunk into his lower lip. His hair was a riot of dark softness around his face, and she wanted to brush it back so badly, she
felt it as an ache. A hard ache deep in her belly.

She tried to breathe. The air between them was thick and hot,
as if the room were filled with smoke. She was still holding his hand.
For a long, long moment, neither of them moved. She could not
stop looking at him. He was normally talking, laughing, gesturing,
scowling. She had never seen him so still. She had never seen that
he had a freckle on his left temple, or the way the colors seemed to
change and shift in his eyes, as they did in the moonstone of his
ring.

When he spoke at last, his voice sounded as if it had been
dragged over gravel. "How serious is it, then, Goddess?"

She felt dizzy. "How serious—?"

"My burn."

"It will heal." She touched it again, lightly; saw the color darken
around his pupils. "But . . . how odd for a spill of candle wax that it
should be in the shape of a hand. Look, here is the palm, and here
the fingers—"

Conor drew his hand away. Lin sat where she was, without moving, trying to hide her breathlessness. She wanted his hand back in hers, wanted his eyes on her again. But she could not consider that. She forced herself to think instead of her dream, of the scorch marks on the walls inside the King's tower, and of what Mariam had said of the cursed King in the time before the Sundering.

"Your father did this, didn't he?" she whispered. "He burned you with the touch of his hand."

Conor yanked his sleeve down hard, hiding the burn. "Why would you say that?"

"In the Sault, I have access to books that speak of magic in the time before the Sundering."

"How illegal." His eyes glittered. "And there is no magic now."

"You have cause to know better," Lin whispered. "There is the magic of talismans, like the one Kel has, that lets him be your Sword Catcher. And there is magic in the healing I do."

"I know." His eyes said: *You healed the whip marks on my back, made them disappear. It should have been impossible.*

"We all say there is no magic when we know what exists: Old magic. Small magic. What we mean when we say magic has vanished is that no new great spell can be created." She took a deep breath. "And yet I think that Fausten's medicine was meant as a cure for an illness that was magical in nature. That *is* magical in nature. If we still have healing magic in our world, might its opposite not also exist?"

Conor rose to his feet. The room had darkened as the moon outside passed overhead, and he was a shadow against greater shadow. *He will throw me in the Trick*, Lin thought dizzily, *for even bringing up magic. For suggesting it could be affecting the King.*

In a low voice, Conor said, "In the moments before his death, Fausten cried out to my father, saying that if he died, my father's sickness would be worse. He said: *You know what is coming, my lord.*" He raked his hands through his hair. "Why would my father want to kill him, then? Why would he want to sicken, to die?"

"Perhaps he did not want to be dependent on him," Lin said softly. "It can be hard to feel you absolutely *require* someone else. Especially if you do not trust them."

His look was a flash of silver, like lightning over the ocean. He reached into his jacket then. When he drew his hand back out, Lin saw something fluttering and pale, like the wings of a bird. He threw it down on the table: not wings at all, but long strips of parchment, on which were scrawled lines of symbols. They were simple as a child's drawings: a wheel, a compass, a rose, a coin.

"Fausten's notes," said Conor. "At least, I have guessed that is what they are. I found them in a lockbox in his room. They seem nonsense, but he must have valued keeping them secret. It is perhaps a code—"

"They are not nonsense, nor a code." Lin pulled the papers toward her, her heart hammering. "Will you let me have these? I will bring them back to you in a few days, I swear it. I should have their meaning by then."

"Really? You can read them?"

"No," Lin said, "but I know someone who can. And I should examine your father again. I cannot test for the presence of magic, of course, but perhaps I can rule out a few other ailments."

He hesitated. "I suppose I must trust you."

Lin folded the papers carefully into a square and slipped them into her pocket. "Why would I lie to you?" she said. "What good would it do me?"

For a moment, he seemed almost angry, but the look was quickly gone. He passed a hand over his eyes, as if very tired. "Forgive me," he said. "Yes. I will arrange for you to see the King again, when it is safe to do so." His eyes were a very dark gray. "You understand— there are not many I can trust."

He looked very young for a moment, and she wondered if she could see in him the boy he had been long ago, when Kel had met him and thought: *This is someone I would give my life to protect.* She wanted to stand up, to go over to him, but at that moment there was a sound like a whip crack, and the sky outside the window lit up brightly.

Fireworks. She could see the sparks of them, dark orange and red and gold, falling past the open window like a rain of flame. She thought of the people in the city, who would be standing in the streets now, admiring the light show exploding over Marivent.

She should be there, she thought. With the people of the Sault, looking up into the sky; not here in the Palace, under a royal order. She felt the weight of a strange sorrow on her shoulders—that, and the shadow of an even odder feeling, the uneasy sense of something sinister not far away . . .

Conor glanced toward the window. "The banquet is ending," he said. "I ought to find Kel. See how it all went. Whether the nobles behaved themselves." He sounded weary. "I would rather stay here."

But Lin was already on her feet, picking up her satchel. "I must go," she said. She paused. "Unless, of course, you require me further?"

She saw his eyes narrow. *It can be hard to feel you absolutely re-quire someone else.* "No, I do not *require* you," he said. "Go, then. Manish will be waiting for you below, with the carriage."

He turned back to the window as the sky outside lit up again, this time in even more brilliant streaks of color: deep golds and blues, struck to violet by the light of the tinted moon.

Lin hurried from the library, pausing only to look back once. She could see him, outlined in front of the window. He held his injured forearm cradled in his right hand, his fingers over the place where the burn was hidden beneath his jacket. Perhaps it was hurting him still.

Elsabet

Imagine you are light as a bird, flying free. Imagine you are soaring over Marivent, with its salt-white walls and its cliffs that fall away to the ocean below, black as the night above and fringed with lacy foam. Below you is a lighted garden, trees hung with lanterns like luminous fruit. As you pass over it, you see nobles below you, dressed in their finery, their gold and silk and satin that shines in the lamplight. How greatly you despise them. Gremont and Seven are no doubt down there, too, currying favor with royalty; you loathe them equally.

You rise, your magic finding purchase on the currents of the air, until you are at the window of the Palace library. Inside, the Prince is watching a red-haired girl read a book with the expression of a starving man staring at a plate of food. You want to stop and watch the scene, the girl in particular, but you have somewhere else you need to go. Tonight, the Palace is busy. Tonight is your best chance. You cannot waste it.

You soar upward, toward the gray spike of the North Tower. High up in the tower is a window, arched and narrow. You aim yourself toward it like an arrow.

In the dark and silent tower room, the King sits motionless, his gloved hands rigid and still on the arms of his chair. He has been this way for hours, days. He no longer eats or drinks. He stares fixedly into the darkness, his gaze never wavering, even when a dark figure appears at the window. Even when it creaks open on its hinges, and Elsabet slips into the room.

She is all in black, though her face is bare, pale as a moon in the gloom. She seems thin and sharp as a black needle, her inky hair bound tightly at the back of her head. Beneath the thin skin of her chest, a dark stone gleams with a bright inner fire that seems to pulse like a heart. An Arkhe.

If the King recognizes it, or her, he gives no sign. He is motionless as she comes close. The pendant at her throat radiates light, illuminating the room, the King's set face and shadowed eyes. "All my life," Elsabet says, coming a step closer, "I have wished to look upon the face of the man who nearly brought my country to ruin."

The King does not respond. He is a statue, carved out of living flesh, barely breathing.

"What do you see when you look at me?" demands Elsabet. "Do you see my mother? She remembers you well—a quiet boy scuttling through the great halls of the palace in Favár. Who would have thought that such an unprepossessing *pilcza* could destroy the source of all our power?" She brings a hand down, hard, upon the nearby desk, causing the astrolabe and other instruments of celestial divination to shudder. "Were you jealous? Did you realize your royal blood did not carry magic, as ours did? Did you wish to make House Aurelian special, as House Belmany is special? You must have thought you were so clever, fleeing with Fausten, he of little magic. As if he could protect you from our wrath, our vengeance. No. He never did that. He was always on our side, even under your very nose, giving you your potion. You were so desperate for it, he said, for it quieted the screaming in your head. The cry of the phoenix."

The King's hand moves, very slightly. In a flash, Elsabet is at his side, peering at him. Had it been a trick of the light? His eyes are blank as ever.

"What did you think would happen?" she muses. "Spilling the lifeblood of magic itself? You destroyed a being whose whole nature is transformation. Did you not think that would change you? We never thought you would be such a fool as to have your own child. Did you truly never realize that the magic you stole runs in your blood now, and that you would pass it on to him? Your boy, your pretty Prince? Perhaps you understood, a little. Perhaps that is why you insisted he have a *Király*. A Sword Catcher."

Elsabet lets her mind dwell briefly on the Prince, the one who is even now in the library nearby, the contents of his heart stamped on his face. She knows he will be hers, in the end, for that is part of the great plan: He might be mindless, enslaved by magic, but he will belong to her and she will do as she likes with him. The thought spreads warmth through her veins.

"The potion slowed your change," she whispers now. Her mother had told her that Markus had been handsome in his youth, though she could see none of Conor's looks in him. "But when it comes upon you—and it will—oh, we will lock you in a cage and sink it so deep in the ground, your screams will go forever unanswered. And as for your son, spoiled and unformed as he is, he is a seed of power—one that will be replanted in Malgasi soil. In me." She grins, not caring now whether he knows she is there or not. "After that, we will have no more use for him. But he is a pretty thing; I will enjoy him before I discard him. And as for your city, of which you are so proud, it will become a second Favár. Clean, quiet, orderly, and under Belmany power." She leans closer to the King, close enough that she thinks she can smell the bitterness of smoke. "All that you have will be taken from you. All that you love, destroyed."

Slowly, so slowly, the King raises his heavy eyelids. And Elsabet takes a step back. He is motionless again, but in his eyes, she sees fire—that same fire that blazes behind her own eyes when she uses the power of her Arkhe. More golden than any ordinary flame: a fire thought vanished from the world with the Sundering. More than that, behind him, she thinks she sees the shadow of wings, cast against the wall—

Her hand flies to the Source-Stone at her throat. It was filled long ago, when House Belmany had what seemed an infinity of magic to draw upon. It is now a pale shadow of that old power, but it is still more than most will ever have access to. If there is another Source-Stone in Dannemore, she does not know of it.

Sluggishly, it calls to the magic in her blood, and her blood answers. Over the years, it has grown weaker, but it is still enough. Elsabet has been raised to one purpose: To reclaim the lost magic of her family. To recover their power. She gazes now at the King, at his burning eyes.

"When I see you again, you will be quite changed," she says. "It will not be long now."

She leaps for the window then, letting the magic of the stone buoy her into the air, letting it carry her through the night.

CHAPTER TWELVE

During the day, the Ruta Maestra was a wide road bordered by rich shops selling to the upper classes of Castellane. She was a beautiful aristocrat, draped in rich silk, toying with the diamonds at her throat. But at night, she doffed her furs and revealed herself as the pretender she was—a merchant's daughter whose jewels were paste, with an ambitious gleam in her eye.

Kel and Conor rode together through the lights of the Broken Market, Conor on Asti and Kel on Asti's brother, a roan gelding named Matix. Conor had his hood up, hiding his identity from the crowds. Occasionally, they passed the flare of a naphtha torch whose sudden illumination would reveal a portion of Conor's face, and Kel would wonder how they did not know him, did not recognize him by the curve of his cheekbone or the sharp flash of his smile. He had the most recognizable face in Castellane, and yet it was as if he were invisible simply because he had donned a homespun linen cloak.

It was as if he had his own sort of amulet, Kel thought as they turned into the Temple District. Those who knew who Kel really was were not fooled; those who expected to see the Prince saw the Prince. It was, above all things, a game of expectations.

When they reached the Caravel, they dismounted, handing the

reins of their horses to waiting grooms. As they went inside, Conor tossed his hood back, looked at Kel, and smiled.

Kel was not fooled by the ease of the smile. In theory, they were visiting the Caravel to celebrate with Falconet, who had made a great deal of money on a shipment of spices that had just come in. Three months ago, it was the sort of thing Conor wouldn't have thought of missing. Tonight, Kel had had to cajole and press him out the door, telling him it would make Falconet furious if they made no appearance.

In truth, Kel cared little about whether Joss was furious or not; he was worried about Conor. When he had come back from the banquet last night, he had found Conor lying flat on one of the divans in their room, uncharacteristically silent. He had not asked Kel about the nobles, or Anjelica. He had been holding his arm as if it were injured, but he snapped at Kel for wanting to see it. And when Kel had asked him about Lin, Conor had only turned away, as if he did not want Kel to see his expression. It was unusual for Conor to conceal his feelings this way, but Kel already knew that when it came to Lin and Conor, everything was unusual.

Then Conor had woken up in the dead of night screaming—a mix of Castellani and Malgasi. Kel recognized some of the words. *Atma az dóta.* Fire and shadow.

He had gone over to sit on Conor's bed, and Conor had rolled onto his back, looking up at Kel with wide gray eyes, as he had when he was a child. "You are the only one I trust," he said, and when he fell asleep, he did it holding fast to Kel's wrist.

Enough was enough, Kel thought. Joss's party was a convenient excuse for a familiar kind of celebration. One that offered a chance to forget, if only for a night. He had talked Conor into it, and now here they were, having made their way into the crowded main room.

All the expected guests were here. Falconet reclined on a couch near the fireplace, his back to the bare chest of a handsome young blond man from Hanse. He was eating an apple. He grinned when he saw Kel and Conor and tossed it in Conor's direction.

Kel's arm shot out; he intercepted the apple automatically. Conor cast him an amused look.

Kel shrugged. *I am the Prince's shield; I stand between him and thrown fruit.* He played it off by biting into the apple with a smirk at Joss.

Montfaucon had already approached them, Ciprian just behind him. "Conor," he said. "What on earth's going on with the art on the walls?"

Now Conor did grin. "Malgasi sent a gift in honor of my nuptials," he said. "One of their most celebrated artists has rendered several portraits of me."

"You didn't give them to the Caravel," said Kel. "Did you?"

"The Queen didn't want them in the Palace." Conor shrugged. In this case, Kel was on her side. The portraits of Conor were alarmingly like him, and showed him engaged in a variety of upsetting pursuits. Some illustrated him standing over the bodies of murdered Princesses with a satisfied look, while others featured him in compromising positions with an elephant that was clearly Sedai.

"Kellian." A light tap on his shoulder. He turned and saw Alys Asper behind him. As always, she was a neat and elegant presence, her dark hair wound into an intricate braid atop her head. "Silla is upstairs, in the Ochre Room. She was hoping for a few moments with you."

Kel hesitated.

"No hourglass," said Alys. "I believe she only wants to talk."

It was odd, Kel thought as he made his excuses to Conor—now involved in a game of Castles with Montfaucon—and headed up the stairs. He had not visited Silla for amorous purposes for a long time now, and given their last conversation, he had thought they were both at peace with it. Perhaps she had something else she wanted to discuss with him, though he couldn't imagine what.

The Ochre Room was on the second floor, the door painted yellow to distinguish it from the other rooms along the corridor.

The door was unlocked, and Kel walked into the room, expect-ing to see Silla posed artfully on the gold-draped bed, her hair fall-ing loose the way she knew he liked it. He was already preparing himself to tell her *not tonight*, and probably *not ever again*, when he was brought up short.

It was not Silla sitting there, hair loose, her expression a mix of determination and panic.

It was Antonetta Alleyne.

Automatically, Kel turned and closed the door behind him, slid-ing the bolt home. Then he turned around again. And stared at her.

Antonetta. *Ana.* She sat on the four-poster bed, wearing a silk dress the color of cream. Her skin looked pink beside it, or perhaps it was just that she had the sort of skin that flushed easily. Her cheeks were a dark pink as she met his gaze almost defiantly.

"Don't blame Alys," she said. "I told her my visit was a surprise for you. That you wouldn't mind if we played a little joke."

"I see," Kel said. He had his doubts as to whether Alys would have believed that this was a lighthearted amusement; more likely, she'd put Antonetta's desire for anonymity down to her position on the Hill. And surely that was part of it. "Antonetta, if you wanted to talk to me, you could have just summoned me to your house."

"And have your visit reported to my mother?" Antonetta asked. "Certainly not. Besides, I don't want to talk to you."

"I don't understand."

She rose to her feet. Light spilled over them both from a gold-shaded carcel lamp. The silk of her dress clung to her hips and fol-lowed the lines of her long legs down to the toes of her slippers. It was clear she was wearing no petticoats, nothing under the silk, so fine it seemed to melt against her skin. Kel could see the curves of her hips, her rounded thighs; heat flickered low in his belly, and he told himself not to be a fool.

Antonetta raised her chin. Her hair was loose, tumbling in curls around her face. Her cheeks looked flushed. "In a few weeks, I will be married to Artal Gremont," she said. "He insists on the ceremony of First Night, and he will make it as unpleasant for me as possible. He will take enjoyment from that."

Kel forced his hands not to curl into fists. "You know what I think. Refuse to marry him, Ana."

"I cannot do that. And if that is all you have to say, then this will be a short conversation."

"But he—"

"Is disgusting," Antonetta said. "I know that. But I can endure it. I can endure much." Unconsciously, her hand went to her throat, to toy with the locket there. "I only want your help."

Kel knew he should leave. This was torture—for him at least, if not for them both. But he could not stop looking at her, could not stop wanting to be in the same room with her. To be closer than that. "Help you how?"

The flush on her cheeks darkened. "I don't want Artal to be my first. I want it to be you."

Kel caught his breath. He had fantasized—somewhat to his own shame—scenarios in which Antonetta said something like this, but he would never have imagined she really would. Yet as he stared at her, wordless, he knew that she meant it. He knew from the blush that spread across her face, from the way her teeth sank into her lower lip. Knew from the determination in her eyes.

There was a roaring in his ears, his blood beating hard in his veins. He wanted to go to her so badly it was blinding; he had never felt this, not even in those early days with Silla when he had known nothing else.

"I can't," he said hoarsely. "I can't be your penance for marrying someone you can't stand."

Her hand fell from the locket. "But if you just knew *why*—"

"Then tell me," he said. "Tell me why. If there's a reason, give me the reason, Ana, because I need it. More than I ever thought I could."

She didn't reply. A moment later, he was at the door, hand on the latch. At last, from behind him, she said, "You are my first choice, Kellian, but not my only one. There are others I can ask."

The roaring in his ears was deafening now. He had never understood what people meant when they said they saw red, but a scarlet mist seemed to pass in front of his eyes. He could hear Antonetta's harsh breathing behind him as he removed his hand from the door and turned to face her.

Her lips were parted, her eyes very bright. One of the slim straps of her dress had fallen from her shoulder, baring the creamy skin there, the arching curve of her collarbone. He imagined kissing her there, at the juncture of her neck and shoulder, and wondered what she would taste like. Sweet and amandine, like marzipan, or sharp and salty, like sweat and perfume?

He stalked across the room to her. He half expected her to flinch away, but she stood her ground, only tilting her head back to look up at him. Her pupils were the shape of hearts.

He said, "Tell me, then. What you want me to do."

"I . . ." He didn't think she could blush more, but it seemed she could. She said, "I told you. I want you to be my first."

"Your first what?" He swayed a little toward her, held himself back. "Say the words, Antonetta. Tell me exactly what you want me to do. Or I won't do it."

"My first—" She caught her breath, widened her eyes. Looked at him hard. She said, "Touch me. Put your hands on my body." She had bitten her lip; she licked the dent she'd made and said, "Make me like it."

He laid his hands on her shoulders. Her skin, hot and bare, felt like satin; he traced his hands down her body, flat-palmed. Gliding over the silk she wore, over the curves of her breasts. The silk was like water, no barrier to the feel of her body. As her nipples hardened against his palms, he circled them with his fingers, teasing and touching until she cried out and pressed harder against him.

"Kiss me," she whispered. "Kiss me properly."

He knew he should hold himself back. Kiss her delicately, carefully. But no sooner had he pressed his mouth to hers than every shred of careful planning was torn away. She kissed him back eagerly, wrapping her arms around his neck, and he was lost—lost in the dark sharp pleasure of kissing her, the softness of her lips, the heated glide of her tongue into his mouth. He caught her in his arms, lifting her up off the floor, and carried her to the bed.

They were still kissing when they crashed onto the mattress, her hands gripping the lapels of his jacket now, tearing it off him. She yanked the hem of his shirt free from his trousers and slid her hands up his bare chest, sighing against his mouth as she explored him with her fingers.

He tore his mouth away from hers. Braced on one hand above her, he said raggedly, "Antonetta. What do you want now? Tell me."

Her lips parted in surprise; they were red with kisses. His kisses. "I don't know," she whispered. "I don't know what to ask for. Only—" She lifted a hand to caress his cheek, her eyes dark with desire. "Don't stop."

He groaned and kissed her again, feverishly. Her hands stroked his back, and he wondered if she felt the scars there through the material of his shirt. But he was too dazed to wonder long; he sucked her lower lip, making her whimper, before kissing his way down her throat. It was the work of a moment to push down the straps of her dress, baring her beautiful breasts, high and round and tipped with stiff pink nipples.

She had gone still. "Kel . . . ?" she whispered.

He wanted to tell her she was gorgeous, beautiful, perfect. But words seemed beyond him. As all the blood in his body seemed to rush downward, he closed his mouth around her nipple. She gave a small scream and arched up and toward him, wordlessly. Her fingers dug into his sides, her hips rising, grinding against his, sending sparks of blinding pleasure through his body.

When she begged him not to stop, he felt something expand inside his chest. A sense of pleasure in her pleasure, he thought, or a pride that he *could* please her; again, something he had never felt before. And as his hand glided downward, he prayed to any available God that what he had learned about pleasure in his life would not fail him now, when it mattered.

His hand glided over the curve of her belly, his fingers gathering the silk of her dress as they went, bunching it up around her waist. He felt her turn and twist under him, gasping as he circled her navel with his forefinger. The muscles in her stomach jumped under his hands, fluttering against his palm.

"Kel," she whispered, almost tearfully. "Kel—*Kel*—"

His name in her mouth, the sound of her pleading with him, nearly undid him. He wanted to be inside her so badly it hurt. He shoved that thought back: It was impossible. Instead he let his hand travel, down and down, finding the softness of her inner thighs. He moved his lips to her throat; she was taut against him as his fingers found the heart of her. The heat of her there made him groan low in his throat; he began to circle his fingers, gently and then with a firmer pressure.

She was pressed tautly against him as he arched over her. He watched her face with a fascination as intense as any pleasure he'd ever felt as she flushed and whitened, her lips parting, her lashes beginning to flutter. She pressed up against his fingers, her body writhing under his, her hands gripping at the sheets of the bed so hard, he thought she might tear them.

Her eyes flew wide open; their gazes locked. He caught his breath as she trembled and cried out, her legs clamping tight around his hand. He could feel every spasm that rocked her and thought for a moment he might lose control of himself, so keenly did he feel every shock of her pleasure.

As the last shudder rippled through her, she went boneless against him. For a moment he just held her to him, marveling at the stillness that surrounded them, the quiet. Even though his body ached with unfulfilled desire, he thought he could lie like that all night.

Then she sat up. Her hair was a wild tangle of gold strands, sweat shimmering on her collarbone. He felt an overwhelming urge to lick her throat.

"I know there's more than that," she said. "What about *you*?"

And she leaned down to kiss him. Caught by surprise, he hummed softly into the kiss, drawing her down against him. Half silk, half naked skin, she melted against him, her hand sliding along his belly, dipping down between his legs—

He sat up, almost hurling her off him. Rolling off the bed, he rose to his feet, though his whole body ached with want. He could barely look at her, with her dress rucked up to her thighs, her hair tumbled all around her shoulders, her lips swollen from kissing. She put a hand to her mouth.

"But, Kel," she said, "I know—"

"That I didn't make love to you—what was it you said?— *properly*? You're right. I can't. I can't be your First Night, Antonetta. Gremont has the right to have you checked by a doctor, to make sure you're a virgin. And he probably will."

She went white, as if Kel had slapped her.

Before he could say more, a series of knocks rattled the door on its hinges. "Kel Anjuman." It was Hadja's voice. "The Prince is looking for you."

He looked at Antonetta. She was already straightening her dress. "You'd better go," she said. "It's Conor. It might be important."

"It probably isn't," Kel said. The ache of desire was leaving him at least, replaced by a very different ache. "Antonetta—I am sorry I couldn't give you what you wanted."

She stood up and took a linen wrap from the ornate yellow-gold bedstand. She thrust her arms into it, flinging the fabric around herself, covering her body. "I asked for pleasure, and you gave me that," she said. "I have never felt that sort of thing before. I probably never will again."

"Antonetta—"

"Just go," she said, turning away to gather the rest of her things. Her tone was clipped, final. Her mother's voice, ordering him to stay away.

Kel went. He seized up his jacket on his way out of the room and was shoving his arms into the sleeves as he started downstairs. Not that he wanted to go downstairs; he *wanted* to go back to Antonetta and beg her—but for what? What could she give him? What could he give *her*, really? Not even his real name.

Halfway down the steps, he heard voices. Recognizing one, he froze, pressing himself back against the wall. A wave of nausea rolled over him. *Gremont.* The back of Kel's neck prickled. Artal had been very clear he intended to take full advantage of the brothels of the Temple District, whether he was engaged or not, but that didn't mean he'd look kindly on Antonetta being here. He'd be furious. Perhaps dangerously so.

"It's a problem," Gremont was saying. Kel crouched down, peering through the banister railings. He could see Gremont, all unwieldy shoulders in a gaudy doublet, standing on the next landing down with his arms crossed. Across from him was Falconet, looking harried. The amulet around Gremont's neck looked even uglier in the bright stairway light. Kel couldn't help but stare at it— it seemed such a small thing to be protecting Gremont from the wrath of so many people. Including himself.

"It is a problem that will take care of itself, Artal," Joss said. "Honestly. I don't see what the fuss is about."

Gremont sneered. "Always angling for an advantage, aren't you, Joss? The great problem solver, Joss Falconet." He spat, narrowly missing Falconet's boot. "Never mind. I'll handle it myself."

"Really," said Joss. "What about Liorada?"

Kel pressed closer to the banister. Why were they discussing Antonetta's mother?

But before Gremont could reply, a courtesan with a thick pile of dark hair and bright spots of rouge on her cheeks—Audeta, Kel thought—appeared on the landing. She was pouting.

"Artal," she said, "I've been waiting for you for simply *ages* in the Persimmon Room. I'm going to start the hourglass whether you come or not."

Good, Kel thought. *Get him out of here, Audeta.*

Gremont's eyes narrowed. For a moment, Kel worried he was going to snap at Audeta, or worse, but a moment later he shrugged and grinned. "See you later, Falconet," he said, and followed Audeta down the steps.

As soon as he was gone, Kel sprang to his feet and hurried downstairs. He passed Joss on the landing. The other man was looking thoughtful, almost inward, gazing into empty air. Kel almost slid past him without a greeting, but Joss started and seemed to wake as if from a dream.

He glanced at Kel, his expression no longer distant, but wry and amused as it always was. "Conor was looking for you," he said. "Nothing important—he was hoping you'd join his Castles game with Montfaucon." He grinned. "Hadja said you were with Silla," he added. "I thought you'd tired of her."

Kel muttered something noncommittal; he was glad Hadja was lying to protect Antonetta, but he felt weary of petty deceptions. He felt weary of everything but Antonetta; he still wanted her, wanted to return to her. Having kissed her, touched her, how could he be able to return to a life in which he could do none of those things?

From this vantage, he could see down into the great room, could see Conor sprawled on a couch, poking listlessly at a Castles board; could see the blond boy Joss had been leaning against now laughing with Ciprian Cabrol. All was as usual in the Caravel, he thought; only he had been changed.

The Broken Market was in full swing by the time Lin returned to the Sault. She had been out late, tending to a woman in the Warren who was slowly going blind. There was little medicine could do for her: The woman was a seamstress, and decades of sewing by inadequate candlelight had damaged her eyesight beyond repair. All Lin could do was beg her to stop sewing at night, which she knew was useless advice. Domna Bondion had three children and could barely feed them with the meager earnings from her sewing work as it was. She would continue to struggle until she was entirely blind.

The inability to help had left Lin in a state of frustration that did not subside when she reached home. Mez was guarding the gate and told her that the Exilarch was in the Shulamat gardens, "answering questions." *Offering judgment, more like*, Lin thought crossly.

"Yes, and?" she snapped, leaving poor Mez to remind her that she'd asked him to let her know when the Exilarch presented himself to the public again. She apologized before rushing off to the Shulamat, determined to intercept Aron.

It was a warm evening, and the air in the gardens was redolent of flowers. To her surprise, she found the Exilarch perched on a bench, cross-legged, dressed casually in blue linen. He was surrounded by children: Scrubbed clean by their parents until they virtually shone, their familiar faces were upturned to Aron, their eyes wide and serious.

Some had been her patients; she had watched all of them grow up. She recognized Sania Dorin, Rahel's smallest sister, whose ears had been so thoroughly washed that they were still pink. "I don't see why girls can't be Shomrim," she was saying earnestly. "We're better at climbing, *and* we pay attention to things."

Aron, who had looked up briefly when Lin came into the garden, smiled. "I do not think it is officially forbidden," he said, "or at least, I see no reason why it should be. I shall speak to the Maharam."

A boy's hand shot up. Lin knew him, too: little Kaleb Gorin, Mez's cousin. "Why do the Rhadanites only go over the land and not over the sea?" he asked. "Are they afraid of being drowned?"

Aron looked up at Lin then. His bronze eyes gleamed as he said, "When the Goddess returns, it is said she will return in Dannemore. For this reason, the Ashkar never want to be too far away."

Kaleb seemed satisfied with this answer, although a faint muttering was passing among the children. Finally, Dara Malke, one of the older girls, put her hand up and said, "Exilarch. Will something bad happen to us Ashkar here in Castellane, the way it happened in Malgasi?"

Lin felt the question like an arrow in her heart. It was so unfair, that Ashkar children should fear such things. She could hardly remember the day she herself had realized that to be an Ashkar was to always be unsafe; to belong nowhere outside the Sault, but to know that walls could not entirely protect you. All she knew was that it had been a very long time ago.

Aron leaned back on his hands. He looked calm as ever, but there was a flintiness in his eyes that suggested to Lin he shared her anger. He said, "Lin Caster is here. Perhaps she can best answer your question."

Lin nearly jumped out of her skin. Oh for goodness' sake. Why was he pressing this responsibility on her? *Because you claim you are the Goddess, responsible for your people*, said a small voice in the back of her mind.

Sixteen pairs of young eyes were trained on her expectantly. Lin said, "In Malgasi, there was no Counselor to the throne as we have here in Castellane. And so the Queen and King of Malgasi forgot the Ashkar were people just like them. But you should not worry," she added. "We have Mayesh here, who is often in the Palace and can speak for us there. The King will not harm us. He would not want to lose his Counselor or his reputation for kindness."

There was a long silence as the children regarded Lin thoughtfully. At last Kaleb put his hand up again and asked, turning back to Aron, "Why do boats float when they're so heavy?"

A smile spread across Aron's face. Lin did not hear his answer; she was too anxious about her own. If she had put the children's minds at ease, she could not tell. They seemed the same mixture of somberness and giggling that they always were, even as Aron bid them goodbye and sent them back out to meet their parents in the Kathot.

"That was a good answer," he said once he and Lin were alone in the garden. He stretched, flexing his long hands. They were freckled on the backs, and freckles showed, too, at the open neck of his shirt. A reminder that unlike the Maharam, he lived most of his life under the open sky, not inside temples and judgment halls.

"Do you get that question often? About Malgasi?" Lin asked.

"In every Sault, I am asked some version of it, and not always by children. In most Saults, there is no one like your grandfather—no representative of our people to speak to the highest power in the land."

"So what do you usually say?"

"I speak of home," he said. He sounded a little stiff; the ease with which he had spoken to the children was gone. She had never been alone with the Exilarch before, Lin realized. It had never occurred to her that it was even possible he might be awkward, or diffident. "How there are others who have their lands, their homes, and they look askance at us because they do not understand a people who have no home. The selfish among them will say in fear, 'But these people have no home; surely they will try to take ours.' And I tell them to remember that those people are wrong. That we do have a home, in each other. We make our homes within, and not without; that is how we are different."

Lin was silent a moment. She could hear the dry scrape of the wind in the leaves. "That is very pretty," she said, "but it is not a promise, is it? It does not say, *You will be safe.*"

"Because I cannot promise they will be," he said. "That is your task, Goddess."

"Not mine alone," she said. "The destiny given to the Exilarch is to walk beside the Goddess. To help her."

"If she passes the test, yes." His gaze was thoughtful. "Is that why you've come here? To speak to me about the testing?"

Lin shook her head. "No. I came because—well, you are a Rhadanite. Can you read their language?"

He looked surprised. Before he could say anything, Lin drew Fausten's notes, much crumpled, from inside her jacket. She brought them to Aron where he sat on the bench.

"My parents were traders on the Gold Roads," she said. "I think you knew that. And my brother is on the Roads now. I recognize this as the code of the Rhadanite traders, but I cannot read it myself. I never learned."

Frowning, Aron took the papers from her. "Where did you get this?"

"In an old trunk of my parents' things. Josit would be able to translate it for me, but he is far away. I have so little of my parents, I just hoped . . . well, that you could tell me what it says."

He was silent, staring at the pages. Lin prayed quietly to herself that Fausten hadn't made any notes that said things like, *Today I have decided to poison the King. Surely a most excellent idea.* She had no idea how she'd explain *that* to Aron Benjudah.

At last, he looked up at her; only then did she realize she was standing over him, looking down at his bent head as she twisted her hands together. She had not meant to come so close.

He said crisply, "I do not believe your parents wrote this. Nor do I understand why you think you must lie to get my assistance."

Lin bit hard at the edge of her lip. *Do not show him he frightens you.* "Not every secret I know is a secret that is mine to tell."

"You are a curious person, Lin Caster," he said, folding the paper in his hand. "I was surprised by your answer to the child's question. Benezar has always given me to understand that you did not like Mayesh's job very much."

"I have begun to understand, in these recent days," Lin said, "that sometimes we are chosen to do things we do not wish to do, but that if we do not do them, there will be no one to take our place."

"You ask two of the Three Questions," Aron said, rising from the bench. In the pale moonlight, his hair and eyes seemed bleached to a lighter gold. "*If not now, when? If not me, who?*" His gaze swept over her, considering. "You are a conundrum. Those I have met before who laid claim to being the Goddess all sought attention and validation. You seem to dislike one and have no need of the other."

"I recall the Third Question," said Lin. "*All the world is a narrow bridge. How, then, to cross it without fear?*" She looked up at him; she'd nearly forgotten he was so tall. "I have no answer to that. I am often afraid. Even now, you make me afraid."

"Do I?" His expression was stern, cool. Distant. "Lin Caster, I will translate these papers for you on one condition. I would like to join you on your physician's rounds and observe your work."

Lin frowned. She did not like the idea of letting Aron come with her on her rounds, but to push back would only make him suspicious when she had nothing to hide. And she did need that translation.

"Is this an order?" she asked.

"More an exchange," said Aron. "But you may consider it an order from your Exilarch, if you wish."

There was at least a symmetry to it, Lin thought as she left the garden. A tense and complicated symmetry, but there it was: She was under orders from two different Princes.

Silla

"Silla," Audeta whispers. "Silla, come here a moment."

Silla approaches the other girl hesitantly. She likes Audeta, she always has, but Audeta has a boldness to her that renders her somewhat insensitive to anxiety in others. Silla has been on her guard all night, since Artal Gremont came into the Caravel with some of the other nobles. He'd been laugh-snorting like he often did—he reminds Silla of a horse that way—and slapping Joss Falconet on the back. He gave no sign of having noticed Silla, but she still didn't wish to risk running into him; her wrist has only just healed. She'd slipped away past Alys's office instead, where Alys sat closeted with the blond girl from the Hill.

Audeta is lounging in an open doorway, wearing a colorful silk robe and smoking a cheroot. Her hair is down around her shoulders. She winks at Silla as the other girl approaches and stands back, letting Silla have a clear view into the room where Artal Gremont is sprawled on the bed, snoring and . . . quite naked. He hasn't a stitch on—not even the gaudy necklace he usually wears.

Audeta blows a smoke circle. "He's drugged. One of Alys's brother's potions. Won't be awake for hours."

"What are you going to do to him?" Silla whispers. She knows she can't wake Artal up, but she can't help herself.

"We won't lay a finger on him, scaredy-cat." Audeta grins. "But Alys said he'll learn what we've done the hard way soon enough."

CHAPTER THIRTEEN

Early the next evening, Kel dressed as Kel Anjuman to escort Anjelica to her meeting.

He was still reluctant to go—reluctant enough that he cursed under his breath as he dressed in soft leather boots, a mossy silk tunic, and a gray-green linen jacket with a wide, lined hood. But Anjelica would go whether he accompanied her or not, and the results could be disastrous if she went alone. They could probably be disastrous either way, he thought, and slid a dagger into the top of his boot. Then added another one, up his sleeve, just in case.

Upon leaving the Castel Mitat, he found Lilibet in the courtyard garden, pacing back and forth. She looked up eagerly when she saw him, only for disappointment to flash immediately across her face. It was a phenomenon Kel had observed countless times: At a glance, Lilibet would mistake him for her son; at closer hand, she would realize who he was, and her face would fall.

She, too, wore green, just as he did. The color of Marakand. Today her dress was velvet, the color of emeralds, and a choker of emeralds circled her throat. She said abruptly, "Where is Conor?"

"With Mayesh," Kel said. He hoped she could not see the shape of the dagger under his fitted sleeve. The last thing he wanted was for her to be too curious about where he was going. "Going over the Solstice Ball invitations. I believe there is an issue of careful wording."

Lilibet's painted eyebrows rose. "They didn't tell me— Well. Never mind." Her dark gaze sharpened. "I had a mind to ask you. What do you think of the Princess?"

"Of Anjelica?" Kel was taken aback. "It is not my place to have an opinion, my lady."

Lilibet sniffed. "And yet you have spent more time with her than my son has, I'd warrant. He sent you to take his place at her banquet. Why? Does he find her too stubborn?" She kicked irritably at a border of roses, drooping in the heat. "I question how fine a Queen she can ever be. A Queen must be able to compromise, and the girl refuses to come to terms on anything."

"She spoke of you only in glowing terms, my lady," Kel lied.

"Then her words do not match her actions. We have only just had a disagreement on the topic of her elephant. I asked when it would be returning to Kutani. Elephants are very expensive to keep, you know."

Kel made a noncommittal noise.

"She said the elephant would not be returning, but would remain here indefinitely. That Marivent was now its home. When I objected, she told me in no uncertain terms that any decision about the creature would be up to Conor, not to me, and that Conor approved of the elephant."

"That's true," Kel said. "He does approve of the elephant. He may be more excited about the elephant than he is about the Princess."

Lilibet made an exasperated noise. If Kel had not been anxious to get away, he would have found the whole business funny. It was rare that anyone got under Lilibet's skin like this. "Is my son bothered that his bride is so excessively pigheaded?"

"I believe Conor considers this union to be for the good of Castellane," said Kel gravely, "which is, of course, his overwhelming concern."

"Of course," Lilibet said, but there was a note of sarcasm in her tone. "I understand my son is determined to marry for the good of Castellane, as I myself was determined to make an advantageous marriage for my country. Such dreams I had then." She glanced over at the North Tower, her eyes narrowed. "But dreams are flimsy things. One cannot build on them." She turned back to Kel. "You said Conor was with Mayesh? Where are they meeting?"

"In the Armory. The Solstice Ball is only a short time away—"

But Lilibet was already flouncing off, her skirts swirling determinedly. Kel shook his head and turned his steps toward the West Gate.

Twilight was falling—the kind of twilight in which the heat of the day seemed trapped under the oncoming shadow of night. The grass of the Palace lawns was dry and crisp under Kel's boots as he made his way to the place he'd agreed to meet Anjelica and Kurame.

The West Gate of the Palace was a postern gate, rarely used, meant to be hidden in the castle's fortifications. Anjelica's gray carriage was already there, inside the walls, when Kel arrived. Only one guard seemed to be on duty: Benaset, who was leaning against the castle wall and greeted Kel with interest. "Her Highness of Kutani is waiting for you," he said, jerking his chin toward the carriage. "Said something about wanting to see the city at night—the Broken Market and such. Is the Prince meant to be joining you?"

Kel smiled easily at Benaset. To be able to smile past his nerves was one of the first things he'd learned in the Palace; now he bent the talent toward reassuring Benaset that there was nothing interesting going on here. "Conor has obligations, alas," he said. "Her Highness needed a guide, and he asked me to step in for him." He pitched his voice low, confidential. "He's been too busy lately—he's worried she'll be bored."

Benaset grinned. "Woman like that probably gets bored easily," he said, and pushed the gate open. Kel hurried over to the carriage, where Kurame was perched in the driver's seat. The fading sun winked off a pair of jeweled spectacles as he greeted Kel with a nod.

The carriage door swung open; Kel stepped inside, sitting down across from Anjelica. A moment later, the carriage started to move, bumping over several large potholes as they rolled through the gate and outside onto the Hill.

"You had no trouble getting away, then?" Anjelica said. She was dressed as plainly as Kel had ever seen her, in severe black, her hair braided close to her head. She wore no jewelry save a silver band on her right hand, set with a scarlet stone. "And you know where we're going? The meeting is on Castle Street—"

She's nervous, Kel thought. Oddly, the thought eased some of his own tension. Anjelica always seemed so poised, it had not occurred to him she could *be* nervous. It meant that she was more desperate than she had let on, and Kel understood being desperate—far more than she could guess.

Kel glanced out the window. They were making their way down the Hill, and the city was spread out before them, its edges softened by twilight. Heat seemed to rise from it, a shimmer in the air.

"I know Castle Street," he said. "And yes, I had no trouble getting away. I have done things without the permission of the Palace before, you know."

"I expect you have." She twisted the ring on her hand. "But I did nearly blackmail you into this."

"I question your use of the word *nearly*," Kel said, but he smiled a little, to take the sting from it. "That's a pretty ring."

She stopped twisting it, looking a little surprised. "It was a gift from Conor. I told him that he need not give me gifts, but he clearly does what he likes. He has given me a fine pair of gloves, though gloves are something I have never needed or worn before. Also a golden headdress for Sedai, and jeweled spectacles for Kurame, as well as for Kito and Isam, although they don't wear spectacles."

"This is the first time someone has complained to me about Conor doing too many kind and thoughtful things for them."

They had reached the city and were wending their way through the narrow streets below the Hill. "You say that," Anjelica said slowly, "but I find Conor is not at all the way he was painted. I was told he was a wastrel, that he lived his life for pleasure, for drinking and gambling, for bedding anyone who caught his fancy. That he was irresponsible and up to his ears in debt. Instead I find him almost grimly responsible. He is almost always in the library or closeted with his advisers or his father. And when I catch a glimpse of him, when he thinks no one is looking, he seems so . . . *sad*."

Kel, too, had seen that sadness, for all that Conor explained it away as weariness or frustration. How strange that Anjelica saw it, too—though he took a moment to thank the Gods that she did not seem to suspect anything unusual about the King.

Kel said, "He has changed since the Shining Gallery. And there are reasons for it."

"I did not realize how responsible he holds himself for the death of the little Princess."

They had turned off the Ruta Magna, down Castle Street, so named for the view of Marivent from its winding path. Castle Street resembled a byway in the Maze—narrow and ancient, with plaster-fronted buildings leaning tipsily together. It was not a wealthy area, but those who lived there clearly cared for their homes and shops. It was spotless and neat, with colorful signs hung above lively public houses and restaurants.

Kel opened the carriage door, and he and Anjelica climbed out into the street. This was the neighborhood where immigrants from Kutani had settled, and like Yulan Road, it carried the scents and color of a land far away. Mixed with the smell of the nearby harbor was the tangy scent of spices: warm cumin and cardamom, hot pepper and roasting cinnamon.

The address she had given Kel turned out to be a plaster-fronted teahouse painted a cheerful shade of turquoise. The sign hanging above it proclaimed it *Naali Canaali*, which Kel was fairly certain meant "The Golden Light."

Kurame waited with the carriage while Kel and Anjelica approached; Anjelica had covered her head with a white shawl that partially hid her distinctive face. Inside the teahouse, a young woman in the traditional black-and-white *geya* of Spice Town greeted Anjelica and Kel, then led them through a room scented with *patoun* where Kutani sailors, missing home, crowded around tables loaded with pots of tea and plates of buttery, flaky flatbread. Most seemed happy to be there, save for a pale man with a viciously scarred face, who sat alone, glaring at his tea as if it had insulted him.

Anjelica kept her head down, but no one really took note of either her or Kel. Kel wished he had told her: Half of disguise was expectation. No one here expected to see the Princess, no one was looking for her here, and so no one would see her.

The young woman led them outside, into a small walled garden with a flame tree growing in its center. It was empty except for a circular stone table at which a tea service for three people had already been laid; clearly Kel had not been expected—in more ways than one, for the two people at the table were the Ragpicker King and Ji-An.

Kel stood frozen in place. He was vaguely aware that the young woman who had brought them to the garden had returned to the teahouse; he was even more aware that Ji-An was staring at him, her eyes wide. Andreyen, of course, was expressionless, his long pale hands folded atop his cane as usual. His eerie green gaze swept over Kel with studied indifference.

Through the rushing in his ears, Kel saw Anjelica step forward, drawing off her shawl. Her long braids fell down around her shoulders as she said, "Greetings, *namimi keyami*. I am Anjelica Iruvai. With me is my guard, Kel Anjuman of Marakand."

Ji-An looked as if she desperately wanted to say something, but Andreyen was stepping on her foot. Smoothly, he replied, "Welcome, *Ayakemi*. And Kel Anjuman. The Prince's cousin. I have heard of you." He gestured to two empty seats at the table. "Come. Join us."

As Kel and Anjelica took their seats, the young woman in the black-and-white *geya* returned, carrying a tray with a samovar. Kel was grateful for the small ritual of the tea service, as it gave him a chance to catch his breath.

Anjelica clearly had no idea he knew the Ragpicker King; otherwise she would never have asked him to accompany her here. The spies of Kutani had not been as thorough as that. And Anjelica had no reason to be loyal to Kel particularly; if she discovered he knew Andreyen, and knew him well, she might see it as a betrayal of Conor. She might even tell Conor—though she would be revealing her own secret if she did.

Still. It was clear Andreyen wished to preserve the fiction that they had never met. Kel could only silently agree that, of all the courses of action open to them at the moment, this seemed the wisest.

Having served the tea in dark-blue glasses, the young woman left them alone again in the courtyard. The last light had washed out of the sky and the stars were beginning to appear overhead. Kel picked up a glass of tea, welcoming the burn of heat against his hand. It was something to concentrate on outside his own agitation.

"I was all astonishment," said Andreyen, addressing Anjelica, "when I received your message. It is not every day I hear from royalty."

Kel nearly choked on his tea. It was heavily sugared, and spiced with cinnamon, cloves, and cardamom. Glancing over the rim of his glass, he saw Ji-An mouth something at him but couldn't read her lips. He glared at her: *Stop it.*

"They say that in Castellane, there is a King on the Hill and a King in the City," said Anjelica in her musical voice. "Only the very shortsighted would take an interest in merely one."

Andreyen raised his tea glass to her. "Although," he said, "one of them will be your father-in-law, whereas I am only an ordinary criminal who has been blessed with extraordinary luck."

"I hope that luck will help me now. Do you know the pirate Laurent Aden?"

Ji-An shot a surprised look at Kel, who gazed back at her with a bland smile.

"Ah, yes," said Andreyen. "An up-and-coming young man, building his empire."

"An empire of piracy and theft," said Anjelica tightly. "He is a man with no scruples."

"Scruples can be expensive," said Ji-An.

Anjelica ignored this. "I have been told that if anyone can reach him, the Ragpicker King can. I need to get a message to him, in hopes that he will meet with me."

"I cannot imagine," said Andreyen, "that the Palace would be too complacent to hear that you are communicating with a former lover who is now hiding out in a sea cave along our coast."

Anjelica flushed. "Not a lover. A *suitor*."

"Regardless." Andreyen spun his cane thoughtfully. "He is a criminal. For a Princess to communicate with him would be alarming to the Aurelians. What matters to those like the Aurelians is loyalty. For you to plan in secret . . ." He regarded her kindly. "Forget Aden. Forget whatever hold over you he may have. You will be Queen of Castellane soon enough. He cannot touch you."

"Aden was never my lover," said Anjelica, her voice shaking. "But there was a time when I believed myself in love with him. I wrote him letters—the kind of letters that would be disastrous in the wrong hands. It was foolish, and he is threatening now that if I do not return to him, he will have those sent to all the nobles on the Hill. It will be an awful scandal, and the Aurelians will be pressured to end their alliance with my family. But my parents will never permit that—they will not now find a better position for me than

Queen of Castellane—and it could result in conflict between our countries, worse than the one you have with Sarthe. For there is no payment that could make it go away."

The Ragpicker King said nothing. Kel was aware of his quick mind working away, his thoughts hidden behind his bland expression.

"Aden wants to cause trouble," Kel said. "The kind of trouble that is bad for the Aurelians and for Castellane. And I have always been told that you care what happens to Castellane."

Andreyen made a thoughtful noise. "Imagine I assisted you with this, Princess. What would your plan be? Shall you beg for your letters back? Men like Aden are not known for their mercy."

"There will be no begging. I intend to offer him money—a fair exchange of gold for what he has."

"And after you have paid him, do you think you will still be able to afford my fee? Because it will not be low."

Kel shot a glare at Andreyen, who ignored it. Could the man really not understand the importance here? The political danger to the Aurelians?

"I had hoped," said Anjelica, "to pay you with information. Information about Prosper Beck."

Kel jerked in surprise and almost spilled his tea. He was aware that both Ji-An and the Ragpicker King were staring at him with a question in their eyes: *Did you know this was what she was going to say?*

"Prosper Beck?" Kel said harshly. "How would you know anything about Prosper Beck?"

Anjelica looked at him in surprise. "You've heard of Prosper Beck?"

"Everyone's heard of Prosper Beck," said Ji-An; it wasn't true, but perhaps Anjelica would not know that. "And everyone knows he's gone."

"Prosper Beck is not gone," Anjelica said calmly. "Prosper Beck has returned to Castellane. There are rumors he is preparing for a fight. Perhaps with you."

Andreyen's green eyes had darkened. "If you are telling lies right now to get your way, Princess, let me make one thing understood. That is not a safe path to tread. Not with me."

He did not raise his voice or change his expression, yet there was something in the way he spoke that reminded Kel that Andreyen was more than the man who was kind to Ji-An and Merren and enjoyed his roof garden. Here was a man who had killed people and done it without a thought.

"There is no lie," said Anjelica. She had placed her hands in her lap; Kel could see they were clasped together tightly. "There is a warehouse, on Arsenal Road in the Maze. One with a blacked-out door. It claims it is for tea storage, but you will find it filled with trunks of hoarded weapons."

"How do you know all this?" said Kel. "Kutani spywork?"

"My country's spywork is excellent," Anjelica conceded. "But I say no more than this until after you"—she glanced at Andreyen—"have made contact with Aden for me."

Andreyen's eyes were chips of green ice. Ji-An rose to her feet. She had not touched her spiced tea. "I'll go to the Key now. Check the warehouse."

"That seems trivial work for such a skilled assassin," said Anjelica.

"I don't believe I introduced my associate," said Andreyen. The words were calm, but he had about him the aura of a waiting cat, its eyes narrowed, its tail swishing.

"You are Kang Ji-An, are you not?" Anjelica said. "Because of you, a whole family in Geumseong lies dead."

Ji-An and Andreyen exchanged a look. *You had better be careful, Anjelica,* Kel thought. He knew she was trying to show that she was a force to be reckoned with; that she knew far more than they guessed. But there was such a thing as knowing too much. "A whole family, you say?" said Ji-An, drawing on her gloves. She flexed her fingers. "That does not sound like assassination. That is a slaughter."

"But you did it for the girl you loved," said Anjelica. "And it is noble to do such things for love."

Ji-An stared; her face was very pale. The Ragpicker King rose to his feet. "There is no need for any more discussion," he said. "If your story about the warehouse proves true, *Ayakemi*, you can expect to hear from me regarding Aden. Until then, tread carefully. A man who blackmails for money is one thing. A man who blackmails for love is far more dangerous."

Lin sat cross-legged at the small table in her kitchen, her books and papers spread out before her. She had taken her books back from Mariam that afternoon, and to her amusement, she discovered that she now had Mariam's notes, which were scribbled in the margins of the ancient tomes in differently colored pencil.

Mariam, it seemed, had chiefly been interested in the great doings of the Sorcerer-Kings, ranging from the impossibly grandiose (one Sorcerer-King had been irritated that a mountain range blocked his view of the sea, so had relocated the entire range to what was now Marakand) to the slightly ridiculous (a Sorcerer-Queen who had magicked up ten thousand cats to be the attendants at her wedding). But Mariam had made other, more useful notes as well. She had found a section in a book that Lin had nearly discarded out of hand that described how Source-Stones were sealed to their owners. *The magician and the stone must then travel together to the caves of Sulemon, where, having passed the Halls of Hewn Stone, the gem must be cleansed in the Place of Bitter Water before it being bound unto the Sorcerer whose power it will hold.*

Perhaps that was the problem, she thought. Perhaps it was that her stone had not been bound to her. But how to accomplish such a binding? Surely all these places had been lost in the Sundering.

Lin was pulled from her grim thoughts by a knock on the door. Surely Mayesh or Mariam, she thought, but when she threw the front door open, she found Aron Benjudah standing on her doorstep. It was dark outside, the moon half hidden behind clouds. Even in the dimness, though, she could see that he looked weary. He wore his Rhadanite trader clothes of coarse linen, and the shadows were plain below his eyes.

"Exilarch," Lin said, "I did not expect to see you again so soon."

"You asked me to do a favor for you, and I have done it." He drew a piece of paper from his jacket. "Here is the translation you asked for."

Lin took the paper from him. "Thank you."

He looked at her with a half smile. "Aren't you going to read it?"

Lin gritted her teeth. She had hoped that if she did not open the paper immediately, Aron would take the hint and go away, but apparently Exilarchs were not ones to take hints. Slowly, she unfolded the paper. It was, as she'd expected, a list of ingredients, printed in neat and careful handwriting. As she scanned the list, she felt a sense of relief. There was nothing here she'd never heard of, nothing that would be impossible to get.

"It seems to be some sort of remedy," said Aron, "but not an Ashkar one. I am not a healer, but"—he tapped his finger on the page—"I do know yellow poppy is a sedative. On the Gold Roads, healers give it to the injured in the hope that they will remain unconscious through their treatment, regardless of how painful it may be. But it is a clumsy drug, and easy to give too much. We Askhar have access to better sedatives than this."

A clumsy drug. He was right, but what could she say, besides assuring him she had no intention of giving this medicine to anyone? But that, of course, was not true. "Might I ask you a question?" she said instead.

"You are a prospective Goddess," he said dryly. "Ask what you like."

"Have you heard of something called the Place of Bitter Water?"

The effect of her words shocked her. His eyes went wide, and he took a half step back, almost as if she had pushed him. "Who told you to ask me that?" he asked harshly. "Was it Mayesh?"

"Of course not," Lin said. "The name appeared in a book I took from the Shulamat. It was in a history of the Sorcerer-Kings. But I thought perhaps"—she looked at him closely—"it was just a story. Not real."

He seemed to relax minutely. "There is nothing you are not curious about, is there?" he said. "Yes, there was such a place, once. It lay on the border of what was once Aram, deep underground."

"Was it destroyed in the Sundering?"

He shrugged. "Much was destroyed in those days. Much was lost and much was hidden, but some things stay hidden for good reason."

"You speak in riddles," she complained. He was already turning to go, but now he paused on the lowest step of her house and glanced back over his shoulder.

"Then puzzle me out," he said, and was gone, into the shadows.

"That is not at all what I thought the Ragpicker King would be like," Anjelica said as the carriage rattled away from Castle Street. She sat across from Kel with her hands folded in her lap like a young girl's. Her eyes were bright, her cheeks flushed. It had been an exciting meeting, Kel supposed, looked at from a certain perspective. He had not found it exciting himself; he had spent most of the time wanting to throw up.

"Prosper Beck," Kel said sharply. "How do you know so much about Prosper Beck?"

She shook her head. "I am grateful to you for helping me, Sword Catcher. But I cannot tell you."

"You owe me that," he snapped. "You should have told me you intended to bribe Andreyen Morettus by dangling Prosper Beck in front of him. Are you mad? To insert yourself into the games played between violent criminals—"

"I did not think *you* would know who Prosper Beck was." Anjelica sounded stung. They were wending their way down the Ruta Magna now, returning to the Hill.

"A Sword Catcher must know many things." Technically true, Kel thought. He hoped he didn't sound pompous. "And you are playing a game with very dangerous men. Aden among them."

"I am doing what I have to do." In the dimness of the carriage, he sensed her looking at him. "But I should have told you more. Warned you. Forgive me. I did wrong."

Despite himself, Kel softened. An apology from royalty was a rare thing, as he had cause to know. Although he still wondered how she had gathered information about Prosper Beck. Kutani spywork *was* famous, and perhaps that was all it was, but it bothered him nonetheless—especially as he knew perfectly well that if he asked her, she wouldn't tell him. Their friendship, such as it was, did not extend that far.

Anjelica glanced out the window. "Is something going on? A festival?"

Kel did not need to look; he could see the light from the naphtha beacons illuminating the inside of the carriage. "It is the Broken Market. Anything can be sold here as long as it is flawed and in need of repair."

"But why would anyone want such broken things?"

"Some people enjoy the act of repair," said Kel. "In Zipangu, they mend broken pottery with melted gold, so that the shattered object is more beautiful when put back together. And some, I would guess, merely wish to be assured that nothing is ever ruined beyond recovery."

"I would prefer it was never broken in the first place," said Anjelica, after a long pause. She leaned forward. "The Ragpicker King," she said. "Is that what *you* thought he would be like? You are the one who grew up in Castellane, hearing stories and legends of Gentleman Death."

"He is just what I expected," Kel said lightly. "Save that he did not fly in on magpie wings or dissolve into shadow at the conclusion of our meeting. No"—he added, as they rolled through the Broken Market—"the one who surprised me was you."

She smiled faintly at that. "I like knowing things. And it does get dull being one of ten daughters in a palace."

"I see. One must turn to espionage to amuse oneself," Kel said. He looked at her steadily. "I've met him, you know. Prosper Beck."

A look flashed across her face—real astonishment—just as the carriage came to a stop, lurching slightly as it bumped into a pothole. The door swung open—Kurame, ready to help his sister down from the carriage. His jeweled spectacles gleamed like the carapaces of rainbow beetles, and Kel could not help but be amused, knowing they were a gift from Conor.

They went back into Marivent through the postern gate, all three of them silent. As they passed Benaset, who tipped a polite nod, Kel wondered if he ought to escort Anjelica back to her rooms. It would be the courteous thing to do, but nothing about the night so far had been normal, and she might prefer to be alone with her brother.

In the end, his musings were irrelevant. After they walked through the archway into the garden of the Castel Mitat, Kel saw Conor, sitting alone at the edge of the tiled fountain. Above him was a darkened sundial, a verse from an old song etched onto its face: ALAS, HOW MUCH I THOUGHT I KNEW OF LOVE, AND YET HOW LITTLE I KNOW.

He looked up at their approach and smiled as his eyes met Kel's. "I wondered where you'd gone," he said. "My best friend *and* my bride-to-be."

And Kurame, Kel thought, but when he looked around, Kurame had vanished, slipping into the shadows of the night as the Bloodguard seemed trained to do.

Conor looked woeful. "I was so lonely I considered drowning myself in this fountain, but the water is full of frogs."

"Kellian wished to show me the famous Broken Market," said Anjelica, settling herself onto the edge of the fountain beside Conor. "Your city is very lovely at night. We also looked at the Night Garden," she added. "Your mother has excellent taste in flowers."

"I'm delighted to hear it," said Conor, "as she believes you do not enjoy her taste in anything else. Don't worry; I don't, either."

Anjelica laughed. It seemed like a real laugh—unstudied, bright as silver.

"I saw Lilibet earlier, Con," said Kel. "She seemed annoyed you and Mayesh were discussing the Solstice Ball without her there."

"Oh, I know." Conor yawned, stretching his lean body. His hair was a mess, as if he'd been sleeping on his desk again. Kel felt that familiar sharp pain that he knew was love mixed with remorse. For how badly he wanted to protect Conor. For the secrets he was keeping.

He listened with only half an ear bent to the conversation as Conor explained the Solstice Ball to Anjelica—a yearly celebration of the reign of Aurelian. That it was approaching in a short time, and Conor felt Anjelica should have a hand in the festivities.

Kel wondered if he should go, slip away as Kurame had done. Leave Conor alone with Anjelica. They seemed to be getting along well; surely that should be encouraged?

"It's a masquerade, is it not?" Anjelica said. "Everyone in costume."

"And every year a theme." Conor nodded. "Last year, the theme was the stars and planets. The year before that . . . ?"

He turned to Kel, a question in his eyes.

"It was tales of the Gods," said Kel. "Montfaucon came dressed as Aigon, God of the sea, and ruined all the carpets."

Conor turned to Anjelica. "My mother will already have chosen the food and decorations. But I think it would be suitable for you to choose the theme for the costumes, my lady."

Anjelica clapped her hands together in delight. "Beasts," she said promptly. "Each person to mask themselves as the animal they feel they resemble most."

"Resemble? I thought masks were supposed to hide who you are," said Kel.

"On the contrary, one's choice of disguise reveals a great deal," Anjelica said. Her expression was unchanged, but Kel thought he could hear the smile in her voice. "Kellian, you could be a chameleon, that creature which disguises itself so well as others. And you, my lord"—she turned to Conor—"you would be a lion, for you are Castellane."

"And you, *Ayakemi*?" said Conor.

"You will have to wait and see." Smiling, Anjelica got to her feet. To Kel's surprise, she leaned in and kissed Conor on the cheek. "It is kind of you," she said, "to think of something for me to do."

She turned and walked away in the direction of the Castel Pichon. A blue-tinged moon had risen, and her pale-white shawl gleamed under the light. As Kel watched, he saw Kurame emerge from the darkness, a fluid shadow, to join his sister.

"Sit with me," Conor said, interrupting Kel's reverie. He had lain down on the broad fountain's edge and was looking up at the sky. "I find I am in an oddly good mood. Let us drink together and count the stars."

Kel did as Conor had asked. He leaned back on his hands, braced against the tile, and gazed up at the sky. The moon seemed to be playing a child's game with the clouds, darting in and out from behind them, never completely seen.

"Is there a reason for this good mood?" Kel asked.

Conor folded his arms behind his head. One day, Kel thought; one day he and Conor would be able to do this again—to lie side by side, looking up at the stars they had known since they were children—without this distance between them, without this space he could not define or name. "I feel as a sailor must," Conor said, "when he has been out at sea for a long time, and now he can finally see the land."

Kel looked down at his Prince. Conor's eyes were unfocused, as if he were not looking at the sky at all, but past it, at something else. "Did you find what you were looking for in the library the other night?" Kel asked.

"You know, I did," Conor said. "I truly think I did."

Lin slept restlessly that night, and dreamed strange dreams. While she did not dream about the man who burned everything he touched, she did dream of burned hills and valleys, land scorched clean by charring heat.

She woke later than usual and put on a dress of plain gray cambric, with the intention of visiting the Etse Kebeth. She could not help but feel that she had been neglecting Mariam, who was overdue for another healing session. Between the issue of the King's medicine and her own worry over her upcoming testing, she fretted that she had not been as diligent in her oversight of Mariam's condition as she should have been. And was not Mariam's health the whole point of everything, really?

She laced herself into a white pinafore to keep away the dirt, and left her bedroom, still brushing her hair. She ought to eat something, too, though she could perhaps prevail upon Chana to let her raid the kitchen at the Etse Kebeth—

"Good morning, Linnet."

She nearly shrieked. Her grandfather was seated at her kitchen table, a thin stream of gray smoke rising from the pipe in his mouth. She narrowed her eyes at him. How had he gotten in? Surely he was too old to have begun a new career as a housebreaker.

"*Zai*," she said, pointing her hairbrush at him accusingly. "You nearly scared me to death! How did you get in here?"

He did not reply, which hardly surprised her. Out of his Counselor's robes, in an ordinary tunic and trousers, he looked older, but the eyes that regarded her beneath bushy brows were as bright and perceptive as always.

"I have a message for you," he said. "From Prince Conor."

He slid a folded piece of paper across the table. Lin didn't ask him if he'd read it; of course he had.

"Did the Prince ask you to deliver it to me?" she asked, picking it up. She could not help but recall what the Prince had said to her: *Not all messengers can be trusted.* Had he trusted the Counselor?

"No," Mayesh said shortly.

Lin knew she could press him on the point; she also knew it would accomplish nothing if she did. Unfolding the paper, she read the message, written in a ridiculously elegant hand:

The Palace will be nearly empty this Tearsday. Come to Valerian Square at noon. A carriage will bring you from the square to Marivent. You know what is required of you there.

The Prince had signed it with a string of initials. His full royal name, no doubt, whatever it might be. Lin glanced up from the paper to find Mayesh exhaling *patoun* smoke in a thick cloud. He said, "Three days from now, in the main square, the Hierophant of Aigon will give his blessing to Prince Conor and his betrothed, Anjelica Iruvai of Kutani."

Ah. Lin had known the ceremony was coming, as everyone in Castellane did. It was part of the long march of festivals, processions, and ritual protocols that preceded a royal marriage. She had not known it was this soon.

She wondered why Prince Conor wanted her in the square. It made sense to bring her to the Palace when it would be nearly emptied out, everyone down in the city. But surely it would be easier to send a carriage directly to the Sault?

"Why is Conor bringing you to the Palace?" Mayesh said quietly. "What does he expect you to do there?"

"So you *did* read the note," Lin said accusingly.

"Either way, you have confirmed my suspicions," he said. "I am not a fool, Lin, and I have eyes everywhere at Marivent. I know Conor had you brought to the library on the night of the banquet. Why? What does he mean about what is *required* of you?"

Lin hesitated. She could not think of a lie he couldn't check easily. He knew too much about the Palace, about the royal family. More than they knew themselves.

She took a deep breath. The Prince had told her not to speak of this to anyone. But there was no way around telling her grandfather something: He would dig and dig at it otherwise, like a dog trying to find a bone buried in a garden. "I cannot say," she told him. "The Prince placed me under a royal order."

Mayesh stared, his pipe halfway to his mouth. "You're not serious."

"I would not lie," Lin said, "about such a thing."

"Then this is about his father." Mayesh stood up abruptly. He paced to the window, staring out at the modest view of the Sault, the cobblestoned street stretching down and away, toward the gates.

"I cannot tell you," Lin said, feeling wretched. "It is not that I do not want to. I have questions; you may know the answers. But I *cannot*."

"I do not like this." Mayesh's pipe was burning away between his fingers; he seemed to have forgotten it was there. "Conor has changed, you know. Since first you met him, when Kel was injured."

"So I've heard," Lin said dryly. "Mostly from Kel."

"He isn't wrong. And yet—how much can a man truly change, when he has only ever been raised to be one kind of person?" Mayesh's pipe had gone out; he tossed it impatiently onto the table. "In the past, his plans have led to disaster. I do not want him to drag you into disaster with him."

"There is only so much I can tell you, *zai*." She could not help but wonder. The worry in his voice sounded real. But that didn't mean his concern was for her, or only her. He might also be concerned for Castellane, for the alliance with Kutani, for the nobles on the Hill and their thoughts about their Prince . . .

Lin sighed. "I can tell you that Con—that Prince Conor has not asked me to do anything I would not have been willing to do anyway, had he not placed me under an order."

"Recall what our sages say. *Live by the Laws, do not die by them.* You must put your own safety first, Lin." When she did not reply, he let out an irritated breath, and said, "Then why did he place you under an order at all?"

"He believes I don't like him," Lin said, and saw her grandfather raise an eyebrow. "I don't think he knows what to do with such a thing. He's never been around anyone who didn't at least have to *pretend* to like him. He has no idea how to ask someone to help him just for the sake of helping him—not because they want something else from him as well."

A look close to amusement flickered across Mayesh's face. "I see you know our Prince better than I thought. Perhaps better than he knows himself." He picked up the note from the table. "He wants you in Valerian Square during the blessing," he said. "Very well. Come, and bring Mariam with you. She'll enjoy the pomp and circumstance of it all. I will make sure for her sake," he added, refolding the note, "that you have a good view."

Jerrod

Jerrod,

*I've considered your warning, and I've decided you're right.
Though it seemed expedient to keep a certain person around, the
danger now outweighs the potential benefit. Please read the following list of instructions carefully, then do what you must do. I
trust you will act with all speed.*

Beck

CHAPTER FOURTEEN

A ndreyen isn't pleased with you, you know," Ji-An said.

"Really?" Kel peered out at the harbor. "Did he tell you that?"

He had to admit that it was a good night for sailing to Tyndaris, despite his general pessimistic mood. The wind was still, and there was little chop to the harbor water. The moon flashed out only occasionally behind a thick scrim of clouds, allowing for a darkness that hid their movements as he, Merren, Jerrod, and Ji-An clustered at the edge of a narrow dock.

As Andreyen had promised, a small skiff waited for them there. (It seemed he maintained a fleet of shallow, quick-moving boats with which smuggled goods were ferried from ships moored far out at sea to the caves along the coastline where pirates like Laurent Aden lurked in wait.)

Ji-An shot Kel an irritable look before scrambling into the boat. Kel, Jerrod, and Merren followed suit.

The skiff was manned by two gruff oarsmen in worn oilcloth who looked as if they'd much rather be knocking back pints at one of the lighted taverns along the Key. But they were Andreyen's men, polite enough as Kel and the others settled themselves in the boat and they pushed off from the shore.

They skimmed across the water, silent save for the rhythmic slap of the oars. The tide was at its lowest, and the drowned island of Tyndaris rose from the water near the harbor mouth, crowned by jagged temple ruins whose outlines stood out starkly against the cloudy sky.

Merren and Jerrod sat in the bow, their heads close together. Kel wondered what they were discussing, but not for long. Ji-An, frowning, plonked herself down on a seat facing him. "Didn't you hear what I said on shore?" she asked, keeping her voice low. "The Ragpicker King—"

"Isn't pleased with me, yes." Kel sighed. "I heard you. I was actually hoping for a chance to talk to him tonight. I didn't realize he wouldn't be with us."

Ji-An turned to look at the oarsmen, but neither seemed to be paying any attention to the conversation in the boat. Turning back to Kel, she said, "Well, what did you *expect*? Turning up like that yesterday with the Kutani Princess, not warning either of us what she wanted, or even that you'd be with her—"

"I didn't *know*." Kel stretched out his legs. He was wearing all black, like the rest of them, and had both his boot daggers, his wrist knives, and a blade strapped at his waist. "All she told me was that she had a meeting and required me to guide her around Castellane."

"Hmph." There was a faint green tinge to the moon tonight; it lent an eerie cast to Ji-An's eyes. "And why does a Princess require contact with a criminal? She's a tricky one, Anjelica Iruvai. I'm not sure how much you should trust her."

"I'll keep that in mind," Kel said. He saw that Merren was blinking around in some wonder; they had reached deeper water, where the tallships were anchored. The great craft rose straight up from the water, dwarfing the tiny skiff. It was as if they were in a dark valley with mountains rising on either side.

Only, these mountains were inhabited. Lights glowed from the ships, and the sound of voices traveled across the waves. The oarsmen rowed close to the ships' sides, doing their best to avoid being seen.

There was something about the vastness of it all that struck Kel with a peculiar loneliness. He had spent all his life in a city, a place where he was rarely more than a few steps from another human being. But the sea was immeasurable. Once you left the harbor, a vast empty plain of bitter water stretched all the way to Kutani, unfriendly as a scorching desert.

"Was Anjelica correct about the weapons cache? In the warehouse?" Kel asked.

"Yes," Ji-An answered reluctantly. "She was. I suppose Andreyen will do as she asked and send word for Aden. He probably already has."

"So she was right about Prosper Beck. He's come back."

Ji-An pressed her lips together tightly. "It seems so."

She almost sounded weary, in a way that was very unlike her. Kel wanted to ask her more—what Andreyen thought of Prosper Beck's return, what Beck might want—but at that moment, the skiff darted out from between the tallships and he saw Tyndaris, rising out of the water.

From the shore, the drowned island had always seemed to shine, a fragment of broken quartz jutting from the waves. Up close, Kel could see that the glow came from the Chapel of a Thousand Doors. The temple columns were the only part of Tyndaris that never sank below the water, and the white marble pillars gleamed like polished bone. Most of its spires had broken, but a few still reached toward the moon like fleshless fingers.

The rest of the island, the earth it sat atop, was a mass of wet dirt and crumbled ruins, now thickly overgrown with blackish-green seaweed. Barnacles clung to the island's sides; what Kel had at a distance taken for trees were in fact branching towers of coral, from which hung damp clusters of sea-moss.

One of the oarsmen muttered; the other made the sign of Aigon's Wheel, a circle over the center of his chest, meant to ward off bad luck. Kel could not blame them, even as they drew closer to the island. There was something forbidding about a place that spent most of its life sunk into an alien atmosphere, where sharks and crocodiles roamed around its ruins, and the sun did not reach.

The skiff came to a halt in a foot or so of brackish water. It seemed they could go no closer to the island without grounding the boat. The oarsmen indicated a set of stone stairs cut into the island's side; that was, they explained, the only way up to the chapel.

"How long before the tide rises?" Kel asked, swinging himself out of the boat. He could feel the cold of the seawater even through the leather of his high boots.

"An hour, maybe," said the elder oarsman, a man whose pale-gray hair stuck out like hay from beneath a flat cap. "It'll take a while to cover the island, but you want to get away well before that. We'll be waiting here for you as long as we can. But if we have to"—he shrugged—"we'll leave you here."

The four of them were all silent as they trudged through the shallow water to the foot of the mossy steps. Kel suspected they were all imagining the same thing: what it would be like to be trapped on Tyndaris as the tide rose until only the very tops of the temple pillars were visible above the water. Until you floated among the ruins, waiting for a green death—by drowning or crocodile—to claim you.

Ji-An reached the steps first. She hopped up, her bow in one hand; her quiver was slung over her back. Jerrod and Merren followed, and Kel came last. When he set his foot down upon the first step, tiny pinkish crabs scattered.

The stairs wound up through what had once likely been a forest and was now a stepped path lined by dead trees whipped to driftwood by years of sun and salt water. It was necessary to step carefully: Not only was the stone slippery, but cracks in the steps held small tide pools in which flashed starfish and hermit crabs.

The sea fell away below them as they ascended. Kel took comfort in the sight of the skiff, a bright lantern-lit dot out on the water. The sea seemed to sigh and breathe and wind about the island like a living thing. By the time they reached the peak of the island, their little boat had vanished below an overhang of rock.

The vegetation changed swiftly, between one step and another. Now there was seagrass and a few hardy bushes, starred here and there with flowers. The steps became a neat path that cut across the top of the island to the Chapel of a Thousand Doors.

"Funny," Merren said as they approached. It was the first thing any of them had said since they'd set foot on the island. "It doesn't actually have *any* doors."

"Hard to have doors without walls," Kel said.

"That's a little unfair," said Jerrod. "There's *one* wall."

Indeed, a rectangular marble floor, lined with marble pillars, was nearly all that was left of the place. The roof the pillars had once supported was long gone, and all but one wall had collapsed. The whole place had likely once been brightly painted. Here and there, faded flecks of color still clung. A well-preserved mosaic still decorated the single wall, showing Aigon in full glory, his blue-green hair and beard flowing. Before him knelt a man presenting him with a sword—the signal of surrender. The man was a Sorcerer-King; one could tell by the pattern of black tiles above his head. A stone glowed in the hilt of the sword, represented by a cluster of golden tesserae.

"*Look.*" Ji-An pointed, and Kel realized why he was able to see the mosaic so clearly. A small storm-lantern hung from a hook in the wall over the ruins of the altar. A flame burned steadily inside it, which meant . . .

"Someone's already here," Kel said in a low voice. He ducked behind a copse of leafless pine, and the others followed.

They had only been waiting for perhaps ten minutes when the sound of footsteps became audible, boots on stone, and then a low clamor of voices. A moment later, Lady Alleyne appeared, tramping through the scrub toward the temple where the lantern hung, a beacon indicating a meeting place.

Liorada was not alone. To Kel's shock, at her side was a large man dressed in black, a gleaming pendant, like a gaudy lamp, glowing around his neck. Kel heard Jerrod's breath hiss out in surprise.

"*Gremont*," he whispered.

"This is absolutely *ridiculous*," Lady Alleyne was fuming. She was swathed in a deep-red velvet cloak, its hem black with dirt and seawater. Her pale hair was dressed high with ruby pins, and the look in her eyes could have melted glass. "Forcing us into a meeting here, in this ridiculous place . . ." She glared down at her shoes, black with mud.

"She must have her reasons," said Gremont, in his gruff voice.

The sound of Gremont's voice made Kel's stomach twist into knots. He heard Merren, beside him, exhale, the breath hissing between his teeth. Kel couldn't blame him; his own hands itched with his desire to strangle Gremont.

"*Reasons*," Lady Alleyne echoed derisively. "She wants to shame me, that's all this is."

The two nobles had reached the temple, and Gremont stepped forward to help her up the cracked steps. Though spiny branches were sticking uncomfortably into Kel's back, he had to admit they had a good view of the temple floor, spread before them like a lighted stage.

Lady Alleyne looked around the ruins of the chapel, her head held high, her lip curled.

"Where are you?" she demanded, her voice pitched to carry. "You commanded me to meet you here. Here I am. Show yourself!"

A shadow swept down from the broken top of the chapel's single wall. Kel thought of a cat leaping, quiet and graceful. And familiar. Even before the shadow landed in the center of the marble floor, silent as if the soles of its shoes were padded, Kel knew exactly who this was.

The Dark Assassin. Who straightened swiftly, like a puppet

snapped upright. The black fabric that covered them head-to-toe shone faintly under the moon's light—a slippery-dark sheen, like the gleam of black powder. Faceless, motionless, the assassin faced Liorada Alleyne, who—for all her posturing to Gremont—took an involuntary, frightened step back.

"Well, fuck," muttered Jerrod. Kel couldn't tell if he was alarmed or impressed. Or perhaps a bit envious.

"That's the assassin," Kel muttered. "The one who killed Raimon. And the Sarthian Princess."

Gremont hadn't changed expression. He watched with his thick arms crossed over his chest as Lady Alleyne drew her dignity back around herself like her velvet cloak. "Good," she said. "You're here. What do you want?"

The assassin's voice was the same gravelly hiss Kel remembered. "I may have called this meeting, Alleyne, but it was you who forced my hand. The message you sent me—"

"I stand by it." Lady Alleyne's voice rose an octave. "This has gone too far. We agreed on a prank, a joke on the Sarthians, not the disaster that was the Shining Gallery. You used that against us, and now you wish us to do even worse."

Us. Kel's whole body tightened. Who was *us*?

"This alliance may have begun in a less-than-ideal manner, Liorada," Gremont said, doing his best to sound soothing. "And I am sure Her Highness here regrets that." He shot a glance at the figure in black—*Her Highness.* Female, then, and royalty. "But think of all you are being offered."

"Offered?" Lady Alleyne's lips twitched. "You have never offered anything to those of us who helped you enact the nightmare in the Shining Gallery—however much we would not have done so if we knew the extent of your plans. We are Charter holders, and you treat us as common criminals." She sniffed. "My own House—though my daughter knows nothing of this—the Gremonts, the Cabrols, the others, all of us have helped you. All we have received in return is your threats to blackmail us by revealing our connections to what you have done."

The Cabrols. The Gremonts. The Alleynes. Kel's head whirled. And there were others, but who?

The dark figure raised her hands to her temples, as if Lady Alleyne were giving her a headache. With a swift movement, she drew away the dark fabric that covered her from her scalp to her neck. Ink-black hair tumbled down around her shoulders, and a pale, intent face was revealed.

It was not a beautiful face, but it was an arresting one. High-arched cheekbones, winged eyebrows, a thin but well-shaped mouth. Hooded eyes, dark as crow feathers. It was a face Kel knew from portraits, though none of them had captured the intensity burning in her dark eyes.

Elsabet Belmany, Crown Princess of Malgasi. The long-ago words of the Malgasi Ambassador echoed in Kel's head. *Perhaps, Prince Conor, instead of our* Milek *Elsabet journeying to Castellane, you could come to us? Elsabet could be your guide to the city.*

He could not imagine the woman standing before him as some kind of placid tour guide. She seemed as if she would be far more at ease burning down towers and bridges than pointing them out as interesting bits of architecture in Favár.

Elsabet chuckled—a low, rich sound. "There is no blackmail in politics, Liorada. Only bargaining. And Artal is right to point out what is being offered to you. Too long have the Aurelians controlled the Charter Families with an eye to their own benefit. We propose a far more equitable division of power."

"Once you have taken the Aurelians out of the game," Liorada said. "That is your proposition?"

"One of your fellow Shining Gallery conspirators there on the Hill is very close to the Prince himself," said Elsabet, her voice just touched by the guttural Malgasi accent. Kel felt himself tense. He knew the others were looking over at him; he could sense Merren's worried gaze. He stayed motionless. "He knows much about the Aurelians. I assure you, theirs is a line that is rotting. They have ceased to be good stewards of this city. The King is mad, the son a wastrel. The Queen is foreign; she should return to her own lands."

"But you intend for the boy to rule," said Artal.

"The people of Castellane will be more willing to accept the new state of things with a familiar face on the throne," said Elsabet. She had raised a hand to her neck, an unconscious gesture; it drew Kel's eye to something that rested in the hollow of her throat. Something that seemed to shine—a necklace, a pendant? "We will soon enough be rid of the mad old man, and the handsome Prince will hold the Lion Scepter. But the real power will be wielded by you, the families. Look what we did for the Cabrols, Liorada. They were ground down, humiliated, and we raised them up in fire. We can do the same for you."

"Those of us loyal to you," said Liorada. "That is what you mean."

Elsabet shrugged gracefully. "For too long, Malgasi and Castellane have been at daggers drawn," she purred. "House Belmany has a chance now to make sure we and the government of Castellane are . . . aligned."

Kel felt the words like cold fingers walking up his spine.

"And there is much we can do to help return tarnished Castellane to her former glory," Elsabet added. "First, the city will be cleansed of the filthy Ashkar. You will see—"

"I think you discount the latest political wrinkle," said Lady Alleyne. "The Prince allies himself with Anjelica Iruvai. Few would dare strike at Kutani."

"I do not fear them." Elsabet threw back her head proudly, and the stone at her neck flashed. It was not a pendant; Kel could see no chain. "When Malgasi controls the Aurelians, no mere army shall stand against us."

"They have ten thousand warships—" Lady Alleyne began.

Elsabet flung out her arm. For a moment, Kel thought it a gesture of exasperation, but it was not that. She stood stock-still, her eyes half closed, her gloved fingers extended. *Black-gloved hands, covered like the hands of the King are covered.*

And at her throat, the stone began to glow. Like a fragment of a star, burning brighter as it fell, its light intensified until Kel could see that it was indeed not a pendant or a necklace. The stone had been inserted under Elsabet's skin and glowed through it, like flame through a lampshade.

"There are other kinds of power, Alleyne, than those that can be bought with gold. Other weapons than blades and powder."

Elsabet uncurled her fingers. A narrow column of fire blazed through the air, striking the temple floor at Lady Alleyne's feet. The marble cracked and splintered.

Lady Alleyne cried out, stumbling back. Artal caught her by the arm as Elsabet brought her hand down in a quick, swooping gesture. Fire burst again from her palm, arrowing up into the sky, a plume of brilliance. The flames spread and scattered, and for a moment, Kel thought he saw them make the shape of a bird with outspread wings.

"Elsabet!" shouted Gremont. "Enough—"

His shout was choked off in a grunt. Kel whipped around to stare. It was easy to see Gremont in the sharp light of Elsabet's fire; he was struggling, his hands flailing at his throat. There was a dark shadow behind him, a flash of something silver against Gremont's neck.

Lady Alleyne screamed.

Gremont fell to his knees, his hands wrapped around his own throat. Blood pulsed between his fingers, and he sank to the ground with a choking gurgle. Behind him stood a figure in a black cloak, the edge of a silver mask glinting from beneath his hood, a scarlet-stained blade in his hand.

"*Jerrod,*" whispered Merren. He looked horror-struck.

Jerrod spun and vanished into the shadows as Gremont's body sprawled bonelessly at Lady Alleyne's feet. With a small shriek of horror, Liorada aimed a kick at Gremont's prone body, causing him to roll onto his back. *He's supposed to be invulnerable*, Kel thought, but Gremont was utterly limp, blood spreading around him in a dark pool.

Lady Alleyne screamed again. This time she picked up her skirts and ran, putting on a burst of speed as she passed within inches of Kel's hiding place.

Elsabet cried out. Liorada was gone, crashing away through the brush, but Elsabet's eyes were fixed on Kel, Ji-An, and Merren: the brilliance of the fire she had conjured had illuminated their hiding place, and now that Elsabet was staring directly at it, it was clear she could see them plainly.

"*Podrot! Siszokti!*" she shouted.

"*Go!*" cried Ji-An, shoving Merren—who had frozen in shock— ahead of her. "Run!"

They ran. As they cut past the temple, more dark figures spilled from the shadows. Elsabet's guards. Kel was in the rear, his throwing dagger in his hand. As he twisted around to hurl it, something caught at his ankle and he nearly fell.

It was Gremont's hand. Kel sank to one knee, staring. Gremont's face was twisted and bloody; he was bone white, and more blood pumped from a wound in his throat as he choked on his last breaths.

"Kel Saren," he gasped. Kel was surprised; it seemed like Gremont's windpipe must not have been cut if he could still speak. He felt sick at the idea that Gremont knew who he really was. But of course he did—he had learned it from the Malgasi. "Help me—" A bubble of blood formed on his lips. "I'll give you anything— money—more than the Prince could ever give you—"

Kel bent down, and for a moment he thought that he saw a spark of relief in Gremont's eyes. He closed his hand around the amulet—which had done Gremont no good at all—and wrenched; it came free, and he held the bloodied jewel in his hand.

"Help me," Gremont gasped again; his voice was weaker now, his eyes beginning to dart and film over. "Please . . ."

"You deserve worse than this," Kel said, almost shocked at the cold remove in his own voice. "You thought you could treat Antonetta as you treat everyone else. You thought she had no one to protect her." He stood up. "You were wrong."

Gremont made a last, choked noise—perhaps a sound of protest, Kel would never know—and went rigid, his blank eyes turned up to the night.

Kel ran. He raced over the uneven ground at top speed, desperate to catch up to the others. He plunged down the ancient stairs as bright pinpoints of light exploded in the darkness all around him. Something whistled through the air, past Kel's left ear; it hurtled into the trunk of a dwarf pine tree, where it blazed like a miniature star.

"*What's going on?*" Merren yelled as Kel caught up to him; Jerrod and Ji-An were there as well, just ahead. Kel shoved the amulet into his pocket, almost tripping as his boot landed in a tide pool with a splash.

"*People are shooting flaming arrows at us!*" Kel shouted back. His boots were skidding on the wet stone. He twisted to the side, trying to right his center of gravity. Ji-An had an arrow in her hand and was struggling to notch it to her bow as she ran.

"I *know* that!" Merren yelled. "It was a rhetorical question!"

"Shut up, the both of you!" called Ji-An, and let an arrow fly. Kel heard a thump and a cry of pain and felt a vicious satisfaction that surprised him. He wished he'd learned archery himself; swordfighting was all very well, but not much use at a distance.

Stumbling, racing, with Ji-An firing off arrows, they made it to the bottom of the stairs, where the tide was licking hungrily at the lower steps. Jerrod was there, his boots half in the water. He had tossed away his knife, but there was still blood smeared on his hands, the sleeve of his jacket. He looked desperately at Merren, who turned away.

"Jerrod, what the hell were you thinking?" Kel demanded. "Who told you to murder Gremont? And where in the name of the Gods is the *boat*?"

"I've no idea," Jerrod scrubbed at his face with his hand; it left a red smear. "They're bloody gone—"

Kel pushed past him and leaped down into the knee-high water, looking around wildly. There was no sign of the skiff or the oarsmen. Above them, the Malgasi guards were getting closer; Kel could hear them, crashing down the steps like falling rocks. He could hear the quick *swish-flick* of their arrows. Several had pierced the twisted columns of driftwood along the path and were burning, beginning to sputter as the flame met damp wood.

"Over here!" called a familiar voice. Kel spun and saw a brightly painted pleasure craft—a narrow boat with high, flaring sides and a sharp stern—glide into view. Sails billowed in the low wind. At the bow of the boat, waving her arms wildly so that the pale-pink shawl around her shoulders fluttered like the wings of a distressed butterfly, was Antonetta Alleyne.

"Quick!" she shouted. "Kel! Kel Anjuman! Over here!"

Merren gaped. "What on earth?"

Jerrod and Ji-An were also staring at Kel, arrested mid-motion.

"She's on our side," Kel said, trying to sound confident and not at all as if he had no idea what on earth Antonetta was doing here, or why she seemed to have sailed one of her mother's pleasure craft to Tyndaris with the express purpose of rescuing him and his friends. "I swear to you—"

A flaming arrow shot past him, burrowing into the shallow water, where it sparked and extinguished.

"Right," said Jerrod. "Let's go."

"Hurry!" Antonetta waved even more frantically. Kel started to wade out into the water. It was already knee-high, slowing his movements, but he did his best to cut a zigzag pattern as he went, avoiding the fiery arrows that continued to fly from the island behind them. They hissed as they struck the surface of the sea, like matches doused in water.

That was when he heard it. The whine of an arrow, flying past his ear. Not close enough to hit him, but too close to Merren. There was no time for him to shout a warning; he caught a blur out of the corner of his eye, and Merren spun around and fell.

Ji-An screamed.

Kel started toward Merren, who was splashing in the shallow water. A dark stain was spreading across the rippled surface, and Kel had an odd flash of a long-ago memory: Conor pouring absynthe into wine, watching the green-black liquor spread slowly through the clarity of the liquid.

"Merren," he breathed, and started toward him, but Jerrod was faster. He barreled past Kel, seized Merren without slowing, and hauled him to his feet. The arrow had not gone into Merren, but it had torn a gash in his arm. What looked like a frightening quantity of blood soaked his sleeve, and drenched Jerrod's hands.

Arms wrapped around Merren, Jerrod dragged him to the ship, heaving him up over the side. Antonetta shrieked as Merren, still bleeding, tumbled into the boat and Jerrod flung himself after. Kel was a second behind, grasping hold of the hull's edge and clambering in. Ji-An followed him, landing lightly in the prow. She spun around, bow in hand.

"*Go, go, go!*" she shouted; the men hastened to adjust the lines. The boat shot across the water, Ji-An firing arrows back at the island even as they pulled away.

Whether she hit anyone or not, Kel could not tell. Half blind with fury and panic, he whirled and caught hold of Antonetta by the shoulders.

She had been looking around her, eyes wide—staring from Jerrod, who was kneeling over a bleeding Merren, to Ji-An. Now she gasped in surprise as Kel, his heart hammering, caught at her shoulders. He knew he was holding her hard, probably frighteningly so, but his heart could not stop hammering in terror. "How did you *know*?" His voice jerked as he spoke, as if he couldn't catch his breath. "And *why*—do you have any idea how dangerous what you just did was? Ana, you could have been killed—"

"Kel." It was Jerrod. He had taken off his jacket and was pressing it against Merren's bleeding arm. His fixed Kel with an icy look. "She saved our lives. Stop it."

They had reached the tallships again. They cast their great shadows down over the Alleynes' small boat as it sailed between them. Antonetta had not tried to pull away from Kel. She stood where she was, her face pale and set with what Kel assumed was shock.

"My mother," she said, her voice eerily calm. "I was following my mother. I knew she had something planned tonight. I was afraid it was some mad thing. She gets—well, you know how she gets." She looked up at Kel, her blue eyes wide. "I followed her to Tyndaris, and I saw she was with Artal. I didn't know what to do then. If they had an assignation, then I didn't want to know it. I thought I ought to just leave, and then I saw *you*, running. And they were after you with arrows, and there was that bright light—*fire*—" She sucked in a breath. "I—they would have murdered you. I had to try to help."

"But you could have been killed," Kel said. He wanted to shake her again. He wanted to pull her close and hold her hard against him so that he could feel that her heart was still beating.

"*We* could have been killed if she hadn't done it," said Ji-An, standing rigid in the prow. She'd stopped firing off arrows, but she maintained her archer's stance, poised and ready, her eyes scanning the horizon.

"My mother—" Antonetta began.

"I saw her flee," Kel said. "But Gremont's dead."

Antonetta sucked in a gasp. "What? But how—"

"I killed him." It was Jerrod, his metal mask gleaming harshly in the light from the tallships. "I drove a dagger into his neck, all right?

Now, Kel, get over here and help me with Merren. I need something to bind up this wound. And he hit his head on a rock when he fell. He's going to need a physician." He sounded as rattled as Kel had ever heard him.

"Here." Antonetta, all worried eyes, thrust her silk shawl at Kel. He scrambled over a velvet-padded bench to reach the spot where Merren rested, propped against the hull. Jerrod knelt beside him, on his knees in half an inch of brackish water; he was speaking to Merren in a low voice, though Kel could catch only Merren's name.

Merren seemed disoriented, his eyes half lidded, his fair hair plastered damply to his forehead. There was a bad cut on the left side of his forehead, already beginning to darken and swell. The sleeve of his shirt was soaked with red, and more red mixed with the water in the bottom of the boat.

Jerrod hunched protectively over Merren, with the general air of a bear hovering over its cub.

"Kel," Merren murmured as Kel knelt down beside him.

"Hush," Kel said, handing Antonetta's shawl to Jerrod. "You must rest."

Jerrod began to tear the fragile silk shawl into strips, clearly intending to bind the furrowed wound in Merren's arm. He didn't look up at Kel.

"What the gray hell, Jerrod?" Kel hissed under his breath. "You killed Gremont— *How?* He had the amulet on." He pulled the heavy jeweled pendant out of his pocket and held it up. "I took it off him as he died. It was supposed to protect him."

Jerrod stared at the winking pendant, then shook his head. "The thing you're holding is a fake," he said. The efficiency with which he tied Merren's arm tightly with the torn strips of shawl made Kel wonder how many times he'd done this sort of thing before. No doubt it was easy to get hurt being a Crawler.

"How the hell do you know that?" Kel snapped.

"I was told."

"By who? The Ragpicker King? But how would he know—"

"Alys Asper," Jerrod said shortly. "The false amulet was switched for the real one while Gremont was snoring at the Caravel."

Merren stirred at the sound of his sister's name. Jerrod bared his teeth at Kel, who decided retreat might be the better part of valor. At least before Jerrod bit him in the leg.

He rose to his feet, shoving the false amulet back into his pocket, and saw that they were drawing close to the lighted shore. The Alleynes had their own dock next to the Key. They drew up to it, and Ji-An leaped out to help Kel and Antonetta secure the boat.

Alys Asper. The amulet was switched at the Caravel. Kel's head spun as he watched Jerrod maneuver Merren carefully out of the craft, Merren's good arm slung around his shoulder. He hadn't realized Jerrod even knew Alys beyond his light acquaintance with her as the owner of the Caravel. And, of course, as Merren's sister. Had he gone to Alys about Gremont? Or even stranger, had she come to him?

"Take my carriage," Antonetta said, indicating a pink-and-white barouche drawn up before a tavern whose swinging sign proclaimed it THE UNLUCKY ROSE. A driver wearing Alleyne livery was half asleep in the driver's seat, his cap tipped forward to hide his face. "I'll be in awful trouble with my mother regardless, and you must get your friend to Lin as soon as possible."

"Are you sure?" Jerrod was looking at Antonetta in much the way he regarded all nobility—half sour, half contemptuous. "We'll likely get blood on your nice white seats."

Antonetta blinked. "I don't care about *that*," she said. "What kind of person do you think I am?"

"Jerrod, be quiet," Ji-An said hastily. "Demoselle Alleyne, thank you for the loan of your carriage. We will have it sent back to the Key as soon as we've finished with it."

Jerrod nodded curtly. "Kel, help me with Merren."

"I'll do it," said Ji-An before Kel could move, and a moment later she had Merren's other arm slung around her shoulder. She glanced back once at Kel and Antonetta before she and Jerrod set off for the carriage. There was something knowing in her expression.

Kel turned to Antonetta. The taverns along the Key were brightly lit, but the Alleyne boat cast a slanted shadow over them. Still, they were anything but private.

"Ana," he said. "I'm sorry. I shouldn't have shouted at you. I should have thanked you. You saved our lives."

She took the front of his jacket in her small hands. The wind off the water bit at them coldly; Antonetta was shivering. Kel wanted more than anything to wrap her up in his cloak. "What happened, Kel?" she whispered. "Who were those people? Why were they chasing you? And the people you're with—"

"Antonetta." His throat ached, hard, as it had not in years—not since that first time she had turned away from him, at her debut ball, and he had forced himself to show nothing, to give no sign that it hurt. *Antonetta, I can't tell you. I want to, but I cannot.*

"Don't ask me," he said. "If you demand an answer, I will lie to you. And I am a very good liar."

"I know," she whispered. She tightened her grip on his jacket; raised herself up on tiptoes. The wind whipped her hair around both of them in a soft cloud. Her lips brushed his—not a kiss, not quite. It was too light, too brief, but the heat of her mouth against his seemed to press into him, a weight on his heart.

She let go of his jacket, stepped away. Without her warmth against him, the wind was like a thousand tiny blades on his skin. "You had better go and join your friends," she said, turning away from him. "They'll be wondering what's keeping you."

Kaleb

Kaleb Gorin, age eight, is chasing a rubber ball through the darkened streets of the Sault. It is his best toy, one he was given for his birthday by his cousin Mez, who is a gate guard. Being a gate guard makes him one of the most important people in the Sault. This, according to Kaleb's mother, makes Kaleb a very important person, too—which is why she also tells him that he must work extra hard to stay out of trouble. The Gorins have a reputation to maintain.

His mother would certainly not have approved of him racing through the streets after dark had fallen, whooping as his ball bounced off the walls of houses and grown-ups leaned out of windows to shake their fists at him. And she would have approved even less of him climbing the wall of the Shulamat garden because his ball had bounced over it. Kaleb thought that probably didn't matter since there was very little likelihood that she would ever find out.

It is easy enough to climb the wall; the crumbly old stone is full of handholds and footholds. He is already at the top when he hesitates. It has never occurred to him that there might be people in the garden; it is late, past moonrise, and most have gone inside after the evening prayer. But there they are: two people sitting together on a stone bench, surrounded by flowers and greenery.

The lamps caught in the tree branches illuminate them. Kaleb freezes when he realizes who they are. One is the big blond man who answered all the children's questions that day. The Exilarch. And the other is the woman who calls herself the Goddess. Lin Caster, wearing a dull-gray dress, her bright, fire-colored hair in braids.

Kaleb has long known Lin as a physician, someone likely to turn up at his house when he is ill and force vile-smelling teas on him. But lately she has become something else, the subject of grown-up whispers and stares. Kaleb does not understand how she can be the Goddess when the Goddess is a legend, a pillar of fire and magic, and Lin is quite clearly a person. But it is the sort of question that might get you smacked, so he doesn't ask it.

He is much more afraid of the Exilarch. His mother has told him that Aron Benjudah is the most important of all the Ashkar, even more important than the Maharam, and that he has come to the Sault to make sure everyone is behaving themselves. If the Exilarch were to look up and see Kaleb now, he would surely report his naughtiness to the Maharam—or worse, to Kaleb's mother.

Slowly, Kaleb flattens himself to the top of the wall, like a lizard hoping to be overlooked by a bird of prey. Below him, Lin Caster tugs on the end of one of her long braids and says, "Oh, I don't know. I don't think it would be so bad to have people be afraid of you, would it? As long as it meant they didn't interfere with what you needed to be doing."

The Exilarch is facing away from her, and Kaleb sees him smile. It's a real smile, the kind that has fondness in it as well as amusement. But when the Exilarch turns back to Lin, his face is a blank. "I am not so sure," he says. "Have you ever wondered why the Malgasi turned against their Ashkar?"

The Malgasi. Kaleb knows this name, a sort of curse, but he is not entirely sure who these people are or what they have done that was so terrible.

Lin seems to consider this. "No. Mariam has told me what it was like, but there seemed no reason in their hatred. More as if they were just—a nest of snakes."

"You know the Queen there is Iren Belmany," he says. "And the heir to the throne is her daughter, Elsabet. But there was a Prince, an heir before Elsabet. Prince Andras of House Belmany."

"But he is no longer the heir?"

The Exilarch shakes his head. He is very blond, his skin and hair all turned to bronze by the sun. Kaleb thinks enviously of all the adventures he must have had. "When Andras was a young man, he fell in love with an Ashkar woman. He was determined to learn all he could about her people, and she was eager to share her life with him. Of course she told him of the Goddess and her promised return. In all innocence he passed what he thought was a charming story along to his family, but they were not charmed. They were horrified."

Lin looks very surprised. "Would they not dismiss the tale as harmless folklore? They have their own Gods, their own tales. They do not believe in ours."

"House Belmany are unusual. They have always been superstitious, always had harsh punishments for the use of magic. Ashkar magic was always strictly regulated in Malgasi. So you might say it was in their nature to believe." The Exilarch leans back on his hands, a disarmingly ordinary human gesture. "They determined among themselves that if there was even a chance that this was true—that an Ashkar woman could rise with the power of sorcery and challenge their authority—they must do what they could to stamp that possibility out."

"But—"

"You must understand the power of legends, Lin. The Goddess is a Goddess if her people believe she is."

Kaleb squirms a little, uncomfortably. He knew his own mother did not believe Lin was really the Goddess Returned. "She's just a little thing, not at all impressive," she would say, even when Mez argued with her that they had all seen Lin use her power to burn the ships in the harbor. (Kaleb had not seen this; he had been sent to bed early that night and was still resentful.)

The Exilarch continues. "The Belmany Court began to target the Ashkar, and you know the rest. Your friend Mariam is one of those who escaped, but most did not."

Kaleb stirs again. He does not know what the Exilarch means, not exactly. He has heard stories of wolf-faced soldiers, of long rows of gallows where the dead hung like drying laundry. He has always thought they were just tales meant to frighten. Not real, like the magical animals that had disappeared with the Sundering: dragons and phoenixes and sea monsters.

"What happened to the Prince?" Lin's face is pinched with real worry. "The one who loved the Ashkar girl?"

"He took his own life after she was murdered by the Wolf-guards. It's not a happy story, I'm afraid."

In a quiet voice, Lin says, "I had never thought this destruction was brought on by love."

The Exilarch looks at her and says something quiet, something Kaleb has to lean sideways to hear. As he changes position, he loosens his grip and nearly tumbles off the wall. For a moment he is dizzy, clinging with his fingers to the stone wall under him. In that dizzy moment, he hears Lin cry out: He looks down to see her with her arms wrapped around her middle, her shoulders stiff with something that looks like pain.

"Fire," Kaleb hears her whisper. "I see a dark woman, and fire on the water—"

Aron Benjudah lays a hand on her shoulder. And in that moment, Kaleb no longer sees before him the familiar figures of the Exilarch and the physician; he sees a woman wrapped in flames, her eyes like blank pearls, and beside her a great raven, with outstretched wings.

A moment later the vision is gone and Kaleb is blinking in terror, his breath coming in small gasps. Looking down in fear, he sees only what he saw at first: the Exilarch with Lin beside him. The roaring in his ears blocks out their conversation. He begins to scrabble his way back down the wall, forgetting about retrieving his ball, forgetting about anything but getting away quickly.

The strangeness of the vision would haunt Kaleb for many weeks. Ravens are not something he sees often, and they are mostly familiar illustrations from pictures in books of history. After all, in Castellane, the raven is a bird of ill omen, but to the Ashkar, the raven is the symbol of Judah Makabi, who had protected the Goddess in her most vulnerable time and led the Ashkar people to freedom.

CHAPTER FIFTEEN

As Kel had promised Merren, Lin was summoned as soon as they reached the Black Mansion. Andreyen had been waiting for them, perched on his tall chair in the Great Room like a watchful bird of prey. He sprang into action the moment they arrived, sending a messenger for Lin, ordering that hot water, brandewine, and linen bandages be brought to Merren's room, and demanding that Merren, weak from blood loss, go and lie down immediately.

Jerrod would not allow anyone else, even Ji-An, to help Merren to his room, but undertook the venture himself, Merren's good arm looped around his neck. Andreyen watched them go, his eyes hooded, before snapping, "You two. Are either of you hurt?" at Kel and Ji-An.

They both replied in the negative.

Andreyen looked Kel over. "So the blood on you is Merren's, then?"

Kel had not realized the state he was in. There were long scratches on his hands and neck—and doubtless his face as well—left behind by the sharp needles of the scrub pine. His clothes were torn and dirty, his boots muddy and stained with seaweed, and Merren's blood had left crimson patches on his jacket and shirt. The metallic scent of the blood mixed with the smell of brine and seaweed, making his clothes smell like one of Montfaucon's worse colognes.

As he examined himself, a small hermit crab crawled out of the top of his boot and dropped to the carpet. It seemed to gaze around for a moment before scuttling beneath Andreyen's brocaded arm-chair.

Andreyen rolled his eyes. "Go clean up," he said, "the both of you. You are dripping on the rugs. Then come back and tell me *exactly* what happened."

"Well, it isn't *our* fault," Kel said to Ji-An as they did their best to tidy up in the small, green-tiled tepidarium. "You send someone to engage in spywork on a drowned island, you ought to expect them to come back wet."

"He isn't upset about the wet, or even the crab," said Ji-An, who had changed out of her wet boots and trousers and into clean linens. Other than some scrub-pine scratches like Kel's, she had emerged relatively unscathed. "He's upset about Merren. And you should be glad he snapped at you. It means he likes you."

"I thought you said he was angry at me." Kel, too, had changed clothes, in the small room off the tepidarium, into the loose cotton tunic and trousers he usually wore during Crawling lessons with Jerrod. How he was going to explain the change when he returned to the Palace, he was not yet sure.

"You can be angry at someone and still be fond of them." Ji-An ran a brush through her damp hair. Unplaited, it hung nearly to her waist, ink black and straight as an arrow. "He just thinks you ought to have warned him—"

"About Anjelica. I know." Kel cut his gaze sideways at Ji-An. She seemed placid enough, though Ji-An was placid the way tigers in cages were placid; there always seemed to be a part of her that was planning what she would do if she were ever entirely free. "Are you sure he's the one who's angry? Not you?"

Ji-An's brushstrokes slowed. "Why would I be angry?"

"Because Anjelica seemed to know a great deal about you." He thought of the Princess saying in her steady voice, *Because of you, a whole family in Geumseong lies dead.* "Or was she wrong?"

Ji-An was twisting her hair up into its familiar knot at the back of her head. "Not about love," she said with surprising calm. "I loved Na Ri. She was the daughter of the House of Nam. And they killed her." She fastened her hair in place with an amethyst pin and turned to Kel. "I swore I would slay each one of them who had spilled her blood, and I did."

How many? Kel wanted to ask, but he didn't. It was not the kind of question he suspected Ji-An would want to answer.

"Is that when Andreyen saved your life?" Kel guessed. "Did he get you out of Geumjoseon?"

Her dark gaze was steady. "You're not so foolish as you look." She caught up her jacket, swinging it around her shoulders. "Now, he'll want to know what happened on Tyndaris."

"Wait," said Kel. "How foolish do I look?"

But Ji-An was already on her way back to the Great Room. Kel followed her, a little sorry for what he had asked. He had grown fond of Ji-An, of her prickliness and protectiveness, her acidic humor and the gentleness she kept hidden.

Back in the Great Room, the fire had been built high, the flames leaping eagerly up the chimney. Andreyen sat in his chair, eyes hooded, his staff across his lap. He stroked the fine grain of the wood as Kel explained to him what had happened on the island: what they had seen and learned, how Merren had been injured, Antonetta's intervention.

When he was done, Andreyen folded his hands in his usual position, crossing them over the raven's head atop his staff. "So," he said, his eyes shining with an eerie green cast. "What you are telling me—and let me make sure I have this absolutely correct—is that the Shining Gallery slaughter was masterminded by the Malgasi, who tricked several of the Charter Families into cooperating under the pretense that it was simply a nasty political prank."

"Not just 'the Malgasi,'" said Kel. "The heir to the throne. The Princess. Elsabet."

"Who is also an assassin," said Andreyen. "And who practices a magic not seen since the time of the Sorcerer-Kings. And in the wake of the Shining Gallery, the Malgasi have found themselves in the position of blackmailing the Charter Families who *were* involved by threatening to reveal that involvement." He leaned his chin on his folded hands. "And since they would rather do anything than relinquish power, they will go along with the Malgasi and their plans to tear Castellane apart rather than speak up with the truth and risk the consequences."

"They believe that when there is a new Castellane, they will rule it, along with the Malgasi," said Ji-An. "The Aurelians will remain as figureheads."

"They are fools if they believe that," said Andreyen. "The Malgasi will discard them like trash after they've marched armies into Castellane."

Anxiety buzzed like a bee in the back of Kel's head. "That doesn't matter," he said. "By the time they realize that, it will be too late."

Andreyen gave a slight nod.

"We know of three families involved with the current conspiracy," he said. "Liorada Alleyne, but not her daughter. The Cabrols were raised to their current position as Charter holders by the Malgasi, who also enabled their revenge, and now they must serve the Malgasi in return. The elder Gremont was a part of the original scheme that led to the bloodbath in the Gallery. He was killed there to silence him about his involvement. And Artal Gremont was working with Elsabet Belmany, but is now dead. As for any other families working with Malgasi, we do not know their names yet." He sighed, sat up. "There is one question, now, that we must answer."

"What do we do next?" said Ji-An.

"No." The Ragpicker King looked at Kel. "Will Kel share what we've learned tonight with Legate Jolivet?"

Kel stiffened. The thought had not occurred to him until this moment. To tell Jolivet seemed impossible, and yet—

"But you must tell him." It was Lin. She had appeared in the doorway, looking weary; she was dressed in a plain gray dress, her hair in two long braids. Her medical satchel was not with her. She must have left it in Merren's room.

"How long were you standing there?" Andreyen said, his eyebrows ticking up a notch.

"A little while." Lin came farther into the room, and Kel caught sight of her expression for the first time. She looked a little sick, which struck him as odd—she'd seen much worse injuries than Merren's. "I've treated Merren for shock and loss of blood. Jerrod is staying with him for the moment, but he'll be fine. If you want to know what I heard"—she glanced from Kel to Ji-An to Andreyen— "it was enough to know the Aurelians are in danger. The Prince is in danger. You must tell the Legate, Kel. It is his duty to protect them."

"Conor is *my* duty," said Kel. "Jolivet has more wide-ranging concerns."

"Jolivet is not subtle, Lin," said Andreyen. "Once he knows, every one of the Charter Families involved will be arrested. They might well end up in the Trick. And they will not stop at the ringleaders. It could mean very bad things for your friend Antonetta."

The buzz of anxiety was back in Kel's head, louder than ever. Lin said quickly, "It would be wrong to blame Antonetta for what her mother has done." She flashed a look at Kel. "But—do you care more about protecting her than protecting Conor?"

"It's not so simple," said Ji-An. "The Princess of Malgasi said one of her conspirators was someone on the Hill, someone close to Conor. For all we know, it *is* Jolivet."

"But then why would he have asked me to investigate?" Kel scrubbed at his eyes. Madness. This was madness. "All right. I'll keep it from Jolivet, but not for long. The Cabrols are far less established than the Alleynes or the Gremonts. If we confront Ciprian, he'll break. We'll find out from him who the other conspirators are."

"Soon," Lin said.

"Soon," Kel agreed.

Ji-An shot Lin a curious look. "I had not realized," she said, "that you were so fond of House Aurelian."

Lin was pale. "It is more than that. The Malgasi wiped out the Ashkar of their country. Killed or drove away all of them. If they come into power here, they'll do the same."

"That's true," Kel confirmed. "The Princess said as much."

Andreyen leaned back in his chair. "Perhaps this is why the Ashkar of Castellane need a Goddess to lead them. Perhaps you were born for such a time as this."

Lin gave him a long, cool look. "There's a hermit crab under your chair," she said finally.

The Ragpicker King swore, though Kel missed the exact words. They were drowned out by the sound of raised voices from within the mansion.

"That's Merren," Ji-An said. "It sounds like he's feeling better."

Kel frowned. "I'll be right back."

It was a relief to get out of the Great Room, away from talk of trust and treason, of Jolivet, of danger to Conor. He'd visited Merren's room before on various occasions: sometimes to borrow a book, sometimes just to chat. The space was overflowing with books and plants, like Merren's flat in the Student Quarter. It had something of the dark aesthetic of the rest of the mansion, but Merren had done what he could to bring in light and color: hanging bright cloths over the dark tapestries, covering a grim stone urn with a pink blanket. ("I always feel like a snake is about to come out of it," he'd said when Kel asked him why.)

Now Merren was sitting up in his bed. He was pale, wearing a loose, unbuttoned shirt, his arm wrapped in Lin's familiar bandages. The rumpled coverlet pooled around his waist. His face was in his hands, his fingers threaded through his blond curls.

On a chair beside his bed was Jerrod. He looked up when Kel came in; Kel could see the silvery wink of his mask. He'd begun to forget that Jerrod wore it; it was simply a part of him, and Kel no longer felt that it hid Jerrod's expressions. He could read him well enough regardless. Now he could see the look of what seemed almost like despair on Jerrod's face.

"You knew perfectly well how important it was to me to take revenge on Gremont with my own hands," Merren said without looking up. His voice was hoarse. "Did you think I was too weak to do it?"

"No. That wasn't it."

"And you barely know my sister. How could she have told you he was wearing a false amulet?" Merren raised his face from his hands, saw Kel. The pain in his expression was clear, and startling. Merren so often wore his own mask, like Jerrod's, but his was not metal: It was geniality, cheerfulness, the ease of his smile.

"I ought to go," Kel said, beginning to turn around.

"No. You should hear this, too," Jerrod said. "Alys approached me. I did not approach her. Since Gremont seemed to be enjoying himself going to the Caravel, flaunting his presence in her face, she had decided to turn that against him. While he was sleeping, she had Audeta remove the real amulet and replace it with a replica."

"And you knew?" Merren whispered. "When we went to Tyndaris, you knew Gremont would be there, that you planned to kill him—"

"No. That was chance. It was an opportunity, and I took it. If it hadn't been tonight, I would have done it the next time he went to the Caravel. That was what Alys had planned."

"I still don't understand why she'd approach you," Merren said.

"Because she knows I'd do anything—" Jerrod broke off, rising to his feet. "Because she didn't *want* you to do it. She didn't want her brother to live with blood on his hands. And my hands"—he smiled a twisted smile—"are bloody enough already."

Merren thumped his closed fist against his thigh in frustration. "She's my sister. Of course she thinks I'm a child. You should know better. I am neither weak nor delicate."

"I never said you were weak," Jerrod growled. "But I think taking a life will change you, and I don't want you to change."

Merren glared at him. "That's not your decision to make."

Behind the mask, Jerrod's eyes flashed. Embarrassed, Kel said, "Merren, I don't think—"

But Jerrod had taken two steps across the room and caught hold of the front of Merren's shirt. He bent and kissed him—a fierce, hot, demanding kiss, his hands rising to cup the nape of Merren's neck. Merren arched back involuntarily, fingers digging into the mattress on either side of him.

When Jerrod pulled away, Merren looked dazed in a way that seemed to have little to do with his head injury. He lifted a hand to touch his mouth. Kel had wondered if anything like this had happened with them before; now he knew it hadn't. The air in the room felt charged like the air after a pulse of lightning.

Jerrod's hood had fallen back. He ran a hand through his reddish-brown hair; it was shaking. "I'm done," he said. "Done with the lot of you."

He walked out of the room, pushing past Kel with his head down, like a defeated fighter leaving the Arena.

Merren sat bolt-upright in bed and cried out, reaching for his shoulder. "Go after him," he said. "Kel—"

"Merren—"

"Just *go*."

Kel plunged into the corridor. Jerrod had only left a few moments before, but he seemed to have vanished. The corridors had twists and turns, and Jerrod was a Crawler. They knew how to disappear. After a quick search, Kel found himself in the Great Room, where Ji-An and Lin, who had been deep in conversation, turned to look at him in surprise. Andreyen, who had not moved from his chair, did not look up. He said, "If you are looking for Jerrod, he's already gone."

"He said none of us should follow him," said Lin. "He said he'd know if we did and—well, the rest of it was rude."

Kel sighed. "What a mess."

"He'll come back," Ji-An said.

"I don't think he will," said Andreyen. "I suppose it is no surprise he wants no part of what comes next for us all."

"What *does* come next?" Kel said. It was the thing he had wanted to know most since they'd arrived at the Black Mansion.

"A game of Castles on a new board," said Andreyen, staring into the fire. "Jerrod was born on the streets of Castellane. Stealing doesn't bother him, murder doesn't bother him, violence doesn't bother him. But we place ourselves now between countries. Countries ready to go to war." Andreyen gestured with a long-fingered hand, as if at a playing board none of them could see. "It is a thankless task, and dangerous. I would not blame any of you should you choose to refuse it."

No one spoke or moved. All around the room, the firelight cast strange and dancing shadows. Andreyen looked steadily from one of them to the other; his eyes came, at last, to rest on Kel.

"Very well, then," he said. "The Solstice Ball is soon, is it not? And Ciprian Cabrol will be there?"

Kel nodded. "It's in four days."

"Excellent." The Ragpicker King leaned forward. "This is what you must do . . ."

Lin returned troubled from the Black Mansion and crawled exhausted into bed. Still, she could not fall asleep. She kept going over and over the events of the night in her mind. After she had left the Black Mansion, she had been surprised to find that Andreyen had followed her quietly out into the night.

Scarlet Square had been dark and silent, the eastern sky not yet touched with dawn. Andreyen had been a shadow beside her, gazing out at the city. "Is something wrong?" he'd asked. "Just now—you seemed troubled in a way unusual for you."

Lin had not planned to tell him. She had not planned to tell anyone. She was surprised to find the words tumbling out, as if she had tripped over something and unexpectedly dropped what she was carrying. "In the Sault tonight, before you summoned me," she said. "I was with the Exilarch, just talking, and I felt something strange."

Andreyen had frowned. "Because of him?"

"No. I knew somehow that I was sensing a thing outside the Sault. That something terrible was happening. As if a voice had called out a warning, and even as it was calling out to me, I saw fire burning across water."

"Ah." The Ragpicker King passed a hand across his forehead. "You felt the magic Elsabet Belmany did on Tyndaris."

"It wasn't the first time I've had that feeling—often I have it just when I wake up from a dream—but it was more powerful than before. More frightening."

"I would guess Her Highness has been in Castellane for some time. Making plans. Working with these conspirators of hers. You have a Source-Stone, and we know now that she does as well. It is possible they can somehow sense each other."

Lin had frozen. "Does that mean she knows about me?"

"I don't think so," he'd said, but slowly, as if he could not be sure. "You sensed her when she drew on her stone, which must be suffused with great power to fuel the magic she can do. You have yet to use yours for more than healing magic—and Elsabet Belmany would expect healing magic from the Ashkar. Even if she sensed it, she would not note it as unusual."

"Should I be—looking for her? Trying to find where she's hiding out?"

"No," he'd said sharply. "She doesn't know about you, and I believe we should keep it that way. The longer Elsabet Belmany remains unaware of Lin Caster, the better."

Lin turned over in her bed. She could not help but wish that the first time she had sensed another magic-user in the world, it had been anyone but Elsabet Belmany. The Malgasi remained, in her mind, a symbol of horror, of vicious wolf-faced murderers who hung Ashkar children from makeshift gallows and proclaimed it a victory over evil. At least now, she supposed, she could begin to understand how the Malgasi had turned their population against the Ashkar people so quickly and so thoroughly when the Ashkar had lived in Favár for generations of peace. They had used their power. Of that she had no doubt.

When Lin fell asleep at last, she tumbled into awful dreams in which a captor whose face she could not see bound her arms and legs with long strips of cloth in different colors: a scarlet rope tied her ankles, while one wrist was bound with blue and the other with black. She cried out as her limbs were dragged painfully in different directions. "Hush," said her captor, "do not struggle, and it will go easier for you."

The voice was Conor's.

The next morning Lin awoke to discover Chana at her front door, carrying the report that one of the Shomrim had been injured on the wall when a ladder had broken. Lin spent a feverish time nursing him through the worst of his recovery, as what was broken in him knitted itself back together with the help of medicine and amulets.

She finally made it back to her own house two days later, where she realized to her horror that today was the day the Hierophant of the city was meant to bless the wedding of Conor and his new bride, and that she was required to be there to meet the Marivent carriage in Valerian Square. She took herself off to the kitchen to find a tisane for her head, glumly wondering if there was anything in the world she wanted to do less than watch the betrothal of Conor Aurelian and Anjelica Iruvai be blessed by the Hierophant. Mayesh had promised a good view, which seemed worse than a bad one. Hopefully the carriage would arrive for her not too late after noon.

She dressed and went to the Etse Kebeth, where she found Mariam on her toes in front of the small mirror, winding silver ribbons into her hair. The moment she saw Lin, her face fell.

"You're not wearing *that*, are you?" she said.

Lin glanced down at her perfectly serviceable gray linen dress. It had a hole near the hem where she'd spilled a preparation of burdock root, but who was looking at hems?

"It's an event, the blessing," Mariam said. "Everyone will be dressed up. And aren't you going to the Palace afterward?"

"Just to see a patient," Lin protested as Mariam—who was wearing a blue dress in sprigged muslin, with fashionable gathers at the wrists and hem—went to her wardrobe and began to look through it, humming.

"Well, the patient will be stunned by how glamorous you look, and meanwhile you will not embarrass our people by turning up in Valerian Square looking like a rag-and-bone seller." Mariam drew a dress of dove-gray satin from the wardrobe and held it out to Lin. "Wear this," she said. "It will make your eyes look more green."

"As though anyone will notice," Lin muttered, but she went to change anyway. In truth, she had to admit to herself she was glad her grandfather had told her to bring Mariam to the square. Mariam's delight in the pageantry of the event was simple and uncomplicated in a world where nothing felt simple or uncomplicated anymore.

"You know," Mariam called as Lin struggled into the slippery gray fabric, "whatever Princess Anjelica is wearing, everyone will be wanting something similar immediately. Did you see her on the back of that magnificent elephant?"

Lin had to admit she hadn't—though not, of course, why.

"She's absolutely stunning. If she chooses to, she'll be setting the fashions for the next decade or so. In fact, it will likely happen whether she chooses it or not."

Lin made a noncommittal noise and rejoined Mariam in the bedroom. She let Mariam tie her thick hair back with a blue silk cord, then hurried the both of them out of the Etse Kebeth, pausing only to hug Chana, who was boiling leaves in the kitchen.

With her satchel slung over her shoulder, Lin made her way up the Ruta Magna arm in arm with Mariam. It was a bright day, the sun high in a cloudless sky. Valerian Square was packed with people, as Lin had expected, but she was surprised to find that a serious mood prevailed. There was none of the festive spirit of the Independence Festival, no food and drink sellers mingling through the crowd, nor any music or impromptu dancing. There seemed a general public feeling that this was a solemn occasion, as if even the children—scrub-faced and neatly dressed, holding their parents' hands—felt they were there to witness an important moment in the history of the city.

A wooden dais, almost a stage, had been erected in front of the Temple. It was draped with cloth-of-gold, and upon it stood an arched canopy of the shimmering velvet Mariam called *luminància*, held aloft by two pillars of marble wrapped with flowers. A crowd of Castelguards was gathered near the Temple steps—Lin recognized Benaset among them—and Lin squinted, trying to see if Mayesh was among the Palace throng.

"Well, *I* think it will be good for Castellane to have this new Princess," Mariam said, and Lin realized with a guilty start that she had been paying little attention to her friend's chatter.

"Really?" Lin leaned against one of the square's gold lions. "Why?"

"Marriages, babies, those are happy things. They lift people's spirits." Mariam stuck her tongue out at Lin. "I'd think a physician would know that."

"Free beer also raises people's spirits," Lin noted. "They ought to be giving that out, if they want everyone in a good mood."

Mariam laughed. "You have no sense of pageantry." She looked thoughtfully at the Temple. "You know, before the Sundering, a king or queen who was to marry might ride to the Temple on the back of a dragon, or accompanied by a phoenix. Can you imagine such a fire?"

Lin thought of the charred earth of her dream. "Such glory brings with it great dangers."

"Gracious," said Mariam. "You are in a bad mood, aren't you? You hate pageantry, princesses, *and* phoenixes. Is it just the letter *P*?"

"Mariam—"

"You *are* glad the Prince is getting married, aren't you?" Mariam asked archly.

"Of course," Lin said through her teeth. "Oh, look, there's Mayesh. He's waving to us."

Indeed, her grandfather had appeared at the foot of the Temple steps and was gesturing to Lin. She pushed her way through the crowd, pulling Mariam with her, until they reached the perimeter of the Castelguards encircling the Temple. Lin nodded at Benaset, who stepped aside to let her and Mariam through with a sour look.

The Windtower Clock began to strike noon as Lin and Mariam joined Mayesh. Lin glanced around but saw no royal carriage that might be searching for her. She could hear Mariam chattering excitedly to her grandfather, who was nodding along with a faint look of amusement. He had always liked Mariam.

Before Lin could greet Mayesh herself, the high marble doors ground open, dragged along their grooves by acolytes in white Temple robes. The great doorway to the Temple loomed before them, black as a tomb.

The Hierophant emerged from the shadows first. He wore the green-gray of Aigon's clerics, and a long cloak, woven with a pattern of waves, cascading down his back. His head was bare, his hair thick and gray. In one hand he held a silver staff, topped with an orb of Sunderglass. Smoke seemed to move inside the orb, puffs of white and gray appearing and disappearing within the vitreous circle.

He began to walk down the marble steps, head high, unsmiling. The crowd was nearly silent. After him came members of the Charter Families, each carrying a banner representing the sigil of their House. First was Ciprian Cabrol, carrying the madder flower banner of the dye Charter. Then Gasquet and Montfaucon, Esteve and Uzec, Falconet and Cazalet. The Gremont banner, with its coronet of tea leaves, was carried by an elderly woman in black with steel-gray hair and an even steelier expression. Lady Gremont, Lin guessed. As for the Alleynes, a servant in livery held the silk banner. Lin wondered what Lady Alleyne's excuse was for not attending.

After the Charter Families came Queen Lilibet, all in green as was her habit, her hair dressed high with emeralds. It was strange to see her at such an event alone, without the King, even for someone who knew, as Lin did, why he was absent.

All save the Hierophant stationed themselves up and down the stairs, leaving the center clear to form a sort of aisle. The square fell silent, a breathless hush, the only sound the footfalls of the Hierophant as he ascended the dais and turned to face the Temple.

Lin felt a hand on her shoulder. Mayesh. It was a calming touch, as if he were worried for her—but why would he be worried? She turned to him with a puzzled expression just as they came out of the doors together.

Conor and his bride-to-be. Not hand in hand, but their shoulders nearly brushing. Whispers rose, scattering the silence. *So beautiful.*

Lin did not know what she had imagined of Anjelica Iruvai, or what it might mean to be rumored the most beautiful woman in the world. She had pictured the sort of curves that seemed the standard of desirability, the kind possessed by Antonetta. Red lips and cheeks, wide eyes. She was almost ashamed at the paucity of her imagination now. She had not pictured Anjelica's poise and lightness, the way every part of her seemed to come together by design, like one of Mariam's exquisite dresses.

She and Conor were both dressed formally, he in a dark-gray velvet doublet and trousers, embroidered with silver silk, she in a deep-violet gown with a train that fanned out behind her on the steps.

Mariam gasped softly. "Tyndaris purple."

During the time of the Empire, the deep-purple dye had been extracted from the shells of sea creatures that had thrived on Tyndaris before the island drowned beneath the waves. They were extinct now, and the only cloth of that color was the property of House Aurelian. When a new member of the royal family was born, a bolt was cut for them, to be used throughout their life. When Lilibet had married Markus, she had been given her own bolt; now, it seemed, Anjelica had, too.

Beside Anjelica, the Prince walked with his head held high. A tooled-leather belt circled his lean hips, a ceremonial sword gleaming in a scabbard at his side. His black curls tumbled over the gold circlet binding his forehead. His expression was set, shadowed. He seemed braced, as if for an ordeal.

As they reached the foot of the steps, the crowd's murmurs rose: how beautiful Anjelica was, how good this would be for the city, what handsome children they would have.

Anjelica's beauty had won them over, Lin thought with a pang, without a word or gesture needed. Beauty had that power. Even in the Story-Spinner tales in which Conor was a murderer or a tyrant or a coldhearted lonely king, he was a handsome murderer or tyrant. Beauty imbued every action with a sort of glamour and made it easy to forgive.

Conor reached out a hand to help Anjelica onto the dais beside him. The two of them faced the Hierophant. They were so close that Lin could not help but wonder if Conor could see her, too, standing beside Mayesh. But if he did, he gave no sign.

"Oh, Lin," Mariam breathed. "This is so *exciting*."

There was a sudden stir among the Castelguards as the Hierophant began to chant the blessings of Aigon. Mayesh's hand dropped from Lin's shoulder; she glanced over and saw Aron Benjudah, the Exilarch, in conversation with one of the Castelguards. To her surprise, the Castelguard, who seemed to be listening close, stepped aside to let Aron into the protected area.

She stared at Aron as he came closer. Here was neither the Rhadanite trader, dirty from the road, nor the solemnly robed Exilarch meting out justice in the Kathot. Aron wore a high-necked black jacket figured with silver, and at his waist was buckled a sword whose hilt was made of black metal and carved in the shape of a raven whose outspread wings made the cross guard. In its center was set a scarlet stone, red as the setting sun. Lin knew it immediately—any Ashkar would. It was the weapon that the Goddess had given to Judah Makabi after the fall of Aram. *All Exilarchs from that day forth would be descended from Makabi, and would carry the name Benjudah and the Evening Sword, the gift of the Goddess.*

The Evening Sword. Lin had never thought to see it. It was a legend, like phoenixes or dragons. She could not help but look at it as Aron came to stand in front of Mayesh. The sword had been a part of Ashkar history for as long as there had been Ashkar. A history that stretched not just into the past but also forward into the future. A tale she had inserted herself into without thought for the consequences.

Mayesh inclined his head, as if he'd expected to meet the Exilarch here. "Aron," he said. "It's good to see you."

"I thought to congratulate the Counselor to the throne," said Aron with only a glance at Lin. Mariam, who was staring at him wide-eyed, he ignored completely. "This clever alliance between Kutani and Castellane, how much of it was your doing?"

"Some of it," said Mayesh. "As you know, an adviser only has the influence he has earned."

"And you have worked hard to earn the trust of these people, these *malbushim*," said Aron. "I recall, I think, you advising me some years ago. I do not believe I took your advice."

Mariam glanced at Lin as if to silently say: *What's going on?* Lin just shook her head slightly. She could not have described the look on Aron's face. Not angry exactly, but something colder and harder than that.

"No," said Mayesh. "You didn't."

"But I was very young then," said Aron, "and inclined to believe in things like loyalty and honesty."

"I didn't lie to you," Mayesh said calmly. If he was upset, Lin couldn't tell it; there was something about him that made her believe he had expected this conversation. Perhaps not for it to happen here and now, of course.

She glanced up and saw that the Hierophant was still chanting, and that Anjelica and Conor both had their heads bent, and their eyes closed.

"You let me believe a lie," said Aron. "Is that better? I believed that when Asher was exiled, he was sent across the seas. Somewhere very far. I did not know he was here in Castellane, starving and alone. I did not know I could have helped him before it was too late."

"You could not have helped him." Mayesh's tone was flat as a desert road. "Had you tried, you would have found yourself exiled as well. And we needed you. You are a Prince of the Ashkar. Your responsibility is not to one single person, but to your people."

Lin could see Aron flush even under his tan. "Is it your own responsibility to your people you are thinking of when you suggest your granddaughter should follow in your footsteps as Counselor? Is it really that no one else is suited for the task, or do you simply wish to keep the power in the hands of your family?"

He looked at Lin then, and she could not tell if the anger blazing in his eyes was for her, or for Mayesh, or for opportunities lost long ago.

"Lin is not going to be the next Counselor," said Mariam, to Lin's surprise. She looked nearly as angry as Aron; her small hands were in fists at her sides. "She is the Goddess."

"Ah," said Aron, his eyes narrowing. "A true believer. Well, we will learn the truth of things soon enough."

And with a last glare at Mayesh, he turned on his heel and walked away, pushing through the knot of Castelguards.

Before Lin could think to stop herself, she darted after him, plunging into the crowd.

Elsabet

"It was a message," Elsabet says. "Intended for me."

She is weary, but she will not show her exhaustion. It is early morning; later today the Hierophant of this city will bless the Prince's accursed marriage—for all the good it will do. Elsabet sits in the priest's chair, back straight, her eyes fixed on the fire burning in the gold brazier. It is always chilly in the old temple, so Janos keeps it lit.

Seven had been pacing back and forth across the cracked tile floor. He stops now and turns to look at her. "Who would be using Artal's death to send a message?" he demands, an edge to his voice. "I thought no one knew that we—that he was working with you."

She smiles into the fire. Little flames lick up around the brazier like bright tongues. Elsabet has always loved fire. It is in her blood to love it, and in her family's blood. "You're worried about your own skin." She doesn't mind; it is one of the things she appreciates about him. He has a relentless self-interest that makes him easy to predict.

He ducks his dark head. "A little," he says. "I like it when my skin is not whipped from my body and displayed outside the Trick to teach the other Charter holders a lesson."

"Calm yourself," she says. "The Palace remains unaware of our activities. The message was from Prosper Beck."

A frown. "Beck? Doesn't he own a string of gambling houses in the Maze?"

"Not everyone important in this city is a law-abiding citizen, Seven. I had thought that if we could win Beck to our cause, he could challenge the Ragpicker King for dominance of the city's underworld."

"The Ragpicker King—?"

"He has too much power. They call him the King in the City. I do not wish there to be a king in Castellane I do not control. But Beck has been . . . recalcitrant."

Seven grunts. "So you wanted to recruit Beck to replace the Ragpicker King, and he refused?"

"He showed me disrespect. I put his messenger in his place. Now, it seems, Beck holds a grudge."

It had not occurred to Elsabet that Beck would mind the death of some low-level functionary all that much; she would hardly have taken it personally if someone had murdered Janos or Bagomer, but it did not seem like a good idea to say that to Seven. "The man who cut Artal's throat was Beck's man. I recognized him. I had the chance to kill him once, and missed it. I will not do so again."

"I don't like this," Seven says. "I don't like the complications."

No one cares what you like, Elsabet thinks. In Malgasi, her mother would have had a minor noble imprisoned for telling the Queen what policies he did or didn't like. The Aurelians had truly let things get out of control in Castellane, all these foolish little Charter members thinking of themselves as the kings of small fiefdoms. She was looking forward to showing them how a real monarch ruled.

And not just a real monarch, but one who reigned as the Sorcerer-Kings of old had reigned. Once she wrested her power away from the Aurelians, she would be able to rule as her ancestors had, with a radiance of power that compelled loyalty. She does not like to think of the unrest of the Malgasi people now, of their treachery, their lack of dedication to the throne. *It will all go back to the way it was*, she tells herself. *As soon as the Belmany dynasty snatches back its power, Malgasi will be great again.*

"Beck was only aware of Artal," she says tightly. "I brought him to a meeting. That's all. No need to fret yourself into an early grave."

"One of us was murdered," says Seven. "Hardly reassuring. And Artal had his amulet. I thought it was meant to protect him."

"It seems Beck was able to replace the real amulet with a false one." Elsabet does not feel as calm as she sounds, but she does not want Seven to know how much it alarms her that Beck had circumvented her so easily. She had made a mistake in trusting Artal not to be a fool. Now the amulet, one of her family's most trusted possessions, is in the hands of someone she does not wish well. Beck will need to be destroyed—but not yet. She needs to establish her position more strongly first. "You're a gambling man, aren't you, Seven? You shouldn't be averse to a little risk when the reward is so high."

"Engaging in high treason is not a little risk," snaps Seven. "Can we even do this without Artal?"

"It will require a change of plans. A closer eye kept on Liorada and that daughter of hers. But most of all—we need the Sword Catcher. We need him out of the game, and where we can lay our hands upon him." She narrows her eyes at Seven. "Did you discover whether the Prince is aware that the Sword Catcher has been arranging meetings between Anjelica Iruvai and the Ragpicker King?"

For the first time that day, Seven smiles. "Conor has no idea," he says. "When it comes to Kel, he has a blind spot the size of the Jiqal desert."

"That might be all we need for now," Elsabet says. "Keep a watch on Saren. Be prepared to bring all of the Charter Families together, and the Prince with them. Once you lay all your proof at his feet in front of the Hill, he will have no choice but to act."

CHAPTER SIXTEEN

All around Lin, people were chanting prayers to Aigon, a sound like the buzzing of bees in her ears.

Aigon, hear me as I pray with my soul for these children of mankind! Give them happiness, riches, children!

"*Oshozo!*" Lin called. "*Wait!*"

The Ashkar word drifted above the rhythmic chant. She saw a movement in the crowd ahead as Aron turned to look at her. A moment later, she had caught up with him. He was standing by the steps to the Justicia, away from the worst of the throng.

"What do you want?"

"What do I *want*?" Lin put her hands on her hips. "You couldn't have confronted my grandfather in the Sault? You had to humiliate him in front of the *malbushim*?"

"He did not seem humiliated to me."

"That doesn't mean you didn't try." Lin's hair was escaping from its fastening; it whipped across her face in the breeze. "You must realize that the damage you do to him is damage you do to all of us Ashkar."

Aron looked at her squarely. "I have attempted to visit your grandfather at his house in the Sault. Repeatedly. He is always conveniently not at home."

"You know that is no excuse," Lin said coldly. "Why is your anger all for Mayesh? Why is it not for the Maharam? You know my grandfather spoke out for Asher Benezar. You know he did everything he could to keep him from being exiled."

"*Everything he could.*" The Exilarch's voice was measured, but his eyes seemed to burn with the shimmer of sun on desert sands. "That covers a wide variety of sins, does it not? How can we measure what a man can and cannot find it within himself to do?" He leaned closer to Lin; he was so much taller that she almost wanted to stretch up on her toes to hear him. She didn't. "The truth is I expected nothing better from the Maharam. But I did expect better from your grandfather. I trusted him."

"And you don't trust him now?" She searched the Exilarch's face. Such a strange face. A calm face, giving nothing away, and yet those eyes, like cuts in a paper mask, showing only a glimpse of a world otherwise unseen, a word of fiery emotion: anger, rebellion, righteousness denied. "You don't believe that he was trying to protect you? You were the son of the Exilarch. What could you have done unobserved? Had you tried to help Asher, you would have been caught—"

He held up a hand, as if half-commanding her to be silent. "Your loyalty to your grandfather is to be expected," he began. "But—"

"*Loyalty.*" She saw that the bitterness with which she spoke surprised him. "Me, loyal to Mayesh? I used to feel the same way you do. I used to *hate* him. I thought he had abandoned me for the royalty up on the Hill."

The bronze eyes narrowed. "And now?"

"Now I understand that he was trying to protect me, in his way, because he was trying to protect us all. Mayesh will always choose the Ashkar as a people over any one individual. It makes him a good Counselor."

"If not," said Aron, "a good grandfather."

"He is our voice on the Hill," Lin said quietly. "We all know what happened in Malgasi. The Ashkar had no voice there, and we were murdered or driven out. I would think the Exilarch, of all people, would care—"

"You imagine that I do not *care*?" He stared at her, wordless for a moment. In the distance Lin could hear the Hierophant, calling to Aigon to surround Anjelica and Conor with safe water, to bless their union with the strength of the sea and the faithfulness of the tides.

Conor, faithful? Lin bit the inside of her lip.

She had half thought Aron was about to shout at her. Instead, he said evenly: "I do not understand you, Lin Caster. When I look at you, I see that you are much more than you seem to be. I look into your eyes and I see the fire in there, and I think, is that the fire of the Goddess? That fire I was born to see? But around you—around you I see only darkness."

Lin could not help herself, she flinched, just as a red-and-gold carriage rolled up beside them. Jolivet leaned out the window. "You were meant to wait by the Temple."

Lin raised her eyebrows. "I received no message with that instruction."

Jolivet looked as if he were feeling hard done by. "Just get in," he said. "There's little time."

Odd, Lin thought, for Jolivet to speak so freely in front of Aron, a stranger—yet when she turned to speak to Aron, he was gone. He had melted away into the crowd like a ghost; search as she might, she could not see him.

But was he watching her? Lin could not shake the feeling of a gaze resting heavy on her; she turned to look toward the Temple and saw that beside the kneeling Princess, Conor stood straight-backed, one hand on the hilt of his sword. He was not looking at the Hierophant: He was staring directly at Lin, and even at a distance she could feel the bladed sharpness of his gaze.

The hot sun beat down on the Hill as Kel made his way to Antonetta's home on foot. He supposed he could have borrowed Asti, but this was something he felt he had to do alone somehow, absent even the trappings of Palace support.

As he neared the Alleyne mansion, his thoughts strayed to Valerian Square. Conor would be there now, receiving the Hierophant's blessing. He, too, would be alone. Of course he would be surrounded by Castelguards, by Mayesh, by the Charter Families (save Alleyne, as Liorada had begged off, citing illness)—but as far as Kel was concerned, if Conor was appearing in public without him, he was alone.

He could feel it, the physicality of Conor unprotected, as if it were a wound as yet unbandaged.

He tried to distract himself with other thoughts. It was not as if he had a paucity of worries. In the days that had followed the events on Tyndaris, Kel had waited anxiously for the news of Gremont's death to break among the nobility of the Hill.

It hadn't.

Rumors were beginning to circulate about his absence. Perhaps Artal was on a three-day bender in the Maze (Falconet's suggestion), or perhaps he had grown bored with what was on offer in Castellane and gone to explore the infamous brothels of Valderan. Perhaps he had been taken hostage by a group of lowlifes to whom he owed money. Some believed he had ingested so much poppy-juice, either on purpose or by mischance, that he had forgotten who he was and begun a new life.

None of them seemed to think he was dead, which felt strange to Kel, who had watched the life bleed out of him. Who had held the false, bloody amulet in his hand, and later given it to Andreyen for safekeeping. He had waited for guilt to come, waited to regret the way he had treated Gremont in the last seconds of the man's life, but it never came. He only wished he, not Jerrod, had been the one to deliver the killing blow.

Of course, Lady Alleyne and Antonetta knew the truth of the situation, but it was to neither of their advantages to mention that. Kel could not imagine the strain Antonetta must be under, keeping such a secret. He had hoped she would seek him out at the Castel Mitat, but she had not; he had sent her a note but heard nothing back. Part of him knew there was every chance that Lady Alleyne had intercepted the message and thrown it away, but the rest of him kept recalling the last interaction he'd had with Antonetta at the docks, the disappointment on her face when he had refused to tell her the truth. It was like a song in his head, playing over and over, wearing a groove into his brain.

He had no clear idea what he wanted to say to her now, but there had to be some way to mend her disappointment, to reassure her that he was the same Kel he always was, someone she could trust—

He brought himself up short. He'd arrived.

He recalled the last time he'd been at House Alleyne, for the engagement party. *An engagement that will now never be a marriage, thank the Gods.* There had been a line of torch-bearing servants lining the path to the front door. Now there was only a single guard in livery dozing off at the gate, who recognized Kel and put two fingers to the brim of his hat, indicating that Kel could continue on to the front door.

Kel could not help but feel that something oppressive hung about the house like cobwebs. It was utterly silent; there was no noise from within. Despite the heat, the windows were shuttered, and when he raised his hand and knocked, he imagined the sound echoing through empty rooms within. A sharp fear seized him. What if they had gone? Packed up the house and fled at Lady Alleyne's insistence, hoping to escape the consequences of her bargain with the Malgasi—

But the door swung open. To Kel's surprise, it was Lady Alleyne herself, not Magali, who stood on the threshold. He could not help but start at her appearance. He had never seen her anything but impeccably turned out—she had worn rubies to Tyndaris—but she wore only a black dressing-gown now, with silk slippers on her feet. Her long hair fell down her back, blond streaked with silver he had never noticed before. Without her usual paint and color, her features seemed strained and gray, her face lined.

She looked at him with something close to loathing. "You," she said. "You've a lot of nerve, showing your face here."

Kel stared. He knew that Lady Alleyne was not overly fond of him, but she was never overtly rude. Usually she ignored him or was coolly polite.

He tried to look past her into the house, but she moved to block him. He dragged his gaze back to Lady Alleyne, to her blazing eyes. "I have come to see Demoselle Alleyne," he said without emotion. "I have a message from Prince Conor."

"Then give the message to me."

Kel shook his head. "The Prince requires that I give it to the Demoselle herself."

"You are a liar." Lady Alleyne spoke dispassionately.

Kel narrowed his eyes. "I understand you are unwell, Lady Alleyne. For that reason, I will not bring news of your outburst to the Prince. But I act on his orders—"

"Do you?" murmured Lady Alleyne. She put out a hand to brace herself against the doorframe. "I have never trusted you, Kel Anjuman. You think you hide your disrespect, your resentment? You have never had a sense of your place. The Prince, in his blind kindness, has given you ideas far above your station." Her gaze flicked over him. "Ever since I told you to stay away from my daughter—"

"I *did* stay away from your daughter," Kel said; it was all he could do to keep his white-hot rage out of his voice. "I stayed away from her for years. You destroyed an innocent friendship between two children. You let her believe I despised her. You have never cared about her happiness at all—"

Lady Alleyne had gone a grayish color. "Antonetta is *all* I care about," she hissed. "For the past nights I have not slept, not since"—he almost imagined she was about to say *since that night on Tyndaris*, but instead she finished with—"since the night Antonetta left our home."

Kel's ears seemed to be ringing. "Antonetta isn't here?"

Foolish, he thought numbly, *foolish to call her Antonetta and not Demoselle*, but Lady Alleyne did not seem even to have noticed. She was fumbling in the pocket of her robe, from which she produced a crumpled bit of vellum and handed it to Kel without a word.

Mama, he read, in Antonetta's familiar scrawl, *Gremont does nothing but humiliate me in public. It is insupportable. If he inquires, I will be at the house of a friend for some time. I do not wish visitors.*

Lady Alleyne's look was hot with fury. "Swear to it," she said. "Swear she is not hiding herself away in the rooms of the Castel Mitat."

Kel's mind was in a whirl. It was clear that Antonetta had told her mother nothing about her own trip to Tyndaris, that she had not revealed to Lady Alleyne her own knowledge of Gremont's death. "I swear it," he said. "Why would I have come here if I knew where she was? Just to be insulted? But then I suppose you imagine those *of my station* enjoy it."

A look of real concern passed across Lady Alleyne's face; it had nothing whatsoever to do with Kel. He was not even sure she had registered his words beyond understanding he did not know the location of her daughter.

"Then . . . where is she?" she said. "With some other friend?"

"I cannot imagine," he said, holding Antonetta's note out to her. His stomach churned. Did Lady Alleyne really know so little about her own daughter that she did not realize there was no one on the Hill whom Antonetta really counted as a friend?

Which was a terrifying thought. He tried to tell himself that perhaps she had fled to Sancia Vasey's, but he could not make himself believe it. So *where was she*?

"Ask the Prince," said Lady Alleyne, snatching the note from him. "If anyone can discover where she has hidden herself—"

"No," Kel said. The rage and terror swirled inside him like a rising whirlpool; he could not force it down, any more than he could stop himself from saying what he knew he should not say: "So Conor can have her dragged back under your thumb? You forced your daughter into an engagement with a man she hates, a man who has done nothing but humiliate her with his repeated trips to brothels in the city, and who plans to humiliate her only more greatly with the ceremony of the First Night."

A look of shock passed over Liorada's face, but she was made of stern stuff. The steel in Antonetta's veins had its roots in her mother, even if in Lady Alleyne those roots were twisted.

Lady Alleyne raised her chin, her look of contempt washing over Kel like dirty water. "My daughter will always have the finest things in life," she snapped. "I have seen to that." Her voice curdled. "Not that *you* would understand. You live off the royal blood. You will never understand the meaning of responsibility or what it means to sacrifice for another."

"Sacrifice?" Kel bit back. "It has always been my understanding that for a sacrifice to have meaning, you must surrender something that matters to *you*. Not sacrifice your own daughter in your stead."

At that, she flinched, and Kel felt a savage pleasure in having hurt her. A pleasure born in the pain of a fifteen-year-old boy who had just been told he had nothing to offer the girl he loved and should stay away from her for her own good.

Lady Alleyne's lips pressed into a thin line. "My daughter will return. She is being foolish and stubborn, that is all. And when she *does* return, I want you to remember that nothing has changed. Keep away from her, Anjuman."

Kel allowed himself the ghost of a smile. "If Artal Gremont wishes me to stay away from his fiancée, he can tell me that himself. Can't he?"

For a moment, a look like fear passed over Lady Alleyne's features. Then she slammed the door in Kel's face.

As the carriage rolled smoothly up the Hill toward Marivent, Lin clenched her hands in her lap. She could sense her heart beating in her palms. She knew, of course, that it wasn't really her heartbeat she felt. The vessels that carried blood through the body were near the surface only in certain places, like the wrist and throat. But the body in distress was like a broken mirror, casting strange reflections: A wound on one side of the body might be felt on the other, or agony might still register in an amputated limb. Aron's words had burrowed under her skin like poison or a sickness.

She had accepted the fact that when Aron looked at her, he did not recognize the Goddess. That he saw she was only ordinary, and perhaps worse than ordinary—silly, a liar, desperate for attention. It had made her squirm inside.

But now he said he saw fire in her. Whether it was the true fire of the Goddess she could not say, but the thought frightened her almost as much as what he had said next. Was the flame he saw some residue of the magic she'd been doing? A sort of bright reflection of her Source-Stone? But then—

Around you I see only darkness.

What darkness could he be seeing? She did not for a moment doubt he saw *something*. He was the Exilarch, the Lion of Judah. Almost unconsciously, she reached into her sleeve, where the brooch with her stone was pinned. The stone was cool to the touch, inert and empty of magic.

She bit her lip as they entered the Palace through the North Gate. The first time she had come to Marivent had been like stepping into a Story-Spinner tale. Now she was beginning to know the place: the Castel Mitat and its courtyard in the center, the towers at each cardinal point, the Little Palace among the gardens, the walking paths near the cliff's edge, where the sea crashed below, sending up spray like an invading army climbing the rocks.

The chaos in her mind had quieted by the time the carriage halted at the North Tower and she let Jolivet lead her up the stairs. She knew how to set aside whatever troubled her so she could concentrate on a patient. And as for her most important patient— Mariam—all that mattered was making Mariam well before the Exilarch and the Sanhedrin could stop her.

They reached the landing. She scrambled to make sure she had her satchel, her notebook, then nodded at the head of the Arrow Squadron. "It would be better if I went in alone," she said. "To see the patient."

"The patient," Jolivet said. He managed to make the two words sound unexpectedly grim. He was an odd man, the Legate, gray and severe apart from the blood-red signet ring on his hand. "You may be alone with him if you like. Good luck to you. He's been in a wild mood these past days."

Lin tried to picture the silent, staring King in a wild mood. "I see. Thank you. For the warning."

"I will await you on the landing." Jolivet did not look at her as he unlocked the tower room door. Lin's stomach was clenched with tension, but there was nothing for it. She went past Jolivet into the King's chamber and heard the door close behind her with an ominous *click*.

At first glance, everything seemed unchanged. Items of the astronomer's science still littered every surface: bronze astrolabes, cosmological maps, gold and ebony octants, a brass torquetum from the time of the Empire. And, of course, the scorch marks on the walls she had noticed before.

The King sat, as he had previously, in the great wooden chair beside the casement window. As she approached slowly, mindful of Jolivet's warning, she noticed something odd about the window itself—the glass seemed warped, as if there were a flaw in it. But she did not remember a flaw . . .

As she drew closer, she saw that the glass was not warped but scratched. Gouged, in fact; narrow channels were dug deep into the clear material. They created the impression that the view beyond, of the Palace and the sea, was of a countryside that had itself been damaged. Lin could see a row of white plaster follies shaped like miniature buildings—a cottage, a farmhouse, a temple—standing guard at the edge of the sea cliffs. The damaged glass made the pillars of the temple folly seem broken, and the Trick, rising in the distance, seemed riven with pale scars.

If the King, staring out the window, noticed any of this, he gave no sign. He sat still as a statue, robed in gray and black. He wore no crown, but the omnipresent dark gloves were, as ever, firmly on his hands.

"Your Highness," Lin said quietly. "I am your physician. I have come to examine you."

She knelt down in front of him. Opening her satchel, she retrieved her lancet, a cannula of hollow reed, and a small glass bottle. It was her own invention, this method of collecting blood.

The chirurgeons of Castellane saw no use in taking blood from patients, save with the use of leeches for bleeding. There was no point in *looking* at blood, surely; what could it tell you? Chirurgeons were fools, Lin thought as she arranged the cannula and the bottle. Blood was a tablet, a book. You could read secrets in it if you knew how.

Lin placed the tip of the lancet against the King's wrist, above the black leather of his glove. She felt him jerk as the cold metal touched his skin; when she looked up, he was staring *at* her—not past her or through her, but directly into her eyes.

"I do not think there is any chance, Fausten," he said hoarsely. "They will never allow us to escape."

Lin stayed very still. She had known he was not incapable of speech—he had spoken in her presence once before—but this was the calmest she'd heard him. Even if he didn't know who she was. "I am not Fausten. I am Lin, Lin Caster. Your son brought me to you before—"

The King shook his head. "I took their greatest treasure. That which made them what they are. But *they stole it*. It was never theirs to begin with." His voice rose. "The House of Belmany was built on darkness, and to darkness it will return."

House Belmany. Lin thought of what the others had told her about Tyndaris. About Malgasi. Fire burning on the sea. She whispered, "What did you take from them?"

His gaze roamed fretfully around the room. "All night I heard it crying out. It was caged. It begged for freedom, but all I could give it was death. They would never have freed it. It was the source of all their power."

"What is *it*? Was it . . . a Source-Stone?" Setting the lancet on the arm of the chair, she folded up the sleeve of her dress, showing the silver brooch pinned inside, the Source-Stone black and lightless—

"*Atma!*" The King roared. His head went back, his eyes flaring, his teeth bared. "*Atma, sur az koval!*"

Before Lin could move to stop him, the King seized up the lancet from the arm of the chair and plunged the blade of it into the palm of his left hand.

Lin cried out. The King's grip relaxed as suddenly as he'd lunged for the blade; the lancet clattered to the ground. Lin caught at the King's wounded hand—blood ran from the cuff of his glove, soaking his sleeve, spattering onto Lin. She felt the hot sting of it, and then a sharp pain at her wrist.

She looked down. The Source-Stone in its brooch was glowing brightly through her sleeve. It was hot. So hot it was searing her skin.

Fire rose up all around her. The room was burning, the papers suddenly alight, the King's chair a flaming funeral pyre. She tried to scramble to her knees, but the smoke was too thick to breathe. Her chest aching, she tried to crawl toward the door, but the smoke burned her throat, choked the air from her lungs. She curled in on herself, gasping as darkness rushed in, smothering her breath.

Lin opened her eyes with the sudden shock that accompanies waking in an unfamiliar place. She was lying on something soft; above her arched a low stone ceiling. A dim light came from somewhere nearby. Her lungs felt emptied of air; she sucked in a breath, struggling into a sitting position.

Memories flooded her mind immediately—memories of fire and falling. A descent into a dark place, the blade of a knife and the bars of a cage. But that had not been real, she told herself. She had been unconscious, dreaming—but the tower room *had* been burning. Of that much she was certain. And she had fallen into unconsciousness, unable to breathe, to think. How had she gotten out?

She was still in the Palace. The room was small, stone-walled, with a single high window. The walls were covered with maps, of Dannemore and the Gold Roads, of Malgasi and Sarthe, dotted with constellations of silver pins. There were maps of the stars, too, and a number of paper constructions with rotating parts: wheels and numbered dials. Volvelles, they were called: spinning die-cut charts that measured everything from distance over land to the orbit of the moon.

She glanced quickly at her hands, her arms, to see if they were burned, but her skin was unmarked. She threw back her thin blanket and sat up. The room seemed immediately to swing around her. She reached for something to anchor her, but her vision had blurred. She dug her fingers into the mattress—

"You're all right." A familiar voice, presence. Her hands were enfolded in a steadying grasp. "Lin. Breathe. *Breathe.*"

She sucked in her breath. She was not alone, she told herself. Nor was she dreaming. Conor was with her. She felt the warmth of him, his presence. His hand brushed back hair from her face. "Look at me, sweetheart," he said. "Can you do that?"

She blinked. He was a blur—a blur of silver silk and gray velvet, of black hair, and of the gleam of his circlet, like the shimmer of water. Gripping his hand, she looked around the room. It was full of heavy, old-fashioned furniture. There were a number of desks, and a wardrobe whose drawers had been pulled out, their contents scattered—everything from gloves to scissors to ceramic hot water bottles. A fine-bound leather book lay on the floor, its cover stamped in gold: OREL VALARATI.

"Where am I?" she whispered.

"This is Fausten's room, or used to be." Conor was no longer a blur. She could see him clearly now. He still wore the same fine gray velvet he had worn in the square, its embroidery gleaming like dull fire in the faint light. His eyes were the same silver, and they seemed to be burning, watchful lights in a face whose skin was too tight on its bones. She had never seen him look like that before. Not—*afraid*.

When he spoke, it was with immense control. "I found you on the floor of the tower. You were unconscious. I carried you in here. Lin—what happened?"

"Your father," she choked. "The fire—the room was burning. Is he all right?"

She tried to get to her feet, but the dizziness was bad. She sank back against the mattress, her head pounding.

"Lin. Stop." Her hair had come out of its braids; he pushed it back again. The feeling was unutterably soothing. "There was no fire. When I came in, my father was sitting in his chair. Everything was as it always is, except you—" He broke off. "I need to know, Lin. Did he hurt you?"

"No," Lin said. When she shook her head, her hair tumbled against her neck, her shoulders, and she thought how strange it was to appear before the Prince with unbound hair. "Nothing like that. The fire may not have existed, but even if it was an illusion, it was of the King's making."

"He is not a magician, Lin. Not a Sorcerer-King of old." Conor's tone was gentle.

"And yet, there is magic here. This is no ordinary aliment, as I said. I know it—" *Because my Source-Stone burned.* But she could not say that. *Because the Malgasi wield true sorcery.* But she could not say that, either. She bit her lip in frustration. "Do you know what happened to your father when he was young? At the Malgasi Court? He left—"

"He fled," Conor corrected her. "Though he has never spoken of his time there." His hand tangled in her hair, the strands winding through his fingers. He watched her sidelong, as if ready for her to pull away, but Lin would not have moved for the world. "Why do you ask me about Malgasi? Because of Fausten?"

"It is not just Fausten. When your father is distressed, he speaks Malgasi. It is clear his mind is fevered with some wound of the past, some memory of his time in Favár . . ."

Conor frowned. "When I found you," he said, "you were babbling in Malgasi. *Atma, atma, sur az koval.* I didn't know you even spoke the language."

"I do not," said Lin. "What do the words mean?"

"'The fire, the fire, the blood and the cage.'"

"The blood and the cage," Lin said. "What did they *do* to him?" Her stone pulsed at her wrist, like the touch of a match tip. She winced.

Conor sat up straight. "You *are* hurt," he said, almost accusingly. "Lin, if this is magic, a curse, it's too dangerous. I should never have asked you to be involved."

"You didn't know," Lin said. "And I am not hurt— *Conor.*"

But he had risen to his feet. He raked his hands through his hair, almost disarranging his circlet. "I should never have let you come here alone," he said. "I wanted you in the square. I wanted you to see me with Anjelica. I wanted you to be—" He flung his hand out, slammed it against the wardrobe, making the remaining contents rattle. "I should never have asked you to fix a problem that is mine and mine alone."

"You didn't ask," Lin said, and though she said it softly, she saw him flinch.

"You mean I gave you a royal order." He was clenching his hand so tightly at his side, she worried his ring would cut into his skin. "Well, I rescind it. You are no longer under a royal order, Lin Caster. I release you from this and any other obligation you might feel to me—"

Lin rose from the bed. She had been worried she would be shaky on her feet, but thankfully she was steady. "What about the obligation I feel to my patient? I want to help your father. To treat him. This is what I *do.*"

"The only reason you are involved at all is because I demanded it," he said. He closed the few steps between them, caught her face between his hands. His thumb brushed along her cheekbone, unraveling something inside her, like Mariam unpicking a row of stitches. "When I found you on the floor, I thought you were dead," he said roughly. "And I realized what that would mean. If you were hurt, even a scratch, because of something I'd demanded you do—" He closed his eyes as if against the vision of something he could not bear. "I rescind the order, Lin. And for the Gods' sake, if I ask you to do something and you know it to be stupid and dangerous, tell me no. Refuse me, the way you like to do."

"Then I am refusing you now," she said. "Not the rescinding of the order. The treatment of your father. You drew me into this; you cannot cut me away from it now."

"I could order you not to involve yourself."

"*Conor.*" She laid her hands on his chest, felt his muscles jump under her touch. He looked at her almost in disbelief. "Not everything has to be orders, demands. I am asking you to trust me."

"I already trust you," he said.

"Then trust yourself." She could feel the beat of his heart under her right hand. It was racing, as if he were running. She wanted to press her hands harder against him, wanted to press *herself* against him, the ache of desire like a fishhook caught under her skin. "You are *trying*," she whispered. "To be a good Prince, a better King someday. I believe you could be a great King of Castellane. You must believe that about yourself, too. You do not want to put me under an order. It is not your instinct. Trust yourself."

His eyes were wide. So beautiful, she thought; he was so beautiful it hurt, black-ink hair and the bones of his face graceful as a soaring heron. "I have never trusted myself," he said. "But I think, if you did—I could."

She did not know what madness seized her then. Only that there was an ache in her chest, in her bones, that she could not understand or explain; only that her body impelled her upward, onto her toes, her hands pressing down on his shoulders as she brushed her lips against his cheek—a quick kiss that was barely a kiss at all.

She drew back to see that his eyes had darkened, the gray almost swallowed up by the blackness of his pupils. His hand curled in her hair, catching at the strands, letting them slide through his fingers. "Lin . . ." he breathed. "Don't do that."

She had never been so close to him; she could see the flecks of lighter and darker color in his eyes, the lighter skin at his temples, the base of his throat, where the sun did not touch, the glint of the circlet in among his curls. The beat of the pulse at his throat, so fast it was visible. "You just told me," she whispered, "not to take orders from you."

His breath hissed between his teeth. "*You,*" he said, and then he caught at her, pulling her against him, her hands flattening against his chest as he drove his mouth against hers.

The force of the kiss would have set her back on her heels, but his hands were already at her waist, pulling her against him, holding her in place. She could taste honey and spice on his mouth, the sacramental wine of blessing. When he sucked her lower lip, running his tongue across it, stars exploded behind her eyes.

The tight coil of control she held around herself whenever she was near him loosened. She slid her hands up his chest, and the pleasure of touching him like that, even without her skin on his, was sharper than pain. She smoothed her palms down his shoulders, took hold of his arms, the muscle of them hard beneath her grasp.

Without her hands in the way, she pressed even closer against him, every part of her fitted against his body. He moaned against her mouth at the touch. Kissed her again and again, each time harder, his tongue curling against hers, her fingers biting into the soft velvet of his jacket. And still she wanted.

People dying of thirst, when they were given water, sometimes drank until they died, unable to assuage the need that had become part of them. She could understand it now, how you could have something and still not have enough of it, ever. He was shaking against her, tremors that curled his clenched muscles tighter, forcing her awareness of the heat of him against her, the strength of him, the pressure of his hand at her hip—

He jerked away from her. It felt like a wound, and not a clean cut: bone and muscle torn apart. Her hand flew to her mouth.

"*Conor*," she breathed.

He stood a few feet from her, his hands half raised, as if to ward her away. His voice shook. "You had better go."

"It's not your fault," she whispered. "I wanted—"

"I stood in front of the Hierophant today," he said. "I was sealed to Anjelica in front of all my people. And now—" There was agony in his words. "Please. I am not ordering you away from the King. I am begging you, for my sake. Go now."

It was the *please* that caught her. Conor Aurelian did not ask, did not request, did not say *please* or *for my sake*. Conor Aurelian did not beg. But he was begging her now.

With shaking hands, she caught up her satchel and fled from the room.

She did not slow down until she had burst from the tower, flinging herself into the carriage waiting there. As it rolled forward across the courtyard, she lifted her arms to wrap them around herself—to stop herself shaking—and it was then that she saw it. The Source-Stone in her brooch, which had been a dead blank eye for so long, was glimmering with a tiny flicker of light deep in its heart.

When Kel came into the rooms he shared with Conor, something struck him as odd. It took him a moment to realize what it was. For the first time in months, the door to the liquor cabinet was flung open, and a row of bottles sat on Conor's desk, atop the papers.

Kel had spent some hours after leaving the Alleyne house wandering the Hill, kicking his way through the *garrigue*, the dry scrubland of tangled lavender, thorny broom, and rosemary that covered the highlands of Castellane. From the higher spots on the Hill, he could see down into the city. There was the dot of the Sault, and to the east of it, Valerian Square turned black with the density of the crowd gathered to see the marriage blessing. He thought of Conor again, but now thoughts of Conor were tangled with thoughts of Antonetta. *Could* he ask Conor to help him find out where she was? But there had been nothing in her note to indicate she was not leaving willingly, and who could blame her? The Hill rumors were poisonous, and she could not tell the truth of what she knew without indicting her own mother.

"Kel?" Conor's voice. His eyes adjusting to the dimness in the room, Kel saw Conor for the first time. He was seated in the embrasure of the arched western window, still in his ceremonial clothes, dark-gray velvet chained with brilliant threads of silver. There was a bottle in his hand. "Kel, is that you?"

"I certainly hope so." Kel crossed the room, glancing at the bottles on the desk as he passed. Dark-red bloodroot liquor from Hanse, pale-yellow ginger wine, pale-lilac elixir made from violets. It seemed Conor had had difficulty choosing.

Kel could sense, more than see, Conor watching him owlishly as he approached and pulled himself up on the windowsill. He swung his legs up sideways so he and Conor could face each other, each at their opposite ends of the arched hollow in the stone. The window glass was cool against the side of his face.

He could not count the number of times they'd sat like this, the dark room on one side of them, the lights of the city a shimmering blur through the glass on the other. Kel could see Conor more clearly now, see his hand wrapped tightly around the neck of a green bottle, see the half-defensive look in his eyes.

Kel said lightly, "It's been a while since you've been at the absynthe, Con. Did the blessing ceremony not go as planned?"

Conor ducked his head. Kel sensed the Prince was vibrating at an unusually tense frequency, like an overtightened viol string. "All was well," he said. "I was blessed and bound, as was the Princess. It is not the ceremony that preys on my mind."

Good, Kel thought. *At least he's willing to admit something is preying on his mind.*

"The Solstice Ball is troubling you, then? Don't tell me. Your costume isn't ready, or they've sent you the wrong one and you're going to have to go as a hedgehog instead of a lion."

"I would make a noble hedgehog," said Conor gravely. "No, it is not the ball. I have simply been thinking on what I bound myself to today, and of all the bindings I have willingly submitted my will to over the past months. I am bound by treaties, by contracts, by promises both explicit and implicit, and by expectations."

"The expectations others lay on you or the ones you have of yourself?"

"I think I no longer know the difference."

"It may not be so bad, you know," Kel said. "All rulers are bound by such obligations, yet they manage. I do not see why you would be different."

"I cannot hope for *not so bad*," Conor said gravely. "Hope is a danger, you know. Hope may raise you up for a time, but when it is disappointed, the fall is all the more acute."

He reached up to press a forefinger against his temple, as he always did when troubled. And at that moment, Kel wanted to tell him everything. About the conspiracy, about Malgasi, about what he had seen on Tyndaris. He would swear him to utter silence. He would tell him no one could be trusted. He would explain that he had done what he had done at Jolivet's bequest, and because the Ragpicker King was not an enemy. *There has always been a King on the Hill and a King in the City—*

Something must have shown in his eyes. Tension, anxiety— whatever it was, Conor sat up straight, shaking his head to clear it. "Never mind," he said with a disarming smile. "I am lamentably no longer used to strong liquor, I think. Take this bottle from me, Kel; there is no point in my being hung over at the Solstice Ball. That's what the day *after* the party is for. Now, I could use your advice on my costume . . ."

Jerrod

Jerrod has only gone a few blocks into the Maze when he becomes aware of the figure flitting across the rooftops overhead. It is clear that the moving shadow is following him: pausing when he pauses, turning as he turns.

For a moment, a cold finger of unease touches the back of his spine. He knows that chilly slide of nerves well; he has grown up with it on the streets of Castellane.

He steps carelessly into the middle of Arsenal Road, passing a series of ramshackle stalls that sell everything from false jewelry to soup (a penny cheaper if you bring your own bowl), then looks up and sideways. The figure is still there, gliding along the tops of warehouses.

He turns a corner abruptly, taking him deeper into the space between the Maze and the Key; he can smell the salt-rot stench of ocean water here, lapping against the shore. The alley is narrow and dirty, lined with stacks of empty, splintered boxes.

It was in an alley like this that Kel had nearly died. It is a moment Jerrod does not enjoy dwelling on. He remembers how angry Prosper Beck had been when he'd returned with the news that they'd caught the wrong fish in their net: not the Prince, but his

Sword Catcher. Beck had kicked the wall with a booted foot. *Kel was never supposed to be harmed, Jerrod, you ought to have known that.*

He looks up now to where a strip of gray-blue sky shows between the roofs above. "Ji-An," he says, "get down from there. I know it's you, sneaking around."

She lands lightly in front of him. She wears a silk jacket and trousers of a violet color so dark, it is nearly black. He remembers catching a glimpse of her on the rooftop that night Kel nearly died, a flick of shadow against a darker sky. "I do have a distinctive manner of sneaking," she says. "Were you worried I was her? The Malgasi woman?"

"Perhaps for a moment. But much as she may dislike me, I doubt I am high on her list of priorities." He cocked his head to the side. "Why have you been following me? Do you miss me that badly?"

She smiles coolly. "I'm just wondering what Prosper Beck plans to do with all those weapons you've stuffed into that warehouse. You are working for Beck, aren't you?"

Jerrod leans his back against a stack of crates. "You knew I was Beck's man when you let me into the Black Mansion."

"You said he was gone."

"Well," Jerrod says. "He came back."

Ji-An slowly shakes her head. She doesn't seem angry, which surprises Jerrod. He would have thought she, of all of them, would be the least forgiving. "How long were you in touch with him before you decided to quit on us?" she says. "You were the least surprised about what happened on Tyndaris with the Malgasi woman. Did you know about her because of Beck?"

"I can't tell you that."

"What does he hold over you?" she asks. "You were perfectly happy with us. I know you were."

"Prosper Beck saved my life." Clouds are gathering overhead, further graying the sky. "I owe him. Like you owe Morettus."

Her expression softens. "Should we be worried about what information you plan to share with him?"

"No. Beck's not your enemy. I don't know what the weapons are for. Selling, probably—"

Ji-An's eyes narrow. "Selling to Malgasi?"

"Definitely not." *I wish I could tell you all of it.* "Malgasi hate every one of us. They're the threat. Not Beck."

"Hmm." She bites her lip. "What are you not telling me?"

"I'm telling you everything I can," Jerrod says, and that, at least, is the whole truth. "That's why I left the mansion. There was too much I couldn't tell any of you. I don't mind lying, but not to people I . . ."

Now she smiles. "Like?"

Jerrod crosses his arms over his chest. "Don't laugh at me."

"Merren misses you, you know," she says. "He isn't even interested in experiments anymore. Just sits around staring at his alembics. Moping." She examines her nails. "Sighing."

Jerrod glares at her. "Why are you telling me this?"

She straightens up, giving him a hard look. "I want you to promise on Merren's life that Beck isn't stockpiling these weapons to use them against the Ragpicker King or any of us."

Jerrod nods. "I can promise you that."

The hard look softens slowly into something else. It certainly isn't a look of trust, but it isn't hatred, either. Jerrod supposes he should take what he can get.

"Good enough," Ji-An says, and—with a flick of shadow—disappears into the darkness, a moment before the sky opens up and pours down rain.

CHAPTER SEVENTEEN

"Are you quite sure you're all right?"

Lin looked anxiously across the table at Merren. They were in the Black Mansion, Merren perched on a stool with a round glass alembic in his hands. The length of the much-abused table was between them, but Lin could still read Merren's expression clearly.

Merren, unlike the Ragpicker King or Ji-An, had never been good at hiding his emotions. Under his tousled hair, his face was set in lines of clear unhappiness. His blue eyes were rimmed in red. She wondered if she dared mention Jerrod's name—it had been days since Jerrod had left, and she still didn't really know how Merren felt about it.

Merren lifted a hand to pat his bandaged shoulder. "Not to worry. I'm healing nicely."

He'd misunderstood her deliberately, Lin thought. But then, she could hardly blame him. It wasn't as if she were eager or willing to spill her confused thoughts about Conor, even to Mariam.

"Well, don't lift anything too heavy," Lin said. She touched one of the packets of ingredients—some from the physick garden, some fresh from this morning's market—that lay in a tidy row on the table. "How long do you think it will take to formulate the altered remedy?"

Merren looked thoughtful. Hopefully at least the new project would be distracting, Lin thought. And that went for both of them. For all she did not want to dwell on Conor or what the kiss between them had meant, it was proving close to impossible. That morning, when she'd set out for the market, she'd found a thick envelope on her doorstep, marked with the royal seal.

An invitation to the Solstice Ball. She'd been standing there staring at it helplessly when Mariam had appeared. Lin had handed over the envelope wordlessly, expecting Mariam to be shocked. Instead Mariam only announced rather gleefully that she'd *expected* Lin to receive such an invitation, and had begun a dress the previous week that only needed a few last touches.

"Argh," Lin had said, or something to that effect. She couldn't be angry at Mariam for assuming; she'd been right. And she wasn't even sure she could be angry at Conor. The invitation was a polite gesture, and one she wasn't even sure was personal. Perhaps it was professional, political? It was formally worded, not signed by him as the letter Mayesh had delivered had been.

Which meant Lin wasn't sure at all whether she should go. If it was personal, surely she ought to stay home. If it was professional—

"*Lin*," Merren said loudly, and she realized, with a start, that he was looking at her with a mixture of amusement and exasperation. "Where have you drifted off to?" He pointed at the pile of ingredients on the table. "When do you require the remedy to be finished?"

"Ah." Lin knew she was blushing. "As soon as possible."

"Hm." Merren set the alembic down and reached for the recipe Lin had written out for him in her scrawling physician's hand. "To make a remedy is not that different from making a poison. But I do have a concern." He rubbed at the bridge of his nose, leaving a faint smear of ash. "The formulation contains a heavy dose of sedative. More than I'd be comfortable giving to someone, and I poison people for a living." He hesitated. "Jerrod . . ."

Lin cocked an eyebrow.

"Jerrod worked in the Maze. He knew a number of poppy addicts. It's possible to survive quite high doses of this sort of thing if you're used to it, but I wouldn't like to say what it does to your mind. Jerrod might know, but he . . ."

Has run off, and didn't seem to want any of us to follow. Merren was looking woebegone. Lin reached across the table to pat his hand.

"Someone else raised a similar concern to me," she said, remembering Aron, his bronze hair shining in the moonlight, standing at her front door. The same doorstep where that morning she'd found the invitation, the red royal seal gleaming like a drop of fresh scarlet blood on white linen.

"Take out the yellow poppy, then," she said, deciding several things in a single moment. "Replace it with two grains of morphea."

Merren sat back. "You're sure?"

"I'm sure. Thank you, Merren." She picked up her satchel. "I'll be back for the remedy . . . ?"

"Tomorrow," he said, looking at her curiously. "What are you looking cheerful about?"

"If you must know, I'm off to the Solstice Ball tonight," she said, pausing at the door on her way out. "Don't worry," she added, as both his eyebrows shot into his hairline. "I'll be sure to take down the monarchy while I'm up on the Hill."

"Don't get my hopes up for nothing, Lin," he called after her. "There's only so much disappointment a man can take."

The summer solstice had been a celebration in Castellane since the Aurelians had come to power, for their symbol was the sun. It was Lilibet, though, who had added the tradition of the masked ball. They were popular in Marakand, as they allowed nobles to enjoy themselves with a certain amount of plausible deniability regarding their actions.

It was a cool night, with rain threatening, but Lilibet had thrown open the doors of the old Armory regardless. Armies might alter their plans because of inclement weather, but Lilibet never would.

Inside, the circular ballroom glowed warmly. The floor was a sheet of gold tesserae. Long alcoves were set at even points around the central circle, like rays of the sun. Each alcove featured some new treasure: a life-sized bronze statue of Lotan with his sun-chariot, a fountain that poured fire, not water, a tree painted entirely gold, from whose branches hung golden apples.

The rounded roof overhead was glass. Through it, Kel could see a thick layer of low clouds, illuminated from below by the Palace lamps. The threat of rain had forced Lilibet to abandon the idea of a golden carpet that would lead people across the threshold and into the ballroom. Instead, yellow and white flower petals had been scattered across the grass and over the stone steps. As guests arrived, they tracked the flowers in on their shoes, and the scent of crushed petals rose to mix with the scent of jasmine candles in a heady infusion.

Lilibet herself was rushing to and fro, directing Dom Valon and his staff as they put the last touches on the groaning banquet tables. Everything was in the colors of House Aurelian: pig roasted with lemons, lamb baked with saffron, turmeric rice, iced sherbets of mango and passion fruit, sugared kalamansi juice.

Conor had decided to be on good behavior tonight: He was making the rounds, greeting guests with extravagant compliments, causing Lady Alleyne to announce that she was blushing behind her tiger half-mask. She wore a matching dress of striped-black-and-gold silk.

Despite the cover provided by the mask, all evidence was that Lady Alleyne was nervous. Kel, seated on one of the long divans stationed at intervals along the wall (Lilibet wanted guests on their feet, dancing and mixing) could not help but notice that her laughter was a little too shrill, her flirting a little too brittle. Kel doubted Conor would see it, but Conor didn't know what he did.

In fact, Kel had not found himself this uncomfortable at a gathering of the nobles on the Hill since he'd been eight years old, and then they had all been strangers. He'd grown up knowing he could trust none of them to do anything but act in their own self-interest, but he had naïvely assumed that self-interest included loyalty to House Aurelian. Now, though, they seemed not just strangers, but a pack of wild animals, circling, waiting for the kill.

It was not *all* of them, he reminded himself, as Conor departed from Lady Alleyne's company and crossed the room to greet Esteve who had come, not unexpectedly, dressed as a horse. Conor himself was all in black, down to his onyx rings. His half-mask was, as Anjelica had suggested, the golden mask of a lion, the eyeholes surrounded by glittering chips of topaz.

Kel, too, was in black, though his mask was silver: plain, save for two ram's horns curling at his temples. He thought of the names mentioned by Elsabet Belmany on Tyndaris: Alleyne, Gremont, Cabrol. So who were the other conspirators? Had there been any families who had been approached by Malgasi, but had stood firm? Old Gremont had regretted his involvement at the last moment, but that was not the same thing.

Cazalet, Kel thought, was far too clever to risk his name and fortune on a wild scheme. And while the younger Gremont had been involved, did that mean Lady Gremont knew anything about it? Her husband had done everything he could to warn Conor before his death . . .

"If you are wondering if the rumors are true, they seem to be," said Falconet, sliding onto the brocade sofa beside Kel. He wore the mask of a Shenzan dragon, its snout wickedly curved. With him were Montfaucon and Ciprian Cabrol. "Artal Gremont has absconded into the night, leaving Antonetta bereft of his name and fortune."

"Lady Alleyne is trying her best to behave as though nothing untoward has happened," said Montfaucon. He wore a peacock mask and a suit of a gold material that crackled like wax paper. "She's claiming he's gone to visit some trading partner or other in Valderan, but I wonder."

"You think she's saving face?" said Kel. What *was* Lady Alleyne's plan, he wondered. But perhaps she was just waiting for marching orders from Elsabet. The conspirators on the Hill would have to account for Gremont's death somehow.

"Well, it reflects on her badly, doesn't it?" said Cabrol. He wore rumpled brown velvet and a jackal mask. "Or at least—let's be plain—it reflects badly on her daughter. If Gremont prefers to leave behind his inheritance and escape Castellane in the dead of night instead of marrying Antonetta, he must have found her very unsatisfactory indeed."

"I rather thought he found her exactly as he'd expected," said Falconet. "Beautiful and stupid. If he'd thought she was anything but decorative, I doubt he would have gone through the effort of exerting his First Night privilege."

"I can't say I'm sorry not to have to watch *that* happen," said Falconet. "Speaking of brides—the lovely Anjelica has arrived."

Kel glanced over and saw Anjelica standing with Conor near the entrance to the ballroom. Conor had her hands in his and was leaning in to speak to her in a low voice—a picture of young love, Kel thought sardonically.

"It must be odd for Conor, having such a lovely bride," said Montfaucon cattily. "He's so used to being the prettiest one at parties."

Anjelica wore the costume of a swan, her mask a confection of glitter, paint, and satin, decorated with long pale feathers and diamond crescents. Her hair was swept up, coiled at the back of her neck and held in place with ivory pins carved to resemble feathers. Her dress was simple: white silk and seed pearls, clinging close to her body. From her back sprouted two white wings, lavishly appliquéd with feathers and diamonds, making them brilliantly gleam.

Together, she and Conor were stunning to look at. But it was all costume, Kel thought—and not just the masks. They were playing a much more careful part. The way they leaned into each other; the way Conor took Anjelica's hand as he led her into the ballroom. Each move practiced, studied, and executed for maximum effect.

"Regard Lady Alleyne," said Falconet, amused. "She looks as if she's just eaten a lemon."

"She had always hoped to marry Antonetta to Conor," said Montfaucon. "But Conor had his sights set higher, and now Antonetta is without any husband at all. It only goes to show that ambition is a vice," he added pompously.

Cabrol snorted. "You *are* drunk, Lupin. Where is Antonetta, anyway?"

"I doubt she could face the crowd," said Falconet. "Too many whispers. Some are even saying she did away with Gremont herself, to avoid the humiliation of the First Night."

"And who could blame her if she did," muttered Kel.

Montfaucon looked puzzled. "Do you think she killed Gremont?"

"Of course not," Kel said irritably. "I think he's probably drunk at the Caravel, and has been for days. I think everyone's hoping this situation is much more exciting than it actually is."

"Congratulations, Kel," said Joss, with a grin. "You have cut to the very definition of *gossip*. Besides, our Antonetta is a simple soul. Not bright enough to execute a murder plan."

Rage stirred in the pit of Kel's stomach. Before he could respond, a hand fell on his shoulder. Looking up, he saw that Benaset, in gold livery for the occasion, had appeared at his side. "If you would come with me for a moment, Mirzah Anjuman," he said. "It has begun to rain."

"And what am I supposed to do about that?" Kel said, utterly baffled.

"You'll have to ask the Queen," said Benaset, giving Kel a hard look. *Ah*. It was *Conor* who wanted to speak to him, Kel realized, and indeed he saw that Anjelica was alone, deep in conversation with Lady Gremont.

To a chorus of amused catcalls from Conor's friends, Kel rose and followed Benaset into one of the alcoves. This one featured a tree made of metal, its trunk gleaming bronze, its foliage hammered leaves of gold and brass and silver. Beneath the tree waited Conor, who waved Benaset away. He held several long moments before speaking, presumably to make sure Benaset was out of earshot.

"You have your talisman with you, don't you?" Conor said at last.

"Yes," Kel said slowly. "Conor, what's happened? Is there some kind of danger?"

Conor reached up to undo the silk cords that held his mask on. When it fell away, his face looked oddly stripped bare, faint grooves marked beside his eyes where the mask had dug into his skin. His hands shook slightly. "Switch masks with me? It'll only be for a few moments."

"Why?"

"There's no danger." Conor looked at Kel steadily, and behind his eyes Kel could see the light he had seen when he was a child, the first time he had visited the Palace. The first time he had ever known what it was to want something you had never realized you wanted. "But I need you to trust me."

"Something's been bothering you all night." Kel reached up to unfasten his mask. "I don't know what it is, but you've been troubled since this party began."

Conor, his mask dangling from his hand by its strings, smiled painfully. "My very observant Kel."

"Tell me," Kel urged him. "Tell me what it is. I can't help you otherwise."

Conor's eyes met his. Gray eyes, the same color as Kel's, though they had not always been the same. "There isn't time," he said. "Not now. I won't make you do it, Kel, but if you trust me—"

Kel held out his mask. They exchanged them quickly, the heavy gold circlet and jeweled lion's mask thumping into Kel's palm. It was followed by a dozen small cold circles—Conor's onyx rings.

Conor tied the silver strings of his new mask neatly behind his head.

"I'll tell you," he said hoarsely. "I swear it, but—I must go now."

Kel said nothing, only nodded. Conor turned on his heel and walked away, leaving Kel staring after him.

When Lin arrived at Marivent, it had begun to rain. A light drizzle that had the carriage driver warning her to step carefully and avoid the mud.

Lin did not mind. The weather only made the Palace seem more magical. Jewel-toned lamps glowed through a softening mist, like puffs of colored air. The driver had told her to follow the path of flowers to find the Solstice Ball; the blossoms were wet and bright, drops of rain trembling on their petals. Crushed under her slippers as she walked, they gave off the smell of bright-green things, lacquered with a sweet overlayer of tuberose and jasmine.

She pulled her thick velvet shawl tighter around herself as she walked. It was strange to be here. There were countless Story-Spinner tales that involved a young girl being summoned to a ball at the Palace—whatever Palace it might be in the story. She had not been charmed by Marivent before when she had made her secret visits to heal Kel and then the King. They had been hurried, furtive expeditions, during which she had always feared that she would be seen. Discovered. Now she was *supposed* to be here.

Mariam had sworn up and down that her iridescent rose-colored dress—a forbidden color for her, of course, but Lin had accepted that no one on the Hill seemed to care—was the height of fashion. That her hair, a fountain of loose curls, looked just as it should. And indeed, when the carriage had come to retrieve her from the Sault, the driver had looked surprised and admiring.

Her confidence took her nearly to the doors of the ballroom. The Armory was a gray stone building near to the place where the green lawns of Marivent dropped away into sea cliffs. A curved glass dome was set atop it; torches burned along this last stretch of the path, sputtering against the drizzle. Through the leaded-glass windows of the Armory she could see flickering candlelight, the figures of men and women in fancy dress, their faces hidden by an array of masks all in the shapes of different animals: cats and boars and foxes, peacocks and phoenixes.

Oh, no. She realized with a start of alarm that she had no mask and had made no plan as to how to get one. The invitation had mentioned that the Solstice Ball was a masked affair, and yet she'd completely forgotten.

She looked down helplessly at her empty hands, as if a mask might suddenly appear in them. There was laughter behind her; something thumped against her shoulder. She whirled around to find two drunken nobles behind her—a woman in a gray mouse mask decorated with sparkling hearts, and a boy wearing a striped black-and-white domino. "*So* sorry." The woman giggled, leaning on the arm of the boy—her son? her lover?—as he led her back to the ballroom.

Lin felt her stomach lurch. The idea of walking bare-faced into the ballroom held no appeal. The nobility, the Charter Families, even the Prince would stare, whisper . . . They knew who she was: Mayesh's granddaughter, apparently too silly to remember the rules of etiquette. By the Goddess, why had she even *come*?

A moment later, she was hurrying away from the yellow light spilling from the ballroom. Across the wet grass to the crushed stone of the cliff path. She could see the ocean to her right, surging gray-green at the feet of the cliffs.

Thunder rumbled overhead, the sound of gray-black clouds colliding far out to sea. The rain was turning from a drizzle to a true downpour. The various follies she had seen from the North Tower—

impermanent structures of white-painted wood and plaster, meant to amuse and delight the eye—had been placed along the path in a row bordering the cliff edge. Most were open to the sky. Lin ducked into one that offered shelter: It was modeled after an old temple, its angled plaster roof held up with fluted pillars. Through the gaps between the pillars she could see the storm moving in from the ocean, churning the water into white-tipped waves.

She leaned against a pillar, letting her head fall back. It was not real marble, thankfully, only wood painted to resemble stone. She knew she was ruining the hair Mariam had carefully curled and pinned; she felt a jolt of guilt for that, and another for her slippers, wet and stained with mud. *So foolish*, she thought savagely. Why had she ever imagined she wanted to come to the Hill, to open herself up to the judgment of the nobility and their hangers-on?

She straightened, smoothing her hands down the front of her dress—a deep satin so close to the true color of roses that she almost expected it to have a scent. The material was cool and slippery under her hands. Around her neck she wore her mother's *magal*, the hollow circle on its thin gold chain.

She recalled Mariam fastening it for her. Her dear Mariam had been so delighted that Lin was attending the Solstice Ball that she had nearly flown around the room like a hummingbird. Lin smiled at the memory and told herself not to be ridiculous. She had come all this way; she was as finely dressed as she needed to be; she had nothing to be ashamed of, whether she had a mask or not. And how disappointed would Mariam be if she found that Lin had not attended the party at all, but merely hid in a folly?

Thunder cracked again overhead. Out to sea, lightning illuminated the horizon, turning the surging waves to moving, silvery mountains. The rain was a steady downpour, rattling the plaster roof. Lin sighed to herself. Well, there was nothing to be done about it; she wouldn't be the only guest arriving at the ball soaking wet—

Movement caught her eye, and Lin squinted through the pillars. Someone was coming down the cliff path. Odd. Who would be out for a stroll in weather like this?

He came closer. It was a he, she could see that now, a tall young man, wearing the mask of a silver ram.

She took a step back as the man ducked into the folly. He pushed the hood of his velvet cloak back and water streamed from the soaked material, pattering to the stone floor.

It was dark in the folly, but not so dark that she was blind. She could see that he was all in black, wet dark curls plastered to his head. The silver mask with the twisting horns on either side was bright as a star. It covered half his face, but she knew him immediately.

It was Prince Conor, looming over her, water streaming from his hair.

"What are you doing in here?" he snapped. "Benaset let me know you'd come through the West Gate. When you didn't arrive at the party, I thought you'd fallen off one of the cliffs."

Lin immediately felt truculent. "I was lost."

She could see his gray eyes widen behind the mask. "You got *lost*? How could you get lost? There is a path of flowers laid down that leads directly to the doors of the Armory—"

Lin crossed her arms over her chest. "Well, how was I supposed to know that? You didn't mention it."

He shook his head, causing a cascade of silver droplets to fly from his dark hair. "I didn't think I had to mention *every single thing*—"

Lin scowled, though she doubted he could see it in the darkness of the folly. "I don't see why you came all the way out here to find me if you were only planning to be rude."

"I wasn't *planning* to be rude— Good Gods." He passed a hand across his face. "It is absolutely unbelievable," he said, to no one in particular. "I have been shouted at by famous ambassadors. Had inkpots and expensive ceramics thrown at me by furious diplomats. Been in more than one fistfight with a future monarch. Yet nothing, *nothing*, has ever infuriated me the way you do."

"I oughtn't to have come." Lin dropped her arms. "Girls in the Story-Spinner tales always end up absolutely triumphing at the royal parties they attend, and everyone marvels and admires them, and that is *never* going to happen to me. I am always going to be odd and awkward and wind up hiding in a folly—"

"So you *were* hiding. You didn't just get lost." She could hear the amusement under the exasperation in his voice, like a vein of crystal running through granite.

"Does it matter? I don't belong here."

"Lin." She turned to see Conor looking at her; he was not wearing his crown she realized. "Your grandfather is the King's Counselor. I invited you myself. You are no interloper at Marivent."

"Why?" Lin whispered. Outside the folly, the rain fell hard enough to strike silvery sparks from the packed earth. "*Why* did you invite me?"

And in that moment, she realized that this was the reason she had come. To ask him this question. To know why he wanted her here.

"Lin." His voice was ragged. Even with the mask, she could see he was staring at her, with almost a fixed look, his gaze traveling from her eyes to her lips, over her body, weighted as the touch of a hand. She felt the heat in that look as it traveled over her, like a scatter of sparks against her skin. "Are you truly asking? Because I should not answer that. For my sake, for yours. For the sake of so many things."

She tilted her head back. "Please," she said, and she saw the shiver that went through him at the word. Her own pulse quickened. "I am not afraid of the truth."

"No. You are afraid of nothing. You have certainly never been afraid of me." He lifted a hand, slowly, almost as if he could not believe what he was doing, and laid it against her cheek, his skin cool against her hot face. "But there are some answers, once given, that can never be taken back. Never forgotten."

She reached up, circled his wrist with her fingers. She felt the hammering beat of his pulse against her fingertips. Imagined his heart, frantic as her own, driving his blood. "Tell me," she said. "Or I will go."

"Why did I ask you to come?" he whispered. "Because I could not do anything else. Even as I sealed the invitation, I raged against myself—my own stupidity and selfishness—and still I could not stop myself." His fingertips stroked her cheek, the lightest touch, but the tide of fire that washed through her veins was hotter than blood, enough to make her lips part, her body tremble. "I asked you because when I am not with you, Lin Caster, I feel as if some part of me has been torn away. I feel as if I am *bleeding*, insensible with the pain of a wound no one can see save myself. When you are with me . . . It is the only time I feel whole."

Lin was outwardly still. But inside, it was as if something had broken—a phial of one of Merren's poisons, the kind that brought sweet death, flooding her veins with fire. And for the first time she understood the Story-Spinner tales, how people could line up week after week to hear the slow progression of a tale that would make them feel even the shadow of the shadow of *this* . . .

"Lin?" Conor whispered, and she could hear the fear in his voice, fear of how she would react, fear that she would turn and run.

She closed the last bit of space between them. She sensed the warmth of his body before she rose up on her tiptoes and kissed him. He froze for a moment before he caught at her, drawing her into him, against him. He made a noise deep in his throat. The sound of a man who has been clinging to a rope by his fingertips for hours, and has finally let go, abandoning himself to the fall.

To kiss him seemed as natural as the rain, and as unruly. Her kiss had been gentle, but he did not return it gently. He slanted his mouth over hers, parting her lips with a hard flick of his tongue. He tasted of fruit and wine. His tongue curled against hers, drawing a moan out of her throat. She stretched up toward him, almost on the tips of her toes. He sucked her lower lip into his mouth, running his tongue across it, making her squirm against him.

His clothes were damp, plastered to his skin. She could feel all of him, feel that he was hard against her. She knew the physiological reasons, knew the whys and hows of it, but had not expected the way her own body would respond to his desire. Her nipples hardened against the inside of her bodice. A hot spike of wanting wound its way from her belly downward. She arched up against him, not caring about anything except that he not stop kissing her.

The rain had become a blanket, a continuous, thrumming patter, holding them inside. Making sure no one came near them. His hands dropped from her face to her body, slid roughly around her waist. She heard him curse, and then his hands were in her hair, pulling at the pins Mariam had so carefully placed there. He flung them away from him as they came free—flung them as if he hated them—hurling them to the stone floor where they clinked like coins. Her hair came down in long waves, tangled by its compression and by the humid air. He buried his hands in it with an animal growl, the strands slipping through his fingers. He kissed her temples, her cheek, kissed along her jaw, down to her throat. Kissed the racing pulse there, the evidence of her own turmoil. Brushed his lips along her collarbone.

He seemed to freeze then. Burying his face in her hair. She could hear his ragged breathing in her ear. He seemed hesitant, as he almost never did, as if he could not decide what to do next. As if he could not imagine she wanted him to continue.

She took his hands in her own, firmly guiding them. Setting them against the bodice of her gown, where it hooked up and down the front. Nothing she had ever done—not even declaring herself the Goddess Returned to the whole of the Sault—had felt as daring as this. She lifted her hands away, heard his intake of breath. Hoped he understood what she could not say aloud.

Touch me. I want you to.

The hooks melted away under his fingers, her bodice gaping open. Not hesitating now, he kissed her again, even as his hand slid under the neck of her chemise, cupping her breast in his hand. His fingers were hot against her skin, his thumb circling her nipple expertly, making her gasp into his mouth. She arched into his touch, wanting more.

She felt him smile. He walked her backward until her spine collided with a pillar. She heard him whisper, *Lin, my Lin,* before he bent his head and took her nipple into his mouth.

She was not prepared for the piercing arrow of desire that shot through her. She moaned, scrabbling at him, pulling the hem of his tunic free of his trousers. Her wet fingers glided over the bare expanse of his belly, silk skin stretched over hard muscle. The air smelled of lightning and she wanted him like she had never wanted anything.

He lifted his head from her breast. She could not see his expression at all, but his breath had gone harsh and uneven. He kissed her hard and deep, seizing her around the waist. Lifting her. She caught at his shoulders, bracing herself. His body pressed into hers. She could feel him shaking. He was using his body to hold her up, even as his left hand slid under her skirts, even as he touched her there, at the heart of herself.

She had only ever touched herself like this, and had not imagined what it would be like for someone else to do it. But the pleasure was like a whirlwind. It took away all other thought. She moaned helplessly against his mouth as he stroked her, circling, and the pleasure of it began to wind tight within her, a coil of intensity, tightening and tightening.

Still gripping his shoulder with one hand, she reached down with the other, undoing the buttons of his trousers. It was too dim to see anything; she worked blindly, in the dark, felt him spring free, hard against her palm. Hard and soft at the same time, skin like hot silk as she began to stroke him, operating almost entirely on instinct, guessing what he would like—her hand wrapped around him, gliding up and down—

"Ah—Gods—*Lin*," he gasped, and she felt a momentary triumph, that she had stolen his words, reduced him to incoherence. His mouth crashed against hers. She arched her hips, guided him toward her. He was lost, far beyond any hesitation, and she was glad. Her legs tightened around his waist as he drove into her.

Time seemed to stop. Lightning illuminated the sea, turning Conor's gray eyes to silver, rimmed with the darker silver of the mask. There was pain, but she didn't care. He was fully inside her, his lips against her throat. She could hear his desperate breathing as he held himself utterly still—for her sake, she knew, so as not to hurt her—though the effort made fine tremors run through him, his hands shaking at her waist.

She dug her hands into his hair, into the fine curling strands, black as raven's wings, black as crow feathers. The ribbon of the mask tickled her fingers. She kissed his mouth, tasted the rain on his skin. "It's all right," she whispered. "Love me. I want you to."

The noise he made in response was barely human. He drew back before sliding into her again, and she sensed he was still trying to hold himself back. To exert control over himself. She would have none of that; she wrapped her legs more tightly about him, pulling him deeper inside her. His eyes went black; she sensed she had driven him over the edge, and was glad for it. Glad for the way he gripped her hips bruisingly, glad for the way he drove into her, and that coiling feeling inside her tightened and tightened until she was sure some part of her would break apart. No book she had ever read had prepared her for *this*—this debilitating, overwhelming pleasure, rising with every movement of his body against hers, and she could understand why people fought and died and wrote poetry about this. And it rose and rose until the pleasure crested and broke, arrowing through her like lightning spearing the sea.

She heard him suck in his breath as the spasms tore through her. A moment later, his mouth fastened over hers as he thrust into her one last time. She felt him break, felt the moment as he came to pieces in her arms, his fever-gasps of pleasure caught between them, and she knew he was wholly hers in this moment. That he belonged to her, to this space between and around them.

The rain had slowed to a soft whisper, though Lin did not know when. She wrapped her arms around Conor's neck as he slowly relaxed, his body warm and hard against hers. He was still holding her carefully, his ragged breath easing. He was so close, cradling her, she could not help herself and let her hands run over him gently, touching his hair, his cheek. He kissed the palm of her right hand lazily. "Sweetheart," he murmured, his voice rich and slow. "Never . . . not ever before . . ."

Suddenly she felt him go stiff in her arms, like a plank of wood.

"Someone's out there." He drew back, letting her slide to the floor, her legs trembling a little as she put weight on them again. She shook her skirts back into place as he looked anxiously toward the folly entrance. "We can't be seen here," he said, and she could hear the anxiety in his voice. "I'll return to the party first, then you can follow."

The ringing in her ears blocked out his voice. She tried to remember the feeling she'd had just a moment ago, of being safely held, of him being entirely hers. But it was gone, and everything she had made herself forget tonight, everything she had shut away, came rushing back like a wave up the harbor beach.

Of course he was terrified that they would be caught. He could lose Anjelica, lose the alliance with Kutani. She could not even blame him. And yet when she tried to imagine entering the Armory after this, pretending nothing had happened—watching him as he danced with beautiful Anjelica Iruvai and laughed with his noble friends, aware at every moment that *this* was his life and she had no part in it—she wanted to be sick.

Her stomach turned over. She realized she was shivering, with more than just cold. *What in the name of the Goddess have I done?*

What pain had she opened herself to feel? How could she have been so *stupid*?

"No," she said, and her voice sounded strange to her own ears. "Go back to the party, Monseigneur. I cannot stay."

He spun around instantly. His damp black curls hung in his eyes as he stared at her. "Lin—"

"Don't." She stepped away from him; he was gazing at her incredulously, arrested mid-motion, as if he had meant to reach for her, to draw her with him, back to the Armory where he would have no problem whatsoever pretending that he did not know her, because nothing about what had just happened was unusual for him.

"Don't touch me again," she whispered, and fled past him, out of the folly, into the driving silver rain.

Mariam

"Who's there?"

Mariam sits up in bed, clutching her woven coverlet around her. She had been sleeping very lightly, her rest interrupted by the loud rumbling of thunder and intermittent cracks of lightning. When she was younger, she had loved storms, loved standing atop the walls of the Sault with Lin, watching the clouds gather at the horizon, the wind driving them across the sea toward the city like an advancing army. The shadows they cast on the ocean, darkening the waves from blue to black, whipping them into peaks topped with frothy silver.

Now it is different. Sleeping is difficult regardless as she tosses and turns, trying to find the least painful position, the one where it is easiest to breathe. Often she dreams that a black cat has come into her room and curled up on her chest, watching her with unblinking gold eyes as she struggles for breath beneath its weight. The thunder is an irritant now, not a reminder of the glorious power of the sky but an interruption of her precious sleep.

Now, as her eyes adjust to the darkness, she recognizes the source of the rustling that has woken her.

"Lin," she whispers. She draws aside the curtain covering the window beside her bed. The storm has cleared, and moonlight floods the room. She can see her friend clearly. She stands with clasped hands just inside the doorway of Mariam's room. She is drenched, her silk dress heavy with rainwater, her hair hanging down her back in bedraggled tails. *What happened?* Mariam wants to demand. Lin had been meant to dance on stars all night, to return to the Sault with a breathless account of glamour and wonders.

But as Mariam looks at Lin, the question dies on her tongue. Lin, the most stubborn, determined person Mariam knows, looks as if she can barely keep all the pieces of herself together.

Mariam puts her arms out. "Come here," she says, and Lin crawls gratefully onto the bed beside her. She is wet and cold, but Mariam holds her, just as she held her all those years ago when she was an orphaned child whose grandfather had not wanted her.

"Did he hurt you?" Mariam whispers. "Did he hurt you, *khum lōq?*"

"No. But I'm such a fool, Mariam," Lin whispers. "Such a fool."

"Hush." Mariam strokes Lin's damp hair, whispering, "Hush, my little sister, my little heart," while outside the window, the rain continues to fall in soft sheets, whispering like silk against the panes.

CHAPTER EIGHTEEN

A s soon as Kel had returned to the main ballroom, he was accosted by an anxious Ciprian Cabrol. "Monseigneur. *Monseigneur!* I need to speak to you."

Even behind the jackal mask, it was possible to tell that Ciprian's eyes were bloodshot with anxiety. He had hold of Kel's sleeve between whitened fingers. *Conor's sleeve*, he reminded himself. He was Conor now. He wished he'd had a moment more to adjust himself to it, but it seemed that was not to be.

"Do let go of me, Ciprian," Kel said pleasantly, and Ciprian snatched his hand back. "Indeed. Let us speak. In fact, I've been wondering when you were going to approach me."

"You have?"

"Oh, yes," Kel said smoothly. "There should not be too many secrets between a man and his sovereign, don't you think? And you've been keeping quite a lot of secrets, dear Ciprian. For example, I had no idea that you were on such close terms with Elsabet Belmany."

Ciprian shrank back a little. With his head hung low, he was beginning to resemble less of a vicious jackal and more of a worried terrier. "Wh—what?"

"The Malgasi Princess," Kel said. "It's unusual, a merchant family having such a close connection to a foreign Princess, don't you think?"

"I . . ." Ciprian reached up to adjust his mask, glancing around as he did so. No one seemed to be paying special attention to them, beyond the regular sort of glances Conor received at any event like this one—a mix of admiration, curiosity, desire. Save that Beatris Cabrol was looking over at her brother, Kel noted, worry very plain on her face.

When Ciprian spoke again, his voice was low. "I don't know what you're implying."

Kel hesitated only a fraction of a second. This was dangerous stuff, he knew. He was out on a ledge, over the ocean. Crocodiles below. He felt no fear, just concentration—that pleasurably careful sense of walking a tightrope.

He said, "I have no need to imply anything, Ciprian. I know perfectly well what I'm talking about." He cocked his head to the side. "Let's talk in private, then. How about the Caravel? Tomorrow at noon? We won't be disturbed there."

Cabrol gave a nervous jerk of his head. "Yes. Yes," he muttered. "Tomorrow afternoon." He stiffened. "Monseigneur," he added, and there was a slight warning in his voice that made Kel turn around.

Anjelica stood behind them, smiling. She held a hand out to Kel. "Dance with me, my lord?" she said.

As Conor would have done, Kel dismissed Ciprian without a word and let Anjelica sweep him out onto the dance floor. The music was lively, the musicians themselves hidden behind a velvet curtain, giving the impression that the sounds of viol and *lior* were divinely provided.

Anjelica moved gracefully as they danced. The pale feathers of her mask provided the no-doubt-deliberate illusion of bridal lace. She was slim and strong in his arms, and Kel was aware that a new emotion had been added to the mix of feeling projected in Conor's direction: envy.

"Come," she said. "Let us move away from the Queen."

Kel had not noticed Lilibet, standing with Lady Gremont, a silver goblet in her hand. She did not seem to be observing them, but he followed Anjelica's lead across the room nonetheless: Lilibet's eyes would pierce the illusion of his amulet immediately, which would result in nothing but trouble later.

"So." Anjelica raised her face to his. Her smile was not for him, he knew, but for all the watching eyes. "I must admit, I am impressed. I did not even see him leave. What was so urgent that he felt obligated to flee this celebration of his own dynasty?"

Him. Neither he nor Anjelica, Kel reflected, felt the need to use Conor's name. He was the planet around which they revolved; there could be only one *him.*

"I've no idea, but I'm sure I'll find out later." The circlet was snagging in Kel's hair; he longed to readjust it. "And I imagine if you ask him, he'll tell you as well."

"No doubt," Anjelica mused. "When I found out the Prince had a Sword Catcher, I never thought I would spend so much time with him. But it is a lucky thing tonight. For I have had a message from the Ragpicker King."

Kel was instantly on alert. "What kind of message?"

"He tells me Laurent Aden will be here tonight. At the Solstice Ball."

Incredulous, Kel said, "But that's madness! He's a wanted criminal."

"Laurent enjoys risk." Her lip curled delicately. "I suppose the masks proved too much of a lure. He intends to disguise himself as a diplomat from Hanse." She sighed. "He will absolutely *delight* in walking unnoticed among a group of nobles who would adore nothing more than to see him swing from the Tully gallows."

"And then what?" Kel could hardly believe her calm. "You exchange money for the letters of yours that he has? And that's the end of it?"

"Supposedly."

"Do you really trust his word in the matter? He is already black-mailing you. Can you put so much stock in his honesty?"

Annoyance flashed in her eyes. "Had you a better suggestion, you could have voiced it when we met the Ragpicker King."

"I speak only out of concern."

"But not concern for me," she said dryly. "Concern for your Prince's precious alliance. Kellian, you must understand. What Laurent wants is to see me. He believes that it is my parents' will that separated us. He needs to hear from me that I do not *want* him, that I am not suffering from our parting. That he must leave me alone for my own good."

"He really believes you cannot bear being parted from him?"

"People believe what they want to believe," Anjelica said. Her slender hands tightened on his shoulders. "He is here," she murmured. "Look—in the eagle mask."

She had gone tense all over, her lips pressed together in a bloodless line. Carefully, Kel glanced across the ballroom.

And there he was, just at the edge of the dancers, dressed in the black and yellow of Hanse. A tall man, fair-haired, wearing the mask of an eagle with a cruelly hooked beak. *He is disguised as a diplomat, but he does not carry himself like a diplomat. He carries himself steadily, flat-footed, like a man used to standing upon the swaying deck of a ship.*

The room was full of rising whispers. For a moment, with a stab of alarm, Kel wondered if Aden had been recognized. *And what do I do if he is? Go to his bloody rescue?*

A moment later, though, he realized he had been entirely wrong. No one was looking at the criminal in their midst. They were all staring at Antonetta, who had just come into the room.

Kel blessed the years of practice that kept him dancing, kept him moving across the floor with Anjelica. All he wanted was to cross the room to Antonetta's side, to catch her up in his arms. To shield her with his body from the narrow-eyed stares cast in her direction, the whispers sharp-edged as blades.

But he was Conor now. And Conor would not go to her. Conor would watch, with a mix of interest and admiration, as she moved into the ballroom, her head held high.

Another woman might have dressed herself plainly, that she might not be remarked upon or stared at, but Antonetta had clothed herself in fire. Her dress was russet silk, the skirt slashed at every pleat so that as she moved, glimpses of her slim legs flashed through the material. Around her shoulders was a cape of gold and russet, and her mask was a clever-featured fox, with burnished orange and gold silk ears. Around her throat gleamed her heart-shaped locket.

Behind Anjelica's back, Kel clenched his left hand into a fist. It was not what Conor would have done, but he could not help himself; he needed the pressure, the pain, to tear his gaze away from Antonetta.

He found Anjelica looking at him, her expression a mixture of sympathy and pity. He could read the thought behind her eyes: *Oh, poor you. As bedazzled and mistaken as Laurent.*

"I see," she said.

"Anjelica—"

She drew away from him. "I'd better go while everyone is staring at Demoselle Alleyne," she murmured, and he knew she was right. "Besides. I believe you have something else to attend to?"

He felt her pat his shoulder gently, and then she had slipped away into the crowd, her pearl pins gleaming amid her dark hair. He waited one heartbeat. A second. A third. And then he was striding across the room, the throng parting for him with murmurs he barely heard: *Monseigneur, I did not see you there.*

And then he was near her. Up close, he could see she was pale, though her lips were lacquered crimson, her cheeks stained with rouge. As she turned to face him, he was about to say her name when a figure crossed between them.

Lady Alleyne, fierce and feral-looking in her tiger's mask. She whirled on her daughter like a cat pouncing on a mouse. "Where have you *been*—"

Beneath the mask and the rouge, Antonetta flushed scarlet. Kel cleared his throat.

"My dear Liorada," he drawled, and never had he let so much scorn drip into Conor's voice. Slow and sour-sweet, like rancid honey. The satisfaction that went through him as Lady Alleyne jolted around to face him was nearly pleasure. "I believe my mother was hoping to speak with you."

Lady Alleyne glanced over at the Queen, who was busy directing a group of servants to relight the tapers outside, which had sputtered in the rain. Lilibet looked impatient behind her mask, which was that of a golden deer.

"My daughter—" Lady Alleyne began tightly.

"Looks stunning tonight. I simply must know who made your dress, Demoselle, as my fiancée has not yet chosen a tailor for her wedding dress, and time grows short." He proffered his arm to Antonetta. "Come, let us dance, and you can tell me all about it."

For someone else, it would have been a breach of etiquette to interrupt Lady Alleyne's conversation with her daughter, but Conor was not required to ask permission for anything he did. It was a privilege Kel could only wear occasionally, like his borrowed crown, but he let himself feel the gratification of it as he led Antonetta out onto the polished dance floor.

"I suppose I should thank you, Monseigneur," Antonetta said as he slid an arm around her waist and began to guide her into the music. "For rescuing me from my mother—the most terrifying of all the beasts in the animal kingdom."

Behind her mask, he could see Antonetta's eyes, the pupils turned the shape of diamonds by posy-drops. "I've been wanting to talk to you, Nettle."

She shot him a surprised look. "You haven't called me *that* in years."

Kel almost missed a step in the dance. *Speak to her as Conor would speak to her. Not as you would speak to her.*

He should not have had to remind himself.

"Regardless, I am surprised you are willing to be seen with me," she added. "I am social poison, after all. Artal Gremont has fled the city rather than marry me."

You know better than that, Antonetta.

"If you have driven him away truly," Kel drawled, "then you have done us all a service."

They were moving among the other dancers, and Kel caught sight of Anjelica in the throng, easy to spot in her luxuriant white dress. She was dancing with Laurent, and to Kel's eye, they appeared to be arguing.

He would have to keep an eye on them, he thought.

"I do not pretend to know why Gremont has left the Hill," Kel said, "but I suspect it has more to do with him than you. The whispers may have made you the scandal of the moment, but they will fade soon enough. We will find you a better match than Gremont ever was."

Antonetta was silent a moment. Then she said, "You are being so kind to me, Monseigneur. You must be very happy in your new engagement." She moved closer to him. Closer than the dance required. Kel caught the scent of her hair, her skin: white roses and honey. It made him think of the yellow room in the Caravel, the way she had shaped herself into his arms, and he felt his blood quicken. "Let me repay the favor, then, with all I have to give you."

Kel wanted to ask her what she meant, but he could not seem to catch his breath. She smiled up at him.

"Advice," she said.

The frantic beat of his blood slowed. "Advice is always welcome from someone I trust."

She tilted her head to the side, letting the rich fall of her hair sweep across her shoulder. "Well, it is an issue of trust, in fact."

"Oh?"

"You have to be careful, Monseigneur," Antonetta said. She glanced quickly about the room before returning her gaze to him. "Careful about what you share with Kel."

Kel felt himself stiffen. "*What?*"

Antonetta's blue eyes were full of concern. "I have seen him with members of the Ragpicker King's coterie," she said. "He seems to know them quite well."

"I see." Kel spun Antonetta in his arms; when she had returned to him, he said, "Kel does many things for me. Sometimes that requires him to meet with unsavory people." He smiled; a rictus grin, he feared. "I can be unsavory myself, on occasion."

"Oh, I believe that Kel loves you," Antonetta said carelessly. "But you will never be equals. You will always have power over him. He may resent that."

"I don't question his loyalty," Kel said in a tone meant to quell future discussion. He wasn't sure he could bear to hear what else she might say.

"I have heard," Antonetta said in a conspiratorial whisper, "that the Ragpicker King has ways of manipulating even those with pure motives. Kel seemed to know Morettus's people well, to trust them. That leaves him open to manipulation. And the Ragpicker King is a master of manipulation. He could turn Kel against you without Kel even knowing it was happening."

Not since he was a child had Kel felt so close to breaking the pretense of being Conor. He wanted to catch hold of Antonetta and demand why she was saying these things. He wanted to shake her. He wanted to press her up against the wall and kiss her breathless. *I am not Conor. I am not Kel Anjuman. I am myself, Kel Saren, and I am nobody's fool.*

"You make him sound like a fool," he said.

"He is not a fool, but he is sincere, and sincerity can be exploited. Think of what's already happened. He was stabbed when someone mistook him for you. He tried to pay your debts to Prosper Beck." She gave a shudder: real or false, Kel was too fevered to tell. "When I think of him lying in that alley . . ."

He tried to pay your debts to Prosper Beck. Kel felt a sudden, awful pressure behind his eyes as myriad disparate pieces came together.

It felt as if the ground were falling out from under him, but he knew he could not show it. Years of training saved him. As if faintly bored, he said, "Enough, Antonetta. I have heard you, and believe me, I will take what you have said into account. But, my dear"—and he looked directly into her diamond-pupiled eyes—"you must not repeat these concerns to anyone else. Under my royal order, I require it. Do you understand?"

It seemed to Kel that she looked surprised beneath the fox mask, but she gathered herself quickly. "I shall be the very picture of discretion." She glanced away, her brow furrowing. "Look, there Kel is now. Where has he been, I wonder? He's soaking wet."

Almost blindly, Kel followed her gaze. She was right. Conor, drenched to the bone and wearing Kel's mask, had just slipped silently into the room.

He was keeping to the wall, his head down. Had Kel not known to look for him, he would not have seen him.

Conor moved along the wall, out of view of most of the dancers, and disappeared into one of the corridors opening off the central rotunda. A quick glance assured Kel that no one else had noted his presence.

"I had better go after him." Kel bowed stiffly to Antonetta before turning away to follow Conor. His head was pounding; he felt lightheaded and a little sick. Had he ever really known Antonetta? He had always thought that she had one face she showed to the world and another she showed to him, but what if neither was the true face? What if there was some other, secret truth he had never guessed at, too dazzled by the thought that he, and he alone, knew the truth of her to imagine that he had been as blind as all the rest?

It was not a pleasant thought, and he carried the bitterness of it as he ducked into the corridor after Conor. It featured a splashing fall of gold-tinted water, contained in a handmade grotto at the end of the hall. Someone had clearly been picnicking here earlier; there was a tray of half-eaten food and a bottle of wine balanced precariously at the fountain's edge.

For a moment, Kel thought Conor had disappeared—vanished into thin air as the Sorcerer-Kings had once been rumored to do.

Then he looked down.

Conor was sitting on the floor. The hem of his cloak, the leather of his boots, were dark with mud. His hair and shirt were wet from rain. As Kel stared, Conor reached up, silently, and undid the ties of his mask. It fell into his lap.

He looked at Kel.

"Con," Kel said, dropping to his knees; he could not bear to be above Conor, gazing down. Any resentment, any anger, had fled. He had never seen Conor look like this before. His pupils were vast and black, rimmed with a thin ring of silver. His face looked as if the bones were protruding too sharply through his skin. There was blood on his lip. He must have bitten it, though it seemed profoundly unlike him. "Conor," Kel breathed. "What happened?"

Conor closed his eyes. He shook his head slowly. "I," he said, "am a fucking idiot."

"Look at me." Kel took Conor's face in his hands. Felt the sharpness of bone against his palm, the familiar slant of Conor's cheekbones, the coldness of his rain-damp skin. "Everyone's an idiot," Kel said. "Some people pretend better than others."

Conor didn't smile, but he turned his face into Kel's hand. It was something.

"Tell me what's wrong. I won't ever blame you, you know that. Just tell me."

Conor opened his eyes. *Tell me*, Kel thought. *Tell me. I will fix it for you. Like I fixed it with Prosper Beck. Like I'm trying to fix it now. Tell me, just tell me, so I can understand you again.*

"Not my secret to tell," Conor said. His voice was flat. "I need something to drink. Wretchedly badly."

"That won't help," Kel said.

Conor bared his teeth in a smile. "It won't hurt."

Kel stood up, grabbed the wine bottle off the abandoned tray—it had been opened but was still half full—and knelt down again. He handed the bottle to Conor, who threw his head back and took several deep swallows.

By the time he lowered the bottle, his hand was steadier. He had spilled a little of the wine onto his hand and the black velvet of his tunic.

"Is this about your father?" Kel whispered. He could hear the fear in his own voice. *Conor, what has happened that's so bad you can't tell even me?*

Or was it worse than that? He thought of Antonetta's warnings. Of all his own lies. Of the house of cards he had built on sand, so precarious a single wrong word could bring it all crashing down.

"No." Conor looked down at the back of his left hand, watching the spilled beads of scarlet wine run between his fingers. In the gold light of the waterfall, they seemed to shine. "Not my father. I want—" He looked up, directly at Kel. "I want a different life than the one I have."

"Oh," said someone softly. A low voice, and familiar.

Kel looked up, as did Conor. Anjelica stood at the mouth of the corridor. It was not far away; Kel wondered when she had arrived there. She would certainly have been able to hear everything.

Conor blinked, looking dazed, as she moved toward them. Because she was beautiful, Kel thought. And because, in her diamond dress, she seemed to blaze like a torch. It reflected back the waterfall's light, turning her from silver to gold. Rings flashed on her fingers as she reached the place where Conor knelt and held out her hand.

"Get up," she said. "Conor Darash Aurelian, Crown Prince of Castellane, get up off the floor."

There was something in her voice Kel had not heard before. She spoke to Conor as if, between royalty, there was a secret language. Conor stared up at her. And then, as if the words were hooks lodged beneath his ribs, he rose to his feet. He straightened his shoulders. He looked at Anjelica, maskless, his gaze direct.

"You heard me," he said. "How much did you hear?"

Kel rose silently. The balance had changed, he thought. Shifted between one breath and another. He was in the background now, as Prince and Princess regarded each other. It did not matter that Conor was clutching a wine bottle, that he was muddy and wet with rain. He was who he was. And so was Anjelica.

She said, "I heard you say you want a different life." She took a step toward him. "I understand you did not choose me, or this marriage—"

"It's not you—" Conor began.

She only shook her head. "And I did not choose you," she said with a small smile. "But it is incumbent upon each of us, I think, to make of our lives something we *would* choose."

"I think you are braver than I am," Conor said.

"You are brave enough," she said gently. "What is more frightening than change? And you have changed a great deal in these past months. I did not know you before, but everyone speaks of it. How much you have altered since the Shining Gallery. It may be a change that had its birth in blood and horror, but it is change nonetheless."

"Perhaps," Conor said. He looked at her. "What do we do now, *Ayakemi*?"

"Our duty," said Anjelica. "We return to the ballroom. We show the Hill we are united. Kutani and Castellane." She stretched out her hand to him, and he took it. "They play the tune. And we dance."

Anjelica

"Don't look at me like that," Anjelica says, almost in a whisper.

"How am I looking at you?" Laurent's voice is soft. His arms are around her, as the dance requires. It is the first time she has felt his touch in months, and she is dizzy from it. She can feel the resonant beat of her own heart, smell the familiar scent of him: ocean and spice. A dash of black powder. The scent threatens to bring back memories in a wave—a dangerous wave that might crash over her, leaving her vulnerable in front of all these people. Leaving her unable to hide what she needs to hide.

She thinks of her mother. *Control your emotions, daughter, or others will use them to control you.* She has always been the least obedient of her sisters, the one who demanded to know why she could not go out into Spice Town on her own, why she could not sit with the King when he dealt judgment or met with Ambassadors. Her father had found it amusing when she was small, and he had been inclined to indulge her. Later, he had regretted that.

How are you looking at me? Anjelica thinks. Like fire. Like his gaze would burn away her clothes, leaving her naked in his arms. *Like I am a person and not just a beautiful object. No one has*

*looked at me like that since I came here—no one but Kel and
Conor.*

"Not the way the Ambassador from Hanse would look at me," she says.

"You can't be sure," he says. "I fell in love with you the first time I saw you. The same might have happened to him, had he been here." Laurent's voice threatens to undo her and all her promises to herself. It is rough and rich, low like the ocean when the tide went out, scraping itself over barnacles and sand.

"Before the message from Andreyen reached me, I thought perhaps I might never see you again," Laurent continues. "Though I had determined to wait until all hope was gone."

"I know." The next part of the dance has come. She places her hands on his shoulders, feeling the flex of muscles under her palms. Memories come along with the feel and shape of him. How she had crept aboard his boat when it was moored in the harbor at Spice Town. How she had professed her love for him in his office aboard the *Black Rose,* and he had only stared at her, blue eyes widening, until she thought she might die of the humiliation, and only then had he gotten to his feet and taken her into his arms— and later, into his bed.

She had not thought of the future, then. Only that she wanted him and would have what she wanted. She had not expected to fall in love with him. She had not known what love would feel like when it came.

"I, too, feared I had lost you," she says now, "when I arrived in Castellane and the *Black Rose* was not there to carry me back to you. I—I thought you were dead." (She recalls the moment Kel had said he was sure Laurent Aden was still alive, and the relief that had gone through her like a blade.)

"Someone told them I was coming." Laurent's mouth is hard with anger. "There was no way to get into the harbor without en- during the death of half my crew, and even then, I would have simply been arrested." He raises his chin; the light of the chandeliers sparks off his cruel eagle mask. But she knows what he looks like without it. She knows what he looks like with nothing on at all, how rough and scarred and lovely he is. Her body feels tortured with a desire that she cannot show.

"My love, you sent me no word," Anjelica says. "All this time—"

His hands tighten at her waist. "I saw no way I could get you free of the Palace, now that you are here," he says. "I could hardly waltz in and steal you from under the nose of a hundred Castelguards—"

"Really?" she murmurs. "Laurent Aden, afraid of a few guards?"

"I am risking my life to be here now," he says, raking her with his gaze. His blue eyes are icy; even so, they make her feel hot and strange. He has always been able to do that to her. "But it is worth it, to see you."

"I didn't even know if you still wanted me."

"If I wanted you?" They spin, as the dance requires. "I thought you might have fallen in love with your fiancé. I imagined you had decided remaining in Castellane offered you the opportunity to be a Queen someday, which I cannot give you. Anjelica—"

"Hush," she whispers. "Do not say my name. Not like that." *Everyone who hears you will know how we feel.* "Neither of those things has happened."

"Good. There are those who are willing to help us. If you still want it, I can get you away, both of us away, and your brothers—"

She feels her eyes widen and is glad her mask hides her expression. "Who would offer to help with such a thing when it would inevitably put them at odds with all of Castellane . . . ah." She shakes her head. "The Malgasi."

"I don't like them much, either, but they're desperate to marry their Princess off to Conor Aurelian. They'll help me—"

"They can't be trusted, Laurent. I've learned more about them since I've been in Castellane. They have done some true evil to their people—"

"I don't trust them," says Laurent. "I do not trust any government, any monarchy. They are all selfish. They all have secrets, dreadful things that they have done. There is no such thing as great power that has never been used unfairly."

"Quite a thing to say to a Princess," Anjelica smiles. She hopes it will not be seen as strange; surely she can smile at an Ambassador without much note being taken?

She feels the low rumble of his laugh. "Obviously, you are different. Which is why I wish to get you away from all this. I'm willing to accept some aid from the Malgasi to free you, but I have my own plan. It involves Sedai—"

"Laurent. I can't do it." The words hurt, though she's known she'll have to say them. "I cannot abandon Conor."

"So you *have* become fond of him." A beat. "I'm surprised. I hadn't heard he had a particularly endearing personality."

"I heard the same. But he is not what they say." She sees Conor's face, his serious eyes, the thoughtful curve of his mouth. He had been straightforward with her. She'd thought he would be full of false expressions of love, which would only have annoyed her, but he had been surprisingly honest. He had not demanded anything she did not want to give, nor had he hidden that he, too, was in pain. "It is hard to explain. I am not in love with him, but he has treated me with honesty and respect. And I understand what he's facing. I understand it in a way you cannot."

Laurent swears softly under his breath. His grip on her waist slackens as he turns her, mechanically, in the next move of the dance. When she faces him again, she says, "If I flee with you now, it will be seen as another stain on his reputation. It will weaken his power—"

Laurent makes an exasperated noise. "He's a Prince. He'll be fine. The Malgasi are desperate for a wedding; they will step in to provide him a Princess and an alliance that will ward off Sarthe, if needed. The nobility hardly care if he marries Kutani or Malgasi as long as their precious trade is protected."

"But he won't marry Elsabet. He hates her, hates Malgasi and the whole Belmany family. What they would do to Castellane—"

"Suddenly you care about Castellane?" She can see the pain in his eyes. How can she explain, how can she tell him that to go with him is all she wants? "Do you truly think it such a wonderful place? Imagine growing up an orphan here, looking up at the Palace, knowing you would never have any of the riches and luxuries enjoyed there—that your only task was to starve and to die?"

"Please," she says. "I love you, the Gods know how much I do, but give me some time. A year. I can stretch out the engagement until the situation is less dire—"

"A year?" Laurent shakes his head as the music slows and stops. "Aurelian won't wait a year to marry you. Nor can I spend a year hiding in a sea cave."

"Laurent, please—"

But the dance is over. Hurt flashes across Laurent's face, followed by anger. Without another word, he turns and stalks off into the crowd.

Just a year, she thinks. *Just a year to honor my promises, before I can come back to you. Laurent, please. Listen to me.*

But she cannot race after him, cannot call out for him and beg him to come back, to hear her out. He is only supposed to be the Ambassador from Hanse, after all.

CHAPTER NINETEEN

When Lin left the Etse Kebeth the next morning, wearing a clean blue cotton dress borrowed from Mariam's stores, she found the day incongruously balmy. She had expected—and perhaps hoped for—rain and thunderclouds to match her mood. Instead, the sun had risen bright and hot, drying the puddles she had sloshed through the night before. The physick garden gleamed green and white in the unshaded brightness. A few white brushstrokes of cloud painted the sky: The storm must have been blown back out to sea. It was probably halfway to Kutani by now.

Lin wished she could say the same about herself. She felt as if a stone had lodged itself in her belly. She had lain awake much of the night, remembering the rain, the folly. The way she had lost herself—lost all the control she had built up so carefully and delicately over so many years. She had wanted Conor too badly to stop herself, and now he knew that—knew her weakness—and would scorn her for it.

She could taste the bitterness of disappointment on her tongue, like the aftertaste of Chana's herbal tea. She was not disappointed in

Conor; she would not have expected anything else from him. She was disappointed in herself.

She heard a voice call out to her. "Lin Caster. A moment."

She was just at the gate of the Women's House. She turned to see Aron in the middle of the street, his arms crossed. He was dressed as he had been the first time she'd seen him, in the clothes of a Rhadanite trader. His desert-colored hair and eyes were bright in the sunlight.

She looked at him wearily. If there was anything she did not have the energy for, it was an argument with Aron Benjudah, or another demand on his part that she try to puzzle him out.

"I do not have a moment," she said. "I am about to begin my rounds, seeing to my patients in the city—"

"I know," he said. Behind him, she could see a group of boys, the same age Josit had been when they lost their parents, at play in the gardens of the Dāsu Kebeth. They kicked up dust in clouds as they chased one another, carelessly happy in the sun. "We had an arrangement, I believe. I translate your text for you, and in exchange you take me with you on rounds and let me watch you tend to your patients."

She had nearly forgotten. "Today?"

He smiled coolly. "There may not be that many days left until the testing."

What an infuriating man he was, Lin thought, as she raced home to get her physician's satchel. But perhaps being infuriated would be a good thing. Perhaps it would take her mind off the Prince.

She rejoined Aron outside the walls of the Sault. He fell into step beside her as she headed up the Ruta Magna in the direction of her first appointment, near Castle Street. "So," she said. "What am I meant to say to my patients when they ask who you are?"

"Tell them that I am learning to become a physician and you are instructing me. Or perhaps I am writing a book on medicine and studying their cases."

"Wonderful," Lin said. "My patients will enjoy having a large, glowering man stare at them while they're treated."

"You could tell them I am to be your husband and insist on following you wherever you go."

"They know me too well to imagine I'd tolerate that," said Lin sweetly, and Aron made a noise that *almost* sounded like a reluctant chuckle. Lin saw someone glance at him as they passed. They were most likely wondering exactly who, or what, he was, with his leather arm straps and Rhadanite tattoos. Or perhaps they just thought he was handsome. He *was* handsome—which was one of his many irritating qualities.

It also turned out that he was not as totally ignorant of medicine as she had imagined. They went first to visit a young mother on Lark Street to make sure she and her new baby were thriving. Aron observed quietly, and did not seem discomfited by a long discussion of getting the child to latch to the breast. After that, a sailor near Yulan Road who was recovering from the bite of a crocodile. While Lin checked his wound, Aron silently handed her instruments and listened as the sailor cheerfully told him that he had been drunk when he had fallen into the harbor, and had been hauled out half naked and bleeding by a boatload of pilgrims on their way to Tyndaris.

A seamstress in the Silver Streets who feared needles was comforted by Aron while Lin stitched up a cut on her hand. On Tower Street, he distracted a fussy baby while the child's mother anxiously watched Lin tend to her older boy's ear infection. Lastly, Lin visited Zofia in the Fountain Quarter, hiding a smile as Zofia flirted shamelessly with Aron.

"*My*, but you are big and handsome," she announced, her eyes gleaming mischievously. "If Lin doesn't plan to marry you, I'll do it myself."

Aron blushed, and Lin looked on in amazement as she set Zofia's tincture of foxglove on her wooden nightstand. She had never imagined the Exilarch could blush. It suited him, she thought; made him look more human, less like a carved statue gazing into the distance, intent on some noble destiny no one else could see.

"Let me feel your muscles," Zofia commanded, and Aron blushed again but obeyed with good humor, letting Zofia squeeze his arm and exclaim that she hadn't felt a biceps like this one since she'd been the lover of Ruthless Nestor, the most fearsome pirate ever to sail the seas until Laurent Aden.

As it turned out, Aron had heard of Nestor, and wanted to know if it was true that he'd left a treasure map behind after his mysterious disappearance off the coast of Taprobana. "Maybe, maybe," Zofia said with a wink. "Now turn around. I want to have a feel of—"

"Zofia, *no*," Lin said firmly. She kissed the old woman atop her messy bun of gray hair and said, "Be good, take your medicine, and I'll see you next week."

"Will you bring *him* with you?" Zofia inquired, pointing a long finger at Aron.

"If you're good," Lin assured her, escaping with a bemused Aron by her side. They walked in silence back toward the Sault. Aron seemed lost in thought, his hands loosely clasped behind his back as they passed the dried fountains that gave the quarter its name, and crossed Elemi's Way, where flowering vines spilled from wrought-iron balconies and down the white-plastered walls of the neat row houses. The air was warm and dry and smelled of oranges and jasmine. It was the sort of day that made people fall in love with the city, though if Aron felt such a thing, he hid it well.

They crossed the Ruta Magna together, where shops were closing for the hour of afternoon rest. Lin couldn't blame them. All she wanted was to return to her house, crawl into bed, and sleep—though just last night she'd thought she would never sleep again. She realized with a faint sense of surprise that for at least these past few hours, tending the sick with Aron, she had not thought about Conor.

x x x

Mez was at the gates and winked at Lin as she passed through with the Exilarch at her side. She made a face at him, though she didn't really mind. At least Mez hadn't changed how he behaved around her since the Tevath.

They had gone as far as the Kathot when Lin, wondering if Aron meant to walk her all the way to her door, paused and turned to him. "I hope," she said, as he stopped as well, a faintly inquiring look on his face, "that you learned all you wish to know?"

Aron took a moment to answer. His gaze swept over her, dry as the desert sands whose color they had absorbed. The trees of the Kathot had burst into almost unreasonable bloom: Lacy clusters of saffron brightened the yellow jacarandas, and heavy green fruit dangled from the fig trees. (She and Mariam had been inveterate fig thieves as children, and had often been chased from the Kathot by one of the elders shaking a stick.) Such a pretty place, she thought, that most of the people of Castellane would never see, just as they would never see the inside of Marivent. But for such different reasons.

"You are an excellent physician," Aron said, startling her—both his words and the fact that it had taken him so long to say them. "Truly skilled with your patients. I admit I thought—well, it doesn't matter what I thought." His expression was gravely serious, as if he were giving her bad news instead of good. "I would hate to see your skill wasted."

"Wasted? What do you mean?"

Aron glanced around as if to be sure they were alone. The Shulamat doors were closed for the afternoon hours, and the square was quiet. The heat seemed to press down on it, like the weight of a hand. "It has always been part of my task to observe and to evaluate you, before your test could be given, and I believe I know you now somewhat, Lin Caster. I understand why you claimed to be the

Goddess. You are an inveterate healer, and you wish to save your friend Mariam, most likely with knowledge you can only access in the Shulamat."

Lin stared at him, feeling sick. How many desperate people must he have met? How many different reasons for making the same claim she had?

"It is a shame you are who you are," he said quietly.

She willed her voice to remain steady. "What does that mean?"

"Your grandfather is Mayesh Bensimon. Should you fail the test—and I don't think you have much confidence you will pass it—your false claim will be seen by the Sanhedrin as a political gambit, not a simple mistake."

"But that's ridiculous. My grandfather didn't even know—"

"Do you hear me, Lin? You will be exiled."

It hit like a blow. *Exile.* "But—I have nothing to do with my grandfather's work—"

"You go to the Hill quite often," he said gravely. "You attend the parties of the nobility. You can see how it will look to the Sanhedrin."

"And to you?" The wind had risen; she pushed her hair impatiently out of her face. "How does it look to you?"

"It looks to me like an easy choice, Lin," he said. "Withdraw your claim, take the small punishment, and that will be the end of it. I have known those who have been exiled. The pain of it is difficult to imagine. Everyone you ever knew, everything you ever knew, taken from you in an instant. And to no longer be Ashkar. To have the Goddess turn her face from you. It is death in life."

"I see," she said numbly. The sun blazing off the gold of the Shulamat's roof seemed to pierce her eyes like needles. "What is the *small punishment*?"

"You will be forbidden from leaving the Sault, or from practicing medicine, for six months," said Aron, and it was clear to Lin from the way he said it that he had discussed this with the Maharam, that they had crafted this together. A rebuke to her independence, to her pride in her skill. And more than that—

"Six months is too long," she said. "I must treat Mariam. She could die by then."

"Mariam's name is written in the Book of Life. Both the date of her birth and that of her death. You are the finest physician I have seen, yet surely you know you cannot save every life."

Lin gasped. "How can you say that? How can you even *think* it?"

"You will not hear me, then." He shook his head. He did not look angry, but more as if he had failed her, and that was somehow much worse. "In any case, you must make your decision. I know all I need to know; the test will be soon, Lin. Do not let it be too late."

Kel's head was pounding. The bright sunlight and loud clatter of carriages rolling by wasn't helping, either; he was very definitely hung over. He felt like vomiting into the green canal water of the Temple District, but somehow he did not want to give whatever malign force seemed bent on ruining his life—Fate? the Gods?— the satisfaction.

By the time the ball had finally concluded, the last of the guests staggering out the doors beneath a cloudy, smoke-thickened sky, Kel had been vilely drunk on nettle wine mixed with honeyed gentian liquor. Like drinking poisoned sugar, sweet and deadly. The irony was not lost on him.

He had not said another word to Antonetta that night, as Conor or as himself. Nor had she approached him. She'd seemed to be having a fine time, smiling as she chatted with Sancia Vasey, with Montfaucon and Falconet, with Beatris Cabrol, even with Lady Gremont. Kel had not wanted to look at her, but he had not been able to *unsee* her. She was so bright in her shimmering dress, a star moving across an otherwise dark sky.

That morning Conor had sat at the foot of Kel's bed, doing up the buttons on the long cuffs of his jacket. He was preparing to join Anjelica at the Royal Docks for the unveiling of Castellane's newest warship. "They are naming the ship after Anjelica," he said. "They never named a ship after me."

"Well, she is prettier."

"Debatable," said Conor. He had finished doing up his buttons and was staring unseeingly at the window. "The people are happy, the nobles are happy—even my mother is happy, when she isn't brooding about curtains. Why am I not happy?"

"Conor—"

"This is the best I could have hoped for," Conor said, half to himself. "I was never going to marry for love. And Anjelica. She is beautiful—I knew she would be—but she is clever, too. Resourceful. She sees the truth of things. And she is honest about them."

Kel thought of Anjelica's secret meeting with Aden the night before. Honesty, perhaps, was relative. Especially his own.

"And she seems to have patience with me," Conor had added, "which, I think you might agree, is unusual."

"It used to be more unusual," Kel said, and when Conor looked at him sidelong, he added, "You are pushing yourself too hard to feel what you think you need to feel. You *like* Anjelica. You seem well on your way to friendship. There are worse foundations for marriage."

He could not remember what Conor had said in reply—and he was distracted now by someone calling his name. It was Merren, waiting with Ji-An outside the Caravel.

The two of them were seated on the barrier wall of a stone bridge over the canal. Merren raised a hand and waved at Kel; Ji-An, as usual, looked as if she were busy thinking about all the people and things that she disliked.

"You look awful," she said to Kel by way of greeting. She wore her usual violet silk jacket, her long hair caught with coral clips at the back of her head.

"I am," Kel informed her, "hung over."

She wrinkled her nose. "Your face is green. It clashes with . . . whatever that color is." She waved her hand at his clothes: a wine-colored frock coat and matching trousers.

"Here, take this," said Merren, sliding off the railing. He rummaged in his jacket and produced a pewter flask.

When Kel unscrewed the top, the pungent odor of tree sap made him wince. "Are you sure this isn't poison?"

"If I were going to poison you, I would tell you," said Merren with an air of injured dignity.

"Hmph," said Kel, and tipped the flask back, swallowing hard. What felt like a small firework burned its way down his throat to his stomach. Tears sprang to his eyes. He was somewhat aware of Merren telling him that they'd only just gotten the message he'd sent to the Black Mansion last night, and how had Kel managed to get Ciprian Cabrol to agree to meet him at the Caravel?

"I think Kel might be dying," said Ji-An, gazing at Kel with interest as he coughed. "Are you *sure* you didn't poison him, Merren?"

"It's as if none of you trust me at all," Merren complained. To Kel's surprise, the burning feeling was fading, as was the pain in his head. *Well.* He handed the flask back to Merren, blinking. A not unpleasant clarity was spreading through his veins. The world around him seemed to have sprung into focus: He felt as if he could count every stone of the bridge in minutes, if he were so inclined. It rather put Dom Valon's hangover cures to shame.

"What *was* that stuff?" he asked. "I could talk Conor into buying literal buckets of it, if you cared to sell."

Merren tucked the flask back into his jacket. "I use it sometimes when I need to concentrate on my studies. And you know I won't sell anything to the Palace," he added. "It's against my principles."

"Of course," Kel said. "I so rarely meet people with principles, I forget what they look like."

"Speaking of the unprincipled . . ." Ji-An nudged.

"Right. Ciprian." Kel looked behind them at the Caravel. He did not want to think about the last time he'd been there; he couldn't bear thinking about Antonetta at all. "He thinks he's meeting Conor. Merren, do you have any of that truth serum you used on Raimon?"

Merren looked dubious. "Do you think he'll willingly take a drink from you once it turns out you're not Conor?"

"I'm not sure he'd even willingly take a drink from Conor." Kel scrubbed at his eyes. "All right. Let's think. We have one chance to get this information from him. What's our plan?"

There followed a flood of suggestions from both Merren and Ji-An. They were still disagreeing on the finer points when Kel left his companions on the bridge and headed to the Caravel, trying not to mind that his mouth tasted as if he had been licking the floor of a pine forest.

When he rang the copper bell, Hadja answered, her gold earrings swinging. She ushered him in, saying only that Domna Alys Asper was expecting him. Kel followed her to the main room, which was emptier than he had ever seen it; he supposed the Caravel did most of its business at night. A group of courtesans, with no one to entertain, were gathered companionably on sofas in the main room. One of them was Silla, her red head bent over her cards.

Kel glanced away just as Alys came into the room. She was unchanged: small and neat as ever, her dark hair loose over her shoulders. She really was surprisingly like Merren, Kel thought, though they did not look alike at first blush. They had the same delicate frame, the same fine-boned hands, the same economical gestures. Kel had not known Merren well enough to see it before.

"Is he here?" Kel said.

Alys nodded and began to lead him up the stairs. As they went up, Kel saw Silla glance over at him with a small, regretful smile.

Kel said, "My thanks, Domna Asper, for helping us once again."

She said calmly, "I wasn't aware that I'd helped you before."

"You deprived Gremont of his protective amulet. Believe me, you did us all a service."

A look of real pleasure crossed her face. There was no regret in it, only the satisfaction of seeing a balance restored. "Who knows that he's dead?"

"Only a few people," Kel said. "For the moment, everyone on the Hill merely thinks he's gone off somewhere. What did you do with the amulet, by the by?"

"It's in good hands," she said as they reached the top floor. He fell into step beside her as they traversed the familiar corridor. Months ago, he had met Merren here for the first time—the same night he'd been kidnapped by Andreyen and offered a job working for the Black Mansion. The second night of his life where everything had changed in a moment's span.

The tension in his back ached now, like a wire winding his spine too tight. "It's a dangerous object," he said. "Something that magically powerful needs to be kept safe."

Alys smiled knowingly. "Just so. Understand, I can't tell you where the amulet is. But we all have our secrets, don't we, Kel Anjuman?"

She paused before the library door. It was very slightly ajar. Kel could smell the scent of *patoun* smoke wafting from within.

"Some more than others," Kel said, and went inside. The sweet smell of smoke was stronger in here, the light dimmer. The room was as he recalled: shelves of books, scattered tables, the archway leading to the reading room. In front of the window where Merren had sat the first time Kel had met him was Ciprian Cabrol.

He turned around just as Kel blocked the doorway behind him. His shoulders stiffened, the look on his face turning from anticipation to surprise. "Anjuman? What are *you* doing here?"

And suddenly Kel was not nervous at all. For so many years he had been trained to read every room as he came into it, to examine the behaviors of those surrounding Conor as a jeweler might examine the fine workings of a watch. Now he looked at Ciprian Cabrol, usually so elegant, and saw that his auburn hair was disarrayed where he must have scrubbed his hands through it more than once.

Under his eyes, the skin was stretched tight and shiny, a clear sign that he had not slept.

He's afraid, Kel knew. *No. He's terrified.*

Kel locked the door behind him, then leaned back against it, his gaze fixed on Ciprian. "Conor sent me," he said easily. "He can't get away, I'm afraid. You know how it is. Busy royal schedules." He grinned, showing all his teeth. "So much to do. Roistering, drinking, looking down on the peasantry, counting all the silver to make sure none of the lesser nobility made off with the spoons last night . . ."

Ciprian stared at him. "I can't tell if you're serious."

"I'm keeping the mood light," Kel said. "Conor said you seemed to wish to unburden your soul to someone. Rest assured, I will happily pass on your unburdening to Conor."

Ciprian flushed angrily. "What I have to say can be heard only by the Prince himself. Not his lackey." He started for the door, clearly annoyed that he would have to push past Kel to get out.

"Stop," Kel said with a quiet menace that stopped Ciprian in his tracks. "You owe House Aurelian for granting you the Charter in the first place, don't you? But you owe Malgasi more."

To Ciprian's credit, he didn't bluster or deny. He only narrowed his eyes at Kel and said, "Conor does seem to tell you everything, doesn't he?"

"What you should be asking yourself," Kel said, "is what I will tell Conor about our meeting today. You seemed to think you had something to share with him, perhaps something that would exonerate you from your part in the Shining Gallery massacre. So what was it?"

"I had nothing to do with that," Ciprian started angrily. "All I ever wanted was to get rid of the Roverges—and the Belmany Princess offered me that."

"Oh, indeed," said Kel. "By giving you the money to buy enough black powder to blow the Roverge fleet sky-high."

Ciprian had gone a sort of putty color. "What," he said tightly, "exactly, do you know?"

Kel shot out a foot and hooked a chair, pulling it toward himself. He sat down, crossing one leg over the other. He leaned back with a sigh and saw Ciprian's eyelid twitch.

He smiled to himself. He had learned from the Ragpicker King how beneficial it was to seem to be at one's ease while others stood around uncomfortably. "I suspect I know more than you imagine," he said. "But let us find out if my suspicions are true, shall we?"

Ciprian nodded impatiently.

"I know the Malgasi Court dreams of bringing down House Aurelian, and of using the Charter Families to do it," said Kel. "I know that a number of families are loyal to them, and that your family is one of them." He was gathering the strands to him as he spoke, weaving them into a tapestry he had not yet seen in its completeness.

The pupils of Ciprian's eyes seemed to have grown larger. "You devil," he snarled. "How do you know all this?"

"Through spying on people, Ciprian. I advise you to concentrate more on what I know, and less on how I know it." From the second library room, Kel thought he heard the squeak of door hinges. He spoke loudly to cover the sound. "I know you're about to tell me that, at first, Malgasi only approached the nobles—the Alleynes, the Gremonts—with a plan to *frighten* the Sarthian Princess. And perhaps that's true. But when that plan became a bloody massacre, the Belmany family used the conspirators' guilt to blackmail them. To paraphrase your own speech to a friend of mine— once the Malgasi have their claws in you, they keep that grip forever. They will never stop demanding more of you. So tell me, what is the rest of their plan?"

Ciprian was panting a little. "Conor can't know all this. He can't. We'd all be in the Trick if he did."

Here Kel would have to step carefully. "Conor has charged me with discovering the full picture of what is going on," he said. "And of course, he has his own plans for the Malgasi." He leaned forward, keeping his expression neutral. Friendly. "Ciprian. I don't dislike you. I know you merely wanted to get rid of the Roverges, and you had justified reasons for it."

Ciprian nodded in agreement.

"You didn't even know of the Shining Gallery plan until it was all over."

"No—no, I didn't," Ciprian said with an almost pathetic urgency.

"You fell into a Malgasi trap," said Kel. "And I would be willing to intercede with Conor for you if you will give me the names of the other conspirators. I can make him understand you should be pardoned."

"But I don't *know* the names of the other conspirators," Ciprian protested. "Only the ones you mentioned—Alleyne and Gremont. First the Malgasi had an agreement with the father—old Gremont, the one who died in the Shining Gallery. But he got cold feet. So they killed him and brought in the younger one."

"Artal."

Ciprian nodded. "Artal Gremont was put in charge of everything. We communicated with the Princess through him. I know there are two more families, but not which ones."

Kel was silent a moment. He'd known it was a possibility Ciprian wouldn't talk, or simply didn't know, but he hated it. More delay. More lying to Conor.

"Really," Ciprian said. He'd pulled his sleeves down over his hands, like a boy, and was worrying at them with his fingers. "I don't know."

"All right." Kel stood up. "Use what contacts you do have. Go to Elsabet Belmany herself if you have to. Charm her. Find out who the other conspirators are, then come back to me with names."

Cabrol hesitated.

"It's the only way to keep yourself out of the Trick, Ciprian. It will be a proof of your loyalty to Castellane and the Aurelians."

Something flickered and faded in Ciprian's eyes. He shook his head. "It's a nice offer," he said. "Believe me, I'm afraid of the Trick.

I'm no fool. But the Malgasi—" He broke off. "The Trick, the gallows, they frighten me in a way I can imagine. What the Malgasi can do to me is unimaginable."

Kel thought of the flame pouring from Elsabet's hand, fire burning out over the ocean. So Ciprian knew something of the magic the Belmany Princess could do. Artal seemed to have known it, too, though Lady Alleyne had seemed shocked. Still, he would need to be careful here. This was dangerous information to trade. "I know they are powerful, the Malgasi," he said. "In a way no one else is powerful—"

But Ciprian, still shaking his head, strode toward the door. It was clear Kel had lost him, so he rose and moved out of the other man's way. Ciprian hesitated a moment on the threshold before unlocking the door and flinging it wide.

Only to find Ji-An and Merren standing on the other side. Merren looked mildly interested in what was happening; Ji-An, holding a dagger in her hand, was smiling.

"This conversation isn't finished," she said.

Ciprian narrowed his eyes. "I know you. You work for the Ragpicker King." He swung his gaze around to stare at Kel. "And you . . ."

"Get inside," Kel snapped, and Merren and Ji-An hastened into the library, Ji-An urging Ciprian back into the room at the point of her dagger. Kel wasn't sure it was entirely necessary—Ciprian looked too confused to want to run—but it added a dash of theatricality.

Merren kicked the library door closed behind him. "We all work for Andreyen, yes."

"That's how you knew about the black powder." Ciprian turned to Kel. "But you're the Prince's cousin. You— Well, all right, I don't know what you do exactly, but you're clearly loyal to the Aurelians. What are you doing mixed up with the rabble of Castellane?"

Ji-An whistled through her teeth. "Watch yourself."

"There is a King on the Hill and a King in the City," said Kel.

"And that is not just a saying; it is the truth. Do not imagine monarchs do not acknowledge each other. If you ally yourself with the Malgasi, you make yourself an enemy of both Kings."

"But if you look out for the King on the Hill, then the King in the City will look out for you," said Merren.

"What does that mean?"

"Andreyen will protect you," said Ji-An. "Get those names for Kel, and the Ragpicker King will take you and your family into the Black Mansion. You know how safe it is there. And the Malgasi fear him. They, too, are not fools. They know that should they antagonize the King in the City, the streets of Castellane will never be safe for them, no matter whether they control the Hill."

There was a long silence that seemed to stretch out like the sea toward the horizon. Kel could not read Ciprian's face; he could only note that his nervous, plucking hands had stopped their movement. At last, Ciprian said, "All right. All right. I'll do it. I'll get the names." He turned to look at Kel. "But there is something you should understand about the Malgasi. They are not like Sarthe. It is not greed that drives them, or the desire for more territory. It is hatred. Hatred of the Aurelians. Why, I cannot say, but it is pure as white fire. They will not rest until the Aurelian line is burned away to ashes."

Lin

"What is your name?" Lin asks gently. She is sitting by the bedside of Domna Delores. It is late in the afternoon, and the shadows are beginning to gather like hungry ghosts in the corners of the room. "Your Ashkar name. If you wish to tell it to me."

The small woman in the bed tries to smile. In the few days since Lin has seen her last, she has gone from being a very ill woman to standing upon the threshold of death. She is refusing food, as the dying often do, and according to the neighbor who had summoned Lin would only take a few sips of water. Her hand in Lin's felt like a bundle of dried twigs.

"Talia," she whispers. "My name was Talia."

Lin nods. "Talia," she says. "Do you want me to pray for you?"

Because the Maharam cannot pray over you while you die, because you have no family to do it, not even an Ashkar friend. That is the cruelty of exile.

It is not specifically forbidden for the Ashkar to pray over non-Ashkar people, but Lin doesn't usually do it. Other religions have their own prayers, and there is often a priest or a family member by the bedside to say those words. This, however, is different. Talia is so very alone.

Talia moves restlessly in the bed. "I fear you cannot pray for me. I fear there is no place for me in the world to come. For I am not really Ashkar."

A great sense of the unfairness of the situation comes over Lin. Ashkar are taught from the cradle to participate in mending the great wounds of the world, which is rife with injustice, cruelty, and prejudice. To strip someone of their faith and their people, of the very fabric of who they are, solely because of who they love, seems to Lin a great injustice in itself. How can a people who have been forced into exile inflict exile on their own?

But what of other crimes? What of those like you and like Asher, the son of the Maharam? Those who dabble in forbidden magic? whispers a small voice in her mind, but Lin banishes it: She is with a patient now, and her own concerns are not to be dwelled on.

"Hush," says Lin. "You loved someone. You made a home for them; since then, you have lived a life of peace and solitude. You have done no harm in this world. I have no doubt that when you pass into the world to come, the Goddess will welcome you."

It is true. She has no doubt, and she can say that now in a way she would never have been able to do even half a year ago.

This time, Talia manages to smile. She watches with sunken eyes as Lin takes a scarf from her bag. It had been her mother's and was embroidered with the words of the Great Prayer.

She puts the scarf in Talia's hand, wrapping the other woman's fingers around the fabric. The prayer had been embroidered in gold thread: THE GODDESS IS ONE; SHE WILL RETURN.

These are the words that are supposed to follow the Ashkar wherever they go, that are meant to be inscribed over the gates of every Sault, that are meant to be held and carried with them from this world into the next.

Talia's eyes are closed. Under the weight of her hand, the edges of the scarf flutter lightly with her shallow breaths. It will not be long now. Putting aside any misgivings, Lin begins to recite the Prayer for the Dying in as soft a voice as she can. "Go, for the Goddess sends you. Go and she will be with you . . ."

CHAPTER TWENTY

After she returned from rounds with Aron, Lin prepared to leave for the Black Mansion to collect the King's medicine from Merren. When she stepped out the door, she found that a folded piece of parchment had been laid upon her front steps. Sure that it was something to do with her upcoming test, she opened it to read three words scrawled in an elegant hand:

We must talk.

And beneath, initials.

C A

Conor Aurelian.

Her heart was beating as if she had been running, and the taste of metal was in her mouth. She crumpled the parchment in her hand and cast it into the fireplace before slamming the door behind her on her way out.

x x x

Kel and Conor were seated on the floor of their room playing Triumph for copper pennies. Kel's luck that afternoon had been abysmally bad. He squinted at the cards in his hand, willing them to improve. He had the Witch, the Vine, and the Ship, but the more powerful cards—the Sorcerer, the Chalice, the Sunderglass Tower—had so far eluded him. Conor was almost certainly going to win.

At another time, this would have pleased Kel. Conor hated to lose but was sensitive to being *allowed* to win. Currently, however, he was playing with very little attention, having discarded both Lotan's Sword and the Tower without seeming to have noticed.

He had been distracted since yesterday's Solstice Ball, which continued to puzzle Kel. Whatever had happened when Conor left the Armory had troubled him greatly, and though he and Anjelica had made a great show of enjoying the rest of the evening together, Kel knew it was only acting—on Conor's part at least.

He had tried to gently inquire as to what had happened, but Conor had only put him off, always changing the subject; Kel supposed Conor would tell him when he was ready. Or he would forget all about it; either eventuality seemed entirely possible.

He set down the card of Gentleman Death, which always made Kel think of the Ragpicker King. Of course, Gentleman Death was smiling, and the last time Kel had seen Andreyen, he'd been exasperated.

Kel, Merren, and Ji-An had been forced to return to the Black Mansion after questioning Ciprian Cabrol and admit that they had offered Ciprian the protection of the Ragpicker King. Andreyen had not been pleased. "*Protection* is vague. Did you specify *what* I was offering him? Am I now to share my home with Ciprian Cabrol and his entire family?"

"There are plenty of extra rooms here, if that's what it comes to," said Merren.

Andreyen looked upon Merren with resignation. "Merren, I do not expect you to understand why this would annoy me," he said. "But Ji-An—you are not usually so liberal with the use of my name."

"I was caught up in the moment," Ji-An admitted. "We've been spending too much time with Kel. He only has reckless ideas."

Kel made a noise of protest.

"Well, don't offer things in my name without consulting me first." Andreyen slumped back in his chair. "Still, it was an interesting gambit on your part. I will be curious to see what comes of it."

Conor threw his cards onto the floor. He was sitting with his back propped against the frame of a divan, his eyes circled in shadows. Kel had heard him tossing and turning through the night. "I give up," Conor said. "I cede victory. Have every penny."

Kel was not interested in the pennies. "But you're winning, Con." He fanned out his pathetic cards. "See?"

Conor's mouth twitched up at the corner. "Those *are* bad."

"I was telling you—"

The door to the apartments burst open. Kel could hear the alarmed voice of a Castelguard in the corridor, but Anjelica sailed past him and into the room.

She looked magnificent in saffron silk, thin gold chains at her wrists and ankles. There was something about her that seemed different from any time Kel had ever seen her before. He had seen her nervous, even worried, but never without a layer of cool control. Even when preparing to deal with Laurent Aden, she had been calm, but now—

Conor waved pleasantly at her, as if out the window of a carriage. "Care for a hand of Sixes?" he offered. "I am a wretched player myself, which should afford you a satisfying and easy victory—"

"You told me," Anjelica snapped, her voice icy, "that you would not humiliate me."

Conor did not move or react. Only the muscles around his mouth tightened—and someone who was not Kel would not have seen it. "You will have to elaborate on what you mean," he said slowly, and Kel could tell he was taking whatever time he could to gather his thoughts. "Is it my outfit? My tailor did warn me against pairing burgundy with teal—"

"You were seen," Anjelica said evenly. "The night of the Solstice Ball."

"It was a public event," said Conor. "I imagine I was seen often, yes."

"When you left the Armory," Anjelica said. "I assumed you had been called away on some matter of state, something that was urgent. Instead, I find out today from Kurame that you were fornicating with some commoner. In public. Where anyone could see you." She bit off each word as if she were snapping at it.

"*What?*" Kel said. He looked at Conor, half prepared for angry denial. It did not come. Conor's expression hovered somewhere between resignation and relief. *This has been weighing on him,* Kel thought, through his own growing anger. *This is what has been troubling him, of all things. Perhaps he is even glad to be caught.*

He wondered, too, who it had been—but he could not ask Conor that now.

"It was an error in judgment," said Conor, "and not planned. Though I understand that may make no difference to you, *Ayakemi.*"

"Do not use that word when speaking to me." Color burned high on Anjelica's cheeks. "You play with honorifics that mean nothing to you, yet you will not treat me with honor."

Conor's eyes flared with anger. "Do you have your brother spying on me?"

"Conor," Kel interrupted. "*Apologize.*"

For the first time, Anjelica looked at Kel, this time with some surprise. She must be wondering if he had known, Kel thought. If he had been protecting Conor at the ball, even when he'd been dancing with her.

Kel rose to his feet. "I should go," he said. "This is personal business—"

Gold bracelets clinked as Anjelica threw up her hand. "No. Stay. For you are part of this."

"Kel is *not* part of this," said Conor. He stood up, facing Anjelica directly. "I only told him I was leaving the ball—nothing more, and certainly not why. I am sure we can all agree it is better my absence was not noted."

Anjelica said, "We agreed that you would be discreet, and I assumed you knew what *discreet* meant. It does *not* mean leaving your Sword Catcher to take your place at a ball so you could meet some courtesan in one of your mother's ridiculous follies, where anyone could see you. It happened to be Kurame this time, and he will tell no one. But it could have been any member of the Charter Families. Then how long do you think it would have been before everyone knew? And the shame would not be yours. It would be mine."

Conor passed a hand across his face. "You have nothing to be ashamed of, Anjelica," he said with a sort of weary self-loathing that surprised Kel. "And my Sword Catcher is right. You see he is not just my guardian, but my conscience. I do owe you an apology."

She narrowed her eyes. "Then make it," she said. "And I will tell you if it satisfies me."

"I know you were told even before you came here that I was weak. Someone who cared nothing for his city, who counted pleasure above responsibility. And those were not just scurrilous rumors. Those were the truth. But it is also the truth that I have changed. And change, I have learned, is not one decision, but many decisions made every day. What I did was a mistake, and I can say that in absolute truth. When I did what I did, it was because it was what I wanted at that moment, and I gave no thought to those I was hurting."

There was a silence. Kel looked out of the corner of his eye at Anjelica. Would she understand, as he did, how unusual it was for Conor to speak this way? To reveal his true thoughts and doubts to anyone?

"Well," Anjelica said. "That was not, quite precisely, an apology."

Conor met her eyes. "I am sorry," he said. "More than I can say."

Indeed, Kel thought. *There is much you are not saying.*

Anjelica nodded slowly. "I will forgive you," she said. "Not this moment—there is something I must do first—but I will forgive you. This time." She turned to leave; at the door, her hand on the latch, she hesitated. "At the ball, I told someone you had only ever treated me with honor and respect," she said, and a deep anger that Kel did not precisely comprehend underlined her words. "Do not make a liar out of me."

The door slammed shut behind her.

Conor looked after her. "I wonder," he said. "What does she feel she must do?"

"*Conor*," Kel said. "Look at me. Who was it? The girl in the folly?"

Conor's gray eyes darkened. "Leave it, Kel. It doesn't matter."

"You would not have done it if it didn't matter. You left a politically important party—and you asked me to change places with you. This is someone you care about, Con."

And I think I may know who it is.

Conor cursed under his breath, turned, and began to climb the spiral stairs that led to the tower. Ordinarily, Kel would have let him go, but nothing about the situation was ordinary. He started up the steps after him.

"Conor—"

Conor glowered down at him from the step above. "If you are correct," he said, "and I am not saying you are, that should tell you why I cannot answer your question."

They had reached the top of the tower. It was another hot, bright day. Not a single cloud marred the porcelain-blue sky. The gardens of Marivent spread out, green and low, around them; the clear edge of the sea cliffs was visible, the ocean a sheet of blue iron.

"I know what you want to say," Conor said, and Kel was surprised by the savagery in his voice. It was a savagery directed not at Kel, but at Conor himself. "*Tell Anjelica you can't marry her. Figure out some other way Castellane can pay its debt to Sarthe and protect itself at the same time. Do not torture yourself.* But you know there is no other way."

"I would not have used the word *torture*," Kel said in a low voice. "But it means something to me that you did."

Conor whirled to face Kel. "I see them," he said. "At night, when I close my eyes."

"Who do you see?"

"The people of Castellane," said Conor. He sounded reluctant, as if he did not want to be saying what he was saying. Which, Kel knew, made it likelier to be true. "Guildmasters, publicans, merchants' wives, shopkeepers, children. I see them put to the sword when the Sarthians break through the Narrow Pass. I see the Palace burn, the ashes of Poet's Hill, our city brought to ruin all because I failed. Because I could not manage this alliance with Kutani." His gray eyes fixed on Kel. "You have always been an idealist, Kellian. But this is not an ideal world. If you knew—"

He was interrupted by a loud blast. The trumpeting of an elephant.

Sedai. Kel raced to the edge of the tower, Conor beside him, and looked over the parapet. The clarity of the day made it easy to see them—Sedai, with Anjelica perched on her back, marching along the cliff path. Despite her size, Sedai picked her way delicately, Anjelica riding her without benefit of the usual wicker seat. Even from this distance, Kel could see her perched by Sedai's head, her legs dangling as she leaned forward to stroke her mount's broad ear.

"Well," Conor said in his normal voice. "At least she's having a good time . . . ?"

Kel rather thought it was more than that. He said nothing, watching as—alerted by the elephant's trumpeting—quite a number of Marivent's servants and Castelguards spilled out into the courtyards. A faint cheer went up from a few; everyone was fond of Sedai. Kel wondered where Kurame was, if he was watching as Anjelica and Sedai bore down on a white folly perched by the cliff edge.

"Is she—?" Conor began just as Sedai reared back and came

down, her two great circular feet landing directly on top of the folly. Kel could hear the noise as it burst apart. Plaster dust rose like smoke as Sedai drew back and kicked out with her powerful legs. More wood and plaster collapsed as the folly's roof fell in, landing like a wobbly plate atop a pile of kindling.

"Well," Kel said, "you always did say you thought the follies ruined the view."

Conor laughed. It was a real laugh—half disbelief, half genuine amusement. "So is *this* what she had to do before she forgave me?"

Sedai had already turned around, and she and Anjelica were moving past the ruins of the folly, heading farther down the cliff path. It would take them to the wooded path that ran along the spine of the hills separating Castellane from Detmarch. As they went, Anjelica turned around and waved in the direction of the Castel Mitat.

"I suppose it is," said Kel. "Be glad she only crushed the folly, and not you personally."

Conor was gazing out toward Detmarch and the mountains. "You have always been the one thing in my life that was real," he said. "But when I become King, I will lose you."

"I will still be here," Kel said, though he knew what Conor meant. He would never *be* Conor again, never need to stand in for him, never need to recall at all moments how he talked and walked and thought, and as the head of the Arrow Squadron he would not be Conor's shield alone, but a shield for all Castellane. "But you may require more than just me." *Anjelica? Perhaps, if you are honest with her, and discreet as she has required.* But he did not say it.

"*Require*," Conor echoed. "There is something I require now. Before I can speak with Anjelica again." He looked at his hands, at the rings glittering there, as if he had never seen them before. "I have to be sure."

And with that he was gone, in a whirl of burgundy silk and teal velvet.

Conor's tailor had been right about the colors, Kel thought, leaning against the ridged parapet. They *did* clash with each other.

x x x

Lin could not concentrate. Having returned from the Black Mansion with the medicine, she had determined to do what she could to prepare for her test, but her mind would not focus. She sat fretfully at her kitchen table, where she usually did her best research, her books spread out around her. Her eyes had blurred from staring at diagrams of Source-Stones and reading various accounts of how they held power.

If only she could *concentrate*. But every time her mind wandered, it wandered back to the night before, to the folly and what had happened there. To Conor: his mouth, his hands, the sound of the rain, the sensation of him against her. Her heart would skip and stutter; she would feel sick and hot all at once, as if her skin were burning.

Trying to pull her mind free of the memories was like trying to wrench her hand back through narrow slats that seemed to want to peel off her skin. But she did it, telling herself to forget Conor, to concentrate on how power was forced into a Source-Stone. Still, the image of the letter he had scrawled to her kept rising in her mind, as did the knowledge that in fact, she *did* need to talk to him about the medicine for his father, regardless of how very much she didn't want to talk to him about anything else.

Focus, she whispered to herself. *Lin, you are facing a trial whose substance you cannot guess at. You must prepare.* It was true that since she had last seen King Markus, she had noted a flicker of power in her stone, but it was only a flicker.

She thought again of those blurred moments in the tower. The King shouting in Malgasi. The stone flaring up with brilliant light when his blood touched it, so hot that the metal pained her. She still had a pale-pink scar from the burn.

Old legends claimed that a king or queen was inherently magical. That they could perform miracles, could heal with a laying on of hands. But Lin had a practical physician's mind. She did not believe in miracles—or at least did not believe they had existed since the Sundering. Nor did she believe there was something physically different about royal blood that made it in any way different from the stuff that ran in ordinary men's veins.

She could hear Aron in the back of her head: *It looks to me like an easy choice, Lin. Withdraw your claim, take the small punishment, and that will be the end of it.*

A knock on the door roused her from her misery. Mariam, perhaps, or Chana, who had been brewing up horrible teas that were supposed to help Lin study.

A second knock. "All right, all right, I'm coming," Lin muttered, hurrying to the door. She threw it open and all thoughts of medicine flew from her mind. It was not Chana standing on her stoop, tea in hand.

It was Conor.

Her heart contracted painfully inside her chest. He looked awful. He was dressed plainly, in a black linen cloak with a hood, no doubt to hide his face. But she could see enough to note that his light-brown skin was ashy, his eyes circled in blue-black. He wore no crown, and his black hair was tangled. The muscles in his jaw were tight, his mouth set.

"If you are wondering how I got through the gates," he said, his voice flat, "the guards are surprisingly sentimental. I told them I was a Gold Roads trader with a lady-love I wished to importune. That, and I tipped them each three crowns. Where sentiment fails, good old-fashioned bribery cannot but win the day."

There was a faint humming sound in Lin's ears. Mechanically, she said, "The Watchers are not meant to take bribes."

"Then you will have to speak with them about it." He regarded her tensely. "Is there someone else at home with you? Or do you simply not want me to come in?"

I don't want you to come in. She was terrified of what it would mean to allow him inside, to be alone with him. She did not trust her self-control. After last night, she knew it crumbled like wet sand in his presence.

But. It would be much safer not to be seen speaking with him. Even if he was disguised, tongues wagged in the Sault, and anyone could see them on the doorstep together.

She stood aside. "Come in."

He shouldered past her, smelling of the city: warm stone, river, and seawater. She closed the door behind him, smoothing her fingers quickly through her hair. She was suddenly aware of how she must look. Her white dress was crumpled, an ink stain on one of her sleeves. She was barefoot, her hair out of its braids and tumbling in uncombed curls down her back.

"I know I sent you a message earlier." He was drawing off his gloves, black kidskin. He seemed to loom strangely large inside her small house, as if his head might brush the rafters. "But I decided that this could not wait."

She almost closed her eyes. The memory of the rain, the folly, his hands on her hips, was too strong. It threatened to draw her back down and under into currents of feeling so bottomless, she feared the depth and force of them. "In the folly— It was a mistake," she whispered. "You knew it immediately. So did I. What else is there to say?"

He had pulled the gloves off and was twisting them between his hands. His head was lowered; she could not see his face. "And that's all?" he said. "A mistake?"

"Are you worried that I will tell someone what happened?" She stared at him. "Mayesh, or—" She swallowed. "I will not tell anyone. I have no more reason than you to want this known."

Twist, went the gloves. "I had not thought you would."

"Then, if there's nothing else . . ."

"Of course that isn't all," he snapped. "Lin. I am not a fool. What we did— That was your first time, wasn't it? If I had guessed, I would never—"

"*Stop*," she hissed, and he looked up at that, surprised at the force in her voice. "It was my choice. I wanted to. I said as much."

"But"—he sounded bewildered—"you said it was a mistake."

"Of course it was!" she cried out, and how could he not understand? "Story-Spinner tales of princes and peasants are just that,
Conor. *Tales.* And I am Ashkar. If anyone were to discover what we
had done—"

"I *know* that, Lin. It is a crime for us to touch each other. I know
the Laws, my family *made* the Laws—"

"Then why are you here?" she demanded. "To apologize to me,
to tell me it was a mistake? You could have sent a letter. Something
on royal stationery, with a seal." Her voice shook, and the backs of
her eyes ached as if something were pressing hard against them.
"Why compound the risk by coming to the Sault?"

"Because." His gray eyes were slits of silver. "I had to see you. I
had to."

"Why?" And to her horror, her voice caught on a sob. The heat
pressing against the back of her eyes became tears, spilling hot
down her face. She could not stop them. Shocked, she covered her
mouth with her hand, hiding the trembling of her lips.

Everything about him changed. His eyes widened. He dropped
the gloves he'd been holding as his hard, stiff, defensive posture
seemed to melt away; suddenly he was frantic to get across the room
to her. He pulled her against him, his hand in her hair, his voice
soft. "Lin, Lin. Don't, sweetheart. Please."

She had never heard him sound like that. Never imagined he
could. He kissed her cheeks, her salt-damp eyes; he curled his arms
around her, burying his face in her hair. His heart beat under her
cheek, fast as hummingbird wings.

"I cannot marry you," he whispered.

Her voice caught on her reply. "I know."

"But I can offer you— Lin, look at me. *Look* at me."

Half unwilling, she craned her head back. His gray eyes burned
with a clear light. He looked almost fanatical, as if he were praying
for salvation—or damnation, perhaps. "I am a Prince," he said. "I
can give you gold. Jewels. A fleet of ships. But you want none of
those things. What I cannot do is marry you—not without smash-

ing the alliances that are keeping Castellane whole. Not without losing the throne, and who then would take it? If there was someone I trusted, I would give it up willingly, but there is no one—"

"Conor." She was half appalled. "You should never give up those things. I would never ask it."

"I want to give them up." His voice was ragged. "But I cannot. I cannot offer you what the lowest peasant in the street could offer you. *Myself.* Because *myself* does not belong to me. It belongs to Castellane."

"I know. I expected nothing else." She started to turn her face away, felt him go rigid against her.

"I cannot offer you what I would wish to, Lin. But I can offer you— I can settle some money on you. A house, a grand one, in the Silver Streets. A carriage, servants. Whatever you needed."

"And I would be your mistress?"

"It would be discreet," he said. "But we could see each other. I would spend nights with you. Not every night, not at the beginning, but some. I would see you as much as I could."

Lin could not speak. She thought of Silla—*The dream of every courtesan is to become a mistress. One gets a house in the Silver Streets, a carriage, and a bit of money to save. Independence. It's a decent living if the man's kind.*

Lin took a step back. "Conor. No."

She saw the hurt bloom across his face and wondered if she would ever be this close to him again. Close enough to see his flickering expressions, pain followed by stubbornness, the quick flash of anger that mirrored hurt. Close enough to see the way the dark curls of his hair lay against his temples, begging for a hand to brush them back. Close enough to examine the exact curve of his mouth. "Why not?" he said.

"You know what I am," she said. "I am Ashkar. My people are here. What you offer me—a life outside these walls, but one penned up in a house, waiting on your visits—means exile for me."

The tops of his cheeks flushed; it was clear he had not thought of that aspect of his offer. "And it is not worth it to you."

"*Conor.*" Her heart ached as she looked at him. Part of her saw only that he hurt, saw the pain in his eyes, the way his hands gripped themselves into fists so that his nails could dig into his palms. How well, how oddly, she knew him. "If I became your mistress," she said, "how long would it take you to tire of me? Once you had enough of my body, once I was no longer something you wanted but could not have, what would you do then? And what would happen to me?"

He whitened. "I had you already," he said harshly. "I doubt you have forgotten. And I want you still. That has never happened to me before." He plunged his hands into his hair, as if he would tear it out in handfuls. "You are a healer," he said with a bitter laugh. "If you could cut this fascination out of me, like a cancer, oh, I would let you. For it has *tortured* me, Lin. I have neglected every duty, every requirement, just to steal another moment with you. I feared that if anyone ever saw me with you, they would see it on my face, that I was an addict, that I would barter my birthright just to touch you—"

"*Stop.*" The word came out more harshly than she had intended. "Please. I *can't.*"

He sucked in a breath. "You are sure of your answer," he said. "You are determined to say no."

He was so close. So close she had to force back the memory: the taste of his mouth on hers, wine and rain. His hands a key that unlocked a Lin inside her she had never imagined: a girl who burned like fire burned, whose heart was thunder, wind, and storm, whose body was capable of feelings as sharp and fine as a blade's edge. She knew she was losing that Lin forever as she spoke, even as she knew she had no choice about it.

"Would you give up your marriage?" she whispered. "Cancel the alliance with Kutani? Make me Queen instead?"

He had been bending over her; now he jerked upright. "You know I can't. Lin. *You know.*"

"It is your life you will not give up, just as I cannot give up my own. I will not be your mistress," she said. "I do not want some part of you, of your time and self." She raised her face to his, wondering if the hot spark of desire and memory she saw in his eyes was only a reflection of her own. "I do not want a lover. I want something more than that, and you cannot give it to me."

She saw a shudder go through him, like a spasm of pain. "There is one more thing," he said, almost as if he hated himself for saying it. "There could be a child."

"No." Lin thought of the early hours of this morning, alone in the kitchens of the Women's House, stirring the mug of oily tea. She had made it so often for other women; never once had she expected to require it herself. The flavor of it had been strong, tasting of mint and bitter pennyroyal. "I made sure no pregnancy could take hold."

It was as if something vital went out of him then, like blood running from a cut. "As easily as that?"

She recalled holding the cup of tea in both hands, hesitating; recalled how for a brief moment, the thought of a child with the most beautiful eyes in the world, silver as storm clouds, had flashed across her vision.

But that was not her child to have. One day it would be Anjelica's. That was the way things worked.

"As easily as that," she said.

There was an awful sort of silence.

"Well," he said finally. Something about his face looked different, as if the shape of the bones had changed—become harsher, sharper, beneath the skin. "Thank you for your honesty."

He moved toward the door, a little unsteadily, as if he were finding his way in a dark room. At the door, he paused without turning back to look at her. "My father," he said. "We have unfinished business there, you and I."

"Oh—yes. Wait a moment." Lin darted into her kitchen and

returned with the stoppered flask Merren had given her. She crossed the room to Conor at the half-open door. She could not bear to look at him, but she held the flask out for him to take. "The remedy," she said. "It is ready for you to administer. And of course I will continue to treat the King," she added. "He is my patient."

His fingers brushed hers as he took the flask from her. He drew his hand back quickly.

"Thank you," he said. "You are indeed an excellent physician, Lin."

And he was gone.

Lin sank into a chair, staring at the still-open front door and the bit of the street she could see beyond it. Dust and cobblestones. She felt oddly too light, as if a gust of wind might blow through her, finding no resistance.

She did not know how long she had been sitting there when a shadow crossed her threshold. Loomed up in the arch of her doorway, eyes bright and narrow behind a tangle of hair.

Oren Kandel. Staring blankly as if it were not at all odd to find her sitting barefoot in her kitchen, staring at an open door.

"Shekinah," he said. "Your test has been set for tomorrow at sundown. Present yourself at the Shulamat at that hour. Such is the instruction of the Exilarch."

She drew in a breath. It was too much, all of this, happening at once. She could not hold it in her mind, could not feel anything beyond a great emptiness.

"Oren," she said wearily. "You do not need to call me Shekinah."

"For now I must," he said, and she saw the hate flash in his small, bright eyes. "But after tomorrow, I will never need to do it again."

Thunk. The sword stabbed into the hay bale with a satisfying noise. Kel pulled it free with a twist of his wrist, spilling loose hay onto the floorboards.

He was in the Hayloft, and the golden light of late afternoon was spilling in through the windows like the slow drip of honey. There had seemed no better place to go, really, once Conor had left on his mysterious errand. Especially as Kel wanted to avoid Lilibet, who would surely be in a rage over the destruction of her folly.

By the time he'd left the Castel Mitat, dressed in his practice linens, crews of servants were already starting to cart the broken pieces of the folly away. It would be gone entirely by evening, no trace left, as if none of it had ever happened. As Lilibet had closed away the slaughter in the Shining Gallery by bolting the doors. *Why not scrub out the blood, clean the place, restore it?* Conor had asked.

Because what is not seen is forgotten, Lilibet had replied.

Thunk. Kel slammed the blade into another hay bale, withdrew it. His arms would hurt tomorrow, but today he didn't care. Anger powered his movements. Anger at Conor, for the nonsensical and dangerous thing he'd done that had nearly wrecked the alliance with Kutani. Anger that the only way to buy Castellane out of its trouble with Sarthe was with Conor's life. He was so clearly wretched, and Kel hated it. He was angry at himself, too. It was his duty to observe Conor, to pay close attention to his moods and movements, and yet Conor's actions at the ball had surprised him—more, he suspected, than they had surprised Anjelica. How had he become so distant from Conor that he could not even guess at the depths of his longing, his despair?

But perhaps it was unfair to blame Conor for hiding his feelings. Hadn't Kel hidden his own? He'd barely slept himself the past two nights. Over and over he heard Antonetta's voice, *You have to be careful about what you share with Kel.*

He had thought she believed him to be the only one she could trust. Now he knew she had never trusted him at all. Not with the truth of herself. He had congratulated himself for being the only one on the Hill who saw through her pretenses, who glimpsed the whip-smart intelligence behind the silk ribbons and giggling. That self-congratulation rang hollow now that he realized she'd taken him in with a different kind of acting.

And he hadn't seen it. Not until she'd spoken to him at the ball, when he'd been pretending to be Conor. He still didn't know why she'd said what she had, what her motivation could be. But he knew she'd been laughing at him for some time now. He wondered about that night, when she had rescued him from Tyndaris. Would it have been any different, he wondered, had he given her a real answer when she'd asked what he was doing there?

Would it? He swung again with the sword—an old one, dented from many practice sessions—and again and again, his arm aching, his hair wet with sweat. *Burn out the rage*, he told himself. *Throw yourself against the wall of it like water crashing against rocks. Break yourself apart like a ship running aground on coral. Spill out what is inside—the cargo of useless feelings, pointless hopes.*

"Your hands are bleeding."

Anjelica.

Kel whirled around. He had created a small tornado of loose straw, drifting in the air along with a cloud of dust motes. She was right, he realized, with some surprise—his knuckles *were* bloody. He didn't know how they'd gotten that way.

"I thought you might be here," she said. "I was looking for you."

She had twisted her hair into braids and looked younger than she usually did. She had changed from her saffron silk into more casual linen.

"Why?" he asked, still breathless.

"I wanted to apologize."

Kel plunged the sword into a hay bale, where it stuck, the hilt vibrating slightly. He turned to her, wiping his forehead with his sleeve. "Apologize for what?"

She raised her chin. "Princesses do not often apologize."

"Nor Princes," said Kel, "in my experience."

"And yet. I have no regrets about shouting at Conor, but I should not have done it in front of you. I should have insisted that Conor let you excuse yourself. You are a Sword Catcher. Your duty is to protect Conor from weapons, not angry words."

"I've done both."

She smiled a little at that. "Still, I should not have put you in that position. You're not just anyone. You have been a good friend to me in a place that I did not expect to find friends."

"It is early days yet, Princess. You will find friends here, ones closer to your station."

"I am not overly concerned about my station." She looked him over thoughtfully. "I will not ask you again to lie to the Prince on my behalf."

"Are you going to tell him about Laurent?"

"I will. I think I might write it down in a letter. It will go better that way." She looked at him solemnly. "I will not forget that you have been good to me."

"I did what I thought was best," said Kel. "Anjelica—I do think you can be happy here. I think Conor will do all he can do to make sure you are."

"You care for the Prince very much," she said. "He is lucky, for you would do your duty whether you loved him or hated him."

"I think perhaps," Kel said slowly, "it is your own duty you are thinking of."

"Perhaps," she said, smiling, and departed.

He wondered if she would ever speak to him again, now that she had no further need of him. She had used him in her plan to rid herself of Laurent; that was over. He wondered if that was how it would be with his friends in the Black Mansion, once they had solved their mystery. Jerrod was already gone; Andreyen, Ji-An, Merren—would they disappear from his life in an eyeblink? It would leave a hole, he knew, one that would be hard to fill, and made harder so by the fact that he would never be able to speak to anyone about it.

Lin

Lin dreams. And in her dream, she sees again the charred land where everything had burned. The earth is black, shot through with blazing rivulets, threads of red and bronze fire that glitter like the gold embroidery thread in one of Mariam's dresses.

Through the haze of smoke, Lin sees a figure, dressed in black and red, wearing a coronet of gold. As he comes closer to her, she recognizes King Markus. He looks younger than she has ever seen him, as if he has just claimed the throne, just begun his reign. There is intelligence in his eyes, and a clear awareness.

He stops before her. They are separated by a river of fire that splits the ground between them. Glassy black rocks float in the red-orange blaze.

"You have opened the way," he says.

Lin shakes her head. She knows it is a dream, and yet it feels real. She can taste the bitter air, feel the burn of it deep in her lungs. "What way? What do you mean?"

"You think that I have seen little," says the King, "but I have seen much. I know of the test you will face soon. I know that your stone thirsts for power. You struggle to fill your stone with power, but without the Word, it cannot be done by any means you might find in a book."

"So it's impossible." Lin feels the words like a blow. "I can never do real magic."

"Not so. The power in my blood contains the Word. The power I gained at the Court of Malgasi, the fire in my veins that they so dearly wish to have back." His gray eyes seem to glitter. Conor's eyes, inherited from his father. "You have done much for me. I wish to give you a gift in return."

A gift. Lin does not trust gifts. "I only treated you as I would any patient. I require nothing in return."

It is the King's turn to shake his head. Sparks fly from his crown as if it, like the land, is burning. "Come to me in my tower," he rasps. "Take of my blood to fill your stone."

He reaches across the burning river, reaches as if to take her hand, and though she would have thought it was impossible, his fingers close around her wrist. Pain flares in her hand, shooting up her arm as if it were lightning traveling along the path of her bones.

Lin sits up with a scream, quickly muffled as she claps a hand over her mouth. A moment later, she is scrambling out of bed. Her arm aches and burns; she hurries to the window, pushing up the sleeve of her nightgown so she can examine her skin in the bright-blue moonlight.

She is unmarked. Lin turns her arm over, stares at her forearm, her wrist and palm, still stinging. Nothing; only gooseflesh from the chill night air.

The silver brooch is on her nightstand. Swinging her heavy braid over her shoulder, she goes to retrieve it, and finds that when her hand closes around it, the pain begins to fade.

She turns it over on her palm. There it is, deep in the heart of the stone, a burning spark.

Her own heart begins to beat in double time. As if she is still in a dream, she pads barefoot into her kitchen. It is cool in here, too, the fire in the grate put out long ago. She gazes at it—at the blackened logs surrounded by gray ash—and says, her hand clasped tight around her brooch, "Burn."

There is a soft rending sound, like tearing cloth. A dozen gold sparks fly up from the half-burned wood, like golden beads flying from a broken necklace. For a moment Lin fears that this will be all there is, all the tiny flicker in her brooch has power for, but a moment later sheets of red and orange join the gold, flames leaping jagged in the hearth like dragon's teeth. Lin can feel the heat flood over her skin, sending her heart soaring.

She glances down at the stone in her hand. The flicker is gone, the stone cool and lifeless again. She closes her hand around it.

CHAPTER TWENTY-ONE

Kel woke up to the sound of voices. He pushed himself upright slowly, his body aching from the pummeling he'd given it in the Hayloft the day before. He'd slept badly, and he guessed Conor had as well, but Conor was already awake, fully dressed, sitting behind his desk, his feet up on a pile of papers. Perched on the edge of the desk was Joss Falconet, wearing a hot-pink frock coat and an animated expression. "They spotted the body last night," he was saying. "But by the time the Vigilants reached the canal, it had sunk out of sight. They're dredging for it now—though the Gods only know what they'll find."

The body. Kel felt suddenly cold all over, despite the sun streaming in through the windows. He glanced down; he was shirtless, but then, it was just Falconet. He cleared his throat.

"What's going on?" he said. "Whose body are we talking about?"

Conor glanced over at him. Kel couldn't remember the last thing he'd said to Conor the night before; Conor had come back silent and withdrawn after his "errand" in the city, and Kel had left him alone.

There was an unusual gravity in Conor's dark-gray eyes. "It's just a report right now," he said, "but it looks as if Ciprian Cabrol has been found dead in the Temple District."

Falconet had a new carriage. He had drawn it up to a stop near the Bridge of Singing Women, not far from the Caravel. The neighborhood was not usually crowded, as the Temple District tended to be less frequented at the height of the day. But word that a body had been seen in the green canal—and was suspected to be that of a noble—had stirred the sluggish interest of various passersby. They stood in uneven clumps up and down the banks of the water, chattering among themselves.

Vigilants, easy to identify in their scarlet uniforms, were dredging the canal with nets made of rope. It was a hot afternoon, the sunlight bouncing off the water as if off a jade mirror. Kel felt vaguely queasy, the light seeming to stab into his eyes as if he had a hangover.

Ciprian. Dead. It could hardly be a coincidence. Just yesterday, Kel had sent Ciprian off with orders to find out which other families were tied into the conspiracy, and now Ciprian had been killed. *We sent him to his death*, Kel thought. He hadn't been innocent, but that didn't matter. Kel should have anticipated the danger.

"Is everyone quite sure it was Ciprian?" said Conor. "Who saw the body last night?" He was leaning back against a satin bench seat, flocked with silver and gold embroidery in the shape of twining grapevines. Falconet's new carriage was so ornate as to be ridiculous. Bronze carcel lamps dangled from hooks, though they were not lit now; the walls of the carriage boasted gold-framed mirrors and diamond-pleated silk tassels, while beneath the seats were padded boxes holding wine bottles and glasses.

Merren would have been outraged, Kel thought. Sometimes he forgot how wealthy the Charter Families really were, each one a royal family in their own right, ruling over kingdoms of porcelain and silk, spices and wine. No wonder Malgasi thirsted to control them.

"I woke up at the Caravel this morning," Falconet said, covering a yawn with his hand. "It was chaos outside, Vigilants everywhere. Alys got me out the back way, said Silla saw a body in the water. That it was Cabrol. Alys wasn't pleased. Noblemen dying in the district is bad for business."

"Well, he wasn't a nobleman all that long," said Conor. He was gazing out the window, just as Kel was, but seemed distracted. "Three months, was it?"

Falconet chuckled. "Not a long time to get someone angry enough to kill you, I grant. Didn't you talk to him at the Solstice Ball, Con? Did he ask you for any royal favors—paying off gambling debts, doing away with an enemy or two?"

Conor shrugged absently. "I don't think I spoke with him at all. He seemed busy keeping Esteve away from Beatris."

Kel tensed. It wasn't like Conor to make a mistake like that. *Oh, Ciprian had nothing of note to say,* he should have answered. Knowing to cover for the time he'd been gone, for the time Kel had been him.

Falconet shrugged. "Well, I was very drunk. I must have misremembered."

"He didn't look particularly troubled," said Kel, thanking Aigon that Falconet liked his wine. "Not that it matters much now."

"I suspect," drawled Conor, "that this was the work of the exiled Roverge family. They had their Charter usurped, after all. They would have been hungry for vengeance."

"They certainly waited long enough to take it," Kel said as a shout went up from outside. Several of the Vigilants appeared to have caught something dark in their net.

"Perhaps Beatris will take over the Charter," said Falconet, resting an arm on his drawn-up knee. "She's unmarried, but with her brother dead, there's no other male heir. An exception could be made."

"You could marry her, Falconet," said Conor. "Then you'd have a Charter to bestow on some fortunate friend."

"I could." Falconet looked amused. "Speaking of marriage, is it true the lovely Anjelica rode over one of your outbuildings with her elephant? Crushed it to powder, I hear."

"It wasn't an outbuilding," said Conor. "It was a folly."

Whatever the Vigilants had found in their net, it was not the body of Ciprian Cabrol. A wave of relief went through Kel, though it only had the effect of making him feel sicker. Kel cracked the carriage window open an inch, inhaling the salty canal-water scent of the Temple District as the Vigilants continued their search.

"The official word is that it was an accident," said Falconet. "But I rather wondered if you'd done something to annoy the Princess. Did she catch you in a dalliance, perhaps?" he asked, with that Falconet smile that was meant to take the sting out of the words.

"There was no dalliance," Conor said in a strangely flat voice. Falconet looked at him with some surprise.

"My mistake, Con," said Falconet. "But—may I make an observation?"

Conor made a *go on* gesture. Outside the window, the Vigilants were dragging a net up the side of the bank again. Kel could not see what was caught in it.

"If you *were* to be caught in a dalliance—and I'm not saying you have been, but who knows what might happen in the future— I would remind you of the wise words my father once shared with me. He told me, 'Never make the mistake of fucking around in the foreground, Joss. You are meant to fuck around in the background.' And that is even more true for you, Con. You are a Prince but she is a *Princess*. She will expect discretion—"

A shout went up from outside. Falconet flung open the door of the carriage and the three of them peered out. The Vigilants had spread out their net. Lying in the center of it, already beginning to bloat, was the corpse of Ciprian Cabrol. Even at this distance, Kel recognized his dark red hair, water streaming from it. His clothes were dank, sodden, clinging to his body.

Kel's stomach lurched. It would do no good to tell himself that Ciprian had been planning treason against the Aurelians; his guilt was another thing that would need to go in the lockbox, down into the depths where he could forget it for now.

"May he pass through the gray door unhindered," Falconet said gruffly. "Alys was right—"

Another shout went up. One of the Vigilants had got hold of something else that had been in the water, something heavy and dark. Others crowded around him to help, and Kel heard gasps of disgust. The faint salt tint carried on the air was tinged with something else now. The smell of rot.

"Another body," Falconet said, hopping out of the carriage. He stood at the canal's edge, his pink coat incongruous against the scene before him: the Vigilants rearranging themselves so that a new corpse could be laid out on the stones. A bigger body than Ciprian's, rotted gray fabric stretching across bloated flesh, a slashed throat gaping like an eel's mouth.

"By the Gods," Conor said, leaning out of the carriage. "It's Gremont."

"I can't help but feel this is our fault," Merren fretted. "We tasked Cabrol with bringing us information, and the next day he was dead."

"I really don't see how that can be blamed on us," Ji-An said. "Not directly, at least."

Merren shot her a dark look. They were all in the Great Room, where a fire was blazing in the hearth despite the heat of the day outside. Andreyen, looking like a very thin, very tall scarecrow, was lounging in his chair, his staff balanced across his bony knees. His sharp green eyes seemed fixed on a point slightly in the distance. He had not spoken since Kel had come to tell them that Ciprian had been murdered and Gremont's body found.

"Not to mention," said Ji-An, examining her nails—currently painted a foxglove violet that matched her coat, "if he had not decided to involve himself in a life of crime and blowing up boats, nothing would have happened to him in the first place."

"*You're* involved in a life of crime," Kel pointed out.

"Yes, but I know what I'm doing. It's not for amateurs, now, is it?"

"I can only imagine that the death of two Charter holders will create chaos on the Hill," Andreyen said, breaking his silence. "Not only will heirs need to be chosen, but the remaining Charter members will be watching their backs lest they, too, find themselves floating in the canals, laid low by an unknown enemy."

"They're going to want to know who did it," said Merren. "Especially since Jolivet never heard about Gremont's death—"

"I stayed by the canalside," said Kel, "after the bodies were found. I was wondering why Belmany wanted these bodies found in the same place, because it was clear she did. She could have buried Gremont's body under Tyndaris, or burned it away to ash, but she kept it to stage this scene."

"What scene?" said Ji-An.

"When they dredged the canal, they found dueling swords. Both bodies had sustained stab wounds, though we know Gremont died of a slit throat," Kel said. "Belmany is trying to make it appear that they killed each other in a duel."

"Duels require seconds, and a witness," said Ji-An. "Won't they be looking for them?"

"King Markus made dueling illegal years ago," said Kel. "No one would come forward to admit they were involved—even if there had been a real duel, which we know there wasn't."

"But will it fool anyone? Were they even known to have disliked each other?" Merren asked.

"Everyone disliked Gremont," Kel said. "Falconet pointed out that Gremont always talked down to Ciprian, thought of him as a lowly merchant's son whether he held a Charter or not."

"For an improvised plan, it's clever," said Andreyen with a trace of condescension. "It will fool the right people. And as for the rest, well, those are the ones she wants to frighten."

"The real problem we have is that with Ciprian dead, we've lost our lead," Kel said.

"We could try to capture and torture Lady Alleyne," Ji-An suggested.

"No," Andreyen said. "She's terrified of Belmany now; she won't go anywhere unless she's surrounded by guards." He looked thoughtful. "How aware do we think Beatris Cabrol was of her brother's alliances? Surely he couldn't have kept his family entirely in the dark."

"He might have," said Kel, thinking of Beatris—though he had never looked closely at her, never really wondered what she knew. "If only we could find Belmany's hideout. We could position ourselves outside and see who goes in and out."

"Jerrod would have been able to find it," said Merren. "He was so good at finding things."

"*Merren*," said Ji-An. "*He* left *us*."

"Only because I shouted at him," said Merren glumly.

"No," said Andreyen, passing a hand over his pained face. "He left to rejoin Prosper Beck's ranks, which he would have done whether you'd shouted at him or not. At least he has promised that Beck will not be using his storehouse full of weapons against us, which gives us one less thing to worry about."

"Then what should we worry about?" said Ji-An.

"Elsabet Belmany," said Andreyen. "I do not know her, but I know people like her. She has lost two of her conspirators, and she will begin to feel backed into a corner. In that position, she will pivot to a more swift and violent solution to her troubles rather than depending on the slow treachery of the nobles." Andreyen looked down at the magpie ring on his finger. "She has said she needs Conor, presumably alive. And that the King must die. I fear, though I cannot say precisely why, that if she accomplishes either of those things, it will go very badly for us."

"I think you are right." It was Lin. She had just come into the room. She wore a cloak of soft blue wool, a brooch pinned to her shoulder. The stone set in the brooch seemed to wink brightly in the firelight.

"Do you?" Andreyen said to her, his sleepy green eyes curious.

"Yes," she said slowly. "The Prince brought me to the Palace to have me cure his father, who has been ill. He put me under a royal order not to speak of it, or I would have told you before. But I have learned a great deal about the Blood Royal. I think—I am almost sure that if the Malgasi get hold of the King and Prince Conor, it will be deadly for the rest of us."

Andreyen's eyes went to the brooch at Lin's shoulder, and then to her face. "But," he observed, "you will not tell us what you've learned?"

"Not yet. I need to go to Marivent. I must see the King. Only then can I be sure." She turned to Kel. "I need you to bring me to the Palace again."

Kel looked at her, puzzled. How many times had she been to the Palace before? "Did Conor not invite you?"

"Today I am not going at his request," she said. "I am going at the King's. But the guards at the gate will not know that."

"The King?" Kel said slowly. "He spoke to you? Lin, he has not spoken to anyone in months."

"He sent a message," she said, though there was something shadowed in her eyes that made Kel think this was not the whole truth. "All this has something to do with his fostering at the Malgasi Court. Something terrible happened there. Something that had to do with burning, with fire. Something he was persuaded to do."

It was not his fault. He did only what he was persuaded to do. Fausten's words, spoken to Kel in the Trick so many months ago, echoed in his head. "*Atma az dóta,*" he murmured. "Fire and shadow." He sat up straight. "She is telling the truth."

"*Well,*" said Lin, looking offended. "As if I wouldn't."

"Kellian, is it safe to bring her to Marivent right now?" Andreyen asked. "If the Prince did not request her presence, he may be startled to find her there. Startled enough to ask questions."

"We will have to be careful," Kel said. "But all the nobles will be closeted in the Dial Chamber, discussing the deaths of Gremont and Cabrol. It is not the worst time to sneak around Marivent."

"And if you find the answers you seek, you will come and tell us?" Andreyen said.

"Yes. As soon as I am done with my trial."

Kel rose to his feet. "We have lost Cabrol. We have no plan. And if what you believe about Belmany's nature is correct, Conor is in danger at this moment. Not at some time in the future—now." He took a deep breath. "I'm going to tell them. Jolivet, Bensimon, and Conor. They need to know everything we have learned."

"Jolivet, maybe," Andreyen said. "Conor may not forgive you for lying to him all this time."

"That may be so, but to save his life, it will be worth it." He heard Lin inhale, a short, sharp breath of relief.

"Thank you," she said in a low voice. She had been twisting a piece of her blue cloak between her fingers. She released it now. "We ought to go quickly," she said. "I will have to get to the Sault by sundown."

No one spoke. Kel glanced at the three inhabitants of the Black Mansion. Andreyen, as always, a closed book. Ji-An staring at the ground. And Merren, his face troubled.

"Are we done, then?" said Merren. "No more investigation? No more reason for you to come to the mansion?"

"I'll be back, Merren," Kel said gently. "Of course I will."

He looked at Ji-An, but she said nothing. He went to join Lin, and as he escorted her from the room, he realized he was pacing along slowly, waiting for one of his friends to call out to him. To summon him back, to ask him when he would return. To wish him good luck.

But they made no sound.

x x x

"Where does he think you are?" Lin said.

She sat opposite him in the carriage. The curtains were open and the hot sunlight poured in, making the small space stuffy. Lin had her medicine satchel on her lap, and Kel caught the faint scent of willowbark and astringent soap that seemed to infuse her clothes.

Where does he think you are? He knew she meant Conor, though she hadn't used Conor's name. Like him, when she said *he*, she meant only one person.

"He didn't ask where I was going," he said. "He's fairly distracted at the moment."

"Oh." Her eyes darted away from his. Kel leaned forward as the carriage lurched on its way up the Hill.

"Are you in love with him?" he asked. "Because he is certainly in love with you."

Lin started so violently that her satchel fell to the floor, spilling ampoules of herbs. "I don't—" She bent over, hiding her face, gathering up the dropped substances. She waved away his offer of help. "Don't," she said. "Why would you ask such a thing?"

"Because it's obvious," he said, remembering the way Lin and Conor had danced at Antonetta's engagement party. The way Conor looked the night after he'd met Lin during the banquet. The way his voice changed when he said Lin's name. "At least, it's obvious to anyone who knows him, and I should have guessed it sooner. I've been an idiot."

"That's ridiculous," she said. "He isn't in love with me. He needed me to help his father. He didn't even want to ask me, but he was desperate. And he put me under a royal order to do it. Does that sound like something you'd do to someone you love?"

"For Conor, it is. Because you make him feel out of control. Do you know how unusual that is for him? Almost everyone in Conor's life wants something from him. They want power, money, proximity to the throne. They want to be near him because to be near him is to be closer to the Gods."

"Conor doesn't even believe in the Gods."

"That doesn't matter," Kel said. "And especially not to you. You have no use for our Gods. You are complete in yourself. You need nothing from him; you never have. And he *cannot understand it.* You might as well put him in a lifeboat and set him adrift. He grasped at that royal order because to him you are like water slipping through his hands. He knew no other way to hold you—and," he added, "I am not saying this is a good thing about him, but it is a true thing. I am assuming he has released you from the order since?"

Lin, having managed to stuff everything back into her satchel, glared at him. "Yes," she said. "How did you know?"

"Because Conor likes to win games, but he doesn't like to be *allowed* to win. If he thought you were only willing to see him because he was forcing you, he wouldn't be able to stand it."

Lin's mouth trembled. "He set me free, but I still felt bound to him. I feel bound to him even now. As if there is some cord that connects us both—and I feel it even when he is not there." She pushed her tumbled red hair out of her face. "He has offered me a house in the Silver Streets, a place as his mistress, his word that he will always take care of me. But is that not also just another sort of imprisonment? A gilded cage is still a cage."

"He offered you all those things? Then he's desperate to keep you with him. I didn't realize how desperate."

Lin spread her hands wide. "I'm sure he's made this offer to others."

"Never," Kel said. "I doubt the thought of such an offer has ever even crossed his mind before. He is the Prince. He has always known that his heart was not really his to give."

"He didn't offer me his heart. He offered me a house."

"It's all he *can* offer," Kel said with a force that surprised him. He thought of Antonetta, and of how little he had ever had to offer her. "It's everything he has."

"I always knew it was impossible," Lin said. "He is the Prince, and I am Ashkar."

"I don't think he gives a damn about that," Kel said. "For the past months, since the Shining Gallery, he has thought of nothing except how he can make up for past sins. And for the first time he has taken it seriously, what it means to be a Prince and a leader. What you owe to the throne and the people who put you on it. You have seen the state of his father. He has had to be both Prince and King. It's not because he loves Anjelica that this is all he can offer you. It's because he loves Castellane, and only through this alliance with Kutani can he keep it safe."

It was all true, he thought, even if Conor didn't understand the full nature of the threats Castellane faced. But he would by tonight, and perhaps they could bring Anjelica into the discussion. Kutani would help them fend off whatever Malgasi might bring.

Lin was very pale. "I don't know what to say, Kel."

"You never answered my question." Kel leaned forward. They were rolling under the North Gate into the Palace proper. "Do you love him?"

She smiled the ghost of a smile. "Sword Catcher," she said. "Are you protecting him now? You know I cannot hurt him."

"I think you can hurt him more than he has ever been hurt," said Kel. "And even if I cannot stand in front of him to block this blow, I can stand beside him while he endures it."

Lin closed her eyes. They were drawing up to the North Tower, where Benaset stood guard by the door. The shadow of the tower fell over them, darkening the inside of the carriage. When Lin opened her eyes again, Kel saw them shine in the dimness.

"I do not want to love him," she said. "It frightens me more than anything has ever frightened me. Can you understand that?"

Kel said nothing. With an impatient gesture, Lin flung the door open and leaped down from the carriage. He watched her run past Benaset into the tower, her satchel bouncing on her shoulder, her red hair flying like a bright banner in the sun.

Elsabet

The fire in the brazier has burned low. Elsabet sits in the darkness of the temple, her hand at her throat.

She can feel the Source-Stone pulsing under her skin, the way it always does. A palace doctor had put the first stone there when she was thirteen and she had nearly fainted from the agony, but now she is used to it. As each stone faded in power, it had been removed, and a new one put in. She's had the operation three times now, and has come to enjoy the pain, even revel in it. For the stones are the source of her power—a power no one else in Dannemore outside her family could hope to touch—and the pain and the power go hand in hand.

The power in this one is slowly dying, she knows, for all that she has tried to conserve it. The night before, she had woken to find it flickering, as if it were warning her of something, but she had felt nothing out in the city save the dull hum of slight magic that always came from the Sault. She will need to reach out soon for a replacement stone; one that malfunctions is worse than no stone at all.

"My lady." Bagomer slides into the room like one of the shadows he likes to hide in. "All is in place."

She flicks her gaze up to him. "The bodies have been found?"

"Yes. We left them in the canal outside the Caravel, as instructed. One of the whores found them." Bagomer grins. "And more good news. I was just with the privateer, Laurent Aden. I have told him which guard he must speak to in order to be let into Marivent. He will retrieve the Kutani Princess and bring her to his ship. She will no longer be in the way."

"I thought she was being recalcitrant?" says Elsabet. "That she no longer wishes to leave her betrothed?"

"Aden said he believes he can convince her. And if he cannot . . ."

"Then we will kill her at Marivent instead of in the sea caves. It will be messy rather than clean, but she must die either way. As must Laurent Aden. Ridiculous of him to involve himself with royalty in the first place. Men in love are so terribly foolish." She shakes her head. "And Seven?"

"The meeting is planned for tonight. He will take full advantage, he assures me."

The stone at Elsabet's throat pulses as if it, too, is pleased. "Everything is in Seven's hands now," she says. "If he pulls it all off, I might just let him live."

She sits back in her chair, feeling—for the first time in some days—pleased with herself. Her mother, she thinks, would be proud. She is pleased enough to be distracted, and distracted enough not to notice the faint sound of footsteps as a cloaked Laurent Aden slips from his hiding place and makes his way out of the temple.

CHAPTER TWENTY-TWO

Golden afternoon light spilled into the North Tower through dozens of slatted, narrow windows. A Castelguard was waiting on the landing outside the King's room and ignored Lin—as if he'd been instructed to do so—as she went through the door.

Once inside, Lin felt her heart sinking. She was not sure what she expected might have happened since she'd given Conor the reformulated medication yesterday, but nothing seemed to have changed.

The room still felt close, oppressive and dusty. The papers scattered on the desk had a yellowed look, as if they were becoming antiques. The King was a shadowy, motionless silhouette in his chair.

As she moved across the room toward him, her skirts rustling as if they, too, were old paper, Lin noticed again that the noon light that lay across the floor looked fragmented somehow, like light seen through stained glass.

She remembered, then. The scratches on the windowpane. She sped up her pace, passing in front of the King—who did not seem to see her or react to her presence—and reached the window, a single heavy square surrounded by leaded glass. She dropped her satchel and ran her fingers across the cold surface of the pane, the ridged scratches scraping against her fingertips.

They were on the inside of the window, not the outside.

Without dropping her hand, Lin turned to look at the King. His eyes were fixed on her. There was no expression in them, and none on his face, but he was looking *at* her. Of that, she was sure.

"You did this," she said. "Didn't you?"

He moved slowly, infinitesimally, turning his body toward her. He was draped all in dark cloth, as he always was, and Lin was struck by the awkwardness with which he moved. As if his own skin were a suit of ill-fitting clothes.

He spoke then, but not out loud. His voice echoed inside her mind, just as it had in her dream. She did not even feel surprised by it.

Take my gloves.

Lin blinked.

Remove them, healer. See my hands.

As if she were still in her dream, Lin went toward King Markus and knelt before his chair. His hands lay unmoving in his lap. She lifted one, carefully; it was deadweight. She wondered vaguely if she would be able to manage this without her physician's training; the sense of something eerie, something awful, pressed at her like a weight. If she had not seen horrors before—snapped bones, crushing wounds—would she have run screaming?

She took hold of the gloves. They felt strangely warm, as if the leather were the temperature of skin.

She drew one off quickly, and then the other, dropping them where she knelt.

The King held out his bare hands, and Lin stared. Her breath felt tight in her chest. She had seen burn wounds before, skin turned to gashes and runnels by blistering fire. Limbs that seemed melted.

This was nothing like that.

The skin of the King's hands was black and cracked, like a burning log just before it collapses into the fire. Yet it was not ashy but *glistening*, scarlet veins of breakage crisscrossing the glassy black surface. Bleeding gashes, she thought numbly, but no—as she looked closer, she saw that it was not blood that seemed to bubble under the surface of the King's skin.

It was fire.

As he moved his hands, turning them that she might see them fully, the skin flexed, the cracks widening, showing the glow of red embers beneath. As for his fingers . . . Once, she guessed, they had been long and graceful like his son's. Now they were *fused* together, reshaped so that each hand sported three curved, angry-looking talons, each one tipped with a wicked, hooked nail.

Claws.

"Oh," Lin whispered. Her voice seemed to echo in the silence. She could not take her eyes off the King's hands—if they could be called such. "What *happened* to you?"

The hands flexed, turned, talons curving inward as the King made two fists. In Lin's mind, his voice crackled like a bonfire.

Long ago, when I fostered at the Court of Malgasi, I heard whispers in the night.

A picture began to form inside Lin's mind. A richly furnished room, a young man tossing and turning on a high wooden bed. All around him, a voice echoed, a pleading chant in an unknown language.

They were the whispers of something tortured. Tormented. Begging for my help. I began to see it when I closed my eyes. A shadowy creature, trapped in darkness.

Lin saw it, too. A thickening of shadows, and within its heart, the glow of two red eyes, too flat and monochrome to be human.

At last, I could bear it no longer. In the dead of night, I went to free it, not knowing who or what it was.

The young man, stocky and tall, his face half hidden by wheat-colored hair, made his way silently down a curved stone stairway, carrying a sailor's glass lantern. It was dark, the walls gleaming with damp. Lin knew he was underground. She saw the dread on his face as the lamplight fell on a cage. A massive golden cage that could have held a man or a great beast, though it held neither. Instead, a burning golden creature the size of a lion, the rush of wings, the curve of a long neck as it turned to look at him . . .

"A phoenix," Lin breathed.

The Malgasi had captured and preserved an ancient power. For generations they had kept it imprisoned, in a huge cage below their throne room. It was from this source that they drew their awful power. Do you see?

Lin saw. She saw scars across the golden skin of the great bird, saw that one of its eyes was blinded, saw the dark stains that mottled the cage's floor where blood had been spilled over and over. How many times had the Belmany bled the magnificent creature to power their Source-Stones? How had they whipped and cut at it until it promised blessings and success? Lin felt the pain of it in her heart—a shattering pity, a rage to see such rarity and beauty defaced, defiled.

Malgasi has never been successfully invaded. The Belmany family has held the country since before the Sundering. It is the power of the phoenix that has allowed them to keep their stranglehold on the land. And in that moment, I realized that, through thousands of years, all their power rested on the torment of this creature. And now it demanded of me that I end its misery.

I found somehow that I had a knife in my hand, and almost against my will, I plunged the knife deep into the chest of the phoenix. The blood covered me, and I felt its fire seeping into my own veins.

Lin saw the knife, the blood. The phoenix crying out in release as it died, its torment ended. A fall of blood like burning rubies.

In panic, I ran to the only person who had ever been kind to me at the Malgasi Court, my tutor Fausten.

Lin saw a much younger Fausten rising from his desk, his expression changing from curiosity to terror.

He feared he would be blamed for having told me of the phoenix, though he had not. But he was one of the few in the Court who knew of it, and they would never believe the phoenix had summoned me itself. So Fausten and I made a bargain that night, and he fled with me, before dawn came, back to my country. To Castellane.

Lin saw the young man, now filthy and disheveled, approach the South Gate of Marivent. He fell to his knees before it and kissed the ground. His wheat-colored hair had turned to a pale yellowish white.

I had expected that as soon as I returned to my birthplace, the Malgasi would take action. Against me. Against my city. They did not. I began to see why when I sensed the changes in myself. I was stronger physically, I healed swiftly from wounds, but my mind wandered often in dreams of the stars and sky, of fire and burning. It was Fausten who told me the truth: Every phoenix dies and is reborn, again and again. The Belmanys had prevented their phoenix from dying and returning, keeping it always alive without rebirth, adding to its torment. It had seen me as its only escape from the hell of its cage—it would not die and be reborn as it normally would, but die and pass its essence into my blood. Over years, through me, it would effect a rebirth through transformation. The Belmany family could not kill me without killing the chance that the phoenix would return for them to reclaim.

It was time for Fausten to live up to his end of the bargain. I had given him safety in Castellane, away from the Belmany family. Now he made for me a medicine that would slow my transformation. I would, he promised, remain human for many years—enough time to marry, to sire and raise a son to follow me.

But Fausten was not loyal. I do not know when he turned back toward Malgasi, or what they promised him to betray me. I know now that he began to alter the formulation of my medicine. My mind subsumed itself in dreams, in the music of stars, in the whisper of wings. I heard them awake and asleep. I began to feel the phoenix stir inside me, and I yearned to let it free.

I nearly lost control of it once, during the Marriage to the Sea. I was out upon the water, and the phoenix called to me to Become, to be free of my mortal flesh. Had it not been for Jolivet, I would have been reborn in flame at that very moment. As it was, my hands were changed; from then on, I hid them from the eyes of other men.

And then the Malgasi came. After years spent lost in fog and dreams, I realized that Fausten had lied to me. He was loyal to the Malgasi Court, not to me. He had promised to return the phoenix to them. It—I—would be imprisoned again. Tortured again. And so I had him executed.

"Yes," Lin said. "But then there was no one to make your medicine."

And without it, I began to change. I saw the massacre in the Shining Gallery. I knew the Malgasi had caused it, but I could not speak of it. I can hardly speak at all. I have now entered the phase of transformation in which the phoenix prepares, body and soul, to become itself anew.

"And is this what you want?" Lin whispered. She thought of the King, crying out to her in Malgasi: *They are trying to prevent me from becoming what I am.*

I? The King's inner voice was soft. *There is no Markus now. I do not think I will ever be Markus again. But yes, a part of me longs for a great, cleansing fire. I dream of the open sky in which I might have the power of flight. I am no longer needed to rule Castellane. My son could take the throne. I could be free.*

The ache of longing in his voice hurt. But something else hurt more. Lin said, "But Conor told me you agreed, when he was very young, that he would marry the Malgasi Princess. Why? Why let them touch your child?"

Because if I had not, they would not have let him live. They cannot kill me; I am the phoenix itself. But thanks to me, Conor also bears its blood in his veins. It is a power he knows nothing of—and a power the Malgasi will always believe belongs to them. I always knew he was in danger. It is why I provided for him the Királar. *The Sword Catcher.*

Lin exhaled sharply. "But Kel cannot protect him from such a force."

There is more to the bond between a Prince and his Sword Catcher than you know. The Malgasi fear it. And as long as they thought they would have Conor one day, that the Belmany line would not lose all the power the blood of the fire-bird has given it . . .

"But they know now they will not have Conor. Not through marriage."

My son is too clever by half. Too clever for his own safety. The voice in Lin's mind was colder now. The way it spoke of Conor—there was a possessiveness there, but none of the warmth of love. And was it the King's possessiveness, or that of the phoenix for its own blood?

Lin thought of Conor healing from the whipping, how it had left no scars. She had thought it was her own power. But perhaps it had been his.

And then he brought you to me, said the King—or perhaps it was the phoenix who was speaking now. *An Ashkar physician. The great fear of the Malgasi—an Ashkar woman of great power. One who could become the Goddess.*

Lin thought of the Exilarch. *You must understand the power of legends, Lin. The Goddess is a Goddess if her people believe she is.*

"But they still have magic," she protested. "Elsabet Belmany can wield fire with her hands—"

You know of the Source-Stones. You possess one. The Belmany have a few they keep in their treasury, still charged with the power of the phoenix, but they cannot last forever. Soon enough they will be gone.

The King opened his hands. His palms were a map of a volcanic land, glassy with onyx-black stone, crossed with veins of bloody fire.

In her mind, his voice was a hissing whisper.

Daughter of Sorah, he said. *You, like me, are becoming. I need you to become what you are destined to be—for should the Malgasi win Castellane for themselves, they will possess the phoenix again. Only another power that existed before the Sundering can tear their armies apart. They know of the prophecy of the Goddess. It is why they will wipe every Ashkar off the face of the earth, if they have their way. Should the Goddess be reborn, she could destroy them forever.*

Lin remembered Aron's tale of the son of House Belmany who fell in love with an Ashkar woman and learned the legend of the Goddess.

"Is that why you summoned me here with that dream?" Lin said. "Because my trial is today? I cannot promise—"

Hush. I can do something for you, and you can do something for me. Lin could feel the heat that rose from the King's hands, as if they were burning sticks in the desert. *When my blood touched you, I saw into your mind, as you saw mine. I saw the trial that you must face, and I saw your fears. I can give you power, child. Power through my blood that will make your stone glow brighter than any in the Belmany treasury.*

Lin lifted her face to his. "But what could I do in return? For you?"

His hands came up; she felt his talons on either side of her face, wands of fire and thorns. Claws scraped her skin gently. Her stomach thumped, half with revulsion, half with desire—not for the King, but for the power promised by his touch. *The Malgasi will come. They cannot be held back without great power. You will be that power. You will protect Castellane. You will protect your people. For without the Goddess, all are doomed.*

He dropped his hands, his blank eyes fixing on her face. And for the first time he spoke, not in her mind, but aloud, his voice cracking and rusty but still the voice of a King.

"The Malgasi fear a legend," he said. "Claim your power. Give them something true to fear."

Kel raced out of the bright sunlight and up the steps of the Castel Mitat, his mind awhirl. However firmly he had told Andreyen that he was unafraid of Conor's anger, of his sense of betrayal, the words rang hollow to him now. He and Conor had so rarely fought, nor could he remember a time when Conor had been truly disappointed in him. The thought of it—

Was brushed quickly from his mind as he looked up and saw Conor jogging down the stairs. He was clearly in a hurry, his expression distracted, a sheaf of vellum papers under his arm.

They reached each other halfway up the stairs. Conor started at the sight of Kel before casting him a distracted smile. He looked much as he had this morning, though he had thrown on a deep-red cloak, made for ceremonial occasions, with gold Aurelian roses embroidered on the sleeves. Binding his forehead was a heavy gold circlet.

"On your way to the Dial Chamber?" Kel asked.

Conor nodded and shifted the papers he was carrying. "Succession documents for the dye Charter," he said. "Beatris will be taking over from Ciprian. Not that she's in much of a state to sign paperwork, but the Law makes no allowances for grief."

Kel thought of Beatris Cabrol, the way she tended to always find her brother at any party or ball, the way she stood beside him as if reveling in his protection. At least, he thought, Ciprian would not go into the gray lands unmissed.

"I suppose not. What of the tea Charter . . . ?"

"It will go to Artal's younger brother, Donan. He's been fostering in Valderan, but a rider has already been dispatched to fetch him back. Where have *you* been, anyway?" Conor added, looking at Kel curiously. "I'd thought you'd be in the rooms."

"I went to speak with Lin," Kel said, taking care with his words. "Her trial is very soon. I wanted to wish her well."

Conor's hand tightened on the papers he held. "How is she?"

Kel hesitated. *I cannot tell you that she is even now in Marivent. That she is with your father, the King. That when I speak your name to her, her eyes fill with a rare light, just as yours do when you say hers.*

Kel said, "She is nervous. But you know how she is. She will not show it."

"No." A shadow flitted across Conor's expression. "She does not show much." He glanced toward the doors of the Castel. "I should go. They'll be waiting for me in the chamber. But, Kel—"

"Yes?"

"It seems long since we have talked." There was something oddly formal in Conor's tone, something Kel could not quite put his finger on. "Shall I come find you when the meeting has ended?"

"Of course. There are things I need to talk about with you as well. I'll wait for you in the room."

Kel could not help but think that the look Conor gave him was a strange one. Perhaps he could not imagine what news Kel might bear. But, "I'll look forward to hearing about them" was all that Conor said. And then he was gone, clattering down the steps, his red velvet cloak flying around him as Lin's hair had flown about her shoulders when she ran into the tower.

The Windtower Clock was striking the hour of six as the carriage wound through the streets approaching the Sault. Lin gripped the edges of her seat, readying herself to leap out the moment they arrived.

She had realized, upon leaving the North Tower at last, that much more time had passed while she was inside with the King than she had imagined. The sky had begun to shade over in preparation for twilight, and her test was meant to take place at sundown. She had little time to return to the Sault.

She could feel the Source-Stone in her brooch, pulsing like a heart. The glow of it had been so bright when she left the tower that she'd had to drape the edges of her shawl over it. The color of it had changed entirely, in a way she had never seen before, from a luminous pearl to a hot and burning red, the color of the King's blood.

She had thought she would need to use her scalpel, but the King had used the claw of his right hand to slice open his own wrist. His blood had resembled molten metal, almost glowing from within. As it splashed onto her brooch, lighting the Source-Stone, she had felt the heat from it and wondered how it did not cause the King agony to have such blood in his veins. There was a hiss as each drop hit the stone, and the smoke within it turned the color of blood and began to swirl under its surface.

She had thought she would need to bandage his wound, too, but it had closed almost as quickly as he had opened it.

"Thank you," she had whispered, but he had withdrawn into himself again. He only watched her as she caught up her satchel and let herself out of the room, breaking into a run as she reached the stairs.

She did not know when she would see the King again. How would he know if she passed her test or not? If she did, or could, become the thing he expected her to be? *You will give the Malgasi something to fear,* he said, but she could not now see past her own fear to imagine that that would ever be true.

The carriage was finally in sight of the Sault gates. Before it had even come to a full stop, she catapulted herself from the open door, nearly tripping over her skirts, and raced through the gates.

As she ran full-tilt through the Sault, bits of its familiar landscape seemed to flash into closer focus, as if placed under the lens of a magnifying glass. The House of Women, with its windows of stained glass, scattering rainbows on the pavement. The almond trees by the west wall, where she and Mariam had climbed when they were children. The physick garden, lush under the fading sun. And finally the Kathot, where she had first claimed to be the Goddess. The flagstones were scattered with clusters of saffron jacaranda petals, the dome of the Shulamat glimmering as the setting sun sparked off its tesserae of bronze and gold.

She had half expected the square to be crowded, but it was empty. Indeed, the Shulamat felt as if it were shuttered for the night, everyone asleep, though it was far too early.

As she neared the Shulamat, she saw a lone figure standing on the steps. It was Mayesh. Lin had almost not recognized him in his *besilon*. It had been so long since she had seen him dressed in anything but his Counselor's garb. He looked older, she thought, and more serious as well.

She met him halfway up the steps, almost expecting him to chide her for being late. Instead, he only looked down into her face and said, "I had thought for a moment you might not be coming at all. I had even hoped it. But of course you are here."

"I am." Lin's heart was beating hard against the inside of her chest, sparking an eagerness inside her. She could feel the heat of the Source-Stone, burning against her chest. She wondered if she looked strange, wild even, but Mayesh did not seem puzzled. Only worried. "This is something I have to do, *zai*."

"The test," he said, and hesitated. "It might not be what you are expecting."

She looked at him hard. What was this about? She knew better than anyone else how ruthlessly practical Mayesh could be. "So you know what it is," she said, "and you think I cannot do it."

For a moment, he looked like the old man he was. "I am not permitted to say what the test might be, Lin. You know that. Only— prepare yourself."

Lin straightened her back. Above them, the double doors were open, only darkness visible within. She held out her hand to her grandfather, and he took it.

"Walk with me," she said. "We will go inside together."

She had not imagined herself ever walking into the Shulamat with her grandfather at her side, even in the unlikely event of her future wedding day. But they went in together now, their hands linked, as if she had been much younger than she was. Mayesh's face was stern, unyielding in the light of the hundreds of candles illuminating the Shulamat's interior. They glowed up and down the roof beams, lined the sills of the diamond-paned windows, burned in candelabras placed at the far end of the room by the raised platform of the Almenor.

Ranged along either side of the aisle were the witnesses. Fifteen women, Chana Dorin among them, on the left side. And fourteen men on the right. All wore the *hesilon;* all bore matching expressions of gravity. Atop the Almenor were three figures—the Maharam, his staff planted squarely before him. Beside him, Aron Benjudah, broad-shouldered in dark blue, a silver circlet binding his brow.

And squarely between them, seated on a wooden chair, was Mariam.

Prepare yourself, Mayesh had said, but the shock was still like being shaken out of a strange dream. Lin had imagined many kinds of tests, but none of them had involved anyone but herself. What was Mariam doing here? She looked up at Mayesh, but he was staring straight ahead, his dark eyes fixed on the Exilarch.

"Lin Caster," said Aron, his voice carrying through the Shula-mat. "Come closer to the Almenor. Mayesh Bensimon, if you please, go stand among the witnesses."

If you please. It was an order, however politely phrased. Mayesh patted Lin's hand once before moving to join the other men. Facing the Almenor, Lin moved with slow deliberation down the aisle. She was aware of the weight of the stares on her as she went, curious eyes in familiar faces. The Sault was small; she recognized each one of them. What did they want, she wondered. To see her succeed, or to see her fail?

Just before the raised platform of the Almenor was a cleared circular space, ringed with candles. In the center of the ring was, curiously, a low divan, covered by a white blanket.

"Lin." Mariam's voice, thin but strong, cut through the silence. "Lin, I didn't know. What the test would be."

Lin looked at her friend, huddled on the hard wooden chair between the Exilarch and the Maharam. Mariam's eyes were wide and dark in her thin face. She was clutching a pink shawl around her shoulders. "Mari," Lin said, "I'm so sorry. I never thought they would involve you—"

"It was the choice of the council," said Aron. "And by that choice we must all abide."

Lin wanted to be furious with him, but she could see the real regret behind his eyes. He might not show it to the Maharam, to the council, but this would not have been the test he would have chosen.

She could not help but think of Conor, of what Kel had said in the carriage. *It's not because he loves Anjelica that this is all he can offer you. It's because he loves Castellane.*

Just as Conor had to put his people above his own choices, so did Aron. They were not so different, the Prince and the Exilarch.

As she watched him, Aron raised his voice and said, "Children of Aram. We are those who wait, but we have not always waited. Once we had our Goddess among us; once we thrived in our own land. Once we did not live within walls to keep ourselves safe, but walked proudly in our own streets, in our own cities, among our armies and our towers, our ships and fleets, our places of worship and celebration."

The eyes of the witnesses were fixed on Aron. As worried as Lin was, she could not deny that he had the ability, apparently inborn, to hold a crowd. The words touched something inside her, too. Something deep and never lost—the dream of a true home.

"Now we live in exile. But it will not always be this way. One day, our Goddess will return. One day, Aram will flower again. The Goddess chooses the vessel by which she will return to us. That is why we hold the Tevath yearly; why we invite the Goddess to speak from the mouth of she who holds our Lady within." His gaze passed over Lin. "Lin Caster has made the claim. The claim that the Goddess resides within her. And we must give her a chance to prove this claim."

Lin held Aron's gaze. She would not look away, however fearful for Mariam she might be. She could not show her fear, her concern, in front of those gathered here.

"We must offer to the Goddess the chance to show us the truth of who she is," said Aron, his voice like honey over thorns. She could not help but wonder who the thorns were for—herself, or those in the council who had chosen this particular test? "The God-

dess healed, they say, with a touch. Your test, Lin Caster, is to heal
your friend Mariam. Put your hands on her and heal her."

It was all Lin could do to hide her shock. *Heal Mariam?* As if
everyone in the Sault did not know that was all she had been trying
to do for years. It felt like a slap—as if they were saying plainly: *You
have never been able to do this before. How can you possibly do it now?*

And yet. They were also giving her a chance. A chance she
would never otherwise have had.

Aron helped Mariam from her chair. He was solicitous, careful
as he led her from the platform to the ring of fire and settled her
onto the white-blanketed divan. He murmured something Lin
could not hear and Mariam lay down, her hands crossed over her
chest, her gaze upturned.

Aron gestured for Lin to approach. As she did, she thought suddenly of the Ragpicker King, of the steady sound of his voice.

*You can lay your hand on magic, Lin. Concentrate not on faking your
way through these tests, or on the time you imagine is growing ever shorter
before you. Concentrate on* passing *the test. I believe you can.*

She was standing over Mariam now. Mariam was gazing piously
at the ceiling, but as Lin looked down at her, she turned her head,
just a little, and winked. And something in Lin's chest lifted. She
took hold of Mariam's hands and drew them apart, laying her arms
on either side of her, and placed her palms on Mariam's chest, flat,
just beside her heart.

She reached down inside herself. Down below her deepest
memories of her mother's laugh, her father's voice. Of Mayesh lifting her, tossing her in the air. Of the enormity of a dark-orange
butterfly landing atop the back of her hand. Of the surge of water
spilling into the harbor after a day of storm.

The Source-Stone grew warmer against her chest, and she
could feel the energy within it, flowing into her. The burning power
in the King's blood—a power more ancient than the Sundering, a
power born in the morning of the world, when wonders were as
common as field mice. It flowed into her and through her; it sur-

rounded her. She reached out and easily plucked a word from the void: *wholeness*. She drew upon it. *Contagion* rose, and she dismissed it. Other words came that she did not know, but that expressed repair and healing, health and strength. She reached out even further then, as the shape of a powerful word revealed itself—one of the most powerful words. One that the knowledge placed in the highest sphere of words, higher than heaven.

Life.

She caught the word and drew it down. There was a bright, sharp feeling within her. She thought she could see her own bones through the skin of her hands, as if they glowed like torches.

Mariam gasped, and her back arched under Lin's hands. A dark fluid was seeping from Mariam's chest—no, not seeping, but pulsing fast, like blood from an artery.

Lin kept her hands glued to Mariam while black fluid pattered to the floor like dark rain. The candles guttered as if in a wind as Aron raced to the edge of the Almenor.

Mariam sat up. She laid a hand over her chest, her expression full of amazement. She looked wildly at Lin. Her face was flushed with healthy color, as Lin had not seen it in years. Lin watched, her heart in her throat, as Mariam took a deep breath—her chest expanding, her mouth opening wide with surprise as her lungs filled. "It doesn't hurt," she said in amazement. "It doesn't hurt—"

The Maharam was pale and staring. From all around Lin came a murmur of rising voices, wonder and horror. They seemed strangely far away, almost muffled.

"Lin," the Maharam said in a terrible dark voice. It was the first time he had spoken since she had come into the Shulamat. "*What have you done?*"

He was staring down at her hands. She followed his gaze, and what she saw was horrifying. She could see clear through the skin and muscle, to the bones beneath, which burned with a bright-red fire.

She thrust her hands out before her. She could still feel magic pulsing through her body, overwhelming, pressing against the borders of her conscious self as if it wanted more than anything else to break free.

She could no longer see the Shulamat or hear the voices around her. She saw instead a massive dark hall, half lost in shadow. Around her loomed grinning statues with skull-like faces. And before her stood a woman—all in black, thin as a whip—who turned to look at Lin, her cold face unforgiving. Lin had never seen her before but knew immediately who she was.

Elsabet Belmany.

She saw Elsabet's eyes widen as if in recognition. Her lips shaped the word, *You.* And then Elsabet was striding toward her and Lin saw the Source-Stone at her throat, embedded under the skin there, pulsing like a second heart. A sneer crossed her pale face. *Of course. You would be a filthy Ashkar.*

Lin thought of the King, of his last words to her. Of the Wolf-guard and the bloody gallows and the terror sowed by the Belmany royals, and she raised her hands, palms out. *Fear me,* she thought, and the fire that had seemed trapped under her skin broke free. It poured from her like water from a broken dam until everything around her was brightness and heat. She heard the crackle of the flames and the shattering of stone, and the power was fading, it was going away, and darkness came like blindness, covering her vision.

Elsabet

Elsabet Belmany, Princess of Malgasi, heir to the Phoenix Throne, sits and gazes into the dark corners of the temple *cella*. It is quiet, the only noise from the Maze outside, and the sound of Janos's and Bagomer's boots as they pace the floor upstairs.

If there is one thing she despises—and in truth, she despises more things than she can count—it is waiting. And the pain of the waiting only grows stronger as the goal approaches.

Soon they will lay hands on the Sword Catcher. Not even his Prince will be able to help him after tonight. The pleasure of that thought buoys her up, as does the blaze of the fire in the brazier. She shivers a little, looking at it from her seat across the room. How warm it would be in the heart of that fire. How glorious . . .

Then she sits up straight as an awful sense of wrongness washes over her. She presses her hands against her stomach, gripped by sudden nausea. *What is wrong?*

All her life she has been alone in her power, her Source-Stone a single burning star in the darkness. But the darkness is beginning to flood with a terrible light, and Elsabet is—afraid. *So this is what fear feels like.* This gnawing, cold dread, like a dying snake thrashing in her belly.

She staggers to her feet, then nearly falls down the steps of the altar. As she weaves drunkenly through the *cella,* her shoulder hits the edge of the brazier, tumbling it to the ground. Hot coals roll across the floor, sparking with fire that spreads quickly to the wooden rows of seats facing the altar. Dimly, Elsabet hears the crackle of flame, but it is lost against the pulse of her own blood in her ears.

It would never occur to Elsabet to warn her guards, even if she were thinking clearly. She is thrashing toward the door to the temple as a diver might thrash upward toward air and light. As she explodes out into the night, the noise and smell of the Maze hit her like a blow. *Yells and cries, the raucous shouts of whores and moneylenders, the stench of liquor and sweat. And above, the sky turned orange by flame.*

Elsabet spins around, trying to locate the source of the blaze. The temple of Anibal is burning, she knows, but no flames are yet visible from the outside. And this fire—this is no ordinary burning. This is magic. And it is coming from the other side of the great wall that rises behind the temple. From inside the Sault.

Elsabet is no longer looking at the Maze. She is in a dark room, and opposite her is a young woman with bright-red hair and a determined expression. Elsabet recognizes her immediately: the girl who had been with the Aurelian Prince in the Palace library. Around her neck glitters a pendant, the hollow circle of the *magal. Of course,* Elsabet thinks, *you would be a filthy Ashkar.*

The young woman's face changes, her eyes hardening. The Source-Stone she wears on a silver pin fastened to her dress seems to blaze up with light, wiping away Elsabet's vision. She is back in the Maze now, and the wall of the Sault is dissolving, great stones crumbling away as an unearthly fire chars them to rocks and dust.

And through the gap they make pours a raging fire that surrounds the temple of Anibal.

Elsabet is sure she can hear Janos and Bagomer screaming, their cries dissolving into the sound of the fire, the avalanche of stones. She turns to run, but the fire is at her heels in seconds, like a hungry animal leaping for the kill.

CHAPTER TWENTY-THREE

K el paced the length of the room he shared with Conor, wearing a track (he was sure) into the center of the expensive
Hindish carpet on the floor.

It was dark; the sun had gone down. Some time earlier, Kel had
seen smoke in the sky and heard the ringing of the city alarms that
signaled a fire that needed to be put out (a not uncommon occur-
rence, but it did nothing for Kel's already jangled nerves).

Though Marivent was alive with torchlight, Kel could see that
the North Tower was dark. Lin would have made her way back to
the Sault for her test. The Dial Chamber was invisible from the
windows, but every once in a while, servants would hurry by along
the paths outside, carrying wine and food in the direction of the
meeting. It was entirely possible it could take the whole night.

Kel prayed silently, to no God in particular, that it would end
soon—mainly because his nerves were being slowly shredded. Over
and over he pictured his confession to Conor. *Should I begin with:
Well, there is a King in the City and a King on the Hill and they communicate. They have Castellane in common, you see. Or: On the night of
the Shining Gallery massacre, Jolivet approached me.*

Thinking of Jolivet brought him up short. Jolivet had insisted

that Kel keep his activities secret; if Kel revealed the truth to
Conor, would Jolivet admit to his part in it? Would he deny all, and
let Kel take the blame? Or would revealing the truth to Conor cause
the Legate to take drastic steps that could put them all in danger?

Reaching the room's northern end, he spun around and began
to pace back the other way. He thought of Antonetta and felt a
surge of sharp pain go through him. He wanted her with him desperately, despite his anger, wanted her voice and her advice. He
changed course, heading to his wardrobe and throwing the heavy
door open. He riffled through the clothes, looking for the plain
brown cloak he wore when he wanted to go unremarked outside
Marivent. It wasn't as if he did not know where to find her—

He hesitated, his hand still outstretched. He might know where
she was, he reminded himself, but he could not trust her. The
thought had a bitter taste; to love someone you could not trust felt
like standing unprotected in the freezing cold. He thought of Lin,
saying, *I do not want to love him. It frightens me more than anything has
ever frightened me.*

He lowered his hand, frowning. It was ridiculous to think of
leaving the Palace, in any event; he had promised Conor he would
wait here. There was something odd about his wardrobe, though.
His brown cloak was missing, and the shelves were also a mess, as if
he or Conor had riffled through them in a hurry, looking for something—

Shh. A whisper of sound. Kel turned to see that something white
had been pushed beneath the door of the room. He darted swiftly
to fling the door open and peer out into the corridor, but he saw no
one there.

The paper fluttered at his feet like a bird's wing. He bent to pick
it up and saw a message that made his blood go cold.

*Anjelica Iruvai is fleeing the Palace tonight. Go quickly and
convince her to remain. Should she leave, I do not need to tell
you how dire the consequences to Castellane will be. —Andreyen*

x x x

The door to the Castel Pichon was locked.

Kel paced back and forth before the blank face of the Little Palace, the feeling of ice in his veins. He had never seen the castle deserted, not since Anjelica had been in residence. Usually two of her brothers would be outside, often playing cards or even relaxing in the grass. Now the Pichon was lightless, the doors sealed, the place utterly silent.

He thought about shouting Anjelica's name, but that would only bring the Castelguards. Who would summon Lilibet, Jolivet, Mayesh—all of Marivent would be roused. Andreyen's note had begged Kel to *convince* Anjelica not to leave, not to bring the weight of the Aurelians and the Charter Families down upon her.

It was then that Kel noticed the window about ten feet from the ground, facing out toward the needle of the Trick. If memory served, it was most likely one of the windows in Anjelica's suite of rooms. Swearing under his breath, Kel summoned up his lessons with Jerrod, flexed his fingers, and leaped to catch hold of the wall.

Fortunately, the Castel Pichon was not made of smooth stone. Its bricks were uneven, offering easy footholds and handholds. Kel scrambled up to the window in a matter of moments and flung himself inside.

He landed awkwardly on the wooden floor, rolled, and came up on his feet. He was in Anjelica's bedroom, which was lit only by moonlight. The bed itself loomed on his right. The colorful tapestries that hung on the walls were drained of color by the dim white light.

"Anjelica?" Kel called softly. There was an air of disuse to the room, a quality that felt empty and abandoned. Surely she could not be already gone? What could have driven her so suddenly from Marivent? None of this was making sense.

It was then that he saw movement in the shadows, at the far end of the room, where double doors opened into a small study. Curtains, he thought, blowing in the wind from open windows. Windows that faced the disused garden at the back of the Palace—

Kel slid his dagger silently from his wrist brace, a flick of silver in the gloom. He took a step forward, only to freeze in place as a shadow emerged from the blacker shadows of the study. For a moment he saw only the outline of a woman in darkness and thought of Elsabet Belmany. Then a lamp in her hand flared to life and he saw her.

Anjelica.

"Oh, Kel," she said sadly.

She was dressed for travel. A linen cloak, fastened in the front, soft leather boots, a dark tunic. The curls of her hair had been gathered into a knot at the back of her head. She carried nothing save the lamp in one hand, and in the other, a short, straight-bladed knife, not unlike Kel's dagger.

"I wish you hadn't come," she said. "There's nothing you can do."

One look at her face told him that she meant it. She was not leaving because she was angry, not stalking away in a temper or even a state of hurt or distress. She was calm and decided.

Before he could ask why, a sound came from outside the window. A man's voice drifted up through the night air, cautious, a little worried. "Anjelica?"

She turned her head. "A moment, Laurent. It's Kel."

Kel heard the privateer swear. Something about his voice was oddly familiar—possibly he had heard him speak at the Solstice Ball? "Kel's up there?" he called. "Well, tell him to get the gray hell out of Marivent, too. There's enough room on Sedai."

"Laurent Aden." Kel kept the knife steady. "You're running away with Laurent Aden."

Her dark gaze was steady. "It's nothing to do with you, Kel. The less you know, the better."

"It does have to do with me. Because it has to do with Conor. You've lied to us since the beginning, Anjelica."

She glanced away. So she wouldn't try to deny it. Memories were running through his mind, everything tinted differently now, as if he had seen events unfolding before only through distorted glass, and now it had become clear.

"It was a lie that Laurent was in love with you and you spurned him," Kel said. "You loved him. You have always loved him. I saw you at the ball—I saw the way he looked at you. I told myself it was nothing, but I was being a fool, wasn't I? He was meant to come get you the moment you landed in Castellane—that's why you were so unsettled when I got you from the harbor. You kept looking around for Aden. Isn't that right?" Kel recalled her tension when he had fetched her from the Kutani ship, the way she had scanned the harbor over and over. Looking for Laurent, but not in the way he'd thought. She'd been hoping to see him, not afraid.

He took a step forward. Anjelica moved only a very little, the knife in her hand flashing, but it was enough to stop him. He could see by the way she held the blade that she knew how to use it.

"You are clever," she said. "Laurent was meant to take me directly from the ship when it docked in the harbor. When he didn't come, I thought he might have been killed."

"I have to applaud you," he said, wondering how long he could keep her here, keep her talking. "You showed none of your distress."

She tossed her head. "I am a Princess. I have the same practice in not showing what I feel as Conor does. And in a way, I was honest with Conor that day. When I told him I did not require him to play-act at love, and that I would not do it myself, I said only what I meant."

"Because you were in love with Aden."

"And Conor, too, is in love with another," said Anjelica. "You must know that." She looked at him speculatively. "We do not have much time, *Királar*. But I thought you should know. I had been told many things about Conor—that he was a monster, selfish, cruel. He is not. He has a gentle heart that even years of politics have not destroyed. And if you asked me, I would say it was because of you. You have kept him human all this time. Perhaps that is not a Sword Catcher's duty under the Law, but it ought to be."

Kel ignored this. He could not touch it, not now. "That story about the blackmail. All of that was a lie. You used me to get in touch with Laurent through the Ragpicker King."

Anjelica only looked at him, blade in hand, unapologetic.

"Why did you not run away with Aden the night of the ball?" Kel demanded. "Why wait until now?"

She set her chin. "That was what Laurent wanted. And it was what I wanted, too, but I told him I could not abandon Conor. I knew what the cost to Castellane would be."

"And then—the folly changed your mind?" Kel recalled what she had said that day.

"I had just told Laurent that I could not go away with him," she said quietly. "That I would not abandon Conor, because he had shown me honor and respect. I was angry—angry enough to let Sedai destroy that stupid folly."

"And that's why you're leaving?"

"Of *course* not," she said indignantly. "I was still going to stay— I was angry, but I understood. I knew Conor was in love with some-one he could not have; how could I not recognize the same situation I found myself in?" She shook her head. "Oh, Kel. You have no idea how bad things have gotten, do you? Representatives of Malgasi came to tell Laurent they would help him spirit me away. That they would marry Elsabet Belmany to Conor in my place, sparing him scandal. But when I refused the offer, they were not deterred. Aden learned they planned to have me murdered to clear the way for El-sabet."

Fucking Malgasi. Again. Their greasy handprints on everything bad that happened in Castellane. "You should have come to us. We could have protected you."

"I'm not sure you can protect yourselves," she said quietly. "If I run away, I'm a Princess who ran away with her lover. The fault is mine. It is far better for everyone if the nobility in the Dial Chamber sees me fleeing on an elephant. Then there can be no question what I did."

"Fleeing to the Malgasi for protection? You can't trust them, Anjelica—"

"Aden isn't really working with them. They think we're taking a carriage, fleeing to his ship. But we plan to be beyond their reach by the time they figure out he's betrayed them."

"Conor is never going to marry Elsabet Belmany."

"I know that. But if I am murdered here, even if he is innocent of my death, do you not think Kutani will want revenge? Do you not think a second dead Princess will make everything worse—for him, for you?"

"Let me talk to Aden," said Kel. "I need to know what the Malgasi have said to him—"

Something crashed against the front doors of the castle. What had been silence exploded in a roar of angry voices; light bloomed outside the front windows. A harsh voice shouted, "*Open! Open in the name of the King!*"

Kel spun to look at Anjelica. She was already at the window to the back garden. Her blade flashed as she slid it into her belt. She glanced over her shoulder at Kel just as the front doors of the castle gave way under the force of the crowd outside. They burst open, and a flood of Castelguards flooded into the room.

Over the noise, Kel could hear Laurent calling for Anjelica, yet she was still hovering, halfway out of the room, her eyes on Kel. He inclined his head toward her, as if to say, *It's all right. Go.*

She flung herself from the window. A moment later Kel heard the trumpet of an elephant and the sound of heavy footfalls on dirt.

A familiar voice echoed in his ears. Kel turned, as if in a dream. The Castelguards were a red tide, surging through the room. A blur. But among them two figures stood out clearly. Conor, in his green coat with the burning yellow roses. And beside him, Falconet, all in black and white like a domino. He looked at Kel with a faint grin, like the look he'd worn that day in the Caravel, when Kel had caught the apple he'd thrown.

"Where is she?" Conor said, his voice flat. "The Princess. Where's she gone?"

Kel shook his head. "She went with Aden. I couldn't stop her."

"Oh, you tried to stop her, did you?" Falconet said with a sneer, but Conor was already turning, rapping out instructions to the guards.

"Go after her—you five!" He pointed at a group of Castelguards. "The Princess has been taken. They're riding that Godsdamned elephant. *Stop them at the gates! Go! Go now!*"

As the Castelguards raced from the room, Kel saw a commotion at the doorway. Several familiar figures pushed their way into the room—Cazalet, his round face unusually serious. Lady Alleyne, dressed in red silk. And Sardou, sour-faced, ducking his long frame under the low doorway.

"Yes, I tried to stop her, Falconet," Kel snapped. "What's wrong with you?"

Falconet didn't bother to answer him. Instead, he turned to the small group of remaining Castelguards, who were watching him expectantly. Kel felt a hard twist deep in his stomach. Something was very wrong.

"Seize Anjuman, Benaset," said Joss, and his smirk was wound all through his voice, a sort of ugly triumph. "Hold him."

Kel waited for Conor to say something. To snap at Joss, to tell Benaset to step away. But Conor said nothing. He was looking at Kel with an expression Kel had never seen on his face before. He struggled to think of anything like it. Maybe when the King had whipped Conor, when the blood had streamed down his back like it would never be stanched. Maybe then.

Kel was conscious of Benaset behind him, catching hold of his arms, twisting his wrist until his knife fell to a clatter on the ground. It should have bothered him more, but all he could think about was Conor.

Falconet said, "So you thought you'd get away? Flee with the Princess before Conor found out you've been working behind his back for the Ragpicker King?"

"I still can't believe it," said Sardou, approaching the center of the room, where Kel stood, along with the other Charter holders. "Anjuman's always been loyal to a fault. Like a dog."

An echo in Kel's ears of Roverge, long ago. *The dog barks on behalf of its master. Bark somewhere else, little dog.*

"The Ragpicker—" Kel started hoarsely before turning to Conor. "Jolivet," he said. "Jolivet can explain."

Conor's lips were white. He said, "So you don't deny it."

"Joss already told us. There are witnesses to your treason all over Castellane," Lady Alleyne said, her rouged lips a red slash across her face. "They've seen Kel go in and out of the Black Mansion. Ride with the Ragpicker King in his carriage."

"I'm telling you," Kel said, "Jolivet—"

Conor put his hands up to cover his eyes. "Stop," he said, almost breathless. "Just tell me none of it's true—"

"He can't say that." Falconet's tone darkened. "You must think your cousin a fool, Anjuman. How many times have you crept off to the Black Mansion, dozens? Hundreds? Did you think you were never noticed? The Hill has eyes all over Castellane. You ought to know that as well as anyone."

And of course he had known it, Kel thought. But he had not been concerned about it. He had always been so unimportant in the eyes of the Charter Families; why would they look at him? And besides, the Hill's spies reported to Jolivet. Jolivet, whom Kel had assumed would protect him. Where *was* the Legate?

But Falconet was still talking. "What did the Ragpicker King promise you in return for information about the Aurelians?"

"I think that much is obvious," said Lady Alleyne coldly. "Gremont's death. We all know how Kellian feels about my daughter. He tried to scheme his way into my house just last week to see her. She was terrified."

This is insane, Kel thought, feverishly. He tried to catch Conor's eye, but Conor wasn't looking at him. *Wouldn't* look at him. He felt breathless, as if he were being squeezed in a vise. He had dismissed them, he thought, looking from Lady Alleyne to Joss, as panicked nobility in over their heads. Being blackmailed by Malgasi. He had not seen the web they were weaving around him.

He thought of what Elsabet Belmany had said to him on that rooftop. *I have a use for you.*

"I had nothing to do with Gremont's death," Kel said as steadily as he could. "And I had no reason to wish ill on Ciprian—"

"No, you did that errand for the Ragpicker King, didn't you?" said Joss. "You were seen meeting with Ciprian at the Caravel, along with several of the Ragpicker King's henchmen. And Ciprian wasn't seen again after that. Not alive, at any rate."

"Conor," Kel said. "You know this isn't true. You know I'm no murderer."

I'm a Sword Catcher. I protect you. I am no assassin.

Conor said, "Are there any witnesses to suggest Kel is guilty of these deaths?"

"Kristof, at the Caravel," said Joss, and Kel remembered the blond man who had handed Joss an apple. "And I doubt even Alys Asper would lie to the Vigilants, if she was made to see how serious the situation was—"

"You fucking *bastard*, Joss—" Kel started at Falconet, but Benaset's grip bit into his arms. Falconet took a nimble step back, grinning. Kel looked around the room wildly. "Don't you see," he said. "This is a trick. He's lying to you. He's trying to cover up his own part in all of it—"

"His own part in what?" Cazalet asked.

"The conspiracy," Kel said, knowing how desperate he sounded. "Gremont, Cabrol—they were working against Castellane. Hand in hand with Malgasi."

"How absurd," said Lady Alleyne loudly.

"We knew there was someone else," Kel said. "Someone close

to the throne, someone who was a danger to Conor. So it was you," he said to Joss. "You're the traitor. And you—" He looked at Liorada. Somehow he couldn't bring himself to call her a traitor; she was hateful, but she was Antonetta's mother. "You're no better."

"So you're not *denying* your association with the Ragpicker King?" said Cazalet, who looked as if he were trying to puzzle through a complex problem of taxes. "Just saying that you didn't murder anyone?" He turned to Joss. "But none of this is treason, you know. You said he'd committed treason."

"It is treason to help the Princess of Kutani plan her escape from Marivent," said Joss coolly. "It is treason to take her to see her lover behind the Prince's back—and we have a dozen witnesses that will say that's exactly what Anjuman did."

Conor turned to Kel. His eyes were wide, dark with shock, a sort of tarnished silver. "Did you bring Anjelica to meet with the Ragpicker King? Did you arrange for her to see Aden?"

Kel couldn't deny it; he couldn't look directly at Conor and lie. "You have to understand—"

"Of course he did," sneered Falconet. "And he was about to run away with them tonight."

"I wasn't trying to run away," Kel said through his teeth. "I came to stop Anjelica—"

"Really?" Falconet said. He went over to the great bed, with its arched headboard, and knelt down. Kel barely had time to wonder what the hell he was doing when he rose to his feet, carrying a leather bag with two straps. It was the kind Gold Road traders often wore on their backs. As Kel stood frozen, Falconet tore the bag open and upended its contents on the floor.

"Then what's this?"

Conor inhaled sharply. Kel could only stare. Spilled on the ground were his own clothes, the ones that had been missing from his wardrobe: his homespun cloak, garments of Marakandi green, his boots. Conor would know them as well as he knew his own.

Falconet bent down and caught up something from the tangle

of Kel's belongings. When he rose, and Kel saw what dangled from his fingers, his heart stopped. "*This* looks valuable," Falconet gloated. "Aurelian property, no doubt. Planning to sell it on the Gold Roads?"

It was Kel's amulet. How had Joss gotten it? Not that Kel had ever been terribly careful with it . . . why would anyone steal it? If they knew what it did, then they knew it would only work for Kel. And if they didn't, well, it was likely the least valuable piece of jewelry in Kel and Conor's apartments.

Kel had never imagined something like this. As the amulet dangled between Falconet's fingers, gleaming softly, Kel felt his heart nearly break for it—for all it represented, for the tie that bound him to Conor, soul-to-soul.

Falconet gazed at Kel, his expression—now that Conor could see his face—one of gentle sorrow. "It's really too bad," he said. "I quite liked you, Kel. But then I suppose you tricked me, just as you tricked everyone."

Kel twisted around to face Conor, who had gone the color of old ashes. "Con. Today on the stairs, I told you I had something I needed to tell you—I was *going* to tell you." He spoke as calmly as he could. "It's true, I was working with the Ragpicker King. Jolivet asked me to. I was trying to uncover who was responsible for the murders in the Shining Gallery—"

Conor said, his lips barely moving, "Joss told me you'd say that. All of it."

"Because he *knows it's true*," Kel gasped as Benaset's grip tightened. "Get Jolivet here, ask him—"

"I'm here." Kel felt Benaset's grip on him loosen in surprise; at some point, Jolivet had come into the room, so quietly none of them had noticed. For the first time, he saw a look of anxiety flicker across Joss's face. It was mirrored on Lady Alleyne's. Had they not known of Jolivet's involvement? Was that possible?

"Jolivet," Kel gasped as the Legate came forward, moving slowly. For the first time, Kel thought he looked old: His face was strained, deep lines at the corners of his mouth. He walked stiffly, as if an old wound hurt him. "Jolivet, tell them. What we know, that you asked me to investigate—"

Conor turned toward the leader of the Castelguard. Kel could not see his expression, but there was a trace of hope in his voice when Conor spoke. So little that he doubted anyone else would have been able to mark it. "Aristide," he said. "Is what Kel's saying true? Did you ask him to work with Morettus?"

Jolivet's gaze came to rest on Kel. The whole room seemed to be holding its breath. Even Joss, who had talked so much until now, was silent. There was something like regret in Jolivet's expression, and Kel thought: *This would be hard for him, too.* He would have to explain why he had hidden his plans from Conor. But Conor would understand. Kel knew him better than anyone. He just had to have it explained to him the right way—

"I am afraid to say that Kel is lying," said Jolivet. "I never gave him any such instructions. It seems he has betrayed us all."

Something seemed to explode in the back of Kel's head. Using all his strength, Kel pulled free of Benaset's grip, and for a moment he saw fear flicker across Joss's face. As Falconet stumbled back, Kel heard Jolivet rap out an order sharply. There was a crack like lightning piercing Kel's skull, followed by a searing pain.

Afterward, darkness.

Aron

To Aron Benjudah, leader of the Ashkar people, from Conor Aurelian, Prince of Castellane.

This letter is to inform you that the royal family of Castellane is aware of the damage done to the walls of the Sault by the recent fire. Know that we will be posting Vigilants at the gap in the wall to protect you from any incursions, until the rebuilding of the wall is complete. I also wish to apologize to you for not acting upon this sooner, but I was informed by my advisers only that there had been a fire in the Maze, and not of the damage to the Sault.

    I understand that there were no casualties, for which I am greatly relieved. Let me reassure you that the Ashkar are among the most valuable citizens of our city, and should trouble arise in the future, feel free to apply to me personally as one Prince to another.

    C.A.

Aron sets the letter down and frowns. From every description he's heard of Conor Aurelian, this is not the sort of message—

generous, thoughtful—that he would have expected the Prince of
Castellane to send to anyone, much less an Ashkar.

Aron is aware that both Lin and Mayesh spend a good deal of
time on the Hill. Is it possible that knowing some Ashkar individually has broken down prejudices the Prince might otherwise be carrying? It is certainly part of the point of having an Ashkar Counselor
to the throne, to be sure, but . . .

"Exilarch, can I speak with you?"

Aron looks up. He's been sitting on a stone bench near the
Kathot; he can see, in the distance, Mez Gorin and some of the
other men laboring on the broken wall. Beyond them, the red coats
of the Vigilants, forming a temporary wall between the Sault and
the Maze. Strange as the whole business is, Aron is grateful for
their presence. The walls that surround the Sault might have been
built to protect the city from the Ashkar, but they also protect the
Ashkar from the chaos and danger of the city.

He recalls himself to the present moment. Standing before
him is someone he knows well by sight but has never spoken to
directly: Mariam Duhary. He cannot help but stare a little. She is
no longer even recognizable as the frail, sallow young woman he'd
first met, when he'd thought: *This one has the hand of Death on
her.* Though she is still thin, the color is bright in her face, her eyes
are clear, and her hair tumbles thickly around her shoulders as if
every strand is alive with health and vigor.

He nods at her. "Of course you can speak with me."

"Good." She takes a determined step forward. A gold *magal*
glitters at her throat. "I wish to speak with you of Lin Caster. I think
you know what I am going to say."

Aron swears silently. Lin. The last thing he wants to talk about.
The reason he barely slept the past night, or the one before. His
greatest challenge and greatest revelation, which seems set to become his greatest regret. "I understand, Mariam," he says as gently
as he can, "why you want to talk to me, and I even agree with you

that Lin's exile is unfair, but it is the decision of your Maharam. I cannot interfere."

Mariam shakes her head. The *magal* at her throat glitters, and Aron realizes belatedly what it means: It had been Lin's. But Lin is no longer Ashkar, and cannot wear it, so Mariam will wear it for her. He remembers the dazed time after Asher's exile, how he had wanted to cling onto the things Asher had owned—his books, his papers, a green shirt that had matched his eyes.

"I know that isn't true," Mariam says. "I saw the way you looked at Lin when she healed me. I know that you saw the Goddess in that moment."

He stares at her. It is not what he expected her to say—perhaps because seeing the Goddess seems to him such a private and personal thing. Perhaps because it is true.

"I saw her, too." Mariam raises her chin. "It may be that because we are a people who have been so long waiting, you have forgotten that your purpose is not to be a politician. Not to keep the Maharam happy and our people complacent. Your purpose is to help mend the world by protecting the Goddess when she returns. And if you fail here, you will render purposeless not only your own life, but also the life of every Exilarch who comes after you." Mariam folds her arms over her chest. "So what are you going to do?"

CHAPTER TWENTY-FOUR

Kel woke up in the Trick.

He didn't realize where he was immediately. He was lying on a hard surface, he knew that much. His head ached and the shadows seemed to crisscross each other at strange angles. For a hallucinatory moment he imagined that this was a dream in which he was locked in a cage, iron bars all around him.

Slowly he sat up. His stomach lurched, bile rising in the back of his throat. He sucked in a gasp of stale air, gazing around him: Bare stone floor. A straw-tick mattress and ragged blanket. A cheap clay pitcher. Three stone walls rose all around him, a gap of light high above—a barred window, through which moonlight spilled. A ceramic pot on the floor, for obvious purposes. And instead of a fourth stone wall, bars ranged from floor to ceiling. They seemed to glow with a dull light.

Kel rolled onto his knees. He did not think he could stand up without vomiting, so he crawled across the floor until he reached the bars. He wrapped his right hand around one, felt the faint vibration pass through his palm, like static electricity.

Sunderglass.

He was in *La Trecherie*. The Trick. Treason Tower. Its various names rolled through his mind like carriage wheels carving bloody tracks, and he barely managed to crawl to the chamber pot before he was sick in it. He coughed and spat, rocking back on his heels, bitterness flooding his mouth.

Conor. It was coming back to him now, in disjointed pieces. Anjelica's room in the Castel Pichon. The Castelguards bursting in. Falconet. The look on Conor's face as Falconet presented his evidence, painting Kel as a murderer, a liar, a traitor.

Kel crawled over to the straw-tick mattress and rolled onto it, seizing the pitcher. Thank the Gods, it was nearly full of dusty water. He drank down half of it before realizing he had no idea when it would be refilled. Reluctantly, he set it down.

First, assess the extent of your injuries, Jolivet had always said. So, in the dim light of the window, Kel set about examining himself. There was a knot at the back of his head where he'd been hit, still sticky with blood. He was still wearing the same clothes he'd come to the Little Palace in, though there were tears in them now, some edged with blood. He imagined he'd been dragged across the grounds while unconscious, and this was the result.

Otherwise, he was unhurt. He wondered how long he had lain here. Was it still the same night, or had he been unconscious for a full day? The thought made him feel utterly disoriented, as if he had become unmoored in time. Then again, now that he was a prisoner, it no longer mattered what hour it was, or what day. It was not as if you had appointments to keep—save the last appointment of them all, the one that all men and women kept in the end.

It was as if he could see the Dark Guide and the gray doorway before him. Kel closed his eyes, but that was hardly better. Printed against the back of them was that look on Conor's face in the Castel Pichon. The look of one who had been dealt a mortal injury. A child abandoned in the dark.

Stop, he told himself. There was no point sitting here having *feelings* about what had happened, what Falconet had done. The ache in his head was starting to recede a little, and he could think.

Ask questions, he thought. *Imagine you are standing in front of the Rag-picker King, piecing together the bits of a mystery, finding the puzzle piece that fits the gap in the picture.*

The first piece. That note. The Ragpicker King had not written it. He had been tricked into going to the Little Palace by someone who had known Anjelica was leaving. Someone who had planned what would happen if he was there when she did.

The obvious answer was Falconet. Someone had also taken his clothes, his amulet, and hidden them in the Little Palace so it would look as if Kel were fleeing from Castellane. He thought of the amulet glittering in Joss's grasp, something so intimate, so personal to Kel and to Conor, used in such a way.

Falconet had pretended well. Pretended that he did not know Kel was not Kel Anjuman, but Kel Saren, Sword Catcher. Kel wondered how long he had known. When had Elsabet told him? How long had he been in league with Malgasi, and when had he decided he needed to rid himself of Kel—the person who was uncovering the truth about the conspiracy, circling ever closer to Falconet's name?

He thought of Joss in the carriage by the canals. *Didn't you talk to him at the Solstice Ball, Con? Did he ask you for any royal favors—paying off gambling debts, doing away with an enemy or two?*

And Conor, replying, *I don't think I spoke with him at all. He seemed busy keeping Esteve away from Beatris.*

Falconet shrugging it off. *Well, I was very drunk. I must have misremembered.*

But he had not misremembered anything. He'd been confirming for himself that the Conor at the Solstice Ball was Kel. Perhaps confirming what Elsabet Belmany had told him: Kel Saren can become Conor anytime he likes. He's probably fooled you a dozen times. Joss was vain; he would have hated that. And he would have wanted to test anything Belmany told him for himself. Such a small mistake for Conor to make; such consequences.

Kel passed a shaking hand across his face. There was more. Falconet had been the one to tell them about Cabrol's death.

Kel's head spun. Ciprian had approached Kel at the ball, wanting to unburden his soul about the conspiracy. Falconet had discovered it was Kel that Cabrol had talked to, not Conor. And that Cabrol, desperate to shift blame, was a liability. Perhaps he had even found out about Kel's meeting with Ciprian at the Caravel. Either way, both Kel and Ciprian had been revealed to be threats to the conspiracy. And a day later, Ciprian was dead and Kel was in the Trick.

Kel almost had to admire the work, it was so neatly done. At the same time, he wanted nothing more than to cut Falconet into small pieces and distribute them around the Maze. He sank back onto the prickly mattress, staring into the dark. All his realizations, he thought bleakly, had come too late. He could not warn Conor. He could not reach the Ragpicker King. *My friends have no idea where I am, or that anything has happened to me. Gods, what do I do?*

Lin woke to daylight streaming across the foot of her bed. No, not her bed. It was *a* bed, the shape and feel of it unfamiliar. Was she in the Etse Kebeth, or a patient's house?

She blinked and sat up. She felt dizzy and tried to breathe carefully as the world swung around her. There was dust in the air, bright motes dancing in the light that came from high windows. As everything stopped spinning, she realized she was in a strange room, bare save for a desk, a trunk at the foot of the bed, and the bed itself.

The walls were smooth and dark. *The Black Mansion*, she thought. *I'm in the Black Mansion.* She swung her legs over the edge of the bed, her head pounding, an ache like a wound behind her eyes. She rested her face in her hands for a moment, struggling to remember the last thing that had happened. *The Shulamat*, she recalled. Images began to filter back into her consciousness. Mariam, lying with her hands crossed over her chest. The elders surrounding her, unspeaking, staring. The look on Aron's face. Mayesh, his expression bleak. Her mind spinning with visions of words, with shining equations. She recalled the feeling of power flooding out of her like a river, her last desperate attempt to control it, to form it into a weapon that might burn away the threatening shadows that had haunted her dreams.

A bright running gold rim of fire. And then silence. And darkness, unpunctuated by light or sound. She thought she could remember the sensation of being carried. She had dreamed in bursts of images: flame and glass, the toppling pillars of a temple, walls collapsing into powdery fragments.

My stone, she thought, then jolted. The Source-Stone. A quick check let her know that it was not pinned to her clothes—she wore a clean tunic and trousers; she could not help but wonder what had happened to the clothes she'd worn at the trial—nor anywhere among the bed linens.

She slid from the bed to the floor. For a moment her legs refused to support her, and she hit the ground on her knees. She crawled across the floor to the trunk at the foot of her bed.

The hinges creaked when she flung it open. Inside were familiar objects. Her clothes, some of them, folded neatly. A scarf Josit had given her. Her father's compass, which he had used on the Gold Roads. The thin gold chain that had born her mother's *magal.* An anatomy book, a pair of gloves Mariam had sewn for her. Several packets of seeds, neatly labeled. She picked through them, a cold feeling growing in her belly. Each was labeled with Chana's handwriting; each a type of medicinal plant that grew only in the Sault.

Someone who knew her well had packed this trunk. Several someones, it seemed. It had been prepared with a knowledge of what Lin herself would take from the Sault, if she knew she was never coming back.

She flattened her hands over her stomach, as if she could hold in her rising panic. She knew she should get to her feet, go out into the mansion, seek Andreyen and the others. But she could not make herself move. *Breathe*, she told herself, as she had told so many of her patients. *Breathe through it.*

There was a knock at the door. Lin raised her head. "Come in," she tried to say, but her mouth would not quite form the words. She frowned, started to try again, but the door was already swinging wide.

The Ragpicker King stood in the open doorway. He seemed impossibly tall and thin, a stick figure with a stick staff in his hand, entirely black save for the white oval of his face. The sight of her on the floor beside the open trunk did not seem to surprise him. He crossed the room and sat down on the foot of the bed.

In a characteristic gesture, he folded his hands over the top of his cane before speaking. "Lin," he said. "I wondered when you would wake. It has been three days." He looked at her, sitting on the floor, the trunk open in front of her. "You must have questions."

What happened? she tried to say, but again, she could not quite seem to form the words. Instead, she said, "Mariam?"

Andreyen's green eyes were sharp. "You may have trouble with speech for a short while," he said. "The *gematry* you performed was so powerful that some of it tore its way free of you, of the Source-Stone. I suspect it nearly killed you—" He broke off at the expression on her face, acknowledging her question with a nod. "Mariam Duhary is well," he added. "As if she had never been ill. She will live a long life, thanks to you."

"*Oh.*" A great tension went out of Lin, one she had been carrying for so long that she'd nearly forgotten the weight of it. "I want to see her—"

"Lin," Andreyen said. He turned the staff around in his hands, his characteristic gesture. "You fainted when the power ripped free of you," he said. "It was like a leashed tiger, suddenly freed. It poured out of you, into the world. A wall of the Sault burned, and an old temple to Anibal in the Maze was destroyed."

Lin's vision swam. *Blood and fire.* "Was anyone hurt?"

"A few minor injuries. Scrapes and burns. You were lucky: The temple has been disused for years, and the Shomrim were not on the walls. And the Ashkar, with customary diligence, are already rebuilding. In the meantime, Castelguards have been posted where the wall is broken. By the order of the Prince."

He searched Lin's face with his eyes. But she was thinking of someone else. *Conor.* Conor, making sure the Ashkar would be safe. But perhaps it had nothing to do with her. Perhaps Mayesh had asked him to do it.

"I need to see my grandfather," Lin said. Her words were coming back at least; they came out clear and stern. As if she could order the Ragpicker King around. "And Mariam—I need to see Mariam."

Click. Andreyen tapped the head of his cane with his fingertips. "Lin, do you understand why you're here? In the Black Mansion?"

She shook her head. Not because she could not guess, but because she could not bear to say it. The pain felt like a bone stuck in her throat, something that stabbed and choked her from the inside.

"You have been exiled, Lin. You are *galut.* Ashkar no longer."

She felt the heat behind her eyes. Tears, anger, refusing to show themselves. "It makes no sense," she said. "They asked to see power. I showed them power. They wanted a Goddess. *The Goddess brings fire.* It is in our lore, our stories—"

"They wanted the idea of the Goddess," said Andreyen. "It is one thing to wish for a Goddess to return; it is another to look upon holy fire. People are terrified of the Gods, Lin, and the Ashkar are no different. The Goddess is a tale of past glory and strength. But she is not in this world; she wanders the outer darkness, and that itself fulfills the human desire to hold one's Gods at a safe distance. For what happens to those who come too close to the Gods? Only ruination."

Lin said nothing.

"If it's any consolation, I understand it was a contentious decision. You do have your supporters in the Sault, but the decision is ultimately up to the Maharam, and he said that the Goddess would have been able to withstand the use of such power and would not have collapsed as you did. That whatever source of power you used, it must have been corrupt and evil."

Lin stared blankly at the objects in the trunk. She wondered again who had packed it. She imagined Mariam's gentle hands folding her clothes, Chana painstakingly writing out the names of the plants in the physick garden.

I cannot say I was not told, she thought. *Over and over Aron tried to warn me. Mayesh, too.* "I do not know what else I expected," she said. "I am not the Goddess, after all. Just a girl with a magic stone."

"Speaking of which." Andreyen drew the brooch from his waistcoat pocket and lightly tossed it to Lin. She caught it in her hands, turning it over, feeling a wave of relief pass through her. Relief, and surprise. For there was still light in the stone. A burning heart, suffusing it with a dark glow.

"I would have thought," she said, "that they would have destroyed it."

"I doubt half of them know what it is," Andreyen said, and there was an odd bitterness in his tone. "Mayesh Bensimon was the one who brought you here."

"My grandfather? But he never knew I worked with you . . . did he? Why would he bring me here?"

The Ragpicker King avoided her gaze. "Do not underestimate Mayesh. He always knows more than you think. And Lin, look." He leaned forward. "The stone still burns with power. After all you did, it is not dead. It *lives*."

She closed her hand around it. "It does not matter. I will not use it again."

Real astonishment flashed across his face. "Why not?"

"All I wanted was to cure Mariam. That has been done. I pretended to be something I am not, and I have been exiled for it. I have lost—so much." She closed her eyes.

"But you have also gained. Perhaps you cannot be the Goddess of the Ashkar people, but you can be a sorcerer, Lin. A Sorcerer-Queen."

"I have never wanted to be a Sorcerer-Queen. I am done with this power."

"That would be a waste. Of everything you have learned and done. I understand—"

"You couldn't *possibly* understand."

"I understand because I, too, was exiled in my youth. I, too, wished to learn the ways of magic and was punished for it. All magic was taken from me, and the possibility of ever controlling it. But you, Lin. You still *have power*."

Lin opened her eyes. His green eyes were burning like a hawk's. She said, "You have only ever cared about the magic. Never about me. Only about power."

"I am the Ragpicker King," he said. "What do you think I traffic in? Crime? Murder? I traffic in *power*, Lin. Power matters. Power like Elsabet Belmany displayed on Tyndaris. But Elsabet is a force of evil. You can be a force for good."

Elsabet Belmany. The vision Lin had had in the Shulamat came rushing back: She saw the dark-haired woman standing on the steps of the temple of Anibal as flame rushed around her like water. *I have destroyed her hiding place,* she thought. *But she is not dead; I can feel the power of her stone still, somewhere near Castellane. And how could I ever defeat her, anyway? I only can use the power of the King, and Belmany has her own power.*

"Stop," Lin said. His words were just that, words. They echoed in the emptiness she felt down to her bones. She was an exile. She would not see Mayesh again, nor Mariam; not Mez, not Chana, not anyone.

And she had lost Conor. She had chosen her home in the Sault over a home with him, and now the Sault did not want her. And here was Andreyen, pushing at her, wanting yet more from her, more things she could not do, could not give.

She closed her hand so tightly around the Source-Stone that it ached. The edges of the brooch cut into her skin.

"Please," she said, barely able to find the energy to speak the word. "Leave me. Leave me alone."

In the past, Kel had looked up at the Trick and thought about the dreadful fate of those consigned to its cells. Trapped behind Sunderglass, knowing there would be no trial, only waiting on His Highness's pleasure until the execution could be arranged. (And then the cold green water, the pinch and bite of teeth, the undignified screaming ceasing only when life ceased.)

He had never imagined how *boring* it would be. Watching the single patch of sun travel across the floor. Awaiting the occasional visit from the guard bringing food and water, not because he was hungry but because eavesdropping on their conversation broke up the monotony. It also allowed him to learn that Anjelica and her privateer had made their escape through the Narrow Pass, where they had been joined by a garrison of mounted guards led by Kurame, Kito, and Isam; the Castelguards had turned back at that point, no longer on their home territory. It was some solace to know that she was, at least, safe from the murderous Malgasi.

He was almost relieved when he heard footsteps outside his cell. He sat up quickly, brushing straw from his clothes. It wasn't a guard, he knew; their boots made a particular noise on the stone floor. Heart roaring in his chest, he said, "Conor?"

A shadow passed in front of his cell. Stopped at the bars. A broad shadow, too tall to be Conor. Disappointment bit at Kel just as light flooded his cell. Standing in front of him was Legate Aristide Jolivet, just as Kel had first seen him all those years ago at the Orfelinat, dressed in his scarlet uniform, his ring gleaming on his hand. In a rough voice he said, "Believe me or don't, but I never wanted it to end like this."

Kel rolled onto his side and glared up at Jolivet. Jolivet, who had plucked him from nothing and brought him to the Palace, who had taught him to fight for Conor, who had ordered him to seek out those responsible for the Shining Gallery murders. "I would spit on you," he said, "but they have not provided me with sufficient water."

"You cannot be so surprised as all that," said Jolivet. "You always knew that one day you would die for Conor."

"I'm not dying for Conor," said Kel. "I am dying for your lies, and Falconet's."

"I lied for the Aurelians," said Jolivet without emotion. "I always will. It is my duty, and yours. If I had come out in that moment in the Little Palace and spoken for you, said that in investigating the Charter Families you had acted on my orders, then we would have lost the only slight advantage that we have over the conspirators. They are not aware of *what we know*."

"Please don't say *we*," snarled Kel. "Why don't you tell Conor, then? Just tell *him*."

"What would be the point?" said Jolivet. "You are a Sword Catcher, Kellian, but you cannot return to what you were. You have been too greatly compromised. You cannot be put back at Conor's side, to live as his 'cousin,' among his friends, his enemies. Not now." He sounded slightly incredulous that Kel did not already see this. "If a shield has been broken, one should no longer cling to it but cast it away in battle. If you were a different kind of soldier, Kel, and this were a different kind of war, you might have a medal pinned to you. Instead, I can offer you only an honorable death."

"Bullshit," said Kel. "You could free me. Send me away in exile. But you won't. I know too much about the Aurelians, about the workings of the Hill. If I am not bound to the Palace, I am dangerous to you. Even if I swear my silence, you would never trust it."

There was a long silence. Jolivet said, "I wonder sometimes if I did you a disservice by teaching you too well."

"That," said Kel, "is not the disservice you are doing me."

"I remember when you were a little boy from the Orfelinat," Jolivet said. "That first night you were at the Palace, they all marveled at how clever you were. I thought, better he were not so clever. That one will know too much to believe in glory and honor. He will always see too much to be at peace with what he is destined to be."

"I will tell you what I see now," Kel said. "I see that you imagine you can manage the matter of the conspiracy, of the betrayal of Falconet and Alleyne and who knows who else, all on your own. Without telling Conor. But it is long past time to tell Conor."

"As you told me what you learned on Tyndaris?" Jolivet said. "And you imagined that I would not find out? That I do not have spies among Lady Alleyne's guards? We all make decisions about what we tell, Kellian."

"So then you know the severity of the threat?" Kel demanded, sitting up. "You know what the danger is? And you won't tell Conor—"

"It is nothing to you what Conor knows, not now," said Jolivet. "You are already a dead man, Kellian. And the Palace of Marivent keeps counsel with the living."

Lin did not know how long she lay on her bed in the Black Mansion, holding her stone in her hand. She knew the patch of sun on her coverlet had faded into twilight, shadows introducing themselves into the pattern from new angles that formed shapes like those one could sometimes see in clouds.

At one point, she heard voices at her door—Merren and Ji-An, she was nearly sure—but she did not call out or make a noise, and eventually the voices faded with their accompanying footsteps.

Lin could not herself have described her emotions. The enormity of what she had lost kept her from feeling it completely. Shock cushioned the blow, as it had when her parents had died, drowning her grief in a cloudy numbness. Every once in a while, a specific aspect of loss would assail her, and then she would feel it, the way her patients sometimes described feeling flashes of pain break through a fog of morphea. (*Josit—oh, Goddess, Josit. What would happen when he returned to the Sault? Who would tell him Lin was gone, that he could never see her again? She could not write to him on the Gold Roads; an exile could not write to an Ashkar in good standing without tainting their reputation. Oh, my little brother,* she thought, *how I will miss you.*)

After a long time, she rose to her feet. She stripped off her clothes, noting with a vague interest the bruises that marked her pale skin. They were worst on her right side. Perhaps she had fallen there; she did not remember her collapse in the Shulamat. She recalled only her burning hands, unmarked now.

The few clothes that had been packed for her in the trunk were the colorful gowns Mariam had made her over the years. Green, scarlet, bronze. Nothing blue or gray. Nothing *Ashkar.*

She put on a dress of flowered muslin, brushed her hair, braided it neatly. She had just slid on a pair of shoes when the sound of a familiar voice pierced the thick wood of the door.

Lin froze. She had not caught the words, but the cadence, the timbre, she knew. Had always known, even when she'd tried to forget. She fastened her brooch inside her sleeve and went out into the corridor, following the sound of voices into the Great Room.

The windows were open, letting in an unaccustomed amount of light and noise from the city outside. The rattle of carriage wheels, wind in the boughs of the trees in Scarlet Square, the sound of birdsong. A reminder that whatever else happened, Castellane went on.

Merren, Ji-An, and the Ragpicker King stood clustered in the center of the room. None looked pleased. Merren seemed genuinely upset and was gesturing worriedly with his hands.

None of that was surprising to Lin. What was surprising was that Mayesh was in the room with them, dressed in his gray robes, his face lined with tension. There was something different about him, though she could not at first tell what.

"*Zai?*" Lin came slowly into the room. "What are you doing here?"

Mayesh nodded in her direction. "Lin. You're awake."

"It's about Kel." Merren looked pleased to see Lin up and around, yet at the same time his tension remained. "They've stuck him in the Trick."

"What? But *why*?" Lin demanded. Her heart had begun to beat very fast. It could not be . . . surely it was not what he had done for Lin, sneaking her into Marivent, into the King's chamber, under the eyes of the Arrow Squadron? But how could anyone have known about *that*?

"The official word," Mayesh said grimly, "is that he stands accused of murdering Artal Gremont and Ciprian Cabrol. We may know that the idea is ridiculous, but there are many who speak out against him. Alleyne. Falconet. Sardou." Mayesh looked at Lin. "Your friends have told me about the conspiracy," he added. "I've long suspected that someone on the Hill was involved in the Shining Gallery massacre, but not that it was so many, or that they had the backing of Malgasi."

"But what about Legate Jolivet?" Ji-An said. "Kel has been acting on his orders all this time. Can't he speak up for him?"

"He has not done so," said Mayesh. "He has denied involvement. Which means that we cannot trust his loyalties in the matter."

"What about you?" said Lin. "Can you not speak up for Kel?"

Mayesh hesitated for a long moment. "I am no longer the Counselor to the throne of Castellane," he said. "I cannot return to Marivent, nor can I speak with the Prince."

It was then that Lin realized what was different about her grandfather. His silver medallion, the one that marked his office, was gone.

"But that's not possible," she said. "Why— Who dismissed you? And why would they ever do that? You have counseled the throne for more than three decades."

"This is worse than I had imagined," murmured the Ragpicker King. "Without Kel, without you—the Crown Prince will stand alone."

"Did Conor dismiss you because you spoke for Kel?" said Lin. "Is that why?"

"It was the Queen and Prince who dismissed me," Mayesh said dryly. "As Counselor, I have always advised the Prince to trust in his Sword Catcher. It seems they felt this advice may have been given in bad faith."

"Bad faith?" Andreyen echoed quietly.

"The rot of the conspiracy has spread more than can be easily seen, I suspect," said Mayesh. "Who knows what poison may have been dripped into the ear of the Queen? She told me to return to the Sault and serve my own Prince, the Exilarch."

"How vile," said Ji-An.

"I knew the monarchy was not to be trusted," muttered Merren.

Lin said, "Conor would never hurt Kel. Never. Kel is one of the only people he cares for in the world."

"Which is why the idea of his betrayal is so destructive," Mayesh said. "And I agree that Conor would not hurt Kel. But the Prince of Castellane might have to. Two nobles lie dead. The alliance with Kutani is hopelessly broken. Conor cannot be seen to have lost control of the situation. Kel is the one who will have to pay the price."

"Then we'll rescue him," said Ji-An. "We can get anyone out of anywhere. We'll get him out of the Trick. We'll need some force to back us up—"

"No," Andreyen said.

Every one of them, save Mayesh, looked at him in surprise.

"No," Andreyen said again. "We cannot enter Marivent. I cannot enter Marivent, nor can any under my instruction or command."

"Kel did," pointed out Merren. "But— I suppose he wasn't in your employ, was he?"

"He was not," said Andreyen. "And he has paid a great price for working with us as much as he did."

"The King on the Hill is likewise forbidden from coming here," said Mayesh, "so the Black Mansion is protected. It has been this way for a long time. The Ragpicker King must stay away from Marivent, and Marivent from the Ragpicker King. I am here only because I no longer represent the Palace."

"That's ridiculous, Andreyen," said Merren. "You expect us to just sit here while they feed Kel to the crocodiles?"

"I don't like it, either," said Andreyen. "But you are asking me to do what only the King on the Hill can do, and I am the King in the City."

"But we *know* things," Ji-An said. "Surely our knowledge must weigh something in balance with Kel's life—"

"Stop." Lin's voice rung out harshly. "*I* will go to the Palace." It was now night, of course, and the Ashkar were not supposed to travel through the city after dark. But she was no longer Ashkar. "I will tell Conor that Kel has never acted against him. I will make him understand who his true friends are." She looked around the room; her gaze lit on Andreyen, who was regarding her with a small, sideways smile. "I will not be acting on the orders of the Ragpicker King. I am making this choice myself."

Mayesh did not seem surprised. All he said was, "I suppose you have a way to enter the Palace?"

"The guards at the North Gate know me," Lin said. "They will let me in." She looked at her grandfather. "Will you accompany me to the door? I know it is forbidden for you even to walk with me, but—"

"Some Laws are foolish," Mayesh said roughly, and joined her on her way out.

As they paced through the corridors of the Black Mansion, Lin could not help but cast a covert sideways glance at Mayesh; his hawkish face seemed hollowed out, lines of sorrow cut like grooves at the sides of his mouth, the edges of his eyes.

"Grandfather." Impulsively, she reached for his hand. "I am sorry. So sorry."

"For what?" he said roughly, though he did not take his hand away. "For getting yourself exiled? I suppose I helped with that. The Maharam was not at all pleased with the way I spoke to him."

"And what of Aron?" Lin asked. "He told me so many times this was a mistake. He must be pleased at how this has turned out."

"I do not think so," Mayesh said. "Not at all."

"But what will you do now?" Lin said. "Now that you are no longer Counselor? Will you be all right?"

For the first time in a long time, he smiled. "I'll be fine," he said. "I will sit on my porch and smoke my pipe and throw *sabra* fruit at the children who try to pick my flowers. In fact, perhaps it is better I have been dismissed." He searched her face with his eyes. "It means I do not have to ask you why you call Conor by his Gods-given name, and do not use his title."

Lin tensed. "I—"

"I knew Conor was not suddenly asking me all these questions about the Ashkar because he was curious about my life," said Mayesh. "I ought to have guessed he was curious about yours." He hesitated. "You truly think he will listen to you?"

"He does," said Lin, "sometimes."

Mayesh nodded slowly. "Then it must be tried."

Kel lay awake, tracking the progress of the rising moon through his single window. He had only just started to doze off when he heard footsteps in the corridor.

And wondered immediately how he could ever, earlier, have mistaken Jolivet for Conor. Even Conor's pace was familiar to him. He would have known it anywhere. *If I were dead and buried and those feet walked over my grave, I would know those footsteps.*

Kel put his back to the wall, slid slowly down it. He was sitting on the floor by the time Conor appeared in front of the bars. There was hardly enough moonlight for Kel to see him clearly, but it did not matter. It was Conor.

Conor regarded him silently. Kel was not sure how long he had been in the Trick now—three days? It was the longest he had gone in fifteen years without seeing Conor Aurelian. Though surely that was not enough time for Conor to have changed in any real particular way. Still, there seemed something different about him—about the set of his mouth, his eyes. In some way he had not before, Kel thought, he resembled Lilibet.

Like her, his outward appearance was perfectly polished. High black boots, a silk tunic and a velvet cloak with a rose clasp at the front. His winged silver circlet holding back his dark hair. A folded pair of dove-colored gloves held carelessly in one hand. But there was a wariness to him, a tension, that was new. He had never been wary around Kel before.

"I knew you'd come," Kel said.

"Why so sure?" Conor's tone was light, emotionless. But that meant nothing, Kel told himself. Conor had been trained for years to use his face, his voice, as tools of diplomacy. To show nothing he did not want shown.

"Because I do not think you can trust Falconet so much as all that. Because I think you must see the holes in the web of lies that he is spinning for you. Because you *know better*, Con."

"Oh, but I don't." Conor leaned his back against the bars of the cell opposite Kel's. "I have learned not to trust my instincts. They seem usually to be wrong."

Kel wanted to kick the wall. "You cannot honestly think I betrayed you for money—"

"Of course not." The words came out as a pained hiss. "The betrayal itself matters more than the reason, don't you see that? And can't you understand, I don't want to believe it? But I cannot let myself be someone who ignores what is right in front of him."

"What is right in front of you is that Jolivet is lying. So is Falconet—"

"Is *everyone* in Castellane lying, then?" Conor began to pace up and down in front of the cell. "At the meeting in the Dial Chamber, when we had gathered to discuss the Gremont and Cabrol Charters, Falconet surprised us all by announcing that he had proof of treason. Of *your* treason. He warned of your secret alliance with the

Ragpicker King. Of your plans to betray Castellane by helping the Princess of Kutani reunite with her lover—"

"Conor—"

"He brought *dozens* of witnesses." Conor's voice rose. "Benaset got up to say that you have been creeping in and out of the Palace at all times and going to the Black Mansion. Falconet had Castel-guards follow you, you know. Then there was the tavern-keeper from Little Kutani who says that you met there with the Ragpicker King, and brought Anjelica with you. And there were more. Are you really saying that Falconet convinced a dozen Castellani citizens to claim falsely that they have seen you in Scarlet Square?"

Kel tried to picture the scene, tried to picture Conor defending him as Falconet paraded before him one piece of evidence after another. Falconet was clever—clever enough to turn truths and half-truths into damning lies—and who knew how long he had been planning this?

And not just him. He was hardly acting alone.

Kel said, "So you believed all forty or so of these people over me?"

"My old friend Falconet and fifty witnesses and the captain of my guard, you mean?" The ghost of a smile flickered across Conor's face. "Don't, Kel. Don't joke about this."

"They really are lying, Con," Kel said, his voice low.

Conor's gray eyes glittered. "It's almost ironic," he said. "You wanted me to be better, a better ruler, and I decided I would be, partly because you wanted it so much. And the person I used to be would forgive you, because he was never interested in being much of a leader. But I cannot forgive you for *treason*, Kel."

"It was never treason," Kel whispered. "I would never break my oath as a Sword Catcher. You know that, too." Kel met Conor's gaze through the gloom. "I *was* meeting with the Ragpicker King. I was working *with* him, not *for* him—"

Conor made a disgusted noise. "Even if that were true, you're admitting you kept so much from me, Kel. Has every word out of your mouth for the past months been a lie? When did it start?"

"I was trying to protect you," Kel said. "I went to the Ragpicker King because Jolivet requested it—"

"He denies that."

"Because he thinks I'm compromised, useless to you now. He's cutting his losses—but he wanted the Shining Gallery murders investigated. You know he did. And the Ragpicker King knows everything that happens in Castellane. Jolivet thought if I worked with him—"

"So you just went to the Black Mansion and offered your services?" Conor said acidly. "And the Ragpicker King, out of an excess of civic duty, wanted to help the Palace? And asked nothing from you in exchange?"

"Something like that," Kel muttered. "There is more to the story of the King on the Hill and the King in the City than you know."

"But you know it, I suppose. And have kept it from me." Conor stared at Kel as if he were a stranger. "Don't you understand? You have lied to me and lied to me and lied to me and you do not even *deny* it. You say you did it for my own good, but you *did it*. And Falconet has proved it to the Hill, to every family; he has made it impossible for me to forgive you. Even if I believed you, I could not forgive you."

"Because of how it would look?" Kel said bitterly. "To these people who are conspiring against you? Working with Malgasi to bring down the House of Aurelian?"

"Because I cannot *afford* to believe you, Kel. I know that my trust in you is a weakness—has always been a weakness that could be exploited." Kel stared; Conor had never said anything like this to him before. How long had he thought it? "In these past months, I have known something was wrong between us. Your secrecy, your silence, your lies—and I knew they were lies. I told myself you had found a girl or a boy in the city, someone you were keeping secret. I did not want to face the truth. I don't want to face it now. But it is my duty. I cannot afford the comfort of lies."

Kel could not stand the look on Conor's face. As if he were breaking from the inside. "Blame me as much as you want," he said quietly. "I knew what I was risking. But Falconet is not to be trusted."

"It does not matter whether I trust Falconet," he said. "I cannot trust *you*. And if I were to forgive you, the Charter Families—whether they are conspiring or not—would all move against me. They would see weakness all over me like blood on a wounded animal." Conor slammed his hand against the Sunderglass bars. The noise echoed through the Trick, a crack like thunder. "If you had only *come to me*," he said with real anguish, "we would have determined something, come to some understanding, but what you did—treason cannot be wiped away or forgotten. Everyone knows of your guilt; everyone has seen it. I cannot stop what is going to happen. I cannot—" He took a deep breath.

"You cannot save me," Kel said flatly. "That is what you mean."

"No," Conor whispered. "All your decisions have brought us here. You have taken yourself away from me. And I can never forgive you for that."

"I don't want to leave you," Kel said. He held out his hands. He knew Conor could not touch him through the bars, but he had never reached out for Conor and found the gesture unanswered. He could not stop himself. "I am your Sword Catcher," he said softly, and he saw Conor's eyes shine in the dimness. "I bleed so that you will not bleed. I die so you can live forever."

"No one lives forever, Kel," Conor said evenly, and walked away.

As the carriage drew close to Marivent, Lin remembered Kel telling her that, when he was a child, his first thought on seeing the Palace had been, *I can climb those walls.*

She smiled a little at the thought of that tough little boy from the Orfelinat. She had been a child then, too, before her parents died. She had stood on the walls of the Sault, looking up toward Marivent. In her mind, it was the palace from every Story-Spinner's tale. She had felt sorry for other cities, who did not have such a beautiful white castle, such a gorgeous royal family. She had seen Conor only in glimpses then, at public occasions—a beautiful scowling boy with dark curling hair like his mother. She had known he existed in the world, and that she would never know him. He might as well have been imaginary.

Now he was more than real. Now she could not think of him without anxiety rising inside her—fear for him, for his safety. For he was surrounded by serpents, and he could not see it. Would not see it.

She had to change that.

Mayesh had let her take the Palace carriage—the last one he would ever ride in, he had observed—from the Black Mansion to Marivent. The driver seemed to have no objection to transporting her. He might not even know that Mayesh had lost his position as Counselor, Lin thought. On the way up the Hill, she had thought about her grandfather returning to the Sault, breaking the news of his dismissal to the Maharam and the elders. Who would they choose to replace him, she wondered. And what would he do with himself now? Story-Spinner tales were about ordinary lives that became suddenly extraordinary, but little was said about what happened when it went the other way.

They rolled under the North Gate into a Palace that felt peculiarly silent. Usually, Lin was aware of servants and Castelguards hastening to and fro, running through Marivent in a steady stream like blood through the arteries of a body. Now, as she dismounted from the carriage outside the Castel Mitat, she heard no babble of voices or sound of hurrying feet, only the buzz of insects and the chirp of trellised birds. Above her, a shutter banged to and fro in the breeze outside an open window.

The moon was bright, and the Trick loomed in the distance like a black spear piercing the sky. *Kel.* A shiver went up her spine. She needed to keep her concentration on helping him, on helping Conor. That was what mattered now.

She made her way inside the castle and up the stairs, noting that even this place seemed deserted. No one in the colorful downstairs rooms, no one in the long stone corridor upstairs. No guards outside the Prince's rooms.

She knocked on the door.

For a long moment, she heard nothing. Then a rustle, the chime of glass, like wine goblets clinking together.

She knocked again.

Conor's voice, raised just enough to penetrate the thick wood of the door. "Jolivet," he said. "If it is you, I told you before—quite clearly I thought—to *fuck off.*"

Lin counted to five, silently, and pushed the door open. She had half expected it to be locked, but it swung wide without a sound. Shocked, she looked around in silence, recalling the apartments when she had first seen them. How beautiful, she had thought, and extravagant, from the rich bed hangings to the marble tables to the cabinet of rare liquors, the bottles gleaming like jewels.

Now those hangings had been ripped down. The bottles had been torn from the liquor cabinet and smashed against the walls and table edges. The room reeked of alcohol, and shattered glass lay in bright heaps on the stone floor. Someone had clearly walked on the broken glass in bare feet; their sharp edges were crusted with dried blood. Tables had been upended, spilling their contents: pens, silver candlesticks, bruised apples.

The lamps were unlit, but moonlight was streaming in through the great arched windows, illuminating the figure that stood in front of them. Conor, with his back to her. She would have known him anywhere—known him at a distance from the way his black hair curled against the nape of his neck, from the way his dark cloak hung from his shoulders. From the way he held the open wine bottle in his hand.

She licked her dry lips.

"Conor," she said.

He turned around. He did not look surprised to see her, not exactly. Somehow she could not read his expression at all. In contrast with the room, he looked elegant, as if he had dressed for an occasion—black velvet tunic and trousers, a silver clasp at his throat, the shimmer of more silver caught among his curls.

"Your grandfather told me you survived your trial," he said. "I wasn't sure if I believed him or not."

The shadows under his eyes were nearly black, and Lin could see the whiteness of his knuckles where he gripped the wine bottle. And though he spoke flatly and without expression, what she heard underneath his voice snapped the cords that held her in place. She could not stop herself. She rushed across the room and threw her arms around his neck.

She felt him sway a little in surprise. Then his free arm came around her and he pressed her hard against him, his fingers digging into the fabric of her dress, bunching it up in his hand. She pressed her cheek to his chest, velvet soft against her skin; she listened to his heartbeat, fast but steady.

He spoke roughly, into her hair. "I knew the wall of the Sault had come down. I pictured you lying among the rubble."

"No. Nothing like that." She tipped her head back to look up at him. He was so young to be all that he was, she thought. He was a grown man, but there was still a boyish softness to the curve of his mouth. "I have been so worried about you."

His brows drew together. "You, worried about me? Why?"

"Because you have sent everyone you could depend on away," she said. "My grandfather. Kel—"

"Kel has committed treason. It is my duty—"

"Your duty." She shook her head. "*He* was doing his duty. He was protecting you. He never had any other intention—"

"You are awfully worried about Kel." There was a quiet something in his voice—not danger and not jealousy. She could not have said exactly what it was, but it felt like a cold finger on her spine.

"Of course I am. He's my friend."

"And you want a favor from your Prince, do you?" His hand slid up her back, cupped the nape of her neck. She felt herself shudder—though not with something that was cold. It was ridiculous that the touch of his fingertips on her skin could catch her breath and make her legs feel as if her bones had turned to feathers. Ridiculous, that she could not control it. "You want your friend freed from the Trick, whether he is a traitor or not."

"He's *not*," Lin said. "And if you hurt him, if you have him *killed*, don't you see what it will do to you? If you let him swing from the Tully gallows, or have him thrown from the cliffs like Fausten? It will wreck you, Conor. You will never get back what you lost."

She felt a shiver go through him; thought for a moment he had heard her. Really heard her. He brushed a kiss at her temple, his lips hot. "What makes you think you know me so well?" he whispered.

"Because," she said, "I love you."

She felt his body go rigid as iron. "Lin," he said. "You sent me away—"

"I know. I couldn't bear it, that all I could ever have was a tiny part of you. That marriage and children with you would belong to someone else, someone who didn't even feel about you the way I do." *And Kel made me see it*, she thought. *He made me understand.* "You said you wished you could cut your feelings for me away, and do you think I have not felt the same? Do you know how often I have thought of you? In my dreams, my waking hours, you never leave me, Conor." She tightened her hands on his shoulders. "Nothing can be perfect. I want you—all of you. You do not know how much." She took a shivering breath. "But I will take what I can have. It is not nothing. I do not think I can bear nothing."

His gray eyes searched her face, and at last there was something in his expression she could read: wonder, bewilderment. And a bitterness she did not understand.

"Conor?" she breathed.

"You are accepting my offer? You are telling me you will be my mistress? Because I cannot offer you anything else, Lin, not even now, with Anjelica gone."

"I told you," she said. "I will take whatever I can have of you—"

She thought she heard him say her name. Then he was pulling her against him, crushing his mouth to hers in a kiss. His mouth was hot and hard against hers, and he had never kissed her like this, not even in the folly, not with such force that she tasted wine and blood on his lips. His hand cradled the back of her head as he devoured her mouth, his tongue flicking between her lips in a way that had her aching for his hands on her body, the feel of his skin against her skin.

And then he pulled back, breaking the kiss abruptly. Lin could feel that he was shaking, small tremors that rocked his body, but his voice was steady when he spoke. "It is ironic," he said, "that I have always known you were an excellent liar. I depended on it when I took you into my confidence about my father."

"What do you mean?" Lin could hear the bewilderment in her own voice; she was not like Conor. She could not keep her voice steady even as her body screamed at her that it was being deprived of something it desperately wanted, even needed.

"You come here and beg me for Kel's life," he said. "You say that you know he was only protecting me. That you knew he was working for the Ragpicker King. And don't bother denying it; I am already aware of your own association with Morettus. You and Kel had this shared world of secrets, it seems. One you both hid from me. Although in your case, at least, it is not treason. Just the ordinary, boring sort of lies."

It was as if he had shaken her or slapped her. She choked, "I was trying to protect you, too. All we ever wanted was to find out who was responsible for the murders in the Gallery, who was targeting House Aurelian. All Kel ever thought about was you and Castellane—"

His lips twisted into a sneer. "All *we* ever wanted?" he echoed. "You seem to be positing a sort of conspiracy of kindness. A group of people who lied to me with the best intentions. All while you warn me of a conspiracy of unkindness, an opposing group who lied to me with *bad* intentions. Pardon me if I see little difference between the two."

"What are you saying?" Lin whispered. "You can't really mean it. You can't be intending to murder Kel—"

He flung her away from him. Lin stumbled back, shocked, as Conor hurled the bottle he was still holding against the far wall; it shattered, releasing a silver rain of glass.

"I never thought I would trust anyone like I trusted Kel," Conor said, and the bitterness she had sensed in his voice before was now at the forefront, turning every word to a curse. "And then I trusted you. You never seemed to need anything from me. I thought that meant I was safe with you, but there is no safety, is there? Not when I am weak, and I have come to understand now, finally, where weakness lies. You are my weakness, Lin—and so is Kel. You are chinks in my armor that can be pierced through."

"Trust is not a weakness," Lin said. "And if you cannot trust me, at least trust Kel. He has only ever tried to help you."

Something flickered across Conor's face, and for a moment Lin thought that he might have heard the truth in her words.

He raised a shaking hand to his face. "Castellane cannot afford me to be weak," he said. "I have to be my own shield now. And a shield must be iron."

"*No*. Turning yourself to stone will not make you strong. Hurting Kel will not cauterize the bleeding—"

"Look at you," Conor said, "so sure I plan to murder him. And yet at the same time you say you love me. What am I meant to believe? For to imagine that you love a murderer, Lin, seems out of the question."

He was white as a sheet, but the mockery in his voice cut at her.

"At least let my grandfather counsel you," she said. "Even if you cannot bear the sight of me, at least let there be someone you can rely on in the Palace—"

"*Stop it!*" Lin took a step back; she did not think he had ever shouted at her before. "Don't you understand? You are deadly to me, Lin, like poison or a blade. I cannot be near you."

"But I—"

"*Leave me,*" he snarled. "Consider it a royal order. Stay away from me. Stay away from the Palace. *Go.*"

He might as well have shoved her. She staggered back, found her way to the door. She could feel the burn of tears behind her eyes; even as she reached for the doorknob, it seemed to waver in front of her.

The door swung open. Lin paused, then turned on the threshold. "Your father," she said. "Order me away if you wish, but he is my patient, and there are things you should know—"

He looked at her from across the room. He was motionless, the icy moonlight striking sparks from the silver clasp at his throat. From the crown half hidden in his tangled hair; she had thought at first, for a moment, that he was not wearing it. But she supposed it changed nothing about him and who he was whether the crown was visible or not.

"The King is no longer any concern of yours," he said. "I release you from your place as his physician. Consider this a binding royal order, Lin. Stay away from the Palace. Stay away from my father. And stay away from me."

Lin took a deep breath. "Then you can throw me in the Trick for this, if you must," she said. "But before I go, there is one thing I must tell you. About your father. And not just about him—about you."

Delfina

Delfina lays the odd and irregularly shaped package down in front of the door to the Prince's apartments and hurries away without knocking.

The last thing she wants is questions about where the package has come from. And besides, the entirety of the Palace staff knows to stay away from the Prince when he is in a bad mood, and he is currently in a *very* bad mood. Nor could Delfina guess whether the contents of the package—such a large, ugly necklace, why would he want it?—or the note would improve his mood or worsen it.

Delfina has been in the employ of the Palace since she was a young woman, freshly off the boat from Detmarch. And for nearly all that time, she has carried clandestine messages to and fro from the city to the Hill and back again, for a few crowns each time. One day she will retire with a *very* comfortable savings.

She rarely peeks at the contents of the messages she is given, but this time she had. She'd been handed the package—along with five crowns—by Jerrod Belmerci, but when she had asked if it was from the Ragpicker King as usual, he had only winked at her.

It had been enough to rouse her suspicions. She was happy to carry messages, but the package was surprisingly heavy—what if it

was something dangerous? She'd carefully undone the twine holding it together and peeked inside. What she'd found surprised her.
It was a sort of necklace, very large and ugly. Certainly nothing
that the Prince would be likely to wear or to admire.

With it had been a small, scribbled note. Delfina had opened
and read it without a trace of compunction, having already decided
that if the contents seemed likely to upset the Prince, she might
give it to him tomorrow, or maybe even next week.

The note, however, had merely been nonsense, or so it had
seemed to her. As she walks down the steps of the Castel Mitat,
she can't help but think about what she'd read: Why was it that
people couldn't just be straightforward these days? Honestly, just
think of all the strife in the world that could be avoided if people
would just say what they meant.

For Prince Conor Aurelian

*Before there were Sword Catchers in this world, there were en-
chanted objects that offered a different sort of protection. With
such an amulet, one could survive a fatal dose of poison or a
blade to the heart. What would you do with such magic if you
had it, Monseigneur?*

*Though I would not have thought so once, I now believe that you
would—that you will—do the right thing.*

—*Prosper Beck*

CHAPTER TWENTY-FIVE

Lin barely remembered leaving Conor's rooms, or leaving the grounds of Marivent. She walked numbly out of the Castel Mitat and across the Palace grounds. Now that she was no longer dressed in Ashkar garb, no one seemed to take much notice of her, even when she passed through the North Gate and made her way down to the city.

Her thoughts were a blur of white noise. She was aware of the dust in the air and the smell of the *garrigue,* lavender and sage and sea salt. Eventually there was the end of the dirt path and the beginning of houses that rose up around her like comforting walls. Like the walls of the Sault, which would never circle her again.

After some time she realized she could see Scarlet Square only a few streets away. She wondered when she had learned to navigate her way to the Black Mansion without thinking about where she was going. She wondered when she had grown grateful to see it rather than wary, when it had become a place of possible refuge.

She tried to imagine what she would say to the Ragpicker King, to the others. She had been so sure she would be able to convince Conor to see the truth.

The guard in front of the mansion stepped aside to let her in.

"Domna Caster," he said to Lin, surprising her; usually he was silent. "Morettus is waiting for you inside. In the Great Room."

"Thank you." Lin hurried past him and through the snaking corridors of the mansion until the Great Room opened up before her.

It was almost as though she'd never left. She saw Andreyen in his chair, his staff in his hand; Ji-An and Merren were both standing near him, though none of them were speaking. Waiting for her, she thought. For news from the Palace.

She took a step into the room. "He wouldn't listen to me," she said. "Not about Kel, not about the conspiracy."

Andreyen held up a hand, as if to stop her talking. "Lin—"

"We are going to have to find another way," she said. "To stop Malgasi. To help Kel—"

"*Lin.*" Andreyen cut his eyes sideways, and Lin realized that there was someone else in the room. He had been sitting in an armchair facing Andreyen, which is why she had not seen him; now he rose to his feet and turned to face her.

Her breath hissed out of her in a shocked exhale. "Exilarch."

Aron Benjudah regarded her from across the Great Room. He wore his Rhadanite traveler's linens and looked much as he had the first time she'd seen him. Only then he had been in the Shulamat, in a world in which the black straps around his arms, the Evening Sword at his hip, the dark markings on his skin, were expected. Here he seemed wildly out of place, the sight of him a sort of shock, as if she'd come across a basilisk in Fleshmarket Square.

He nodded stiffly. "Lin."

"How did you know where I was?" she said, her gaze darting to Andreyen, then to Ji-An and Merren. Merren shrugged, palms up, as if to say he'd no idea and doubted the others did, either.

"Your grandfather," said Aron. "He understood it was important that I speak with you."

She felt a brief surge of almost painful hope. "Has the Maharam changed his mind about my exile?"

There was a flash of something like pity in Aron's eyes, and she hated him for it. "The Maharam is not one to change his mind," he said, and looked at Andreyen, whose green eyes were blazing. "You remain exiled."

Disappointment laced her voice with bitterness. "Then you shouldn't be here," she said. "Speaking to an exile is forbidden even to the Exilarch, I imagine."

"There are some things more important than the Maharam and even the Law," Aron said. There was something in his voice Lin had never heard before. Unease, hesitancy—even something like desperation. It wasn't a tone she'd ever have expected from the Exilarch. She half expected him to tell her something terrible: that something had happened to Mariam—that the cure she had effected had not been permanent. That Mayesh had been lying, and that when the wall of the Sault had collapsed, someone had been hurt, even killed.

Instead, Aron crossed the room to her. She almost flinched away from the intensity in his eyes, the emotions that seemed to pour off him like water. To her shock, he dropped to his knees in front of her, his head lowered, his hands extended toward her, palms up.

"I acknowledge you," Aron said, "as the Goddess who has been promised. And I present myself as your guardian, as my ancestor Judah Makabi guarded the Shekinah Adassa during the fall of Aram."

Lin felt numb. This was the very last thing she would have expected him to say, and now that he'd said it, she had no idea how to feel. "What?" she said, feeling foolish for not having a more composed, Goddess-like reaction. "*Now?*"

He remained on his knees, but looked up slowly, as if he could not quite believe the sight of her. "I have been blind," he said. "I have been blind because it served me to be blind. For years, I have tested those claiming to be the Goddess, and each time I met a new claimant, I hoped for it—for that sense of recognition that was promised to me. That when I saw her, I would know her. I have awaited that knowing and have felt nothing. I grew used to that lack of feeling, and when I met you, I saw you with the eyes of my mind, not of my heart. I was determined to doubt, and so I doubted."

Lin remained stock-still, barely able to breathe. She was waiting for him to stop, to stand up, to laugh and say he was only mocking her, that he'd come to ensure she knew how far from the light of the Goddess she truly was.

But he didn't. "When you healed Mariam," he said, "I saw a fire within you. I saw the tower burning. I was myself and I was also my own ancestor, looking up at the tower, seeing the Goddess at work. I felt what he felt. I felt that sense of knowing. I felt a perfect faith, a perfect rightness. I could not have described the feeling ahead of time, but now that I know it, it is undeniable. You are the Ancient of Days. You will change the course of history. The Maharam does not see it, but he is a small and petty man. I see it. I *know.*"

"I am not sure," Lin whispered, "that I am worthy of a perfect faith. I do not even have perfect faith in myself."

"That is because you are not ready," said Aron. "The destruction you caused in the Sault was because you have not yet connected to your full, true power. It was a lack of control, and that is what you next must master. The ordeal will grant you that control."

"What ordeal?" said Merren. "I don't like the sound of that."

Lin had nearly forgotten that he and Ji-An were there. Both were looking at Aron warily. Andreyen's expression as he gazed at the Exilarch was unreadable.

"The Ordeal of Bitter Water," said Aron. "It will connect the Goddess Returned to her Source-Stone. Having passed through the ordeal, she will rise up in fire and power. She will be invincible."

And Lin remembered suddenly what she had read: *The magician and the stone must then travel together to the caves of Sulemon, where, having passed the Halls of Hewn Stone, the gem must be cleansed in the Place of Bitter Water before it being bound unto the Sorcerer whose power it will hold.*

But that had been a thousand years ago, when she had been

determined beyond reason to master magic, to cure Mariam. And she had done it. Mariam was well now. She was no magician, whatever Aron might say. She had tried to compass magic and had nearly lost everything. Her home, her best friend, her community.

"What are you asking of me?" she said, almost in a whisper. "No one believes I am the Goddess. Will this ordeal force that faith upon them? Perhaps all you saw in the Shulamat was the power of my Source-Stone. Perhaps the Maharam is right. The Goddess would not return in such a weak vessel."

Slowly, the Exilarch rose to his feet. Without taking his gaze from hers, he said, "Asher. Tell her."

Lin's head spun. Did he mean Asher Benezar, the Maharam's son? Why was he invoking the name of someone exiled so long ago?

The Ragpicker King sighed. "I am not sure she can be convinced, Aron. Lin is very stubborn."

Lin stared at him. "Asher?" she whispered.

Andreyen laid his hand atop the head of his blackthorn staff. "*Tahe Asher Benezar,*" he said in Ashkar. "*Sape zenevet altah wakhahe. Pekanwa kol qemzo zawahena.*"

I am Asher Benezar, I was exiled by my father. I think you know my story.

Lin's head spun. As if she were recalling a Story-Spinner's tale, images flashed before her—the silver incantation bowl on the shelf in this very room, with its Ashkar inscription: DESIGNATED IS THIS BOWL FOR THE SEALING OF THE HOUSE OF BENJUDAH. She had thought he had simply collected it, as he collected so many pretty things; now she realized otherwise. His obsession with magic—the very subject that had gotten Asher exiled. That he had known there were books in the Shulamat, books he wanted. She had wondered why her grandfather had brought her here after her trial: It was not because he had known she was working with Andreyen, she realized, but because he had known Andreyen was really Asher, and would look out for another exile.

Asher Benezar. She had never seen a hint, never guessed. In her world, there had been Ashkar and *malbushim*, and one could not be the other. And yet . . .

"Does your father know? That you are the Ragpicker King?" she demanded, turning from Andreyen to Aron. "How did *you* know?"

"Indeed, Aron," said Andreyen, with a slightly foxlike grin. "How *did* you?"

Aron spread his hands wide and spoke not to Lin, but to Andreyen. "Asher, I tried to stop it when it happened. I spoke to my father when you were exiled; I beseeched him to intervene. He said he could not, that it was in the Maharam's power and neither the Law nor mercy would justify interference. But I could not let it lie. I searched for you, for whispers of you on the Gold Roads, and when I heard there was a new Ragpicker King, and I heard of his doings, I recognized your cleverness, the labyrinthine paths of your mind. I knew— You were always resilient, Asher. I knew you would not simply disappear. I knew you would find your way."

For a long moment, Andreyen said nothing. His clear green eyes were opaque, like milky jade; Lin could not guess what he was thinking.

Then, to her immense surprise, he swung his beloved staff up over his knee and snapped it unceremoniously in half.

Ji-An jumped as if a cannon had gone off. They all stared as Andreyen dropped one half of the cane and lifted the other. It was hollow as a reed. He reached his fingers inside and drew out a long length of parchment vellum, carefully rolled into a hollow circle, like the symbol of the *magal*.

He handed it to Lin. "Read it," he said.

She began to unroll the paper, careful with the old vellum, which threatened to crack in her careful fingers. At last she had it open, a narrow banner upon which was written in a careful hand the Great Prayer: *Hear, oh Aram, She is One, She will return.*

"You gave me that," Andreyen said to Aron, who was gazing at the paper with a stunned expression. "And I have kept it all these years. I never blamed you, Aron; you were a child. And I have never accepted that because I am exiled, I am not Ashkar." He turned to Lin. "If Aron believes that you are the Goddess, then you are the Goddess. If *you* believe it, then you are the Goddess. I may be a heretic and an exile, but I have always thought that the Goddess is the one who has the courage to stand up and claim the name and all that comes with it."

"But I am exiled," Lin said. "What could I even do with such power, if I am not accepted by my people?"

"Then you make them accept you," said Ji-An. She had her arms crossed over her chest. "You make them see the truth."

"Come with me," Aron said, "to the Halls of Hewn Stone. The place of the ordeal. And when you return from the ordeal, you will return with the power of lightning in your hands. They will have no choice but to see, Lin."

The Halls of Hewn Stone. Lin felt lightheaded. She had never been out of Castellane, and Aron was asking her to come with him to what had once been Aram. The stony desert of Jiqal, far in the northeast of Dannemore.

"The Malgasi have magic," added Aron. "Only another who wields magic can face them down. But Lin, you must choose soon. The *Black Rose*, the ship that will take us to Jiqal, will sail at dawn. And it will not wait."

In that moment, Lin heard the voice of the King, burning with the fire of the phoenix inside him. *The Malgasi will come. They cannot be held back without great power. You will be that power. You will protect Castellane. You will protect your people. For without the Goddess, all are doomed.*

"But I am needed here," she said. "Kel and Conor, both of them need our help. The conspiracy will close its net around House Aurelian very soon. The Malgasi—"

"Let us worry about Castellane," said Andreyen, and glanced over at Merren and Ji-An, who nodded. "About Kel, and about the

Prince. If Prince Conor must be made to see the truth, we will find a way."

Lin slowly closed her hands at her sides. She could feel her heart beating in her palms. She did not say that there was no use telling her not to worry about Conor; she had never been able to stop herself thinking of Conor. And she would not forget her last glimpse of him, alone in his rooms with a pile of glass shattered at his feet. She did not say she doubted her own ability to withstand the ordeal, or to return with the power to strike down an army.

She did not say any of those things, because they did not matter. What mattered was not that her chance of success was small, but that it did not seem that Castellane had another chance as good. And it mattered that those in the most danger from the Malgasi were all those she loved—even if they had cast her out. Even if they did not want her.

She had chosen to claim the title of the Goddess, and with it she had claimed a destiny. She did not know if she could see a fire within herself, as Aron could, but she could see it reflected in his eyes, and she could see the road to Jiqal spread out before her like a beacon. At the Tevath, she had made a promise to her people, and she would keep that promise. Even if it took her away from her friends, her family. From Conor. From all that she loved.

She turned to Aron, who was watching her with his desert eyes. "It is up to you," he said. "As the Goddess chooses, I will do."

Lin looked to her friends. Ji-An and Merren regarded her steadily, as if to say that whatever she was leaving was safe in their hands. And Andreyen—Asher—sat holding the broken pieces of his staff, the staff he had carried everywhere with him for years because of the prayer it contained: an invocation and a vow, a statement of faith and belief. In the Goddess. In Lin herself.

She turned to Aron.

"I have made my choice," she said. "I will go with you. I choose the ordeal."

x x x

Hours passed after Conor's footsteps had receded into silence, and Kel didn't move. He stayed where he was, his back to the wall, watching the small patch of moonlight travel across the floor before it dimmed and vanished.

He was not angry at Conor, he realized. He couldn't be. Falconet and the others had lined up the evidence against Kel like Castles pieces, arranged on a board by a master of the game who left his opponent no way out. And Kel knew better than anyone who Conor had to be, and what his responsibilities were. The Malgasi and their allies had made sure it didn't matter whether Conor believed in Kel's guilt or not; his hands were tied.

And there were other, deeper reasons, Kel knew, why Conor could not afford to let himself be convinced of Kel's innocence. He remembered Conor sitting opposite him on the windowsill in their room, saying, *Hope is a danger, you know. Hope may raise you up for a time, but when it is disappointed, the fall is all the more acute.*

Kel knew that Conor feared the fall, the tumble into the vast empty abyss of despair. Anger was better than despair—even anger against someone you loved. Anger was fire, and despair was darkness. And Conor had for years been afraid of the dark.

Kel woke from a fitful sleep plagued by dreams in which he was once again bleeding out in that alley near the Maze, only when he called out for help, Falconet came and, grinning, pushed the knife in deeper.

He sat up, rubbing at his sore eyes. He ached all over, probably from shivering. It was cold in the Trick. He turned to mark the place of the moonlight, wondering what time it was.

He stared. The moonlight fell upon the bars of his cell—and upon the wooden tray placed in front of the door. Usually it contained an unpleasant meal of porridge or flavorless bread. This time, though, something on the tray sparked the light.

A key.

Kel barely had time to think; he was on his feet and kneeling down by the bars within seconds. He slid his hand through them, feeling around on the tray until his hand closed on the heavy silver key. When he fitted it into the lock, it turned silently, without a creak, as if the hinges had been recently oiled.

The door sprang open. A second later, Kel was through it. *A trap,* he thought. *This has to be a trap.* But he was moving anyway, down the corridor, past empty cell after empty cell. At the end of it, before the steep spiral stairs leading down, a dark, huddled figure crouched behind Sunderglass bars. Moonlight illuminated the path ahead; Kel could barely see into the occupied cell, see anything save two bright dark eyes regarding him from behind a tangle of hair.

He paused, just for a moment, then threw the key he was holding into the cell. If this was a trap, he thought, he might as well create as much chaos as he could before they took him down.

He had just made it to the top of the steps when he heard voices below: guards, headed upward. He looked around. There was nothing here. No weapon to lay hands on, no stairs going up. Only a single casement window through which moonlight spilled like blood.

Kel yanked the window open. Turning his body around, he wriggled through, bare feet first. He turned as he went, grasping the sill, his head disappearing below it just as the guards reached the top of the stairs.

He could hear them shouting as he lowered himself slowly, his feet searching for purchase on the smooth wall. There was some cursing, too, and the sound of blows. Apparently the prisoner he had just freed was creating an excellent distraction.

Not that he could let himself think about what was happening inside the tower. Nor would he let himself think about what he was doing right now; nor that no one escaped from the Trick, that it had never been done. *But surely no one who knows how to Crawl has ever tried it*, he told himself.

He was high up, so high that the wind tore at him, whipped his hair and his clothes. He seemed to be hovering among the stars, and it ought to have been terrifying, but somehow it was not. Being in the cell was terrifying. This was freedom, and his own salvation in his hands.

He began to climb, leaning into the side of the tower, remembering what Jerrod had told him, remembering to imagine that he was Crawling across a flat surface. That gravity did not exist, was not trying to draw him down.

There. A slight impression, a dent in the marble side of the tower. And there, a crack, minute but textured. He dug in, fingers and toes bearing his weight. The shouts and cries of the guards receded as he made his way down.

He glanced up at the ever-changing moon, its wine-red light weaving patterns on the surface of the ocean. He saw the sea itself, a black shield stretching to the horizon. He was part of the tapestry, part of the night, moving down and farther down.

The tower rose above him now, a vast black pillar. His hands and feet were aching. He moved his foot down, seeking another toehold, and hit a solid surface instead.

He had reached the ground.

He sprang away from the tower, his blood roaring triumphantly in his ears. He had done it, what no one else had ever done. He had escaped the Trick. He was on the rocky ground of the *garrigue* now, the walls of the Palace rising in the distance, the tower and sea cliffs curving away to his right. He could hear the crash of the surf far below, taste the brine on the air.

He was alive.

In the distance, Marivent rose like a galleon at sea, glowing from every window. Keeping to the shadows, Kel crept around the side of the tower, the uneven gravel digging into the soles of his feet. His heart was slamming in his chest like a door in a high wind.

He was hidden, but they'd be looking for him, and there was no-where to run. He was pinned between the guards on one side and the sheer cliff-edge drop to the sea on the other. He could hope that the prisoner he had freed would at least be leading some of the guards off in another direction, but there would still be plenty of others to hunt him down.

Could I climb down the side of the cliff? he wondered. He'd made it down the Trick; surely a natural rock wall offered better purchase for his hands and feet. But then, there was nothing at the bottom—only the dark water filled with snapping green death.

He heard more shouts. He peered around the corner; Castel-guards were approaching from Marivent, a wall of red uniforms, torchlight gleaming off their swords. Kel jerked back, away from the sight, only to find himself seized in a strong grip.

He struggled, but the hold on him was hard as iron. He was dragged several feet away from the tower before being spun around.

The face that looked down at him was as familiar as his own face in the mirror. It very nearly was his own face in the mirror. Gray eyes, black hair, set jaw. The spark of moonlight off a gold chain around his neck.

"Conor," Kel said blankly. "What in gray hell—"

"Shut up," Conor said. "I don't want the guards here yet." With that bizarre pronouncement, he grabbed Kel by the back of his shirt and pulled him after him as he edged away from the tower.

Kel went. He had never fought Conor in his life; he wasn't going to start now. His mind was buzzing. Had *Conor* left the key for him? Had he been planning to get Kel out?

They had reached the cliff edge. The Trick loomed directly above them; below was churning white water that spilled over the rocks at the cliff's base.

Conor swung Kel around to face him. Behind Conor were the lights of Marivent and the Hill, the glow of windows, the shimmer that came from the white walls of stone—all the places where Kel had grown up, and where he would never have a place again.

He could see a group of Castelguards coming from the Palace, heading for the Trick; they were too far away for Kel to make out their faces, but they would arrive soon enough.

Kel's back was to the sea, to the drop below. He could hear the crash of the water. Feeling oddly calm, he looked at Conor. He wished he could memorize his face, but how much did it matter now? "I had not thought we would end like this," he said. "That you would kill me as your father killed Fausten."

Conor gave a sort of gasping laugh. "You know me well, too well," he said. "I, too, was thinking of Fausten tonight."

"I do not know how Fausten may have felt," Kel said, "but I would rather that you ended my life than that you let anyone else do it. My life was always yours anyway."

Conor closed his eyes, just for a moment. When they fluttered open again, they were wide, piercing—haunted. Conor took hold of the lapels of Kel's tattered jacket, fingers whitening with the tautness of his grip.

He said, "You are my unbreakable armor. And you will not die."

He pulled Kel closer for a moment; Kel felt Conor's lips brush his forehead and something cold settle around his neck. Conor let go of his shirt—Kel could see the Castelguards, not far behind him now, staring with wide eyes—and Conor's hands struck Kel's chest, flat-palmed, a hard shove. Kel stumbled, felt the ground under him crumble and give way as he fell, toppling headlong from the cliff edge toward the sea below.

For a long and breathless eternity that lasted less than three seconds, he fell. The stars were under his feet, the sea a sheet of rumpled glass below.

Kel struck the glassy surface as if striking the surface of a mirror. The sea shattered soundlessly around him, sending up shards of jade laced with white foam. He saw the stars wheel away overhead and then he was sinking into a numbing cold.

Icy black liquid seemed to swallow him. For a moment, it was all he wanted. He sank as if in a dream, silver bubbles tracing a path above his head.

Something moved past him. A shape in the water, dark against a greater darkness, slipping past with a sinuous flick.

Crocodile.

Kel choked, kicked upward. He broke the surface with a gasp, spitting bitter water. Looking up, he could see he had already drifted some way past the Trick. The lights of Marivent glowed atop the cliffs, a string of fiery pearls.

His fall had been an implosion, leaving a trail of silver-white foam across the water. A few feet away, he thought he saw something break the surface. The glint of moonlight on scales.

He kicked out as hard as he could, toward the harbor. Thank the Gods Jolivet had insisted he know how to swim. He swam for his life now, his arms pistoning, legs scissoring, cutting an arrow's path through the water. His eyes stung, the harbor a blur in the distance. He could think of nothing but the gape of distance below him, the depth of the ocean, and the sharp-toothed creatures that swam and swarmed in it.

He thought of Fausten. His blood spreading across the water like scarlet dye. The crocodiles had devoured him in an instant. It was madness that Kel was still alive. Certainly he could not outswim them, but that did not matter. He would not float aimlessly, waiting to be devoured.

Conor, he thought, and waited for the sense of betrayal to hit him in the guts, but there was no space for it. Something hard and slimy struck him in the side. He swung around in furious terror, only to see a rotting log. He kicked at it, pushed off, swam harder. He was finding a rhythm now, the strokes of his arms interrupted only when he turned his head to breathe. Salt water ran stinging down his throat.

He could see the Key now. And music; he could hear music spilling from the taverns. The water had begun to turn gray as the light from the city fell upon it. *Gray hell.* Kel's legs and arms were burning, each stroke forward an agony. The water underneath him rolled, and rolled again. He had reached the wave break.

He let himself go limp, let the next wave catch him and carry him in. It slammed him down on the edge of the beach, shoving him up the rocky, pebbled slope. He rolled over onto his stomach, retching salt.

And then he saw them. They slid up out of the water, two—no, three—green crocodiles, slithering, low to the ground. Kel tried to stand, but it was no use. His legs did not work. They were useless as wet string. He managed to push himself up onto his elbows, gasping, wet hair in his eyes.

In the moon's red light, they were enormous. Lurching, scaled, massive jaws hanging open, row upon row of jagged, prehistoric teeth. He had heard of such things—of crocodiles slithering up on land, fast, to snatch up a child and drag it back to sea before the mother even had a chance to scream.

He tried to push himself up to his knees. It was too late, regardless; they were on him, rearing over him. They stank of salt and rot and the deep places of the ocean, and their eyes glowed red in the moonlight, blank scarlet marbles without feeling or depth. Kel raised a hand to his face, as if he could ward them off—

And something cold brushed against his wrist. He glanced down and realized to his shock that a gold chain was looped around his throat, and from it dangled a glimmering medallion. He recalled Conor settling something cold around his neck. Conor's words to him. *You are my unbreakable armor. And you will not die.*

He knew now what Conor had meant. The medallion was big and bright, gaudily familiar. The last time Kel had seen it, it had been worn by Artal Gremont. The amulet that had so frustrated Merren; the one that kept Gremont safe from any kind of harm. Conor had given him the amulet then thrown him from the cliff— knowing that the fall would not kill him. That the crocodiles could not hurt him.

That he would live.

Kel let his hand fall, slowly. Around him, the crocodiles had gone still. They crouched over him, motionless, jaws agape. They were staring at him—no, not at him. At the amulet. Kel felt pinned beneath the gaze of malicious statues, only statues did not drip water, they did not breathe hot, stinking breath, they did not rear back and turn around, tails whipping. They did not slide back into the ocean like ghosts, one after another, humped dark shapes disappearing into the churn of the waves.

The pebbled beach was utterly still and empty. Somewhere in the distance Kel could hear water running. There was a ringing in his ears, a darkness at the edge of his vision. He slumped motionless onto the ground.

Elsabet

"My lady, is there anything else you need?"

"No." Elsabet dismisses the soldier hovering outside her tent with a curt word. He hesitates a moment before scuttling off, half frightened and half relieved.

She lies back on the hard ground. She has been provided with a feather-tick mattress and a camp bed, of course, but she does not want to sleep. Too many thoughts burn in her mind for rest to come.

Beyond the fragile enclosure of her tent, she can hear the Malgasi soldiers moving around their encampment, deep in the sea caves outside Castellane. She knows she had terrified the men when she'd appeared in the night, bloodied and covered in plaster dust, only to collapse in their midst.

The shame of it—for her, a Belmany, to collapse among peasant soldiers—but her legs had no longer been able to hold her up. Kalman, the captain of the guards, had barked orders for a medic to attend to her burns, but Elsabet had waved him off. She wanted the pain, wanted to feel it. It was the pain of her failure.

The scope of that failure became clear to her over the next days. Seven—Joss Falconet—had done all that she asked, but the

Sword Catcher had escaped from the Trick and been executed by the Prince. The Temple of Anibal had been destroyed, and Bagomer and Janos had been killed. Elsabet's stone had saved her life, but the effort had cost it nearly all its power. It is cold now beneath her skin, cold as a dead man's skin. It will need to be replaced by one of the Belmanys' few remaining Source-Stones before Elsabet can use her power again.

Worst of all, Elsabet now knows there is another magic-user in Castellane—the red-haired girl who caused all of this. Somehow, one of the filthy Ashkar, that class of diseased vermin, has gotten her hand on a Source-Stone and used it to unleash a power that rivals Elsabet's own.

But Elsabet is not beaten yet. As she listens to the sounds of the sea crashing against the inner walls of the cave, she feels her own fury pulse inside her, stronger than any magic. She has lost her guards, but she still has her army. She has drained her stone, but there is still power to be accessed, behind the walls of Marivent. The blood of the Belmany phoenix runs in the veins of both the King and the Prince of this city.

She will reclaim her birthright. She will take Castellane for her own. And when she does, she will destroy the woman with the Source-Stone. She knows her name already, the name of the Ashkar woman she had seen first in the library at Marivent. It had come to her with the fading power of her stone, which had recognized a fellow sorcerer and whispered its dying alarm into Elsabet's ears.

Her name is Lin. Lin Caster.

CHAPTER TWENTY-SIX

When Kel regained consciousness, the red moon had changed positions in the sky. It hung lower now, a coral pendant on an invisible chain, descending toward the horizon.

Gingerly, he pushed himself into a sitting position. His limbs seemed to work again, though his body ached. He wondered how long he had lain here unconscious. Long enough for the moon to change positions, and for his clothes to dry, stiff with salt, against his body.

Kel rose to his feet, the heavy necklace Conor had flung around his throat bumping against his chest. He looked out at the ocean, at the blood-red horizon. He had half thought the Arrow Squadron would be out looking for him, but he knew now it was unlikely. The approaching Castelguards would have seen Conor throw him from the cliffs of Marivent into the ocean, and that was a death sentence. That he had survived it due to the amulet's magic would not be something they could guess.

Kel turned back toward the city. He was bedraggled and filthy. He had just escaped from the Trick. He could, he guessed, go to the Black Mansion, throw himself on Andreyen's mercy, but if Jolivet or the Vigilants were to look for him even perfunctorily, that would be the first place they would seek him; they already had people watching Scarlet Square.

There was still, by his accounting, one other place he could go. Even if he didn't know exactly where it was.

Kel began to walk toward the Key. He could feel every pebble of the beach against his bare feet, but louder than any pain was the sound of Jolivet's voice in his ears: *You are a Sword Catcher, Kellian. Your life belongs to the Palace. But you can never return to what you were.*

Kel felt strangely calm. Perhaps this was because if he let the tide of recent events wash over him fully, it would drown him. In thinking of his own mistakes, of the danger to Castellane, of the way he had let down his friends in the Black Mansion. In thinking of Conor and the fact that wherever Kel woke up tomorrow, it would be the first time in more than a decade that he had woken up outside of Marivent, and far from Conor.

But he would wake up. And for the first time, when he did, he would not be playing a part. He was Kel Saren now, and he knew who his friends were. His enemies had removed their masks, so he knew them, too. He knew what to expect from all save one person, and the need to see that person thrummed through his blood, propelling him as he shouldered through the crowds of the Key, taking no heed of whether they stared at him. Though why should they? He might be ragged and damp looking, but that was not unusual, and if his hands were bloody where he had dragged himself up the beach, he kept them at his sides where they would not be seen.

He turned into the Maze, heading down Arsenal Road. It was crowded, as it always was at night, the usual mix of foreign sailors, beggars, and painted prostitutes hooting and calling from the balconies of tumbledown houses. The occasional burst of naphtha light seared Kel's eyes. He found it at last: the warehouse whose windows had been blacked out with paint.

The front door was not locked, but it seemed stuck in its frame; wood warped often here, so close to the sea and the humid air. Kel shouldered it open and stepped into the long corridor. It was light-less, illuminated only by the street outside.

He made his way to the enormous main room. It was empty, the glass lanterns swaying unlighted over a dusty floor stacked with un-marked wooden boxes.

If he closed his eyes, he could imagine what this place had been like the first time he'd visited it: filled with the sons of nobility gam-bling and carousing with poppy-juice addicts and masked courte-sans. Where there had been music and glowing naphtha torches, now there was a profound silence, the only illumination the pale-red moonlight that spilled through the cracked windows.

"Kel."

He turned. Standing in the entranceway was a familiar figure in a black cloak. His silver quarter-mask gleamed, as did his boots. His hood was up, drawn close about his face. Kel could not see his ex-pression.

"Jerrod," Kel said.

"I have to admit," Jerrod said, "I didn't think it would work. No one's ever gotten out of the Trick."

"I suppose you taught me well," Kel said. "I Crawled down the side of the tower. Though I can't brag about it without getting ar-rested. Unfortunate."

Jerrod said nothing. His eyes gleamed, brighter than his mask.

"I just have one question," Kel said. "How in gray hell did Conor end up with Gremont's amulet? Beck must have given it to him, but I'm having a hard time picturing *that*."

"Beck has his reasons for doing what he does—"

"I'm not interested in hearing about Beck from you, Jerrod," Kel said. "When I think about how long you've been lying to me, I just—" He shook his head. "I just need to see Prosper Beck. The *real* Prosper Beck," he added, before Jerrod could interrupt. "Not some goon you dress up and sit behind a desk to fool me."

To Jerrod's credit, he didn't try to deny the ruse. "Beck's done enough for you," he said. "Keep the amulet. Get out of Castellane. Don't ask for anything else. I'm telling you this as a friend."

"Really?" said Kel. "Whose friend? Because I know who Beck is now. Who *she* really is."

Jerrod did not move or make a sound; only his expression changed. Even under the shadow of the hood, Kel could see his face harden. He wondered for a moment if he'd picked the wrong strategy. Perhaps the truth would only make Jerrod angry, defensive, more inclined to keep Kel away from his employer.

And then Jerrod smiled. There was little amusement in it, and a great deal of wryness. "I wondered if you'd figure it out someday. She was always a little careless with you." He beckoned to Kel, indicating he should follow. "Come with me, then."

They made their way through the narrow curving streets of the Maze, Jerrod silent at Kel's side, which didn't bother Kel, as his mind was buzzing. Rather abruptly, as they turned onto a narrow alley that twisted off Arsenal Road, Jerrod said, "Does Merren hate me?"

"No," Kel said. "He was angry at you. It's not the same thing. You could go back, you know. And see him. It's not as if Andreyen would stop you."

"He hasn't tried to see *me*," Jerrod said crossly.

"I would point out that he doesn't know where you are," said Kel, "but I see you are committed to your own obstinacy."

Jerrod muttered something that Kel suspected to be uncomplimentary, and then stopped at a tall, battered-looking town house that tipped slightly eastward, as if slowly lurching off its foundations. A scratched plaque by the red-painted front door indicated that this had once been the harbormaster's house, before shipbuilding had moved to the Arsenale and the Maze had become what it was.

"Wait here," Jerrod said coldly, and disappeared through the red door.

It was a warm night, but still Kel shivered, standing alone in the alley. It was late—two in the morning, he would guess—and he could not help but wonder what was happening at the Palace. The Castelguards would have seen Conor push him over the cliff; Conor would have told them Kel was dead. They would have no reason to disbelieve him.

He wondered what Jolivet would think. If anyone would mourn him.

The door opened. Jerrod, in the doorway, said, "She'll see you," in a tone that indicated that he had advised against that very thing. Kel climbed the front steps, brushed past Jerrod, and found himself in a clean, plaster-walled house, with low ceilings and wooden floors. A stairway disappeared up into shadow. A single lantern hung on the wall, spilling very little light.

"That way," Jerrod said, pointing down a short corridor to a closed door; a bar of illumination was visible below the frame. "And Kel—"

Kel, halfway down the hall, turned. "Yes?"

"If you hurt her . . ."

Kel spread his arms wide. "I'm unarmed."

"I didn't mean—" Jerrod broke off, shaking his head, half disgusted. "Just go."

Kel went. Down the narrow hall, through the door, into a room illuminated by a leaping fire in a soot-blackened grate. The greenish tiles of the fireplace surround were cracked, the walls newly painted white, the furniture oddly dainty, as if it had been pilfered from the house of a noblewoman. Kel suspected that, in fact, it had.

She sat on a spindly gilt chair near the fire—if *sat* was the right word. She was sprawled in the chair, her legs up over one arm, her feet, in knee-high leather boots, dangling over the side, dangerously close to knocking a cut glass decanter off the side table. Tight trousers with a sheen like oilskin were tucked into the boots, and over those she wore a half-buttoned admiral's coat, dark blue with yellow piping and brass buttons down the front. Her blond curls spilled down her back, over her shoulders, a sharp contrast with the stiff masculinity of her starched collar.

"Antonetta," Kel said. "It's good to see you."

She looked at him without expression. "You're soaking wet."

"I fell in the ocean," Kel said dryly. "After escaping from the Trick."

Her red lips curved into a smile. "And you don't look the least bit chewed on by crocodiles. It seems that amulet really *does* work."

Kel's heart was pounding, but he'd had years of practice masking his feelings, hiding his physical reactions to stress and shock. "You gave the amulet to Conor," he said. "How sure were you that he'd use it the way he did?"

"You forget, I know him, too. Not as well as you, but well enough. He never has cared about anything more than he cared about you." She rose to her feet, the admiral's coat swirling around her legs. The coat must have been cut to fit her. It skimmed distractingly over her curves. Kel reminded himself that he was furious with her and had been since the Solstice Ball. "You figured it out," she said, and there was a strange note in her voice, something he couldn't quite define. "I wondered if you would."

Because you think I'm a fool. Because you think you can lie to me and I'll never realize it.

She came toward him. Kel stood still, very conscious that he was barefoot, still wet from the sea, his damp hair stiff with salt. None of that seemed to bother her. She came closer to him—close enough to put her hands against his chest. Close enough that he could smell her perfume, soft and flowery, intriguingly at odds with her masculine attire. She said, "Now you know." She raised her eyes, wide and clear, her pupils unchanged by posy-drops. "Now you know. Do you hate me?"

"I could never hate you, Antonetta," Kel said.

She took hold of the lapels of his ragged shirt. Pushing herself up on her toes, she kissed him, not gently, and he could not help himself; he kissed her back. He slanted his mouth against hers and kissed her until his heart was beating like a drum through his body. In the last moment when he still had control, he felt his hands rise to clasp her shoulders. As if in a dream he broke the kiss, pushing her away, setting her back on her heels, her hair tumbling around her flushed face.

"Antonetta," he said. "*No.*"

She stared at him for a moment with a mixture of shock and hurt. A slow dark-red color stained her cheeks. "But you said— I thought you weren't angry?"

He thought of Jerrod warning him not to hurt Antonetta. As if Jerrod did not understand that all the power to cause pain was Antonetta's. That she could hurt him far more than he could hurt her.

"I said I didn't hate you. And I don't. I couldn't hate you. But you lied to me, Ana. You lied to me about who you are, you lied about what you know—"

"You know now," she said. "You guessed. Isn't that better than if I'd told you?"

A flash of anger went through him, coupled with the desire to do something, say something, that would make her understand. "It is not," he said tightly, "*better.* I have no reason to think, Ana, that you would *ever* have told me, no matter what happened between us. You did not just lie by omission. You manipulated me. It was useful to you, and why would I imagine you'd ever stop doing something that was useful to you?"

"I would have told you—"

"No, you wouldn't. You were enjoying yourself too much, Ana. You like being Prosper Beck. And it's been years, hasn't it? To build up a reputation like Beck has—to grow your power in the Maze—"

"You will not make me ashamed of what I've done—"

"I would never assume anyone could make you feel shame, Antonetta," said Kel, and watched the color change in her face as she realized the double meaning in his words. "I don't even know you. That's what I've realized. I cannot guess at why you became Beck—

perhaps because you were bored and spoiled and wanted your life to have some sort of meaning and purpose—"

She took a step back from him, and even through the blinding pain that had made him lash out, he ached to see her pull away. "I became Prosper Beck out of a sense of self-preservation," she said, almost spitting each word. "I became Prosper Beck because my life was so small, and the choices available to me on the Hill were nothing I wanted. I became Beck because there was a real Beck once— a man I hired to teach me how to use a sword. Because I *was* spoiled and bored and I wanted to know how to fight, and he was a shoddy, minor sort of criminal, and when he got himself killed, I saw the chance and took his place."

"There was a real Beck?" Somehow Kel hadn't expected that.

"I *am* the real Beck," she snapped. "He was nothing. Drank himself to death in the Maze. I took his name and made him a legend."

"You think a lot of yourself," Kel said, "for someone who was careless enough to mistakenly reveal their secret to me."

Antonetta's eyes flashed. She picked up a blackened fireplace poker and jabbed savagely at the logs in the fireplace, not looking at him. "Fine. Tell me. Tell me how you guessed. Tell me my *mistakes.*"

Kel gritted his teeth. He had not expected to be so angry. He had imagined confronting her calmly, ticking off the ways he had guessed who she was, explaining to her how at last he saw through her. Instead he felt as if he were looking at her through a haze of fire.

"It wasn't one thing," he said. "It was several. And if it makes you feel better, I thought I might be going mad at first."

"Go on," she said.

"When I went to see whoever that was—the man you had playing Prosper Beck—"

"Bron," she said, a darkness flickering across her face. "He was one of my couriers."

"He acted well enough," Kel said. "It was the boxes of wine in his office. *Singing Monkey*. Not a name you'd forget easily. Then later, at the Roverges' party, you deliberately got us lost on the way back to the main room."

She swung on him with the poker in her hand. "Did I? Or was I just being foolish? Maybe I have no sense of direction. Maybe I'm just absentminded—"

"You are none of those things," Kel said furiously. "That's a part you've been playing all these years, no more real—"

"Than the part you play?" She looked over at him, the firelight dancing across her cheek. "As the Sword Catcher?"

Kel did not react, despite the racing of his pulse. He had wanted her to know at the Shining Gallery party, when she had looked at him as if she saw through his disguise as Conor, saw who he really was. There was nothing more intoxicating than being seen. He had wanted it so badly, and had let the dream go; he had learned long ago that dreams like that only caused pain in the end.

He had wondered again at the Solstice Ball. Her words had seemed so pointed, designed to hurt him. Even as he'd grown more and more sure she was Prosper Beck, he hadn't been able to decide: Had she known she was talking to him and meant to wound him? Or had she thought it was Conor, and meant to betray him?

"No more real than that," he said. "For instance, you know the Roverges' house as well as you know your own. You brought me into the cellar, so I could see there were boxes of the same wine there. I asked Charlon about the bottles later. He said they'd been a gift. I tend to believe him. You knew I was looking for Prosper Beck's funding on the Hill, and you wanted to throw suspicion on the Roverges."

"Very good," she murmured. "But not enough. You didn't guess, not then."

"Conor told me about the tunnels under House Alleyne," he said. "That's how you've always gotten in and out without being noticed, isn't it? And then there's the amulet." He tugged at the gold chain around his throat. "Jerrod stabbed Gremont to death on Tyndaris— Why? He knew that the amulet Gremont was wearing was false; he'd been working with Alys Asper. But not *for* Alys Asper. Jerrod has always been your right-hand man. Loyal to Beck, which means loyal to you, Antonetta. And you were determined to marry Gremont. Jerrod wouldn't have raised a hand against him unless he thought you wanted him dead, not when he knew how it would upset Merren. What changed your mind?"

She hesitated before saying, almost reluctantly, "I had not known of Gremont's association with the Malgasi until it became clear that while he did not know I was Beck, he had somehow learned I *knew* Beck. He demanded I arrange a meeting."

"Did you fob him off with the same stand-in you sent to meet me, when I thought I was meeting Prosper Beck?"

"Yes," she said. Only the one word, leaving Kel a bitter taste in the back of his throat. The bitter knowledge that she had treated him, when it came to Beck, no differently than she had treated Artal Gremont. "But Gremont came to the meeting with the Malgasi Princess. Jerrod was there. It became clear Gremont was under her thumb, completely. He would do anything she wanted. If she demanded he slit my throat in the ballroom at House Alleyne, he would have done it and not worried about exile. It was too dangerous to marry him. I had to abandon that plan."

"I see. And then—there was the Solstice Ball. When you told Conor I wasn't to be trusted."

She bit her lip. "Kel—"

"Don't," he said. "At first, I thought you were indeed speaking to someone you believed to be Conor. Until you started listing off all the ways in which you felt I'd endangered myself for Conor's sake. You said, *He tried to pay your debts to Prosper Beck.* But there was no way you would know that. No one knew that—except for Beck."

She half closed her eyes. "Stupid," she murmured. "So stupid—"

He took a step toward her; she didn't move. "Do you remember in the cellar at the Roverge party? When I helped bandage your cut?" He put a hand on the swell of her hip, where the cut had been. He could feel the warmth of her through the fabric of her trousers, feel the curve of her under his hand. "You told me you'd been injured learning how to use a sword."

"No one becomes Prosper Beck without a few injuries on the way," she said, but her voice was a little unsteady. She looked up at him, the firelight darkening her eyes. "What about the locket?"

"Yes. You sent me to steal your own locket," he said. "You knew I'd open it and find the grass ring there. You knew I'd torture myself over what it meant."

She looked up at him, her eyes glittering, a little narrowed. "I never thought you'd be tortured," she said. "I never wanted to hurt you at all—"

"I don't believe that," he said savagely. "I have puzzled over it and puzzled over it. What I could have done to make you so determined to strike at me—with the locket, with what you did to Conor, with the things you said to me at the Solstice Ball? If you had planned for a thousand years, you could not have come up with words that would have crushed me more—"

Antonetta had gone white. "I was *trying to get you to lie low*," she said, her voice rising above the crackle of the fire. "You stupid, stupid man. I knew you were lying to Conor, working with the Ragpicker King, doing favors for the Kutani Princess, acting as if you believed you'd never get caught. I thought if I made it clear how much danger you were really in, you might stop before you got yourself *killed*. And I knew you'd hate me for saying what I said, but I thought it would be worth it if it meant you'd live—"

She broke off. Kel stared at her. She was flushed with rage. He wanted to believe that she meant it, that she had only been thinking of his safety. But she had lied to him and lied to him, and he felt now the danger of wanting to believe in her—in her, of all people.

Antonetta threw the poker, which clattered into the fireplace. "I told you at the Roverges' that I wanted the silk Charter," she said. "I wanted Gremont's Charter, too. Not for myself—I couldn't have held it, I know that. But I could have given it to someone."

"You would have . . . sold it?" Kel said. "I don't—"

"No, you don't," she said furiously. "I can't believe you came here thinking you had everything all figured out, Kel Saren. You don't understand anything. I wanted it for *you.*"

Kel caught her by the wrist. She started to twist away before turning to glare at him. "*Why?*" he demanded.

She took a deep breath. Desperately he searched her eyes with his own. For a moment, he thought he could see the truth of her in her eyes, see through the layers of pretense and lies and history, through the defensive wall that he himself had had a part in building up so long ago.

Tell me, Ana, he thought. *Tell me the truth. Tell me what you feel.*

But her gaze flicked away from his. "So you could be free of being the Sword Catcher," she said in a flat voice that let him know that whatever her real reason was, she had no intention of revealing it. "I know what it's like to be trapped by duty and expectation. I suppose I wanted to see power in the right hands for a change."

Kel's heart sank. She would never be honest with him. It was more than concealing her identity as Prosper Beck. He could have lived with that. But to know that she would never tell him what she really felt about *anything*—

"All those years ago," he said roughly. "You shut me out. It wasn't just your mother—though Aigon knows I blame her for many things. You are the one who told me we were not of the same class. That there was no point in closing our eyes to reality."

Almost unconsciously, she put her hand to her throat, where her locket would usually rest. "You remember what I said?"

"Every word," Kel said. "You put me exactly in my place. I thought you hated me. And then later, just these past months, when

I realized what a part you were playing, I thought: *Perhaps she is showing her real self, only to me.* It made me think I might be different in your eyes. But you have lied to me just like everyone else."

"And you have lied to me, Sword Catcher," she said. "You stand there so angry that I never told you I had a second life as Prosper Beck. Yet you have only ever been Kel Anjuman with me, and while I may have hidden my false self, you hid your real one. You *are* Kel Saren, Sword Catcher, and I had to learn that name from others."

Kel sucked in his breath. "It was not my secret to tell," he said. "I took an oath, a vow to protect Conor. A vow never to tell anyone that such a thing as a Sword Catcher even existed."

She smiled almost sadly. "Jerrod knows," she said. "Ji-An. Merren Asper. The Ragpicker King. Lin Caster—"

I never told any of them. They already knew, or found out. But did such things matter? Especially now, when he was demanding honesty from her, demanding she strip herself down to the bones of what she really was and show that self to him?

"I think I always knew, Ana," he said, "that you were hiding some truth of yourself from me, and so I did not trust you with who I really was."

"And I," she said, meeting his gaze levelly, "always knew you were hiding some truth of *yourself* from me, and so I did not trust you with who I really was."

They were both silent for a moment, the only noise the fire crackling in the grate. At last, Kel said, "Perhaps, then, it is time that we finally introduced ourselves to each other. As we truly are." As she watched in surprise, he laid a hand over his heart, where it beat under his ragged jacket, and made a bow. When he straightened, he said, "My lady. I am Kellian Saren, born an orphan of Castellane. I have no blood family, but I am the Sword Catcher, the protector of the Prince of Castellane, and though I am exiled from Marivent, I will always be that."

Her eyes bright, Antonetta crossed the room, picked up the decanter sitting on the table beside the chair, and, with practiced economy of gesture, poured two full glasses. She turned to Kel, offering him one. "Kel Saren," she said. "I am Antonetta Alleyne, heir to the silk Charter, and I am also Prosper Beck, a criminal of the Maze. I am pleased to make your acquaintance."

Accepting the glass, Kel took a drink, letting the harsh tang of the brandewine burn its way down his throat.

"Very well," Antonetta said, settling herself back into the spindly gilt chair. She looked at him over her drink. "Now we know each other. For the first time, it seems. Which means I must ask you: Why are you here? You could have gone anywhere after you escaped the Trick. I had thought you would flee the city. Why come to me? Just because you were angry?"

Kel thought—he could not be sure—that her voice trembled slightly on that last, rising question. But he could not be sure, and he could not ask. Not now. *It is not her fault if you see what you want to see, hear what you want to hear. Somehow, you have fallen in love with a person you do not know, a person who may still be only a dream or a figment. You must come to know her, this new Antonetta; you must know your own heart before you can know hers.*

"I came here because you have a storehouse full of weapons we can use against Malgasi," he said, "and I have a plan."

If a flicker of disappointment passed across her face, it was too swift for him to be sure of it. "What makes you think I would want to be part of your plan?"

"Because the Malgasi will bleed Castellane dry and kill everyone on the Hill, and whatever your feelings about most of them, I know you don't want that, either. Because we have a common goal, Antonetta, and I need you on my side."

She tucked her hair back behind her ear—an old gesture that meant that she was considering what he'd said. Something about the familiarity of it bit at him like teeth. And that's how this would be, he knew, if she agreed. He had known it would hurt to be away from her, but not how much it would hurt to be close: to be always reminded that he knew her and did not know her at the same time.

But this was the only chance Conor had; the only chance Castellane had. He needed her brilliance, her clever ruthlessness, even as that ruthlessness was part of what held them apart with the force of steel doors.

"Your side means the Black Mansion?" she said. "Andreyen and the others? You're suggesting we all work together?"

"Yes," he said. "That's exactly what I'm suggesting."

"But do you want me as Beck," she said, "or Antonetta?"

I am not sure I even know myself, Kel thought. Aloud, he said, "Both. The task ahead is impossibly hard. But if we are to have a chance of success, we need you. *I* need you. Exactly as you are."

Her smile was faint but real. She gazed down at her glass, the light from the fire turning the dark liquid within into a burning amber. "Very well, then," she said. "I'm listening."

Epilogue

As Conor made his way up the steps of the North Tower, he could not help but remember that long ago, when he and Kel had both been children, they had taken astronomy lessons here with Fausten.

At the top of the tower, they had studied maps of the stars, the movements of the spheres, and the legends of the planets, each ruled by a different capricious god. They had promised each other that one day they would visit the far south, where the stars were different.

But much had changed since then—the kinds of great sweeping changes that made a long-ago promise between two boys feel small and insignificant. He could not think of Kel without pain, despite all he had tried to do to save him. There had been no way to keep Kel with him, and not to know when he might see Kel again—if ever—felt as if Conor walked a narrow bridge over a yawning chasm below, its recesses lost in shadow.

And then there was Lin. Like Kel, she would be safe *because* she was away from him. He had to believe that, or die.

He forced his mind back to what she had told him just before she'd left Marivent. What had seemed at first like a Story-Spinner tale. The young Prince at a foreign Court, the discovery of a magical creature long thought to be lost, an exchange of blade and blood and fire, and a secret kept for many years by a King who seemed to be turning into a madman but was changing into something else altogether.

And yet he felt it to be true. Conor had always inhabited a world in which he only trusted a few things: his connection to Kel and, later, his feelings for Lin. In that same fashion—more instinct than logic—he trusted this, with a trust that went as deep as his own blood and bones.

Conor reached the landing, where a Castelguard stood at attention in front of his father's chamber. Conor passed him with a nod, and once he was inside the tower room, he locked the door behind him.

King Markus sat in his customary place, his chair, though its position was different now. Rather than gazing blankly into space, the King was facing the narrow window as if he were looking out at the world beyond. And when Conor came close, although he did not otherwise move, he inclined his head in greeting.

"Father," Conor said. In the sunlight, the change in the King was very apparent. His eyes were clear and focused, and the color had come back to his skin. The anger that had seemed to grip him before was gone, though there was still about him the sense that he was waiting—not impatiently, but with anticipation—for some great future event.

Conor knelt down before his father's chair. He knew what he had to say; the words came clearly and simply, as if there were no other words he could use. "Father," he said again, "Lin has told me everything. Everything that you told her about Malgasi, the phoenix, and what is happening to you—all of it." As he spoke, he saw Lin's face, the tears in her eyes as she left his room. He remembered her telling him that she loved him, and though he knew it might never matter, he might never see her again, it gave him strength. "I sent her away, far from here. I told her never to come back. And she's not the only one. Kel is gone, too. *My Királar.* Everyone in the Palace thinks he's dead. And I sent Mayesh away. I know you told me that he was the one I could always trust, that every Aurelian King has always depended on his Counselor. But I had no choice. They have to think I'm all alone. Can you understand that? They must believe that I am at my weakest, completely undefended. That there is no one in Marivent who will lift a hand to protect me. It will make them overconfident, and when they strike they will do so because they think I am alone. But I am not alone, am I? Not entirely."

He could no longer hold his father's gaze. He looked down at the floor. "They think you are weak, Father," he said. "But I believe they are wrong. I believe we can defeat them, together."

He heard a rustle as his father moved, and a moment later the sharpness of needle points against his scalp as the King reached out and ran a clawed hand through Conor's hair.

"Yes," Markus rasped. "Together."

ACKNOWLEDGMENTS

It takes a village to create a book. I'd like to thank my husband, Josh; my mother and father; Elka Cloke; my in-laws: Jon, Melanie, Helen, and Meg. My critique partners, Kelly Link and Holly Black, and my crew that cheers me on: Robin Wasserman, Marie Rutkoski, Leigh Bardugo, and Maureen Johnson. My assistants, Emily and Jed and Daisy. My super agents, Suzie Townsend and Jo Volpe, and everyone at New Leaf. My editor, Anne Groell, a legend in her time. The teams at Del Rey and Pan Macmillan. Heather Baror-Shapiro and Danny Baror. With many thanks also to Matthew Abdul-Haqq Niemi (Ashkari language design), Nicolás Matias Campi (Malgasi language design), Margaret Ransdell-Green (Kutani language design), Melissa Yoon (sensitivity reader), and Clary Goodman (sensitivity and research).

ABOUT THE AUTHOR

CASSANDRA CLARE is the author of the #1 *New York Times,* *USA Today,* *Wall Street Journal,* and *Publishers Weekly* bestselling Shadowhunter Chronicles and the *New York Times* bestselling *Sword Catcher.* The Shadowhunter Chronicles have been adapted as both a major motion picture and a television series. Her books have more than fifty million copies in print worldwide and have been translated into more than thirty-five languages. Cassandra lives in western Massachusetts with her husband and four fearsome cats.

CassandraClare.com
X: @cassieclare
Instagram: @cassieclare1

ABOUT THE TYPE

The text of this book was set in Janson, a typeface designed about 1690 by Nicholas Kis (1650–1702), a Hungarian living in Amsterdam, and for many years mistakenly attributed to the Dutch printer Anton Janson. In 1919, the matrices became the property of the Stempel Foundry in Frankfurt. It is an old-style book face of excellent clarity and sharpness. Janson serifs are concave and splayed; the contrast between thick and thin strokes is marked.